IRON PIONEERS

Enjoy!

Tyler R. Tichelaar

IRON PIONEERS

The Marquette Trilogy: Book One

a novel

Tyler R. Tichelaar

Marquette Fiction
Marquette, Michigan

IRON PIONEERS

Marquette Fiction
1202 Pine Street
Marquette, MI 49855
www.marquettefiction.com

ISBN-13: 978-0-9791790-0-6
ISBN-10: 0-9791790-0-9
Library of Congress PCN 2007932348

Publication managed by Superior Book Productions
www.SuperiorBookProductions.com

"The beginnings, therefore, of this great iron industry are historically important and are of interest to every citizen in the United States, for there is not a man or woman today living who has not been, directly or indirectly, benefited by the great mineral wealth of the Lake Superior country and the labor of winning it and working it into the arts . . . . Has it not the elements in it out of which to weave the fabric of the great American novel so long expected and so long delayed? For the story is distinctly American. Indeed there is nothing more distinctly American."

—Ralph Williams, in his biography of Marquette's iron pioneer *The Honorable Peter White: A Biographical Sketch of the Lake Superior Iron Country* (1905)

PRINCIPAL FAMILIES IN IRON PIONEERS

The Bergmanns

Fritz Bergmann - a German immigrant
Molly Bergmann - his wife, an Irish immigrant
Karl Bergmann - their son
Kathy Bergmann - their daughter

The Brookfields

Lucius Brookfield - family patriarch, partner to Gerald Henning in building a
    forge
Rebecca Brookfield - his wife, a staunch Methodist
Omelia Brookfield - Lucius and Rebecca's daughter who remains in New York
Darius Brookfield - Lucius and Rebecca's son who disappeared years ago on
    the Oregon Trail
Sophia Rockford - Lucius and Rebecca's daughter, second wife of Gerald
    Henning
George Rockford - Sophia's first husband
Caleb Rockford - George and Sophia's son
Cordelia Whitman - Lucius and Rebecca's daughter, proprietor of a boarding
    house
Nathaniel Whitman - Cordelia's husband
Jacob Whitman - Nathaniel and Cordelia's son
Edna Whitman - Nathaniel and Cordelia's daughter

The Dalrymples

Arthur Dalrymple - family patriarch, born in Nova Scotia
Charles Dalrymple - his son, a carpenter
Christina Dalrymple - Charles's wife
Margaret Dalrymple - Charles and Christina's daughter, born in a boarding
    house
Sarah Dalrymple - Charles and Christina's daughter
Charles Dalrymple Jr. - Charles and Christina's son

The Hennings

Gerald Henning - a wealthy businessman from Boston
Clara Henning - his first wife, from a Boston high society family
Agnes Henning - Gerald and Clara's daughter
Madeleine Henning - Gerald's daughter by his second wife, Sophia

The Varins

Jean Varin - a French Canadian
Suzanne Varin - his wife
Amedee - Suzanne's brother

Other Principal Characters

Ben - logging partner to Karl Bergmann
Lazarus Carew - a stable boy, son of Cornish immigrants
Patrick McCarey - an Irish immigrant
Joseph Montoni - an Italian saloonkeeper
Therese - Montoni's sister

HISTORICAL PEOPLE IN *IRON PIONEERS*

Captain Atkins - captain of the *Jay Morse*
Frederic Baraga - "the Snowshoe Priest" - missionary and first Marquette
    Diocese bishop
Mrs. Bignall - mother of the first white child born in Marquette
Pamelia Bishop - the Mother of Methodism in Marquette
Captain Bridges - captain of the tug *Dudley*
The Calls - prosperous family who owned a house on Ridge Street
Father Duroc - Catholic priest
Cullen Eddy - Justice of the Peace
Heman Ely - early Marquette businessman
Sam Ely - first president of the First National Bank
Philo Everett - Marquette businessman and banker
Robert Graveraet - a founder of Marquette
Amos Harlow - principal founder of Marquette

Olive Harlow - his wife

Martha Bacon - Olive Harlow's mother

Charles Kawbawgam - Last Chief of the Chippewa

Charlotte Kawbawgam - his wife

Father Kenny - pastor of St. Peter's Cathedral

Jacques LePique - Kawbawgam's brother-in-law

Chief Marji Gesick - Charlotte's father, who led the white men to the iron ore
    in 1844

John Munro Longyear- landlooker and real estate agent

Father Jacques Marquette - seventeenth century Jesuit missionary

The Maynards - passengers on the *Jay Morse*

Captain Samuel Moody - builder of Marquette's first dock, Civil War soldier

Jay Morse - Marquette businessman, owner of a pleasure yacht

Bishop Mrak - second bishop of the Marquette diocese

Colonel Pickands - partner of Jay Morse

Edmund Remington - Civil War soldier

Joe Roleau - passenger on the *Jay Morse*

Reverend Safford - Episcopalian minister

Alfred Swineford - owner of the *Mining Journal*, later governor of Alaska

Bishop Vertin - third bishop of the Marquette diocese

Mrs. Wheelock - proprietor of one of Marquette's first boarding houses

Jerome White - Civil War soldier

Peter White - Marquette businessman, early settler, and civic benefactor

Preface

Iron Pioneers Ten-Year Anniversary Edition

Creating a Literature for Upper Michigan

It's hard to believe ten years have passed since I published my first book, *Iron Pioneers: The Marquette Trilogy, Book One*, and it's even harder to believe how Upper Michigan literature has flourished since then.

Iron Pioneers was published in 2006, but when I began writing it in March 1999, very few novels had been set in Upper Michigan, and most of those were for children. I had long felt that Upper Michigan deserved its own literature, and as early as June 4, 1987, the summer of my sixteenth year, I put pen to paper to begin writing my first novel, which I titled *Marquette: The Life and Times of Robert O'Neill*, a book that eventually would become *The Only Thing That Lasts*, published in 2009. When this first book failed to find a publisher, I went on to write other novels, some of which eventually evolved into published books while others today remain manuscripts stuffed in desk drawers.

The earliest version of what would become The Marquette Trilogy was one of those manuscripts, titled *Tales of the Marquettians*. "Marquettians" was a word I coined because I wanted to create a whole mystique and culture set around my hometown, and I believed we, its residents, deserved a moniker of our own. Since then, I have occasionally heard a person use the same word, but it has never caught on and has been overshadowed by the more universal "Yooper," which describes all of us from Upper Michigan, while I tend to refer to myself as simply a "Marquette resident" today.

In any case, Tales of the Marquettians was intended to be a short story collection, although I never got past writing the first story. Later, that story would become part of the opening chapter of *Iron Pioneers* in which Clara Henning arrives on a schooner in Marquette's harbor during its founding year of 1849. But the vision for Iron Pioneers was still in my future at this time, as I continued to write novels that I chose not to publish until I became better at the craft of writing.

Realizing I would not be able to support myself anytime soon by writing novels, I went to college, and in 2000, I earned a Ph.D. in literature from Western Michigan University with the intent to become an English professor. In 1999, while I felt I was in exile attending graduate school in Lower Michigan, Marquette celebrated its sesquicentennial, and that, coupled with my homesickness and my ability to appreciate Marquette even more by being separated from it, made me believe the time was right for me to write a novel about Marquette that celebrated its history. In fact, I strongly felt that my life purpose had been to write such a book.

Little did I know what a task I had before me. My initial plan was to go back to the intended structure for *Tales of the Marquettians* and write fifteen stories—one for each decade of Marquette's history—that would carry the cast of characters forward generation after generation. I quickly realized that plan could never do full justice to the richness of Marquette's history. There were simply too many fascinating events to depict, so how could I choose just one per decade? For example, could I focus on the devastating fire of 1868 and completely skip mention of the Civil War's effect on Marquette? I couldn't, and the more research I did about Marquette's history, the more stories I found that I wanted to tell. As I researched and began writing drafts for various scenes, I quickly realized how unwieldy the book was becoming, and finally, I decided it would need to be three books, which eventually became *Iron Pioneers, The Queen City*, and *Superior Heritage*, each just under 200,000 words. Even then, it was difficult to decide what to leave out.

In writing the series, I was inspired to make Marquette the overarching protagonist of the novels. While the trilogy's pages are filled with countless characters who span seven generations, ultimately, they compose the biography of the main character, the city of Marquette, with its supporting players being Upper Michigan's forests, Lake Superior, and the seasons.

As for trying to decide what to depict as a scene and what to leave out based on the plethora of historical events and fascinating details I had to choose from, I set the following three rules for myself:

1. The novel's scenes should never stray outside of Marquette County—I only broke that rule once in the second book when I showed Karl Bergmann's death in Calumet.

2. Every chapter must contain something significant about Marquette's history or culture.

3. Every chapter must develop the characters and through their development advance the plot.

Being a native of Marquette, I was also heavily inspired by the role that family and the passage of time play in one's life. I had grown up hearing stories about Marquette's past, especially from my grandfather, Lester White, and his brothers and sisters. After my grandfather's death, I became very interested in genealogy, and I learned that my ancestors came to Marquette the year the city was founded. I was actually a seventh generation Marquette resident on two branches of my mother's side. I began collecting family stories and thinking about how Marquette and its history had influenced my own family. For example, I would walk past where the Marquette Opera House had once stood, where my grandfather had proposed to my grandmother. I would mail packages at the Marquette Post Office that my grandfather had helped to build. I would drive past the First Methodist Church where my great-great-great-great grandfather, Basil Bishop, had been an early member and helped to found Marquette's first temperance society. Houses sprinkled all over Marquette's east side had been built by my great-grandfather, Jay Earle White. Another great-grandfather, John Molby, had worked at the Marquette Branch Prison. These family associations go on and on so that I have always felt connected to Marquette, its past and present, in so many ways; this sense of place and connection to the past heavily inspired so many of the scenes in The Marquette Trilogy, and my ancestors and relatives fill the pages, thinly disguised as many of the main characters.

I also was influenced by my great love of literature. I read widely as a child and teenager, and once I knew I wanted to write novels, I grew especially fond of the classics because I felt my best teachers would be the great novelists—Jane Austen, Charles Dickens, the Brontë sisters, Anthony Trollope, Nathaniel Hawthorne, Mark Twain, Margaret Mitchell, and so many more. Their novels were set in places far from Marquette—England, Boston, Atlanta, the Mississippi River—places I had never been to when I first read their books. However, I had been completely engrossed in their fictional worlds, so I felt strongly that if people would read books set in places with which they were unfamiliar, there was no reason why they wouldn't read books set in Upper Michigan, and therefore, there was every reason to create a literature for Upper Michigan.

I felt vindicated in this desire to create a true Upper Michigan literature when in my research I came across the following quote from Ralph D. Williams' *The Honorable Peter White*, a biography of one of Marquette's city fathers:

> The beginnings, therefore, of this great iron industry are historically important and are of interest to every citizen in the United States, for there is not a man or woman today living who has not been, directly or indirectly, benefited by the great mineral wealth of the Lake Superior country and the labor of winning it and working it into the arts.... Has it not the elements in it out of which to weave the fabric of the great American novel so long expected and so long delayed? For the story is distinctly American. Indeed there is nothing more distinctly American.

That passage eventually became the front quote to *Iron Pioneers*, and I feel it is the manifesto for The Marquette Trilogy. While I don't claim to have written the great American novel, I was determined to tell a very American story about the growth of a community that was a microcosm for any city in the country—a tale of pursuing the great American Dream, a tale of pioneers and immigrants and everyday hardworking people, with their successes and failures. At the same time, I would depict what made Marquette and Upper Michigan unique and special so people elsewhere would come to realize why this land was so extraordinary.

I was also very aware of the regional fiction of other areas that had preceded me, so as I wrote The Marquette Trilogy, I sought inspiration from reading all the regional novels I could, especially the works of Willa Cather. The front quote to *The Queen City* is from Cather speaking about her reasons for writing—a reason I could definitely identify with:

> I had searched for books telling about the beauty of the country I loved, its romance, and heroism and strength of courage of its people that had been plowed into the very furrows of its soil, and I did not find them. And so I wrote *O Pioneers!*

Ultimately, my choice of the title Iron Pioneers was both a tribute to those pioneers who first came to Marquette to begin its iron ore industry and a tribute to Willa Cather and her novel *O Pioneers!*

Finally, for the quote for Superior Heritage, I borrowed a passage from Helen Hooven Santmyer's novel *Farewell, Summer*:

> Solitary women like me, old men like Cousin Tune: in every day and time there have been many of us, clinging with all the strength of our memories to the old ways—old men and old maids who eye each other on meeting, and in that silent interchange promise to hold fast, by their futile stubbornness, in their own minds—who when they see the life they know not only doomed, but dead and very nearly forgotten, sit down alone to write the elegies.

I felt this quote fitting because as I wrote the novels, I realized how much Marquette had already changed from the town I had grown up in, and I wanted to capture that past so future generations would get a glimpse of the world I had known as a child. I was only about twenty-eight at the time, but I already felt I was part of Marquette's past.

And so, that is how The Marquette Trilogy came to exist. Today, the first book of the trilogy, *Iron Pioneers*, remains my most popular book, so I felt a special ten-year anniversary edition was deserved, and I thought a new edition could serve not solely as an anniversary celebration for the book but also as a celebration of how Upper Michigan literature has grown and flourished since I first set out to write about this wonderful region in 1987.

The advent of digital printing and the self-publishing revolution began about the same time I started writing The Marquette Trilogy. The year prior, in 1998, the Upper Peninsula Publishers and Authors Association was founded, which I joined in 2006 when *Iron Pioneers* was published. At the current time, I am the president of this organization and we have eighty members, all of whom are writing in or about Upper Michigan. I think that's a sign that we all felt the time had come, as James Joyce's Stephen Dedalus says about his own writing, "to forge in the smithy of my soul the uncreated conscience of my race," which is reflected in the creation of Upper Michigan literature. Indeed, we Yoopers are a people to ourselves, and we have a rich and vibrant history, a strong work ethic, and a closeness to Nature that few people in other areas share. We know what it is to endure economic hardships, blizzards, and lack of recognition by others; we also know what it is to live close to the land, to feel akin to trees and lakes and wildlife, and even if we leave the U.P., as we fondly call this peninsula, many of us feel haunted by the Great Lakes and the rugged landscape and long to return. And most importantly, we have a story—with many stories woven into it—that is rich and powerful and deserves to be shared with the world and preserved for future generations.

I, for one, am proud to be a regional author of Upper Michigan literature and even prouder to be one of its pioneers. I hope to live many more years and see it continue to grow and flourish, and I thank all my readers, whether or not they be Yoopers, for supporting me in what has always been my chosen vocation.

Tyler R. Tichelaar
Marquette, Michigan
January 1, 2016

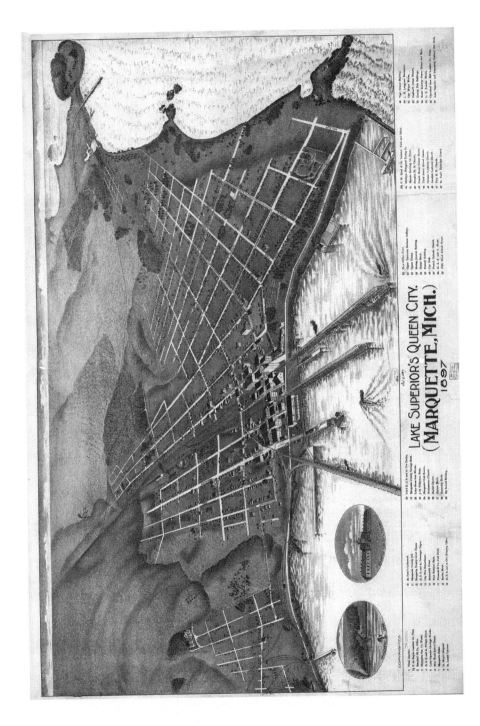

Lake Superior's Queen City.
(MARQUETTE, MICH.)
1897

Prologue
1671

For millions of years the land waited, unconscious of its waiting. Then came the glaciers. Massive ice sheets moved down from the Arctic and spread steadily farther and farther south over what would one day be the region called Michigan. The glaciers moved rapidly, pushing the mile thick ice into the earth and carving out the continent of North America. Only after tens of thousands of years did the great ice blanket begin to withdraw, and only eight thousand years before the birth of Christ, it left behind a large peninsula projecting out into newly carved lakes.

One day, this new land would be the Upper Peninsula of Michigan, but for now, it was a virgin, pristine country, untouched by man. Again the land waited, waited for people to cross the lakes and rivers that served as its borders. When they came, these people would discover a splendid and mighty forest, through which ran streams rich in fish, among whose trees hid deer, bear and squirrel, chipmunk and beaver, and deep beneath the earth was the mineral wealth of iron, gold, and copper. The people would claim the land's bountiful riches, but the land demanded a price in return—it protected itself with harsh winters that only the truly courageous men and women, those who admired Nature's magnificence, were willing to face. The climate would drive many a coward away, while many a true child of Nature would find here a richness of spirit surpassing all the earth's minerals.

In prehistoric times, this land may have had many visitors, but no record is left of them. First remembered are the Anishinabe, who called themselves "the People." They became the People of the land, claiming it as their own, not by government deeds, not by belief in property, but by their appreciation of this splendid wilderness, their respect for its stern strength, and their gratitude for its bounty.

Then came the white men, and with them they brought their religion, their Christianity, their belief in the one God. The white men told the People it was their own God who had created this magnificent wilderness land. The People, the Anishinabe, or the Ojibwa as the French would name them, the Chippewa as the English would mispronounce their French name, would largely come to accept the religious teachings of the white men. The Christian God was not dissimilar to the Great Spirit the People believed was Creator of the world. But they would find it hard to believe this precious land was not guarded by many spirits, spirits similar to what the Christians called guardian angels. The People believed there were spirits in the beasts and the berry bushes, in the clouds and the waterfalls, in the sun and the seas, in the rivers, the rocks, and the great oak trees. Here in this garden paradise, each branch of Nature was individually blessed. These guardian spirits hid themselves away from white men's eyes, but once in a great while, a white man might hear a spirit's voice mixed in with the wind, or he might feel a pleasing tingle as a water sprite brushed against him during a swim in a lake. When white men loved the land as well as did the People, the spirits welcomed, befriended, and protected them.

The white men and their religion came to this land in the seventeenth century of the Christian era. Among them came a Jesuit priest, a man short, strong, and devoted to spreading the word of God among the People. He found they had a strong faith, as strong as the beliefs of his own civilized French brothers and sisters. On this day, when our story begins, the Jesuit, the Black Robe, as the People called him, Father Marquette, as history has recorded his name, had come to the land with a couple of the People for his guides and a few French voyageurs who had traveled with him from Quebec. He had come to preach God's kingdom on earth, to convert the land and its people to Christianity.

The People held great festivities to greet the Black Robe, festivities culminating in celebration of the Mass. Surely, this day had seen the greatest conversion of the People in the New World. Hundreds from throughout the peninsula had journeyed to this central location along the shore of Lake Superior, the shore of Gitchee Gumee. They had come, the men and the women, the elders and the children, the chiefs and the lowliest members of the great People. Some four or five hundred of these new but devout Christians were present. They had traveled from over a hundred miles away, from all along the shores and even miles inland from the other Great Lakes. They had come by foot and by canoe to be present. Two hundred canoes lay along Lake Superior's beach, and each person brought in them was eager to attend the Mass.

The Jesuit felt truly blessed. He was thousands of miles from his native France, hundreds of miles even from Montreal and the last real outposts of civilized man. He had once been told the native people of this lake region were savages, but they had embraced him as one of their own, even as an elder to whom they showed great respect. Here as he never could have elsewhere, he was reaping God's plenty, bringing to the Mother Church the souls of hundreds who without him would never have heard the Gospel or received the sacraments. And how attentive the People were when he said Mass! Most of them did not understand his French tongue, much less the Mass's Latin words, but they had the faith of children, the innocent faith Christ had proclaimed necessary to enter the Kingdom of Heaven; the priest did not doubt these good people would enter that kingdom. Yet even he could not foresee their faithfulness in the retelling of this event in their legends for generations to come. Most of them would never see another Black Robe, neither would their children or grandchildren, but the stories of how this priest had loved them would be remembered until another would come, a hundred or more years from now, and that future servant of God would find the People still steadfast in their faith and longing to be baptized as once had been their forefathers by this honored Black Robe.

All seemed fruitful to Father Marquette this evening. He loved this faithful, goodhearted people, and he saw God present in their beautiful land. There was nothing in France to compare to this wilderness splendor; he admitted to this land's superiority even when he felt most homesick for his native French village.

"Come, we climb Tadosh," said an Ojibwa chief to the priest who rested upon the beach. Father Marquette took a second to translate the meaning of this request. The People wished to honor him for his kindness by showing him the splendid view of their land from the nearby mountaintop. Quickly a band of the Ojibwa gathered to form the excursion, and Father Marquette, joined by one of his voyageurs, accompanied them along the shore to the mountain called Tadosh.

It had been a warm, fatiguing day, but the Jesuit felt energized by the successful conversions he had made, and he could not refuse this gracious invitation. It was a long hike along the beach, and then a strenuous climb up the mountain called Tadosh. The mountain rose up, a towering granite summit nearly five hundred feet above Lake Superior. The overgrowth was so thick that the party had to travel in single file. The tree branches snapped in the Jesuit's face, and the bushes scratched at his long robe. Up the party climbed for half an hour, panting yet never resting. Fifty feet from the top, the trees almost disappeared and the soil turned into solid rock. One of the People offered Father Marquette his arm, but the Jesuit declined, determined to show his own strength; his many difficult journeys made this climb one of little effort. Jesting, he offered to carry the Ojibwa up on his back. Then smiling, they climbed up together, side by side, while the French voyageur followed.

Upon reaching the summit, Father Marquette found his efforts well repaid. He could see several islands lying spread out along the lakeshore, and to his right was Presque Isle, the most beautiful little peninsula on Lake Superior. Out across the lake the view was spectacular as the water gradually faded into the horizon; dark indigo blended into light shades of blue revealing shallow water that in the distance appeared like clouds with little islands poking up through them. The Black Robe imagined he was viewing Heaven spread before him among the cloud-like waters. For years he had been traveling on the Great Lakes, but at such moments as this one, he never failed to experience awe as the lakes changed hourly from being bathed in rays of sunlight to being darkened by overcast skies; each lighting revealed a new wonder upon the waters. Father Marquette had never seen the lake look so placid as today's cloudy appearance. What a contrast from the rolling waves he frequently experienced while plummeting over the water in his canoe. The beach was golden and warm while the water looked refreshing as its breezes blew inland, cooling the thick forests. Behind him, the Jesuit could see the towering pines, birches, maples and oaks that spread into the horizon. It was an uncharted region, a bountiful country reminiscent of the biblical promised land flowing with milk and honey. He saw that the bay would provide shelter and that it served as an outlet from the two nearby rivers. It would be an ideal settlement in years to come. He imagined his own French people would someday settle this land, and he hoped they would do so peacefully, sharing it with the People whom he loved.

The wind rustled through the leaves, like a whispering voice, almost like the voice of God uttering a blessing; silently, the Jesuit prayed the land would always know peace and fellowship among its inhabitants, whomever they might be.

"It is a beautiful country, isn't it, Varin?" he said to his voyageur friend.

Pierre Varin looked all about him, agreeing with the Jesuit. He was pleased to be in this good land with this good man. Like Father Marquette, he felt more at home here than in his native France.

"I do not know whether Heaven could be this beautiful," Varin replied, patting his friend on the back. "But come, Father, we should go so we can travel yet before nightfall."

The party descended the little mountain. They walked back to the lakeshore and the waiting canoes. The Jesuit paused to give a final blessing to the newly faithful Christian People while Pierre, his fellow voyageurs, and the Ojibwa guides prepared to leave.

As the canoes pushed off from the shore, Father Marquette could not know how well his prayer would be heard. Nor could he foresee that someday an important city would be built along this bay. The city would be remote from the troubles of the world, yet play an important role in the history of its nation. Its name would honor this holy man, and its people would bravely love this land as much as he had.

1849

The schooner swept over the stunning blue waves of Lake Superior. On board, Clara Henning looked across the water to the forests of Michigan's Upper Peninsula. All she had seen since the boat had left the little port of Sault Sainte Marie was mile after mile of water and wooded shoreline. As the wind lifted a chilling water spray off the lake, Clara reflected that there was nothing here but wilderness, miles and miles distant from roads, trains, and civilization. In a couple hours, the schooner would arrive at its destination, the new settlement of Worcester, Michigan—a handful of small, hastily constructed wooden buildings sheltered along a bay. Clara suspected this cramped schooner was the most comfort she would know for months to come.

Gerald had warned her about what their new home would be like, but at nineteen, she had let her youthful determination convince her she could overcome any obstacle and handle any hardship. Gerald had been determined to come here, and as his wife, she must follow. Back in Boston, the thought of settling in a new land had seemed a romantic adventure to share with her new husband. Now, despite the lush green trees, and the sandy golden beaches, she began to fear what wild animals or unfriendly Indians might lurk in those woods, and she sensed the loneliness to come of being so far from her family. All she now had was Gerald; she loved him, but she had only known him as a member of Boston society, not as the adventurer and entrepreneur he wished to become.

Clara looked across the deck at her handsome husband; he was engaged in conversation with Mr. Harlow, the founder of the new settlement. Clara admired Gerald's manly figure, its strength reassuring her she had made the right decision to come here. She had known, even before he proposed to her, that there could be no other man in her life; she would follow him wherever he led her, even though it meant abandoning the only world she knew, including her family and all the advantages of Boston society. She drew upon an inner strength formerly repressed by a world of tea party etiquette; she told herself to revel in this new freedom, to prepare herself to experience the greatest adventure of her life.

Three months ago, she had never dreamed of a life in the wilderness. She and Gerald had just then been engaged, with a wedding date set for mid-June. Clara had imagined herself continuing her role in Boston society as a wife and mother. But one May evening, just as the Wilson family finished dessert, Gerald had called with an unexpected announcement.

"In all fairness to Clara before the wedding, I wanted to let you know my future prospects have dramatically changed," Gerald had said, standing awkwardly as the family remained seated at the dining room table.

"Is there something wrong?" Mrs. Wilson had asked, fearing scandal or loss of fortune would deter her daughter's marriage.

"No, please think of this as an opportunity," Gerald had replied. "You may have heard that great deposits of iron have recently been discovered in Northern Michigan. My father has had some business dealings with a Mr. Harlow of Worcester, and he and a few other businessmen—a Mr. Edward Clarke and Mr. Waterman Fisher, also of Worcester, and a Mr. Robert Graveraet of Michigan, have proposed establishing a settlement on the south shore of Lake Superior to provide a harbor and to set up forges so iron ore can be shipped to the major industrial cities. My father wishes to be involved in these enterprises, and consequently, I'm going to the region to bring the plans to fruition."

"But when are you going?" Mrs. Wilson had asked. "We can't postpone the wedding after all the preparations we've made."

"No, it won't affect the wedding," Gerald had replied. "I won't leave until the end of July. What it does means is that Clara and I, if she'll still have me, will be moving to Michigan."

"Michigan!" said Mrs. Wilson, while Clara's grandmother looked astonished. Mr. Wilson was so surprised he lay down his dessert fork.

"I need to live there to oversee the business," Gerald had said. "My father and Mr. Harlow believe there's a fortune to be made in the iron industry—that whole area could develop into a great industrial empire to out rival any now existing in this country. It's an opportunity we cannot afford to pass up."

"Yes, I've heard there is great potential in that region," Mr. Wilson had said, always interested in business.

Mrs. Wilson, however, while she reaped the benefits of abundant money, was ignorant of the commercial details that produced her husband's wealth.

Gerald Henning's arguments made no impact on a woman who felt only the loss of her daughter and the social status planned for her.

"You cannot expect Clara to travel hundreds of miles from home to some wilderness," she said. "Why there must be savage Indians there! It wouldn't be safe. It's unthinkable. You're foolish even to think of going."

"Eveline," her husband reprimanded.

"Well, it is foolish," Mrs. Wilson repeated.

"There are Indians in the area," said Gerald. "They are Chippewa, and by all accounts, they're friendly to settlers. Clara has nothing to fear. I'll build her a good home, and while I can't give her all the advantages and niceties of Boston, I'll provide her with all necessities, and I'll care for her to the utmost of my being."

"I know you will, Gerald," Clara said, feeling safe whenever her lover was near.

"It would be beneath Clara's station," Mrs. Wilson said. Clara and her grandmother exchanged smiles; they both knew her mother's words would lead to a recital of the family history. "No member of the Wilson family would go trudging through the wilderness like some Indian squaw. And my own family, the Lytes, have been leaders of Boston society since before the Revolution. No one in this family would think of living such an existence. If my father were alive today, he would roll over in his grave at the mere thought."

"If he were alive," chuckled Mr. Wilson, "he wouldn't be in the grave to roll over."

Mrs. Wilson flashed indignant eyes at her husband. Generally, he gave way to her temper, but on matters of business, he would not be superseded, and Clara's financial interests were uppermost in his mind, even over concern for her physical safety or social mobility.

"Like Mrs. Wilson," he said, addressing Gerald, "I am concerned for Clara's welfare, and it will be difficult for us to have our only child so far from home, but she is an adult and capable of making her own decisions. If she agrees to the proposition, then you have our blessing."

Clara's heart beat heavily for a moment. She looked about the room, at the painting of her ancestor Governor Bradstreet on one end, on the other wall the painting of her Grandfather Lyte, who had made his fortune in shipping. Across from her was her mother's china—really her great-grandmother's—imported from France just before that country's revolution, locked up in the hutch cabinet like Marie Antoinette protecting herself from exposure to the everyday world. The cabinet itself was a great, heavy, polished mahogany piece, bought during her parents' honeymoon from the finest furniture manufacturer in New York City. Could she leave all these priceless possessions? When her parents were gone, would she regret if these items were not hers? But they were only things—nothing more. They were not life; they were not love; they would not keep her warm at night like Gerald's strong arms. Her heart still beating, she made her reply.

"I told Gerald I would be his wife, so I will go wherever he thinks best."

She was not without some inner hesitation, but once her words were spoken, she knew she would not change her mind. When Gerald's face lit with a tremendous smile, she felt confirmed in her decision.

"Clara, don't be foolish!" Mrs. Wilson had replied. "You don't want to live in the woods with a bunch of grimy miners and lumberjacks. And what about your children? How will they be educated there? They'll be deprived of all culture, and they'll never know their grandparents."

Clara felt confused. She simply wanted to go with Gerald. The thought of children had not been included in her decision, but secretly, she believed her own education had been a waste of time; what practical purpose was served by learning to play the piano or to write rhyming couplets? With Gerald, she might find real work to do, similar to the work so many women in Boston already did, but which she was forbidden to join in because of her social station. She did not know how to explain that she did not want her life to be an imitation of her mother's, but she knew she must leave before she suffocated in Boston's society.

"May I speak my mind?" Grandmother Lyte had then asked.

"Of course," said Mr. Wilson.

"I think Eveline is partially correct; it will be difficult for Clara to leave Boston and start a new life in a wilderness a thousand miles away. I can understand Eveline's fear of never seeing her grandchildren since Clara is my only granddaughter, and I will be sad to see her leave. But Eveline is wrong to think it beneath Clara's social station to make such a journey. That's just a lot of nonsense. It's true the Lytes are a prominent family in Boston with a long family heritage. But if we are to be proud of that heritage, we should embrace the courage of our ancestors, not become complacent." Mrs. Lyte's glowing face and succinct words recalled generations of family puritans and patriots who had struggled bravely, not just for the fancy china teapot on the dining room table, but for the freedom to choose a teapot or a log cabin or both.

"My grandfather," Mrs. Lyte continued, "did not say we couldn't defeat the British, though in his heart he may have feared it was true; like countless brave colonists, he fought for what he believed in so we could be Americans. And what of our ancestors who came before that? They came over on the *Arbella* to help found the Massachusetts Bay Colony in 1630. One of them was our ancestress, Anne Bradstreet. When she arrived in the New World, she wrote that she feared the wilderness, but she trusted in God and herself. She and her family had a dream of freedom, and they lived and fought for that dream everyday of their lives. In her poetry, we can read how she daily faced every adversity, from the death of loved ones to the burning of her house, but it did not break her trust in God. After the sacrifices of such ancestors, we cannot be cowards; we must carry on their work for the betterment of this country. If an adventure lies before Clara, and if her heart says another life will make her happier, then she should go with Gerald and my blessings shall go with them."

"Thank you, Grandmother," Clara had replied, her eyes tearing up to be so well understood by the dear old woman.

"I still don't think Clara will have a better life than here," grumbled Mrs. Wilson, but no one was listening to her now.

Gerald was asked to stay for dessert, and he remained long after to discuss his and Clara's future. Clara listened as he described the far away region that would be her home; she imagined it would be exciting to live in that wilderness land, to help build a new community, just as her ancestress, Anne Bradstreet, and so many others had done when they came to Massachusetts Bay.

That dinner conversation had been three months ago, but as Clara caught the first glimpses of the land where she would now live, she still did not regret her decision to marry Gerald; she was proud of her husband's courage to come here, even though he knew little about mining, or iron forges and blooming, or how to build a house and survive a winter in the wilderness. He had determination and intelligence, and those traits would provide a home for them. And Clara promised herself she would be not just a wife but a helpmate, doing whatever necessary for their survival and prosperity. She still had her doubts, but she would not let fear overcome her resolve; before this strange land could defeat her, she would befriend it.

"Clara, there it is!" Gerald exclaimed. She turned in the direction he pointed as he came and linked his arm in hers. She dimly made out a few logs floating in the water; in another minute, they were discernible as a small dock. Then between the trees a couple wooden structures became visible.

"There's Worcester," said Mr. Harlow, joining them on deck.

"I'm sure your wife will be pleased to see you," Clara told him. Mr. Harlow had met them in Sault Sainte Marie, where he had come to fetch more supplies and then return to the settlement. Meanwhile, his wife and mother-in-law had traveled on to the settlement alone and taken up residence in an old fishing hut Mr. Harlow had found to serve as their first house. Clara already hoped the Harlow women would be her friends; she would need the tender sound of female voices in this rugged land, and if Mrs. Harlow and her mother could do so much on their own, Clara knew she could succeed with Gerald's support.

"Yes, I've missed my wife," said Mr. Harlow, "but now we'll be together, ready to begin our new life here."

The schooner turned into the bay and drew up to the dock, from which rose a little uphill path surrounded by lush green trees that stretched miles and miles inland to create a near impenetrable forest. On the dock was Mrs. Harlow, waiting for her husband to step off from the boat. Clara and Gerald waited politely as the long separated husband and wife embraced. Then Mr. Harlow made introductions all around. Twenty people—half the community—had shown up to greet the boat, enough people nearly to fill the dock. Clara felt overwhelmed and immediately forgot everyone's name, except that of Mrs. Wheelock, who had just started a boarding house.

"You must be tired," Mrs. Wheelock said. "Come with me. I'll make you a good supper and then you can go to bed early. There'll be plenty of time in the morning to find your plot of land and start building a home."

Clara and Gerald followed the kind woman to her little wooden structure where they would stay until Gerald had built them a house. After supper, the newlyweds went to their chamber, a corner of a room with sheets for walls. There were a few other boarders, but Clara was so tired she simply undressed, then waited for Gerald. When he climbed into bed, she cuddled into his arm. She loved that he already smelled like the surrounding pine trees. She was exhausted yet content to have arrived here, and in the morning, she told herself she would be well rested and prepared to face the opportunity before them.

When Clara woke, it took her a few seconds to remember she was no longer on a boat, or a train, or in her comfortable bed back in Boston. Above her was a wooden roof with a crack that revealed the sky. She crawled out of bed and onto boards laid across a dirt floor. Since Gerald was already gone, she feared she had slept later than she should; from the crack in the ceiling, she could tell it was already daylight. Last night, she had been relieved to have a roof over her head and a bed to sleep in, but now this dingy little partition of a room made her hope Gerald would not be long in building her a decent house.

Last night, she had hardly more than glanced at the other buildings in the village. She had noted the rough exterior of the Harlows' house and that of Mr. Harlow's assistant. Both buildings had been rundown fishing huts moved from farther down the lakeshore to serve as temporary residences. Clara was surprised to find herself envious that Mrs. Harlow had her own house, no matter how dilapidated its condition. Even if at this moment, Gerald were purchasing them a plot of land to build on, she knew she could not expect more than a small one-room cabin this first year. Winters here were supposed to be long and harsh and to arrive early, so Gerald would have to build soon and spare no time for fancy details if they were to have a shelter before the first snowfall. It was August, but as Clara emerged from her makeshift bedroom, she could already imagine the fierce winter winds.

She found Mrs. Wheelock in the kitchen cooking breakfast.

"Your husband went to look around the village, but he told me to let you sleep," said Mrs. Wheelock. "I know how tiring the long journey here can be."

Clara thanked her hostess as Mrs. Wheelock placed eggs and bread before her. She wished Gerald were here, but she understood he had work to do. Mrs. Wheelock said he had promised to return by noon, and he had suggested she call on Mrs. Harlow that morning.

"I'll visit her as soon as I finish eating," Clara replied. Mrs. Wheelock planned to go wash up the dishes, but Clara asked her landlady to stay and talk while she ate, in return that she help her with the dishes. Clara had never washed a dish in her life, but she was not so spoiled that she did not understand she would have no servants here as she had in Boston.

Mrs. Wheelock gladly sat down to rest a few minutes. She told Clara how quickly her boarding house had filled with guests, and that she had her hands full cooking and doing laundry for the inmates. She was thankful to have a female guest if only to have someone to talk with. Clara had nearly finished her breakfast when a young man stepped into the house. He was about her age; Clara assumed he was Mrs. Wheelock's son until he introduced himself.

"Hello, I'm Peter White," he said. "I'm a boarder here. You must be Mrs. Henning."

"Yes, I'm pleased to meet you," she replied, taking his offered hand.

"Peter is one of the youngest and most active members of our settlement," said Mrs. Wheelock. "In fact, he helped to build the first dock. Peter, why don't you tell Mrs. Henning about it?"

Peter laughed as Clara prepared herself for a humorous tale.

"Well, any city needs a good dock," began Peter, "and we were determined ours would be one of the best. Captain Moody was in charge, and in no time at all, he had us hauling entire trees into the water and piling them crossways until we had built two tiers from the lake bottom up level with the water. Then we covered it all with sand and rocks. In just two days, we had the dock finished. We believed we had accomplished the first step in transforming Worcester into a future industrial metropolis. We imagined a hundred years from now our descendants would look upon the dock and praise us for our ingenuity."

Clara smiled at Peter's self-mocking tone.

"Next morning, imagine our surprise when we discovered one of Lake Superior's calmest days had been enough to wash the dock away. Not a single rock or log was left behind to mark where it had been. The sand was so smooth you never would have known the dock existed. How easily man's grandest schemes succumb to Nature's power."

There was a moment's pause while Peter smirked. Then Mrs. Wheelock scolded, "Peter, be fair. Finish the story."

Peter grinned but obeyed.

"The entire episode was so comically tragic I could not help but feel some record of it should remain for the city's future annals. I took a stick and wrote on the sand, 'This is the spot where Capt. Moody built his dock.' Well, Captain Moody took one look at that and wiped it away with his feet. He was apparently not as amused as I was, and he told me I would be discharged from his service at the end of the month."

Clara had been smiling, but the story's conclusion saddened her.

"What a shame. You didn't mean any harm by it, and it was as much your work as his that failed."

"I was sorry to offend him," Peter confessed, "but he hasn't dismissed me yet. Either he quickly got over his temper or he's forgotten about it. I'm certainly not going to remind him."

"I'm sure Captain Moody has forgiven you by now," said Mrs. Wheelock. "He realizes what a blessing you've been lately. Mrs. Henning, I don't wish to scare you, but there's been an outbreak of typhoid fever here. Nearly everyone has now recovered, so there shouldn't be anything to worry about, but we can all thank Peter for his hard work. He has bravely cared for the sick, even bathing them at risk to himself."

Peter ignored the praise to explain further. "We recently had a large number of foreigners arrive in the settlement. Mr. Graveraet brought them up by boat from Milwaukee to work. Most of them are German, but there are a few Irish and French among them. Almost all of them got typhoid on the trip here and several died before they arrived. It's a sad situation, so I did what I could for them. Everyone has been taking turns helping."

"It isn't as bad as we first feared," Mrs. Wheelock told Clara. "We thought it might be cholera; that was enough to scare the local Indians into deserting the area, but then Dr. Rogers determined it was only typhoid, though that's bad enough."

"There's only a handful still recovering," Peter added. "And no one else has contracted it, so it can't be contagious anymore. I'm sure it's nothing to be concerned over, but we could use a little more help caring for the sick."

"Oh," said Clara, terrified at the thought, yet anxious to do her share of work in the new community; she knew she would need friends to lend her a hand in future hardships. "I'd be happy to help with the nursing."

"We wouldn't want you to become ill too," warned Mrs. Wheelock.

"Oh, but I can't let those people suffer if I can help them," Clara said to mask her fears.

"I could show you the building we're using for a hospital," Peter offered. "Then you can decide if you want to help."

"All right, I should be free this afternoon," Clara replied, "but I promised to call on Mrs. Harlow this morning."

Peter agreed to come fetch her after dinner and thanked her in advance for her help; Clara felt a sudden fondness for this young man who seemed so bright and capable. She did not believe even typhoid could lessen his liveliness.

After Peter rushed off, Clara helped Mrs. Wheelock wash up the breakfast dishes. She also inquired more into Peter's history.

"Oh, Peter is quite an adventurer," replied the landlady. "He's been all over the Great Lakes working on boats, doing various types of work."

"How old is he?" asked Clara.

"Only eighteen," said Mrs. Wheelock, "but he's already an old timer in terms of knowing this country. His family is from New York, but when he was nine, they moved to Green Bay, Wisconsin. Then when he was fifteen, he basically ran away from home and went to Mackinac Island; ever since, he's been exploring the Great Lakes and working at whatever he can find. Last spring, Mr. Graveraet hired him to help with the iron company, and he's been living here since."

"What an adventurer," Clara said. Even Gerald's courage in coming to this region seemed small beside a fifteen year old boy traveling all over these dangerous lands.

Once the breakfast dishes were finished, Mrs. Wheelock went to start the laundry before she needed to prepare lunch. Clara decided to act on her promise to visit the Harlows. Mrs. Wheelock pointed the way to their dilapidated hut; then Clara started down the path through the little settlement. Along the way, she glanced at the tall, unfamiliar trees that surrounded the few scattered buildings. She had never before seen so many trees stretching for so many miles. She wondered what ferocious beasts might lurk in those woods. Even in the forests of Massachusetts, it would only be a mile or two until a person saw a house or farm, but here one could walk for days without seeing another human being. Worse, a bear might be encountered. Frightened by the thought, Clara scurried to the Harlows' hut, wishing someone were in sight in case of danger.

She found Mrs. Harlow and her mother, Mrs. Bacon, occupied with sorting the new supplies Mr. Harlow had brought from Sault Sainte Marie. After introductions, Clara's first remark was about how nervous she felt to be outside alone, but Mrs. Bacon assured her she was perfectly safe. "No one will harass you here, and we aren't established enough to worry about such social proprieties as a woman walking without her husband. You're as safe here as on the streets of Boston."

"But are there any Indians nearby?" Clara asked.

"Yes, but the Chippewa are perfectly friendly," Mrs. Harlow added. "They've been very kind to us since we arrived a few weeks ago."

"Olive, tell her about your first meeting with a Chippewa," laughed Mrs. Bacon.

"Oh," Olive laughed. "My first morning here, I was determined to see everything I possibly could about my new home. I stepped out my front door and practically the first thing I saw was a wigwam. I'd never seen one before, and I was just so curious it never suggested itself to my brain that it might be someone's home. So I went over and opened up the blanket door, and to my amazement saw two squaws. At first I was surprised, and a little frightened, but they smiled and giggled, and then I giggled back and retreated."

"I would have been terrified!" Clara gasped. "You're lucky they weren't male Indians."

"Oh, the male Indians are just as kind as the women," replied Mrs. Harlow. "They've already assisted us a great deal. Chief Marji Gesick has been very kind by stopping to inquire how we are all coming along, and Charley Kawbawgam has an Indian village not far away on the Carp River. He's been showing the men the best hunting and fishing grounds, and some white men are even staying in his lodge house. Granted, we've only been here about a month, but so far, there's been no need to worry, and our hearts are strong. Now that my husband has brought us some more supplies, we should have little trouble getting by for several months. I don't think it's going to be easy, but I feel this little settlement will grow and prosper faster than one might suspect."

"Yes," said Mrs. Bacon, "the men had the dock built in just three days, and the sawmill and forge should be finished before winter arrives. It may not be until next year that we really become a businesslike town, but it will happen soon enough."

Clara smiled, but she was presently more concerned about the settlement's safety than its prosperity.

"I can't believe how this country is changing," added Mrs. Bacon. "I was born just about the time President Jefferson made the Louisiana Purchase, and since then the country has more than doubled in size. When I was a child, no one ever would have imagined Michigan becoming a state, and here it's already been one for a dozen years. Just imagine, Mrs. Henning, how much this town will have grown by the time you're my age."

"Yes," said Clara, "but I'm afraid it will be a lot of work along the way."

"Hard work is what we're put on this earth for," replied Mrs. Bacon. "Besides, we have it easier now than any of our forefathers ever did, and after how they struggled to make this nation what it is today, we have to carry on the tradition of that hard work."

Clara recalled her grandmother uttering similar sentiments. She thought again of her ancestress, Anne Bradstreet, trembling upon arrival in the New World, only to become a famous poetess and one of the first ladies of the land, daughter, wife, and sister to colonial governors. Clara wondered whether someday she might equally be remembered as a pioneer of this rugged place. If the iron ore recently discovered made them all as rich as predicted, and Worcester grew as large as Boston, she might delight her mother by becoming a leader of Worcester society.

But Clara had not come to gain wealth or social position. She reminded herself she had come to support her husband, and to prove she had the courage to surmount challenges rather than settle for the dull social rituals of Boston. For the first time, she felt excited to be living along the shores of Lake Superior. Her travel fatigue was lifting, and she felt anxious to see the rest of her new home, despite what dangers might exist in the forests. So Mrs. Harlow and Mrs. Bacon could return to their work, she soon excused herself.

"I think I'll go for a walk along the lake before Gerald returns at noon."

"Go ahead," said Mrs. Harlow. "You might as well enjoy your first day here."

"Yes, I told young Mr. White I would go to the hospital this afternoon to help."

Mrs. Bacon and Mrs. Harlow exchanged approving glances. Clara's heart glowed inside her—she had been afraid people would think her some frail young miss from high society, but already she felt she was proving herself.

As she stepped out of the wooden hut, she scanned the other log cabins under construction. A few wigwams and a lodge house were in the distance; she wondered whether Indians resided in them or had white men taken possession. Scarcely enough buildings existed to qualify as a village. She looked down to the lake where the lone dock stood. The schooner had already disappeared from sight, leaving no chance to escape. Lake Superior stood before her—the only source of communication with the outside world—so large she could not see Canada across it. How long before another ship would come, before ships would come regularly? It might be years before there was a railroad or even paved streets, before there would even be stores in which to buy trinkets, or cloth, or even food. There wasn't even a butcher—Gerald would have to hunt for their meat, and they would have to plant their own vegetables. She wondered how much land they would have to plant to feed themselves. Mr. Harlow had told Gerald sixty-three acres had been purchased for the village to expand upon, but only a few acres were now cleared. She could not imagine the settlement ever growing enough to cover that much land. The trees would only encroach back in. All around her were towering pines, oaks, and maples. So many trees—a giant unexplored forest all around, full of mystery, perhaps horror.

"Clara!"

She turned to see Gerald walking toward her with Mr. Harlow. He was beaming.

"I've found the perfect place for our house. A few of the other men have agreed to help build it, and when they heard I had a wife, they said we could raise our roof first, and then I can help them later. We should have our own shelter within the week."

"That's good," Clara smiled. "Then I'll have a place to put my china."

"More than that," said Gerald, "we'll have a home, and I'll fill it with homemade furniture. Isn't it exciting, Clara? It's a whole new world for us."

She hesitated to reply, but Gerald's enthusiasm won her over; he was so free from self-doubt, so charismatically able to make others believe in him; she believed in him. His confidence was what made him most attractive to her. If they did not survive here, it would not be through the fault of this brave man she loved.

Clara took his hand.

"It's a fine land, Gerald. I'm sure we'll be happy here."

Mr. Harlow smiled in recognition of the same courage his own wife possessed. Maple leaves rustled in the breeze, as if confirming Clara's words. Gerald once more felt he had made the right choice in his bride, in this brave, beautiful young woman.

During lunch at the boarding house, Clara introduced her husband to Peter and mentioned she would be visiting the hospital that afternoon. Gerald was displeased by this news, thinking his kindhearted wife too delicate to expose herself to sickness. After all, she had been raised in the lap of luxury, had never known any hardship; while many hard days were before them, he wished to shelter and protect her whenever possible.

"I don't think you should go, Clara dear," he said.

"Gerald, why not?"

"I don't want you to overstrain yourself. We've had a long journey here, and I think you should rest this afternoon. You'll need your strength for the work ahead."

If she were in Boston, Clara would have deferred to her husband's wishes, but here she could not succumb to such social proprieties. She would not sit back while others labored, and Gerald had to realize that from the start. If they were to survive here, she had to familiarize herself immediately with all the community's needs.

"Dear, you're not resting today," she replied. "Besides, it can't hurt me simply to visit the hospital and meet some of the other settlers."

"I'm just afraid that if you wear yourself out, you'll be susceptible to disease," he replied.

"Oh, Gerald," Clara dismissed his worries. "Mr. White says the epidemic is over and the patients are no longer contagious. I'll be fine. I promise I won't stay long."

When Gerald began to curl his lip in surprise at his wife's dissension, Peter boldly entered the marital dispute.

"I assure you it's perfectly safe, Mr. Henning. I've been nursing the sick for several days without becoming ill; nor have I passed the sickness on to anyone here."

"That's true," said Mrs. Wheelock.

"I promise I'll only stay a short while, Gerald," Clara continued. "Then I'll come home and rest before helping Mrs. Wheelock with supper."

Gerald felt he should object again. They were paying Mrs. Wheelock for room and board, so why should his wife help her like a common maid? Yet he was proud of Clara's enthusiastic spirit. She was obviously determined to have her own way; in one sentence, she had appeased him by promising to rest, yet added to her demand to visit the hospital by offering to help Mrs. Wheelock. Gerald wished his mother-in-law could see Clara visiting a hospital and working in a boarding house; the droll thought won Gerald over.

Mr. Harlow now entered the boarding house; he had promised to spend that afternoon helping Gerald find lumber for the Hennings' new home.

"I'll be with you in just a moment, Mr. Harlow," Gerald promised, swallowing the last of his coffee and rising from the table. "Very well, dear. You go ahead, but don't tire yourself out. I'll see you this evening. Take good care of her, Mr. White."

Realizing her victory, Clara flashed Gerald a radiant smile. She was determined to be her husband's partner in their marriage, not to be subservient to him, but neither would she rule over her husband as her mother ruled her father. As for Gerald, he admired his wife all the more in her beautiful glow of triumph. Were it not improper before all the others, he would have kissed her right then. Instead, he wished his table companions a pleasant afternoon and departed.

"Are you ready to go, Mrs. Henning?" Peter asked. Clara fetched her bonnet, then joined him outside.

Ten minutes later, she found herself entering the little building that had been rapidly constructed to serve as a hospital when the typhoid crisis broke. She was surprised to think anyone could get well here when the building looked as if it would not stand for long; she could imagine winter's freezing gusts creeping through cracks in the walls; she hoped all the patients would be long recovered before that fierce season arrived.

"I need to help bathe a couple of the patients," Peter said as they entered. "I've been bathing them in cold water. I didn't know what else to do, and Dr.

Rogers was too ill to instruct me, but he says I've helped save many lives by doing so. Only a few are still ill, but they've entered the recovery stage. Still, I wouldn't advise you to follow me when I visit a couple of them."

"Oh," said Clara, disappointed to be separated from her guide, although she understood he had work to do.

"Let me introduce you to that couple over there," Peter offered, pointing toward a woman sitting beside her husband's bedside. "Many of the patients are German immigrants, and they only speak broken English, but this couple, the Bergmanns, speak English fairly well because the wife is Irish. Mrs. Bergmann is about our age, so perhaps you ladies will find something in common."

Clara recalled her mother's many complaints about the horrid, dirty Irish who had flooded into Boston, taking over the city, and crowding its streets. They were Catholics and uneducated, and Clara's mother thought them little better than the dirt they used to grow their potatoes. But Clara reminded herself that in this little settlement, if everyone were to survive, there could be no social class distinctions. "It's thoughtful of you, Peter, to think I might want a female friend my own age."

"Come then; I'll introduce you," he said, leading her across the room.

Mr. Bergmann was sitting up in bed, while his wife sat beside him, attempting to feed him some broth. Upon seeing Peter, both husband and wife broke into smiles.

"Mr. and Mrs. Bergmann, allow me to introduce Mrs. Gerald Henning. Mrs. Henning and her husband just arrived last night with Mr. Harlow."

Mrs. Bergmann extended her hand to Clara, while her husband nodded a polite welcome, his arms still too weak to be lifted.

"Hello," said Mrs. Bergmann, "please call me Molly. It's nice to see another woman brave enough to come here."

"I'm Clara. Actually, I'm surprised by how many women have come here," Clara replied, shaking Molly's hand.

Clara knew her mother would disapprove of her adopting a first name basis with a foreigner, but Clara felt independence surging in her, a desire to rebel against her mother and all the old constricting social rituals she had learned. Each hour, she reaffirmed that she had made the right decision to travel to this rugged, distant land.

"I think you women stronger than we menfolk," Mr. Bergmann remarked. Clara noted his English was better than she had expected.

"I understand you are from Germany, Mr. Bergmann?"

"Saxony," he corrected. "I come to America last year to work. My country have bad political problems, so I no stay there. Safer here, and here better chance to make money. I meet my pretty wife when I get here, so am glad I come."

"Did you meet here in Worcester?" asked Clara.

"Oh no," laughed Molly, "but we're still newlyweds. Fritz and I met in Boston last Christmas, and then we got married in March when he decided to go to Milwaukee where he had some German cousins. My family is from Ireland. We came to this country a few years ago because of the potato famine there."

"Then you are still newlyweds," said Clara. "I'm one myself. My husband and I were just married in July before we began the journey here. And we're both from Boston."

"We'll have to help each other raise new families in this wilderness land," Molly smiled.

"Yes," Clara replied. With so many friendly, kind people, Worcester would be a good place to raise her and Gerald's children.

"But you must miss Boston?" said Molly.

The two women discussed familiar places in Boston, but in the end, Clara confessed she did not miss her native city. Then the three of them discussed their journeys to this new land. Clara suggested the journey to Worcester from Boston, while difficult, must have been nothing compared to Molly's journey a few years earlier from Ireland to America. Molly agreed but appeared reluctant to speak of Ireland. "I try not to think about that," she said. "The future is the only thing worth thinking about." Fritz drifted to sleep during the conversation, but the women continued to chat, each relieved to find someone of her own age and gender with whom to discuss her dreams and anxieties about this new land. After an hour, when Peter came to fetch her, Clara promised Molly she would visit again the next day. Already she felt they were friends.

For the next several days, Gerald labored to build the small cabin that would serve as his and Clara's home during their first Upper Michigan winter. The Hennings had been warned the winters here would be cold and severe, if not worse than those in New England; Clara shuddered to think of such a winter without all the comforts of Boston, but Gerald told her they would not lack for heat when surrounded by such thick forests of birch, pine, oak and maple to use for firewood. Gerald was fortunate to receive help from the other men in building his cabin, and he helped them finish their shelters before the first winter snow flew. Meanwhile, Clara continued to help Mrs. Wheelock prepare meals, to visit the Harlows and Bergmanns, and to assist at the hospital. Mr. Harlow occupied himself in supervising the construction of a sawmill and forge, as well as building a larger home for his family; this house would include a large single room in which the community could hold church and village meetings. By the second week, Clara had met everyone in the little village of Worcester and even memorized their names. She enjoyed the closeness of the friendly settlers, so different from the vacant, unfamiliar faces of the thousands she had constantly seen on the streets of Boston. Realizing her own integral role in the community gave her a sense of belonging and importance she had never felt before. The pioneer spirit of these brave settlers remained cheerful as they watched autumn come with its burst of magnificent colors; such beauty was a reminder of winter's approach, but it also confirmed what a fine land they had chosen.

By mid-September, the Hennings' cabin was finished. Clara could scarcely restrain her pleasure at finally being mistress of her own home. It was a small house—only two rooms that could have fit inside her mother's Boston parlor—but it was as fine a house as any in the village. On a brilliant fall morning, with sunshine breaking through the trees and onto the new kitchen floor, Gerald brought Clara to her new home and insisted on carrying her over the threshold. Once through the door and then back on her feet, Clara took to admiring her husband's workmanship in every detail from the wooden door to the window frames. Then unexpectedly, she was overcome by queasiness and bolted back outside.

Gerald ran after her. He found her behind the house, bent over and making unladylike noises.

"Clara, what's wrong? Are you ill?" Instantly, he blamed himself. How could he have consented to let Clara nurse at the hospital? For that matter, how could he have brought her to this wilderness land? And this house—why it was nothing but a shack! He could not expect his precious wife to survive in this savage place. He did not even deserve her when he had been so thoughtless regarding her welfare. "Clara, what's wrong? Please, answer me," he begged.

He was close to tears by the time she lifted her head and wiped her beautiful lips with her handkerchief. "Clara, is it—the typhoid?"

"No, Gerald," she smiled, despite her queasiness. "I think you're going to be a father."

"What?" He was too worried to understand. "A father? A—you mean—a child?"

"Yes. I've suspected it for days now, but I wanted to be sure before telling you."

"But are you all right? Do you feel well otherwise?"

"I believe such sickness is natural," she replied.

"You have to see Dr. Rogers right away."

"There's no rush. I'm sure I'll be fine. But I will stay away from the hospital, so I don't endanger the baby. Everyone has recovered from the typhoid, so I don't imagine there's anything to worry about, but I'll be careful from now on."

"Come inside the house and sit down," Gerald urged. "Let me carry you. You should drink some water."

"I'm fine, Gerald. The feeling passes after a few minutes. I can walk."

"A baby," he repeated, taking her arm and leading her back inside. He sat down in their only chair, then pulled her to him. "Come, sit on my lap. A baby! What a splendid start to our life here. Clara, I love you."

And this time, he did kiss her. No one was watching, but he would not have cared if anyone were.

As the autumn evenings grew cooler, Clara was glad to be in her own home, no matter how small compared to her parents' brick colonial house back in Boston. She was sure she was happier here than her mother had ever been. She had great pride in her little home, and great respect for the strong man who had built it and assisted in building so many others. The sawmill and the forge were being raised, and a meeting house established, and with each pounding of the men's relentless hammers, the wilderness was being pushed back to reveal a substantial little village. Already noticeable changes had occurred, and by next year, more people were sure to come and make it a true town.

Clara's major source of happiness this season was the child growing in her womb. She would be mother to the first child born in the settlement, and already she could imagine the pleasure of showing this child the rich, beautiful land its parents had chosen. Here her child would roam, free to explore the world in ways Clara had never imagined possible amid the crowded city streets of her childhood. As precursor to the long summer walks she planned to take with her little boy—she wanted a boy for Gerald's sake—she had begun to roam along the lakeshore or to venture for an hour or two into the thick yet inviting forests. She usually walked alone without hesitation; she never went so far she could not have shouted for Gerald to come to her rescue. She had not yet seen a bear or wolf, and the occasional deer would flee at her approach. She felt no fear of the local Indians who had been nothing but friendly to the settlers. She did not know any of the Chippewa personally, but Charley Kawbawgam was a familiar sight around town. She knew Kawbawgam had provided shelter for many of the settlers in his lodge house until they could build their own homes.

Clara believed these afternoon walks would be beneficial to the baby; her excursions kept her spirits up as she took in the immense beauty of this land along this marvelous blue lake. She had never understood the Nature worship poems she had read in school, but she realized that growing up in Boston, she had had little experience with Nature save for an occasional weekend excursion to the country. Now in this silent forest, far from sound or sight of another human being, she learned how a solitary hour with Nature can rest the spirit and restore peace to the soul. Here amid all this beauty, she could praise God in a way she had never done in a Boston church. Nor had she ever seen such a feast for the eyes as she saw that autumn. The trees were rich in reds, oranges, purples, yellows, browns, greens and every shade in between, often with multiple colors upon the same leaf. She learned the names and distinctive shapes and leaves of each tree—maple, oak, birch, pine, evergreen. Many a New England autumn she had seen, but never had she known acre after acre of color. When the leaves began to fall, Clara was overcome with childish joy, and reveling in her freedom, she danced between the trees, trying to catch a falling leaf for good luck. She caught many leaves that October; in the afternoons, she would come home with a collection of colors to cheer her plain little house, and she would arrange them in the single china vase she had brought from Boston.

Gerald was astonished by his wife's wholehearted embrace of her new life. And while Clara had always been beautiful, now a deeper redness marked her cheeks, perhaps from the cold autumn weather, but more likely from her sheer pleasure in this new land. Since they had arrived, he had not seen her put on the face powder or cosmetics she had worn in Boston, and she had quickly dismissed her jewelry as simply cumbersome while she worked; it was pointless to wear silk or bombazine when carrying pails of water or placing wood on the fire, and not wanting her frilly laces to tear on forest bushes, she took up a more modest dress that made her appear more capable and ultimately more attractive to Gerald. When she decided that curling her golden locks was a waste of time, he did not disagree with her, but told her he liked her hair mussed, as when she took her bonnet off after a walk in the woods, and when she sweated over the fire to cook supper and found her husband would still kiss her, she wondered what had ever made women resort to so many false behaviors to attract a man. But Gerald knew most other women, especially those expecting, would have refused to work in this rugged environment, and so he was well pleased with her.

As winter approached, however, Gerald began to worry about the coming baby. When the child would be born in June, they would have little medical help. Dr. Rogers was quite capable, but he lacked many of the fine medical instruments available back East. Gerald knew nothing about childbirth, so his ignorance made him overprotective; he worried less that Clara was active than that she might be upset by anything. When November arrived and the village inhabitants began to fear the approach of winter, he warned his neighbors not to voice their concerns to Clara, and when town meetings were held, he insisted Clara stay home to rest.

Winters in Michigan's Upper Peninsula can demand herculean survival efforts, and the tiny village knew its chances were far more grim than usual. In November, the last expected supply ship failed to arrive; when weeks passed without word of it, the settlers feared there would not be enough food to support them through the winter. People began to talk about butchering the livestock while others suggested a party be formed to snowshoe to Green Bay, a hundred and eighty miles south, to bring back whatever supplies could be carried. During these anxious days, Clara remained unaware that a desperate situation was developing.

Never had Clara seen so much snow. New England was famous for its severe winters, but Clara was stunned by this powerful wind whipping across Lake Superior to drop a foot of snow at a time. Boston might receive as much snow as Worcester, but Boston was so large its buildings blocked the wind and limited the level of snow in the streets. With so few buildings in Worcester, the snow piled up steadily, then blew into enormous drifts. Clara pitied Gerald and the other men, who now added to their regular daily workloads an hour or two of shoveling, just to carve out paths so they could walk to each other's cabins. Yet Clara delighted in the dazzling whiteness of her new home. It was like living in a fantastic new land of make-believe. Snow blankets covered the hills and trees, and even wedged between the boards of the houses until the buildings looked as if they had white stripes. The lake was placid, too cold to stir, and in the mornings there was often crystal thin ice upon it. At other times, the waves roared, keeping her awake at night. The winds were bitterly cold, and she had to protect her fingers and face from frostbite, but it was always a delight to come indoors to a cozy fire. She doubted anything could be more comforting than the crackling sound of logs in the fireplace when outside fierce winds whipped through the trees and shook the shutters of the house's two windows. At night, the Hennings were content with the peaceful quiet of being alone together, warm and safe from the storm's fury. Then they would sit and read a book out loud, or just hold hands while they listened to the wind and dreamt of the baby to come.

Clara did feel Gerald worried too much. She was almost relieved one day in December when he came down with a bad cold and finally had to stay home to rest. It was a good day to be sick; the wet snow that morning was too miserable to walk in and too heavy to shovel. Gerald slept through the morning. After lunch, he sat up to read for an hour; then went to lie down again. The snow let up by late afternoon, and when the sun began to peek through the clouds, it created a blinding reflection off the freshly fallen ice crystals. Clara was sewing and gazing out at the splendid scene when she saw Molly Bergmann trudging a path to the Hennings' door. Clara was glad to see her friend, but she could not imagine why Molly would clump through unshoveled streets just to visit.

"Molly, what is it?" she asked, opening the door and extending her hand to help pull her friend in over the foot of snow packed up in front of the door.

"Is Gerald here? I need to talk with him."

Clara was surprised that another woman would ask for her husband.

"Why?" she asked.

"It's important. Is he here?"

"Yes," said Clara, "but he's sleeping. He isn't feeling well."

"Fritz is sick, too," said Molly. "He can't seem to get over the weakness left from the typhoid. Men think being sick means they don't have to work, but it's never stopped me. Anyway," she said, brushing snow from her dress, "a town meeting is being held this evening. Gerald had better come if he can. It's important."

"I'm surprised there'd be a meeting with all this snow," said Clara. "Can't it wait until tomorrow?"

"There won't be many tomorrows left if we don't do something," said Molly. Gerald had asked her not to tell Clara about the village's lack of supplies, but Molly's own fear now overcame her; she had known the horror of starving before, and having a sick husband only frightened her more.

"What do you mean?" Clara asked.

"I think you better wake up Gerald," Molly repeated.

Clara saw the desperation in her friend's eyes; thinking better of asking for an explanation, she went to wake her husband. Gerald, however, had woken when Molly entered, and when Clara asked him if he were keeping something from her, he crawled out of bed, took her hand, and led her back to the kitchen.

"It'll be all right, Clara," he said, but the haggard look in his eye made her doubt it would be.

Since Gerald had made two more chairs in the past month, one for each of them, including the future baby, they both could sit down with Molly at the table.

Gerald explained to Clara the extent of the crisis. The boat intended to bring the village's winter supplies had never come; now that it was December, it was unlikely any boat would arrive until spring, after the ice had broken up. There would not be enough food for everyone to get through the winter. When Gerald mentioned they might have to slaughter and eat the horses, Clara felt sick to her stomach, but she was also annoyed that everyone had thought her too fragile to know the truth.

"We'll manage somehow," she tried to smile, "but we better go to the meeting tonight."

"I'll go," said Gerald, between coughs, "but I want you to stay home."

"No, everyone's been protecting me too much. I knew beforehand that life here would be rough, and you can't carry all the burden. I'm supposed to be your partner in marriage, and I need to be informed so we can make the best decisions together."

Gerald looked surprised, as if to say, "How can this city girl be so brave?" Clara glowed, feeling his admiration and wishing she had words to tell him how much she drew upon his own strength.

"Very well," Gerald told her, "we'll go together."

"I better get back to Fritz then," said Molly. "I'll see you at the meeting."

"All right," Clara replied. "Tell Fritz we hope he feels better soon."

✤   ✤   ✤

Courage aside, Clara did not fully realize the seriousness of the situation until the meeting. From the moment she and Gerald arrived, everyone was talking at once, frantic and anxious, but without any solution for the situation—there was little anyone could do. Clara had stayed indoors so much in the past few weeks because Gerald did not want her out in the cold; she had not seen several of her neighbors all that month, and now she was struck by how gaunt so many of them looked from lack of food. Worse were the faces where fear had already been replaced by reconciliation with starvation. The only consensus among the settlers was that they would never make it through winter without the supplies the schooner *Swallow* had failed to bring. Clara pitied her neighbors and worried for her unborn child. Gerald, recognized as a village leader, sat silently, feeling miserable from his cold, and knowing he could say nothing to solve the crisis.

In the back of the room, Mrs. Stonegate started crying that her little girl would starve to death; understanding the mother's fear because of her own expected child, Clara tried to cross the room to go and comfort her, but before she could take a step, a sudden warm feeling flowed through her; when little black spots formed before her eyes, she realized she would faint if she did not get some fresh air. She grasped Gerald's arm, but she did not want to draw attention away from the meeting, so rather than ask him to walk her outside, she whispered she was stepping out for air. Gerald offered to go with her, but she refused, not wanting him outside when he had a cold. Trembling, she made it through the crowded room, then stepped out the door, barely finding strength to shut it behind her. She stumbled a few steps in the snow, trying to lean up against the side of the building, but when her legs collapsed beneath her, she fell into the snowbank.

Fortunately, another settler felt the need for fresh air; within a few minutes, he discovered Clara's prostrate form. The meeting was interrupted as Gerald rushed to his wife, followed by Dr. Rogers. They carried her back into the meeting hall while her neighbors stepped aside to make room. When she was laid down, Clara screamed from the sharp pain coursing through her body.

Four days later, she woke in her own bed, aware she would not be a mother anytime soon.

This was the first day Clara was able to do anything more than sit up for a few minutes to drink. She had been struggling against a fever, perhaps from the same virus Gerald had caught. The unsuspected weakness of her immune system and the sudden worries of the village had fueled an already problematic pregnancy into dangerous realms. The doctor assured her she probably never would have given birth anyway from how it now looked. He feared she was too delicate ever to undergo the labor of childbirth. Gerald had wanted to keep the baby's loss from Clara until she felt better, but she had known instantly she would not have a child. Now, she sat, exhausted and despairing. Gerald's kind words did little to ease her pain. He tried to console her, but she saw how badly shaken he was from the loss of the child and the near loss of his wife. Finally, Clara asked to be left alone, preferring to suffer in silence. She loved Gerald, but men were little comfort; for the first time since coming here, she missed her mother; she wished another woman could care for her, but Molly had Fritz to tend, and Mrs. Harlow was busy consoling a husband who felt the terrific strain of being founder of the doomed community.

In her stronger moments, Clara told herself the loss of her child was insignificant compared to the greater worries of her neighbors. But her personal worries were difficult to cast aside. Now she and Gerald would have no son to help his father, no daughter to share in Clara's feminine world. Instead, they would starve before winter was over; her mother had been right; they had been fools to come here.

But after a week, a sunny day invigorated Clara to get out of bed. She moved about the cabin that morning, cleaning up after her husband, who had tried to keep everything tidy, although, being a man, he had no idea of what constituted proper housekeeping. When Gerald returned at lunch time—although nothing was left but some dried up bread they had been stretching out for days—he was concerned she would overstrain herself, but Clara paid him no attention. Her self-reliant spirit had returned, and after so many days of being cooped up in the lonely cabin, she informed him she would go that afternoon to visit Molly and Fritz. She knew Molly worried about her but was unable to visit because of Fritz's chronic illness. Clara told Gerald she needed fresh air and exercise, and the walk to Molly and Fritz's house was only a few hundred yards. Gerald begrudgingly gave approval, and Clara, warmly dressed, went on her visit.

Christmas was only a few days away so Clara wanted her visit to be a merry one, without discussion of her lost child or the village's desperate situation. She hoped having a visitor would brighten Fritz's spirits, and if she could do any little work for Molly to ease her burden, that would be a fine Christmas present.

She felt cheered when she knocked on the door and heard Fritz holler, "Come een." His hearty tone made her suspect he felt better.

But when she entered, Clara was not prepared for the sight before her. Two bundles lay on the makeshift table, both severely packed until they were nearly bursting. Molly was rushing about, collecting their few belongings while Fritz had been set to folding blankets.

"Why, what are you packing?" Clara asked. At first she thought the giant bundles were Christmas presents; she was surprised anyone would have presents in these desperate times.

Molly took her hand, while Fritz sat down and lit his pipe.

"We're leaving," Molly said.

"Leaving? But where will you go? There are no boats this time of year."

"We will go on foot."

"But where?" Clara asked.

"To Milwaukee for winter," said Fritz.

Clara stared at her friends, completely aghast. "But how can you? Milwaukee must be three hundred miles away. You'll die of frostbite or starvation on the way."

"People will starve here if we don't go," said Molly.

"But—" Clara felt speechless. "But—but the two of you will scarcely make a difference when there are so many of us. Your share of the food won't feed the whole settlement."

"We not only ones who go," said Fritz. "We all go, all us Germans, Prussians, Saxons. Back to Milwaukee. Many of us, we come here to work, not to live, so we no right to stay. Others, then, get better chance."

"All of you!" Clara felt close to tears at the thought. "Why, you can't all go; you're just abandoning us to starve! How can you?" She knew her accusations were unreasonable, but she could not bear the loss of her friends at such a time.

"No, Clara, this way the food will hold out longer," Molly replied. "The sooner we go the better. The walk to Milwaukee will only be harder if we wait until the heavier snows. When we get there, we can send help back—by sleigh, rather than waiting for the lake to thaw so the ships can get through."

"Oh no," Clara said, so upset she sat down on the bed. She started to feel sick again. This was all too much. She suddenly hated it here.

"It's the only choice," Fritz said. "Everyone know. Gerald should have told you. It's decided. The whole town agree."

"I haven't been out of the house since I was ill," said Clara, struggling not to cry. "I've been so lonely that I couldn't wait to visit my friends, and now you're leaving."

"We'll come back," said Molly. "Fritz can find work this winter in Milwaukee, and then we'll have money to return in the spring and make a better start. And Milwaukee is warmer so it'll be better for Fritz's health."

"Walking to Milwaukee won't be good for his health," Clara replied.

"It's decided," Fritz repeated. "Best for everyone."

Clara understood they were sacrificing for the community's well-being, but she could not overcome the selfish notion that her friends were abandoning her. "It's very kind," she forced herself to say. "You Germans and Irish must be the most warmhearted people in the world, but it still seems unfair, especially since Gerald and I arrived after you did. We're the ones who should go."

"You can't travel in your condition," Molly replied, "and Gerald has business concerns here. Not like Fritz and me, who are only laborers, so not as necessary."

Clara did not know what to say. She doubted Fritz was any more able than herself to walk three hundred miles. The Germans and the Irish might be kind, but they were also stubborn; she could not argue with them; all she could do was help them finish packing, and that only took a few minutes. The German party would take only what they could carry on their backs. They would travel by foot or on snowshoes, without even a horse, since the animals would be needed as food by the remaining inhabitants. They would leave the next morning, but Clara could not bear to see the Bergmanns off, so she said goodbye now. She felt Molly was her closest friend here, and already that friend was leaving. Everyone else in Worcester was kind, but only Molly had been close enough in age for a real bond to form between them.

Clara went home to wait for Gerald to return. Since they had no food, she could not even occupy herself with making a meal. She knew she needed all her energy to endure the rest of this terrible winter, but slowly, between the loss of the baby, and now the loss of her friends, she found her spirit hardening, and she was frightened for the first time by her own potential desperation if the horses were eaten and then there still was no food.

The German immigrants left the next morning, taking the Indian trail east then south on their three hundred mile trek to Milwaukee. By the second day, Molly's legs ached from walking through heavy snow, and sleeping in the cold night air. Still, she did her best not to complain, knowing everyone suffered from the same difficulties; nor did she want to worry about Fritz worrying about her; she already had enough to worry about with his poor health. She loved Fritz dearly, perhaps all the more because he had been so sick; he was all she had in the world now. She would not go back to Boston, though her parents and brother were there—she had come here for a better life than she had known in Boston or in Ireland, yet it did not seem to matter where she went, she always ended up poor and desperate. Before coming here, she had asked everyone she met what they knew of Upper Michigan. She had heard tales of harsh winters, a climate like a tundra, a land of glaciers, an impenetrable wilderness, completely uninhabitable. But she had also heard the land was rich with iron and copper and that the plentiful forests could be logged to make a thousand men rich. Perhaps here, she had thought, she could escape the constant fear of hunger and want she had known since her childhood during the great potato famine, and she could overcome the prejudice she had known against the Irish in Boston.

In Europe, both she and Fritz had been told any dream could come true in America, but after Boston and now Worcester, Molly was beginning to lose faith in this new world. Each dream she had tried to follow only seemed to lead her down a worse path, until now she was trudging through three hundred miles of snow; her heart became as bitter as the cold winds biting her cheeks. She felt guilty for lying to Clara; she knew they would never return to the settlement, and she was sorry to lose the only female friend she had found since her arrival in America. But it could not be helped. Fritz could never make this trip back, if he even made it to Milwaukee; and what would they do when they reached Milwaukee, except starve in its streets? She would not go to his cousin again for charity—the cousin had made it clear they were not wanted. Fritz would probably die before he got there, and then she would be alone. She tried not to think what would become of her then.

They seemed to be walking forever. They had to travel east until they reached some place called Au Train, and then they would turn south. They had walked all of yesterday, and now today, and yet they were still following along the shore of Lake Superior. A piercing wind blew off the lake, while beneath her clothes, Molly sweated from the strenuous walking. Then the sweat froze until she had ice against her skin. If she were alone, she wondered whether she would have had the courage to walk into the lake and be done with it all. That sudden cold shock of an ending would be better than this prolonged bitter cold. Such an act would be a sin, but could even God blame her when she was so terribly cold? Still, she kept putting one foot before the other, while watching that her husband did not collapse in front of her from exhaustion.

Then she realized her companions had halted. She looked around to see a man running and hollering behind them; the wind howled so loud she could not understand what he shouted until he was only a few feet away.

"Stop! Stop!"

Molly had been near the front of the party, and by the time she and Fritz turned around and returned to where half the group had stopped, everyone was shaking hands, clasping each other around the shoulders and shouting for joy.

"What is it? What is it?" she asked, stunned by the transformation in her formerly morose companions.

"The supply ship is in L'Anse!" a man shouted. He had run on snowshoes from Worcester, and though he had to keep pausing to catch his breath, he quickly told the news. "An Indian came to tell us, and now a couple men have left to snowshoe back to L'Anse. The ship was forced to take shelter there, and it's locked in by some snow and ice, but the men are determined to bring the ship back with them. There'll be enough supplies for the entire winter, so you can all return."

Molly could scarcely believe it. Everyone started to talk at once.

"Praise the Lord!"

"But it's eighty miles from L'Anse to Worcester."

"Even if they get the ship into the lake, it will never be able to sail in the winter storms."

"Why don't they haul the supplies overland by sled?"

"No, that would take days."

Molly doubted the news was hope enough to cling to, was reason enough to walk back to Worcester, but they were only a tenth of the way to Milwaukee. If they went back, they would have lost three or four days, but what did it matter when they had no food for their journey anyway? When her companions turned back toward Worcester, she and Fritz did the same; they could not go on to Milwaukee alone.

As the group walked, everyone spoke excitedly in mixed German and English while clapping the messenger on the back. Fritz smiled and linked his arm in Molly's. She saw how exhausted he looked despite his smile. For the moment, he felt invigorated, but she knew he never would have made it to Milwaukee. Better they return to starve in Worcester—at least there he could die in bed. She reconciled herself to whatever fate was before them.

Molly soon learned she had no reason to dread for the immediate future. The good news was true; it seemed like a Christmas miracle to the settlement. The *Swallow* and its precious cargo had been prevented by a storm from reaching shelter in Worcester's Iron Bay, so the crew had sought shelter in the L'Anse harbor. An Indian had then been sent from L'Anse to Worcester with word of the schooner's whereabouts. When the news was heard, Captain Moody and his sailor companion, Mr. Broadbent, snowshoed their way to L'Anse, following an Indian trail along Lake Superior. After three days of long hiking over soft and consequently difficult snow, they arrived to find the *Swallow* trapped in the harbor's ice. They also found another schooner, the *Siscowit*, the same size as the *Swallow* and able to sail. With determination, Captain Moody took charge, had all the *Swallow*'s supplies transferred to the other vessel, and pointed a shotgun on the *Siscowit*'s owner when he objected to the proceedings. Captain Moody, knowing the supplies meant life or death to the settlers of Worcester, refused to back down, until finally, its owner begrudgingly agreed to let the *Siscowit* sail to Iron Bay.

And if any doubt remained of their friendliness, the Chippewa now received the praise of the white folks, for they took their axes and went out on the frozen lake, chopping the dangerously thin ice for three miles out on L'Anse Bay so the *Siscowit* could move into Lake Superior's open water. Then, fully supplied and with her sails lifted, the *Siscowit* was dragged by the Chippewa out into the lake until it broke free of the ice and reached rolling waves. Yet all this human effort was no match for winter's fury; soon after leaving L'Anse, the *Siscowit* sailed into a snow squall and lost sight of the shore.

In Worcester, the people waited, praying the ship would arrive, unaware of how the snow squall had effected the schooner's journey. Winter on Lake Superior is always dangerous, and with ice floating on the lake, the danger of crashing into invisible ice floes was as serious as a heavy wind that could toss over a ship. The sailors aboard the *Siscowit* knew they might capsize, but they were determined the settlers of Worcester would not starve that winter. Through that snowstorm they sailed, the entire eighty miles, despite cold and ice, fierce winds and threatening waters. The lake's mist froze on the sails, and the deck became a skating rink of inch thick ice. The hulls and masts were so encased with ice it was feared they would crack and break. The sailors did not know whether they were even following the south shore of Lake Superior or whether they were heading straight across the lake to Canada, but they sailed on nevertheless. Sometimes the frozen ice caused the ship to tilt sideways, nearly overturning. At any moment of the journey, all could turn futile, the brave sailors and the desperately needed supplies being claimed by Lake Superior's frigid depths.

Then on Christmas Day, on the distant horizon, a sail was spotted by a Worcester man. A holler went up. People gathered to look. Cheers rang out. Every man, woman and child in the village rushed to the shore, the ship clearly in view. In came the *Siscowit*, in it came to Iron Bay! Safe again were the courageous mariners; saved was the settlement of Worcester! The schooner docked at Ripley's Rock, its brave men, their bodies frozen, forgot the cold as they were warmly hailed as heroes. The village burst with good will as each person helped to unload the supplies and praise the men who had saved them all. This Christmas was the finest any of them had ever known. This Christmas was the one they would remember when all others were forgotten. This moment had been the most vital in the village's history. Not a single heart failed to give thanks that day. Worcester would survive through this winter, to face many more winters to come.

Clara felt how splendid it all was. What an adventure it had been! And the ship arriving on Christmas Day, like something straight out of a fairy tale. That night, she and Gerald invited Molly and Fritz for supper; Fritz, despite the long walk, looked like a new man, and Molly told herself he would get well now, and Clara could already imagine herself being a mother by this time next year. They all thanked God for the good fortune that had come to them, and they imagined only future happiness and prosperity in this dangerous but exciting land they now called home.

1850

September 1, 1850
Mr. Lucius Brookfield
Marquette, Lake Superior, Michigan
My Dear Daughters,

You will be happy to hear of our arrival hear in Marquette which we reached last month. You may not have heard, however, that Worcester, Michigan has been renamed Marquette to honor the priest who first explored Lake Superior & converted the Indians. We had a long journey of it hear over the many months which is why I have not had the chance to rite you since we were in Ohio when we were staying with your mothers cosin, now several months back. But we are happy to be hear now & I have already bot land & am starting to build a small hous for your mother & me to shelter us through the winter until spring when we can think of building a larger & stronger one.

It was a long journey from your cosin Stephens hous in Ohio. There was much to see along the journey but if you come out hear next year as I hope you will then you will see many of the same sites so I will not describe them all to you now. You will be most concerned to learn what kind of place this is where we have come to live & if the land is good & if there is a proffit to be made hear. My children, it is a beautiful contry we have come to & I feel everyday that the good Lord has blessed us by bringing us to this land which looks as if it will fulfill all its many promises. It will be a good place for your mother & I to live. The air is fresh & the contry is the most beautiful I have ever seen. It is all virgin forest as it must have looked when our ancestors first came to New England from the Old Contry. There were only Indians hear until iron was discovered but now this little viledge will soon be an important city. The stories we heard along the way about the richness of the area—that there is more iron hear than there is gold in Californee—all seem to be true. The day we arrived I stood on the Iron Mountains & there was Sea to Sea Millions upon Millions of the Richest ore I Ever Saw piled up 200ft above me, & miles of Maple timberland below. It was the most delightfull Seen I ever experienced & I have no doubt but you would be equally pleased to see it, as I have hoaps you will next Season if you move hear. Already there are now a dozen large uprite houses & over fifty small log houses. There is a forge 130 ft long, a machine Shop, a Shingle Mill & grist mill all under one Roof, & the largest Cole house I ever saw. I have already been inspecting the Iron hear & it is the best I Ever Saw. Not the ore from any other contry seems equal to it for what you can make of it. I am already setting up my forge & soon will take up my old task of blooming as I did back home. There is talk that a Rail Road will be coming through hear soon as a company from Ohio & Pensylvanee make contracts hear to ship the ore to the docks in Marquette's harbour & it seems as if the ore will never run out so we can only hope to get rich off it. Roads are planned to many of the nearby cities of Lanse about eighty miles northwest from hear & to Green Bay in Wisconsin so we will not be cut off from the rest of the contry for very long. Once the Rail Road comes through we will have easy transport to anywhere in the United States. There is talk that a stage coach will come every week from the Menominee River when the roads are better. Even if the Rail Road does not come through soon, I still think my forge will prosper because a canal will probably be built soon at the falls at Soo Saint Marie where Lake Superior meets Lake Huron so all kinds of freight will come through & go out & it will save me the expense of teams to carry the ore. I am confident I will get richer hear than doing any farm work or even running my forge back in New York. I think you could not find a better oppertunity than to come hear, so please consider my advise.

Your mother will not be pleased if I rite only of busines, so she wants me to tell you we are very happy. We have met nothing but kind people since we came hear. Even the Indians are friendly & they helped the first settlers hear who otherwise might not have lived through the first harsh winter. The Indian Chief hear is named Kabagum & he allowed people to live in his lodge hous while people built houses but our hous will be built before winter snows fly. We have already become familiar with many of the viledge leaders including Mr. Peter White, Mr. Amos Harlow & his family, Mr. Graveret, & a nice young couple, the Hennings—all of whom came when the viledge was founded. Mr. Henning has become my busines partner in the forge. Everyone hear helps one another because the winters are harsh & we are still not connected hardly to the rest of the world. We must all depend upon each other, but the viledge grows so quickly that in no time we will be comfortable as if we had never left New York state. I do hoap my daughters that you & your families will come hear next summer, & I will continue to send you letters with favoring reports to convince you & your husbands to do so.

Give greetings from your mother & me to all our family & friends back home.

Your father, Lucius Brookfield

Lucius hoped the letter would be convincing. He had described everything as well as he could, and now he must hope for the best. He had never been much of a letter writer; he knew his penmanship and spelling were extremely poor—he was constantly asking Rebecca how to spell words, but he had always been too busy working to pay much attention to education except what would benefit his forge. Lucius was an industrious man and an adventurer. He had spent all his life working, beginning as a boy when he helped his father amass a fortune by farming, owning a brewery, and operating a forge. Then his father had fallen into drinking and gambling, and the fortune had been lost. Lucius, by then with a wife and four children to feed, had also been forced to support his broken old father. But eventually, his daughters had married, his father had died, and his only son had gone West on the Oregon Trail, never to be heard from again. Lucius found himself relieved of his responsibilities, but he also found himself bored. He had never known the freedom of youth, but in his old age, he longed for adventure. When he heard of the possibilities to gain wealth in the Lake Superior region, he and his wife, both past their sixtieth year, had packed up their belongings and made the long journey west to Marquette.

His daughters had told him he was crazy to go. They argued it was unfair to their mother at her age to be so far from her children and grandchildren. But Rebecca did not complain. She loved her husband, and she supported his dreams. Even more, she believed she was needed to spread God's word in the new settlement of Northern Michigan. As for Lucius, he could not understand his daughters' complaints that he and Rebecca were too old. Over six feet tall, broad shouldered, and all his life no stranger to hard work, Lucius was hardier and had more capacity for endurance than most men half his age. He had always had a wandering spirit, probably the same spirit that had sadly caused his son Darius to vanish out West, but while Lucius missed his son, he knew he would have done the same if given the chance. And now, he would rather wander and start anew than sit in New York State, a doting old grandfather. There was still work he could do, and a fortune he might make.

Once settled in Marquette, Lucius felt in his very bones that nothing but prosperity could come to him; here he believed he would regain the wealth his father had lost, but he was also sad that his children would not witness his prosperity. And he knew Rebecca equally missed their girls. So he had written to them, hoping to convince them to come. In his letter, he had not stretched the truth about this marvelous new land. The soil was so rich he had never seen such well grown turnips, carrots, and tomaters as his neighbors were growing, and the iron ore was spectacular, a sure ticket to wealth with a little hard work.

Two of his daughters had married farmers, while the third had married the owner of the town's general store. None of Lucius's son-in-laws were wealthy; their land back home was not the best for growing crops, and the general store had little chance for growth in such a small town. By comparison, the rich land of Upper Michigan would produce bumper crops, and Marquette was sure to grow so rapidly any store owner would quickly prosper. In twenty years or less, Lucius was certain this little village would rival Chicago and Detroit in its wealth, and he wanted his family to enjoy that prosperity.

Lucius's success seemed predestined from the first day he arrived in Marquette. He had barely arrived in town before he heard Mr. Henning was planning to build a forge, and leaving his wife at the boarding house, Lucius set off to forge a business partnership. Gerald and Mr. Harlow had both talked of starting forges, so Gerald was eager to snatch up Lucius's expertise. Gerald thought a little rivalry between his and the Harlow forge could not hurt, and the iron ore was so abundant and of such fine quality that if demand for it continued to increase, neither man need fear competition.

Gerald immediately took Lucius to the river bank where the forge was to be built. The old man heartily approved, and he made several suggestions until Gerald was thoroughly impressed with his knowledge and experience. As they walked back to town, Lucius keeping up with Gerald's swift gait, Gerald described the hardships to be expected from a life in this wilderness.

"They can't be any worse than when I was a boy," Lucius replied. "My father uprooted us from Vermont to go into upstate New York, which was all wilderness at the turn of the century, but now it's so built up my father wouldn't recognize it if he were alive."

Gerald felt the true pioneer spirit in this man, and Lucius had an incredible knowledge of iron ore; he had made blooms out of ore shipped from all over the world, even as far away as Russia. Then as Gerald and Lucius passed the little blacksmith building, Lucius suggested they peek inside. They watched the blacksmith for a minute; then Lucius started to ask the man questions. Gerald stood silently, knowing nothing about the work, while Lucius rolled up his shirt sleeves, picked up a hammer and tongs and struck some blows, showing the blacksmith himself a trick or two. Gerald watched the veins of Lucius's arms bulge as he swung the hammer with the strength and dexterity of a man half his age. Gerald knew he personally lacked such physical power. Lucius appeared a veritable Vulcan come to bring civilization to the pioneers. Yet what most impressed Gerald was the man's eagerness and his apparent enjoyment in getting his hands dirty; such earthiness would prove the foundation of his shrewd business mind. Gerald's father was brilliant at bookkeeping and business deals, but the actual labor itself—never would he have stooped to such work. But Lucius did not stoop; in labor, he manifested his mastery of Vulcan's art. Lucius would be a strength to Gerald's business ventures and to the entire community, and if Rebecca Brookfield had the least bit of her husband's spirit, Gerald suspected she might serve as a replacement for Clara's sorely missed Grandmother Lyte.

When Gerald got home that day, he could hardly hold in his excitement. He quickly told Clara how fascinated he was by his new partner. He was so brimming over with enthusiasm that Clara could barely get him to sit down to supper. Finally when he paused to eat his potatoes, Clara asked, "Did you say Mr. Brookfield is sixty years old? I can't imagine coming here at that age to start over."

"Sixty-one," Gerald corrected. "But what's even more amazing is that his wife has come with him."

"His wife!" said Clara. "The poor thing. Is she as old as him?"

"Yes," said Gerald. "But she sounds quite capable. I would like you to call on her tomorrow, Clara. She's staying with Mrs. Wheelock right now."

"Certainly," said Clara. "Did you meet her as well?"

"No, but if she's anything like her husband, she must be remarkable."

Clara called on Mrs. Brookfield the next day. She was always happy to welcome another woman to the settlement, and she imagined that without any children to assist her, the elderly Mrs. Brookfield would need all the neighborly support available. At the same time, Clara felt she could always use an older woman's advice.

She found Mrs. Brookfield in the dining room of Mrs. Wheelock's boarding house. The old woman was seated in a corner, engaged in her sewing, but when she heard Clara's step, she lifted up her head and smiled.

"You must be Clara."

"Ye-es," Clara replied, surprised by the first name basis, but respectfully not resenting it from an elder. "Are you Mrs. Brookfield?"

"Please, Rebecca. In this small community, we must all be friends if we are to survive."

"Yes, that's true," said Clara, remembering she and Molly had instantly adopted a first name basis, and this past winter, everyone in the settlement had supported one another. But Mrs. Brookfield looked so frail that Clara did not wish to alarm her by mentioning the community's past trials.

Despite a scrunched up chin and wrinkled cheeks, Mrs. Brookfield's eyes glowed when she smiled. She looked far beyond the sixty years Gerald had guessed as her age, but her eyes declared she was still firmly active.

"Your husband stopped by earlier to say you would call this morning," Rebecca said. "Mrs. Wheelock had to step out for a bit, but she let me make tea for us. Would you care for some? I brought it from New York."

Clara had not had tea since she left Boston. Gerald preferred coffee, and as a result, her tastes had turned toward it when it was available.

"Yes, thank you," Clara replied. She continued to marvel at this woman's face, never having expected someone who looked quite so old, yet Rebecca was spry in her movements. Clara followed her into the kitchen and offered to help.

"Oh, no, I'm quite capable," Rebecca replied. "I hope you like tea. I know coffee is more popular these days, but I always find tea much more comforting to my nerves."

"My grandmother used to say the same," Clara replied. "She was the only tea drinker in our family."

"Yes, your grandmother is probably of my generation," said Rebecca, lifting the teapot from over the open fireplace. "We learned to drink tea from our parents, but our children seem to have turned to coffee. I daresay the Boston tea party had something to do with it. Americans decided it's unpatriotic to drink tea, but somehow, my parents never lost the taste for it, and I've followed in their footsteps. Funny, considering my grandfather helped throw the tea into Massachusetts Bay."

"Really?" said Clara. "Then you must be from Boston? Gerald told me you were from New York."

"My family is from Boston," Mrs. Brookfield said, pouring the tea and handing Clara a cup. She set the teapot down and led her guest back into the dining room. "I was born there, but left when I was a little girl. My father decided to buy land in upstate New York, which was as much a wilderness then as Marquette is now, so I already feel right at home here."

"I lived in Boston all my life, so at first I found the transition difficult," Clara replied, "but now I'm learning to love it here."

"You've been here a year now?"

"Almost. We came at the end of August."

"I imagine it would be difficult for a young girl like you to leave her family."

"Yes, but Gerald is my family now; he takes good care of me."

"He seems like a smart, capable young man."

Clara was always pleased to hear her husband complimented. The two ladies sipped their tea, trying to think of another subject for conversation. Clara noticed the book on the table.

"What are you reading, Mrs. Brookfield?"

"*The Scarlet Letter* by Mr. Nathaniel Hawthorne. Have you read it?"

"No, I've read a couple of Hawthorne's other books, but I've never heard of that one. Is it new?"

"Yes, it was just published before we departed for Marquette. It is a great masterpiece I think. Some people claim it is an immoral book, but they are too obtuse to realize its wisdom."

Clara was surprised that such a simple little woman would make such an opinionated statement. She soon realized Mrs. Brookfield was not at all simple.

"I guess I wouldn't know," said Clara. "We don't have any new books here."

"Would you like to read it, my dear? I'd be happy to loan it to you?"

"That's kind of you. Perhaps when you've finished it."

"I already have. Actually I'm halfway through my third reading. I could bring so few books with me, and it's such a fine novel it deserves multiple readings."

Clara was doubtful. Last year, she had tried to read Hawthorne's *Grandfather's Chair*, but the historical details had bored her, so she doubted *The Scarlet Letter* would be much better. Still, she agreed with a "Thank you," to please the old woman.

"I do think Mr. Hawthorne is our greatest writer. Don't you, dear?"

"Oh, certainly," said Clara, never before having considered the question.

"He is really the only author we can truly call American in his writing. All the other authors try to copy the British, but Mr. Hawthorne is an original. Of course, there is Mr. Cooper, but his stories I find rather tedious. No, I think someday Mr. Hawthorne will be considered the first great American writer. But then, being from Boston, perhaps you know more about current trends in literature than myself."

"No, I'm sorry, but I'm afraid I'm not much of a reader."

"Well, with all the hard work to do here, I don't imagine you have much spare time. Once my own work begins, I'll have little time to devote to literature."

"Keeping a house is a great deal of work," Clara agreed, "even if only for a husband."

"Yes," said Mrs. Brookfield, "but that is not the work of which I speak."

"I'm afraid I don't understand," Clara replied.

"Have you ever heard Mr. Wendell Phillips or Mr. William Lloyd Garrison speak in Boston?"

"No, I'm afraid I don't know who they are," said Clara.

"Really?" Mrs. Brookfield half-rose from her chair, spilling her tea in her astonishment.

"Are they politicians?"

"No, they are leaders in the righteous cause of abolition," Mrs. Brookfield stated. Her four foot ten inch frame suddenly seemed to tower over the table as though she were speaking from the pulpit of a great cathedral. "I'm surprised you have never heard their voices raised to decry the sins of the South. Why it was in Boston itself, when I was there ten years ago, visiting a cousin of mine, that I first heard them speak at Faneuil Hall; then I was converted to the cause. They are marvelous speakers and great men, my dear. Their voices boom out over the audience like lightning and thunder, bringing the wrath of God upon the South for its sin of slavery. Because of these men, I am sure it will not be long before the injustice of slavery is brought to an end. Why, even with the compromises made in Congress, slavery cannot survive many more years."

"No, I don't think so either," said Clara, although she did not know enough to hold an opinion. Her father had business concerns in several of the Southern states, so he had often told her slavery was an economic if sad necessity. As for Clara's mother, she gave no thought to questions that did not concern her status in society. Clara had grown up uninformed about the great issue slowly dividing the nation.

"My other great concern," Rebecca stated, setting down her teacup, "is temperance. Has it become an issue here yet, my dear?"

"Uh, no, not really," Clara replied. "I believe the men are all too busy to drink much."

"Yes, but I understand the settlement is growing rapidly. Soon there will be drunken sailors coming in from the ships, and the miners will come into town to waste their paychecks on drink rather than using the money to support their families."

"Well, I don't know of any who have done so yet," Clara replied.

"There must be some," Mrs. Brookfield insisted. "There always are. We need to take a firm hand to civilize this area by building churches and making strict laws to dissuade vagrants and all manner of drunkards from running loose in the streets."

"Certainly," said Clara. "I know there's much talk of building churches."

"Are there any Methodists here? I am a Methodist."

"I believe so," said Clara. "Gerald and I are actually Episcopalian."

"It makes no matter so long as we all do the Lord's work," Rebecca replied.

"Yes," said Clara. She was growing tired of hearing about Mrs. Brookfield's causes. She had actually hoped the old woman would bring her news of the Eastern fashions. She thought it best to change the subject. "Have you seen much of the town? I'd be happy to show you around this afternoon."

"Thank you, dear, but I'm afraid I'm not up to walking much. I caught a bad fever when we passed through Ohio, and it's still lingering, though it's been several months. In fact, we had to stay in Chicago for a couple weeks until I got back my strength."

"I'm sorry. I hope you feel better soon. Perhaps I should leave you then so you can rest," said Clara, relieved to find an opportunity to end the visit.

"Thank you. I do need a rest, but I appreciate your coming," Rebecca smiled. "It was nice not to have to drink my tea alone. I really should rest now to keep up my strength so I can do the Lord's work here."

"Yes, um," said Clara, trying to make her departure politely, "I hope Gerald can help find you and Mr. Brookfield a home."

"I'm sure he's been very helpful," replied Rebecca. "You must stop by again when I'm more settled. By then I can probably find some tracts on abolition for you to read. We really must all concern ourselves with it if this nation is to persevere in its goals of freedom and equality for all people."

"I'd be happy to read them," Clara fibbed. "Have a pleasant afternoon."

"Thank you, my dear. It was nice to meet you."

With that, Clara took her leave.

During supper that evening, Gerald asked Clara about the visit.

"Yes, I met Rebecca. She insists we be on a first name basis."

"Really? That's friendly of her," Gerald said. "But then, her husband is friendly; quite the grandfather type I would say. But what did you think of his wife?"

"I think," Clara fumbled. "I think—frankly Gerald, I think she is the most opinionated woman I ever met."

"Opinionated? About what?"

"Everything—especially abolition and temperance. She's convinced Marquette will be flooded with drunkards, and she wants me to read a bunch of tracts against slavery! I mean, I'm a Christian too, but she's a zealous crusading missionary."

"I gather you did not care for her?"

"I respect her for having strong opinions," said Clara. "It's good she wants to do what she perceives as her duty, but I'm afraid we'll never be close friends."

"You're already close friends with Molly; it's rare we find more than one or two close friends in life," Gerald observed. "Just be polite and pay her an occasional visit, dear. Her advanced age will make it hard for her to get around and participate in the community."

Clara would be kind, but she doubted Rebecca would have any difficulty making herself a felt presence in the village.

Had Rebecca given herself time to think about it, doubtless she would have felt homesick for her children and grandchildren and the familiar surroundings of New York. But she was a woman of determination. While her husband pursued the financial success Rebecca perceived as a sign of God's favor, she pursued her Christian duty. She had brought from New York a great deal of literature on abolition and temperance, and she was willing, despite her recent illness, her unfamiliarity with the community, and her advanced years, to sacrifice her own well-being for the Lord's work.

On a weekday in September, one of the last fine days of the year, Rebecca put on her bonnet and set out to convert the villagers to the cause of temperance. She knew the men would be working, but she also knew women were the moral influence in the home, so she went door to door to make mothers, wives, sisters and daughters into disciples of her cause.

A few women were willing to hear her out, and most took the pamphlets she offered, but she only found a couple who thought their husbands would take the pledge of abstinence from alcohol. Mrs. Brookfield felt frustrated to achieve so little success in such a small village, but she remained persistent. At the end of the day, she knocked on the Bergmanns' door.

Fritz Bergmann was home that day. He had suffered another relapse of his illness that left him weak and dizzy. Molly was busy baking, and between the hot kitchen, and her constant money worries caused by Fritz's unsteady work, she had stirred herself up that afternoon into a fine Irish temper. Fortunately for Rebecca, Fritz was the one who opened the door.

"Hello," said the elderly crusader. "I'm Rebecca Brookfield, and I'd like a moment of your time to talk with you about the Lord's work."

"You're welcome to come in," replied the man of the house. "I'm Fritz Bergmann and this is my wife, Molly." Molly wiped her hands on her apron, then shook hands with her visitor. "You must be a newcomer to Marquette. I don't believe we've met."

"My husband and I have only been here a few weeks," Rebecca replied, sitting down in the chair Fritz pulled out for her.

"What did you say your name was?" asked Molly, wiping her sleeve across her perspiring forehead.

"Rebecca Brookfield."

"Oh, her husband is Gerald's new partner," Molly explained to Fritz. She tried to recall what Clara had told her about Mrs. Brookfield, but she was too hot to remember anything today, so she explained, "Mrs. Henning and I are good friends; she mentioned your arrival to me."

"Oh, you know the Hennings? Aren't they a nice young couple?"

"Yes, they're very good people," said Molly.

"My health has been poorly," Fritz explained, "but Mr. Henning has helped me find work when I'm able."

"You are not ill from drinking, are you, Mr. Bergmann?" Rebecca asked.

"I have drink now and then," said Fritz, "but my health is poor from typhoid last year."

"Drink will not help that," Mrs. Brookfield stated.

"Fritz is German and I'm Irish," Molly laughed, "so it's hopeless to think we won't enjoy our liquor, and nothing's wrong with drink in moderation."

"But that's where you and so many are wrong, my dear," said Rebecca. "Even the smallest drink can be a bad influence on others. Think of your children."

"We haven't any," said Molly.

"I'm sure the Lord will bless you eventually."

"I hope so," said Molly; she longed for children, but with Fritz's poor health, she had begun to wonder whether she would ever be a mother. "But just why have you come, Mrs. Brookfield?"

"I am forming a temperance society and looking for people to take the pledge."

"What is that?" asked Fritz. "I only been in America a few years and do not know all your ways yet."

"I see," said Rebecca, harboring a secret belief that foreigners were increasing drunkenness in the United States. "A temperance society has members who swear not to touch a drop of liquor, and they encourage others to do the same."

"Why?" asked Fritz.

"To set a good example," Rebecca replied, thinking it a foolish question, "and to prevent drunkenness from spreading in the community."

"We're not drunkards," Fritz stated, "and if I do not drink, it not change anyone else's mind."

"Indeed, but it may," said Rebecca. "As a baptized member of the Methodist Church, I can assure you I firmly believe temperance—"

"We're Roman Catholic," Molly interrupted. "We can't join your society since we drink communion wine at Mass."

Rebecca did not know how to reply to this. Suddenly temperance became less an issue than the need to convert these people away from the blasphemy of popery.

"Perhaps you would like to come to one of our church services when we begin having them," Rebecca suggested. "Then you will understand better."

"We're not interested," Molly stated.

"But thank you for the visit," Fritz said.

"Very well," Rebecca replied. "May I leave you some pamphlets?"

"No," said Molly. "I don't have time for them, and Fritz can't read English."

Seeing her efforts were fruitless, Rebecca departed for the next house.

"Molly, your tongue is too sharp," Fritz said when their visitor had gone.

"I don't have time for people who tell me how to live my life," she replied.

Others in Marquette felt the same. Rebecca was surprised to find Marquette filled with so many Germans and French Canadians, all Roman Catholics, an obstacle she had not expected to encounter. She had known only those of the Protestant sects in New York. But these Catholics had a false faith; they worshiped idols and did not read the scriptures. Rebecca suspected the Lord had sent her to this wilderness land to carry out a greater work than she had first imagined.

She returned home, exhausted in body, but invigorated with the glorious task before her. After all, the Catholic Church promoted imbibing alcohol in its very services as Mrs. Bergmann had admitted. By preaching temperance, she could weaken the devil's hold in that sacrilegious church. And if God had given her such a trial, how much greater would be her reward in Heaven! When Lucius returned to the boarding house that evening, she informed him of the great responsibility before her.

"Perhaps," he said, "these people do not feel a need for temperance. After all, the population here is so small, and alcohol is not readily available all the time, considering it must be brought in on the ships."

"Alcohol finds its way into every community," Rebecca replied, "and if it has not yet caused serious trouble here, it will if we do not hinder it now."

"I understand that, dear, but how will you make these people understand?"

"They'll understand when it becomes a problem," Rebecca stated. "You, Lucius, know how drunkenness can destroy a person; look what it did to your father; you must speak upon temperance to the men you have business dealings with here."

"I'm sure Mr. Henning is a temperate man," said Lucius. But his thoughts were less of Gerald than of his own father who had drank and gambled away the family fortune; after years of hard work, Lucius had yet to regain that fortune. He had long ago forgiven his father, but he wished his wife would let his father's misdeeds rest with him. He changed the subject.

"How long do you think it will be before our girls write to us?"

Rebecca had a relapse of her illness when the first snow fell. By then the Brookfields had moved into their own home on a large piece of property a few miles from town; there Lucius planned to farm when not busy at the forge. Clara visited Mrs. Brookfield as often as she could during the old woman's illness. She feared the zealous woman would not survive the winter, so she kindly sat through many a dull lecture upon the evils of slavery. She suspected Rebecca rallied around her social causes to keep at bay the loneliness she felt from being in a community of strangers where few sympathized with her. When Lucius mentioned to Clara how he and his wife missed their daughters, Clara tried to fill that role for Rebecca, but the two women were so different that no true understanding could exist between them.

A few times, Clara tried to convince Molly to join her on her visits to the Brookfield farm so she would not have to be alone with Rebecca; Molly always found excuses, until one day, she finally said, "Clara, I cannot tolerate that woman. She hates that I'm a Catholic, and if her definition of Christianity does not contain charity toward people of different faiths, then I won't be doing her any favor by visiting her."

That was the last time Clara asked Molly to accompany her. Clara continued to visit Mrs. Brookfield until Christmas, but then the community was struck by new worries. Again, a supply ship did not arrive; again the settlers feared starvation, and again good fortune relieved their fears at the last possible moment. Then just after the New Year, Clara learned she was expecting another child. Gerald now became overprotective, refusing to let her walk to the Brookfield farm in the heavy snowdrifts. By spring, Clara's condition was too apparent for her to be seen outside; she would not have ventured out anyway from fear of creating any strain that might endanger the child she carried. She would not give birth to the first child in the settlement—both Mrs. Everett and Mrs. Bignall had now given birth—but if her child were healthy, Clara would be content.

That midsummer, little Agnes Henning was born. Enraptured with her newborn daughter, Clara lost any semblance of concern for social causes; her tie with Rebecca then became nonexistent except for their husbands' partnership. Also by midsummer, enough Methodists had arrived in Marquette to organize a congregation. Rebecca Brookfield befriended Pamelia Bishop, a woman to be remembered as the Mother of Methodism in Marquette; now with such Christian sisters to help promote her beliefs, Rebecca did not seek out Clara's company. As for Lucius, he continued to promote his new home; he wrote numerous letters to his children, assuring them if they would come to Marquette, they were certain to become immensely rich.

1853

April 6, 1853
To: Mr. and Mrs. Lucius Brookfield, Marquette, Lake Superior, Michigan
From: Mrs. Nathaniel Whitman, Essex County, New York
Dear Father and Mother,

I hope this letter finds you both well and prospering, and that the long winter there has come to an end. We are all fine here and look forward to seeing both of you. You will be happy to know that after many months of work, of packing and selling our land, we are prepared to leave here in a few weeks and begin our journey to Marquette. Sophia and George have been busy buying up all sorts of supplies, or rather luxuries, which Sophia hopes she will be able to sell in Marquette—everything from jewelry and cloth to buttons, china, and silverware. They hope to open up a mercantile store and plan to have more goods shipped directly from New York to Marquette before next winter if the store can be built by then. Nathaniel and I are equally busy with packing. Nathaniel is so excited he avidly searches the newspapers for any news of the iron industry there. He looks forward to helping Father in the forge and starting up a new farm. I wish Sophia and George would also farm because I do not know that many people there will have money to buy the items they intend to sell, but time will tell I guess.

You will be disappointed that I have not been able to convince my sister Omelia to come with us, but you know her husband is the only child of his parents and they are aging rapidly. His parents could never travel to Marquette, and he cannot leave them. Perhaps when his parents are gone, Omelia says she and Ebenezer will join us, but I do not think they will ever come because now her eldest daughter is engaged to be married, so they won't want to leave her behind. I will say no more of that though, but let your granddaughter write of her happiness at being engaged. I hope, at least, that you will find comfort in knowing that two of your daughters will be near you again.

Jacob is well and looking forward to seeing his grandparents. He is a strong boy of ten now and already a great help to his father in the farm work. He is equally good at helping me in the house and keeping an eye on his younger sister. Little Edna will need to be reacquainted with you since she was only a few weeks old when you left. But soon we will all be together as if we had never parted, and you will be able to get to know your grandchildren all over again. I know our neighbors are sorry to see us go, and Aunt Thetis is especially saddened for she says she will never see any of her brother's family again, but she notes your frequent letters ease the pain she feels at your absence. She is well and planning a great party this week to celebrate her seventieth birthday. She remains very active with the church, and her sewing circle, as well as spending much time with her own grandchildren.

I have little else to say so will close now as we will be seeing you soon if God wills it. Sophia asks apologies for not writing because she has so much to do for the journey, but she sends her love, as do we all.

Your daughter, Cordelia

Less than two months after this letter was written, Lucius and Rebecca Brookfield rejoiced when their two daughters and their families arrived in Marquette. Cordelia was less pleased, for while delighted to see her parents, Marquette did not appear as promising a town as she had imagined from her father's glowing letters. The land was certainly green enough, the forests were lovely, the lake stunning in its ever changing shades of blue, and so much larger than even Lake Champlain back home. She could not imagine this lake would ever freeze over, but if it did, it would be breathtaking. She could not complain about this land's beauty, and she was impressed with what the settlers had accomplished—her father's farm had never been so prosperous in New York, and the cool, gentle climate here seemed to have kept him from aging at all, but it was so very far from home, from New York, and her sister Omelia, whom she had always been closer to than her sister Sophia. And she felt so isolated here.

In New York and New England, even towns smaller than Marquette were linked by the railroads, but no trains existed here. The journey to Upper Michigan, both by land and water had seemed neverending. Their husbands had wanted to travel overland the entire distance, but Sophia and Cordelia had insisted they travel by boat, thinking it would be less tiring than the noisy rattling of stagecoaches and engines. The journey by train to Lake Ontario had been trying enough. Then they had embarked on the boat, and everyday the cold spring winds had blown as they made their way to Lake Erie, then Lake Huron. With each mile that had brought them farther north, they had only seemed to become colder. The women had soon hated to leave their cabins on the ship, tired of the spray soaking their faces, yet they had stepped out every few minutes to be sure their boys, Caleb and Jacob, had not fallen overboard, or dared each other to jump for that matter. Sophia had been seasick from the first day, and when they had reached Detroit, they had postponed the remainder of the journey for three days while she declared she could not continue. But the journey over land would have been lengthier yet, so finally Sophia was persuaded to board the little schooner heading for Lake Superior. They had made it to Sault Sainte Marie, and they had managed to cross the land around the rapids and then enter the greatest of the Great Lakes. It had constantly rained after that, and Sophia had never ceased complaining that the view was abominable. Cordelia thought it all beautiful, if monotonous. When it quit raining and a sunny day appeared, Sophia whined that her eyes hurt from the bright reflection off the glistening waves. By then, Cordelia well recalled how poorly they had gotten along as girls, but she bit her tongue; she would not fight with her sister before they had even reached their destination, and she did not want her parents to think she was sorry she had come. Even long after she was settled in Marquette, Cordelia would not know how she had endured that voyage; she marveled that her mother had endured the journey overland which had been so much longer—but then her mother had not listened to Sophia whine for a thousand miles.

The men had managed the trip much better. They had hardly said a word, except to talk or rather grunt with the sailors, pretending they understood the marvels of modern shipping. Cordelia had often secretly laughed at them since neither had ever been on a boat before. At least the boys, Caleb and Jacob, were not ashamed of their ignorance; in place of grunts, they had pestered the sailors with questions ranging from what island that was and why they could not stop at Fort Mackinac to speculating over the likelihood of being scalped by Indians, an event it almost seemed they wanted to happen. When Jacob had told his little sister Edna that the wolves in Michigan might eat her if she were not good, his sister had not stopped screaming for an hour; at that point, Cordelia had been ready to walk into the forest and let any wolf eat her if it would free her from her family.

But all the trouble of traveling she forgot when the schooner pulled into Iron Bay, and she saw her parents on the shore, waiting for her. She greeted them with open arms, and because they had made the long journey at twice her age, she refused to complain. Sophia did enough complaining for the entire family.

A small band played at the dock to welcome the new arrivals. Many of the settlers turned out for the occasion to cheer the brave souls who had come to join in their wilderness enterprise. From that moment, Cordelia felt the warmth and friendliness of her new community. But what won her most to this land was when she embraced her mother, then watched the tears stream down her mother's face as she embraced Sophia. Cordelia had missed her parents terribly, and now that they were elderly, she vowed she would not be separated from them again. She was surprised by how tall and strong her father remained, though he was in his sixty-fourth year, but her mother seemed to be shrinking and shriveling; she thanked God she had arrived before her mother had completely faded away.

The new arrivals followed Rebecca and Lucius to their farmhouse, where they would stay until their own homes had been built. In the three years of their residence in Marquette, the Brookfields had expanded their house until it now had six rooms. Separate bedrooms existed for each of the three married couples, while the children could sleep on the dining room floor. The quarters would be cramped, but spacious compared to some of the original structures in the village; already many of the one-room shanties built during the village's first year were being replaced by respectable homes of three or four rooms. Sophia and Cordelia's families did not mind being a little crowded until they had their own houses; the family's reunion was enough to keep everyone in good spirits.

Once arrived at the farmhouse, a true family celebration began. Cordelia found everything to commend about the house and its layout. The men and the boys followed Lucius about the farm, approving of all the family patriarch had so far accomplished. Rebecca made a tremendous meal, fit for Thanksgiving dinner, and everyone sat down to feast. Once stomachs were filled, conversation ensued about the family and friends left behind in New York, and then about the promises of this new land. Cordelia could have spent all evening talking to her parents, but Sophia eventually complained of fatigue, and the boys, for all their excitement, were already nodding off on the dining room floor before the fireplace. Their first night in Marquette had passed uneventfully, but being with her parents once more was event enough for Cordelia. Before she fell asleep to the wind rustling the pine trees, she thanked God for their safe arrival and for the family being together again.

The following morning, Lucius set off early with Cordelia's husband, Nathaniel Whitman, to show him the piece of farmland he had purchased for him, as well as the forge where Nathaniel intended to help his father-in-law in his spare time. Sophia and her husband, George Rockford, went into town to meet with Gerald Henning at his newly established office. Gerald had promised Lucius to help his daughter and son-in-law find a piece of property upon which to establish their mercantile. The Rockfords intended to build a store that would include upstairs rooms for living quarters. Meanwhile, Cordelia remained home to watch the children, her son Jacob and daughter Edna, and Sophia's son, Caleb. The two boy cousins were both ten years old and the best of friends; Cordelia felt grateful Sophia had come to Marquette if only so the two cousins, more like brothers, would not be separated. Cordelia happily spent the day with her mother, listening to her detail her progress in establishing a temperance society in Marquette. While her mother's eyes shone with fervor for the cause, Cordelia could not believe how haggard her mother looked compared to three years before; as she listened to the boys running about outside, laughing and shouting with delight at the discovery of each new tree, or the little creek on the edge of the property, Cordelia hoped having children and grandchildren near would bring comfort to her mother's last years. New York was nearly a thousand miles away, but sitting with her mother, Cordelia felt she was home again.

During several evenings in the next couple weeks, Gerald Henning came home from his office to tell his wife about fussy Mrs. Rockford.

"Of course, I was happy to do everything I could to help her start her store," he told Clara, "but she drives a hard bargain. She pulls her purse strings so tight I'm surprised she even lets her husband eat because it costs money. They'll have a nice little store once they open it, and a couple fine rooms upstairs, as fine as ours, but I'd rather live in a one room shack with you, Clara, than in a palace with that woman."

Gerald's comments were unlike him; he was typically generous in his opinions toward others, but Sophia had hounded him to get ample building materials as cheaply as possible, until for Lucius's sake, he had used all his business contacts in the village to satisfy her. Gerald was no misogynist, but he could not approve of how George Rockford followed his wife around town, always a step behind Sophia's skirts as she scurried intently about her business; Gerald admired the woman's spunk, even if he thought it a bit unnatural, but he also recognized her husband had no head for business; he wondered if Sophia had been forced to take the financial burdens on her shoulders.

What Gerald could not know was that George Rockford had been a capable if not spectacular man of business at the time of his marriage. He had inherited a store from his father, and the small social stature he had acquired from this acquisition had been enough for Sophia to choose him as the most eligible bachelor in their little New York town. Once she had married a man of business, she had married the business itself, and once she became frustrated that her husband did not seek to make as much profit as possible, she had deemed it necessary to take over all aspects of the store's operation except to stock the shelves, which was delegated to George because of his strong back.

Sophia came to the Lake Superior region with hopes that the growth of the iron industry would lead to Marquette's growth, and thereby, increase her own prosperity. If she were a money hungry woman, it must be argued that she had once known wealth and then known what it was to lose it. She remembered a childhood when her father owned a fine carriage, and her mother had servants so she could devote herself to being a great lady, which she manifested in her many charitable deeds. But the family's wealth had not belonged to Sophia's father; Grandfather Brookfield had been a self-made half-millionaire, who in his old age, had become a gambler and an alcoholic, and through several bad investments, had lost his fortune. Sophia had grown up assuming she would someday be partial heir to her grandfather's fortune, but upon entry into womanhood, she found herself no better off than the local farm girls. She had never known hunger or true poverty, but she feared both greatly. She had married George both to protect herself from sliding into the lower classes, and as the first step in her plan to restore the family to its past grandeur. She now believed a mercantile store in Marquette would increase her wealth and give her the opportunity to achieve stature in the town; in her heart, she harbored deep hopes that one day she would be leader of Marquette's vast metropolitan society.

The day of Rockford Mercantile's grand opening, half of Marquette's population passed through its doors. Gerald had asked Clara to attend the store's opening out of politeness to Lucius Brookfield, as his business partner. Clara and Molly made plans to visit the shop that morning, then to have lunch afterward. Clara would have been enthusiastic about the new store if it were not for the trial she had brought upon herself that day. Molly was her closest friend, so Fritz's constant bouts of illness alarmed Clara as she watched the couple struggle to get by; Clara knew Molly was proud, but she also wanted to help her friend, and today she was going to ask if Molly would become her housekeeper so she could make a little extra money. She dreaded the thought that her friend would be upset at being treated like a servant, but Clara could think of no other way to help her, other than to give her money directly, which Molly would refuse as a form of charity. The day before, Clara had explained this delicate situation to Mrs. Bacon, who had agreed to watch little Agnes until after Molly and Clara's lunch. Clara brought Agnes over to the Harlows' house that morning, then waited nervously for Molly to arrive, while she rehearsed numerous ways to broach the subject tactfully.

When Molly knocked on the front door, Clara opened it to find her friend wearing the same dress she had worn constantly for the past four years. But Molly did not let a shabby dress dampen her spirits. She could not afford to buy anything at Rockford Mercantile, but she looked upon its grand opening as a pleasant diversion from her daily cares. That her husband had felt well enough to work that day had also lifted her spirits. Sensing her friend's festive mood, Clara nervously scrambled to put on her hat, then walked with her friend to Superior Street; Clara tried to control her anxiety as they chatted about the treasures they anticipated finding at the new store.

Rockford Mercantile had been in business for just over an hour when Clara and Molly entered the store. Sophia had already made several sales, but Clara's entrance seemed the climax of her morning. The Hennings were already one of Marquette's most successful families, and while the village's settlers still depended on one another so much that differences in wealth were not readily apparent, Sophia had no doubt Gerald Henning's intelligent mind would make him prosperous, and that his pretty wife would be her rival as leader of Marquette society. Sophia hoped that because of her father's partnership with Gerald Henning, she and Clara might be friends; otherwise she feared a rivalry between them which might not lean in her favor.

Leaving the other customers to her husband, Sophia fluttered over to greet Clara and the unknown woman who accompanied her.

"Hello, Mrs. Henning, how are you today? I'm so pleased you could come to our grand opening."

"Hello, Mrs. Rockford," Clara replied. "Of course we had to see the new store. Anything new is such a novelty here. Have you met Mrs. Bergmann?"

"No, I—haven't had the honor," said Sophia, her eyes sizing up Molly's tattered clothes. "What can I interest you ladies in? Would you like to buy some new dresses perhaps? I have several that are in fashion this season back East."

"I think we'll just look around," said Molly, knowing she could not afford a dress so it was pointless to depress herself by looking at them. She left Clara's side and walked farther back into the store. She had promised herself she would only focus on necessities like sugar, salt, coffee, and flour.

"Feel free to look around," replied Sophia, not to be daunted. "Perhaps you would like some new hair ribbons or some jewelry, Mrs. Henning? Let me show you what I have."

Clara followed Sophia across the store to a shelf full of hair ribbons. Sophia selected several and spread them out for Clara to view, while praising the colors and making assurances of the merchandise's excellent quality.

"I bet you haven't seen such fine things since you left Boston," said Sophia.

"No, I haven't," Clara replied. "That's why we're all so pleased to see your store open."

Clara hoped kind words would excuse her from making a purchase. If she were to employ Molly, she would need to be economical, although she doubted she could be more so than she was already.

"I'm sure Mr. Henning likes to see his wife wearing pretty things," said Sophia.

"They certainly are pretty," Clara said, "but I just came to look today. I'm afraid I don't have money to spend at the moment."

"I assure you, Mrs. Henning, all our merchandise is the most reasonably priced you'll find north of Chicago. I'm certain we'll be sold out of handkerchiefs and hair ribbons before the week is out. I wouldn't want you to miss your chance."

"Yes, everything is reasonably priced, but I do need to consult Mr. Henning before I buy anything. Molly, have you found anything you want?" Clara called to her friend to avoid Sophia's badgering.

"No, I guess not," Molly replied, deciding to wait until they were outside to inform Clara of how overpriced everything was compared to the village's general store.

"Could I interest you ladies in some new undergarments?" asked Sophia.

"No, I'm all set with those," said Molly.

"Anything I might order for you then? Of course, we don't have room in the store for everything, and we are still trying to learn our customers' tastes, but I assure you, I can have anything shipped here that you might find in Milwaukee or Chicago."

"No, but thank you, Mrs. Rockford," Clara replied. "I've enjoyed seeing the store; you have everything laid out so beautifully. I'm sure Mr. Henning will stop by later this week. I know he's looking for some new tools."

"Very well," Sophia replied, "but remember, the ladies of Marquette will soon be wearing all the Eastern fashions, and you won't want to fall behind your neighbors; we women must keep ourselves attractive for our husbands."

"I'm not worried," Molly smiled. "Mr. Bergmann spends most of his time in bed anyway."

Sophia looked aghast at this private information.

Clara, realizing Sophia had misinterpreted Molly's words, explained, "Mr. Bergmann had the typhoid fever our first year here. He's never fully recovered from it."

"I'm sorry to hear it, Mrs. Burger," Sophia muttered. "Please excuse me while I help my other customers."

Seeing no profit would be derived from these two women, Sophia disappeared into the store's depths. Clara and Molly returned outside.

"Don't buy your sugar or flour there," said Molly as they walked down the street. "It's nearly twice what it is anywhere else."

"Well, it's still nice to have a new store in town," said Clara.

"Yes, but too bad somebody else don't own it," Molly grinned. "Funny that with all Mrs. Brookfield's preaching, her daughter's so attached to worldly things."

Clara was usually amused by Molly's irony, but today her thoughts remained focused on her dreaded task. She changed the subject by inquiring more specifically about Fritz's health. A few months earlier, Fritz had become a clerk for Mr. Harlow, a position Gerald had secured for him. Gerald would have hired Fritz himself except he feared Fritz would think taking the job an imposition on their friendship. When Fritz realized Gerald had gotten him the job, and how lenient Mr. Harlow was about his frequent bouts of sickness, he said nothing to Gerald, knowing his friend would not want gratitude.

"He's doing fine," Molly replied to Clara's query. "He's gone to work everyday this week. I think he feels better just because he's appreciated at his work. I'm hoping he's on the road to recovery so we can start to save money and pay off our creditors."

They had now arrived back at the Hennings' house; Clara insisted Molly sit down while she prepared lunch. Molly had wanted to bake a cake for the occasion, but Clara had refused, knowing Molly could not afford to make special desserts. Determined to be useful, Molly set the table. Once they sat down to eat, Clara decided to make her offer. Molly started to comment on the weather, but Clara persisted.

"I'm glad it's sunny after all the rain we've had," said Molly.

"Rain doesn't matter if there's sunshine in your heart," replied Clara, trying to hint at her proposed topic and instantly realizing she sounded ridiculous.

"I'm Irish," said Molly. "There's always sunshine in my heart."

"But it's hard to be sunny," said Clara, "when you have lots of worries."

"Is something wrong, Clara? You sound troubled."

"Oh no, it's not me," said Clara, feeling she was making a mess of everything.

"Do you mean there's something I should worry about?" asked Molly.

"Oh no!" said Clara, not wanting to alarm her friend.

"Good because things are going better now that Fritz is back to work."

"Yes, I know and I'm glad, but—"

"But?"

"But you don't know how long he'll be able to work."

"Well, there's no sense in worrying about something I can't control," Molly replied.

"No, but you need some security in case he gets sick again."

"I doubt we'll ever have security," Molly frowned. Her glum tone gave Clara courage to blurt out her idea in one breath.

"Molly, what I'm trying to say is that I know you and Fritz have money problems, and as your friend, I thought maybe I could help. Now I know you won't take charity, so I was wondering if I could help you some other way. Please don't be insulted, but I talked it over with Gerald, and we thought maybe you could help me around the house a little, and I could pay you for it. I could use the extra help since Agnes is such a handful. I know it's not a perfect idea, but I only ask because we're friends, and I don't know how else to help you."

"Oh, Clara," was all Molly replied.

Clara did not know how to interpret this reaction. She had expected an argument, but Molly's blank expression did not say whether she were pleased or insulted. Awkwardly, Clara picked up the coffee pot and refilled their cups. Then she boldly looked into Molly's face, steeling herself for the bite of Molly's sharp Irish tongue.

"Clara, I'm afraid I can't," Molly said.

"Oh."

Clara waited for a reason.

"I just can't," Molly repeated.

"Please don't be angry," Clara apologized. "I didn't mean to insult you by suggesting you be my servant. I just want to be a good friend, and I don't know how."

"I'm not angry," Molly said.

"Then why won't you let me help you? Won't Fritz like it?"

"No, Clara," said Molly. "I don't need Fritz's permission for anything. It's just that—well, Fritz and I recently had some unexpected news."

"Not bad news? Is Fritz's health worse?"

"No, nothing like that. Actually, it's my health."

Clara was afraid to ask more. Molly was her only true friend in this wilderness land. She feared losing her.

"Clara, I'm going to have a baby."

Then the two women burst into laughter.

"Molly, you've wanted one for so long! I'm so happy for you," Clara said.

"Thank you," said Molly as Clara tried to reach across the table to hug her friend. Molly stood up. Then the women were in each other's arms sharing their joy.

After they had cried and laughed and cried some more, Clara insisted Molly sit back down because of her condition.

"Oh no, I'm fine," said Molly, but she sat anyway.

"How far along are you?"

"Three months."

"Is Fritz happy?"

"He's beaming with pride. We've tried so long, and because of his poor health, we feared it might never happen. I would have told you sooner, Clara, but I wanted to wait until I was absolutely certain."

"I'm so happy for you," Clara repeated.

"Thank you," said Molly, "and I do appreciate your kind offer, but you understand now why I have to turn it down."

"Yes, but you will allow us to help you with the baby."

"We won't take charity, Clara."

"There's a difference between charity and friendship," Clara replied. "I know you'll let me be like an aunt to the baby, and if Fritz is too proud to let us help, well, you just leave him to Gerald. We'll see the baby has everything it needs."

🍁   🍁   🍁

That night, after she had told Gerald the good news, and they had talked it over, and he was asleep beside her, Clara thought back on the day, and when she could think of the expected child no more, her thoughts ran back to the morning visit to the mercantile. That store now seemed to her like the infringement of civilization upon this independent land. What a fuss Mrs. Rockford had made over those silly hair ribbons! Clara did not care whether she ever saw a hair ribbon again. She had almost forgotten about fashion now; she always wore her hair down and she enjoyed the freedom of it, rarely even restraining it inside a bonnet. Neither did she restrain her body in those torturous corsets or heavy, warm crinolines. This land had no place for them when you never knew from one day to the next whether you would have to shovel snow or work in the garden. In Marquette, fashion was impractical, and those who tried to ape Eastern ways found themselves looking foolish when their fine clothes met the village's dusty streets and muddy spring snowbanks. Clara regretted all the time she had wasted back in Boston fussing over gowns and shoes; now she much preferred to collect agates along Lake Superior's beach or to walk among the giant maples and jack pines that flourished about her. Her soul had blossomed in this land, and she was pleased that her daughter, and now Molly's child as well, would grow up surrounded by the natural beauty that brought serenity and self-reliance to an individual, while proclaiming God's majesty more fully than all of New England's churches. She was thankful to be here, where she was Gerald's partner rather than just an ornament in his Eastern mansion. As she cuddled against her husband, Clara wondered whether Mrs. Rockford, with all her hair ribbons and lace undergarments, would like Marquette; Clara somehow doubted it.

1855

On July 4, 1855, Marquette held its first official Independence Day celebration. The grand master of ceremonies, Mr. Heman Ely, had gone all out for the festivities in the belief that Marquette had plenty to celebrate. Despite many doubts regarding the settlement's survival, now its success seemed determined. In this year, the locks had been completed at Sault Sainte Marie, resulting in ships making easy travel from any of the other four Great Lakes through the locks at the Sault and into Lake Superior. Until now the differing water levels of the lakes had made it difficult for ships to travel into Lake Superior, but the locks allowed for adjustment of water levels so ships could pass through without difficulty. Trade would now be easier for every city along Lake Superior, and for Marquette, it meant the iron ore would not have to be shipped overland but could be transported by water to the other great ports, such as Chicago, Detroit, Cleveland, and Buffalo. With this easier ore shipment, the iron industry would soar to prosperity and Marquette's harbor would bustle at the center of this activity. Finally, Marquette was realizing its dream of becoming a great industrial metropolis. With such a promise for success, the Fourth of July, until now ignored as a holiday because everyone had so much work to do, was set aside as a day of civic rejoicing, a day of reward for years of pioneer dedication and ingenuity. Mr. Ely, as organizer of the celebration, invited all of Marquette's citizens to be his guests at a massive barbecue on his property.

At the party, Gerald had never felt so proud of his role in the birth of this fine community. He gazed with appreciation at the fine estate Mr. Ely had built, with what would soon be among many prosperous homes in Marquette. The Ely land included a two acre lawn with flower gardens and rustic bridges crisscrossing a small brook that meandered through the grounds. For today's festivities, Mr. Ely had added a bandstand and a pole to fly Old Glory. The entire community of seven hundred residents—for Marquette had grown until it was almost impossible to know everyone's name—flooded into his yard. Mr. Ely began the festivities with a welcome speech, followed, to everyone's astonished pleasure, by the boom of a hidden cannon that would fire continually throughout the day. Fireworks were not yet available for celebrating, but they were scarcely missed amid all the day's other splendors.

Gerald admired all these signs of prosperity, as he and Clara strolled about the property with their little girl. While some of the women and children plugged their ears during the cannon blasts, Clara was delighted to see Agnes laugh, her excitement surpassing even that of her parents. The Hennings were raising no dainty little daughter but a courageous native girl of the great North.

They were soon joined by Fritz and Molly, carrying their baby boy, Karl. Fritz claimed the warm weather put him in good health today, but Clara thought he had looked better ever since the couple's fear of being childless had been relieved.

"I've not seen a party like this," Fritz said, "since last Oktoberfest I saw in Saxony."

Little Karl struggled to see where the cannon's boom came from, and he babbled away inquisitive, unintelligible questions.

"He's more curious than frightened," said Gerald. "He'll be a brave boy."

"We hope so," said Fritz. "You need be brave to live here, but today is worth it, yes?"

"Well worth it," Clara said.

"Air is fresh and healthy here," said Fritz. "I never see boy grow like Karl. Lake Superior is what does it."

Fritz was prone to exaggerate his son's strength and health, but after his own many years of illness, he could not be blamed for his pride.

"And now that he's been baptized, he has God's favor," said Molly, who had been overjoyed when the October before, a Catholic church was established in Marquette. The Upper Peninsula had now become a separate diocese of the Catholic Church with its own bishop, Frederic Baraga, stationed in Sault Sainte Marie. Bishop Baraga had come to choose the site of Marquette's first Catholic church himself, and this year, the building had become functional. Now with a priest in Marquette, the Bergmanns felt they had more cause to celebrate than over the opening of the locks at the Sault.

But across the lawn, not everyone was enjoying the party. Sophia and Cordelia were deep in argument with their husbands. Tomorrow, Caleb and Jacob wanted to camp overnight by themselves at Presque Isle. Their fathers had approved the plan, but their mothers were convinced the boys would be eaten by bears or accidentally plunge off a cliff to drown in the lake.

"When I was their age, I had plenty of such adventures and came to no harm," Nathaniel Whitman told his wife and sister-in-law. "They're levelheaded boys with ample experience in the woods. If you don't want them to grow up to be cowards, they need to learn independence, and Presque Isle is the perfect place. They can't get lost there because it's surrounded by water on all sides except the narrow land bridge, and it's close enough that they can run home if there's trouble."

"If anything happened to Caleb, I would never forgive myself," Sophia objected. "George, how can you agree to this trip? Aren't you at all concerned of the danger to your son?"

"Danger," scoffed George, supporting his brother-in-law. "Ain't no danger."

"What about the bears?" asked Cordelia.

"Bears are more scared of us than we are of them," Nathaniel replied. "The boys know better than to rile any wild animals. They were out deer hunting with us last winter so they know how to survive in the woods. And it's only for one night. They'll be just fine."

"You don't know how nervous I was when they went hunting last winter," Cordelia said.

"It's a ridiculous idea," said Sophia. "I don't want my son growing up to be some wild mountain man. There's no need for them to go."

"Well, George and I already told them they could," Nathaniel said. "We can't go back on our word now."

Cordelia was angry the men had consented without asking her and Sophia. But she knew further objections were pointless. Men were stubborn creatures who would argue with a woman just to spite her. Cordelia turned away and walked to the picnic table while Sophia remained to glare at her brother-in-law. She hated men who tried to boss her. George knew better than to argue alone with her, yet with Nathaniel, he would always side against her, and Nathaniel was impossible to reason with. She was also angry that Cordelia had given in so easily. When Nathaniel ignored her glares, Sophia also turned away, seeking someone whose society was more desirable than her family's.

Peter White stood nearby, engaged in talking to a young couple who had arrived in Marquette on the most recent ship. Ever the storyteller, Peter was recalling how he had rescued Marquette's mail by hoodwinking the United States Post Office. The mail had constantly been delayed during the winters because of the village's isolation and a lack of transportation. During the summer, a villager would have to hike some seventy miles south to the shore of Lake Michigan to collect the mail and carry it back to Marquette, but in winter, the only way to cross this distance was by snowshoe, and the constant blizzards and freezing temperatures made such excursions nearly impossible. In January 1854, Marquette had received no mail for three months, so Peter had been elected to go to Green Bay to fetch it. With Indian companions and dog sleds, he set out on the one hundred eighty mile journey. Halfway, he met sleighs coming north with the village's mail. Eight tons of Marquette's mail had accumulated in Green Bay, and it took three months for the postmaster to find someone willing to carry it north. Peter sent his companions and the mail back to Marquette, but intent to resolve the situation, he continued on to Green Bay.

Upon his arrival, he discovered Marquette's mail was accumulating at the rate of six bushels a day. Frustrated, Peter traveled another fifty miles to Fond du Lac so he could telegraph Senator Cass about the situation. Determined to receive a response, he bombarded the senator with telegrams until a special agent came to Green Bay to investigate. The postmaster in Green Bay, as upset about the situation as Peter, agreed to act as accomplice. Together the two men filled all the post office's empty sacks, claiming, when the agent arrived, that every bag contained mail for Marquette. Thirty bags of actual mail now appeared to be four times as much. The agent, overwhelmed by the sight, quickly authorized weekly mail delivery to Marquette from Green Bay. Marquette had not lacked for its mail since, and Peter had been hailed as a town hero.

Peter's listeners laughed at his story, while feeling relieved to know they would receive their mail in winter. Sophia had listened carefully to Peter tell his tale, all the while admiring the young man's ingenuity. He had become a jack-of-all-trades in Marquette, not afraid to try anything; recently, he had even become a real estate agent. When Marquette was founded, he had hardly been more than a boy, but now at twenty-five, he seemed destined for a large share of the community's prosperity. Grimly, Sophia reflected how her mercantile was only making a small profit, while her husband did little to improve their welfare. She almost wished—but Peter was ten years younger than her, and she could not change the past now. But she just wished something . . .

"Ma!" Caleb shouted, running up to her. "Did you talk to Uncle Nathaniel? Can Jacob and I go?"

"Yes," Sophia said, pursing her lips in annoyance and shooing the boy away.

"Great!" Caleb yelled and ran to tell his cousin; Sophia turned back to hear more of Peter's interesting conversation.

✦   ✦   ✦

Presque Isle, a peninsula just two miles north of the little village of Marquette, is fondly regarded by the locals as perhaps the most beautiful and scenic place ever known. Its sublime cliffs, its sumptuous forest, the geological novelty of its Black Rocks, the variety of its wildlife, and its breathtaking views of Lake Superior's deep blue splendor—whether in raging fury or pristine winter iciness—all make it one of Michigan's many wonders. For hundreds of years, the Chippewa had prized this little peninsula as a favorite hunting, fishing, and camping ground. A few years prior to Marquette's founding, a silver mine had been established here, although it was soon abandoned. A few of the silver miners' huts had later been transported down the lakeshore to serve as temporary shelter during Marquette's first difficult winter. In another thirty years, Presque Isle would be preserved as a park and become the favorite spot of Marquette's natives and visitors. But in these early years of the village's history, Presque Isle was still an uninhabited place, difficult to reach without a struggle through the thick forests north of town. Access was primarily by boat since the swamp that connected the peninsula to the mainland was difficult to cross; Nature seemed to protect the little peninsula from all save the most deserving who attempted to see its beauty.

Jacob and Caleb had visited Presque Isle a couple times before on fishing excursions with their fathers, but those trips had been made by canoe. Now that they were both twelve years of age, they believed themselves men enough to visit the island on their own. Even when Jacob's father had offered to bring them by boat, they had scornfully refused, feeling that crossing the swamp would somehow be a mark of their independent manhood. After the two mile trek through the wilderness north of Marquette, the boys felt their arrival at the bog was little less significant than the Hebrews' emergence from the wilderness and across the Jordan River into the Promised Land. The boys had no sacred ark to part the waters, but no promised land would seem so promising if the journey were easy. With bedrolls and food satchels strapped to their backs, the boys waded through the mucky, mosquito infested swamp, and when they reached the other shore, although dirty, tired, and sweaty, they felt exhilarated by their achievement. The great reward of this noble crossing was not milk and honey, but freedom, the glory of being alone on this uninhabited island where they would be completely undisturbed by the outside world—here would be no chores, no cows to milk, no store shelves to stock, no little sisters to annoy them, no mothers to fuss at them about taking baths. The only difficulties would be deciding when to fish, when to swim, and when to do absolutely nothing at all.

Greatly pleased with themselves, they walked onto Lake Superior's sandy beach and prepared to clean the bog's muck off their clothes. On this warm July morning, they removed their shirts to wash them in the lake, then hung them to dry in the nearby trees. Now barechested and feeling manly, they sought out a place on the forest's edge to erect their camp and build a fire in full view of the brilliant summer sky. An old tent, some tree branches, and some tattered blankets were enough to raise a crude shelter the feminine sex would have shuddered to sleep in, but the two cousins found it as sumptuous as the tent of an Arabian sheik.

Their work now done, they were ready to abandon themselves to pleasure. Jacob suggested they go swimming to cool off, but Caleb insisted they could go swimming anytime so it would be better to go exploring. Finding a rough path once blazed by a Chippewa hunting party, the boys stepped into the forest, thinking it the most uncivilized and delightful wilderness imaginable; they tried to picture what adventures might have occurred here, long before the white man settled in Upper Michigan. They imagined themselves as French voyageurs, coming to explore this forest for the first time, only to confront a band of Indian braves thirsty for their scalps.

They had no acquaintance with the local Chippewa, despite the presence of several in the area; the boys' knowledge of Indians was chiefly derived from reading the novels of James Fenimore Cooper, or rather, for Caleb, from hearing Jacob recite the stories he had read in the novels. Youthful imagination made the excitement of the Leatherstocking Tales scarcely distinct from the reality of the boys' lives. They had known several of the places in New York where the stories were set, although the eighteenth century wilderness Cooper described had largely vanished from New York before they were born. When they had first come to Marquette, they had believed every day would bring an adventure. Today they saw no Indians, but as they stumbled among the lush ferns and over the tree roots, they caught glimpses of a raccoon or a deer, a chipmunk or a squirrel, and such noises sufficed for imaginary Indians shrinking behind the trees, waiting to attack, waiting solely so the boys might kill them to prove their immense bravery.

"You be Magua, and I'll be Hawkeye," Jacob suggested. "You go hide in the woods and then jump out and try to scalp me when I'm not looking."

"I don't want to be a dirty Injun," Caleb objected.

"Well, what's the point of playing if one of us isn't an Indian?"

"Then you be Magua."

"I don't want to be Magua either," said Jacob. "How about you be Uncas then. He's a good Indian. We can just pretend we're chasing Magua."

"I said I don't want to be a dirty Injun."

"But Uncas is a Mohican. He's a good Indian."

"I don't care. I don't like Injuns. The only good Injun is a dead Injun."

"That's not true," said Jacob; he suspected Uncas was more noble and strong than Hawkeye, but he never would have dared voice such a subversive thought.

"Then why," asked Caleb, "are there so many bad Injuns in the Leather-stocking Tales, and why do they always get killed?"

"There are good Indians too," said Jacob. He tried to remember what Cooper had written at the end of *The Last of the Mohicans* about the Indians' plight, and how unfair it was for the white men to steal their land; but Jacob did not have an eloquent tongue. Neither did he wish to fight with his cousin when they were supposed to be enjoying their camping trip.

"Then I'll be Hawkeye and you be Major Duncan," he compromised. "We'll pretend Magua has kidnapped the general's daughters, and we have to rescue them."

"All right," Caleb said.

The boys now actively explored Presque Isle in their literary roles. At times they climbed a tree to look out for Magua and the kidnapped sisters, or they stopped to search the ground for footprints to aid their quest. After half an hour, however, they tired of their game and simply walked along until Jacob suggested they take a break. They had brought along some fruit, so finding an overturned log, they sat down to eat.

When Caleb acted bored, Jacob asked what was wrong.

"I don't know. I just don't feel like playing Last of the Mohicans anymore."

"Well, we don't have to," said Jacob.

"I think we're getting too old for those games. I mean, we're both twelve now."

"Yes," said Jacob, not wanting to be thought childish, but he suspected he had a more active imagination than his cousin. "Then what do you want to do? Go back to camp and rest?"

"No, I just wish something exciting would happen. I thought Marquette would be full of adventures, but it seems as if there's nothing more to do here than in New York."

"We can go fishing," said Jacob. "Let's go back and get our poles."

"All right," Caleb agreed, although fishing fell short of the excitement he craved.

They hiked back to their camp, but when they came out of the woods, they saw a man on the beach. Neither boy felt fear for Marquette was without crime, but they did not want their solitude invaded. Hiding behind some trees, the boys spied on the intruder, who seemed to be inspecting the arrangements of their camp.

"It must be your pa," said Caleb.

"No, I don't know who it is," Jacob replied, straining his eyes to identify the figure.

"It's that Injun chief," Caleb whispered. "What does he want?"

"Maybe he just wondered who we were?"

"He's probably trying to steal something," Caleb seethed.

"I doubt it. Chief Kawbawgam is—"

"Hey, you, get away from our stuff!" Caleb yelled, running into the open to scare off the stranger. But then Caleb remembered this was a real Indian, so he came to a standstill, a bit afraid the man might attack him and carve out his heart. Last winter, a little girl in Marquette, Annabella Stonegate, had died in a snowstorm and rumor was one of the Indians had chased her into the woods until she got lost. Jacob's father had told Caleb that story was not true, that the Indian had been trying to help the little girl, but Caleb still had his doubts. He hated the Indians, almost as much as he feared them.

Charles Kawbawgam stared for a moment at the boys, then shook his head and turned down the beach. Once he had gone far enough that the boys felt safe, they ran to their campsite.

"Caleb, you shouldn't have yelled at him like that," Jacob said.

"Why not?" Caleb replied. "You can't trust Injuns."

"Chief Kawbawgam can be trusted," said Jacob. "Everyone respects him."

"Their kind shouldn't even be let into town."

"If it wasn't for him," said Jacob, "many of the settlers wouldn't have made it through the first winter. He and the other Chippewa welcomed the people here the first year and many of them stayed in his lodge house through the winter."

"How do you know?"

"My father told me. He heard it from Mr. Henning who was here the first year."

"Hmmph, well, the chief probably had no choice. He knows better than to mess with white men," said Caleb.

"Why didn't he have a choice? All this land belonged to the Indians until we came here." Jacob wished he could remember that passage from Cooper.

"Well, it belongs to white people now."

"But think about it, Caleb. We're the ones who took their land."

"Are you saying my parents are thieves?" asked Caleb, twisting his cousin's words rather than admitting he could be wrong. "My mother says all Injuns are thieves. Are you calling my mother a liar? If you are, I'll beat the tar out of you."

Jacob said nothing. He could think of many choice names to call his Aunt Sophia, but he dared not utter them; not that he was afraid of Caleb; they were close in height and build, yet Jacob was certain he could pin Caleb to the ground. What Jacob feared was his father's belt, and his mother washing his mouth out with soap, and most of all, the look of sorrow in Grandmother Brookfield's eyes if she learned he had said something unkind.

When Jacob remained silent, Caleb looked around the camp for a moment, then said, "Guess we scared him off before he could steal anything."

Jacob said nothing, even when Caleb picked up his fishing pole.

"You coming?" Caleb asked.

"No," said Jacob.

"Why not?"

"I'm hot and tired," Jacob fibbed. He wanted Caleb to leave him alone.

"Oh," said Caleb, sitting down on a log beside his cousin. He could not understand why Jacob was mad over that dumb Injun, but he did not want to fight with his best friend despite his challenge.

"Want to go swimming instead?" he asked.

Jacob knew Caleb was trying to apologize. He also knew it was pointless to explain how he felt; his cousin would not listen. He hoped he had made his point by showing his silent anger.

"Okay."

"Come on," Caleb yelled, smacking his cousin on the shoulder and then stripping down to his underwear. A couple minutes later, the boys were splashing each other in the water, all hard feelings forgotten.

They stayed in the lake until they were nearly shriveled—something that does not take long in Lake Superior's frigid waters—but young boys are tough. Not until the sun began to set would they admit they were cold. They had stayed in longer than normal to convince themselves of how much fun their special vacation was.

After emerging from the water, they wiped themselves dry, dressed, then proceeded to build a campfire. Their mothers had dreaded the thought of this moment, but their fathers had taught the boys the danger of fire and how to use it cautiously. And what would camping be without a campfire?

The fire warmed the boys' shivering bodies, and it provided great amusement as they poked their sticks in it and heated lake water over it to make the coffee Caleb had sneaked off the shelf at the mercantile; he apparently did not equate such pilfering with that of 'thieving Injuns.' Neither boy knew how much coffee to use, so it turned out to be black as tar, but they eagerly swallowed it down after Caleb remarked it might make hair grow on their chests.

When they were finally so tired that even thick black coffee could not keep them awake, they put out their fire and lay down on the beach, the night too warm and beautiful for them to suffocate inside a tent. Then, as many a youngster before them, they found that in the dark, with only the stars as silent witnesses, they could say many things they could not discuss in the daylight. They shared their dreams, confessed their deepest longings, and spoke what only one best friend can confess to another.

"I wish we could stay here always," said Jacob. "Wouldn't you like to live free like this always, just hunting and swimming and camping? What do we need with anything else?"

Caleb was not the philosopher his cousin was, but he agreed, "Yeah, no school, no parents telling us what to do. That would be the life."

"At least we can always remember today."

"Yeah, tomorrow night'll come too fast, and I'll be home doing chores again."

"Well, we're twelve," said Jacob. "It won't be that much longer before we won't have to do chores. We'll still have to work, but we'll be our own men and work at whatever we want."

"What are you going to do, Jacob?" Caleb asked, turning to look at his cousin's dreaming face, though the night made it only a white blur.

"I don't know," said Jacob. "I want to have adventures."

"Don't you want to stay in Marquette? I thought you loved it here?"

"I do, and I imagine someday I'll die and be buried here, but there are lots of other things in the world I want to see before I settle down."

"Like what?"

"Lots of things—like California. Wouldn't you like to go there and find gold? We probably wouldn't find any, but wouldn't you like to try at least?"

"Yeah, California would be great. Anything else?"

"I'd like to be a sailor. To sail around the world and see the Tower of London and Paris and the pyramids of Egypt and the pygmies in Africa and all sorts of things."

"That would be great too," said Caleb.

"What do you want to do?" Jacob asked.

"I don't know. I don't imagine my parents would like it if I left Marquette, but if you were gone, I wouldn't want to stay around here."

Jacob had thought out their departure many times; he knew how controlling Caleb's mother could be, but he thought he had the solution. "Grandmother says someday soon there'll be a war to end slavery. If we're old enough to fight in it, then maybe you could leave Marquette that way."

"It would be fine to fight in a war and become a hero," Caleb replied.

"Maybe we could go together—be in the same company," said Jacob. "And then when the war is over, we'll go out West to explore and have adventures all the way to California. Then we could sail around the world until we came to New England and then sail up the Great Lakes and right back to Marquette."

"Wouldn't that be a lark!" said Caleb. "Imagine—people from Marquette who have sailed all the way around the world. That'll be the day."

"It would be a fine day," said Jacob.

They both imagined such a grand possibility for the next few minutes.

"Jacob?" Caleb's voice quivered.

"Huh?"

"If you do go out West or off to war, you will take me with you, won't you?"

"Course, Caleb. You're my best friend. Who else would I go with?"

Caleb smiled to himself.

After a few more minutes, Jacob heard Caleb snoring. He thought some more about journeying around the world; he could hear the waves lapping against the beach, then rolling out and back in, making a quiet roar. He fell asleep to the sound of those waves, and he dreamt he was sailing on a giant ship, but at the end of the dream, he sailed into Iron Bay, returning home to everyone he loved.

🍁   🍁   🍁

The boys woke shortly after dawn as sunlight flooded their eyes. They sat up, shaking the sand out of their hair, and shivering from the cool lake breeze.

"We ought to go for a swim," suggested Jacob.

"I'm cold already," said Caleb.

"A swim'll make us warmer. The water's so cold that when we come out, the cool air will feel warm."

Caleb thought this idea logical enough that two minutes later, the boys had run into the water, dunked themselves beneath the waves, then run back to shore, their arms filled with goosebumps and their heads aching with numbness.

"That wasn't a good idea!" Caleb grumbled.

"Well, it got the sand out of my hair at least," laughed Jacob. "Let's go for a hike. That'll warm us up."

"All right. Why don't we bring our breakfasts and fishing poles?"

"Hey," Jacob said, "if we catch any fish, we can cook those for breakfast, or for lunch anyway."

They collected their fishing poles and the bread and apples they had brought for breakfast. Then they trudged along the wooded cliffs overlooking the lake. After half an hour, they sat down to eat. Then they decided to trek through the interior of the island. They easily hiked up the large hill that dominates the center of Presque Isle; from there they found a view of the lake through the trees. Caleb wanted to see better, so he climbed a giant maple. When he was a couple dozen feet in the air, he shouted down to Jacob, "I can see the Black Rocks from here!"

"That's where we should go fishing," Jacob hollered back.

"Okay!" said Caleb, shimmying down the tree. Once Caleb was on the ground, they hiked back down the hill to the rocky shoreline, their feet sure as the hooves of mountain goats.

The western side of Presque Isle hosts one of the world's geological wonders. While the scientific name of its four billion year old stones is Keweenawan Peridotite, their color has made them locally known as the Black Rocks. Unlike the sandstone that composes much of the island, they are the only rocks at Presque Isle upon which nothing grows, and by jutting out into Lake Superior, they are easily distinguishable from the rest of the forest-covered island. Historians have suggested these rocks provided black dyes for the early Native Americans, becoming the source for the name "Blackfoot Indians." Caleb and Jacob only knew they were a wonder to behold. They were especially intriguing to the boys because they were so low the waves would wash over them, trapping fish in their small indented pools. A live carp trapped in a rocky swimming pool would be easy fishing, and even if the boys were not lucky enough to find such a pool, they were certain the Black Rocks were the best place to catch enough fish for their lunch and have leftovers to bring home for supper.

Despite all their enthusiasm, the boys had little luck catching anything that morning; by lunchtime, they had gobbled down their bread, and munched on their apples, and still found themselves hungry. Jacob patiently wanted to keep trying, but Caleb insisted on returning to camp where they had left some food.

"I'll make some sandwiches for when you get back," he said.

"Okay," Jacob replied. "I'll come in about twenty minutes."

Caleb began a leisurely walk back to camp, deciding to meander up one of the cliffs to look out over the lake. When he noticed the wind was picking up and the waves were becoming stronger, he shook his head, thinking Jacob would never catch fish with the lake so rough.

What happened next Caleb would never forget. Perhaps it was just the bright sun or the spray from the waves, but as he stared at the water, Caleb thought he must be hallucinating. Out in the lake was a small rock poking its head above water. Only a seagull might have landed there, but what Caleb saw was no seagull. A woman was sitting perched on that rock—a naked woman!

Caleb could not believe his eyes. Who could she be? She was too far away for him to recognize if she were someone from town. He could not imagine any woman would dare swim out into the rough lake, especially not as far as the rock, and certainly not naked. For a moment, he wondered whether she were shipwrecked, and then he wondered whether he had sunstroke and was seeing things.

The woman jumped into the lake. A flash of white, followed by two pointed tips, broke through the water, then disappeared. It had looked like a fish tail! But now Caleb could only see the ripple and the foam where it had sunk. He had not imagined it. Could it have been a small whale perhaps, or an otter—but there were none of those in Lake Superior. Could it be a . . .

He stepped closer, peering out at the white crests of the waves, straining his eyes in hopes the creature would resurface. He was so busy seeking white flesh amid the foam that he failed to heed his footing until he had tripped over a root. He plummeted forward. He reached out to grab onto something but missed the cliff's edge. His foot stayed caught in the root, and he found himself dangling over the lake. His hand desperately grasped a small bush growing out of the sandy cliff. He used it to pull himself up and reach for the tree root.

Then the bush broke. Only a few of his fingers clutched the root; he knew it was too weak to support him for long.

He looked down. The waves were ten feet below him. They struck at the cliff, furiously smashing against it. The water was so cold that even if he could fight the waves, he would freeze before he could swim to the beach and climb back onto land. The root began to crack. He flung his free leg at the cliff, only to kick off sand and rock.

A frantic scream instinctively shot from him; he was too frantic to form words. He knew Jacob would never reach him in time.

"Oh God, my poor mom," he sobbed, thinking of how grieved she would be. He kicked up his foot again, seeking to wedge his shoe into something, but instead, rocks tumbled into the lake.

"Jacob! Help!"

The tree root snapped. He felt himself falling backward.

Then a tight grip seized his wrist. An amazing strength pulled him up. Before he could see what was happening, he was swung up into the air and dropped onto the ground. He collapsed, gasping for breath. He was dazed, yet marveled that Jacob was so strong. Several seconds passed before he opened his eyes.

Jacob was running toward him, still some twenty feet away.

"Caleb! What happened? Are you okay?"

Caleb was confused. Jacob was so far away, so who had saved him?

Turning his head, he saw a smiling Charles Kawbawgam looming above him.

"Boy should be more careful," said the chief.

"Are you okay?" Jacob repeated.

"Yeah, yeah," muttered Caleb, rising to his feet.

"You're lucky Chief Kawbawgam was here to save you," said Jacob.

Caleb slowly struggled to his feet. He looked at the chief, then realized he had mud on his hand. He wiped it on his pants, then held it out.

"Thank you, Chief," he said.

Had another moment passed, Caleb might have reflected on whose hand he was about to shake, but his extraordinary rescue had momentarily obliterated his prejudice.

"You're welcome," said the Indian. "Be careful now."

"I—I will," Caleb said.

"Thank you, Chief," Jacob added.

"You catch fish?" asked Chief Kawbawgam, ignoring their gratitude.

"No, nothing," Jacob replied.

"No good day for fishing," said the Chief. "Rain soon."

"Sorta looks like it," Caleb muttered.

"Safe journey home," nodded the Chief, turning to go.

"Thank you. You too," Jacob replied.

The Chief turned back and grinned. "Maybe someday, I teach you real way to fish."

Jacob smiled. "We would like that."

"Thank you," Caleb repeated, still feeling dazed.

Charles Kawbawgam slipped back into the forest. He smiled to think he had a full day's catch compared to those boys.

"You sure are lucky," said Jacob after Caleb's rescuer had gone.

"Yeah, lucky Chief Kawbawgam was here. Did you see him pick me up like nothing? He must be really strong. I bet if there were still Indian wars around here, he'd be the greatest warrior in his tribe."

"Maybe," said Jacob. "Let's go eat lunch, and then we better pack up and head home. Chief Kawbawgam said it looks like rain, and Indians know these things."

"All right," said Caleb. "Did you see how tall the chief is?"

"Yeah, he's really tall."

"Handsome too, for an Indian I mean," said Caleb, his admiration conflicting with his prejudice.

"How'd you fall over the cliff?" Jacob asked.

"I—" And then Caleb remembered what he had seen out in the lake. He could not tell his cousin about it. He was sure it had been a woman, and she had been naked, and he thought he had imagined it because thinking of naked people was wrong, just as many similar thoughts he had were wrong. Maybe his falling into the lake was intended as punishment for his sins. Jacob would not understand; Jacob was good compared to him, and if Jacob had those kinds of thoughts, he would have told him because they were best friends. Caleb felt he was not as good a friend since his shame kept him from being honest with Jacob. Caleb felt maybe he had been saved because God had wanted to scare him into turning away from sin. Still, he would not tell Jacob what he saw. "I was watching a big fish I saw out in the lake, and I guess I just didn't look where I was going."

"What kind of fish?" asked Jacob.

"I don't know. I didn't get a good enough look at it," Caleb replied.

"Anyway, at least you're safe," said Jacob.

It began to sprinkle when the boys reached their camp. They crept into the tent to eat lunch, hoping the rain would let up so they could pack and walk home. Jacob found the weather a disappointing end to their adventure, but Caleb paid it no attention. He was still thinking about what he had seen. Finally he had to ask, "Jacob, do you think anyone ever saw a mermaid in Lake Superior?"

"Why?" Jacob had not expected such a question from his unimaginative cousin.

"Just wondering. They say sailors have seen mermaids in the oceans, so I wondered whether they've ever been seen in lakes."

"Caleb, there's no such thing as a mermaid."

"I know; I was just wondering."

"Well," Jacob said, "my pa once told me the Chippewa believe that if you see a mermaid, it means someone you know is going to die, so that must mean the Chippewa have seen mermaids in the lake."

Caleb was silent. He had nearly died by falling off that cliff. Maybe the mermaid was a sign of his approaching death, and because she had been naked, it meant he would die because of his sinful thoughts. He resolved not to think such evil thoughts anymore.

The rain soon passed; then the boys packed up their belongings and crossed back over the bog. They were leaving a few hours earlier than planned, but Caleb, still feeling shaken, was relieved to go home.

The boys followed the lakeshore until the village came into sight. As they reached Iron Bay, they saw a man walking toward them.

"Maybe it's the chief again," said Caleb. He had begun to idolize the chief, whom he hoped would make good on his word and take them fishing.

"No, it's a white man," Jacob replied. "Actually, I think—it's my father."

Jacob ran forward, excited to tell about their trip, but Nathaniel greeted the boys with a grave face.

"I was coming to find you," he said. "Caleb, I have bad news."

"What's wrong?" Caleb grew pale for the second time that day.

"It's your father; his appendix burst early this morning. He had some pain last night but thought it was just indigestion. The doctor's there, but he says there's nothing he can do. You better hurry. Your mother hopes you'll be home before he passes away."

Caleb spent a second taking in the news. Then he tore down the beach, recalling what Jacob had said it meant to see a mermaid.

But Caleb arrived too late. George Rockford had died just minutes before, leaving his wife a widow and his son without a father. The burden was a heavy one for a twelve year old boy; Caleb wondered how he would ever learn now to be a man without his father to guide him, and he wondered how he would handle his mother without his father to defend him. He loved his mother, but he feared she would never let him go off to see the world with Jacob. He did not feel he had done anything so sinful to deserve such punishment.

1856

"But Cordelia, do we really want a Catholic in our society?"

Sophia asked the question as she and her sister walked to the Varin house. The sisters were on a quest to find members for their newly organized women's literary society. So far, besides themselves, only their mother, Clara Henning, and Molly Bergmann had joined. The society had been their mother's idea, and Cordelia had agreed to help, although she feared neglecting her tasks at the boarding house she and Nathaniel had begun to operate that past fall. She need not have worried, however, because Sophia had willingly taken over command in hopes a role in the society would allow her to shine in the community's eyes. Nine months had passed since George's death and Sophia remained in mourning, but Cordelia thought it time for her sister to be active again in normal life and this literary society might help; for her sister's sake then, Cordelia reluctantly drew up a list of potential members and accompanied Sophia in paying calls to recruit women.

"We need more members," Cordelia insisted. "Five will hardly do, and so many of the other women have refused that we cannot be choosy."

"But we don't even know the Varins."

"But because they're newcomers to Marquette," Cordelia said, "we want them to feel as welcomed in the community as we were when we arrived here."

"But they aren't even Americans," Sophia replied.

"They are now that they live in the United States, and since they're from Quebec, they must speak French, which can only enrich the culture of our society."

"That's true," said Sophia. She tried to recall some of the French she had learned at the girl's academy before her grandfather's loss of the family fortune had ended her studies.

"Besides," said Cordelia, "Molly Bergmann joined, and she's Catholic and wasn't born in the United States either."

"We wouldn't have asked her to be a member," Sophia frowned, "except that Mrs. Henning insisted, and now Mrs. Bergmann insists we call on this French woman."

"Mrs. Henning is loyal to her friends," said Cordelia.

"Maybe so, but Mrs. Bergmann is a woman completely lacking in tact. Just because this Mrs. Varin is her next door neighbor doesn't mean Mrs. Bergmann can decide who's in our society. There are enough French-Canadians around here; why, they've even started a church of their own, so why don't these Varins befriend their own kind?"

"Sophia, you know in an isolated community like this, we all need to be neighborly if we're to survive."

Sophia was silent. She did not mean to be rude, but foreigners made her uncomfortable.

They had now reached the door of their prospective member's home. Mr. Varin was at work, but his wife gladly greeted them.

"Hello," said Cordelia when the door opened.

"Allo," replied Madame Varin. "May I help you?"

"Bon jour," said Sophia. "Nous sommes ici bienvenu vous."

Sophia stumbled a bit over the words, but she thought she had spoken them correctly.

"Pardonne?" Madame Varin replied, scrunching up her face.

"We're here to welcome you to Marquette," said Cordelia.

"Ah!" replied the Frenchwoman, instantly enlightened. She understood English better than someone slaughtering her own language. "Please, come in."

Cordelia entered, remarking, "We know you've been in Marquette for several weeks now; I'm sorry we didn't have a chance to call earlier."

"I will make us coffee. Please, have a seat," Madame Varin replied, showing them into a dark little room, where the curtains were still drawn. A small sofa and two comfortable if well-used chairs made up the only furniture. "Oh, the baby is sleeping, so be careful you do not wake him. I'll be back in a moment."

The mistress of the house disappeared into the adjoining kitchen, which looked more like a little closet from where Cordelia and Sophia had seated themselves.

"She seems happy to see us," Cordelia whispered.

"She's not much of a housekeeper," said Sophia, noting dust everywhere.

"Shh, she'll hear you. Besides, they're probably still getting settled, and she didn't expect us."

"How can they live in this cramped little place, especially if they have children?"

"They only have one baby so far," replied Cordelia. She looked around for something pretty to point out to Sophia, but seeing it was rather a dismal parlor, she decided to be silent until their hostess returned.

Madame Varin soon came in with coffee, cream and sugar.

"Thank you," said Cordelia. Sophia gingerly picked up her cup to sip the coffee, nervous about the degree of hygiene the French might practice in washing their china.

"Madame Varin," began Cordelia.

"No, please, Suzanne," she said.

"Suzanne," smiled Cordelia. "I'm Cordelia Whitman and this is my sister, Sophia Rockford. We want to invite you to join our new ladies' literary society. We wish to bring some culture to Marquette, and we feel your French background would be a great asset to our little club. We would love to have you share your opinions with us upon the books we intend to read."

Suzanne strained her ears and twitched her face while listening to this speech. Cordelia spoke slowly, hoping Suzanne understood her English. Sophia was convinced Cordelia's use of "literary" and "asset" had gone over the Frenchwoman's head.

"Literature. It is my passion!" was Suzanne's surprising reply. "Ah, and I have so few books. Mama would not let me read novels as a girl, and the convent school I attended in Montreal strictly forbade them. But my Jean, he does not mind what I read. Only, we cannot afford many books."

"That's understandable," Cordelia said. "Books are limited here, but Sophia owns Rockford Mercantile, so she can order books we can all share."

"I can share my books too," Suzanne said. "I have several novels of George Sand, whom I adore. You have read her, yes?"

"I'm afraid not," Cordelia replied. Sophia frowned in disgust. George Sand! Wasn't that the Frenchwoman who wore pants and had a man's name! God forbid. What would their mother say?

"We intend," said Sophia, "to read good moral books. *Pilgrim's Progress* for example."

"Ah, George Sand is moral," said Suzanne. "She believes women should be free, not slaves to men. Do you not agree with this philosophy, Mrs. Whitman?"

"Call me Cordelia," smiled her new friend. "I'm sure we could consider reading a George Sand novel. But we thought we would begin with *Uncle Tom's Cabin*. It's been very popular these last few years and we have a couple copies. You may enjoy it because it's about the wrongs of slavery, but for the Africans, not women I mean. We also might read something by Mr. Dickens or Mr. Hawthorne."

"I do not know these writers," said Suzanne, "but I have heard of this *Uncle Tom* and long to read it. I feel great sorrow for the slaves. My heart bleeds, for they are more oppressed than us women. I feel akin to them, but I am lucky. I married a kind man who does not beat his wife, unlike some men I have known. I would never submit to being treated like a slave."

Sophia frowned. Men beating their wives? Only the lower classes indulged in such bestiality. Where did this woman grow up to have known such brutes?

"Good, then you will join us," said Cordelia.

"Oh, yes, I will be delighted."

"Fine," said Cordelia, rising from her chair. "I'll stop back then to inform you when we'll hold the first meeting."

"I will look forward to it," Suzanne replied.

"We must go now. We have to enlist more members, you understand. Thank you for the coffee and welcome again to Marquette."

Cordelia shook Suzanne's hand, receiving a warm response.

"Good day, Cordelia. Good day, Mrs. Sophia."

"Mrs. Rockford, if you please," Sophia replied, fumbling with her hat to avoid shaking the Frenchwoman's hand. Having succeeded in taking only one small sip of coffee, she felt she had escaped from this little hovel in as sanitary a manner as possible. "Adieu, Madame Varin."

Clara and Agnes had climbed the hill early that morning. They were now up on the forested ridge north of Marquette, which provided one of the two hills that sloped down to form the valley where the little harbor village was nestled. The ridge was still largely woods, but Clara climbed up it regularly for its spectacular view of the lake and harbor. Today the view was especially gorgeous. June had just arrived, and after a long winter of cold weather and heavy snow, the warm air was scented with spring flowers. Trees were budding, everything turning green, and through the boughs of the trees, framing the view, was the deep blue lake.

Agnes was thrilled to skip about the woods. At age five, she was enraptured by every tree with a gnarled face, eager for every branch low enough to be climbed, and delighted especially with white may flowers and budding lady's slippers.

"Why are they called lady's slippers, Mama?" she asked as they filled a basket with the delicate rare flowers.

Clara stood up, her back aching; she was expecting another child, and her stomach was starting to protrude, but she had been unable to resist this visit to the woods, and it was so early in the morning that few people were likely to see her. She did not think she looked like she was expecting yet, just a bit over-weight, but in another week or two, she would not feel comfortable venturing outside. She had to get out and enjoy spring before she had to spend summer cooped up in the house; but she would spend everyday inside if it meant this child would be born. Clara had suffered another miscarriage last year, and she wanted Agnes to have a little brother or sister. Not that Agnes was not enough to love, but already Clara was sad to see how quickly her little girl was growing up.

"They're called lady's slippers because they look like the fancy pink slippers a lady would wear."

"Do you ever wear slippers, Mama?"

"Well, sure, but mine are knitted. These look like silk slippers, like the kind a ballerina would wear."

"What's a ballerina?"

Clara was surprised. She had known what ballerinas were when she was Agnes's age, but then, her mother had taken her to the ballet in Boston. Marquette had no ballet.

"Ballerinas are beautiful girls who dance in a show called a ballet in a big theatre with hundreds of people watching."

"Dancers? I can dance."

Agnes began jumping up and down and waving her arms.

"No, dear, ballerinas dance far more slowly and gracefully."

"How? Show me!"

"Well," Clara hesitated, then set down her basket. "Like this."

She spun around on one foot with her arms raised in the air; carefully, she did two pirouettes, feeling ridiculous because she was pregnant, but laughing nevertheless.

"Mama, are you a ballerina?" asked Agnes, amazed by the graceful sight.

"No, dear, but I've seen them dance many times so I can copy them a little."

"Where can we see one? Are there any ballerinas in Marquette?"

"No, dear. We'd have to go to Boston, or at least Chicago."

"When can we go see one?"

"I don't know," Clara replied. "Maybe in a few more years. If transportation to Marquette becomes easier or they build a railroad, then maybe a ballet company will eventually come here."

"I want to see one now," Agnes said. "Can't we go to Boston to see one."

"No, dear, Boston is about a thousand miles away. It would take us a long, long time to travel there."

"But aren't your Mama and Daddy there, and Daddy's Mama and Daddy too?"

"Yes."

"When can we see them? I want to see my grandparents."

"Soon, dear. Your father is very busy with business right now, but someday we'll take you to Boston. I would like to see my parents again, and my old grandmother too before she's gone."

"You have a grandma too, Mama?" asked Agnes in astonishment.

"Yes, dear, but she's very old now."

"I don't see anymore lady's slippers here," Agnes said. "Where else can we find them?"

"We'll look some other time. We have to go home now, dear. Mama has company coming after lunch."

"Mama also has a book she's supposed to have read," Clara thought. She had agreed to join the Ladies' Literary Society only because Mrs. Brookfield had been so insistent, and Gerald was Mr. Brookfield's business partner. Then before she knew it, Clara had volunteered to hold the society meetings in her home because her parlor was the largest and fit all the members.

Mother and daughter climbed down the hill. Clara tried to remember the little she had read last week in *Uncle Tom's Cabin*. She knew they never would have picked the book except for Mrs. Brookfield's obsession with abolition. Clara had lost interest after the first few chapters. She wondered if she could just skim over the rest of the pages before the ladies arrived. She knew the book was incredibly popular, but she found it too sentimental—at least the little of it she had read. She imagined slavery was a horrible institution, but how could any of them in Marquette know the truth when none had ever been to the South? Clara hoped Mrs. Brookfield would not next choose a novel railing against the evils of alcohol. Why did they have to read silly novels anyway?

Why not something like one of Mr. Emerson's essays, something that contained some good Yankee common sense?

"Mama," asked Agnes, "will Mrs. Bergmann bring Karl over to play with me?"

"Yes, dear, but you must be gentle with him. Remember he is only two."

"Do any of the other ladies have little boys or girls?"

"Mrs. Whitman will bring over Edna."

"Oh yeah, Edna. Okay."

"You don't sound pleased. She's only a year older than you; I would think you would have more fun with a girl close to your age than you would with Karl."

"Edna's okay, but she's really quiet. I'll play with her though if she brings over her doll. It's really pretty."

"You'll be nice to her, whether she brings her doll or not."

"Yes, Mama," said Agnes.

The women arrived for their meeting soon after Clara had washed up the dinner dishes. Karl, Agnes, and Edna were relegated to a corner of the dining room, while the ladies seated themselves in the parlor, the mothers finding strategic chairs from which to watch their children.

A total of nine women attended this first meeting—Sophia Rockford, Cordelia Whitman, Rebecca Brookfield, Molly Bergmann, Suzanne Varin, Clara Henning, and three others Clara did not know, all of them Methodists Mrs. Brookfield had recruited; doubtless, these women were interested in abolition and temperance; their presence made Clara wish she had not offered her parlor for meetings.

"Our first order of business," Sophia called the meeting to order, "is to choose a chairwoman. She will draw up the reading lists and organize whatever activities we plan, primarily to raise money for charities and to sponsor cultural events."

"I nominate Clara," said Molly.

When Suzanne Varin seconded the nomination, Sophia glared at the Frenchwoman, who then felt it necessary to explain, "She has been so kind to let us meet in her home."

"I nominate Sophia," Mrs. Brookfield said, knowing her daughter wanted the position.

One of the Methodists seconded the nomination; she did not know Clara, and she was hoping to extend her credit another month at Rockford Mercantile.

Slips of paper were then dispersed, marked, and folded. Cordelia silently tallied the votes, then announced, "Clara has five votes so she will be chairwoman."

A little cheer of congratulation ended when Mrs. Brookfield suggested, "Then we should make Sophia secretary so she can fill in if Clara is ill or unable to perform her duties."

No one disagreed. Sophia graciously consented, although she envied Clara. Being chairwoman did not make Clara any happier about the organization. She did not want any extra duties when she already had to care for a house, husband, daughter, and soon another child.

The women now decided they would meet for two hours the first and third Thursday afternoon of each month. Next they discussed what activities they would promote in Marquette. Suggestions were made for the establishment of a lending library or a museum. Suzanne suggested an opera house, but Mrs. Brookfield remarked that theatres were immoral places. Clara did not see how they could accomplish any of these dreams with so few resources. Mrs. Brookfield suggested a lecture hall where they might host a series of speeches on abolition and women's rights, but the other women felt this work would be too time-consuming.

"I have plenty to do now," said Molly. "Fritz is sick so often I can't commit to other activities outside the home."

"Gerald has to work," Clara said, "so I have to stay home with Agnes."

Sophia adamantly backed her mother by declaring women should not depend on men for their incomes. As a widow, she declared she was responsible for earning her own income at the mercantile, and she still had to care for her home and son, yet she was proud to be independent.

"She wouldn't feel that way if she still had a husband," thought Molly. "She just says that to hide the fact that no other man in this town will look at her."

"I thought we were just a literary society," said Suzanne.

By the time all the ladies' suggestions were discussed and postponed for future discussion, as is typical of meetings, only twenty minutes remained to discuss *Uncle Tom's Cabin*. Clara gave a couple head nods and inserted an "I agree" to pretend she had read the book. Then she thanked everyone for coming, and they thanked her for her hospitality before making their departure.

"That wasn't so bad," Clara said to Molly, the last guest to leave.

"I don't think I can spare two afternoons a month to hear about social causes," Molly replied. "If I wanted to do that, I'd become a Methodist."

🍁   🍁   🍁

Sophia arrived home that afternoon, tired and irritated. She had campaigned to organize the literary society yet her efforts had only gotten her elected as secretary. She was glad to have the use of the Henning home for meetings, but that hardly meant Clara deserved to be chairwoman. Who would accept such a position, then state she did not have time to promote cultural activities? And then there was Molly Bergmann and Suzanne Varin—hardly desirable members.

Sophia sat down in the kitchen and pulled off her shoes, bemoaning that she would never meet anyone in this village who appreciated her culture and intellect. The women were all jealous of her fine clothes and brains. As for the other sex, the few who could aspire to being gentlemen were all married, except Peter White, who was too young for her. She could not find a suitable husband anyway until she completed her two year mourning period; George had not been a bad man, but two years of mourning was a harsh sentence for a husband who had never been much good at supporting her; she was no worse off without him, but she wanted more from life, and she resented that she lived in a world where a woman needed a man to get ahead. Neither George nor Caleb nor her grandfather had ever understood what the fear of poverty was to a woman, especially when a man is usually a woman's only defense against it. She told herself she had the mercantile, and a son who might someday care for her, but for now she was still burdened with having to be self-reliant.

"Mother, look at the huge trout I caught!" Caleb shouted. He came in the door, followed by Jacob, both boys carrying fish dangling from lures.

"Don't let it drip on the floor," she replied, feeling annoyed that now she would have to cut up the fish. She hated fish, but at least eating it would save a little money. She decided to make Caleb cut it up.

"Where did you catch it?" she asked, pretending to share her son's excitement.

"Down on the Dead River," he replied.

"Chief Kawbawgam, he showed us how to catch them," Jacob said. "I caught one too, but Caleb's is three whole inches longer."

"I thought I told you to stay away from that Indian," Sophia said. "You can't trust his kind."

"He's a chief, Mother. He's the most trustworthy Indian ever. Why I told you how he saved my life last year."

"I told you to stay away from him, Caleb. I don't want you to disobey me."

Caleb's face fell. Jacob said, "I better go home. Ma will have supper soon. I'll see you tomorrow, Caleb."

"When did you go fishing?" asked Sophia after Jacob was gone. "You were supposed to watch the store this afternoon. It's only thirty minutes since you should have closed it up."

"Business was slow today, Mother. We only had two customers between one and three, so when Jacob came to see whether I wanted to go fishing, I didn't think—"

"So you closed early? How do you know whether we might not have had more customers after three? How do you know how much money we might have lost?"

"But there wasn't anyone—no one was shopping today, and—"

"I ask you to watch the store for one afternoon," Sophia snapped, "and you can't even do that for me."

"But Chief Kawbawgam had promised to take us to a special fishing hole, and I forgot it was today. I couldn't disappoint Jacob."

"So an Indian and Jacob matter more than your mother having food on the table?" said Sophia. "I can't rely on you, Caleb. Go to your room until supper-time."

"What about my fish?" Caleb asked. He wondered why his mother could not understand that the fish he caught saved money by putting food on the table.

"Clean your fish then and cook it for supper. I need to rest a few minutes. Since you can't obey me, you can make supper."

"Yes, Mother."

"And don't you let me catch you around that Indian again. I'm going to have a talk with your Aunt Cordelia; she probably doesn't want Jacob around him either."

Sophia went upstairs and lay down on her bed. That boy made her so angry. She knew he was just a boy, but already he took after his father, irresponsible and undependable. She prayed for patience.

Downstairs, Caleb asked, "God, why does she always have to ruin everything?"

The summer passed uneventfully. Sophia hatched schemes to expand her business and to make herself socially prominent in the village. Since Caleb was not in school, she saw no reason why he should not work daily. Jacob helped at his grandfather's farm, and he helped his mother in the boarding house, but he was always allowed time to go fishing—his father saw to that. The couple times Caleb managed to get away, Jacob had already made plans to fish with Chief Kawbawgam, and Caleb feared his mother's wrath too much to join in these expeditions. Another time, Caleb tagged along when Jacob went fishing with his father, but then Caleb returned home, sadly reminded that his own father could not take him fishing.

Only once that summer were the two boys able to go fishing alone together. Most of that trip, they scarcely spoke a word, simply watching their lines for a fish to bite. Then to Jacob's surprise, Caleb said, "You're the only friend I have now, Jacob. I thought I might be friends with Chief Kawbawgam, but my mother spoiled that, just as she spoils everything."

After a second, Jacob said, "There are other boys you could do things with."

"No, my mother doesn't like other boys. She says they're too noisy and wild—she probably wouldn't even like you except that you're her nephew."

"You can't let her choose your friends."

"None of the other fellows like me anyway," said Caleb.

Jacob did not ask why Caleb was unpopular. He knew his cousin tended to complain, even whine. Caleb was like Aunt Sophia in that way.

"You'll always be my friend, won't you, Jacob?"

"Course," Jacob muttered, casting his reel again. Such questions did not help Caleb's popularity. Whenever the cousins had played with another boy, Caleb had been ornery because he wanted Jacob's complete attention, and he feared Jacob would throw him over for another friend; he could not imagine the possibility of having two close friends. The cousins had been more like brothers since the time they could walk and talk so Jacob had long since learned to tolerate Caleb's temper and faults, not unaware that he had his own shortcomings. But in the last year since Uncle George had died, Jacob thought Caleb had become more frightened and controlled by his mother than ever before, and Jacob did not know how to improve the situation.

♦   ♦   ♦

While boys mark summer's passing by the number of their fishing trips, Clara marked it by the months of her pregnancy. She expected her child in late October, but already she was convinced she had never been so fat before. She thought the child would be a boy since it was so heavy, and she had never felt this uncomfortable when carrying Agnes, but then, Agnes had been born in June, before the intolerable heat and humidity of July and August. Clara felt constantly warm these days; the slightest movement made her perspire.

One humid afternoon, she was doing her baking. She had put it off for a couple days, hoping for a cooler morning, but finally, she had to bake or they would have no bread, and she refused to pay the ridiculous price for bread that Rockford Mercantile charged. She had been baking since long before any store in this town sold bread, and even though Gerald's business had finally begun to prosper, she had found it hard to break her thrifty habits. She would not mind baking at all except that the house was so awfully hot. Not even a hint of a breeze existed when she opened the kitchen window. She was certain today would reach ninety degrees.

"I better sit down for a minute," she told herself once the bread was in the oven. She grasped the back of a chair, and lowered herself down, but missed the chair bottom. Once she found herself on the floor, she had no strength to pull herself up. Then she felt her stomach cramp until she could not help but scream.

"Mama, what's wrong?" asked Agnes, running into the kitchen.

Clara could not breathe for a minute. She grimaced in pain, waiting for it to stop so she could try climbing into the chair.

"Mama!" cried Agnes, becoming frightened.

"It's okay, dear," Clara panted between contractions of pain. "It's the baby. I think it's coming. Go—go get the doctor."

"Where, Mama? I don't know where he is."

"Go, get your father—no, oh, oh, your father's too far. Go to, oh, oh, Molly—Mrs. Bergmann."

Agnes stood petrified.

"Hurry. Go to Mrs. Bergmann. She'll know what to do."

Agnes hesitated, afraid to leave her mother alone, but more afraid of the writhing pain on her mother's face. She turned and ran out the door. She was only five, and it was across town to Mrs. Bergmann's house, but Agnes reached it in five minutes. Forgetting her manners, she just burst inside without knocking.

"Agnes!" exclaimed Molly at the sight of the red faced, perspiring child. "What are you doing running like that in this heat?"

"Mama. The baby. She needs my daddy. She needs the doctor. Hurry. Help. Please! Help!" Agnes babbled.

Molly did not wait for further explanation.

"I'll fetch the doctor, then run right over to her," she promised. She picked Karl up from where he was playing on the floor. "I'll have to bring Karl with me since Fritz is at work. But someone will have to fetch your father. I think he's at the forge today. Can you do it, Agnes? Do you know the way?"

"Yes," said Agnes, although she had her doubts. She had been to the forge a few times, but never by herself. It was okay if her daddy were in the office, but she was afraid of the forge itself. And it was much farther than even Mrs. Bergmann's house.

"Drink a glass of water so you don't overheat," Molly told her. "The pitcher's on the counter. Then hurry to your father. Don't lose any time." Then Molly rushed out, Karl wiggling in her arms while Agnes was left behind to shut the house door.

Less than fifteen minutes later, Molly and the doctor were with Clara.

Meanwhile Agnes ran until she thought her legs would fall from under her. She ran all the way to the Carp River, and when she reached the property, she still ran around the forge to the office building. At the door, she met old Mr. Brookfield; usually his scraggly grey beard frightened her, but she knew this was an emergency, so she had to be brave.

"Where's my daddy?" she asked the scary old man.

"I don't know who your daddy is," Mr. Brookfield replied; he was too involved in his work to remember any little girl except his granddaughter Edna.

"Mr. Henning's my daddy."

"Oh, he's over there," said Mr. Brookfield, pointing outside. Agnes wished she had not wasted time asking because she would have seen her father in another second.

"Daddy!" she shouted, her little legs bolting toward him. She sprinted so fast across the yard she could barely stop. When Gerald saw her coming, he picked her up to prevent her from colliding into him.

"Agnes, why are you here? Where's your mother?"

"The baby," Agnes gasped. "The baby's coming."

"Oh!" Gerald was too startled to know what to do. He was looking for something. His hat. There it was. Oh, better tell someone.

"Lucius," he shouted across the yard, "my wife seems to be in labor."

"All right," replied his partner, too busy to be interested. "I'll keep an eye on things."

And then Gerald, half running, Agnes still in his arms, headed for home. It was a long walk, and to run it, while quicker, was exhausting because he had to climb a hill, then go down another hill to enter the valley Marquette nestled in. When he reached the hill, he set Agnes down for a moment so she could climb on his back.

"You better not run anymore in this heat," he said. "I'm very proud of you to come all this way. Did you tell anyone else?"

"Yes, I ran to Mrs. Bergmann, and she went to get the doctor."

"Good," said Gerald. That was a relief. Molly would know what to do better than he would. And she didn't live too far from the doctor. Gerald now broke into a trot, Agnes riding piggyback with her arms wrapped around her daddy's neck. Several people laughed to see the distinguished Mr. Henning running with his child on his back, but they knew he was an affectionate father. Most people were too busy with their own concerns to consider something might be wrong at the Henning house.

Mrs. Brookfield was an exception; Gerald arrived home to find her in the parlor. She had seen Molly running down the street and followed. Now she sat in the parlor watching Karl while Molly and the doctor helped Clara.

"I can watch Agnes for you," Mrs. Brookfield said, wanting to be useful. Gerald muttered a quick "Thank you" before surrendering his child and running into the bedroom.

Clara was moaning and writhing in the bed while the doctor tried to examine her and Molly tried to hold her down.

"Clara!" Gerald rushed to her side.

"Gerald, I'm so sorry," she said when she saw him. "I'm so sorry; it's happening again."

The baby was in danger, and she was apologizing for it. She still felt guilty that she had failed to give him the other two children.

"It's okay," he said, taking her hand. "It'll be okay."

"Please, Mr. Henning," said the doctor, gently touching his shoulder. "You need to leave. Mrs. Bergmann and I can handle this."

Gerald squeezed his wife's hand. "I love you, Clara. Be brave. Everything will be all right. I don't need any more children so long as I have you. Be brave, dearest."

He stepped backwards to the door, waiting until the last minute to break from Clara's loving gaze. Then he turned around to see the terror in Agnes's eyes. He picked her up and smothered her face against his shoulder.

"The Lord will care for her," Mrs. Brookfield told him. Karl had amazingly fallen asleep on the sofa, leaving Mrs. Brookfield feeling useless. She wished she were not here, but she knew someone had to help, and the Lord had chosen her for the task.

"I left Lucius in charge of the forge," said Gerald, trying to be polite despite his quaking insides. "I'm lucky Lucius is there. He's a good partner."

"Yes," said Mrs. Brookfield, too distracted by Clara's moans to say more.

Gerald and Mrs. Brookfield were silent after that. They quietly prayed the doctor would come out and tell them everything was fine.

Molly had shut the bedroom door after Gerald left the room. When it finally creaked open again, Gerald continued to stare at the floor. But he knew he must look up when he saw the doctor's shoes before him.

"I'm sorry, Mr. Henning. There was nothing I could do."

Mrs. Brookfield let out a little shriek while Molly came into the room, her cheeks full of tears.

"She's with the Lord now," Mrs. Brookfield muttered.

"The—the baby?" Gerald asked.

"Both are gone," said the doctor, placing his hand on Gerald's shoulder.

Too overwhelmed to know what to think, Gerald simply said, "Thank you, Doctor. I know you did your best. Thank you."

Molly knelt beside him.

"I'll take care of preparing her for the funeral, Gerald. I think I know which clothes she would have liked best to be buried in."

"Buried," Gerald muttered. Everything that had just happened was unimaginable. He had always known women could die in childbirth; he had feared it with each of Clara's pregnancies, but he had never really believed it would happen. His worst nightmare had come true. He had thought Clara was frail, but when he brought her to this wilderness land, he told himself he could protect her; how could he have protected her from this?

Molly sat down beside him. She held his hand and spoke words of comfort. He made halfhearted replies. At some point, the doctor left, although he sent Reverend Safford over to talk with Gerald. Molly and Mrs. Brookfield then went into the bedroom to prepare Clara for viewing at the wake. Molly could scarcely find presence of mind to touch the lifeless limbs of her friend. Mrs. Brookfield was silent, but she had no qualms over touching the dead. Molly had always thought the woman overly opinionated, but now she saw how strong the old lady was, capable of doing whatever necessary without fear or complaint.

The minister tried to comfort, but Gerald found little consolation in his words. He blamed himself for bringing Clara to this rough land. Reverend Safford told him it was not his fault, but Gerald preferred to consume himself with guilt than face the gaping void of the life before him. How could he write to tell Clara's parents? Even when the minister remarked that Clara could just as easily have died in childbirth back East, Gerald refused to be comforted.

Somehow that night, Gerald managed to sleep. Fritz came to stay overnight with him, while Molly took Agnes home. The next day, Molly went to choose the burial plot in the Episcopalian cemetery where only a handful had yet been buried in the community; Gerald had insisted he did not feel well enough to choose the gravesite. When Molly returned, she tried to cheer him by describing Clara's final resting place as a serene spot on the forest's edge, where daisies grew and chipmunks scampered about.

"Clara would have chosen it herself," Molly said. "She'll be at peace there."

"She did love the forest," Gerald replied.

"I never saw anyone who loved to walk in the woods so much," Molly added, sensing Gerald was now ready to be consoled.

"Do you think she was happy here, Molly? Would she have been happier in Boston?"

"I think Boston was too small a world for her, too crowded and constrained. Here she was free." When Gerald did not reply, Molly kept talking to fill the terrible silence of a house without its mistress's laughter. "Clara often told me how beautiful it was here—not just the scenery but life itself—the freedom and the sense of community. She never had to worry about her dresses being fashionable, or being polite to snobbish people just because they were rich, as back East. I don't think Clara could have been happier anywhere else. When I first met her, she seemed so innocent and childlike. Nothing like me—headstrong and with a sharp tongue. She seemed frightened that first day she met Fritz and me at the hospital, but she was trying to be brave, and I liked her right away because of it. She was a little delicate, but that just made her all the more courageous; I think she was stronger than any woman I've ever known. I can't say how much I'll miss her."

"She was happy here," Gerald agreed. "Last night I thought maybe Agnes and I should go back to Boston, but I think now Clara would want us to stay. Agnes is a lot like her mother; she loves the forest and the lake. And since Clara will be buried here, I guess we'll stay, if only to be near her."

"Nobody would ever want you to leave," Molly confirmed.

1857

Gerald did not want to attend a wedding. It was September 29th, over a year since Clara's death, yet he still felt awkward attending a social function without his wife on his arm. For the first several months, people had shown concern for him, but now they had moved on with their lives, finding little time in this industrious settlement for elaborate mourning rituals or extended grief. So when Gerald received an invitation to Peter White and Ellen Hewitt's wedding, he reluctantly attended, partly for business reasons, partly because Clara had always liked Peter.

Gerald brought Agnes to the church so she could see the bride; then he left his daughter in Molly's care while he attended the reception. There he sat largely alone and wondering how soon he could escape without being impolite. He was relieved when Lucius came to sit with him; Lucius was old and cantankerous, but Gerald believed him an eccentric genius, and the two men had prospered both in business and friendship. Since Rebecca was sick at home, Lucius was feeling equally awkward at the reception. He had brought Sophia with him, but she did not mind socializing her way around the room on her own, so with relief, Lucius joined Gerald in the corner.

"What do you think about all this talk of statehood?" Lucius asked.

Gerald had not thought much about it. He was less concerned with politics than with business, but he had considered that if the Upper Peninsula should become a separate state from Michigan, then Marquette would be the likely choice for its capital. With the recent completion of the new county courthouse, a grand Greek revival structure, the first of its kind in Upper Michigan, complete with a portico and four columns, and built at the substantial price of $4,300, no one could deny the village's prominence or its future promise. Gerald could well imagine a glorious state capitol built beside the courthouse. And living in the new state's capital city was sure to be good for business.

"I don't know whether we'll ever see a state of Superior," Gerald said, choosing his favorite from among the suggested names for the potential state. "I'm hopeful, however; we shouldn't have to be at the mercy of a legislature down in Lansing, especially when our long winters make it inaccessible to us six months of the year."

"Yes," replied Lucius, "and we deserve our own local representation now that the Upper Peninsula has about ten thousand inhabitants; that number's enough for statehood as far as I'm concerned."

"Yes, and the federal government needs to recognize we are now one of the richest and most important areas in the country due to our mineral wealth. That should make statehood happen soon if the legislators downstate don't fight to keep our wealth in their own hands."

"We men of business think alike," Lucius smiled. "Rebecca wants our statehood because she figures it'll add another free state to the Union. If we can make the free states outnumber the slave states, maybe the South will be intimidated into ending slavery without a war being needed."

"I don't think we need to worry about a war," said Gerald. "The South could never last long if there were one since the North has all the industry; they're just backwards farmers down there."

"That's what Edmund O'Neill told me the other day. He says he's glad he moved here from the Carolinas because the South will fail if it doesn't become industrially advanced like the North. Industry is the future of this country. I tell you, these are marvelous times we live in. As a child, I never would have dreamt of such a thing as a locomotive, or that the United States would grow as it has—I remember back when President Jefferson made the Louisiana Purchase, how astounded we were by the new size of the country, and yet look how the nation has expanded since then. Look at the trains we have, and the locks, and now this new pocket dock. The ship captain who came up with that idea was a true genius."

"Yes, the arrival of locomotives sure has made things easier," Gerald said.

Marquette's first steam locomotive, the *Sebastopol*, had arrived in August 1855 to the opposition of mule drivers who were paid to transport the iron ore along a plank road from the mines almost ten miles inland all the way to Lake Superior. Meanwhile, the railroad had been built from the mines to the docks, and when the locomotives came, the mule drivers became angry from fear they would lose their jobs. When that past June the second locomotive had arrived in the harbor, a mob formed to prevent it from being unloaded from the ship, but the little riot had been squashed. Since then, the ore transportation had been done by train, making it far easier and more cost-effective. "With the plank road, we could only transport thirty-five tons of iron ore a day, but with the steam locomotives, there's twelve hundred tons being shipped daily to Marquette's docks."

"It's unbelievable," said Lucius, shaking his head. "I never would have imagined it could be done so quickly and efficiently."

"Same with the Soo Locks making things easier," said Gerald. "And now we have that new pocket dock so we can dump the ore right into the hold of a ship rather than shoveling it on top from the dock—it's amazing. We live in a time of true industry, and Marquette will be great because of it."

"I hope I live to see more of these marvels," Lucius said. "If there is a war, I guarantee you there'll be even more inventions. Not that we want a war, but this is supposed to be a free country. Problem is the young people these days don't know what it means to be free. Not like when my father's generation was alive to remind us constantly about the Revolution; even my generation knew about freedom after the British attacked us a second time. Did I ever tell you I fought at the Battle of Plattsburg? I had to walk—"

"Father," Sophia interrupted, approaching the two men, "would you mind getting me a glass of punch. I'm so warm. I need to sit down for a moment."

"Certainly," Lucius said, thus relieving Gerald from hearing the old man reminisce again about his service in the War of 1812.

"I hope you'll forgive Father for rambling on so," sighed Sophia, sitting down beside Gerald. "He always feels lost without my mother at these types of functions."

"I perfectly understand," said Gerald, wishing Clara could be with him.

"Oh, yes, it must be so difficult for you," said Sophia. "Clara was such a good wife and mother. I know, when my dear George died, I felt lost for months."

Gerald felt himself insensitive to reference his pain when Mrs. Rockford had known the same grief. He had never considered how many widows and widowers existed until he was included in their number. He had always considered such people to be elderly, but he was only thirty-three and Mrs. Rockford but a few years older. Neither of them should be forced by death to spend the rest of their lives alone.

"It has been difficult without Clara," he confessed. He suspected he irritated people when he spoke of his grief, but he felt Mrs. Rockford might understand. "How have you coped with your loss?"

"It gets easier with each passing day," Sophia replied. "But it takes time. I still think of George constantly, but it hurts less. I mostly have pleasant memories now."

"I feel that way sometimes—at first, everything that reminded me of Clara brought pain, but now those things just recall happier times."

"It's good to have known love, even if it's only a memory," said Sophia. "Let's hope Peter and Ellen will know the happiness we've had."

"I'm afraid I'm not adding to the merriment of the newlyweds," Gerald replied. "Perhaps it would be better if I just went home."

Lucius returned at this moment with his daughter's glass of punch.

"Thank you, Father," said Sophia, "but I'm afraid I'm too tired to drink it now. Would you mind going home with Cordelia and Nathaniel? Mr. Henning is leaving and if it's not too much trouble, maybe he'll walk me home since it's on his way."

"It's no trouble," Gerald replied, although surprised by the suggestion. "You don't live too far from me anyway."

He was actually relieved not to leave the party alone; he hated the empty feeling of walking out the door without anyone noticing, and he saw no harm in walking home the widowed daughter of his business partner.

As she stood up, Sophia glanced over at the bride and groom.

"Sometimes I think I'd like to marry again," she said, "if I could find a husband who would be a good father to my son."

Her comment sent Gerald's head spinning. He worried constantly about Agnes not having a mother, but to marry again—no, that seemed beyond his ability.

Sophia took Gerald's arm, thankful to escape the rest of the reception. She had secretly harbored a hope Peter White would take an interest in her, but now that he had found a bride, she had almost reconciled herself to living alone. She had thought no other suitable men lived in Marquette, but somehow she had overlooked Gerald Henning, perhaps because she kept forgetting he was no longer married, or perhaps because she had disliked his deceased wife. Now she noted he was her father's business partner, and financially well off, and close to her age. His arm felt strong and capable as she held onto it. She decided Peter White's wedding had not been such a waste of her time.

She encouraged Gerald to talk about Clara on the way home. She listened and inserted little anecdotes about her own marriage to show she empathized with him. Gerald's spirits lightened as he spoke of his pain. He had no one in Marquette to confide in, except a daughter whose youth made her more resilient than her father; even the Bergmanns had their own troubles, so he hated to unburden his morbid thoughts on them. Sophia was an unexpected but welcomed companion.

"Thank you for walking me home, Mr. Henning," said Sophia when they had reached her door. "I couldn't stay any longer; the happy couple was making me think too much of George."

"I'm glad to have been of assistance," Gerald replied.

"I enjoyed the evening more than expected since I had a sympathetic listener."

Gerald was surprised by this remark; he had done most of the talking and thought she had been the sympathetic one. Sophia smiled, knowing a man liked to be thought gallant, and she was willing to flatter men when it suited her purpose. "I'm sure I'll see you in my store, Mr. Henning. Stop in this week to buy something for your little girl."

Gerald tipped his hat and wished Mrs. Rockford good night. He needed to get home to relieve Molly from watching Agnes, but his steps were slow and nervous. No woman had held his arm since Clara, and he wanted that feeling to linger a moment.

In the morning, Gerald awoke with the chronic anguish of realizing Clara was not beside him. Then he remembered Mrs. Rockford and how she had suggested he stop into her store to buy something for Agnes. In pondering what he might buy his little girl—while denying to himself that he really just wanted to talk to Mrs. Rockford again—he realized he had been neglecting his daughter who was definitely outgrowing her clothes. Clara would have long ago bought or made the girl new garments; he wrote down the sizes Agnes wore, then went to the mercantile, intending to surprise his daughter with a new dress.

Afterwards, Gerald was never quite sure how it happened. He found himself struck by Mrs. Rockford's capability from the moment he entered her shop. He scarcely needed to explain why he had come before she overwhelmed him with her knowledge of dresses, female undergarments, hair ribbons, and fashion in general. She was so cheerful as she waited on him; such a woman would be a good mother to a little girl who deserved better than a moody, depressed father. Then he remembered Mrs. Rockford had a fatherless son;

Gerald had never given the boy much thought, but now he decided he liked Caleb, and hadn't he always wanted a son?

Sophia had put on one of her prettiest dresses that day. Fine clothes never hurt in catching a husband, and today she wore a purple silk that rustled when she moved, and complemented her green eyes and raven black hair. Later, she told herself the dress was what had clinched the bond. Actually, Gerald had never really looked at Sophia until that day, never realized how much she was a woman. She seemed mature and maternal, and yet somehow she retained a sensuousness in the way she catered to him, helping him pick out the very best items and flattering his tastes. She was not Clara, but she struck him as a strong, healthy partner, who could make him feel like a man again.

"Agnes is lucky to have a father so concerned even for her smallest needs," Sophia said as she wrapped up the dress, locket, and hair ribbons she had picked out for him. "It's admirable of you, especially when I know how hard it is to be parent to a child of the opposite gender. I never seem to know what to do for Caleb."

"I'm sure you do just fine with your son," Gerald replied. "Any boy would be lucky to have such a loving, pretty mother."

Gerald was embarrassed to hear himself flirting, but the remark helped seal the bargain as much as Sophia's silk dress.

When Gerald saw Agnes's delight over the presents, he felt grateful to Mrs. Rockford. He knew no woman could replace his Clara, but he was lonely, and all the other unmarried women he knew were hardly more than girls or very old women. He was frightened to spend the rest of his life alone, and Mrs. Rockford had a good business mind for a woman, plus he was already partners with her father. If he and Sophia—it was a beautiful name—didn't it mean wisdom—if he and Sophia should have children, Lucius would probably leave his share in the forge to his and Sophia's child. Somehow, everything suddenly seemed to fit together like a jigsaw puzzle.

Never did Gerald consider what woman Clara might have chosen to take her place.

The courtship did not last long. Gerald visited the mercantile again to buy items for Agnes, and each time he flirted with Mrs. Rockford, and she flirted back; by the third visit, they were on a first name basis, and a few visits later, while leaning across a roll of muslin, he asked whether she would ever consider remarrying, and she admitted she would if the right man asked her; he asked whether he might be the right man, and she said she thought he might be, and he said he was asking, and she said in that case the answer was yes, she would marry him. Five minutes later, a wedding date was set for the week before Christmas.

"I can't believe it!" Molly told Fritz after hearing the news from Gerald's own lips. "It was all I could do not to argue with him. How could he choose that woman? Poor Clara. It's a good thing she can't know about this."

"Don't you say anything to him," Fritz warned. "Even if you were Clara's best friend, Gerald knows his own mind, and we don't want to lose his friendship."

"But why did he pick her?" Molly asked.

"Maybe they'll be happy," said Fritz. "Besides Agnes needs a mother, and that Rockford boy needs a father."

"Agnes needs a mother, not a wicked stepmother!"

Fritz could not help laughing, but he told Molly once more to hold her tongue. She did, but it was not easy.

The wedding went as planned, with a reception as fine as Peter White's. Sophia Rockford became Mrs. Gerald Henning to the consternation of Marquette. Few could imagine how such a match came about, but Gerald was too well liked in town for anyone to comment openly.

Children usually fair the worst in second marriages. Agnes had read fairy tales about wicked stepmothers, but if her new stepmother were not altogether motherly, Sophia did address her as "dear" and "daughter" and bought her dresses far prettier than the ones her real mother or Mrs. Bergmann had sewed for her. Sophia was proud of the young girl, who was a bit plain but might someday be as beautiful as her mother. Agnes found her stepbrother to be kind and protective toward her; despite the age difference, he even enjoyed playing with her.

As for Caleb, Sophia had already considered that as Gerald's stepson and her father's grandson, he was likely to inherit the forge and mercantile. Someday Caleb might be the richest man in Marquette. With such wealth, he could also make a fine marriage; perhaps she would send him back East to college where he would meet a young lady of family and fortune.

Caleb did not consider his mother's reasons for remarrying. He only knew that after the wedding, his mother was kinder to him. And his stepfather was willing to take him fishing. He felt triumphant the day his stepfather told his mother to "quit nagging the boy." He loved Gerald after that. Finally, he thought that like his cousin Jacob, he might live a normal life.

1861

April 3, 1861
Mr. Lucius Brookfield
Marquette, Lake Superior, Michigan
Dear Daughter Omelia and Family,

Thank you for your last letter. Your mother & I are both well, as are your sisters & their families & I know they would all send their love but it is spring & we are all busy becos the last of the snow is melting & there is work & planting to be done. I know you thought I was some sort of half-crazed visonary when I first thought of coming to this contry, but now after over ten years of experence hear, it proves I was rite in all my predictons. More busines seems to be done hear each year & new buildings are going up all over. I would not recognize the town had I only visited it the year we arrived, & then returned now. No, we have not yet become a seperate state but we still believe that will happen some time in the near future. Marquette will doubtless be the state capital if we ever do seperate from Michigan becos now we incorperated as a viledge a couple years back, but we are more like a city I think for the sensus last year numbered us at over one thousand in population.

You & Ebenezer sound concerned about the posibility of war. I fear you are rite, & I do not wish for such a crisis for our nation, but if it does come, this region of the world will provide great resorces to the nation to defeat the South so I do not think the war will last long, & it will be very good for our busines hear. I do not like to value money over human lives, but after the events of the last few months, it seems unlikely the war can be prevented. Now that the Southern States have opposed the Union by forming their own government, I cannot see them ever coming back into the Union except by force. I also do not like war, for I remember when in 1814 I fought at the Battle of Plattsburg. I served only eight days for that one battle, but that was enough & all I ever hope to see of war. But if war does come, hear in Marquette it will only affect us in positive ways by making busines thrive. Still, I say even for increased wealth, I do not want war, but if it is to be fought, it is only because all else has been tried & failed. The democrats have misruled the contry for too many years now & the new president will put an end to that & free the slaves. Everyman deserves the chance to have his own home, support his family, & earn his own living & not be forced to do it for someone else. I have been blessed in my life, & especially since I have come to this marvelous land. I feel everyone should have the same good fortune whether he be white or negro. Your mother, you know, feels the same since she has always been for abolition.

A war could not last long for the South has nothing compared to the Northern states, & hear we will get rich for there will be a need for our ore & copper for the railroads & machinery & weapons needed in the war. I think even without war this area will only prosper—anything seems posible in this wonderful place. Already the ore furnaces hear are making nearly twice as many tons a day as do those back East. Ores are in the Iron Mountains close to the furnaces so it is easy to bloom them. The quantity of ore hear seems inexzostible for a thousand or more years. It is packed in the mountains & in the land for 80 miles up along the lake, & then it meets the copper veins which appear just as rich. Marquette now has three large docks in the harbour & there are two locomotives that run to the Iron Mountains. Who can doubt this is soon to be the richest place in the United States? Espesly since the soil is equally rich & the timber so numerous. The climate may be the best of all, despite long, cold winters, for your mother & I both feel as strong & healthy as when we were half our ages, & with spring now hear, the scenery is so beautiful it makes our hearts glad, while our pockets become filled with dollars.

The only concern we have is that all the foolish young men will join up with the army if it comes to war, & then there will be no one to work in the mines or on the trains & boats to haul the ore. I have told Jacob & Caleb that if they are wise, they will stay hear becos men will be needed for work, & wages will increase if workers become scarce. I could use one of them in my blast furnace perhaps—I believe I told you that I & Mr. Henning have built a blast furnace now. Forges have been found unprofitable hear & there is talk that eventually we will simply ship the ore raw. My grandsons are more headstrong than brave I fear, & I think they dream of fighting for their contry rather than staying home & helping the family busines. But if they go to fight, they would serve their contry so I can not argue with them.

I will close now, for my hand gets soar from too much riting. Otherwise, we are all well. I only wish you could all be hear to join in our prosparity. Your mother promises she will rite to you soon. We give you all our love.

Your Father, Lucius Brookfield

Nine days after Lucius wrote to his daughter, war was declared with the firing at Fort Sumter in Charleston Harbor. The firing was over a thousand miles away from Marquette, but it would drastically effect the little harbor town.

1862

When the war began, the people of Marquette, like everyone else in the North and South, hoped it would be short, perhaps only a few months. Jacob and Caleb were anxious to enlist, but their parents convinced them it would be pointless—by the time they reached the training grounds for the troops, the battles would all be fought and the South defeated. For a year, Jacob and Caleb followed news of the battles and the serious losses to the Union army, and they waited out of respect to their parents' feelings.

To help the Union win victory, men were needed to work in the mines so iron could be dug and shipped to make weapons. At the war's beginning, however, Jacob was working as a farmer, helping on both his father and grandfather's property. Caleb had been replaced in Rockford Mercantile by a hired shopgirl; Sophia had insisted Caleb be given a position in Gerald's office so he might better learn business and bookkeeping; Caleb would have preferred to work outdoors with his cousin, but he did not complain since his stepfather had persuaded his mother not to send him away to college. Gerald had told his wife that with the country in such turmoil and so many going away to fight, it would be frivolous for the boy to attend school; he was needed at home to help with the war cause.

Yet the call for volunteers did not cease. In July 1861, some of Marquette's men had joined the Michigan First Infantry. Peter White himself tried to organize and lead a fighting company from Michigan, but the citizens of Marquette rose up in protest that the town needed him more than did the nation. Other young men, however, could not claim to be so valuable to the community; after a year, Jacob and Caleb felt they could no longer detain themselves from enlisting. In August 1862, Captain Moody arranged for the Michigan 27th Infantry Regiment to enlist volunteers in Marquette. Peter White contented himself with serving as Notary Public to authorize the enlistments. Upon learning of the company's formation, Caleb and Jacob decided they would join the next day.

By now the boys were both nineteen. They had been inseparable since childhood and the war would be no barrier to that friendship. If anything, they felt the war would strengthen their bond as they marched, bunked, and fought together. (Neither boy imagined death, but they did daydream of dangerous situations where they would heroically rescue one another to prove their undying friendship). For years, they had longed to see the world. They had long reminisced upon their childhood journey from New York to Marquette as the greatest adventure they had yet known, an adventure that had fueled a desire to see more of America. Jacob's yearnings for adventure were natural for a young man, but his cousin had more personal reasons to enlist.

Caleb had been happier since his mother's second marriage; he and Gerald had become good friends, and Caleb looked up to and respected his stepfather. Still, he felt being employed in his stepfather's office simply because of their relationship was distasteful. His mother still nagged him, and gradually Gerald had started to protect the boy from his mother. Caleb did not want special treatment because he was Gerald Henning's stepson; he felt annoyed when people treated him like the heir to a fabulous fortune that neither of his actual parents had earned. He did not even want the mercantile his parents had established. He wanted to go where he could stand alone proudly as a Rockford. He saw this war as his chance for liberation.

He knew it would be difficult to leave home, but that August afternoon, he steeled his nerves to face the inevitable fury of his mother. He was going to enlist and no one could stop him. He considered letting his stepfather break the news to his mother, but decided that would be the coward's way. No, he would be bold and announce his decision to everyone during supper.

Once the family was gathered at the table, Caleb had difficulty getting anyone's attention; first Agnes spilled her milk, which made Sophia scowl, and then Madeleine, Gerald and Sophia's two year old daughter, decided spilled milk was so delightful she had to clap her hands, thus knocking over her own cup and sending milk all over the floor as she sang nonsensically. The kitchen girl was summoned, but having someone else to clean up the mess did not improve Sophia's mood. Seeing his mother was already angry, Caleb figured he might as well blurt out his news to get it over with.

"Jacob and I are going to enlist tomorrow."

Silence. He thought maybe no one had heard him; they were all so busy moving their feet so the maid could wipe the floor.

Then his mother fixed her eyes upon him. "That's the most ridiculous thing that's ever come out of your ridiculous mouth," she said. Gerald had long ago realized his wife had her moods, but these were the harshest words he had ever heard her say. Of course, after he had added three rooms to the house and hired a girl to help her, Sophia had little reason to chide him.

Caleb tried to explain why he had made the decision, but then Sophia only laughed derisively. Gerald asked whether he were serious, and Caleb assured him he was. Agnes said she wished she were a boy, so she could kill the Rebs. Gerald told her that was no way for a young lady to talk. Sophia told Caleb to eat his supper and quit upsetting his sisters. Caleb replied he was enlisting tomorrow and that was that.

Then Sophia turned on the hysterics. First she burst into tears that infuriated Caleb enough to say, "Stop it, Mother. I'm not a child you can manipulate."

"How am I supposed to react when my son is so cruel to me," she replied. Then she ordered the maid to bring her smelling salts, and she asked Gerald to help her upstairs so she could lie down.

"I'm going to die of a broken heart," she sobbed as she climbed the stairs. Gerald told her to rest while he talked to Caleb, but before he could return downstairs, the children all appeared in Sophia's bedroom. Madeleine began to sob at the sight of her mother lying in bed during the day. Caleb picked up his little sister to calm her. Agnes went to her stepmother's side and consolingly patted her hand, but this attention only encouraged Sophia to say, "Agnes is not even my real daughter, yet she loves me more than my own ungrateful son." After Gerald sent the girls downstairs to finish eating, he told Caleb to wait in the hall while he talked to Sophia. When Gerald reemerged five minutes later, shutting the bedroom door behind him, he asked Caleb again whether he were serious. Again, Caleb asserted he was. "Then I'll talk to your mother after she's rested some," Gerald replied. He did not want to lose his son anymore than Sophia, but he was proud of the boy for taking a stand.

Caleb retired to his room and tried to control his anger over his mother's selfish behavior. He could not wait until Jacob and he were in the army, far away from here.

But the next morning, Sophia would still not give way. When Caleb tried to speak to her, she complained she had heart palpitations until Gerald agreed to send for the doctor. Caleb and Gerald then sat in the upstairs hall while they waited for the doctor's prognosis.

"She always has to control me," Caleb seethed.

"Perhaps," said Gerald, "but only because she loves you."

"If she loved me, she would understand why I have to go."

Gerald put his hand on his stepson's shoulder. Caleb knew his stepfather did not want him to go either, but at least he would let him make his own decision.

"I have to go, Father. It's my duty to serve my country and end slavery. Grandmother Brookfield would understand."

"It would be a great sacrifice for you to make, but so would it be for your mother," said Gerald. "You have a duty to your nation, but you have a greater one to her."

"I won't let her control my life forever."

"You don't need to. You can find freedom here and still not upset her. We can find you a job outside the family business. You could even get your own house now that you're old enough. But try to understand what a horrific blow it would be for your mother and me if we lost you."

"You told me," said Caleb, "that you came to Marquette even when your first wife's family opposed it. You didn't let them stop you."

"No, I didn't," Gerald said, "but that doesn't mean I did the right thing; maybe my first wife wouldn't have died if we had stayed back East where she would have had better medical care. I can't tell you what's right or wrong. I just know your mother and I need you more than the army."

Caleb was glad his stepfather cared so much for him, but he had also watched his mother manipulate Gerald into compromising about nearly everything in their lives. He did not know how his stepfather could claim freedom might exist for him in Marquette; even if he did not live and work with his parents, everyone in town knew his family and labeled him accordingly. At the same time, Caleb's conscience told him he was not being honest about wanting to serve his country; he wanted to escape his family, and perhaps that was insufficient reason to join the army.

The doctor emerged before Caleb could think what to reply.

"How is she?" Gerald asked.

"She seems fine. She says she's having chest pains, but those are probably just from anxiety. Try not to let anything upset her for the next few days and she'll be fine."

Gerald recalled how he had tried to protect Clara from worry their first winter here, but she had insisted on going to the town meeting, only then to lose their first child. He would protect Sophia, even if he had been unable to protect his first wife.

"Thank you, doctor. If you'll follow me, we'll see about your payment."

Gerald led the doctor downstairs. Caleb went to his room, too angry to talk to anyone. Caleb knew his stepfather would not broach the situation again with his mother. Jacob would be here in an hour, and Caleb knew he would tell Jacob why he could not enlist. It would be unfair to leave Gerald to care for his mother; she would be hysterical if he left. He would stay because he loved her, but he was sick of her selfishness; sometimes he thought she was little better than a parasite the way she fed off Gerald's success and expected everyone to follow her dictates. He did not care about the war against the South; a war raged in his own home, in his own heart, and he had to fight it, not run away. He hoped Jacob would understand; Jacob knew by now what his mother was like.

When Jacob arrived, he did not share Caleb's view of the situation. He saw Caleb had let his mother manipulate him again. He wanted to tell Caleb he had to break free from his mother, but his cousin looked so strained that he did not want to appear as if he were blaming Caleb for his mother's behavior.

"I'll stop by later then," was all Jacob said, afraid if he stayed, he would make a comment he would later regret.

Caleb felt like a coward after Jacob left. A couple hours later, when Jacob returned, he tried to steer the conversation away from himself.

"Did you know anyone else who enlisted today?" he asked.

"Jerome White and Edmund Remington from our church were there," said Jacob, "oh, and Mr. Varin; he said his family needs the money with all the babies his wife has had in the last few years; I guess the army pays better than what he makes now. I feel sorry for his wife, though, being left with all those kids."

"He has five children, doesn't he?" Caleb said. He felt like a coward when Mr. Varin could make such a sacrifice. Now Madame Varin would be left without any help, even if the army paid her husband a steady income.

"Yes," said Jacob. "Those French Catholics multiply like rabbits."

"I want to help the war effort, but I just can't leave my family," Caleb said. "I wish I could help some other way than being a soldier."

"I hear they need hands down at the ore docks," said Jacob. "With so many men going off to war, it's hard for them to keep up with the work, and we can't win this war without the iron ore being shipped to places where it can be made into weapons and ships."

"I don't know," said Caleb. "All I've ever done is office work."

"But you hate that, and you've only done it because your mother wants you to. Wouldn't you rather work outdoors than be cooped up in an office all day?"

Caleb knew his mother would think such work beneath his social position, and the idea rather pleased him. Being on the docks would keep him from under his mother's thumb, yet she could not complain since he had not gone off to war. Gerald could convince his mother that the office did not have much work for him, and if he worked on the docks, he would gain more knowledge of the iron industry so one day he could better manage the family business. He would be out of the expensive clothes his mother insisted he wear; he could be like other young men, dirty but strong, filled with the self-respect gained from hard physical labor. It would be a new kind of freedom as his stepfather had suggested.

"I think I will try to get a job on the docks," Caleb said, "but I do feel like a coward not to go to the war."

"There are battles everywhere," Jacob replied. "We can't fight them all at once; you need to fight the one that matters the most to you."

Caleb was relieved that his cousin understood.

"How about I go over to the docks with you?" said Jacob. "I don't have anything else to do right now, and that way, you can get the job before your family has a chance to protest."

"All right," said Caleb. He feared if he did not go now, he never would. Once he made this first break from his family, the rest would be easy.

The cousins walked across town to the Lake Superior Iron Company's dock. There men were busy loading iron ore from railroad cars onto ships. The cousins climbed to the top of the dock, twenty-five feet above the lake. Built in 1857, it was the world's first pocket dock. The dock's chutes released iron ore from its pockets into the hull of the ship. Several men with long poles poked at ore caught in the pockets to push it through the chutes. The cousins watched this innovative process until a foreman was free to talk with them.

"Do you think you can handle this kind of work?" asked the boss after Caleb explained why he was there.

"It doesn't look easy," said Caleb, "but I'm willing to give it a try."

"What kind of work have you done?"

"Just office work, but I'd rather work outdoors like this."

"Where'd you do office work?"

Caleb told him. The man put two and two together and realized Caleb was Gerald Henning's stepson. He had great respect for Mr. Henning, most of the town did, but he did not respect sons, much less stepsons, of rich men. He assessed Caleb's size, build, and air of capability; he found them all lacking, but he was shorthanded, and he did not want Mr. Henning as an enemy.

"All right, I'll give you a chance, but you make sure you're here on time each morning and ready to work hard all day."

"Yes, sir," Caleb replied.

The boss walked off. A man who had overheard the conversation said, "Don't worry; 'tain't hard as it looks. Your muscles'll be sore the first few days, but then you'll get used ta it. I've been workin' these docks nearly ten years now, and I tell ya the work is easy compared ta when I started."

"You must have been here before the railroad and the pocket dock were built," Jacob said.

"Yup. Those days it was a downright primitive procedure. Why these last five years or so have been marvels of ingenuity."

"How's it different?" asked Caleb. As a boy, he had watched the pocket dock and the railroad being built, yet he hardly understood their significance.

"Why, before the railroad, we had ta haul that ore in carts with mules down the plank road. Then, since there weren't no pocket docks for the ore ta pour inta the ship from, and no ships yet built just ta carry ore, we had ta unload the cars and shovel the ore onta the dock. Then we shoveled it inta wheelbarrows and pushed those up the gangplank, strugglin' and strainin' all the way. From them wheelbarrows, we shoveled the ore onta the ship's deck or hold, depending on the ship's size. It used ta take nearly thirty men and several days ta load a ship with just a few hunderd tons. Now we can do it easy in a day."

"I guess I won't complain about the work then," said Caleb.

"You'll do jus' fine," replied the dockhand, patting Caleb on the shoulder. "I'll keep an eye on ya."

Caleb thanked the man. Then the cousins returned down the twenty-five feet of stairs.

"Congratulations," Jacob said at the bottom. "You've got a new job."

Caleb was less elated, but he felt determined to carry through on his decision. He decided his parents would not know what he had done until tomorrow night when he returned home in his work clothes. Gerald would be surprised when he did not show up at the office tomorrow morning, but Caleb was sure he would understand.

The next evening, Caleb came home with his pants and shirt covered in red iron ore dust. He knew his mother would be furious when she saw him, but he did not care. He was exhausted and that made him ornery and determined to defend his decision. Even with his legs about to drop from beneath him, he steeled himself for an argument.

Gerald met him at the door. He understood instantly—he had made inquiries to find out where Caleb was that day, and he admired the boy's sudden self-reliance. But he asked Caleb to go in the back door; he wanted to talk to Sophia before she had a chance to see her son. Caleb was too tired to argue, although he felt it would be more manly to tell her himself. He went around to the kitchen door. His room was just off the kitchen so he carried in water from the well so the maid could heat it and draw him a bath in his room. Once the tub was filled with water, he went into his room, took off his clothes, and scrubbed off the red dust.

In the middle of his bath, he heard a noisy pounding overhead. Someone was running down the upstairs hall. Then he could hear his mother screaming. He could not distinguish her words, but they were loud and hysterical. He quickly finished his bath, dried himself off and dressed. Then he stepped into the kitchen where he found his stepfather waiting for him.

"Your mother wants to talk to you," said Gerald.

"Is it bad?"

"Not as bad as I expected. I tried to convince her that your working on the docks was a lesser evil than your joining the army, but she's still not happy."

Caleb hesitated, then went to the parlor. Sophia would barely look at him. He made several unsuccessful attempts to speak. Then her wrath broke forth.

"Caleb, how could you? After all I've done to give you a better life."

"But, Mother, it's for the good of the country. So many men have enlisted in the army that there's a shortage of workers on the docks. I thought you'd be happy that I was doing my duty and still remaining at home."

"Why can't you work in your stepfather's office?" Sophia asked. "You'll learn the family business better that way."

"I'm not needed in the office. I'm needed on the docks, and since the iron industry is our business, I can learn more about production and shipment there."

"There are other men who can do that work."

"Sophia, there's nothing wrong with physical labor," Gerald said. "After all, President Lincoln got his start splitting rails."

Sophia thought the country would be better off if Lincoln had stuck to splitting rails; he had not ended slavery as hoped, and the Union only seemed to be losing the war. If he knew how to run the country, the war would be over by now and her son would not be disgracing her by being seen in the streets covered in filthy red dust.

"You knew I'd disapprove," she told Caleb, "yet you deliberately chose to spite me. I hope you're happy that you've embarrassed the entire family with your behavior."

"I need to do what makes me happy," Caleb replied.

"Happy? As if you have reason to be unhappy when your stepfather and I give you everything you could possibly want."

"I'm needed there, Mother, and I like the work and the other men."

"They're low, dirty men. I wanted you to go to college, to become a businessman or a lawyer, to make contacts with people who could help you; you won't meet anyone who matters on those docks."

"Grandmother will be proud that I'm helping the war cause," said Caleb. "I don't know why you can't feel the same way."

Sophia would not reply. Gerald said, "I'm sure the war will be over soon and then we can all go back to our normal lives."

Sophia was infuriated that Gerald took Caleb's side. She would not speak to either of them.

"It's just until the war is over, Mother," Caleb said.

But Sophia remained silent. If she could not win with this obstinate boy, she would not give her verbal consent. Caleb, seeing it was pointless to argue, went to his room until the hired girl called him for supper. Scarcely anyone spoke at the table that night. Caleb was too exhausted from the day's work to talk anyway. The entire family tried to escape its gloom by going to bed early.

In the morning, Sophia refused to get out of bed.

"She'll come around eventually," Gerald told Caleb. "We just need to give her time. As for me, I'm proud of my son."

By the time Jacob Whitman enlisted, Michigan had already sent over twenty-five thousand of her brave sons to fight for the Union. Consequently, it took the Michigan 27th Regiment nearly a month to recruit enough soldiers, but by September, Jacob sailed with Captain Moody's company of ninety-six men from Upper Michigan. They arrived in Port Huron where they would train until April, a long impatient time to wait for orders. But when April 1863 came, they would be boarded on trains heading to Kentucky, and then they would join in some of the Civil War's fiercest battles. Michigan would be proud of their bravery, and many courageous young men would make the ultimate sacrifice to save the Union.

For those who remained at home, bravery was equally needed. Caleb Rockford dutifully went to work everyday, finding the labor less exhausting and more stimulating as the weeks passed. His back grew stronger, his stamina greater, and soon he could climb the twenty-five feet of stairs to the top of the dock without feeling out of breath. He diligently worked while constantly concerned for his cousin. He and Jacob had never gone more than a day without seeing each other; it was strange now not to talk with Jacob, not to know what he was doing or where he was. He wished he had gone to the war if only to look out for his cousin, but he also knew that working on the ore dock provided a vital service to the nation. The iron ore he loaded onto ships made its way to Cleveland and Toledo, then was transported overland to the furnaces of Pittsburgh. That iron ore would win the war—it would be made into Union Ironclad ships, into swords and bayonets, rifles and cannons, cannon balls and iron slugs to fill canisters for shrapnel; it would empower the railroads that brought the men to the front line; it would create the bullet that shot the rebel soldier who otherwise might shoot Jacob. Caleb was helping to win the war, to bring Jacob and thousands of other soldiers home all the sooner. He was proud to be a part of something greater than himself, and proud to do it without his mother or stepfather's help.

Jacob's parents were proud of their own son, although they feared terribly for his safety. They were not alone in their pride and fear. Throughout Marquette, fathers and sons, brothers and cousins, mothers, daughters, fiancees and wives, even grandparents and neighbors prayed every morning and every night for the protection of their young men; often the war was worse for those who stayed home than for the soldiers in the fields, for the soldiers were safe when not in battle, but their loved ones were never free from worry, never knowing whether their men were safe. Yet they were all proud of their soldiers. Some declared they hated the war; others said it was a necessary evil. They all said the Union would prevail because the war was just; they feared to think otherwise.

Suzanne Varin worried every minute. Her husband had gone to the war to provide money to feed their growing family, now of five children. If Jean did not come home, she would never be able to support all the children on her own. When Jean enlisted, Suzanne had written to her younger brother, Amedee, in Montreal; her and Amedee's parents were dead, so Amedee, who had been living with an uncle, agreed to come to Marquette to help his sister. He was only fifteen, and she scarcely knew him, not having seen him since he was a small child. But he was a loyal brother, and she found him a great help with the children; still he was one more mouth to feed. Suzanne tried to keep her temper all that autumn so she would not upset her children, but the day came when she could no longer hold in her pain.

"The Lord's work is being done," Rebecca Brookfield stated one Thursday afternoon when the Ladies Literary Society gathered for its meeting in what was now Sophia Henning's parlor. "God blessed this nation at its founding, but Satan whispered in the ears of the Southerners not to abolish slavery. Now God's righteous cause will prevail."

"Oh what do I care?" said Suzanne, tired of the old woman's pious moralizing about the war. "I know nothing of this nation and its history. I am from Quebec, and there we never had slavery as you Americans have. And why should I care about those slaves anyway? They are not my people. I do not know them. I only know I have five children and a brother to feed, and if my husband is killed, we will all starve."

"We all have to make sacrifices, my dear," Rebecca replied.

"What sacrifice have you made? You have not sent a son or husband to fight?"

Rebecca tried to explain that the Lord vindicates the Oppressed and raises up the Humble. Molly Bergmann tried to speak more to Suzanne's concerns by saying, "Suzanne, I also have a husband and we are also poor, but I know if Fritz were in better health, he would have gone to war, and I would have supported him. We will all get by if we help each other. Be proud your husband is fighting to free people, and tell your children to be proud of him."

Suzanne said nothing; she remained irritated. It was easy for Molly to say she would be proud to send her husband; he could not go, so she need not worry, and Molly only had one child to feed—not five.

Cordelia wanted to say something to comfort Suzanne, but she was so worried about Jacob that she needed consolation herself. Sophia was sick of hearing about the war; she called the meeting to order. Discussion began on Nathaniel Hawthorne's *The Marble Faun*, a novel set in Italy, far away from America's battlefields.

"It's not Hawthorne's best novel," Dolly O'Neill said. She was the society's newest member, invited to fill Clara's place. She and her husband had moved to Marquette from South Carolina a few years before the war began. The O'Neills favored the Union's cause, yet since the war began, their Southern background had made them largely shunned by the community. Sophia thought it bad enough Dolly was a Southerner, and worse that she was another Catholic in a female literary society predominated by Methodists.

"I thought the scene where Hilda goes to confession when she's not even Catholic was completely preposterous," Rebecca said. "No 'Daughter of the Puritans', as Hawthorne calls her, would ever do such a thing."

But if Rebecca Brookfield were prejudiced against Catholics as a group, she did care about individuals. She remembered Suzanne's outburst throughout the meeting. Rebecca had felt it unfair that Suzanne accused her of not having made any sacrifice; Rebecca knew she had sacrificed years of her life for the sake of this righteous cause; first she had devoted thousands of hours to promote abolition before war could result, and now she was praying desperately that her grandson Jacob would return safely. But if she mentioned these facts, they would not bring Madame Varin any consolation. Perhaps she might do something more to their mutual benefit.

"Madame Varin," she said, touching Suzanne's arm as the meeting recessed. "I am sorry I upset you. None of us want this war, but neither do we want those poor slaves to suffer any longer."

"I know. It is not your fault. It's just—I miss my husband, and I worry he will not come back."

"I know; my grandson Jacob has gone also. The war is a burden on us all, but perhaps I could lighten your burden. It may not be the best solution, but my husband and I are getting old; we cannot operate the house and farm by ourselves. Jacob used to help us and we had a farm hand too, but now both have enlisted. I would be willing to pay you wages if you cared to come help me around the house now and then. I know you have your children to look after, but you could bring them with you. I like children—their laughter might keep me young a bit longer."

Suzanne's eyes widened at this good fortune.

"It is kind of you."

"Wait, I'm not finished. I know your children are small, but your brother— he's about thirteen, isn't he?"

"Amedee—he just turned fifteen."

"Perhaps he could help Lucius bring in the harvest. Do you think he'd be able?"

"Oh yes. He is a big strong boy, almost a man, and I have told him he should find work. He has been going to school, but we need the money more, and he can already read and do figures, so I do not think he needs more schooling."

"Well, we don't want to neglect his education," said the true daughter of New England, "but perhaps he could come work after school and on Saturdays."

"Thank you," Suzanne replied. "We will both come."

"That's fine," said Rebecca. "Is tomorrow too soon? I'll talk to my husband to see what we can pay you, but please do come; we all need to help each other in these times, and you will be helping us most I think."

"Thank you," Suzanne repeated. "You are a good woman." Then she hurried home to tell her brother, who was watching the children.

Rebecca Brookfield felt God smiled on her for helping a neighbor. After seventy-two years, she could still find ways to accomplish the Lord's work.

1863

A couple days after the New Year began, Cordelia arrived at her parents' house to bring the news. President Lincoln had signed the Emancipation Proclamation to free the slaves in all the Southern States.

"Glory be," whispered Rebecca, pleased but unable to exult in a louder voice. She had been ill since Christmas and was still confined to her bed. Her enthusiasm was less than Cordelia expected, but her heart beat with joy.

"Some say," Cordelia remarked, sitting down at her mother's bedside, "that emancipation is just a war strategy so the slaves will rebel against their owners."

"No, the President is a good man," said Rebecca. "He knows this proclamation will not only help defeat the South, but will be a transition toward abolition even in those slaveholding states that remained in the Union. Abraham is a fine biblical name, but Moses would be more fitting for a president who has liberated an oppressed people. I thank the Lord for letting me live long enough to see this day."

"I'm thankful it's been done before Jacob has seen conflict," said Cordelia, her thoughts never far from her son's danger. "Perhaps now the war will end before he has to fight."

"Is he still stationed in Port Huron?" Rebecca asked.

"Yes, he and Jean both," Suzanne replied. She had entered the room with tea for the three of them; in the past few months, she had become more a companion than servant to Rebecca. "My Jean just sent me a letter. He says they are both fine. I only hope you're right, Cordelia, that the war will end now, for I want my Jean to come home."

"Both will come home, my dears," said Rebecca, taking their hands. "Trust in the Lord. He will provide."

Suzanne squeezed the old woman's hand. She trusted Rebecca was right for after a number of long talks, she now understood how many trials the old woman had seen, and that she had learned patience from them.

"How are you feeling today, Mother?" asked Cordelia.

"Still rather weak. I've been sleeping a lot—it's mostly exhaustion I guess; I think I'm over my cold, so I just need to get back my strength. I hope to be up in a day or two so I can finish making that quilt for Edna; I feel awful not to have finished it in time for Christmas."

"That's all right; she understands," Cordelia replied. She suspected Edna would have a long wait for the quilt. Her mother had been looking thinner and weaker each year, and while her hardy spirit kept her going, her constant activity had become more than her frail body could handle. Cordelia feared her mother would not be with them much longer, and she did not know how she would manage without her. She had her own family of course; she loved them all dearly, but she was the caretaker for all of them, while her mother had continually been the one she turned to for help; she had no better friend than her mother.

"Hello," called a female voice from the front door.

Suzanne went to the door, returning a moment later with Molly Bergmann.

"I heard you were ill, Mrs. Brookfield, so I made you some chicken soup—I gave it to Suzanne, and she can just reheat it for you."

"Thank you, dear. You're too kind."

Molly felt it was kind of her; she was still not fond of Mrs. Brookfield, but she remembered how Clara had tried to befriend the old lady; sometimes, she wondered whether Clara would have been so kind if she could have foreseen that Mrs. Brookfield's daughter would one day marry Gerald. Poor Gerald! Molly still had to shake her head over that strange marriage. Gerald rarely seemed cheerful since he had remarried, and Molly was certain Sophia's petulance was the cause. Fritz had tried to tell her, "It's not Sophia's fault; Gerald changed because Clara died." But Molly thought a good second wife would have brought back Gerald's old spirit.

"How is Mr. Bergmann feeling?" Cordelia asked Molly.

"He's ill as usual. Since I was making chicken soup for him I thought I'd make enough for both our sick patients."

"I won't be sick for long," Rebecca said. "Have you heard, dear, about the Emancipation Proclamation? Isn't it wonderful?"

"Yes," said Molly; her sympathies were always with the poor; she had witnessed plenty of poverty in Ireland, and she imagined the slaves' lives were just as miserable if not worse.

"Mother, what will you do now that your favorite cause has been achieved?" Cordelia asked.

"There is still plenty to do. We will need to start organizations to clothe and feed the former slaves. We must teach them to read and how to farm for themselves. I'll do whatever I can to support efforts to educate them."

"I never realized there would be so much work after slavery ended," Cordelia replied.

"There is always work. Our Lord said the poor will always be with us. And now that the slaves have freedom, I will also devote myself to women's suffrage."

"What's that?" asked Molly.

"Why, allowing women to vote," Rebecca replied.

"That will never happen," Molly stated. "Men will never let it happen."

"It will happen," Rebecca declared, squaring her lips in determination. "Perhaps not in my lifetime, but I believe in your lifetimes."

A few minutes later, Molly said her goodbyes, and Cordelia, having to get home to do her boarders' laundry, offered to return with her to town.

"I hope Fritz will be well soon," Cordelia said as the women stepped over little snowpiles in the road. Already two feet of snow had been shoveled up along the road, and no one doubted another two or maybe four feet would cover the ground before winter ended. Cordelia wished it were spring so she would not have to worry so much about her mother's health.

"Fritz will be fine. He always gets better," said Molly, although she knew Fritz had never fully recovered from the typhoid of so many years before. Molly could not complain though because Karl was growing up to be a great help to her. Her only complaint was that she had not had more children. But she would not dwell on her own misfortunes; she looked over and saw Cordelia glumly staring at the ground.

"You're very worried about your mother, aren't you?" she said.

"Yes, she seemed better today, perhaps from joy over the Emancipation, but she just keeps getting thinner and more pale all the time. Last time I spoke to the doctor, he told me to prepare myself that if she does pull through this winter, she probably won't make it through another."

"She's a remarkable woman," said Molly, admiring if not liking Rebecca. "She has more determination than any woman I know. I'm sure she'll be supporting her causes for years to come."

"I hope so, but she will be seventy-three this year. I don't know what my father will do without her." Cordelia worried more how she would manage without her mother's support. She did not know she was the least of her mother's worries.

Rebecca Brookfield loved all her children dearly, and she worried how they would get along after she was gone. Her heart had ached most for her son, Darius, who had gone West, never to be heard from again. And she missed her daughter, Omelia, back in New York, whom she had not seen these thirteen years. She worried about Sophia, who claimed she was always too busy to come visit her mother. Rebecca worried least about Cordelia, for she felt this daughter most like herself, hardy and determined. She only worried how Cordelia would bear the pain if Jacob did not return from the war; Rebecca knew what it was to lose a son, and she knew a mother could barely live through such grief. She hoped the Emancipation Proclamation was a sign the war would now take a turn. She hoped she would live to see her grandson return home.

"I think I should take a little nap before supper," Rebecca told Suzanne, after her visitors had departed. "I guess I overexcited myself about the slaves being freed."

"All right," said Suzanne. "You rest, and I'll have some of Molly's chicken soup ready for you when you wake."

"I'm not really hungry, dear. Why don't you save the soup for Lucius's supper?"

"You have to eat," said Suzanne.

"Maybe after I take a little nap," said Rebecca. Suzanne lifted the quilt over her and adjusted her pillow. "I'm so glad Cordelia brought me the news of the proclamation. She's always such a thoughtful daughter. Thank you, dear. The pillows are fine now. You're so good to me. You're just like another daughter."

"That's very kind of you," said Suzanne. "I'd be proud if you were my mother."

"Be sure to wake me up when Lucius gets home, dear."

"I will," Suzanne whispered as she closed Rebecca's bedroom door.

For two more weeks, Rebecca was confined to her bed. She made a couple attempts to sit up and even eat at the table, but afterward, she complained of weakness and was escorted back to her room. She scarcely slept at night and wheezed constantly. Lucius resorted to sleeping in a spare bedroom so he would not disturb her rest. One morning, he did not go to work because she had a fever.

"I'm sure she'll be fine," Suzanne told him. "If she gets worse, I'll send Amedee to the blast furnace to fetch you."

"No, I won't go to work today," said Lucius. "I don't think it'll be much longer."

"You must keep your hopes up," said Suzanne. "Let's send for the doctor."

"Go ahead and send Amedee; perhaps the doctor can make her passing more peaceful, but the time is near. I can hear the death rattle in her breathing."

Amedee returned an hour later with the doctor. Rebecca was given morphine for her pain; she slept more easily then, but the doctor agreed her end was near. She lingered through the day, while Lucius and Suzanne took turns sitting with her. Lucius did not want to leave her bedside, but at certain moments, Rebecca's suffering seemed so intense he could not bear it. She was too sleepy even to know when he was beside her. But he was holding her hand late that afternoon when her spirit left its mortal frame. He did not doubt she was with her Lord now.

He was still holding her hand a few minutes later when Cordelia arrived, having heard by word-of-mouth that Amedee had come to town to fetch the doctor. Lucius was not an emotional man, but he released his wife's limp hand to embrace his daughter, and he held her tightly as she wept. Suzanne marveled that the old man cared more to comfort his daughter than to indulge his own grief. She suspected Rebecca would not have accomplished so much in her life without this self-reliant man beside her. She wondered which of the two elderly Brookfields were the more remarkable.

Winter passed slowly that year. Marquette's winters are always long, and they depress many a soul; this particular winter, sadness and gloom was more common than ever. Cordelia felt a darker mood settle over her than she had ever known before. She was constantly worried about Jacob, and the loss of her mother was an irrecoverable blow. She carried on for Nathaniel and Edna's sakes, but her heart seemed to have gone out of living.

Suzanne also grieved Rebecca's loss; the women had only been friends a short time, but they had become intimate. Few women who came to know Rebecca did not feel she was a motherly or grandmotherly figure to them. With Rebecca to care for, Suzanne had been able to forget her own troubles, as well as confide them to Rebecca, the only adult she had to speak to. She loved her brother and her children, but they could not understand her worries and fears. Until she had Jean back again to share her life, she knew she would struggle to maintain her composure. She missed Jean terribly and prayed he would be sent home to her.

Caleb's heart ached all that winter and into the spring. His best friend's absence became near unbearable at times. He had no one to tell his daily frustrations, or to share his small triumphs. His stepfather was kind, but Caleb felt he could not be completely open with the husband of the woman he blamed for many of his misfortunes. He was also saddened by his grandmother's death, mainly because he saw how hard his grandfather took it. Lucius had lost much of his enthusiasm for life after his wife's death. Gerald had admitted to Caleb that Lucius's enthusiasm for the business was diminishing. Caleb was saddened that after his grandfather had labored so many years, now his life should come to this decaying existence. He had always admired his grandparents for their dedication to their work and for their charity to others, but now what personal good had it done them? When he noticed one winter day how feeble his grandfather's step had become, Caleb suggested he might stay awhile with his grandfather.

Caleb found himself somewhat happier once he began living at the Brookfield farm. He would work all day on the ore dock, then go straight to his grandfather's house, and in doing so, he avoided his mother and decreased a great deal of the strain in his life. At the same time, he found himself bored. Physical labor had little excitement to offer, even if his work aided a good cause. He loved his grandfather but soon discovered they had little to say to one another. Caleb felt he had little to say to anyone; he was lonely. Most men his age were thinking of marriage, yet he did not want to be tied down with a wife; perhaps he feared he would marry a woman who nagged like his mother. He suspected if a girl did marry him, it would be because he was Gerald Henning's stepson and could give her wealth and social position.

If Jacob would only come home, Caleb thought he might be released from his mundane life. As he worked on the docks, he would occasionally stop to stare out at the vastness of Lake Superior. The lake faded off into the horizon as though it were neverending. Caleb wondered what life on its far opposite shore was like; he envied the men on the ore boats, those men who could sail away from this small town. If he were one of them, he might see Chicago, Green Bay, Milwaukee, Detroit, Cleveland, even Buffalo. There were multitudes in those great cities whom he might befriend, with whom he might feel he belonged. Instead he was here, alone.

If only the war would end, then Jacob would return. Then they could leave Marquette together and have the adventures they had dreamed about—to see San Francisco, or the Sandwich Islands, or even Europe. To go anywhere. It did not matter where if he could only escape from here. When Jacob came home, then he might begin to live.

Whenever Cordelia received a letter from Jacob, the first thing she did was look at the postmark to see when he had last written. The postmark always told her the last date she could be certain he was alive. Today when a letter arrived, she was too anxious to wait until Nathaniel returned home before she read it. She quickly ripped the envelope open, then found two separate letters inside. When she saw the first was addressed to her and Nathaniel, she did not look at the second, assuming it must be for Edna. She unfolded the first letter, disappointed to see it was so short.

July 11, 1863
Corporal Jacob Whitman
Michigan 27th Infantry
Dear Father and Mother,
    I am alive and well. As you may have heard, my company is in the midst of a great campaign here in Mississippi. We believe there is little doubt now that we will win the war, but it could still drag on for many months. I hate to worry you, but I admit I fear for my life daily. Today I saw the first of my comrades die in battle. I will keep this short because I must write to his wife. It was Mr. Varin who was killed. I saw him fall the moment he was shot. It was a quick death, and I do not believe he suffered more than a second. I know my letter may be slow in coming, but the government can also be slow in identifying bodies and contacting people. If Madame Varin has not

already received the news, please Mother, will you break it to her and give her the letter I am enclosing? I am sorry to ask you this, but the news may be softened if it comes from a friend. I have never had to write such a difficult letter in my life, and I pray I never will again.

I promise to be careful and to do my best to come through this war alive. For now, take comfort that I am well. I pray for all of you every night as I know you do for me.

Love, Jacob

Cordelia read the letter over several times. Again she felt how unfair it was that the letter was so short when she seldom heard from her son. He made no mention of the last two letters she had sent him, so she feared he had never received them. But he was still alive; that was enough. Then she asked herself how she could be so selfish when poor Suzanne had just lost her husband. Cordelia had scarcely known Jean Varin, but she pitied his wife and children. She went upstairs to fetch her bonnet, while rehearsing in her mind how she would tell the poor woman. She knew Suzanne would be at home today rather than at the Brookfield farm.

Half an hour later, Cordelia found Suzanne at home surrounded by a mob of screaming children among whom she was trying to maintain peace. The mother wanted to put the baby down for its afternoon nap, but Gervase and Francois were fighting up a storm, and Hortense, who had been making mud pies, was trying to change into a clean dress, which she was only muddying in the process.

When the children saw Cordelia, they ran to her, for she had brought them treats a couple times in the past. She had none today, but after promising not to forget next time, and after Suzanne scolded them for begging, the children agreed to go outside so Cordelia could speak with their mother alone.

"You have a way with them, Cordelia. It's a pity you did not have more children."

"I'm sure if I had, they would give me as much trouble as yours are giving you," Cordelia half-laughed. She tried to sound lighthearted, but she felt deathly sick now that she was alone with Suzanne.

"You look faint, mon ami. Sit down please," said her hostess.

"Thank you. I—"

"I will make us some coffee."

"No, please, sit—I don't really feel like coffee, but thank you."

Suzanne sighed with relief. She was almost out of coffee and had hoped to stretch it out a couple more days, but she would not be so impolite as not to offer it to her guest, especially when she knew how hard Cordelia had taken her mother's death.

"How are you, mon ami?" asked Suzanne, lightly tapping her on the knee. "Have you finished our book reading for this month?"

"No. Suzanne, I need to talk to you. It's something very serious."

"You do look serious. Is something wrong?"

"I just got a letter from Jacob."

"Oh, how funny. I just got one from my Jean yesterday. He always mentions what a good soldier your son is."

Cordelia would have been pleased with this praise if she were not focused on her task.

"Jacob wrote because—well, he's written you a letter. It's Jean. He—"

"Is he hurt?" asked Suzanne, now recognizing Cordelia's somber tone; she jumped up from her chair in agitation.

"No, he's not hurt—he's—" Cordelia's inability to speak made her message apparent.

"Oh, no, not my Jean. My sweet, sweet Jean. Anything but my Jean!"

Cordelia feared Suzanne would become hysterical. A desperate wildness flashed in the Frenchwoman's eyes; then she grabbed her apron to hide her sobs.

Cordelia moved to the sofa and pulled the newly widowed mother onto it. She held her. She tried to console her, although she did not know how.

"I believe it was quick. Jean couldn't have felt much pain. Jacob said he died instantly. He'll tell you so in his letter, I'm sure. I'm so sorry, Suzanne. I don't know what to say. I would change it if I could."

"Jacob wrote me a letter?" Suzanne asked, wiping her eyes with her apron.

"Yes. I have it here," said Cordelia, reaching into her pocket.

"It was—kind of him to think of me when he must suffer himself from fear of being there," said Suzanne, taking the letter. "Oh, my Jean. My sweet Jean. If only I had treated him better. I wish I could just see him one more time to tell him I am sorry for every little thing I ever said or did to hurt him. I loved him more than anything. I was never good enough to him."

Her eyes flooded again.

"What can I do for you, Suzanne? Should I go get the priest?"

"No, no, just stay with me a little while. I'll be fine."

"All right."

Cordelia gave her handkerchief to Suzanne and waited as she blew her nose. "Will you read Jacob's letter to me?" Suzanne asked.

"Certainly."

Cordelia unfolded the letter and read aloud.

July 11, 1863
Corporal Jacob Whitman
Michigan 27th Infantry
Dear Madame Varin,

I hope you have already heard the sad news, for I hate that I must be the bearer of it. Your husband and my good friend was killed in battle yesterday near Jackson, Mississippi. It was a sudden death. He was shot in the chest and died instantly. I am sure he did not suffer. You have my fullest sympathies on his loss.

Jean was a good man, one I was proud to serve with. We developed a close friendship these last months, often comforting each other with memories of home. He told me he considered Marquette and the United States as his home even though he was born in Quebec, and he felt great pride to fight with the Union army to help end the dreadful crime of slavery. He told me often whatever good was in him he owed to his wife's influence; he always spoke of you with great fondness. He said he never understood how he could deserve such a good wife or such beautiful children. The day before he died, he told me he could not wait for the war to be over; he looked forward to coming home with his money from being a soldier so he could make his family more comfortable.

He was always kind to me. We often shared a tent at night. He always looked out for my needs and was willing to share with me any letters he received with news from home. He even insisted on sharing his food so the younger men would have more. He spent many of his free hours reading the French book of Catholic prayers he had brought from home, so rest assured he was at peace with God.

I am greatly grieved at his lost, and hope my letter will bring some little consolation. I am sure my family will help all they can to lighten your loss.

With deepest sympathies, Corporal Jacob Whitman

"It is kind of him to write," Suzanne repeated.

"Can I do anything for you, Suzanne?" asked Cordelia, refolding the letter.

"My children. What will become of them without a father? They are so young they will not even remember him."

"They can be proud that he died for a noble cause."

Noble causes cannot console a grieving wife; Cordelia suspected if Jacob were killed, the noble cause would not comfort her either as a grieving mother. This death made the war stunningly real, and not so far away as it had seemed.

Cordelia was relieved when Amedee soon came home; the boy turned pale when Suzanne broke the news to him, but he put duty first and took his sister's hand to comfort her.

"Do not worry, Suzanne. We will miss Jean, but all will yet be well. I will support the family now."

Amedee was little more than a boy, but Cordelia saw he was a brave and good one to take such a burden upon himself. She saw now why her father spoke of him as such a dedicated worker.

"I think I better go lie down for a while," Suzanne said. "Thank you for coming, Cordelia."

"If I can watch the children or help with the funeral," Cordelia said, glad to do anything if only now she might escape from the grieving woman's presence.

"We will let you know if we need anything, Mrs. Whitman," Amedee spoke for his sister. "Thank you for your kindness."

Cordelia escaped from the house of mourning, shaken by the horror of war. The death of Mr. Varin made her fear all the more that Jacob might not return home.

Lucius Brookfield felt old. Since his wife's death, he could feel himself slowing down. Without Rebecca, there seemed less purpose in life, less reason to work so hard. Gerald was able to run the blast furnace just as well as he could. His children had their own affairs to concern themselves with. Jacob was far away and he missed the boy. Caleb, he was sure, did not enjoy playing nursemaid to his grandfather. He had told Lucius he was glad to be at the farm where there were "no women fussing over me like at home" but Lucius suspected Caleb really wanted the freedom of his own home. No one seemed to need him anymore. He had begun to wonder what purpose remained for him.

Then Jean Varin's death made Lucius realize others were suffering. Suzanne had been good to Rebecca, yet now she knew grief like his own. Rebecca had asked Suzanne and Amedee to work for them as a way to help the Varins without giving them charity. Now with her husband gone, Suzanne would have difficulty supporting all her children. Amedee would help, but he was a boy who did not deserve such a burden.

Lucius did not understand why the Lord took away good people, only to leave the weak behind. Rebecca had spent her life caring for others; he had supported her, always feeling his work was scarcely meaningful beside hers. Rebecca used to tell him his business success resulted from his being a righteous man; now he questioned whether he had not spent too many years pursuing wealth when he might have done more for others. He believed in the Puritan work ethic of his forefathers, and now their Puritan guilt welled up in him for not helping his neighbors as much as he could have.

Suzanne still came over to clean the farmhouse a couple times a week. One afternoon, a month after Jean Varin's death, Lucius sat her down and said, "Suzanne, why don't we get married?"

A young man, proposing for the first time, fears rejection, but Lucius's heart could not be broken since he had no romantic delusions. He asked boldly without nervousness.

Suzanne blushed. She did not know what to respond. First, she thought the old man was losing his mind. Then she feared he sought something else, but she quickly dismissed this idea, knowing he had always been a gentleman in the past.

"Mr. Brookfield, I don't understand."

"I want you to marry me," he repeated.

"Ye-es," Suzanne said, "but I don't understand why."

"I'm not foolish enough to think you could love an old man like me," he said. "After all, I'm nearly three quarters of a century old. I could almost be your grandfather—I suppose. But you are a good girl, Suzanne; I can see that. You've been kind to me and you were kind to Rebecca. I want to be kind to you in return. And to Amedee. He's a good boy and a hard worker. Both of you are honest and never rude to your elders. I know you'll have a hard struggle now that your husband has passed away, so I want to help you."

"But you do help; you pay us good wages."

"There's more I could do, but to do it, I need to be more than just your employer."

"Mr. Brookfield," she replied, slowly standing up. "I'm flattered, but what would your family say?"

"Please don't go. Hear me out," Lucius replied. "My family does not matter. I still have my mind about me, so I can do as I please."

"But I—I wouldn't—Mr. Brookfield." She didn't know what to say, or how to object. She was simply too surprised. So surprised she sat back down.

"I don't need reasons for why we should not marry, Suzanne. I just need to know whether you're willing to be my wife for the few remaining years of my life. I don't ask for love, just that you stay and care for me. I'm an old man now, and you know I'm lonely without Rebecca. I love my daughters, but I don't want to burden them with caring for me. If you will be a companion to me in my last years, when I'm gone, I'll make sure you are well provided for."

"It's very kind," Suzanne replied, "but I do not know whether it is right for me to marry a man I do not love."

"People do it everyday, people who do not know each other as well as we do," said Lucius. "And we love each other in the Christian sense as brother and sister. We will be great friends. That can be enough."

"Mr. Brookfield, you have caught me off guard. I—"

"Then you are not refusing me?"

"I—"

"No rush, my dear. I'm sure I'll live a while yet. Why don't you give it some thought and discuss it with Amedee if you wish? It's Friday afternoon now. Give me your answer when you come back on Monday. That's all I ask."

"I—I," Suzanne stumbled for the right words. How could she possibly say yes, or say no for that matter? "Mr. Brookfield, whatever answer I give you, I thank you for the honor you have done me."

She got up from her chair, and although she felt like running from the house, she composed herself enough to walk to the coat hook, remove her shawl, and then pass out the back door, muttering "Goodbye." As she left the house, she saw Amedee working out in the field. He waved to her, and she raised her hand in return, but she was too confused to tell him yet of her dilemma. She trod down the road, her mind utterly boggled as she weighed the choice before her, although she felt she had already decided her answer.

An hour later, Amedee finished his daily work. Mr. Brookfield paid him his wages on Friday, so he went to the house to receive his compensation and exchange a few pleasantries before departing for home. Lucius had more than a few pleasantries for the boy; rather than remaining five minutes, Amedee and Mr. Brookfield talked for an hour, as one man to another; it was an odd meeting, perhaps the first time an old man asked a boy young enough to be his grandson for permission to marry that boy's sister. At the end of the talk, however, the two understood each other. Amedee went home that evening, feeling freed from the burden that had fallen upon him when his brother-in-law had been killed.

A December wedding was agreed upon. Suzanne had requested a wait of several months to mourn her Jean. Lucius consented, not intending to die anytime soon; he hoped the extended engagement would give his daughters time to adjust to the thought of a stepmother. Being in New York, Omelia could make little objection. When Lucius broke the news to Cordelia, she instantly understood her father's generous intentions and recalled Suzanne's kindness to her mother; she knew her father would not forget his children or grandchildren in his will. Then Lucius asked Cordelia whether she would inform Sophia for him. Perhaps he should have made the announcement himself, but even Lucius was a little nervous about his third daughter's reaction.

Sophia was occupied with planning a dinner party that evening. She had invited the Everetts and the Whites, two of Marquette's wealthiest families. She was now scrambling about to have everything prepared in time, and Cordelia's appearance annoyed her; she did not have time to listen to her sister's worries about Jacob. She bustled about the dinner table as Cordelia tried to explain why she had come, but Sophia would not stand still to listen. Finally, Cordelia blurted it out, causing Sophia to drop the silver she was polishing.

"Mary!" she shouted, too stunned even to pick up the fallen knife, "Come finish the table for me. I have to go out!"

"Sophia, please," Cordelia cautioned.

"Please what? Please let our inheritance be handed over to that gold digging Frenchwoman?"

"But if she makes father happy—"

"Don't be stupid, Cordelia!" said Sophia as she stormed out the front door, too angry even to wait for the buggy to be hitched up. Cordelia watched her sister rush down the road, then turned toward her home, hoping her father would not give way. Sophia marched through town and down to the river where her father was working at the blast furnace. She looked about the place for him, then barged into the office where she found Gerald and Lucius looking over some plans for expansion.

"Father, do you have any idea what a mistake you're about to make? Don't you realize that woman is only after your money?"

Lucius set his jaw, angrily trying to find an appropriate response, but at his age, words came slowly to his lips. Gerald raised his eyebrows to ask Sophia what was wrong.

"Has he told you, Gerald, what he intends?" Sophia asked. "He thinks he's going to marry that French-Indian woman."

"Who?" Gerald asked.

"That Suzanne Varin with all her snotty nosed little brats."

"Her children are perfectly healthy," Lucius replied, his eyes flaring, "and she's French-Canadian, not French-Indian, not that it would matter."

"I don't want any half-breed siblings," said Sophia, "but that's not the point."

"Siblings?" scowled Lucius. "Don't be ridiculous. I'm too old to have more children."

"Lucius, do you really intend to marry her?" Gerald asked.

"Yes," Lucius replied. "I have asked Suzanne to marry me, and she has accepted. We've set the wedding for December so we have ample time to mourn our deceased spouses."

"But why?" Sophia whined. "I admit she's pretty, Father, but at your age, you should have more sense."

"I have plenty of sense," said Lucius. "And it seems you have forgotten how to respect your father."

"She's only after your money so she can feed all those children."

"It was I who asked her to marry me. I wish to help her out of gratitude for her kindness to your mother and me."

"Then give her a few dollars, but not your children's inheritance!" Sophia replied. She stepped beside a desk chair, then waited for Gerald to pull it out before she collapsed into it.

"Sophia, you seem more concerned about my money than my happiness. Your mother and I taught you long ago that love of money is the root of all evil. I don't need to leave my children anything; you're already well provided for. Not that I will forget you, but you should be able to understand when I want to help the less fortunate, especially someone as deserving as Suzanne."

Sophia did not respond. In her heart she may have known the truth of her father's words, but she was a stubborn woman. She turned her attention to her husband.

"Gerald, talk some sense into him. Are you going to let him lose this business by putting it into that Frenchwoman's hands?"

"I don't think there's anything I can do," Gerald replied.

"Sophia," Lucius said, "nothing will change my mind, but whether or not it's any consolation, I have stated in my will that my share in the forge will pass to you and Gerald when I'm gone."

Sophia felt little gratification on that account; she wanted to justify her anger and prevent this marriage, whatever its financial implications.

"It's not about money, Father. It's about your happiness. I know you'll regret this because no Frenchwoman can make a good wife."

Then Sophia hindered any chance for Lucius to reply by popping out of the chair and stomping from the office. She returned to town and headed straight for the ore dock where she demanded one of the workers to fetch her son because of a 'family crisis.'

The laborer was stunned to see a woman in all her finery approach the dust covered docks, but after a minute, he recognized her as Mrs. Henning and told his boss that Caleb's mother was there to see him. After Sophia finished her ranting, Caleb said little about the situation. Finally, he pacified her by agreeing to talk to his grandfather. Sophia then went home to finish preparations for her dinner party, although she felt the evening was now ruined.

Caleb was a bit stunned by the news. As he finished his shift that afternoon, he felt an impish glee that Grandfather should spite his mother rather than let her control him as she did the rest of the family. He would talk to his grandfather, but he would say little to dissuade him. He felt so cheerful that he agreed to accompany his coworkers to a saloon for an after work drink.

Caleb had been early indoctrinated into his grandmother's temperance beliefs. He had never touched a drop of liquor before that day. But after one drink, which he drank swiftly to wash away the dust in his parched throat, he found his spirits rising even more. After the first drink, he still thought his mother should not control his grandfather's life any more than she had a right to control his own. After the second drink, he still did not want his mother to tell his grandfather what to do, but he began to think her right; no Frenchwoman should have a share in his and the family's inheritance. His happiness turned to a sense of how mistreated he was by all the family and a determination that for once he would get what was his.

Then the saloon proprietor came out of the back room and stepped up to Caleb.

"Looka who's here!" said the proprietor, a middle-aged Italian named Montoni. "I thought you Brookfields didn't believe in drinking?" He laughed as Caleb finished downing his third whiskey.

A couple years before, Montoni had ordered his bartender physically to remove Rebecca Brookfield from his saloon after she had entered, stood in the center of the room, and begun to preach against the "evils of drink." From that moment on, whenever she was seen walking down Superior Street, Montoni would step into the doorway, making it apparent she would not be allowed inside.

"I'm not a Brookfield," Caleb told Montoni; if his grandfather were going to disinherit him, he saw no sense in claiming the relationship.

"Why," Montoni mocked, "you're notta saying then that you're a Henning?"

Caleb knew the entire town thought he freeloaded off his stepfather. He despised being called a Henning more than anything.

"My name is Rockford," he stated.

"Rockford, you say. We see how much of a rock you are at holding your liquor."

"Go ahead," said Caleb, letting Montoni pour him a fourth glass. He was sick of being controlled by his family, of being mollycoddled by his damn mother, of being pitied by his stepfather, ignored by his grandfather, deserted by his cousin, and alienated from the men he worked with because of his family's money. He was damn sick and tired of it all; so damn sick he had an insatiable urge to drink himself out of his mind. Montoni poured him a fifth and sixth glass. Then Caleb wobbled out of the saloon, vomited behind a bush, and somehow managed to stumble all the way to the farmhouse where he collapsed in his bed, telling Lucius he did not feel well.

He never did discuss the prospective marriage with his grandfather.

Lucius and Suzanne's wedding went as planned in December. The ceremony was held in the Brookfield farmhouse where the couple was married by Justice of the Peace, Cullen Eddy, himself a Methodist. Lucius and Suzanne had discussed converting to each other's religion and decided it was pointless because Lucius would only live a few more years, and then Suzanne would return to the Catholic Church. The celebration was a small affair. The guests consisted of Suzanne's five children and her brother, Amedee, Cordelia's family, Gerald, Agnes, and Caleb. Sophia refused to attend. She said she had to stay home to watch Madeleine, but the maid could have done so. Cordelia, assisted by Edna and Agnes, prepared a supper large enough to feed the entire party of fifteen, including Mr. Eddy and his wife, who were prevailed upon to join the festivities. Gerald had suggested a fiddler be hired for after dinner, but Lucius protested he was too old to dance so dinner sufficed. The ceremony took place at four in the afternoon, and by seven, the married couple were left alone in their new home.

"Wasn't it beautiful, Mother?" sighed Edna as she walked home with her parents. "It was just like something out of a storybook."

Edna had read so many fairy tales she was prone to romanticize the most common daily events. Cordelia was more cynical since she understood the reason behind the marriage, but for her daughter's sake, she agreed the ceremony had been lovely. Edna raved all the way home about the bride's beautiful dress, about the delightful treats at the wedding supper, about the "entire fairy tale atmosphere."

"I'm going straight home to write Jacob all about it," she said. "He told me to write and tell him everything so it would seem as if he'd been at the wedding."

"That's good, dear. You do that," said Cordelia, glad her daughter would keep herself occupied. After the work of preparing the wedding banquet, she was too tired to listen to a thirteen-year old girl's chatter.

Suzanne and Lucius sat up and talked for two hours after their guests departed. Their conversations had tended to be friendly throughout their engagement, but tonight their words were strained and nervous. Lucius continually mentioned how Suzanne could redecorate or remodel the house as she pleased so she and the children would be comfortable. Suzanne expressed concern that her children would disturb him. Lucius insisted their youthful joy would keep him young. Both husband and wife kept sneaking glances at the clock, secretly dreading the hour for bed. The day's excitement had deprived Lucius of his afternoon nap so he yawned through much of the evening. Finally, Suzanne felt she had better suggest they go to sleep. After exchanging awkward glances, Lucius picked up the candle and led the way upstairs and down the hallway.

"Here is your room, my dear," he said, opening a door. Inside was a pleasant chamber with a large bed covered in a pink quilted spread. Pink curtains hung from the windows. It was charming, but confusing to the new bride.

"But—" she began.

"There's another bedroom for the girls, and there's a room in the barn that Amedee can share with your boys. I'm afraid that's all the spare bedrooms there are in the house, but I think it is perhaps more than what you had in your last home."

"Yes, there's plenty of room," she said. She imagined Cordelia must have snuck up here to give the room all its little feminine touches so she would feel at home. Still, this room was not where she knew Lucius and Rebecca had slept.

"What is wrong, dear?" her husband asked.

"Well, the children aren't here yet tonight. You know they're staying with Amedee at my old house because this is our wedding night."

"It is, dear."

"But then, are we not—" Her voice shook as though this were her first wedding night. "Are we not to share a room?"

Lucius cleared his throat. "I'm afraid I'm very restless at night, and I talk in my sleep. I think—" He saw the dazed look in his new wife's eyes. "I'm sorry. The truth is, I am so used to Rebecca that I don't know whether I could bear being with another woman, and I'm much too old to have any more children. I hope you understand."

"Ye-es," she said and forced a smile; he was a gentleman, placing the blame upon himself to save her from any obligations as a wife beyond caring for the household. "I understand," she said, kissing him on the cheek. Lucius knew she meant "Thank you." He went down the hall to his own room.

🍁   🍁   🍁

December 12, 1863
Miss Edna Whitman
Marquette, Michigan
Dear Jacob,

I am writing to wish you a happy Christmas. I hope you are well and safe and you know we are all thinking of you. I know Mother and Father wish you could be here and they worry about you, but all our prayers are with you, as are all those of the Church and Sunday School, and many of our neighbors and acquaintances ask after you. Even your little sister misses you—I wouldn't even mind you tossing one of my books or dolls around— though I'm too old for dolls now—because I miss you so much. It is hard that this is now your second Christmas away from us. We thought you'd be home by now. I hope you shoot twenty rebels a day until this war is over and until you can come home safely to us all. Mother would say that's not a good Christian thought, but the rebels are not good Christians to have kept all those people as slaves all these years and to have turned against the Union which God willed to be established. I am very proud of my soldier brother and hope you will not forget what a hero we all think you are.

We are all fine here. I have been busy with school and helping Mother when I'm able. She thinks I spend more time reading than I should, but I can't help that because books are so much more interesting than ordinary life, don't you think? Right now I'm busy reading *A Wonder Book for Girls and Boys* by Nathaniel Hawthorne and it is full of wonderful stories of the

Ancient Greeks, so very important for my education I tell Mother, but she still thinks I should play or do my needlework instead.

I said we are all fine, but that is not really true. Mother says not to tell you this but I think I should because he's your best friend—cousin Caleb that is. Since you left he has been very strange. He's been quiet, and he doesn't come around much, and now he has taken to drinking. I think he is mad about Grandfather's getting married again, but I don't understand why because Grandfather's new wife is very pretty, and oh, the wedding was so lovely. She had such a beautiful white gown on, and even Grandfather looked handsome in his new suit. Mother and I made a wonderful turkey dinner for the reception, and we let Agnes help a little. Mother bought me a beautiful new dress to wear as well, all blue with a lace collar. Aunt Sophia refused to attend the wedding, but Mother says she will come around sooner or later. But what I have to tell you is this. I heard Mother and Father talking last night, and they said that Grandfather was very angry because Caleb got really drunk one night when he was staying with Grandfather; he got sick all over Grandfather's parlor, and now Grandfather does not want him in the house—though he let him in for the wedding. Since Grandfather has remarried, now Caleb is living again with Aunt Sophia and Uncle Gerald, but I think they are just as angry with him. I think, Jacob, you should write Caleb a letter and tell him that drinking is a sin and will lead to his soul going to Hell if he does not turn from his evil ways and return to the Lord. You know you are the only one he listens to.

I have to go now because it will be my bedtime soon and I want to finish reading my book tonight. Have a very happy Christmas with lots of love from all of us.

Your Sister, Edna

1864

A decade had passed since Marquette's first Catholic church had been built. Its founding had been reason to celebrate in the eyes of Fritz and Molly Bergmann. Little could they have then imagined Marquette would become a cathedral town and home to the first bishop of the newly established Diocese of Marquette and Sault Sainte Marie. Prior to the discovery of iron ore in 1844, Upper Michigan had contained only a few Catholic missionaries; most notable among these good men was Frederic Baraga who had constructed many a church out of birch bark for his Chippewa congregations; these simple buildings had never exceeded a cost of fifty dollars. Now Marquette had been named as future site of the diocese's cathedral, with an estimated cost of twelve thousand dollars and a two-year construction schedule. Frederic Baraga had been chosen as the first bishop of the new diocese, and after a quarter century of serving the Chippewa and then the white settlers of Upper Michigan, he was regarded as a near saint by Catholic, Protestant, and unbeliever alike.

Bishop Baraga had been born in 1797 to a wealthy family in Slovenia, part of the Austrian empire. When Baraga entered the priesthood, he could have received a comfortable livelihood for the remainder of his days. Instead, at the age of thirty-three, he followed the Lord's call to go to America. After four months in Cincinnati where he worked as a missionary and learned English, he traveled to Arbre Croche in Michigan's Lower Peninsula to serve the Ottawa Indians. Lower Michigan had many missionaries, so Baraga soon felt called to spread the Word of God to the Chippewa of the Upper Peninsula. In 1837, he traveled to La Pointe, the first missionary to visit there since Father Marquette nearly two centuries before. Then he traveled on in 1843 to Keweenaw Bay to found another mission in L'Anse. After that, he never failed as a true missionary, constantly moving from one community to another; he preached and established congregations throughout the peninsula, often helping to build birchbark churches with his own hands; he converted the locals and said masses for them, then moved on to find new converts, but always he returned to help each congregation grow in its faith. When he made a trip to Europe, he found himself a celebrity; he held audiences with the pope, dined with royalty, and became the most talked about man on the continent, but his visit and all the attention it gave him only made him homesick for the natives of Michigan who needed him. He loved the Chippewa so much, he learned their language and wrote their first dictionary and a large collection of religious and moral instructions for them. After years of self-sacrificing dedication, he humbly accepted the title of Bishop in 1853 in Sault Sainte Marie. The title did not alter his determination; he continued to preach, to walk or snowshoe through all types of weather from one parish to the next, to spread God's love to His people, now both the Chippewa and the white settlers who had arrived because of the iron ore. Upper Michigan's fierce weather had worn his face until he came to resemble the natives; some said this change was a mark of his saintliness. Now this great man had decided to honor Marquette, centrally located and named for Baraga's missionary predecessor, by building his cathedral there.

Molly Bergmann was especially pleased that Marquette was to be a cathedral town. For ten years she had prayed for a second child, but her prayers remained unanswered. She loved her son, Karl, who had grown to be tall, strong, and sturdily built. Fritz beamed with pride to see his son climb trees, play rough games, and never fall sick. Molly was grateful for her fine son, but he was now ten years old, and she had begun to fear he would eventually move away and leave her and Fritz alone. Fritz tried to console her by insisting the boy would marry and enrich their old age with grandchildren. But grandchildren were far in the future. Molly wanted another child now. She longed for a little girl. She longed for a house filled with boisterously happy children to make up for the loss and deprivation of a childhood so sad she would not even speak to Fritz about it. Now, she hoped her prayers would be more effective when whispered inside a cathedral.

Molly was not an intellectual woman. True, she belonged to the Ladies Literary Society, but she did not read half the books assigned, mainly because she found them dull. Nor did she understand the awesome mysteries of the Catholic Church. She was satisfied that there were mysteries, even if her Protestant neighbors dismissed them as superstition; she believed God's saints and the Holy Spirit would intercede and work miracles for the faithful; since her prayers for another child had not been answered, she blamed herself for not yet having attained great enough faith. That the heretical Protestants who surrounded her should prosper with eight or ten children in their families was something she could only understand as one of God's mysterious ways; she confessed she felt envy toward such families; she struggled with that envy, fearing it was further reason why God did not make her womb fruitful.

The day of the cathedral's groundbreaking ceremony, Fritz was too ill to attend, but Molly was determined to be present, especially since Bishop Baraga would be there to lay the cornerstone. Molly revered the holy man; she felt all her life's hardships were nothing compared to this man's triumphs amid adversity. During the ceremony, she strained her ears to hear the prayers asking God to bless the new St. Peter's Cathedral. Her heart tried to be intent upon the prayers, but her eyes strayed about the crowd. She saw other mothers, women surrounded by three or four children, while her only son had stayed at home to watch over his sick father. All she wanted was one more child, perhaps a little girl; soon she would be too old to have more children; she had tried for ten years now; she told herself she should give up hoping—that she was only bringing herself pain, but she could not control the ache inside. She fought now to hold back tears as she looked at the kindly bishop; she would like to talk to him; she somehow felt he would understand. He looked as if he could hold the weight of the world on his strong shoulders. If he would give her a blessing, pray with her for a child—but why would he say anything different than what Father Duroc had said—that if she did not have a child, it was God's will and she must accept it. She knew Father Duroc intended to comfort her, but she could not accept his reasoning. She had obstinately begun to pray to the Virgin Mary to intercede for her. If God could make a virgin bear a child, why could He not give her one in the natural way? Even the Blessed Virgin did not answer her prayers.

When the ceremony was over, Molly quickly turned to leave. She did not want to talk to the other ladies in the crowd while their children stared at her. She turned onto Superior Street; she had barely walked a block before she met Gerald. She rarely saw him these days, despite the great friendship that had once existed between their families; Clara's death and Gerald's marriage to Sophia had made communication between them nearly nonexistent. Molly had always known the Hennings were in a social sphere above her; that distinction did not matter while Clara was alive, but now that Marquette had grown into a bustling city of over one thousand people, class differences were becoming felt. Gerald always spoke to her when she met him, but little more than pleasantries were said.

Today she attempted to pass him with only a quick hello, but when we least wish to speak to someone is when we find ourselves caught in conversation.

"Molly, how are you?" asked Gerald, taking her hand.

"I'm fine," she said, trying to compose her face. "You seem as if you're in a hurry so I won't keep you."

"I'm never in too much of a hurry to talk to an old friend," Gerald smiled.

Seeing he was determined to chat, she tried to distract him from personal questions by asking, "How is your business?"

"Fine, just fine. The war has been a great help to its prosperity. I was just now on my way to make a deposit at the new First National Bank of Marquette—can you imagine anything so fine as Marquette having its own bank?"

"It is hard to believe," Molly said. Her eyes hurt; she was certain they were red, but she dared not rub them and draw attention to her sorrow.

"After all these years of storing my money in a safe," said Gerald, "I'm not so sure I see the need for a bank account, but my partner, Mr. Brookfield, thought it a good idea, and Sophia absolutely insisted. She even talked me into signing the bank's Articles of Incorporation. Peter White is the one really in charge of it, although he talked Sam Ely into being president while he acts as cashier. Peter's got his hands in so many pots now that he seems to be a success at whatever he does. Clara always did think he had ingenuity, and between this bank and his real estate and everything else, I don't doubt someday he'll be the richest man in town."

"Probably," said Molly.

Gerald had been talking to himself more than to Molly until the tone in her voice made him look closely at her.

"Why Molly, it looks as if you've been crying. Is everything all right?" He silently chastised himself for mentioning money when he knew Molly and Fritz were poor. He expected the way the war had doubled and tripled prices on so many items, their situation was worse than ever.

"Yes, I'm fine," she fibbed.

"No, you're not. Let me give you my handkerchief." Gerald pulled it from his pocket and handed it to her. "What's upset you?"

"Nothing," she replied while wiping her eyes. "I just came from the laying of the cornerstone for the new cathedral."

"It sounds as if it'll be quite a building. You Catholics are putting us Methodists to shame."

Gerald and Clara had been Episcopalians, but when he married Sophia, Gerald had started to attend the Methodist church.

"It will be a grand building," Molly replied. "I'm thankful for it."

"But why are you upset, Molly? You can tell me; we're old friends."

Molly knew they were old friends, but not close ones anymore; she felt she wanted to go home and have a good cry but that would only upset Fritz; he would see her sorrow as critical of his chronic illness, and then she would feel guilty for upsetting him. Gerald would not repeat her words, and she had no woman to confide in.

"It's just that there were so many children at the ceremony, and I want another child, and you know how ill Fritz is. I know it's not his fault, but—"

The tears started again. Gerald took the handkerchief and carefully wiped her eyes, ignoring the stare of a nosy passerby.

"Come home with me and tell me all about it," said Gerald. "We can have some tea, and Sophia has gone out so we won't be interrupted."

"No, no, I should go home," said Molly, imagining how Sophia would react if her husband invited another woman home.

"Then let me go home with you; I haven't talked to Fritz in ages and maybe my visit will cheer you all up a little."

Molly consented, not wishing to be rude, but she felt foolish to have cried. When she apologized for her outburst, Gerald told her, "Such a little thing doesn't matter between friends," and then she suddenly felt as if the old days were back. As they turned toward Molly's home, Gerald said, "I think you are luckier than you know to have just one child. Karl is a fine boy; I can't imagine he gives you any trouble. I have three children, and I love them all, but most days they give me more sadness than pleasure. Caleb is not really my son, but I would do anything for him; still, he's constantly threatening to run off and join the army, or else he's coming home drunk; I would not speak of that except I'm sure it's no secret; everyone in Marquette must know by now since I've gone down to the saloons several times to bring him home." Gerald paused and shook his head. "Agnes is a good girl, but since she's blossoming into a woman, I don't have any idea what to do for her, and Sophia doesn't pay her much attention. Madeleine is a beautiful little girl, but she's already headstrong and spoiled; that's probably my fault since I let her get away with too much, but it's hard to reverse the situation when she already knows how to get her way. See, there's something to be thankful for in having only one child. All those parents with eight or ten children—I don't know how they do it."

They had now arrived at the Bergmann house. At the sight of Gerald, Fritz's face instantly lit up. The men talked while Karl listened politely. Molly retreated to the kitchen and brought out lemonade and freshly baked cookies for everyone. She did not feel comforted by Gerald's words; she would have welcomed the worries of another child in place of the loneliness sure to come when Karl was grown. But she was glad for Gerald's visit; his presence seemed to rekindle some of the old cheer from the past.

"Come over sometime to visit," Gerald said as he passed out the door that afternoon. "I know you and Sophia haven't always seen eye to eye, but you and Fritz are always welcome in my home. We shouldn't let our friendship lapse, and since you don't have a little girl of your own, you could be aunt to my girls. I know Clara would have wanted it that way."

Molly agreed to stop by in a few days, but before she could, Gerald sent over a dinner invitation for next week to include all three of the Bergmanns. However much Sophia controlled the house and business affairs, Gerald would have his own way in choosing his friends. Molly was nervous about the dinner, but she looked forward to seeing Agnes. She had long since noticed the girl's striking resemblance to Clara, even though she had Gerald's dark hair. Perhaps if Agnes would look upon her as a second mother, then Molly thought she might find some comfort even without another child.

Edna Whitman had spent most of her fourteen years with her nose stuck in a book. She might well be considered the product of the literary society her mother, aunt, and grandmother had helped to found. On this hot July afternoon, Agnes and Madeleine found Edna buried beneath a three-volume novel in the parlor of the Whitman boarding house.

"I don't know how you can always be reading," said Agnes. "My stepmother says girls who read too much deform their minds."

"How can she say that when she's Chairwoman of the Ladies Literary Society?" Edna asked, although she understood her Aunt Sophia's ambitions were not literary but socially focused.

"I guess if she's the chairwoman, she would know," Agnes replied. "Anyway, please come for a walk. Madeleine's been annoying me all day so I need a break from watching her."

"I am not 'noying," four year old Madeleine replied. "I'm gonna tell Mama you said that."

Agnes was an even-tempered girl, but the sticky humidity made her irritable. She would have snapped back at her little sister, except she knew Madeleine was a tattletale and her stepmother's favorite.

"It's too hot to do anything," said Edna.

"Well, it's too boring to sit and read all day," said Agnes.

"Some of us want to improve our minds and have some culture."

"I get enough culture at home," Agnes replied. "I study the piano two hours a day."

"I thought you liked the piano? I wish we could afford one."

"I don't like anything when it's so hot, especially when my stepmother only wants me to play Bach and Mozart; I prefer Stephen Foster. Besides, who can play in this heat? Why don't we go wading in the lake?"

But there would be no wading that day; Edna's mother returned home at that moment with a letter from Jacob. Cordelia never opened her son's letters at the post office from fear of bad news; if he were killed or wounded, she feared not being able to compose herself enough to reach home, and she did not want to faint at the post office and cause a scene. Instead, she let her heart palpitate until she was back at the boarding house. When she saw the three girls in the parlor, she retreated to the dining room to read the letter undisturbed. She pulled out a chair from the table, then sat down.

First she looked at the postmark. June 30, 1864. "That was so many days ago. Why does the mail have to be so slow?" she wondered. This letter was the first in three weeks, and she had worried everyday since then; she knew her son was often too fatigued or occupied to write, but trying to think logically about why she did not receive a letter did not end her fears. Once she unfolded the letter, she was instantly confused—the writing was not Jacob's—it looked like a woman's hand. Had someone written it for him? But his name was at the bottom. Then he could not be dead. Trembling, tears springing to her eyes, she read quickly, anxiously.

June 28, 1864
Corporal Jacob Whitman
Michigan 27th Infantry
My dear Father, Mother, and Sister,
    I am sorry to write to you of ill news. Please sit down before you read further. I am still alive, but I have been sorely wounded. I was shot in the stomach near Petersburg, Virginia on June 19th.

Cordelia gasped. She was glad to be sitting. She could feel the blood drain from her head as if she would faint. She breathed deeply, trying to focus on the blurring words. She read on. She read it twice before she could digest it.

I was shot in the stomach near Petersburg, Virginia on June 19th. The bullet entered my right side and passed out through my left. The doctor says it's a miracle I'm alive and that the bullet did not hit my spine and completely paralyze me. I don't want to alarm you but only to tell you the truth so you will be prepared when next we meet. The doctor says I may suffer from some slight paralysis on my left side, and I will be limited in the hard work I can do or in lifting much weight, but eventually I will be able to walk and move about fairly normal. I am in a hospital in Washington and the doctors and nurses are taking wonderful care of me. I may have to stay here for many months before I make a full recovery, but I am able to eat, sit up, and even write a little, although a kind nurse, Miss Hester Katherwood, has agreed to write this letter for me. Keep me in your prayers as I keep you in mine every day and night. Hopefully this war will soon be over and I will be able to return to you whole again. Do not worry over my wound, but instead, feel comforted that I am safe in a hospital. I hope the war ends soon, but if I can fight again, I will go out in the fields to aid my fellow soldiers who bravely fight for the Union and the end of slavery. I know this news is hard for you, but be proud that I have done my duty toward my country, and trust in the Lord for the best.

Cordelia set down the letter. She could not read further until she wiped the tears from her eyes. She cried for her wounded son; she cried for his suffering, but mostly, she cried because he was so brave and still willing to serve his nation. And here his main concern was consoling her. After a couple minutes, she read on.

Mother and Father, do not grieve for me; I am one of the lucky ones. I have worse news. Major Samuel Moody died on June 20th, the day after I was wounded. He was first hurt on May 6th and bravely continued to fight, despite his wound, until a few weeks ago, when in battle he lost his right hand. He was brought to the hospital here in Washington. Everything possible was done for him, but to no avail. I only heard of his death a few days ago and since then made inquiries to send the news home in case it has not yet reached Marquette. I know he has many good friends there and that you remember him well from Uncle Gerald's business dealings with him. He was the bravest man I have ever known, and he never failed to rally the men who served under him. Time and again he would fight in the most frightening and hopeless battles, never failing in his duty to his country. I confess his passing gives me greater sorrow than my own wounds. Please tell everyone in Marquette that he was a great hero and well respected by his men.

I will close now as I am tired, and my nurse has other patients to attend. God bless you all. Please do not worry too much. I will write again and in my own hand as soon as I am able.

Love, Jacob

"Poor Major Moody," Cordelia muttered. Then, "My poor boy," and a great sob broke from her. She began to shake all over, then felt like collapsing on the floor as she imagined the agony her boy must have suffered. "He's still alive. He's still alive," she told herself, trying to stay calm until Nathaniel came home, so she could cry on his shoulder. How could God let her only son be wounded? Other mothers had many sons, so they might spare one, but she should not be made to suffer like this. She had somehow never believed, no matter how she feared it, that he would be killed or wounded. But Jacob was alive. He was safe. He probably would not return to the battlefield despite what he said—surely the war would be over before he could fight again. Better he be wounded and return home than go into battle again.

She had to get control of herself. She had a brave son, and he had partially inherited that bravery from her. She was proud to be the mother of a Union soldier. She would focus on that pride. Now she could look Suzanne and other women in the face. Now she was one of those brave women who had felt the great sacrifice. She needed to be strong so she could tell Nathaniel and Edna. Nathaniel was at the farm; she looked at the clock—he wouldn't be home for two hours. Edna was in the parlor. Cordelia could hear her and Agnes arguing about going to the lake. She hoped they went; she did not want to tell anyone yet. Let them enjoy one more happy afternoon before they heard the news. She looked out the window. Mr. Harding, one of her boarders, was walking down the street. He expected her to finish his laundry that afternoon. All her boarders needed clean sheets on their beds. If she did her work, it would take her mind off her poor, dear son.

She tucked the letter in the pocket of her apron and went to find the laundry basket. She kept her hands busy as she washed the sheets, but her mind was reeling. She wished she could go to Jacob in Washington; she wanted to see him, to assure herself he was all right, that he was not holding back the full truth to keep her from worrying. But she had no money to go to Washington;

it would cost a fortune to travel that far; and who would look after the boarding house? Edna was too young to do the work, and Nathaniel, or any man, could not do the job. She could not afford to lose her boarders. How did God expect a mother to endure this? Wasn't it hard enough to be a thousand miles from her child without knowing he lay suffering in a hospital among strangers?

How would she ever tell Nathaniel? He would be heartbroken. And what if Jacob were not able to work at all when he got home. Nathaniel was not young anymore—he depended on Jacob to help him with the farm. They could not afford another hired hand, and with so many men gone to the war, help was hard to find. She wondered whether there would ever again be a day in her life free from worry. It seemed as if once you quit worrying about one thing, another trouble came along. It had been that way since she was young—ever since Grandpa Brookfield had lost everything. She almost wished she were a man; then she could have gone to the war in Jacob's place, and if she had been killed, well then she'd be dead and not have to worry anymore. But then she would have worried about the family she left behind.

"Mama, I'm going down to the lake," Edna said, stepping into the dining room.

"All right, dear." Cordelia was ashamed to hear her voice choke up.

"Mama, what's wrong?"

She was angry with herself; she had wanted to tell Nathaniel first. For a second she tried to hold it in, but then it swelled up in her throat.

"It's Jacob! He's been shot. He's still alive, but he's been shot!"

She wanted to bury her face in her hands, but instead, she waited for Edna's reaction. Then she noticed Agnes and Madeleine were in the doorway, staring at her. She reached out and Edna came into her arms. Agnes came forward and put her arm around her aunt's shoulder. Madeleine just stared; she was too young to understand.

Cordelia tried to stop crying. Edna stood in her mother's arms, feeling a cloud descend on her happy childhood. Agnes had enough presence of mind to fetch her aunt a glass of water. When she returned, she asked Cordelia, "How did you find out?"

Cordelia pulled the letter from her pocket. Edna read it while Agnes peered over her shoulder.

"It's okay, Mama," Edna said, although she did not feel it was okay. "He says he'll recover."

"How will I tell your father?" Cordelia asked.

Neither Edna nor Agnes could answer such a question.

"He'll be heartbroken," said Cordelia. "Oh well, I'll have to do it."

"It doesn't sound that bad," said Agnes. "Jacob says he'll be able to walk still. He's luckier than many I guess."

"Is he dead?" asked Madeleine.

"No, be quiet!" Agnes snapped. Cordelia saw the little girl was about to cry when she was shouted at so she said, "No, Madeleine dear, thank goodness. You don't need to worry."

"Is there anything we can do for you, Aunt Cordelia?" asked Agnes.

"No, thank you. I better go finish the laundry. I'll be fine. You might go tell your stepmother for me. Ask her whether she'll break the news to my father."

"All right," said Agnes. "Caleb will want to know too."

"Oh, poor Caleb," Cordelia sighed. "I hadn't thought of him; he'll be devastated."

"Madeleine and I should go then," said Agnes. "I'm so sorry."

"Thank you, dear," Cordelia replied.

"I'll walk you home," Edna said to Agnes.

Cordelia was surprised her daughter would not stay to comfort her. She did not want to be alone right now.

"That way on the way back, I can stop at the library," Edna added. "I'm going to check out *Hospital Sketches* by Louisa May Alcott."

"Don't be gone long," said Cordelia, too tired to argue with her daughter. She did not understand how Edna could go to the library at such a time. She had never heard of *Hospital Sketches* so she could not know it was about the wounded soldiers in the Washington hospitals. She did not understand that Edna thought the book would bring her consolation and an understanding of her brother's suffering.

🍁   🍁   🍁

July 18, 1864
Mr. Caleb Rockford
Marquette, Michigan
Dear Cousin Jacob,

I cannot tell you how upset and worried I have been since I learned you were wounded at Petersburg. I'm so glad you are still alive, but I cannot help but cry to think of the pain you must be suffering. I feel as if it is my fault you were shot, and that you can only be alive because you are such a good Christian man. Jacob, you have told me several times now in your letters not to drink, but now when I think about how you must suffer, I cannot help it. I get so depressed without you to talk to. You don't know what it's like to be alone without any friends and all the family thinking I'm worthless. I know they think it of me. Only my stepfather is sympathetic to me, but even he does not understand how I feel. I thought life would be better, and I would be more independent when I started to work on the docks and then went to live with Grandfather, but now I am living again with my stepfather and a mother who hates me. I know she does. She will never forgive me for being a Rockford. She wishes I were Gerald's son, or that she had born him a son to carry on the Henning name she is so proud to bear. She hated being a Rockford; I even think she hated my father. She treats Gerald so much better than she treated him. When I would not help her try to stop Grandfather from remarrying, she told me I was just as weak and useless as my father. I think even Grandfather despises me—he obviously prefers his new brother-in-law, Amedee, over me, and Amedee is hardly more than a boy.

Jacob, when no one understands me, what else can I do but try to forget my miseries in drink? If you were here, I could talk to you to relieve my depression, but without you, I have no one. Writing letters to you is some comfort, but it takes so long for you to respond sometimes that it seems pointless. You are my only true friend, the only one I ever had. I have tried to stop drinking for your sake, but I guess I'm not a good enough friend to you to stop. I am sorry. I know that drinking is a road to sin. Mother and Grandmother have told me that enough times, but sometimes I think I do not care whether I burn in Hell if it would burn me into being unconscious. You will be angry with me for writing such blasphemy. I am sorry. I do not wish to upset you when you should be recuperating so you can come home. I do not understand why God allowed you to be hurt except as a way to punish me through your suffering. Perhaps He thinks that hurting you will be enough to frighten me into goodness. It is cruel and unfair punishment for you, except that I know you are so kind and such a perfect friend that you would even sacrifice your health and happiness for me. But Jacob, I feel all the more guilt then because I know I am not worthy of your friendship, much less your great sacrifice. You know I would lay down my life for you, but that seems an easy sacrifice compared to my giving up drinking. Forgive me. Write and tell me you are well and that you do not hate me. You are my only true friend.

Your cousin, Caleb

❦   ❦   ❦

July 31, 1864
Corporal Jacob Whitman
Columbian Hospital, Washington DC
Dear Caleb,

I received your letter of the 18th, and as always, I was happy to hear from my old friend. Do not worry, and do not blame yourself for what has happened to me. God has a reason for everything, and while we cannot understand His ways, I do not believe He would punish you by hurting me. Rather, I think He has reminded me of His care by preserving my life and letting me earn this honorable scar in the best and most American Cause of Freedom.

You would have been proud to see how I fought the day I was wounded. I had my sword unsheathed and was running at the head of my company onto the battlefield. I had to cross over a fence, and just as I came over it, I felt a stinging sensation and then a great shock that knocked me over onto my back. Our company's flag bearer was near me, so that as I fell, over me rose our glorious starry Banner whose striped folds waved above my head. I felt it an honor and a sign of God's protection that I should fall beside that good flag of freedom. I uttered a prayer then as I lay on the ground that God would care for all my loved ones back home, including my best friend, and that He would bring me home again to see them. Then I called to a fellow soldier who fetched the captain. He had me carried off the field to a hospital tent, and the next day, I was placed on a train for the hospital in Washington D.C. They are taking great care of me here, Caleb. The many kind nurses think very well of me, I believe. I wish I were well enough to go courting with some of them, they are so pretty. One of them was kind enough to help me have my photograph taken, and I am enclosing it for you and sending another to my parents so they will see I am well.

Do not worry, Caleb. I am getting a good rest here. I will be well again soon, and perhaps then I can go back into the field and help to finish this war. I do not want you to worry about me or to blame yourself for anything. We have been friends for so many years, and I have no reason to be angry with you. You say you are proud of me for being brave enough to fight, but I am just as proud of you for working on the docks. I have heard many men say that if it were not for the iron coming from Michigan, we could not win this war. I am so proud of all my family for our involvement in producing the iron ore to aid our glorious cause.

On these warm summer days I wish I could be home so we could go fishing and hunting as when we were boys. But soon this war will end, and then we can again do all those things we used to enjoy so much. Remember me to everyone.

Your proud cousin, Jacob

Successive letters from Jacob detailed that he would undergo several operations and always suffer from some slight paralysis. He continually wrote from the hospital where he continued to recover without any idea of when he would be released. Caleb gradually grew bitter when he realized Jacob might not be active or able to have adventures because of his injuries; he knew if his cousin could not accompany him, he would never find the courage to leave Marquette on his own.

Caleb's depression added little to the family's cheer. Gerald worried daily that Caleb and Sophia would lose their tempers and wreak havoc on each other's emotions, and he pitied his two daughters who lived under such tension. The one time he tried to talk to Sophia about the situation, she accused him of implying she was a bad mother. For solace, Gerald turned to his renewed friendship with Molly and Fritz.

Gerald was good on his word to invite the Bergmanns frequently for dinner, and Sophia consented to having Molly and Fritz at her table in deference to her husband; despite what she thought of Gerald's odd taste in friends, the social advantages Gerald had given her kept her mute on this point.

For Gerald's sake, both the hostess and her guests tried to make these dinners as little awkward as possible, but they were awkward anyway. Karl was inbetween the ages of Agnes and Madeleine and found no interest in playing with them so the children all sat quietly. Molly and Sophia had nothing to say to each other; Molly had quit attending meetings of the Ladies Literary Society, and the two women shared no other interests. Fritz and Gerald would not talk about work from fear of excluding the women from the conversation, while Caleb's constant frowns dampened everyone's spirit.

One evening, Gerald tried to enliven his family and guests' spirits by telling a funny story he had recently heard.

"Did you all hear of Marquette's recent illustrious visitor?" he asked.

"Who?" asked Karl.

"I was talking to Peter White yesterday, and he told me the Secretary of War for the Confederacy came into his bank."

"The Secretary of the Confederacy!" exclaimed Sophia.

"Who's that?" asked Agnes, who was always afraid to read the war reports.

"John C. Breckinridge," Molly told her.

"Here in Marquette?" said Sophia. "Whatever for?"

"He was on his way to join a hunting party in Canada, but his ship docked in Marquette," Gerald replied. "I was surprised he's allowed in the North, but he was granted parole here upon his honor."

"Honor!" scoffed Caleb. "Those rebels have no honor."

"Hush, Caleb," said Sophia as if he were a child meant to be seen and not heard. "Let your stepfather finish."

"Breckinridge wanted to exchange his paper currency for gold, but it was a Sunday so he was directed to Peter White's house for help. When Peter understood the situation, he said he would open up the bank for Breckinridge, but when they reached the bank, they found the teller who lives upstairs sitting in the bank and reading. When Peter asked the teller to open the vault, he refused."

"Good," said Caleb. "We shouldn't do those rebels any favors."

"He refused because it was a Sunday," said Gerald. "The teller said he would not transact any business on the Sabbath, even when Mr. Breckinridge explained he could not wait until Monday because his steamer was about to leave. But the teller could not be persuaded, so Peter asked him for the safe combination so he could get the money himself. The teller refused this as well, saying that writing down the combination numbers would be the same as opening the safe."

"How silly," said Agnes. "He's like those people in the Bible who wouldn't help their cow out of a hole on the Sabbath."

"So what did Peter do?" asked Sophia, naturally siding with the wealthy banker, despite her strict religious upbringing.

"Peter went to borrow the money from a friend who lives nearby and then he sent Mr. Breckinridge on his way. The teller, fearing Peter White's anger, then offered to resign, but Peter would not let him. He said he respected the teller for his principles, but not for his judgment."

"That's the first bad thing I ever heard about Peter White," Caleb stated.

"Why do you say that?" asked Fritz.

"If I had seen that Johnny Reb, the only thing I would have given him was a good thrashing."

"Caleb, that's another of your typically stupid comments," said Sophia.

"If it weren't for those damn Rebs," Caleb replied, "Jacob wouldn't be lying in a hospital."

"Caleb, watch your mouth in front of the children," said Gerald.

"Breckinridge would have knocked you down like the foolish boy you are," Sophia replied. "They say he's a tall, handsome man, and even if he's a rebel, he's made something of himself which is more than I can say for you."

Caleb fumed inside, but he would not embarrass his stepfather before their guests by replying to his mother's remark.

"I don't imagine Breckinridge's visit hurt anyone," said Gerald. "With the war almost over, I doubt we'll see any more Confederates in Marquette."

"I hope it's almost over. I wish the war had never started," sighed Molly.

"Wars never solve problems," Fritz added. "Look at Revolution in Germany. It did not change anything. That is why I left—because I saw it was hopeless cause."

"Mr. Bergmann, what did you do in Germany?" Agnes asked.

"I worked as weaver."

"He helped the weavers fight for improvement of their working conditions," Karl bragged. Because Fritz stayed home sick so often, the boy had spent many hours hearing tales about Germany until he had practically memorized every incident of his father's life. He wished his mother would tell him such stories about Ireland, but she remained tightlipped about her past, always saying she had too many present worries to think about what happened long ago.

"You must have had a hard life in Germany," Gerald said.

"Yes. My brother still does. He says so in letters he sends."

"Papa, I wish we could go there to visit your family," said Karl.

"No," Fritz replied. "We are better off here. In America, we are free."

"That's why we're fighting this war," said Gerald. "To make sure freedom exists for everyone in this country; only then can the nation be stable."

"I don't know," said Fritz. "No wars in Europe ever seemed to accomplish anything, but in America maybe so. It makes me wonder still to live here where ideas work and accomplish things. Yet it's better if they are done without war."

"Let's quit talking about the war," said Sophia. "My cook has outdone herself by making us a wonderful cherry pie for dessert."

Talk turned to the scrumptious cherry pie, and then to other kinds of pie, and then to the good blueberry-picking season, but try as they all might, no one's thoughts were ever far from the war.

1865

March 30, 1865
Mr. Lucius Brookfield
Marquette, Michigan
My Dear Omelia,

Please excuse my long absence in riting to you. I have been very ill most of this winter & am only starting to get back my strength. I am hopeful the long winter is now over & soon the snow will begin melting & then I may be going outside again & getting fresh air since I have been nearly bedridden this last month. My old complaint of the ague has been acting up again, but this is the worst I recall it being since I first caught it that year in Ohio when your mother & I traveled to Michigan. I have been feeling soarely sad ever since your sweet mother's passing these two years now. I am as one who is lost & does not belong in this world since she left me. We were married fifty years, & much as I love all of you, she was the true companion & helper of my youth & all my life to me & it is hardest that now when I am old & most need her that she is gone. I think now that despite how rich I have gotten in this new land that I spent too much of my life thinking upon money & would have been wiser to spend more of it praying & preparing for that other world. Your mother was a good wife & a helper to all who sought her aid so I do not doubt she is gone to Heaven & now I must do all I can so I deserve to be there with her.

I hoap my wish to be with your mother again does not make you think I am not happy with my wife Suzanne. I know you must have heard stories from Sophia that Suzanne has given me much trouble, but they are simply not true. She is a good wife who waits upon me as if I were a king. I do not deserve the comfort she gives me in my old age. She says she owes me everything for marrying her, but I do not know whether that is true for plenty of men would be fortunate for such a good wife. Sophia is concerned that Suzanne only married me for my money & that she will get all that should to go to my children, but Sophia need not worry. I have saved enough money to provide for Suzanne when I am gone, & I hope she will still marry again someday as I cannot last much longer in this world, but she is a good wife & I am thankful to have her with me now. There will be plenty for all of my daughters & their children when I am gone & I say that how I leave my money is my own busines. Not that I would slight my own family, but neither would I slight my new wife when she is so good to me.

I hoap to recover from my illness so I may come & visit you all this summer. It would be good to see my old familar haunts & all of New York & my fourfather's lands again before I am gone. I will bring Suzanne with me most likely, & then you may meet her & judge for yourself.

I hoap by the time I come that this dreadful war will have ended. It has been going on for 4 years now, & while it has made us all very rich hear in Marquette because of the need for iron ore, I worry for all our young men who fight in it, not just from the North but the South as well, for we are all Americans & will be again when the war is over. I worry most, of course, for my grandsons. I am proud to hear that your son Israel has joined the Union Army. I pray he will be safe & that this war will have ended before I come to visit so I can see him. He was only 4 years I think when I left New York, so we would be in much need of being reacquainted, and now I will not see him becos he will be off fighting. I daresay he no longer re-members me anyway, and your other children must be so grown up I will not recognize them. As for my grandchildren hear in Marquette, Caleb & Edna are well. Jacob remains in the hospital in Washington although he is able to go out now for walks. He talks about joining the Invalid Corps, but I think the war will be over before that is necessary. I know I have told you before that Jacob reminds me most of my father, who was also a soldier. I have often thought of my father during these last 4 years, wondering how he would feel to know the nation he fought so hard for in the War of Inde-pendence should have been split in less than a hunderd years. My father's rifle still hangs above our mantelpiece hear as it did in New York. I know you remember your grandfather well, & if you met Jacob now that he is grown to manhood, you would instantly see the resemblence between him & your grandfather.

I must close now. As you can see by my handriting, I still feel weak & shaky when I rite long. Give my love to all the family & our old friends & neighbours. I pray to our Lord that I will see you soon.

Your Father, Lucius Brookfield

♦   ♦   ♦

Two days after Lucius wrote to his daughter in New York, General Grant's army broke through the Confederate lines and the next day Petersburg fell. At Petersburg, where Jacob Whitman had been wounded, the war had nearly reached a standstill, but now victory was achieved. The Union Army marched into Richmond, Virginia, capital of the Confederacy. Then on April 9, 1865, Confederate General Robert E. Lee surrendered to Union General Ulysses S. Grant at Appomattox Court House. The North rejoiced while the South, stunned by defeat, licked its wounds and hoped President Lincoln's immediate display of goodwill toward the Confederate states would bring healing to the reunited nation. Lincoln traveled to Richmond himself to see the damaged former capital. He walked the streets in safety, a sign the nation would now have peace.

Then on April 15th, at Ford's Theatre in Washington D.C., President Lincoln, the nation's savior, the man compared to Moses for liberating an oppressed people, was assassinated by John Wilkes Booth. The Nation fell into shock and mourning.

♦   ♦   ♦

April 18, 1865
Corporal Jacob Whitman
Michigan 27th Infantry
Columbian Hospital
Washington D.C.
Dear Father, Mother, and Sister,
   I am sure you have heard of the terrible tragedy that has struck our nation just when the Great Cause has achieved victory. The President's funeral is tomorrow and people are flooding into Washington to pay their last respects to the great man who has led our nation through these horrible four years. I write now because I have just returned from the White House and thought you would like an eyewitness account of the situation. You might want to report my words to the Journal as well to inform their readers.
   If ever this nation had a great leader, it was President Lincoln as was apparent from the long lines of people stretching for a mile from the White

House and down the street, all waiting to pay their respects. I marveled but was not surprised by the long lines; the newspapers have reported that thousands have poured into Washington by train since the President's assassination, but never could I have imagined the solemnity, the sheer melancholy of the scene. I stood in line nearly two hours, listening to women muttering prayers and old men shaking their heads in grief. A large number of us wounded soldiers from the military hospitals in Washington went to pay our last respects to our Commander In Chief. The wait was long, making me feel the strain upon my war wounds, but I would have stood many more hours just to glimpse the President.

The line passed in through the White House, through the darkened Green Room and then into the East Room where the President was laid out. People filed past the coffin on both sides because so many had come to mourn, and even by the end of the day, not everyone could be admitted. The coffin was on a raised platform, and we had to walk up the steps and then pass by it. We only had a few seconds to see the President, but I tried to memorize the moment as much as possible so as to report it to you. The coffin was very long to fit the President's great height; it was made of walnut with metal insignias along the sides. The President's head rested on a silk white pillow. Most moving was the look of the great man. He was not handsome, but his face looked peaceful. His death is a great tragedy, but we can all be comforted to know he sacrificed himself and did not die until he knew he had succeeded in preserving the Union. I know he must be in Heaven now for his many pains. I was overcome with emotion at the sight of him, not because of his murder, but simply to be in his presence and silently thank him for the great sacrifice he made. Many people were quietly weeping as they passed him, but my heart beat with pride and best wishes toward him and his family. It is for Mrs. Lincoln and her children I most grieve now.

When I left the White House, I returned to the hospital with several of the other soldiers. Many of them had insisted upon seeing the President, even though they needed canes or crutches just to walk; they said they wanted to remember this moment so they could one day tell their grandchildren of it. I am fortunate that I now have the use of my legs again; I limp somewhat and may sometimes need a cane, but I would have gone to the White House today even if I had to be carried there.

Tomorrow is the funeral. All of Washington will be draped in mourning. Since the Michigan 27th is to arrive in Washington for guard duty, I look forward to seeing some of my old comrades, but that is small compensation for the loss of our President. Even so, I feel my wounds are a blessing now, not only as a mark of courage and honor, but because my wounds have allowed me to be in Washington for this historic event. I hope now the man who committed the grievous act of treason by slaying the President will be captured and hung. I try to love even my enemies, but I find it hard to forgive this crime.

I hope all is well at home. I am glad to hear Grandfather feels strong enough to travel to New York. I hope he has a wonderful visit with Aunt Omelia's family. I am sure his wife will take good care of him on the journey, and I think you very good, Mother, to be willing to cook meals for Suzanne's children while she and Grandfather are gone, especially when I know you have so much to do already.

I will close now. I hope to be home soon and will let you know when that will be once I know myself. The doctors say it should not be more than a few weeks. I am walking about almost as if I had never been wounded, although I do have pain that comes and goes, especially when I sit or stand up. The doctor says the pain will continue all my life, but I will manage. I am thankful just to be alive and to have served my nation. Give my love to all the family and friends back home.

Your affectionate son, Jacob

Upon receipt of Jacob's letter, Cordelia brought it to the Brookfield farm so her father and Suzanne could read it before they departed the next day for New York.

"It's so sad," said Suzanne after she read the letter aloud to her husband. Lucius's old eyes found it hard to read small print, and Jacob had crosshatched the lines to save paper so even Suzanne had difficulty deciphering each word.

"Imagine seeing the fallen president," said Lucius. "That's two members of this family now who have met presidents. I met Martin Van Buren once. Got to shake his hand. He was from New York you know."

"Yes, Father," Cordelia replied, having heard the story many times. Suzanne, not being American born, was clueless about who President Van Buren had been, so she remained silent.

"It's a blessing your mother didn't live to see this day," Lucius told Cordelia. "I doubt the President had a more sincere admirer than your mother."

"I wouldn't be surprised if the two of them were in Heaven talking to one another right now," Suzanne replied. "Now Lucius, you still didn't tell me which coat you want to wear on the boat tomorrow."

"The grey one," he replied, resting in his rocking chair while his wife fussed over packing the luggage.

"I hope you both have a safe trip," Cordelia said. "Don't overdo it, Father. All that traveling by boat and train will be tiring, so when you get to New York, you make sure you take it easy for a few days."

"I will. You don't need to worry about me," he replied, unwilling to admit how shaky his long spindly legs had become in recent months. He was actually a bit afraid of traveling, but he longed to see his daughter one last time.

"I wish I could go," said Cordelia, "but I have a boarding house to run, and I'll be cooking for Suzanne's children. Suzanne, you tell Amedee if he needs anything not to hesitate to ask Nathaniel and me. I know he's a capable young man, but watching over five children and working here on the farm won't be an easy task."

"He'll manage," Suzanne replied. "He constantly reminds me that since he's eighteen now, I shouldn't be worrying about him, and the children are good at minding him."

"Well, if there's nothing I can do for the two of you, I guess I'll go over to Sophia's and show her Jacob's letter," said Cordelia, placing the letter in her pocket. "Caleb will want to read it too. Have a safe trip, and I'll see you both again in June."

Cordelia kissed her father's cheek and hugged Suzanne goodbye before walking to her sister's house.

May 23, 1865
Mrs. Nathaniel Whitman
Marquette, Michigan
Dear Jacob,

I just wanted to write you a quick note to say we received your letter of May 12th and are glad to hear you will soon be released from the hospital and then accompanying your regiment to lower Michigan to disband. I hope to see you then before the summer is over. You are right; you will scarcely recognize Marquette anymore after nearly three years absence. The Catholics are raising their cathedral and it should be completed next year. We have our own bank headed by Peter White. The harbor looks amazingly different from when we first came to Marquette. The new Bay de Nocquet and Marquette Railroad's dock is as high as the LS&I dock that Caleb works on plus Caleb says the new dock has a capacity for 8,000 tons. Then there is the village at Chocolay that has been rebuilt since the fire a couple years ago and is now renamed for Charles Harvey. It seems hard really to believe

Marquette is the same city we moved to a dozen years ago. Now there is talk of starting up a Furnace and Rolling Mill—I believe your Uncle Gerald is going to be involved in it. The war, despite its many terrors, has really been an advantage to the growth of our community.

Everyone here is fine. Caleb continually asks me when you will be home. Edna looks forward to hearing all your stories about the war. Your father has been busy with the farm, and I have had a full number of boarders for the last month. Your grandfather has written to say he and Suzanne arrived in New York without trouble and are enjoying their visit. Your Aunt Omelia sends her love to all of us.

I will close now so this letter can be mailed today. Forgive me for writing such a short letter, but I must get to work because Amedee and the children are coming for supper. I know you always complain that my letters are not long enough, but there is little interesting to say when my days are spent working and caring for the family. Instead of complaining about your mother's short letters, think about how you need no longer worry about the war, and that you will soon be home with the family that has missed you so much for so long. If you will not recognize Marquette, I daresay I will not recognize my little boy in the man you have grown into, especially since you say you have grown whiskers now. Write again when you reach lower Michigan.

Love, Mother

July 29, 1865
Corporal Jacob Whitman
27th Michigan Infantry
Detroit, Michigan
Dear Mother and Father,

I am writing a quick letter to let you know my regiment and I left Tannallytown on the 26th and arrived in Detroit today where we will soon disband. I do not know exactly what day I shall return to Marquette, as I have not yet made inquiries about travel, but I should be home by the middle of August I imagine. I am fine and looking forward to seeing you all. I hope you will not be too disappointed in the sight of me. Yes, I do have whiskers now, but I also limp some when I walk. I occasionally have some pains and a couple times have coughed up some blood, but that should improve with time. My back will give out now and then, but after a day or two, I am fine again. I imagine I will never fully recover from this bullet wound, but just being in Marquette with my family will help me feel better. Even if I never fully recover, my wounds were a small price to pay for saving the Union and liberating so many people.

I was glad to hear in your last letter that grandfather enjoyed his trip to New York. I am sorry to hear he came home with a bad cold, but I imagine he is just exhausted from traveling. I know he is advanced in age, but he has always been strong and vigorous so I am sure he will recover soon. Tell him and everyone I look forward to seeing them.

Your affectionate son, Jacob

Lucius was relieved to come home. He had enjoyed seeing his old New York haunts, but Marquette was his home now. New York had changed so much he scarcely recognized it anymore, and while there, he had often felt like a stranger in a foreign land. It had been good to see Omelia and the multitude of his grandchildren and great-grandchildren, but except for his daughter, they were all strangers to him. Most of the kindness directed toward him had seemed forced, only making him feel lonely, especially lonely for Rebecca to confide in. He wished she could have lived to see all their family. Their four children had multiplied into ten grandchildren and six-great grandchildren. That was a total of twenty descendants. But not one of them would carry on the Brookfield name—only their son Darius might have done that and since he had disappeared out West so many years ago, Lucius had reconciled himself that there would be no more Brookfields. He had long ago made his peace with his name not continuing, but he still missed his son. He imagined Darius had been killed by Indians or died of sickness while crossing the mountains, now lying buried in an unmarked grave somewhere along the Oregon Trail. If he did not have his son any longer, Lucius consoled himself that the rest of his family were good people, hard workers, and faithful in the Lord. He was glad to have a sizable fortune to leave them comfortable, far more than what his father had left him. He would also provide for Suzanne and her family, perhaps the greatest good deed of his life.

Lucius's father had died at seventy-six, and now Lucius was the same age, and he resigned himself that his end was near. Since Rebecca had passed on, he had not enjoyed life as much. Suzanne was a good wife, but not equal to Rebecca, his wife of fifty years. Still, he hoped his children would be good to Suzanne when he was gone.

Yes, he was relieved to be home in Marquette. He went to bed early that night with his bedroom window open. As he fell asleep, a cool wind rustled the trees; it sounded like Rebecca calling his name.

❦   ❦   ❦

"Has it been awful for you, Suzanne?" Jacob asked. He had arrived back in Marquette that morning, and just walked over to his grandfather's farm, meeting Suzanne at the kitchen door. His homecoming was bittersweet for his grandfather was dying.

"It's been awful," Suzanne replied, "but the worst will soon be over."

Jacob had scarcely known Suzanne before he left for the war, but his friendship in the army with her husband Jean now made him think of her as an old friend, and he was extremely grateful for her kindness to his grandparents. Suzanne, by contrast, had scarcely given Jacob a thought until the strapping, whiskered young man stood in her kitchen.

"Grandfather was the last one I ever suspected would have a stroke," Jacob said. "He's always been so active and youthful. I wish I could have come home before it happened."

"What's important is that you're here now," said Suzanne. "I know he'll be happy to see you."

"Do you think he'll know me?"

"Oh yes, he's perfectly lucid. He just has difficulty speaking."

"And his mind isn't effected at all? I'm afraid after my being absent for three years, he might not recognize me."

"He'll know you, Jacob. He's so proud of you for being a soldier that he speaks about you all the time. He's been napping for a couple hours, but he should wake up soon if you want to sit beside his bed and wait."

Jacob assented and followed Suzanne into his grandfather's bedroom. He sat beside the bed while Suzanne pulled the blanket up so her husband would not feel a chill. As she turned to leave the room, she saw Jacob take from his pocket a medal he had been awarded for courage so he could show it to his grandfather. The medal made Suzanne sad for another brave soldier who had not come home.

"Let me know if you need anything," she whispered as she left the room and closed the door behind her. She needed a few minutes alone.

Jacob stared uncomfortably at the closed door then turned to look at his grandfather, who was unconscious of his presence.

Through long days of marching under the hot Southern sun, through short nights of freezing in inadequate shelter, even in fleeting moments on the battlefield, Jacob had thought of his grandfather. How often he had imagined what their next meeting would be like. How many times he had replayed in his mind how he would tell his war stories to his grandfather and then listen again to the old man's story of his service in the War of 1812. But he had never imagined their reunion would take place while one of them slept.

Jacob's thoughts were interrupted by a spasmodic cough and wheezing. A chilling fear that superseded battlefield terror spread over this nervous grandson. He wondered how much pain his grandfather suffered; he would have taken another bullet if it could give the old man relief. His grandfather had spent his life raising a family, caring for an aged father, sympathizing with his wife's causes, helping to found an iron industry in the north, and finally caring for a poor young widow and her children. After such a life, what a shame his grandfather must end it helplessly in bed.

Jacob felt his grandfather was a model of how the human spirit can prevail despite any turmoil. He vowed his own battle scars would make him stronger. Like his grandfather, he planned to raise a family, build up a business, or make the family farm prosper. He would be a guide in helping others to endure their trials. He had big dreams for a young man who presently had trouble just to walk, but the physical wound would heal, leaving a scar as testimony of his perseverance. He wished he could thank his grandfather for the inspiration he had given.

After an hour, Suzanne returned with tea and biscuits to see whether Lucius would eat, but Jacob told her his grandfather had not yet woken.

"Do you want to keep waiting?" Suzanne asked.

"No, I think I told him what I needed to. I'll come again tomorrow."

"All right," said Suzanne. "I'm glad you're home, Jacob. I'll be sure to tell him you came."

That night, Suzanne fell asleep in the rocking chair beside Lucius's bed; she did not hear when he stopped breathing. When she woke, she was thankful to find he no longer suffered. She hoped he was with Rebecca now; she did not begrudge him the love he had for his first wife; she would not have wanted it otherwise. She thanked Lucius one last time for his care, then sent Amedee to inform her late husband's family.

✦   ✦   ✦

Following the funeral, the Last Will and Testament was read. Lucius had bequeathed sums of one hundred dollars to each of Suzanne's children and three hundred dollars to her brother, while each of Lucius's grandchildren had been bequeathed five hundred dollars. The remainder of the cash estate was equally divided between Lucius's three daughters and Suzanne, an amount that the lawyer estimated at three thousand dollars each. Lucius's share in the blast furnace had been left to Gerald and Sophia, with the understanding it would then pass to Caleb. The Brookfield farm was bequeathed to Jacob in lieu of a cash bequest, Jacob being the only grandson who knew anything about farming.

After the reading, Jacob told Suzanne she could remain at the farm as long as she needed, and he wished to retain Amedee's services there. Suzanne had rented out the house she and Jean had owned before his death, but she decided she would give her tenants a month's notice, and then with her children, return to their old home.

Lucius's daughters and their families met at the Henning house for supper that evening. Conversation was slow and stilted during the meal, all feeling the absence of the family patriarch. Once supper ended and the grandchildren had gone outside, Sophia, Cordelia and their husbands had a private conference in the parlor. Sophia began the council by demanding, "How are we going to solve this problem?"

"What problem?" Cordelia asked.

"We can't let that Frenchwoman and her children share our inheritance."

When everyone recovered from the initial surprise of Sophia's words, Cordelia said, "I think Father was fair in what he left Suzanne. He married her with the intention of providing for her when he was gone, and I think she deserves what he left her for the good care she took of him, as well as how she cared for mother."

"He gave her and her children free room and board for two years; isn't that enough?" Sophia asked. "I think we should contest the will. We can testify that Father's old age made his mind not right when he wrote that will."

"Sophia, you know that isn't true," said Cordelia.

"Yes," said Gerald. "Your father was in his right mind until his last few days. He wrote that will two years ago right after he married Suzanne."

Sophia glared at her husband. "I don't think he was in his right mind from the minute he let her pretty face make a fool of him. It would be a crime if that woman received a portion equal to my sisters and me."

"She already has," Nathaniel observed.

"What does it matter, Sophia?" Cordelia sighed. "We don't need the money; what he left to Suzanne would not make a huge difference in our lives, and it was Father's money to leave as he chose. She was his wife, after all."

"In name only. They never consummated the marriage; I can tell you that."

"Sophia!" Gerald was truly embarrassed by his wife's vulgarity.

"You can all think what you like," Sophia said, "but tomorrow I intend to consult a lawyer."

"You're just wasting your time," Gerald replied.

"I'll ask Peter White for advice," said Sophia. "Since he left his law practice to focus on his insurance business, he can't profit from the lawsuit so he'll be sure to give me an impartial answer, and then he can recommend to me the best lawyer."

Cordelia stated she would have no part in contesting the will. When no one else would side with her, Sophia turned and stomped upstairs.

♣   ♣   ♣

An equally serious conversation was taking place on the Hennings' back porch.

"So when will we be going off to have our adventures?" Caleb asked the returned war hero.

"I don't know," Jacob replied. He exhaled smoke from one of the cigars he had become fond of during the war. He found that smoking gave mental relief from the occasional jolts of pain emanating from his wound.

"Are you going to sell Grandfather's farm?"

"No. Why would I?"

"Well, if we move from here, what good will it be, unless you rent it out?"

"I don't know. I haven't decided yet."

"I don't think you should tie yourself down here just because Grandfather wanted you to," said Caleb.

"I want to spend a little time with the family before I make any plans."

"How long is a little time?"

Jacob had missed Caleb, but despite their letters, he had forgotten how demanding his cousin could be. "I don't know," he replied. "Summer's almost over, and I've spent the last three winters away—even that first winter I was in Port Huron, there wasn't enough snow to mention compared to our winters here."

"I'd love a winter without snow," said Caleb. "I'm sick of shoveling it."

"I used to think that way until I experienced Southern winters where it can reach eighty degrees in February. All the trees and plants were dead and brown there in winter, and no snow to brighten the landscape. I'd rather live through a hundred Upper Michigan winters and shovel snow everyday than spend another summer down South where you can literally feel your skin burning, and you get so dehydrated you think you'll die from exhaustion and sunstroke."

"I wish I had gone with you," Caleb muttered.

"It's good that you stayed," said Jacob. "If men hadn't been working here to mine and ship the iron ore, the Union probably would have lost the war."

Caleb said nothing. His wartime task had not rewarded him with a medal for bravery.

"Now that the war's over," he said, "I'm not going to work on the docks anymore."

"Then what will you do?"

"I assumed," Caleb said, "that we would go away somewhere. But in any case, I won't go back to that dirty, filthy job. I'll find something better even if it means using my stepfather's name to do it."

"Now that Grandfather's gone," said Jacob, "I'll need help with the farm at least until the harvest is in. Why don't you come work there with me?"

Caleb did not relish the idea, but at least he would be with his cousin.

"Maybe until spring," he said. "Then we could head out West."

"We'll see," said Jacob, putting out his cigar.

Caleb stared into the growing darkness. His stomach gurgled with anxiety. For ten years he had longed to escape from this little town, and now Jacob was homesick. Caleb felt if Jacob did not leave with him, he would lose his mind. He felt suffocated. He doubted the war could have been more terrifying.

1867

Sophia had no success in contesting her father's will. Peter White told her nothing could be done, and he infuriated her by adding, "Your father was in perfectly good health when he wrote that will as everyone in this town knows, and I would testify to myself." Since Peter White was one of Marquette's most prominent men, Sophia dared not argue further, but she decided he was not as clever as she had thought. She considered finding another attorney for her proposed lawsuit, but Gerald eventually talked her out of it. "Even if we take the combined $3,800 left to Suzanne, Amedee, and the five children, once we divide it up between you and your two sisters, it's only about $1,266.66 you would receive, and from that, we would have to pay court costs. We don't need the money so badly that it's worth the trouble." Then Gerald reminded Sophia that he was his parents' only son and would someday inherit the entire Henning fortune, so they need not worry about money. When Sophia saw she would receive no support from her husband or sisters, she grudgingly gave in, but she warned Gerald, "I'll die first before I ever acknowledge that Frenchwoman as a member of my family."

Six months later when Amedee opened a feed store, Sophia knew Suzanne had funded the enterprise with the inheritance from her late husband. Sophia forbade Gerald to purchase a single oat from the store. Then she licked her wounds and returned to her social efforts where she was equally having little success; Suzanne had followed Molly in leaving the Ladies Literary Society; soon Sophia and Cordelia and two Methodist women were all that remained; within a year after the war, the society disbanded. Sophia joined other organizations, but when she was not elected as chairwoman of these groups, she sought other avenues to impress people.

Sophia had never forgotten the shame of her grandfather, Major Esau Brookfield. She had despised him for wasting his talents by becoming a drunk and losing the family fortune; she had been a young girl then and unable to prevent the failure, but she had not forgotten the comfortable life prior to his disgrace. What she best remembered of that simpler time was the grand house her grandfather had owned, the grand house he had let burn down one night when he fell asleep drunk with a cigar in his mouth. After that night, he had become a slobbering, alcoholic old man, whose son had to support him to the neglect of that son's children. Sophia had been relieved when her grandfather finally passed away, although she wondered why he could not have done so before he lost his fortune and burnt down the family home. It had been a grand house in the Federal style, complete with pillars, perhaps old fashioned by post-Civil War standards, but impressive nevertheless.

Sophia had always wanted to live again in such a grand home. George had never provided her with more than a few rooms above a mercantile. When Sophia married Gerald, she had a real house again, but it had originally been Clara's home. Gerald had expanded the little cabin into four rooms by the time Clara died; Sophia had convinced him to add an upstairs with additional bedrooms, while downstairs a new kitchen was added and a front and back porch. Once the war started, however, Gerald refused to spend further on home improvements.

Sophia suffered through the war years in what she still considered cramped quarters. Five family members and a maid were huddled in that ramshackle house where uneven floorboards creaked, and the exterior looked disfigured from its multiple additions that failed to complement one another in style and structure. Other people in Marquette were building decent homes, and Sophia felt she deserved as much. Between her inheritance and the money Gerald had made during the war, she felt she could now show Marquette she was a grand lady. She needed a fine home in which to entertain and impress others with Gerald's business stature. Visiting businessmen could stay with their families in her new mansion, and her children would then make contacts that might lead to suitable spouses beyond what they could find in Marquette's limited social circles; after all, the time had come that Caleb and Agnes think of marriage.

She had her doubts Caleb would ever be the rich, leisured gentleman she had hoped. That was his father's bad influence and his growing up during her less than prosperous years. She loved Caleb, but the traits he had gained from his father made him somewhat of an embarrassment to her; she might still find him a good wife, however, who could further his prospects. Agnes was not Sophia's daughter, but Sophia felt a duty toward her since Gerald apparently

gave no thought to his daughter's marital prospects. Sophia would do the bes
she could by her, but while Agnes was a sweet girl, she lacked the social graces she might have attained in a more metropolitan area, so Sophia had little
hope of marrying the girl off to anyone more substantial than one of the local
businessmen.

Madeleine, the daughter who shared both her and Gerald's blood, was the
child Sophia intended to concentrate on. Madeleine was only seven years old,
but that gave her time to cultivate the manners of a fine lady. Madeleine would
have the best of everything—French gowns, her own carriage, and her parents'
fine home to live in. She would grow up, accustomed to elegance and determined to settle for nothing less. She might even be sent East to a girls' finishing
school; back East she would meet the right people, perhaps a fine gentleman for
a husband, a member of an old established family—maybe even a member of
the European aristocracy.

A grand new home was the first step in improving the family's social
standing and furthering the children's prospects. Sophia searched the town
until she found the perfect location to build. North of Marquette's harbor was
a high, almost unscalable cliff, but one easily accessible up a hill from downtown Marquette. At the top of this hill, Peter White had decided to build a
house, and other well-to-do businessmen were speaking of building there
as well. If Peter White built a fine new home there, Sophia would build a
house to out rival his, a house to testify that the Hennings were the leaders of
Marquette society. It would be a substantial mansion, built of Lake Superior
Sandstone, as formal and imposing as the cliff on which it stood. Sophia hired
an architect to make sketches, then repeatedly showed them to Gerald until
she wore him down and he finally consented, despite concern they could not
afford it. But Sophia knew how to pinch pennies and still make an ostentatious display—she had been doing it for years—she would have her showcase
home. Her only real distress was that the stone mansion would take a year
to complete, a year during which she would have to remain in Clara's shack,
but that sacrifice would be worthwhile once she had the respect and envy of
everyone who mattered.

Not everyone in Marquette was prospering. The Bergmanns, already
fraught with so many cares since they first arrived in Marquette, were to
experience their worst blow that summer. At the year's beginning, Molly

thought their lives had begun to turn around; after years of prayers and tears, she was expecting a second child. Once the doctor had confirmed her pregnancy, she scarcely moved about from fear of losing the baby to a miscarriage. Every night when she went to bed and every morning when she woke, she thanked God for her womb's fruitfulness, and she prayed for her child's health. Fritz told Molly he hoped for her sake they would have a girl. The couple looked forward to many years of enjoying their children even after Karl was old enough to live on his own. By the seventh month of her pregnancy, Molly was certain she would soon hear a baby's cries again.

Then in early spring, a chilling wind blew across Lake Superior, and Fritz caught a violent cold. He was already gaunt from years of fighting the effects the typhoid had wrought upon him; soon his cold gave way to pneumonia and bronchitis until he resembled a skeleton. The doctor was so alarmed by the extremity of Fritz's illness that he ordered Molly out of the house to protect the unborn child. Karl insisted that at age thirteen, he was responsible enough to care for his father. The boy was stubbornly loyal and almost unnaturally attached to his father from years of caring for him. Finding it pointless to argue, the doctor admitted Karl was healthy and faced little risk by staying with his father.

When Gerald heard of Fritz's illness, he insisted Molly stay at his house. Sophia was not pleased with this decision; she was too occupied with designing her new home to be troubled with an unwanted guest, but she knew Gerald would not change his mind; he had always been strangely fond of that Bergmann woman. If Sophia were scarcely tolerant of her guest, Gerald and Agnes were extraordinarily attentive to Molly, and even Caleb and Madeleine endeared themselves with kindnesses to the expectant mother.

Yet all the Hennings' kindness could not console a woman who dreaded widowhood, and Molly had many empty hours to let fear prey on her mind. Sophia busied herself with social calls and planning her new home, Gerald and Caleb went to work, and Agnes and Madeleine went to school. Molly spent her days alone, moaning quietly, praying the rosary to bargain with God to spare her husband. When the girls returned home in the afternoon, Agnes would make tea for Molly, then sit and tell her the local gossip she had heard at school, or she would read aloud and play the pianoforte for her guest. These moments were a happy relief for Molly, who was fond of the young girl who so resembled her old friend. Agnes's memories of her mother were dim and she feared losing the few she had, so one day when Molly mentioned Clara, Agnes asked to hear more because her father would seldom talk about her mother.

When Molly gladly reminisced, Agnes began to trust her mother's old friend. The young girl had no female confidant, but now she began to think of Molly as one.

Agnes revealed her secret to Molly one afternoon after school. She was reading aloud, but inattentively stumbling over the words. Molly asked whether she felt ill. Agnes blushed and said she was just tired, but Molly doubted Agnes ever grew tired of reading their mutual favorite author, Mr. Dickens. Not wanting Uriah Heep's rebuking spoiled, Molly suggested Agnes go lie down.

"No, I'm sorry," said Agnes. "I'm not really tired."

"Then something must be troubling you?" Molly replied.

"No, I—um—well—no, it's nothing," said the girl.

"What's wrong, Agnes? You can tell me."

Agnes hesitated, smirked, then confessed, "I've been wanting to tell you for two weeks, but I'm sure Father and Mother won't approve, so I've been afraid to say anything."

"I'm sure it's nothing that bad," said Molly.

"No, but Mrs. Bergmann," she hesitated. "I hope you won't tell my parents."

"Only if it's something harmful to you, Agnes. I would have to tell them then."

"I don't think it's anything like that," said Agnes, "but they still might not like it."

"Well, perhaps I can help you talk to them about it, but first you have to tell me what it is."

"I suppose my parents will have to know eventually, unless—it's silly of me even to think I could ever—but, oh, Mrs. Bergmann," said Agnes, her calm demeanor giving way to girlish excitement, "I think I'm in love."

The girl expected shock or surprise from Molly, but her confidant smiled and said, "It's about time. I was starting to wonder whether you had noticed boys at all."

Agnes blushed. "But Mrs. Bergmann, he's not a boy. He's a man. That's why I think my parents will disapprove."

"A man?" laughed Molly. "Well, just how old is he?"

"Eight years older than me," said Agnes.

"Eight years. That's twenty-four," said Molly. "Twenty-four is still a boy where I'm concerned."

"Oh no, he's definitely a man," said Agnes in reverence.

"But will you tell me who he is?"

Agnes hesitated, but she felt she had to trust someone. She wanted to trust Molly. She wanted just once to speak his name, to acknowledge her love.

"It's Jacob Whitman."

Now Molly was surprised. Jacob certainly was a man—a big, strapping man with full-grown whiskers. She had to admit he was even more handsome than Fritz.

"My," said Molly. "Does he feel the same way about you, Agnes?"

"I don't know. I only see him when he comes over to visit Caleb. We don't say much to each other, but he's always polite to me."

"Being polite and being in love are separate things."

"But when I talk, he listens as if he really cares what I'm saying. Most people don't listen to each other—they're just waiting to talk. You know what I mean, don't you? Oh, but Mrs. Bergmann, I don't mean that you don't listen."

Agnes looked mortified. Molly laughed, "It's okay. I know what you mean."

"I feel so silly," said Agnes. "Do you think my parents will be angry?"

"They have no reason to be as of yet."

"Then, you won't tell them?"

"What is there to tell?" Molly replied. "Jacob hasn't asked to court you."

"No, but I wish he would. I love him so much."

"I think most of the girls in town think they love Jacob Whitman. Are you sure it's love and not just attraction? He is handsome."

"No, it's more than thinking he's fine to look at, although he is. I can't explain it except that I remember every word he's ever said to me. I know his face better than any other because I think of it so often. I was at church last week, sitting in the pew, and when he entered, I didn't even see him, but I knew he had entered from the sound of his footstep. Don't those feelings mean I'm in love with him?"

Molly remembered being only a couple years older than Agnes when she had felt the exact same way about Fritz, and he was ten years older than her. They had married and been happy all these years.

"You sound as if you're in love," Molly said, "but since Jacob limps from his war wound, his step is fairly recognizable."

"I know, but I love that he limps. Somehow it makes him seem so much more manly."

Molly could see Agnes was clearly far gone in love.

"The question, Agnes, is how you'll make Jacob fall in love with you?"

"Do you think he ever could?"

"Yes. You're an attractive girl, and Jacob Whitman is intelligent; he'll see beyond a pretty face and flirtation. If he listens when you talk, then he probably already realizes you have character, and unlike most men, he's probably wise enough to acknowledge and appreciate that women have brains."

"I don't know," Agnes sighed. "Sometimes I think he's only polite to me because I'm Caleb's stepsister. But he did seem impressed the time I told him I wanted to be a teacher. He said most girls only want to get married. Only, now that I love him, I think I only want to get married as well."

"There's nothing wrong with being a wife or a teacher," said Molly. "What's important is that he respects you for your mind; a good man knows it's an advantage to have an intelligent wife who will help him and not just sit at home while he supports her."

"But Father and Mother—do you think they'll—"

"Why should they object? I can't imagine your stepmother would disapprove of her own nephew."

"My stepmother doesn't even approve of her own son," said Agnes, "so I don't know how she'll feel about Jacob."

"Do you ever talk to Caleb about Jacob?"

"No. Caleb thinks of me as his little sister; he looks out for me, but we don't talk about intimate things."

"If you tell Caleb how you feel, he might find out whether Jacob has feelings for you."

"Oh, but what if he tells my parents, or worse, what if he tells Jacob? I don't want people to think I'm chasing after a man."

Molly could hardly repress laughing at the look of horror Agnes gave her.

"Agnes, you're hardly chasing after anyone."

"But, I—"

The front door opened and in came Caleb, slamming the door behind him. He was in a strange mood, whistling as he stepped into the parlor, and not knowing whether he should laugh or scoff over the news he had just heard.

"Agnes, there you are!" he said as he removed his hat. "Hello, Mrs. Bergmann."

Molly nodded. "You seem in a cheerful mood this afternoon, Mr. Rockford."

"Yes, I've just had a fine laugh," he replied, bursting out again.

Agnes frowned; Caleb interpreted it as a reprimand for his whistling.

"Now don't frown at me, Agnes," he said, "or I won't tell you what's so funny."

"Is it decent for a young lady's ears?" Molly teased.

"Well, that's questionable," he grinned.

"Well, then perhaps you shouldn't speak it, Caleb," Agnes frowned again.

"Oh, but it concerns you, sister."

"Me?" She suddenly feared for her reputation.

"Yes, you. Jacob asked me whether—" Caleb broke out laughing again. To spare the reader further suspense, Caleb's additional outbursts are omitted. Somehow he managed to make clear that Jacob Whitman had asked him whether he thought "Uncle Gerald" would be "displeased" if he were to "court Agnes" with her permission of course.

"I couldn't help laughing," said Caleb. "I told him Agnes hasn't even thought about love yet, and she's much too young."

Molly could not hold back a giggle then, but Agnes was terrified by the news. She jumped from her chair, *David Copperfield* falling from her lap to the floor. Brushing past Caleb, she ran upstairs and locked herself in her room.

Caleb was stunned by his stepsister's reaction. He had expected she would simply laugh as Molly had.

"What's wrong with her?" he asked.

"Agnes," Molly replied, "is in love with Jacob."

"No!" said Caleb. "That is funny. Funny, but also strange."

He sat down to collect his thoughts. He wished there were a drink in the house.

"But—I just laughed at Jacob when he told me," he said. "I didn't think Agnes would be courting for years. She's just a girl."

"She's sixteen now, Caleb, but since she's your sister, you may not have noticed her as other men might."

"Well, I—but they're so many years apart."

"I'm ten years younger than my husband," said Molly, "yet we've been married for eighteen years."

"Agnes and Jacob. I can't imagine it. I—but—maybe!" he said, his words coming in a flood now. "I mean, she's my sister right, and Jacob, well, he's the best of men. Why shouldn't they be together?" Caleb jumped up from his seat. "Yes, why not? Nothing could make me happier."

Molly shared his enthusiasm, but she knew Agnes would still have reservations.

"Do you think your parents will approve?" she asked.

"My parents. Well, my stepfather, he—why I expect he'll be as pleased as me; he thinks very highly of Jacob. My mother, she—"

He knew his mother would not like it. She had never said anything to him about Agnes's future, but he had an inkling she expected Agnes to make a prosperous marriage. His mother would not think Jacob good enough for Agnes; he suspected she did not like Jacob, partly because he was treated like a wounded hero, and partly because Jacob was better looking than him, and his mother did not like to compare her son to others and find him wanting. Caleb knew she compared the two cousins; sometimes he wondered whether his mother did not wish Jacob had been her son instead. But his mother's envy only made him all the more Jacob's loyal friend.

"If you talk to your stepfather," Molly suggested, "he might talk to your mother."

"Ye-es," said Caleb. "There's no real reason for her to object, especially since Agnes isn't her actual daughter."

"Then talk to your stepfather as soon as you get a chance," said Molly. "I should go upstairs and check on Agnes."

Molly found the lovesick girl crying, but once she joined in, both wept joyfully.

❦   ❦   ❦

Caleb spoke to his stepfather early that evening. Gerald and Sophia were going to a dinner party, and while Sophia finished dressing, Gerald waited in the dining room. Sophia was so busy primping her hair he hated to trouble her to button his cufflinks, so he sought out Caleb for help; his stepson was pleased by the opportunity to talk to him alone.

Caleb kept his eyes focused on the cufflinks while he spoke.

"Father, I need to tell you something. I don't think it'll upset you, but you might find it unexpected."

The last time Caleb had talked privately to him, Gerald remembered the boy had gone to work on the ore docks. He steeled himself for another family crisis.

"Out with it then, Caleb. It's nothing bad I hope?"

"Oh no, good I think," said Caleb, smirking uneasily. "It's that Jacob wants to court Agnes, and she seems to be in love with him."

Gerald said nothing until the second cuff link was fastened. Then he sat down at the table.

"Agnes in love with Jacob," he muttered. "And Jacob loves her?"

"I believe so," replied Caleb, pulling out a chair.

"When did this happen?"

"Jacob told me only this afternoon. I thought it was funny so I told Agnes, but after she ran upstairs crying, Mrs. Bergmann told me she had just confessed she loves Jacob. Agnes had no idea Jacob felt the same toward her."

"My little girl," Gerald said. "She's still so young. I know some girls marry at sixteen, but I had hoped for a couple more years with her. I didn't think romance had even crossed her mind; somehow she seemed too mature for all that love nonsense young girls worry their heads over."

"But I don't think it's love nonsense," Caleb replied. "If Jacob loves her, I can't think of a finer man for her to marry."

"Marry!" Gerald was still trying to realize what might happen. "But they'll have to be engaged first, and it'll have to be a long engagement. I won't let her marry before she's eighteen, so she has time to be certain of her feelings."

"Jacob and she will probably think that's sensible."

"Tell Jacob," said Gerald, "to come talk with me. After I know how serious are his intentions, then I'll talk to Agnes. I guess if it's what they both want, I don't see any problem."

"Then you're pleased, Father?"

Gerald frowned. "No father is pleased to learn his daughter has become a woman, but I think Jacob will make a good husband, at least better than most."

"Do you think Mother will approve?"

Gerald sighed. "She isn't Agnes's mother, but of course, she'll have her say. I'll talk to her tonight, but now I have to go or we'll be late. Hand me my hat, Caleb."

"Thank you, Father," said Caleb.

"I'm glad you told me. I imagine Agnes would've been too shy to say anything."

Gerald felt too shy to tell Sophia. One could never tell how she would react. But he saw no reason to forbid the marriage; the more he thought about it, the more excited he became.

Sophia was highly annoyed. All that evening she and Gerald had eaten and spoken pleasantly, and he had expressed support and interest as she told their friends at dinner about her plans for the construction of their new home. Then they had shared a pleasant walk home; she had let him hold her hand, sensing his desire for her that night. She was tired, but he was so sweet this evening and so generous about her plans for the house, that she did not refuse him. He was gentle and kind to her then as well, and later, when she lay cuddled against his chest, she told herself she was lucky to lie in the arms of such a good man.

"Sophia, there's something I forgot to tell you earlier," he had then said.

She knew from his tone that he had not forgotten; as he spoke of Agnes and Jacob, she realized he had kept it from her all evening, waiting to butter her up until the moment when he could easily sway her. Had he told her right away, she might not have minded, but he had given Caleb permission for Jacob to come speak to him, without asking her first. His tone insinuated he did not want her to interfere in the proposed courtship. Sophia could make little reply except that she thought Agnes too young; Gerald concurred, stating he would expect a two-year engagement. Sophia silently hoped those two years would result in an end to this foolishness. After Gerald drifted asleep, she lay sullenly awake until the early morning hours.

She was less angry with Gerald than with Jacob. Why should Agnes marry him? Granted, Jacob was her own nephew, and he was prosperous, and she knew he would be kind to Agnes. But she had never liked him. Gerald had tried to persuade her by remarking that the marriage would keep the money in the family. But Gerald missed the point; he was as good as telling her that Jacob and Agnes would be heirs to the Brookfield and Henning fortunes. She wanted Caleb to prosper, and he would have his share of the blast furnace, but that did not seem adequate enough. She already envied Cordelia for having the more handsome, prosperous, and likable son; now Jacob would again surpass Caleb by marrying one of Marquette's finest young ladies. She doubted Caleb would even find a wife; he was so lazy, so brooding and liable to mood swings.

No matter how she worked for the family's best interests, nothing worked out as she planned. But there was no use protesting against Jacob and Agnes's marriage; Gerald would not give way, and he would probably resent her if she meddled with his daughter's happiness. Madeleine was her only hope now. She would tell Madeleine about how her own Grandfather Brookfield had lost the family fortune, and the horrors of the poverty that followed. The girl would have to be scared into being ambitious. Years of hard work had been wasted on Agnes and Caleb, but Madeleine would make a grand match and raise the family's position. Sophia would not let Gerald or anyone interfere in her youngest child's future.

🍁   🍁   🍁

The following morning Sophia was combing the knots from her hair when the doorbell rang. It was Saturday morning, and a glance at the clock showed it was only five minutes past seven. She was not even dressed yet. Gerald had just gone downstairs so he would have to greet their caller. Sophia peeped through the drawn curtains, but could see no carriage in sight, and the roof of the porch blocked her view of who stood upon it. Knowing the maid would call her if necessary, she started to dress.

Fifteen minutes later, Gerald knocked on the bedroom door. Sophia pulled her dress down over her slip, then admitted her husband.

"Who was at the door?" she asked, returning to the vanity to powder her face.

"Young Karl. It's bad news I'm afraid."

"Oh?"

She spoke coldly; Gerald's presence made her recall his duplicitous behavior the night before.

"Fritz just passed away. Karl is here for his mother. Caleb is going to drive them home. Molly's packing and will be leaving in a few minutes. I thought you'd want to give her your condolences before she left."

"Of course, if I can be ready in time," Sophia replied. "How is she taking it?"

"I haven't spoken to her yet; Agnes said Molly wanted a minute alone; I'm sure she's been expecting it, but it must be hard anyway. Agnes is keeping Karl company in the parlor while Molly packs."

"I don't know why Molly didn't just stay home when she knew it was coming. I never did like the idea of Madeleine seeing her in her condition. You know, I wouldn't be a bit surprised if Molly's talk about babies is what put the notion of marriage into Agnes's head. Now that Molly will be gone, maybe Agnes will forget about Jacob."

Gerald did not want to argue about his daughter's marriage the same morning his old friend had died. He had something more important to argue about.

"Would you fasten my earring?" asked Sophia. "I can't seem to clasp it shut."

"Sophia," said Gerald, clipping on her jewelry. "I want to pay for Fritz's funeral. Molly won't be able to afford it, especially not with another baby to feed."

Sophia paused, searching for the right words. "Gerald, you know the Bergmanns won't take charity; they're much too proud."

"Fritz was the proud one," said Gerald. "Molly will be sensible enough to let us help."

Sophia understood; Gerald had already decided the matter. He seemed to be making many decisions without consulting her. She knew he was unhappy about the expense of building the new house, so she dared not argue with him now, but she hated having to submit to a man's every whim.

"If we make it a simple funeral," she said, meaning a cheap one, "then maybe Molly won't mind so much our intrusion into her affairs."

Gerald stood behind her where, in the mirror, he saw reflected, despite her tone of disapproval, a face of resignation. He had won the issue. That was two scores within twelve hours. He would have a long wait before he dared thwart his wife again.

"Are you ready to see Molly, dear?"

"Yes," she sighed.

Gerald kissed her cheek when she stood up. She gave him a halfhearted smile, then led the way downstairs.

In the parlor, they found Karl talking to Madeleine, who had been woken by the doorbell. She sensed Karl's sadness, but too young to understand about death, she tried to cheer him by showing him her doll. Karl tried to humor her, but his heart was breaking inside.

"Agnes went to help my mother," he told Gerald and Sophia as he rose to his feet in deference to his elders.

Gerald gave Karl's hand a firm squeeze. "We're so sorry, Karl. Your father was a good friend to us."

"Thank you, sir. He always spoke highly of you."

The stairs creaked. Everyone turned anxiously to await Molly's appearance.

The widow's eyes were red from weeping, but she bravely tried to keep her face calm. She carried her bundle of clothes while Agnes followed behind her.

"The maid could have carried that down," said Sophia.

"It's all right," said Molly. "I could do it faster myself. Thank you for everything."

"We're so sorry," said Gerald, clasping her hand, and causing her more tears.

Agnes handed Molly her handkerchief. Sophia, overcome by the awkwardness, selflessly muttered, "Let us know if there's any way we can help."

"Thank you. You're all so kind. But right now I just need to go home. I'm too confused to know what else to do."

"I'll come by this afternoon," said Gerald, "to help with the funeral arrangements."

"Thank you, Gerald," she half-whispered.

"Ma'am, the carriage is waiting," said the maid, appearing in the parlor door. Everyone followed the widow and her son to the front porch; they were glad just to move and relieve the moment's awkwardness. Caleb helped Molly into the carriage, then drove mother and son home to where lay Fritz, the shell of a man who had suffered far too long, and with little complaint.

"She barely seemed grateful when you offered to help with the funeral," said Sophia once she and Gerald had returned inside. "I'm sure she understood you mean to help in a pecuniary manner."

Gerald did not reply. He hid himself behind the *Lake Superior Journal* at breakfast.

The funeral was a simple one, held in the Bergmann home. Gerald paid for all expenses from the cemetery plot to the coffin, even giving the priest a little something for his trouble. The services were over before Molly could accept her husband was gone. For years he had been ill; for years she had tried to prepare for this loss, but she never could have prepared herself for the sudden loneliness.

Friends told Molly to rejoice that Fritz no longer suffered. They spoke almost as if she should be relieved he was gone, and that she no longer had to care for him. He had caused her much worry because he could not always provide for his family, but he had also been her best friend. She had never spoken to him of her impoverished Irish childhood or the discrimination she had experienced in Boston, yet she felt he understood these sadnesses by intuition, by his own difficult experiences in Germany, and together they had muddled through many a frugal season in Marquette. And now her partner was gone.

She promised herself she would not despair. She had to look after Karl, and then, a few weeks after Fritz's passing, Molly gave birth to a little girl. She named her Katherine after Fritz's mother, but she called her Kathy because it sounded more Irish. She wished Fritz had lived to see their daughter.

On a beautiful summer evening, just after the Fourth of July, Sophia attended one of those social gatherings that were the great interest of her life. She and Gerald, included among Marquette's elite, had been invited on a pleasure cruise. The invitation had come from Mr. Jay C. Morse, a prosperous local entrepreneur. When the Civil War had ended, Mr. Morse and his former commanding officer, Colonel Pickands, had gone into partnership in the iron industry. Mr. Morse had purchased a new steamship to carry ore, and when it arrived in Marquette's harbor, he was so proud he dubbed it the *Jay Morse* and arranged a pleasure party to show it off. Forty of Marquette's leading citizens were invited on an evening cruise around Presque Isle. Among the elite guests were Peter White, the Ely brothers, the Calls, the Maynards, and of course, the Hennings.

Sophia, who had completed plans for her new home, and was enviously watching the raising of Peter White's new house on Ridge Street, saw the excursion as the perfect opportunity to inform her wealthy friends of the intricate elegancies that would declare her future residence Marquette's grandest home. Construction of the house would begin that month, but with the early winters of Upper Michigan, and the extensive work to be accomplished, a year would pass before the Hennings could move. Gerald remained alarmed at the house's expense, but he knew once Sophia discussed her plans with the neighbors, he had no choice but to pay for every last detail and ornament she desired. He had long ago accepted his second wife's shallowness, but he still sought to please her; his love for her had replaced his intense loneliness after Clara's passing, and he would not suffer her anger by holding her back from the social esteem she craved.

Sophia, uninterested in the *Jay Morse's* grandeur, scarcely glanced at the ship as she climbed aboard. She immediately sought out the Whites to engage them in a conversation on interior decorating. She had not yet seen the inside of their new home, but she hinted for an invitation so she might spy out its contents, only to make certain she designed her home to surpass its glories. Gerald willingly let others be troubled by his wife's decorating concerns while he conversed with Mr. Morse on the power and size of the new ship, which measured seventy-nine feet long and eighteen feet wide. Mr. Morse explained the ship's role of towing ore barges and assisting schooners in entering and exiting harbors. While not a premier ship, the *Jay Morse* symbolized hopes for future fortune, thus making itself worthy of the austere guests upon its deck.

When the ship prepared to leave the harbor, Sophia seated herself beside Gerald on the deck. The Hennings and their neighbors were seated along a railing to attain the best scenic view, yet Sophia saw less of the lake and sublime cliffs than of wallpaper and chandeliers in her imagination. Gerald loved the water; he felt he could never be on a boat too often; he envied the sailors who passed through Marquette's harbor—envied their great freedom, including the longtime absence from their wives. When he had first come to Marquette, he found Lake Superior lacking in the salt water scent familiar from a childhood spent on Massachusetts Bay, but tonight the lake's refreshing breezes provided relief from his family and business worries. Tonight even Sophia's clinging to his arm and fidgeting because "Boats make me nervous" made his heart beat excitedly. He knew she liked to cling to him for attention, as though he were some status trophy she had won. Gerald had no misconceptions about why she had married him, but he also knew she loved him. She was his wife, the mother of his youngest child, and when she wanted to cling to his arm, he was happy to have her do so.

The *Jay Morse* pulled out from the dock into Iron Bay, then turned west along Lake Superior's southern shore. Gerald and Sophia had not viewed Marquette's shoreline from the lake for many years. While they were familiar with the nearby sublime towering cliffs, the sandy beaches and the glistening blue lake, now this new perspective made everything look more enchanting. Sophia admired the lake's changing shades so much she pondered decorating Gerald's study in blue, thinking he might like a nautical theme.

The ship passed Marquette's new lighthouse; built three years earlier, it provided safety for all who traveled into Iron Bay on Lake Superior's rough, rolling waves. Then the *Jay Morse* drifted along the miles of sandy beach where Marquette's hardiest citizens would dare to swim only for brief moments since even in summer, Lake Superior's waters are chilly, and patches of ice have been seen floating on it as late as June. Next the boat passed Presque Isle, its sandstone cliffs rising up, an inspiration for the sandstone buildings that were becoming a favorite of the local architects. The red, brown, and orange cliffs contrasted with the colors of evergreens and birches rising another hundred feet above cliffs already a hundred feet above the water. As the boat slowly wound around Presque Isle's circular peninsula, caves became visible in the cliffs, marks of where silver had briefly been mined in the years before Marquette was founded. Then completing its curve around Presque Isle, the ship came into view of the Black Rocks, and everyone strained to marvel at their uniqueness. "This place really is a geologist's paradise," remarked one of the ship passengers while another added, "A fisherman's paradise as well."

The evening was so pleasant, the scenery so stunning that Captain Atkins received permission to take the ship beyond Presque Isle to circle nearby Partridge Island. Joe Roleau took the wheel so Captain Atkins might enjoy the view.

Then it happened. As the ship came around the island, without any warning, it ran against some hidden rocks and came to an immediate halt.

The sudden lurch catapulted several passengers over the ship's rail. Sophia, having momentarily released Gerald's arm, found herself thrown overboard with several other ladies. Panic-stricken, she scrambled in the waves, fighting to keep her head above water while her skirts quickly soaked through, growing so heavy they threatened to pull her under. The lake was calm that evening, the waves nearly indistinguishable, yet Sophia was terrified. She had not swum in twenty years, and she sadly lacked for exercise. The sudden surprise and the biting cold water nearly sent her into shock. Gerald was almost as surprised as he stood clasping the rail and trying to spot his wife. After a few initial screams, the other women thrown overboard began to swim toward the ship. One man, Mr. Maynard, had also been pivoted overboard, and like Sophia, he struggled to stay afloat. Sophia's terror increased when she saw Mr. Maynard's head sink beneath the waves. She instantly feared he had drowned, and his failure to resurface made her splash and scream frantically until she began to swallow water. Hearing his wife's screams, Gerald spotted her and dove to her rescue. Meanwhile, the other women were pulled onboard. When Gerald reached his wife, he faced an ordeal trying to hold onto her while she struggled against him; exerting all his strength, he pulled her toward the ship. Once they were close enough, a rope was tossed to them, and despite Sophia's shrieks, she was pulled back onto the boat. Gerald treaded water, panting to regain his breath until Sophia was on deck. Then he pulled himself up the rope.

By this point, it was apparent the ship was sinking. Captain Atkins, having suffered a terrible tumble from the ship's collision, was incapacitated. Joe Roleau took command by turning the boat toward the rocky shore of Partridge Island; he hoped to land the passengers before the ship was submerged. Meanwhile everyone else stared out into the lake, hoping to spot Mr. Maynard. Sophia began to sob as she related how she had seen his head disappear underwater. A few men suggested swimming out to search for him, but the general consensus was that too many minutes had passed for him to be alive, and they could not risk their own lives further by postponing the ship's journey toward shore.

Fourteen feet from Partridge Island, the ship anchored in shallow water. Mr. Roleau could not be blamed for running into invisible rocks, yet he felt responsible for the catastrophe. After constructing a makeshift raft of debris, he went out on the lake to search for Mr. Maynard. Meanwhile, the *Jay Morse* sunk until only the bow deck remained above water; there the passengers crowded together; none wanted to wade to Partridge Island because they would be wet and then chilled in the cool night air. If the ship sunk further, they were close enough to reach land if necessary.

Sophia remained frenzied for a quarter hour, sobbing because she had nearly drowned and bemoaning how long Gerald had taken to rescue her. The other passengers were too somber from Mr. Maynard's loss to object to her wailing. Gerald held her, trying to keep her warm, while two of the ladies gave up their cloaks so she would not catch a chill in her wet clothes. When Mr. Roleau returned, he admitted Mr. Maynard's rescue was hopeless; it was best they look to their own situation. Sophia broke into a couple shrieks at the news that Mr. Maynard had definitely drowned, but Gerald soothed her to sleep, her head resting against his shoulder.

Meanwhile the other passengers debated what action was best to take. The evening was still warm, so they had little fear of freezing; even those who had fallen into the lake found their clothes were drying. They could not remain long on the sinking ship; with darkness approaching, none wanted to swim to shore. Mr. Roleau proposed taking the raft to the mainland; it was hardly seaworthy and unlikely to support more than one passenger so he bravely volunteered to go alone. Some of the women protested the potential danger, but Mr. Roleau was determined. He vowed to reach the mainland, then walk to Marquette; the only difficulty would be crossing over the Dead River. Once in Marquette, he would find a boat to rescue the unfortunate passengers before morning broke. No other solutions existing, he departed.

During the night, Sophia slept on Gerald's shoulder. The other women tried to sleep as well as possible in their crowded conditions while the men comforted them and tried to keep them warm. A few stayed awake to watch for the rescue ship, but they knew several hours would pass before Mr. Roleau could reach town and return. Everyone was distrait over the loss of Mr. Maynard. Peter White had been the man's law partner, and worse, the Maynard family was aboard the ship; many a tear was shed that night over the drowned man's fate.

In the early morning hours, Sophia woke to find herself leaning against Gerald's chest. She shivered in the cool morning air until Gerald hugged her and asked whether she felt better.

"Yes, but I told you I hate boats. They've always made me nervous. We never should have come."

"Well, we can't foresee the future. It seemed like a harmless little venture."

"Oh, Gerald," she whispered so the others would not hear her, "if you had seen the look on Mr. Maynard's face before he sunk underwater. I felt so helpless, but what could I have done when I can barely swim myself?"

"No one blames you, dear."

"I know, but how horrible to drown like that. I swallowed so much water I thought I would drown myself."

"It's okay. Soon you'll be home and safe in your warm bed."

But home was still several hours away. Mr. Roleau was good as his promise, but it was a long voyage to the mainland on a ramshackled raft, and then he had to hike through the forest, and bravely struggle through the Dead River's strong current before he could walk the remaining miles to Marquette. In the early morning hours, he reached the town, where he tracked down Captain Bridges of the tug *Dudley*. The captain agreed to rescue the stranded passengers, but first he had to find his engineer to build up the tug's steam so his boat could leave the harbor. Twelve full hours after the *Jay Morse* had fatally hit a rock, and just as daylight broke, the *Dudley* charted Lake Superior's waters and pulled up beside the unfortunate *Jay Morse*.

Sophia, shivering and still badly shaken, joined the elite of Marquette in climbing aboard the tug; even she was too fatigued to note that a tug was beneath the dignity of Marquette's society queen. An hour later, the ill-fated excursion party returned to Marquette's harbor, and Gerald and Sophia stumbled home in exhaustion. Sophia immediately collapsed on the parlor sofa, not even caring that her dress was damp and dirty. When the children appeared, she declaimed her plight until she had worked up their utmost sympathies. Then after making Sophia drink some soothing tea, Gerald escorted his wife upstairs and to bed. She would remain tucked under her covers the remainder of that day and throughout the next, constantly complaining that she had been taken ill. Mr. Maynard had no such comfortable bed, only the sandy floor of Lake Superior. His body was never found, and as a result, Sophia suffered from nightmares for several weeks. Still, she found the strength to attend the drowned man's funeral and to send an impressive flower arrangement to the Maynard family.

1868

One morning, during a January blizzard, Molly trudged through the driving wind and whirling snowflakes. She pulled a blanket tightly around her baby who protested being out in the cold. But Molly would go out today no matter what she had to face. She refused to miss this event, and she wanted her children present to pay their respects, for Bishop Frederic Baraga, Marquette's saint, had entered into eternal life.

"I'm sorry, dear," Molly cooed as Kathy fidgeted in her arms. "Just a couple more minutes and we'll be inside the nice, warm cathedral." The Mass would soon begin, and Molly could not bear the thought of being late as she stepped quickly but firmly to prevent slipping on any ice. Karl tried to keep up with his mother, not daring to complain because he understood the solemnity of this day; tardiness would be utterly disrespectful to the deceased man—the last man Molly would ever choose to offend; she had not even respected her dear Fritz as much as the man now fondly named "the snowshoe priest."

Bishop Baraga had died eleven days earlier following a two-year illness, doubtless brought on from old age and physical exhaustion. He had passed away at age seventy after thirty-seven years of serving the faithful throughout Michigan. First as apostle to the Indians, then as missionary to the white settlers who came for iron ore and the nearby Keweenaw Peninsula's copper, he had never shirked his duties; his dedication was never less than remarkable, his devotion surpassed the capabilities of most mortal men. His endurance, his many acts of kindness, his overwhelming love, all resulted from his tremendous faith. Clearly the Holy Spirit had chosen him to be a voice crying out in the wilderness to prepare the way of the Lord, to spread the gospel, to bring the peace that passeth understanding to all he met. The great bishop had fulfilled his mission, through snowstorms, on snowshoes, over hundreds of miles from Indian village to white settlement, through mosquito infested humid summer forests, through spring floodings, and in beautiful balmy autumns, caring for the sick, the lonely, and those hungry for God's love; never did he discriminate against native or foreigner, rich or poor—all were equal in God's eyes. Everywhere he went, Masses were said, infants baptized, the dying comforted, and the faithful uplifted to hope in this harsh land.

Tales of Baraga's deeds were circulated among his many admirers in Marquette. Now that the bishop was gone, stories spread of his ability to work miracles. Just days before the bishop's passing, a woman had visited the rectory with the request to borrow his stockings. She had long suffered from sore knees and her pain was diagnosed as incurable. After she wore the saintly bishop's stockings, she claimed her knees were suddenly healed.

Some doubted the truth of this miracle, but Molly was among the believers. All her life, she had believed in miracles; inwardly, she had long pined for one. As a child in Ireland, she had prayed to the Blessed Virgin to end the potato famine and to bring prosperity to the faithful. Her disappointment was nearly inconsolable when no miracles occurred, and the famine forced her family to abandon their home. Only years later did she realize God had answered her prayers in a far better way through her parents' decision to migrate to the United States; at the time, she had been skeptical, but now she knew her life was far better in America than it ever could have been in Ireland. She understood God works mysteriously but always in the best interests of His servants. But days still came when Molly severely doubted God. On one such day, Bishop Baraga himself had proven God's love when a miracle was worked for her.

Molly entered the somber cathedral, now completed and functioning for two years. She clutched Kathy to her, glad to be inside the warmth of the church lit by candles to dispel the gloom of the blizzard raging outside. She felt privileged to attend the saintly bishop's funeral mass, and when she saw his coffin, she replayed in her mind the day of her miracle, the day she was convinced Baraga was a living saint. It had happened a few months earlier, not long after Kathy's birth had relieved some of the pain of Fritz's loss. Molly had found it hard to understand why God had taken Fritz from her, but He had sent her someone equally precious in her long awaited little girl. Then one cold autumn day, Kathy had contracted pneumonia, and Molly was terrified. That day was the worst in her relationship with God; she had never dared be angry with Him before. But even in her anger, she struggled to keep her faith and pray.

"Lord, I don't understand," she had pleaded. "I pray and trust in You and the Blessed Virgin with all the faith I can muster, yet You keep sending hardship my way. I try to believe my sufferings are a sign of Your favor, and that You will make good on Your promise that the meek shall inherit the earth, yet after all these years of praying, there seems no end to my difficulties. I do not wish to complain, but please, dear God, do not take my little girl from me. I cannot bear her loss."

That same evening Kathy's pneumonia had turned into a dangerous fever. Although Molly could scarcely afford the expense, she had sent Karl for the doctor. Kathy's fever raged for two seemingly endless days. Finally, the doctor had admitted Molly should send for the priest to give last rites. But Molly had adamantly refused; she would not give up hope. And then, the thought of the priest had made her think of the bishop. Ignoring the doctor's protests, she had quickly bundled Kathy up in a blanket, then run through an October rainstorm to the church rectory.

When the housekeeper opened the door, Molly demanded to see the bishop; the housekeeper replied he was in a meeting with the Ursuline nuns who had recently started a Catholic school in Marquette; could Molly possibly return in the afternoon?

"No, I can't. It might be too late then," Molly had cried.

"I cannot disturb His Excellency," said the overly dutiful housekeeper.

"Please. My little girl is so sick with a fever. I need the bishop to pray over her. I can't bear to lose her. Only he can save her. You don't understand. My husband is dead, and I waited so many years for this child. I'll never have another. Please."

Molly sobbed as she spoke, and the housekeeper had pitied her, but she also feared Molly's cries would disturb the bishop.

But His Excellency had heard the disturbance and stepped out to the doorway.

"What's the matter?" he had asked, although he need not have; he clearly saw a wretched mother clutching the child she loved better than herself.

"Your Excellency, I tried to tell her to come back later," the housekeeper had apologized, but the Lord's servant calmly dismissed her with a wave of his hand.

"Molly, your little girl is ill," Bishop Baraga had said. Molly had never spoken to His Excellency before, save a few times when he gave her communion at Mass. She had not realized he knew her name. Overcome with fear, she heard herself babbling in desperation.

"Yes. Oh please. She has a fever. The doctor said I should have a priest give last rites, but I can't. I can't bear to lose her. Please, if you pray over her, maybe—"

The words had scarcely left her mouth before Baraga had taken Kathy in his arms.

"The doctor has given up hope?"

"Yes, he's attended her for two days and says he can do nothing. But I thought—if you prayed—God would hear your prayer and heal her."

"You have great faith," Baraga had said, placing his hand on Kathy's forehead to feel it burn like hellfire. "Let us pray, Molly."

She had bowed her head while Baraga whispered, "Lord God, we pray you to heal this child. Cure her sickness that she may grow up like her mother, a faithful servant who does Your will."

He had then spoken several sentences in Latin. Molly had not understood the words, but she was comforted merely by his gentle voice, his kindness, and the sacred language.

"Now go home and care for her, but remember her soul is saved, and that is what matters most. God bless you."

Molly had then felt a bit let down, even as the bishop placed the child back into her arms and made the sign of the cross over her. She had muttered, "Thank you" and turned to leave.

Then Kathy had let out a cry.

"She hasn't cried in two days!" Molly had said as she felt Kathy's forehead, now soaked with sweat. "The fever has broken! Thank you, Your Excellency."

"Thank God, Molly. I have done nothing. He must have some great plan for her to heal her so rapidly. Perhaps someday she will be a loving mother like you and bring many servants to the Lord."

Molly had scarcely heard these prophetic words; she had only had eyes then for her child.

"Thank you," she had repeated.

"Go home now and keep her warm. Do you have medicine for her?"

"Yes, the doctor has helped with that."

"Very good," the bishop had replied and bowed to dismiss her.

She had rushed home to share the miraculous news with Karl. She found him seated with the doctor, both still surprised by her hasty, unexplained departure.

"The fever broke!" she told them.

"Impossible, so suddenly," muttered the doctor, placing his hand on Kathy's forehead. He found it cool and drenched with sweat. "Why, she's breathing regularly now and the color is returning to her cheeks."

"It's a miracle," Molly had said.

The doctor was not a Catholic, but an Episcopalian. More so, he considered himself a man of science. "Often it is at the most critical moment these fevers turn. Perhaps taking her out in the cold air made the sudden difference."

"It was a miracle," Molly repeated.

"It doesn't matter so long as she is better," smiled the doctor, collecting his bag. "I'll stop by tomorrow to check on her again."

It had been a miracle. Molly refused to believe otherwise. Now months later, she knelt in a pew waiting for Bishop Baraga's funeral to begin. She wondered why God had not prolonged his servant's life longer, that more souls might come to Him. Then Molly remembered the Bishop's words that many might come to the faith through Kathy. Perhaps Bishop Baraga had served his purpose on earth and now was rewarded, and it was left to those, like her, whose lives he had touched to win souls for the Church.

The funeral was beautiful. So many mourners had never before been seen in Upper Michigan. Priests and nuns, town dignitaries, the poorest parishioners, the local Chippewa, people who lived miles from town and walked through the blizzard before daylight, and people who rode half a mile in a fine carriage, all were there to pay their respects. All these people testified to the great love felt for Marquette's first bishop. Molly had arrived in time to find one of the last empty seats in the cathedral. Minutes later, the mourners were crowding the aisles, streaming out the door and standing in the street, regardless of the winter storm; discomfort, crowding, and cold were small sacrifices in exchange for what this saintly man had done for so many of them. They had come to commemorate his soul to God after he had saved so many of theirs.

Molly thanked God for the life and holiness of his servant Bishop Baraga. She went to communion, highly emotional, recalling the times she had received the Blessed Sacrament from the bishop's own hands.

As she returned from communion to her seat, she spotted Gerald in one of the front pews. She was glad to see even non-Catholics were present at this august event.

When the Mass ended, the stream of mourners moved patiently out the door. Molly stepped outside where Gerald found her.

"It's a sad day for this community," he said.

"We won't see his like again," Molly replied.

"Everyone realizes that. Every business in Marquette closed today for the funeral." Gerald was as stunned by the outpouring of emotion in the community as by the death of the great man himself.

"He was a saint," said Molly, "and I'm glad so many people realize it."

"Did you hear what he did at the very end?" asked Gerald, so moved by the bishop's generosity he did not wait for her answer. "Just before he died, a priest from L'Anse came to give a report on his church. When the bishop heard how badly money was needed for the L'Anse Indian school, he gave the priest twenty dollars from his personal funds. It was all the money he had left in the world, but he said he would not need it anymore. Even in his last moments, his final thoughts were for the Indians he loved all his life."

Molly wanted to tell Gerald about Kathy's miraculous healing, but she could not; Gerald might understand the Bishop's generosity, but she doubted a Protestant would believe in a miracle.

"There aren't many like him," said Gerald. "We're all brave to have come to this wilderness land, but we did it for personal gain, while he came selflessly to serve."

"We can all learn from him," Molly replied.

Gerald turned to Karl, standing beside his mother. "Don't forget this day, Karl. You'll find no better role model than Bishop Baraga, though your father was a good man too."

"Thank you, sir," said Karl, who loved any mention of his much missed father.

"I think," Gerald added, "that sometimes I am completely blind to what's important in this world. It seems money and material things are all Sophia and I think of these days. I imagine you've heard we're building a house on Ridge Street. It was Sophia's idea, but I'm guilty of having sanctioned it."

"You deserve a fine home," said Molly.

"But I don't need it," Gerald sighed. "I think I was happier when Clara and I lived in our little cabin, but I guess the world must progress."

"Be thankful you no longer have snow leaking through your roof like in those cabins we hurriedly built that first year," said Molly.

"Are you getting along all right, Molly?" Gerald asked, placing his hat on his head. The blizzard continued to rage as the mourners passed by.

"We're fine," Molly nearly shouted into the fierce wind. "Karl found a job after school in a dry goods store, and I take in fancy work while I'm home with Kathy."

"That's good," said Gerald. "Don't be a stranger. Stop by soon."

"All right. Goodbye," she replied as Gerald turned homeward into the wind.

"Mr. Henning doesn't seem very happy these days," said Karl as he walked home with his mother.

"He's just sad. We all are because of Bishop Baraga's passing," Molly replied.

With spring's arrival, preparations ensued for Jacob and Agnes's wedding. Gerald had insisted on a two-year engagement, but after six months, Jacob was so impatient he asked whether the waiting period could be reduced to a year. Seeing the lovers had remained steadfast, Gerald consented to a June ceremony.

"It'll be a large wedding," Sophia decided the night Gerald gave his permission.

"No," Agnes replied. She was seldom outspoken, but in planning the happiest day of her life, she can be forgiven for a pinch of selfishness. "Jacob and I want a small ceremony with just the family."

"How small?" asked Sophia. "We need to invite all our close friends, but we can probably keep it under a hundred people."

"No," Agnes replied. "We only want the immediate family."

"But Agnes dear," said Sophia. "This is the most important day of your life. Don't you want it to be special?"

"It will be special because Jacob will be there."

"Well, but think of our—"

Gerald knew "social position" was about to come from his wife's mouth, so he quickly interrupted. "Why don't we have the wedding in the new house, Sophia? That will be a happy beginning for the newlyweds and our new home."

Gerald knew Sophia would think it a good way to show off the new house, while it would definitely limit the number of guests.

"Oh, that would be splendid," said Sophia. "We could have the ceremony in the East Parlor, since it's going to be light blue, a most appropriate church-like color for a wedding."

"Agnes, do you like the idea?" Caleb asked.

"Yes, it would be fine, just so long as it's kept simple. I think that's how my mother would have liked it."

Agnes rarely mentioned her mother, out of respect for Sophia, but she strongly felt her mother's absence as she prepared for her wedding. Sophia was now so set on the new house as the location for the wedding, that she used Clara as an argument to get her way. "Yes, your mother would have thought a house wedding most appropriate," she said. "We must consider what she would have wanted for you on this day. Why, we might even order you a beautiful wedding dress from Boston, where your mother would have bought hers."

"Where is my mother's dress, Dad? Could I wear it?" asked Agnes.

"Your mother didn't have a fancy dress," Gerald replied. "We married so quickly because we were moving here, that she picked one of her newer but regular dresses. I don't think she kept it, and anyway, we did get rid of her clothes after she died."

"Oh," said Agnes, "well, Molly's a good seamstress so maybe she could make me a dress."

"Oh, dear, no," said Sophia. "You want a decent dress; one made by a professional dressmaker."

"I'm sure Molly does fine work," said Agnes.

"Yes, she sews well enough for everyday clothes, but you want a special dress for your wedding. We'll order you one, and Molly can always fit it to you if necessary."

"I just thought," Agnes began, but she stopped herself. She had been going to say that if Molly made her dress, it would almost be like having her mother make it. But she did not want to sound insulting toward her stepmother, even if she truthfully preferred Molly to Sophia.

"We'll go to the mercantile tomorrow," said Sophia, "and we'll find a lovely dress in the catalog for you."

"Can I get a dress too?" asked Madeleine, perhaps more excited than the adults about the wedding.

"Of course, dear," Sophia replied. "You can be Agnes's flower girl."

Caleb noted how downcast his stepsister looked about ordering her dress. Boldly, he suggested, "Agnes, why don't you ask Molly to make your veil then?"

"That's a great idea," said Gerald.

"Oh, yes," Agnes smiled, "and she can dress it with Michigan flowers to give it a local touch."

"That might be pretty," Sophia replied begrudgingly.

"I will ask Molly. I bet she'll make me a beautiful veil," said Agnes. "But then I'll have to invite her to the wedding; I know, I'll ask her to be my matron of honor since Caleb will be Jacob's best man."

"I'm sure Molly will like that," Gerald replied. "You and your stepmother pick out the dress tomorrow, and then you can tell Molly what you want so the dress and veil match."

"All right." Agnes's eyes sparkled. "Thank you everyone for all your help."
"You're welcome, dear," said Sophia. "That's what mothers are for."

❦   ❦   ❦

The wedding was set for June 11th. Sophia ordered the workmen to have the house finished a week beforehand so she could decorate. She purchased an excessive amount of flowers for the east parlor, but Agnes was too nervous to notice. Gerald was equally nervous; he knew Jacob would make a fine husband, but Agnes seemed his last link to the happy old days, and now he would only see her occasionally because she would be living with Jacob out at the Brookfield farm. Caleb also suffered from anxiety that the marriage would intrude on his friendship with Jacob. Only Jacob did not tremble; he had not one doubt that Agnes was the woman he wanted to spend the rest of his life with.

The wedding morn, Agnes dressed in what had been intended as her bedroom in the new house. Molly and Sophia both assisted her, although Molly politely deferred to Sophia in every detail. The Whitmans arrived an hour before the ceremony. Edna, annoyed not to have been asked to be maid of honor, brought a book to read until the ceremony began. To please Edna, Cordelia had suggested she might help with the wedding dinner, but Sophia rejected the idea, having hired a new cook for the new house, along with an extra girl to come in just for the day to assist with the festivities. Feeling left out, Edna retreated to a corner, more interested in the love story of Cosette and Marius Pontmerci than that of Agnes and Jacob Whitman. Cordelia and Nathaniel sat in the parlor, awkwardly making small talk with Gerald while they waited for the minister to arrive. Jacob's parents could not be happier about their son's choice of a wife, but formal occasions made them nervous. As Cordelia often remarked to her husband, "We are not fancy people, which is why Sophia and I do not see eye to eye on so many things."

The new house became the center of conversation since the Whitmans were inside it for the first time. The house was magnificent, far surpassing Peter White's residence; for days now, the people of Marquette had been walking up and down Ridge Street just to stand and gawk at it.

"I haven't seen the like of this since I left home," many a transplanted New Englander remarked while Marquette's European immigrants often commented it looked like a miniature castle or chateau from the old country.

"I love all the stonework," Cordelia told Gerald.

"It's Lake Superior sandstone," he replied. "I thought it would look distinctive if we used all local materials. The stone came from the new quarry at the Pendill farm."

"What a wonderful idea to use local sandstone," said Cordelia. "It's really made the house the showcase of the city."

The house truly was the grandest Marquette had ever seen. The entire structure was built of sandstone and rose two stories with a central tower to serve as a third floor. Its Victorian Gothic style dominated the landscape with its emphasis on vertical lines in its tower and elongated windows. The windows were embellished with stained glass patterns along their edges. The front porch curved around the side with intricate carvings and trefoil arches. The house's interior was composed of the finest black walnut woodwork. Several tall chimneys rose from the roof, providing warmth and comfort to each of the major rooms. Compared to Marquette's early pioneer cabins, the Henning mansion seemed to have countless rooms. Downstairs was an east and a west parlor, a dining room, a kitchen, a dayroom for Sophia, a smoking room that Gerald would also use as an office, and a small room with an upright piano for Madeleine to practice upon while a grand piano graced the east parlor for social occasions. Upstairs was the master bedroom, individual bedrooms for Caleb, Agnes, and Madeleine, a guest room and two bathrooms. The tower and attic provided two servants rooms, plus a large linen closet and storage space.

Gerald gave Nathaniel and Cordelia the downstairs tour. Edna obstinately remained in the east parlor; she was disillusioned by all the splendor when she learned there was no library. Cordelia and Nathaniel politely praised everything from the expensive oak dining table to the carpets; they daringly touched the silk wallpaper; they were dazzled by the dining room's glowing chandelier, and they admired the stately grandfather clock. Many pieces of furniture came from the Hennings' previous home, but the new house was so large several empty spots remained where newly bought furniture would be placed.

Cordelia could not comprehend the expense of building and furnishing such a mansion.

"Is the work finished now?" Nathaniel asked.

"Not quite," Gerald replied. "The upstairs bedrooms still need wallpapering, and of course, we're going to build a carriage house out back."

"It's magnificent," said Cordelia, and when her sister came downstairs to oversee the wedding preparations, she graciously praised her taste.

"Thank you," said Sophia. "You must come back when the upstairs is finished. Of course, it won't be as grand as the downstairs, since this is where we'll entertain. Did Gerald tell you we imported the east parlor's wallpaper from France?"

"Yes, it's lovely," said Cordelia, although she preferred the pink paint of her own bedroom. But anything from France was extravagant, and she knew extravagance was Sophia's great purpose.

"I came downstairs," said Sophia, "to find the groom and best man."

"They went up to Caleb's room," Gerald replied.

"Why didn't you warn me?" said Sophia. "What if Agnes had accidentally stepped into the hall? It's bad luck for the groom to see the bride before the wedding."

"Well, it didn't happen, dear," Gerald replied. "Why don't you go tell them not to come out until we're ready for them."

Sophia sighed, and returned upstairs; she would be glad when this wedding was over; the full weight of the preparations had fallen on her shoulders since she was apparently the only one with any taste to arrange such matters.

"Oh, Jacob," she frowned when she found the groom. "Is that your best suit?"

"Why?" he asked, looking at himself in the mirror.

"It looks so old."

"I've only had it for a year."

"Oh dear, I never thought about the groom's clothing. I just assumed you would have sense enough to find something decent. Caleb, do you have anything else he might wear?"

"He looks fine, Mother."

"This is the same suit I wore the night I proposed to Agnes," said Jacob, "so I thought it appropriate to wear today; Agnes has always liked it."

Sophia looked doubtful as she glanced out the window. "I suppose it must do since I can see the minister coming. Stay here now until I call you. You can't see the bride before the wedding."

"Just ignore my mother," Caleb said after Sophia had left. "You look terrific, and I'm so happy for you. You'll be a great husband and father. I wouldn't want anyone else to marry my sister."

Caleb smiled encouragingly to compensate for his mother's dislike of Jacob; he felt he had to compensate since the dislike sprung from his being a failure compared to his cousin.

Jacob patted Caleb's shoulder. "Thanks, and you know what they say. The best man is the next to be married."

"I'm not the marrying type," Caleb replied. "I imagine I'll be a bachelor all my days. I'm too much of a wanderer in spirit. I come by it naturally since our family left England for the New World and then kept moving West from New England to New York and then to Michigan. Someday I might just leave and never come back. No woman wants a man that unsteady."

"I don't believe you," Jacob replied. "I don't think we inherit tendencies like that from our ancestors; we each do what is best for us in each generation. You're just young and restless now, but settling down with a wife will solve that."

"No, Jacob, I've never been responsible like you."

"Don't be so hard on yourself," said Jacob; he was slightly annoyed that even on his wedding day his cousin had to take this melancholic tone. "You've always been a reliable worker for me at the farm."

"Not for much longer," Caleb said. He had kept a secret for several days now, and he had promised himself he would not spoil the wedding day by announcing it. Now he felt he was too nervous about his decision to keep it any longer from his best friend.

"I've decided to become a sailor," he said. "When I worked on the docks, I watched the ships go in and out of the harbor, and I longed to be off on one of them. Now I've finally found the courage to do so. I talked to a captain a few days ago to settle it. I'm shipping out tomorrow."

"Tomorrow!" Jacob was stunned; he wanted to spend this day thinking about Agnes, not about losing his best friend. All he could think to say was, "Have you told your mother?"

"No. It'll be easier just to let her find a note after I'm gone."

"I hope you know what you're doing," said Jacob, not wanting to argue today. "I'll sure miss you."

"Once you're married, you won't have time to miss me," Caleb laughed.

Sophia popped her head in the door.

"You two can come downstairs now. Jacob, tell your mother to start playing the wedding march. As soon as I hear the piano, I'll send Agnes down."

The groom and best man followed orders; in the ensuing hours of happiness, Jacob had no time to think about the conversation with his cousin.

The ceremony was held in the east parlor, mainly because of the elegant blue silk French wallpaper, but it also helped that the grand piano was there. The Methodist minister waited with the groom and the best man at the far end of the room while Gerald waited at the foot of the stairs to give away his daughter. First Madeleine carried in the flowers, Sophia having decided she would not have rosepetals smooshed into her new rugs. Then appeared the bride; Agnes was not a stunningly beautiful girl; she lacked many of her mother's charms, but she had an entrancing way about her that her timidity only enhanced. Her eyes were hidden behind the veil Molly had arranged for her, yet Jacob could feel their warmth as his future wife approached him, trailing clouds of satin as she came. She took her groom's arm with assurance; she felt shy from being the center of attention, but she felt no doubt in her choice of a husband. The moment she held his arm, Jacob felt the weight of the war lift from his shoulders; a new life began and his youth returned to him. The lovers stood together, their souls calm in the certainty of future happiness. They scarcely needed to hear the minister's words for their marriage vows had long been engraved in their hearts.

The ceremony was short and simple. Everyone was too happy to hold back tears. When it was over, the minister was prevailed upon to remain for dinner. The photographer was told to spare no expense in taking pictures of the couple together, individually, and then with various members of the family. Sophia and Molly ignored differences and congratulated each other on the gown and veil. Gerald passed out cigars to the men. Edna caught the wedding bouquet despite looking afraid of it.

Sophia's new cook, determined to prove her worth, overdid herself with a banquet table full of elegant dishes. The cook was an Irishwoman who had informed Sophia she knew nothing of "French cooking," but Sophia had insisted she make some French recipes, to which the cook added her ham, cabbage, and potatoes, and Sophia, ignorant of the difference between French and Irish cooking, never noticed. Molly was herself not a grand cook, but her praising the meal, and the minister politely joining in, was enough to satisfy Sophia's vanity and secure the cook's position.

Dinner conversation centered on Jacob and Agnes's honeymoon to Chicago, and then their return to take up residence at the Brookfield farm.

"For Agnes's wedding present," Sophia told everyone, "Gerald and I have given her money to purchase a new wardrobe in Chicago. We want our daughter to be the best dressed newlywed Marquette has ever seen."

Cordelia and Nathaniel gazed at the newlyweds and fantasized about grandchildren. Edna made certain everyone signed the wedding book she had purchased as her gift to the couple. Madeleine kept jabbering about how one day her wedding would be even more grand while Caleb good-naturedly listened to her, then told her she would never marry because no man would be good enough for his baby sister.

When dusk approached, the newlyweds departed in the Hennings' carriage for Marquette's finest hotel, the Northwestern, with its three floors and one hundred rooms. Here the happy couple would spend their wedding night before embarking by ship tomorrow for Chicago. Jacob and Agnes were cheered halfway down the street before the wedding guests disbanded. Then Gerald tipped the cook and maid and Sophia went to lay down. The Whitmans and Bergmanns said their goodbyes, and Madeleine went upstairs to play "wedding" with her dolls.

Caleb was left to wander listlessly about the house. He would be leaving in the morning; he had to pack his clothes, and he needed to write a letter to his parents. But right now, he wanted a drink. He had a splitting headache from all the day's merriment, merriment he had joined in while hiding his inner depression that he could not find similar happiness. He did not begrudge Jacob and Agnes their joy; he just could not bear being around it any longer. Neither could he bear to remain with his family and let their lives continue to consume his. Still, he knew he would miss them all. He wished he knew whether he were making the right choice; he thought a drink might give him courage to go through with his plans.

Sophia followed her parents' belief in temperance, so no liquor was kept in the house. Consequently, Caleb slipped out the backdoor, hoping his absence would go unnoticed. In the growing darkness, he made his way toward Superior and Lake Streets where the number of Marquette's saloons was growing steadily. This section of town was frequented by sailors on shore leave, and here many a lumberjack sought camaraderie after a long, lonely week in the woods. Here many a drunkard gave his fellow man a broken nose. It was a Thursday night; the saloons were not as crowded as on a Friday or Saturday, but plenty of roughnecks were swilling down liquor.

Caleb did not seek trouble that night, only relief. He kept imagining Agnes tonight in Jacob's arms—he wanted to hold a woman like that, but he also distrusted women; he feared he would end up with a controlling shrew as his father had. Yet he knew Agnes would not behave that way. Perhaps he also knew whatever his mother's faults, he unfairly used her as an excuse for his own weaknesses. He pushed the thought away by telling himself, if he left Marquette, he would find the courage to stand on his own. He didn't need a woman, a mother, a best friend or anyone.

Caleb stepped into Montoni's Saloon, filled with sailors actively playing cards and guzzling down whiskey.

"Give me a gin," he ordered at the bar.

"Whatever ya say, Mr. Henning," Montoni sneered.

"Montoni, you know that's not my name!" Caleb replied.

"This is my place, so I'll call ya what I want. You're lucky I don't call ya worse."

"Just give me a drink," Caleb scowled.

Montoni poured him a glass while Caleb settled onto a barstool.

"You a Henning?" asked the man sitting beside him.

"No, I'm a Rockford."

"He thinks he's a Henning," said Montoni, pushing Caleb's drink across the bar.

"You seen that house them Hennings built?" asked Caleb's neighbor. "What they think they is? That woman, she thinks she's Queen Victoria the way she acts. I wouldn't give two cents for one of that clan."

"Do you hate the Hennings just because they have money?" Caleb asked.

"No, 'cause they think they're better than everyone else. That Mr. Henning done fired me last month just cause I was a little late for work one day."

"And a little drunk I bet," Montoni smirked. Whatever Montoni's faults, he was the master at insulting a man and still retaining his business.

"Ain't no crime to have a drink. A man's gotta have a little enjoyment in life."

"Henning probably fired ya," said Montoni, "just so his son here could have a job."

The drunken man turned and glared at Caleb.

"I'm not his son," said Caleb. "I'm his stepson."

"Same difference—no actually, worse," replied the man, spitting tobacco juice on the floor. "Your mother's a bigger snob than Henning is."

Caleb gulped down his drink, tossed some coins on the bar, and said, "I'm taking my business elsewhere."

He walked a block down the street, but once at the next saloon, Montoni and the other man's comments continued to irritate him; Caleb's solution was to get stone blind drunk. But he had picked the wrong bar. A crowd of workmen were there who had helped build his parents' new home; the extravagance of the Hennings' Ridge Street mansion was enough to make the Henning name stink among many of Marquette's working class. Caleb kept drinking to drown out the maligning voices.

"That Henning daughter, there's a pretty thing. Quite the tart she is, I bet," said one rough voice.

Caleb might tolerate his mother insulted, but not his stepsister. He turned around to confront the evil tongued man.

"Ya wanna step outside?" he asked, slurring his words. "No one's gonna insult my sister, ya hear, my sister, that's who you're talkin' 'bout."

Caleb could barely stand up as he challenged, but the man was ready to strike Caleb anyway. The bartender quickly interceded by tossing Caleb outside before a fight could ensue.

Once out in the cool night air, Caleb decided to go home and write his goodbye letter to his parents. He would need to sleep off his stupor before his boat left early in the morning. He inhaled the cold, fresh air as he walked along the harbor toward home.

In the moonlight, he saw the whitecaps washing toward shore. He saw the ore boat he would embark on tomorrow. His head ached. He walked a bit up the dock, then stopped a moment to consider again what he was about to do. Tomorrow he would be on that boat, out in the middle of the lake, with nothing around but miles and miles of water. He thought he would feel free out there. Drunk and daydreaming, he turned and collided into a sailor.

"Hey, watch it!" the man belched and gave Caleb a shove.

Normally Caleb would have ignored such rudeness, but tonight he felt the world and all in it were his enemies; he was too weak to lash out against his family, but the liquor told him he was strong enough not to let a stranger push him around.

"Watch yourself!" he told the sailor. Then he sized up the man and saw how burly he was, a full fifty pounds heavier than him. The sailor's size made him unused to backtalk, not even from his captain who feared him.

"What did you say to me?" he bellowed.

"Give him a socking, Joe," said his buddy, stepping up to him.

Caleb was immediately engaged in a brawl—if it could be called that. He dodged the first swing, then raised his arm to retaliate, but the sailor was an old hand at fisticuffs and quickly struck a blow to Caleb's jaw.

Caleb was too drunk to feel it. He boldly lifted his arm to swing again. He was no coward and no weakling. Few men who grow up in Northern Michigan's tough climate fail to be hardy, and despite his family's social position, Caleb's physical labor had not left him soft. Many a log he had chopped, many a rock carried to clear a field, and many a mile walked. He would have been a good match even for a roughnecked sailor. But alcohol had debilitated his coordination. In swinging his arm, he lost his balance. He stumbled, then stepped back to gain his foothold, only to dangle his leg over empty air. Before any of the three men were aware of what was happening, Caleb had plunged off the dock and into Lake Superior's fierce waves.

"The fool done fell over," said Joe in disbelief. "I barely even touched 'im." "Joe, we gotta help 'im!" said his friend.

But Caleb had already vanished into the dark waves. The night made it impossible to find him, and the two sailors were too drunk and frightened to rescue anyone. They quickly scurried into town, immediately sobered by their fright, and swearing to each other never to say a word of what had happened. Within a couple minutes, Caleb had swallowed enough water mercifully to drown him before he felt the waves smash his lifeless body against the dock's pillars.

Jacob and Agnes spent a tender evening in their bridal suite. Agnes was confirmed in her belief that Jacob was gentle and thoughtful, as he hid his own anxiety and comforted her. She had imagined the joy of being with Jacob everyday, but not until that night did Agnes know the full glory of marriage in those passionate moments when they embraced one another. Afterwards, they lay together, resting content in one another's arms.

"I love you," the bride whispered. The groom was about to reply when the glorious stillness of their souls was destroyed by alarming shouts of, "Fire! Fire!"

The cries spread quickly through the streets of Marquette; people threw on their shoes and coats, ran out of their homes, and asked, "Where is it?" Their eyes answered before anyone could reply.

The fire started in the machine shop engine room of the Marquette and Ontonagon Rail Road at Front and Main Streets. The night watchman had checked the rooms at 11:30 that night when he smelled smoke. Seconds later, he saw the fire. He ran for water, but the flames had already engulfed the room. Grabbing the whistle, he blew it several times before scorching heat drove him from the building. The flames and stifling air made it impossible to reach the pump engine, water reservoir, and hose placed for emergency use. This fire-fighting equipment was quickly swallowed by the flames, extinguishing all hope of stopping the fire before it spread to the rest of Marquette. A hundred buildings were crammed between Ridge Street to the North, Rock Street to the South, and Third Street to the West, while Lake Superior served as the East border of the city's business district. Through this area, the fire spread while people scrambled for safety, too terrified at first to try saving anything.

When Jacob heard the cries, he threw on his clothes, kissed his alarmed bride, and rushed out the door with a warning to Agnes to get out of the hotel and head as far as possible away from the downtown, although the hotel was still a good distance from the fire. Jacob then ran toward the blaze to help fight the flames. He joined the men of Marquette's three volunteer fire departments, but the brave firefighters were nearly incapacitated by a swift breeze blowing up the valley to spread the fire throughout downtown. The firemen found their hand pumps ineffectual because they were designed to put out a blaze in only one or two buildings, not one hundred. The lake was several blocks from the main business buildings so hauling water uphill in buckets from the harbor was almost pointless. The steamer *Northwest* was moored in the harbor, and its men quickly sprayed hoses across the Cleveland dock to prevent the fire's spread, but their hoses could not reach far enough to save the other docks, much less the city.

Peter White, at the first cry of fire, rushed to the First National Bank, broke into the vault, and began to rescue the money. Other bank employees soon came to his aid. The bank was inside the new Burt Building, the finest office building in the Upper Peninsula. As the money and bank documents were removed, the magnificent Burt Building began to cinder and crumble. Peter White ordered the documents carried down to the harbor, where they were placed on a boat and floated out into the lake to keep them safe. Peter White's quick thinking meant the bank would be one of the few businesses fortunate enough to save anything.

Gerald Henning arrived on the scene in time to see the fire spreading to the Burt Building. Seeing the bank employees' valiant efforts, he rushed inside to save his own company's documents, but after one mad dash, he could not return inside. With what little he saved, he rushed home to give Sophia the documents to safeguard. Then he ordered that she, Madeleine, and the servants soak the outside of the new house with water and wet blankets to keep it safe. He now returned to the downtown to help fight the fire. Meanwhile, Rockford Mercantile had been consumed by the flames, no one thinking at the time to save it.

Jacob found himself hard at work on Washington Street, pausing only once in fighting the flames when he saw his mother and sister running uphill from the boarding house on Superior Street.

"Mother!" he called.

She was too overcome with fear to hear his cries. She and Edna were dodging cinders that floated in the air, fearing their clothes or hair would catch fire before they were out of danger's path.

"Mother! Edna!" Jacob shouted again.

Edna saw him, grabbed her mother's arm, and pulled her toward her brother.

"Are you okay?" Jacob shouted above the roar of the crackling flames. "Where's father?"

"He's helping to keep the fire from reaching St. Peter's Cathedral," said Edna. "The Bergmanns are there too. They've lost their home."

"What about the boarding house?"

"It's gone too," sobbed Cordelia, as her son hugged her.

"We're going to Aunt Sophia's," said Edna. "We'll help keep the fire from reaching there. We have nowhere else to go."

Jacob felt devastated. He wanted to sit down, feeling overcome by the tragedy, but there was no time. The fire had reached Washington Street and must be stopped. His mother and sister had barely escaped before the blaze as they climbed the hill. He told them to be careful, then let them go on to Aunt Sophia's house. He was afraid to ask after Agnes; he prayed she was safe.

"Whitman, we need you over here!" shouted a fireman.

Jacob ran to assist, while his heart ached to think of the boarding house gone, and the Bergmanns' house, and the possibility that the cathedral would be next. Gritting his teeth, he fought to save what was left of his city; losses would have to be dealt with later when there was time.

Hours passed before the fire could be extinguished. The blaze continued into early morning, with cinders and sparks floating through the air, then great gusts of smoke choked and blinded many until daylight broke to reveal the devastation of the terrible holocaust. One hundred buildings were reduced to little more than charcoal. The harbor had turned into a floating pile of firewood, with only the Cleveland dock left standing. Forty families were homeless. Tales of destruction spread by word of mouth; there would be no official news because the Lake Superior Mining Journal's offices were completely burnt. In the heart of the fire, only the Tremont house on Superior Street was saved by people throwing wet carpets at the roof, and the Chicago and Northwestern Railroad office was equally spared. The wideness of Superior Street as the main thoroughfare in the village prevented the flames from spreading to the street's south side where the cathedral stood. All the city's other businesses were lost except a drugstore and a meat market where Superior and Front Streets met. The bank, the Burt Building, the mercantiles and homes, the saloons and shops, stables, docks, and ships—all were gone.

Even after the flames were doused, Jacob and many of the other men wandered among the charred ruins in disbelief, checking to make sure the fire would not reignite. Then as dawn broke, Jacob remembered he should look for his bride. He found the Northwestern Hotel still standing and their belongings still in their room. He learned from the clerk that after the fire had ended, Agnes left to check on her family. Jacob knew the fire had stopped before it climbed up the bluff, so he hoped Agnes was safe at her parents' house. He gathered up their valises and carried them up the hill, stepping over the rubble and remains of Marquette. He doubted Rome had been such a shocking sight when it had burnt. He tried not to weep over the destruction of everything he had watched be built since his childhood. He plodded up the hill, afraid if he stopped, he would break down. He needed to reach the Henning house to confirm all his family were safe.

"Jacob!" cried Edna, running out the door to hug him.

"Is Agnes here? Is she safe?"

"Yes, she's upstairs sleeping. She's been here a couple hours. Aunt Sophia insisted she rest before you left on your honeymoon."

"I don't think there'll be a honeymoon now; even if we wanted to go, the ships have all burnt," he replied as he stepped into the entry hall, too tired to consider that the smell of his smoke-filled clothes might hurt his aunt's expensive wallpaper. "We'll stay here to help rebuild the city."

"Do you think we will rebuild?" asked Nathaniel, greeting his son in the hall.

"Of course," said Gerald. "We won't let a fire stop us. The bank managed to save nearly everything so that will help."

"Oh Jacob," said Edna, burying her face in his sleeve, so glad he was safe, "the library is completely gone. Fifteen hundred volumes, and the boarding house—"

Mention of the boarding house made Jacob think of his mother. He found her in the west parlor. Cordelia's entire domestic world was upset by the loss of her boarding house, but she smiled when she saw her son. "I'm fine now that you're safe," she said, thankful to hug him. "I won't have to cook and clean for a while. I needed a little break anyway."

Jacob smiled at her courage.

"I'll tell Agnes you're here," she said. "She wanted me to wake her up when you came, although she already said she didn't imagine you would be going to Chicago for the honeymoon now."

"No, I don't think we will," he replied.

Sophia now came downstairs; in the last hour, she had first heard that her mercantile was lost; then she had gone to her room to look out the upstairs window at the ruins of the town in the early morning light. Now she intended to make coffee so they could all get through the day. Gerald had let the maid and cook leave to check on the safety of their own families, and Sophia found herself relieved to have something to occupy herself, even if it were only making coffee.

"Hello, Jacob," she said. "Did Caleb come back with you?"

"No, I haven't seen him."

"We think he went out to fight the fire without telling us."

"I don't know," said Jacob, suddenly remembering his cousin's plans to depart on an ore boat, and deciding it best to say nothing until he knew where Caleb was. "I'll go wake Agnes."

But Jacob first went to Caleb's room, wondering whether his cousin could have left town despite the fire. Several of the ships had been burnt, and the few remaining were unlikely to leave immediately. Until he knew for certain Caleb had left, Jacob did not want the family to find Caleb's goodbye letter. But Jacob found nothing changed in his cousin's room—even Caleb's clothes were still there. Maybe Caleb had gone to fight the fire before he could pack. Jacob searched the dresser, the desk, and even looked under the bed, but he found no indication Caleb had gone. "If he did leave, he would have left a letter," Jacob told himself, "and with the harbor such a mess, he couldn't leave today. I won't say anything yet."

He stepped back into the hall just as Agnes came out of her bedroom. He greeted her with a kiss.

"Did you get here safely?" he asked.

"Yes, my only problem was worrying about you."

"My clothes are a bit smoky and singed, but I'm fine," he replied. "Let's go downstairs. Aunt Sophia's making coffee."

"It's all right about the honeymoon," Agnes told him. "I know you'll want to stay and help the family now."

"You're a wonderful wife," he replied, taking her arm as they went downstairs.

"Jacob," Sophia asked when everyone was having coffee, "will you go out and look for Caleb?"

"Let him rest, Sophia," Gerald replied. "Caleb will show up. Jacob's been up all night and can't be expected to go out again."

"I just want to know Caleb's safe," Sophia replied.

Jacob had been so occupied with wondering whether his cousin had left on a ship that only now did he consider his cousin might have been hurt in the fire.

"I'll go look for him right now," Jacob said, after swallowing down a cup of coffee. "You stay and rest, Agnes."

Mrs. Jacob Whitman did not want to spend her first day of married life alone, but she understood her husband's concern. She also wanted to know her stepbrother was safe, so she kissed her husband goodbye, then let Cordelia pour her more coffee.

"It's just like Caleb," Sophia muttered. "He probably was thirsty for a drink after helping out, so he went to the tavern rather than come directly home."

"I don't think there's a saloon left standing," Nathaniel replied.

Jacob walked quickly down Front Street toward Washington, then turned east to the harbor. A few boats were anchored there without docks to be tied up to. Jacob did not know which boat Caleb had signed on, but he had no success asking about his cousin from the men cleaning up the harbor.

"Ain't gonna be no ore boats sailing out until the harbor gets cleaned up," one captain informed him. "Only way out of this town today is by horse or foot."

Jacob continued to search by walking to Superior Street. Here, everything on the north side of the street was in shambles, while the south side stood untouched. Since St. Peter's Cathedral had been spared, he went inside it, where he found the Bergmanns and several other now homeless families.

"We've lost everything," Molly told him.

Jacob related his own family's losses, then said, "Why don't you go up to my Uncle Gerald's house? I'm sure you can stay there."

"No, the parish will help us," Molly replied. She did not wish to experience Sophia's inhospitality again as she had during Fritz's final illness. "Tell your parents I'm sorry about the loss of their boarding house."

Jacob thanked her, then walked to the Brookfield farm, wondering whether his cousin might be there. Along the way, he thought how sad it was that Molly Bergmann and her children had no roof over their heads. His family would have to do something for them; he would speak to his Uncle Gerald and his mother about it when he got home. At the farm, he found only the hired hand busy with the morning chores. Jacob told him about the fire, the man's first news of it. Then Jacob took one of his horses from the barn and rode back to town, too tired after his sleepless night to walk anymore.

He returned to the Henning house and apologized to his Aunt Sophia for not finding Caleb. Agnes fixed him breakfast, and then he went upstairs to nap.

"Caleb is bound to show up soon," Gerald told Sophia. "Perhaps he went to Negaunee to get assistance in bringing clothes or food to Marquette."

The family stayed together all that day, too exhausted to make decisions for the future after a sleepless night and their devastating losses. Throughout the day, neighbors stopped by to bring further sad news. The supplies to build the new Presbyterian church had been reduced to ashes, the majority of the businesses destroyed did not have insurance, looters had stolen from abandoned stores during the melee, cars on the docks filled with iron ore had plummeted into the lake, Peter White had held business hours for the First National Bank in the railroad yard that morning, insisting the city would persevere. People had taken relatives, friends, and neighbors into their homes until homes could be rebuilt. One after another, the sad tales poured in, and the occasional story of heroism was told. Sophia listened and congratulated herself that even though her mercantile and Gerald's offices were gone, her own beautiful home had survived. Gerald, however, felt guilty to have such a mansion when so many were homeless. After Jacob told him about the Bergmanns' tragedy, Gerald walked down to Superior Street to find Molly. On the way, he discovered his and Sophia's old house still standing. He had not yet succeeded in selling the house, so when he found the Bergmanns at the cathedral, he insisted they live in it, and he gave them permission to let anyone else in need stay there. Glad to have done a good deed, he returned home, grieving at the ruined city, and glad that Clara and Lucius had not lived to see this disastrous result of all their dreams. He hoped a decent supper and a good cigar would give him strength to begin rebuilding tomorrow.

When he reached home, Gerald found the front door wide open. Several men in sailors uniforms were standing in the front hall. He pushed his way in until he glimpsed Sophia sitting in the parlor, weeping into her handkerchief while Cordelia sat holding her hand and Madeleine cuddled between Agnes and Edna. Gerald looked at the sailors until he spotted one he recognized as a captain.

"We're very sorry, Mr. Henning," said the man.

"For what?" Gerald started to ask. Then he noticed the body lying on the couch across the room. It took him a minute to recognize the blue lips and pale cheeks as those of his stepson. His knees weakened and black spots appeared before his eyes. The captain grabbed him before he could fall, and then Jacob led him to a chair Cordelia had vacated. Gerald's sister-in-law dabbed his forehead with water while Sophia's red eyes stared at him in despair.

"How did it happen?" he asked. He was overwhelmed, in disbelief; he instantly felt this unexpected death was the hardest blow of his life. He thought of Clara, but he had had time to prepare for her loss. He felt guilty; he had scarcely thought of Caleb that day, yet he had loved the boy as his own son, and now to no purpose.

"We were dragging the lake to recover some of the items that sunk in the harbor," the captain said. "We pulled him up with a piece of wood from a dock. We think he drowned by being on the dock when the fire made it collapse."

"He couldn't have saved himself," one sailor added. "Me and Harry here, we seen him down at the saloons last night. He was pretty drunk."

"That's enough, Lyman," the captain snapped. "A fellow down at the docks said he thought he saw your son helping carry things out there last night during the fire. We think he must have tripped and fell in the water, or the dock caught on fire and collapsed under him and with all the commotion, no one heard his cries."

Sophia did not doubt her son had been drunk the night before, but she felt a little comfort to think he had been helping during the fire.

"I'm sure he died a hero," the captain added. "As I said, he must have been helping on the dock when it collapsed. He was trying to save other people and their things rather than thinking about himself. A man told me he saw him down there. Said he'd swear it was your son he saw helping out. It was a tragic accident."

"Thank you," said Gerald. "It—it's just such a shock."

"We'll leave you in peace now," the captain said. "Would you like us to send the minister over?"

"Ye-es, that would be good of you," Gerald replied, too tired to see them out.

"What denomination are you all?" asked the captain.

"Methodist," Cordelia answered. Gerald and Sophia could not speak; their faces were buried in their hands.

The men dispersed, but Jacob heard Lyman say as he went out the front door, "The boy was drunker than a horse when I saw him."

Sophia was distressed enough by her son's death; she was further aggravated that the fire made it impossible to find proper mourning clothes in Marquette. She did not care whether the entire city had burnt down; she would wear proper mourning to demonstrate that Marquette would remain civilized despite the fire. Until mourning could be ordered, she made due with leftovers from when she mourned her father, although the clothes were three years old.

Agnes and Madeleine had to wear the darkest clothing they could find until their mourning arrived. Gerald and Jacob still had mourning suits that would fit them. The Whitmans had nothing they could wear, having lost everything in the fire, but since they were staying at the Brookfield farm, where Sophia could not see their clothing and consider them disrespectful, they mourned silently, their grief not visible to the outside world.

A few days after the fire, Cordelia and Agnes were sitting quietly in the farmhouse kitchen when Suzanne Varin Brookfield knocked on the door.

"I've come to give my sincerest sympathies on Caleb's passing," she said.

"Thank you," Agnes replied.

"I'm sorry also to hear about the loss of your boarding house," Suzanne told Cordelia.

"Thank you," said her former daughter-in-law. "We hope to rebuild soon."

"And congratulations on your wedding," Suzanne told Agnes. She hesitated then because so much ill had recently come to the Whitmans that she felt almost guilty to tell them her good news. "I've come to let you know there's also a wedding in my near future."

"Really? Oh Suzanne, who is he?" asked Cordelia. She was momentarily stunned that her father's widow would remarry, but she reminded herself that three years had passed since his death, and Suzanne was still young.

"Mr. Frederick Rothstein of Green Bay."

"How did you meet him?" asked Cordelia, not recognizing the name.

"Amedee orders supplies from him for the feed store. A couple times I accompanied Amedee to Green Bay and met him there. Last month he proposed to me, only I didn't want to move away and leave Amedee here by himself. But now that the fire destroyed the feed store, Amedee's decided he might as well move to Green Bay as well. Frederick has agreed to make Amedee his business partner."

"That's wonderful," said Cordelia, "although it seems so sudden."

"At least one good thing then has come from the fire," said Agnes.

"Yes," said Suzanne. "I was sorry to see the feed store lost, but there's a bigger market in Green Bay. It's really rather liberating for us, and Frederick is so good to me, and he adores all my children. I couldn't ask for more, not that he's any kinder than Lucius was to me."

She added the last phrase for Cordelia's sake, but Cordelia did not mind about the marriage. "Tell us about your future husband," she said.

Suzanne's tongue rattled gladly as she described her new lover, a successful businessman and a German bachelor without family who longed for a wife and children. She told them what a fine city Green Bay was, and how excited the children were to move there, especially since the fire had destroyed Marquette.

"Well, I better be going," Suzanne said after half an hour. "I told Amedee I would start packing today."

"I was just going to walk over to my sister's house," Cordelia replied, "so I'll go back to town with you."

At that moment, Jacob came inside from the barn. His shoulders drooped and he looked pale. The weight of the war, lifted by his wedding night, had returned with the added weight of the city's destruction and the loss of his best friend.

When Agnes told him of Suzanne's good news, he congratulated her although he did not feel very merry. Then his mother asked whether he wanted to go to town with her.

"No, I have work to do," he muttered. He had no desire to see his Aunt Sophia; her melodramatic grief over Caleb's death annoyed him when she had never shown such affection for her son while he was alive. She kept declaring Caleb had died a hero, but Jacob felt his cousin might have been a greater hero if his mother had allowed him a little freedom.

"I just thought I would go sit with Sophia for a while," Cordelia said. "Gerald is so busy helping to plan the city's reconstruction that she gets lonely. She's taken Caleb's death very hard."

Jacob made no reply. Agnes knew how her husband felt, so to avoid argument, she asked him to come upstairs and help her get something off a high shelf.

Suzanne told Cordelia more about her prospective husband as they walked to town, and Cordelia told Suzanne to write often from Green Bay.

After they parted, Cordelia climbed up Front Street's hill and turned onto Ridge. She found Sophia and Gerald arguing in the west parlor.

"Am I not suffering enough," Sophia demanded of her husband, "without you taking more from me?"

"We can get more lumber later," Gerald replied.

"I said 'No.' Why do I have to keep repeating myself?"

"Cordelia," Gerald turned to her, "talk some sense into your sister. I want to donate the lumber for the carriage house to help build a home for one of the families who lost theirs in the fire."

"That's kind of you, Gerald."

"Don't you interfere, Cordelia," said Sophia. "I'm in no mood to have the two of you siding against me."

"I have to get back to work," said Gerald, and he passed out the door.

Cordelia sat down. "How are you taking it today, Sophia?"

"The same," sighed the grief-stricken mother, wiping her eyes with her handkerchief. "I cried for two hours this morning. Poor Madeleine. I had the maid take her for a walk because I couldn't bear for her to see me like that."

"You need to be strong for her sake, Sophia. Madeleine and Gerald need you."

"Gerald only cares about rebuilding his business. He doesn't care that I suffer."

"That's not true. Men just express their feelings differently. If he doesn't keep himself busy, he'll start to mope."

"I suppose you think I'm moping, but you don't know what it is to lose a child."

Cordelia felt guilty for thinking Sophia was overreacting. Apparently, her sister's grief truly was enormous. "Is there anything I can do for you, Sophia?"

"Yes, I'm glad you came actually. Follow me."

Sophia rose and gathered up her skirts, then stepped up to the fireplace. Above the mantel hung the rifle of their Grandfather Brookfield. When her father had died, Sophia insisted she have the rifle. It had hung in the farmhouse since it had been built, so the rifle should have belonged to Jacob, but he had allowed his aunt to take it. Sophia had no interest in rifles; she despised her grandfather's memory, but the rifle was an antique and looked fine above the mantel so she had wanted to display it in her new home.

Now, pointing to the family heirloom, Sophia said, "I never want to see that thing again. I'd sink it in the lake except that it was our grandfather's, so you take it, Cordelia."

"Nathaniel has always admired it," said Cordelia. "It would look wonderful in our dining room when we rebuild the boarding house. But why don't you want it anymore, Sophia?"

"Our grandfather was a drunk and he passed that on to Caleb. Caleb might have been able to save himself if he hadn't been drinking that night. I don't want any reminders of our drunken grandfather in my house."

"Oh, Sophia." Cordelia remembered only a kindhearted grandfather whose faults she had long ago forgiven. "You can't blame Grandfather for Caleb's death."

"Then who is to blame?" asked Sophia. Her tone made Cordelia wonder if she blamed herself.

"No one. Caleb's death was an accident. He fell off the dock during the confusion. We don't know if he was drunk, just that he was helping to save people."

No one knew what was true; that Caleb had died heroically was what the family had chosen to believe.

"All I know," said Sophia, "is that my son is gone and liquor played a part in it. I don't want that rifle, and I don't care what you do with it."

"All right," Cordelia said. She lifted it from above the mantel. "I'll hang it in the boarding house, and then Jacob can inherit it when I'm gone."

Sophia blew her nose into her handkerchief. She did not like being reminded that Cordelia's son was still alive.

"You don't know, Cordelia, how awful it is for me, especially to know Caleb drowned," Sophia said. "You remember, I saw Mr. Maynard drown—I saw the horror on his face when he knew he was going to die. I hate to think Caleb went that way. I hope, Cordelia, that you never know the pain I'm feeling."

Cordelia felt she had known her own pain. She thought the instant loss of a son could not be much harder than to watch your son go off to war, then spend every minute for years worrying that he might be dead or wounded. Sophia had offered her little consolation during those war years as she pined for Jacob's safe return. Cordelia knew her sister had always been self-centered, but now she hoped this blow might make Sophia more sensitive; perhaps they would be closer sisters now.

"Let's have some tea," said Cordelia. She went into the kitchen to ask the cook to make tea, then returned to the parlor and distracted Sophia from her grief by asking her for advice on rebuilding and decorating the boarding house.

"You've always had such good taste, Sophia; even Nathaniel said I should ask your advice."

For an hour, Sophia forgot her sorrow as she dictated on decorating. Now that the horrid rifle would be out of the house, she felt life might continue.

1873

Marquette rebuilt after the fire, and it rebuilt for permanence in defiance of all future blazes. Before the fire, Marquette's downtown had been composed of ramshackled buildings, hurriedly built in the village's early years, then added onto or left standing for other businesses to occupy when the original owners moved to a larger office or went out of business. Now the city planned for a more definite future, and to prevent future disasters, a city ordinance required all businesses be built of stone; South Marquette's quarry flourished with orders for its solid, distinctive Lake Superior sandstone to rebuild the business district along Front, Superior, and Washington Streets. The First National Bank, despite the loss of the impressive Burt Building, found itself a new home. The Hennings prospered by the rebuilding of Gerald's business offices. Local real estate was selling rapidly, and Gerald, who had bought up a lot of land in Marquette's early years, now sold it and made a great profit from people seeking better locations for their businesses than what they had owned prior to the fire. At the same time, Sophia decided not to rebuild the mercantile since its profits were small, and Gerald let the blast furnace close down because the cost of smelting iron ore had been found too expensive. Iron ore was instead shipped raw out of Marquette, but Gerald had plenty of other business endeavors to occupy him, and between his real estate and shipping the ore, he found himself more prosperous than in the years before the fire, more prosperous than he had ever dreamt when first he came to this wilderness land. The Whitmans also rebuilt and expanded their boarding house. Rather than farm his own land, Nathaniel sold it to prospective farmers and helped his wife with the boarding house or assisted Jacob at the old Brookfield farm. The Whitmans began to feel they were comfortable for the first time in years, even if they could never aspire to the ostentatious wealth of the Hennings.

Molly Bergmann recovered from her losses in the most surprising manner. In the years following the fire, she lived in the Hennings' old house, but she refused to live on charity; she took in washing and did what seamstress work she could, paying Gerald what she was able. She could not afford to build a new house. She scarcely would have managed if Karl did not take on odd jobs to help them out. Then Karl met Mr. Montoni. Montoni had lost his saloon during the great fire, but he had soon rebuilt, and since then, no shortage of loggers, sailors, and miners had sought out his establishment in their quest for good whiskey. Montoni might be contributing to "the devil's cause," as Rebecca Brookfield had once told him, but as an Italian Catholic, he still attended Mass when his conscience irked him. One day at a church picnic at St. Peter's, he offered Karl a job tending bar, which Karl readily accepted.

Molly was a bit concerned to have her son work in a saloon. What would the neighbors think? Yet she and Fritz, being Irish and German, liked their beer, and she trusted Karl to stay out of trouble. She did not realize Montoni would cause her trouble. He was forty-five with a bushy mustache and a desire for a wife. Molly Bergmann was a fine looking woman in his opinion, and knowing how her family struggled, he thought giving the son a job would place him in the mother's good graces. At age forty, Molly found herself being courted again.

After years of caring for her husband and children, Molly's widowhood made her begin to feel the toll the years had taken on her. Now without her husband's loving compliments, she started to notice her wrinkles. She also realized that for a woman, especially an aging one, to earn money and support her family was nearly impossible. Neither did she expect Karl to support her when he would soon want to marry and have his own family.

Molly Bergmann did what any self-respecting nineteenth century woman would have done in her situation. She decided to remarry, not for love, but for financial security. She hoped Mr. Montoni would be a man she could grow to love, and if love failed, one who would support her financially and be tolerable to live with. She felt the meanness of her reason to marry, but marriage was more respectable than living off Gerald's charity in a house she did not own while her children nearly starved.

By the time she walked down the aisle, Molly had convinced herself that Joseph Montoni would make a good husband. His stern Italian brow was a marked contrast to Molly's sparkling eyes, but if his brow were harsh, it resided above a handsome, dark complexion. He looked strong and healthy and ten years younger than his age, and even though he ran a saloon, he appeared moderate in his drinking. He had been born in Italy but had come to America twenty years before and to Marquette just before the Civil War. He had spent his entire life working to make his fortune until he had amassed enough money for his own comfort and to send gifts home to his family in Italy. Molly did not ask him why he had not yet married, assuming he had been too busy working to think of marriage until now. Perhaps she should have asked, but she was in too much of a hurry to marry. The only marriage condition he required was that she learn to cook Italian food as his mother had made; she promised to do her best.

The relationship could have been perfect, but Montoni's years of bachelor-hood inclined him to having his own way, and Molly was used to being in control from years of caring for Fritz. This strong-spirited groom and self-reliant bride met at the altar in the spring of 1870, and by the summer, they found they were ill-suited for each other, both wanting to hold the reins. As usual, brute strength won out. A month after the wedding, Molly lashed her husband with her sharp Irish tongue. She had made ravioli three times to please Montoni, and each time he had said it was inedible. She told him from now on he would get ham and potatoes. Then he threw his right fist at her. Kathy began to cry. Karl was no small lad at sixteen, but when he tried to protect his mother, he got a harsh beating.

Molly told no one about the beatings. She knew if she complained to her neighbors, she would be labeled as a bad wife who could not please her husband. She swore Karl to secrecy and tried to make Kathy promise never to mention what had happened. She did not want her children to be known as having come from a bad home. Seeing no other choice, Molly learned to submit to her husband; holding her tongue was against her nature, but she managed not to let it erupt more than a couple times a year, when she was reminded to hold it by receiving another beating. She lied to herself, believing her misery was worth having food on the table for her children.

For three years, this situation continued until Karl finished school and began to work full time in his stepfather's saloon. That was the beginning of the end for Karl. As Montoni's stepson, he expected respect from the other two employees, a cook and another bartender, but Montoni constantly mocked him in front of the other men; one day when Karl shot back an insult, his stepfather socked him in the gut.

By now, Karl was as tall as Montoni and growing everyday. But years of his stepfather's abuse had made him afraid of the older man. Karl did not understand Montoni was so hard on him from fear his stepson's increasing size would make him lose control over the boy. Montoni also feared his employees liked Karl better than him, and that Karl might use this favoritism against him. Rather than befriend Karl, he beat the boy to keep him down. But Karl, unlike his mother, would not let his spirit be broken, and his father's ability to endure suffering had been inherited by the son. Karl took the beating that day in the saloon, but he also heard the fear in his coworkers' laughs. He knew then the other men hated his stepfather as much as he did; courage now rose in Karl's heart, waiting for the proper moment to prove itself. Karl knew money kept these men working for his stepfather, just as money had caused his mother to marry him. Karl also knew he had a better head for figures than Montoni. He had caught errors in his stepfather's books several times. As the days passed, Karl noted how Montoni moaned over unloading supplies for the saloon, supplies under the weight of which Karl felt nothing. Karl began to despise Montoni, and he knew he could find a better life for himself, so he began to look for the opportune moment to break free.

One night, Karl came home late for supper. He had been at the saloon, waiting for Montoni to relieve him. Little fuss was made about the family eating together, and Karl and Montoni often ate and worked in shifts during busy evening hours. Montoni had returned to the saloon from supper, then told Karl to go home and eat, but when Karl arrived home, he found his mother crying as she cleaned lasagna off the wall.

"What happened?" he asked.

"Nothing," Molly muttered, refusing to look at him.

"I told Papa the lasagna tasted good," Kathy said, "but he threw it anyway."

"Mother, did he hurt you?" Karl asked.

"No," she said. "What does it matter?"

"He threw the plate at her head," Kathy said.

"I'm not going to let you put up with him one more minute."

"Oh, Karl. You know I can't leave him. It would be against God's will. And I'm sure plenty of women have worse husbands. He doesn't lose his temper that often."

"You don't deserve this kind of treatment," said Karl.

"Just sit down and eat your supper."

"I'm not hungry," he replied and stormed from the house.

"Karl!" Molly cried. "Where are you going? Don't cause more trouble."

But Karl ignored his mother's cries, walked out of Montoni's house, and returned to the saloon. Many times Karl had controlled his anger for the sake of a roof over his head, clothes on his back, food in his belly, all provided by his stepfather. But tonight love for his mother superseded concern for his own welfare.

"I want to talk to you," he said, stepping into the saloon and walking behind the bar where Montoni was counting the register drawer.

"I'm busy," Montoni replied.

"If you ever lay a finger on my mother again, I'll make sure you—"

"Do this?" Montoni said, suddenly ramming his fist into Karl's abdomen. He had long dreaded the day his stepson would try to overthrow him, and long ago he had decided he would beat the boy senseless if he dared to rebel. Karl staggered and grasped the bar. Smirking, Montoni turned and walked into his back office.

Karl stood dazed a few minutes, thinking over what had happened. Then he straightened up and followed his stepfather. The other workers stared after him in silence; they feared Karl would be hurt, but secretly, they hoped Montoni would get what he deserved. Both men had dreamt of giving Montoni a good thrashing, but neither dared risk his job. Karl did not care about his job; he only feared retaliation against his mother, but at that moment, even concern for her could not stop him.

Montoni's back was to the door when Karl stepped into the office.

"You won't ever do that again," Karl said.

Montoni turned around, stunned by Karl's threatening tone. Before he could reply, Karl added, "I don't work for you anymore."

"Ya wanna eat, ya work for me," Montoni replied. "I put roof over your head and food on table, so ya do what I say."

"I won't be living under your roof anymore. You're not my father and from this day forth, I'll have nothing to do with you."

Then Karl turned and started to walk toward the door.

"Ya come back here if ya know what's good for ya!" Montoni shouted, but Karl kept walking. "Wait till your mudder hears this. She'll be upset by your disrespect."

Karl wanted to turn around and strike his enemy, but he held his temper. He needed to stay calm if he were to carry out his threat. He stepped outside, slamming the saloon door behind him without regard for the patrons' stares. He knew Montoni would not leave until closing time, so he returned home to collect his belongings before searching for a hotel room to spend the night. He had already decided he wanted to get as far away from town as possible; he knew there was always work in the lumberjack camps. It was autumn and logging would be in full swing soon because the winter snow made it easier to move the logs out of the woods on sleighs. He knew logging would be more strenuous than bartending, but physical work would help relieve the burning anger he now felt.

Molly broke into tears when Karl told her he was leaving. He omitted telling her Montoni had hit him so he would not give her further pain. Finally, she admitted it was best he escape their unhappy situation. She feared not having a son to look out for her, but neither did she expect him to ruin his life for her sake. He was intelligent and strong enough to survive on his own, and she had long known this day would come. Kathy cried that her brother was leaving home, but he promised to visit when he could. Although he could ill afford it at the moment, he gave his little sister a dime and told her to hide it from their stepfather so she could buy some candy. Then he left with only two shirts, a pair of pants, a hunting knife, and a dollar to his name. Molly hated to see him go, but she was proud of his self-reliance. She knew Fritz would have been just as proud.

Gerald had not had a good day. In fact, he had not had a good day for several weeks. He had known years of prosperity, but now everything seemed to be falling apart. He should not have expected business to continue with such rapid growth—he had weathered through some smaller financial downturns in the past, but the economy was becoming seriously strained now. He dreaded getting out of bed in the mornings, dreaded reading the stock listings. All that money he had invested in railroads—all of it was gone! The market had crashed on September 19th, and since then, business had been slowing to a halt. People said it was too soon to panic, that the market would rebound, but Gerald doubted it. Jay Cooke's banking house, one of the greatest in the nation, had failed; everywhere people were withdrawing their money from the banks. Gerald feared Marquette's banks would also fail; he had money in both Peter White's First National Bank, and in Philo Everett's bank. His real estate business was also slowing down—no one could afford to buy land during a depression, and Gerald suspected a depression was where the country was headed.

He knew worrying would not help. The best remedy was to be cautious and frugal until this financial panic was over. He needed to convince Sophia to cut down on her spending. He went home that afternoon, hoping to catch her alone so he could explain the situation before she made another exorbitant shopping excursion.

But Sophia was not home. Instead, Gerald found thirteen year old Madeleine in the east parlor entertaining her Aunt Cordelia by playing the piano.

"I just called to ask Sophia whether anything were needed for this evening," Cordelia explained. Today was the third birthday of Mary, the eldest of Jacob and Agnes's two daughters, and an evening party had been planned at the Henning house.

"No, I'm sure we're all set," Gerald replied. "Do you know where Sophia is?"

"She went out making social calls," Madeleine replied. At that moment, Sophia's carriage was heard pulling up, and a minute later, Gerald's wife entered her showplace home.

"Hello," she said. "I'm sorry I wasn't here when you got home, Gerald, but Mrs. Harlow did insist I stay longer."

"Were you just visiting the Harlows?" asked Cordelia.

"Yes," Sophia replied. "Since Gerald has business dealings with Mr. Harlow, I try to stay friendly with them."

"They have been good friends," Gerald said. "Especially when Clara and I first came here, they were very helpful to us in purchasing land to build a house."

Sophia frowned as she unpinned her hat. References to Clara still annoyed her after all these years.

"What is the inside of their new house like?" Cordelia asked. "It looks so grand, especially with that large park surrounding it."

"I personally don't know why they built there," Sophia replied. "Not when all the fashionable people are building on Ridge Street."

"It's convenient to the main part of town," Gerald replied, "and Mr. Harlow believes it will be on the edge of the city square."

"I suppose since Mr. Harlow is so involved in city politics, he thinks he has to be closer to the courthouse," said Sophia. "Well, it is a fine house. I'm not saying it isn't, but our house is far more comfortable and stylish."

"Is it nice inside?" Cordelia asked again.

"Oh, it's grand enough. The porticoes have Corinthian columns and the entire building is rather Italianate with high windows. There are high ceilings inside and the fireplaces have Tudor arch styles. The floors are pine, and Mrs. Harlow copied us in making hardwood window and door moldings. I don't care at all for the spiral staircase; I think a central staircase like ours is much more grand in appearance."

"I bet it would suit me fine," said Cordelia, "though I think the Calls' house looks more charming."

The Call house, owned by the President of the Lake Superior Powder Company, was a Carpenter Gothic and extremely original in style. Sophia equally admired it, although she would never have acknowledged doing so. She always insisted, and not without reason, that her home was the finest in Marquette.

"It's hard to believe how many beautiful homes are being built here now," said Cordelia. "Everyone has become so prosperous in recent years."

"Yes, well, we can't expect that to last forever," Gerald replied.

"Oh, Gerald, you men are always so worried about money," said Sophia. "What could happen? We have assets spread all over the place, and the economy has been good since the war. Granted there have been some slowdowns, but this little slump will pass as well."

"Mother, did you pick up my new dress for the party tonight?" Madeleine asked. She had been playing the piano during the adults' conversation until she had finished her piece.

"Yes, dear, it's in the hallway."

Madeleine ran to find her package while Gerald said, "She doesn't need a new dress. She has plenty already that she's scarcely ever worn."

"Oh, Gerald, let her have all the dresses she wants," said Sophia. "I only wish I could have had such nice clothes when I was her age."

"You spoil her too much," Gerald replied. "We can't afford anything else new for a while."

Cordelia did not want to hear a marital dispute. Getting up from the sofa, she said, "I'll be going now. Are you sure you don't need anything for the party?"

"No, we'll be fine," Sophia replied.

Cordelia said goodbye until later that evening.

"Gerald," said Sophia once the front door had shut, "I do wish you would not mention our financial matters in front of others. You don't know how people in this small town talk. Soon they'll all think we're impoverished."

"I would hope your own sister doesn't gossip about us," Gerald replied. "And we aren't impoverished yet, but we do have to cut back on our spending. No more new clothes for a few months. You and Madeleine have plenty to wear as it is."

"I only buy what I feel is necessary for Madeleine. I want her to have all the advantages possible. You know how deprived I was at her age, and it hurts me not to have provided better for Caleb when he was younger. Perhaps if I had been able to do more for him—but I did the best I could considering how lazy

George was, and then there were those hard years when I was alone and trying to support us."

Gerald got up and walked out of the room. He was in no mood to hear Sophia whine about Caleb. He wished she would take off the ridiculous mourning ribbons she insisted on wearing five years after the boy's death—she still used the situation to gain attention, rather than from any sincere sense of loss. He understood she had loved Caleb, but she always overreacted; she had probably spent more on her mourning clothes than she had spent on Caleb his entire life.

Gerald went upstairs. He breathed deeply to release his frustration while he changed his clothes. His granddaughters would be coming over tonight; they always cheered him up. His children and grandchildren seemed the only reason to go on sometimes, and now he feared he would not be able to leave them comfortable when he was gone. "And it won't be much longer now," he found himself thinking as age fifty approached. "What have I done with my life? Built a little mansion and made a lot of money. Tried to love my family. I could be more charitable with my fortune; maybe if I were a better steward of my money, God would not be taking it from me now. But does God understand how hard it is to be charitable when your wife is Michigan's biggest spendthrift?"

❦   ❦   ❦

September 21, 1873
Boston, Massachusetts
Dear Molly,

I'm writing to inform you that our father died yesterday. His heart failed in the morning as he tried to get out of bed and he died instantly. I think he suffered little pain. Mother wished me to write to you. She said she wished she could write to you herself, but you know she has never learned how. She has been crying ever since and wishing she could join Father. She keeps saying she wishes she could go back to Ireland to see the family, but we cannot afford such a trip, or even to come visit you. She has a tendency to be forgetful now, and she is always talking about the good old days in Ireland. She reminisces about the green grass of the farm and the smell of the peat, and she seems completely to have forgotten the horrors of the potato famine that drove us from there. I am glad she scarcely remembers those horrible years that are so vivid in my memory, even though I was only a child in those days. I do not think she'll be in this world long, but I promise I'll take the best care of her I can until then. Otherwise, we are all well here. My children are grown and married now so it is just Mother and me at home. My first grandchild is due next month. Can you believe I am to be a grandfather? Sometimes I can understand mother's longing for the past, for the years have flown by so quickly I don't know where they have gone. I am very sorry to bring you such sad news. Write when you can and give my love to your children. I hope to see you all someday.

Your affectionate brother, Michael

Molly did not cry at the news of her father's death. She felt glad his long, difficult life was over, and she hoped her mother could soon join him. When she had not seen her parents in so many years, death made no change in how she missed them. She understood her mother's feelings about the old days before the famine when Ireland had seemed a beautiful land. She thought Marquette beautiful, but it was not home like Ireland. She had thought she hated Ireland when she first came to America. Now she wondered what her life would have been like if she had not left. If she had remained in Ireland, even to starve to death, she would not be married to that beast of a man who had driven away her son, but neither would she have had that son. But what good was a son who was far away? She was lonely. Sometimes she thought she would be glad for the day she would join her father and Fritz.

Kathy came and asked her mother to fix the dress on her doll. Molly smiled, set aside the letter, and remembered she must keep living, no matter how hard life was; she still had her little girl, preserved by her prayers. Bishop Baraga had told her God had a purpose for this little girl. She must not forget that. She must live for her children, not for herself.

She placed the envelope and letter in the fire. She would not tell Kathy or Karl their grandfather had died; neither had known their grandfather, and Molly rarely mentioned her parents because it only made her miss them more. Even back in those hard days in Ireland, she had had someone to suffer with, but now she was suffering alone. Sometimes it seemed her whole life had been suffering, but she would willingly suffer now for Kathy, to ensure that the beast never harmed her daughter, that Kathy would have a better life than she had known.

Karl first became a lumberjack out of desperation. He had no idea logging would become his passion, that he would spend his life in the great Northern woods.

His first logging job was in Marquette County, close enough for visits to his mother and sister while far enough away he need not see or think about Montoni. He took the job because he did not know what other work he could do—he did not want to work in a saloon anymore, and he did not want to move far from Marquette until he decided what he wanted for his future. He fantasized about finding a profitable job so he could support his mother and sister and free them from Montoni. But he also knew his mother would never leave his stepfather; she was a Catholic who could not consider divorce or separation; she would rather let the bastard pound her to death. Karl loved his mother, but he could not understand why she would be unreasonable enough to stay with such a man. How could she follow a religion that told people to submit to abuse? Karl believed in God, but not in a church that kept people in bondage. The God Karl believed in wanted His children to seek joy. Karl intended to find that joy, and when he did, when he was well off, he would share it with his mother and sister.

He went to work in the woods with enthusiasm, thankful to be out of his stepfather's house. He was a good-sized man now—five-ten and a hundred seventy pounds, but he was young and soft, and soon became intimidated by these men of the forest; most of his lumberjack companions had started working in the woods when little more than boys; they could swing an axe from dawn to dusk, and beside them, Karl felt like a downright, puny weakling. His first morning, he tried to saw down a tree with another, seasoned logger, each man on one end of the saw, but all morning, Karl could not get the rhythm of the sawing, and the presence of his three hundred pound companion terrorized him. Moose, as his partner was called, bellowed and growled and grunted at Karl between saw strokes, belches, and streams of tobacco juice. Karl kept expecting Moose to lose his temper, to pick him up and hang him on a jackpine branch. Instead, Moose worked out his frustration by ramming the saw back and forth through the trees until Karl felt pummeled by the mighty man's jerking motions.

Moose kept his temper, but he must have complained to the boss because when the crew broke for lunch, Karl was informed he would have a different partner that afternoon. He dreaded who his new partner might be, but for the moment, he was relieved to rest and eat. He had been starving all morning; now lunch made him lose his appetite. He was used to his mother's home cooked bread, a slice of her pie, and fresh milk. Instead, the biscuits were harder than the tree trunks he had been cutting down. He put so much effort into sawing at them with his knife that he felt as if he had never quit working. The potatoes were cold by the time they were placed on the table, and the meat so stringy he could have tied up his Christmas packages with it. At dessert time, he walked over to the table where the pies were laid out. He started to cut himself a slice, only to discover the buttocks of a cooked mouse sticking out among the chopped apples. He quickly turned away, fearing he would vomit; he managed to get back to his seat and muttered to the other men he was too stuffed for dessert.

"Dag nab it!" yelled one of the loggers, reaching into his shirt. "Damn cooties is bitin' me."

The man pulled out a louse nearly as long as the mouse in the pie; again Karl felt he would vomit, but he was instantly distracted by the men's laughter.

"That critter ain't fat enough yet to eat," said the louse's owner, and then to Karl's amazement, he stuck the creature back into his shirt.

Karl could not believe how rough and dirty these men were. His mother would be worried to know he kept company with them. His father had been as poor or more so than these lumberjacks, but his father had been a gentleman, who never swore and who believed cleanliness was next to godliness. Karl suddenly felt homesick.

Maybe he should have stayed home. Was it really possible he could make a decent living as a logger? Did he even have the strength for it? And did he want to spend his life in the woods with these tough men? But after the defiant words he had spoken, his stepfather would not let him back in the house. Nor would he admit defeat and return home a broken man to become his stepfather's slave. Decent food and lodging were not worth his own self-contempt, and if he returned home, he feared his anger would grow until he either went crazy in his misery, or worse, he lost his temper and killed the man he hated. He was certain either path would hurt his mother more than his absence from home; better he suffer in the woods than make her suffer.

"Come on, pardner; it's time we get back to work."

Karl looked up at the young man standing over him.

"I'm Ben. I'm your new pardner."

Karl nervously stood and shook hands.

Ben was a year younger than Karl, though he had a baby face that made him look no more than fifteen years. His height and build were similar to Karl's, but his arms were corded with muscles, and his chest appeared so hard that Karl could not help but feel envious. Ben looked as if he could rip a tree barehanded from the ground. Montoni was a mouse beside this boyish man who had mastered the forests. And Ben had a smile that instantly won Karl over, removing any fear he might have of a new partner.

That afternoon, Ben guided Karl through his work with a tolerance for his greenness. Karl marveled at how Ben's superior strength and skill allowed him to work so rapidly; he began to idolize the young man, especially when Ben made it clear he liked Karl and would look out for him. At supper, he made sure Karl got a place beside him at the table, and that Karl got decent helpings dished out to him. This mealtime, the other men did not grumble at Karl, and Moose, who had shot him dirty looks all morning, turned away his eyes when Ben glared at him.

After supper, the men continued to work until darkness fell. Then Ben told Karl it was time to "knock off."

"I know they gave you a bunk in the building there," he said, laying down his axe, "but that place is infested with lice. There's plenty of room in my tent—I ain't got a bed mate, so you're welcome to share it with me. I wouldn't ask most, but you seem a neat, clean fellow. I'll warn ya I snore a bit, but you'll find after all your hard work that a little snoring won't keep you awake, and in these rough woods, even a big guy like Moose sleeps better knowing he's got a pardner by his side in case a bear comes into camp looking for food."

The thought of bears made Karl again feel he had chosen the wrong kind of work, but Ben seemed so indestructible, and Karl was relieved to share a tent with the only man in camp who had befriended him. Once they were in the tent, wrapped in their blankets and the lantern blown out, Karl wanted to ask his new friend some questions about his past, since he could not get over how boyish Ben looked despite his size. He imagined Ben must have started working in the camps at twelve or so to become so large and muscular. But by the time Karl got up the courage to ask for Ben's story, Ben was already snoring. Karl tried to sleep too, but he felt dirty and itchy—he could feel tree sap and sawdust on his hands and clothes; he badly wanted to take a bath. Then physical exhaustion overcame him, and dirty or not, he slept soundly for the first of many nights in the great forests of Northern Michigan.

♦   ♦   ♦

Karl woke the next morning to sunlight shining in his eyes through a crack in the tent's opening. He rolled sideways and squinted to see whether Ben were there, but his partner's bedroll was already empty. With all the noisy birds chirping, Karl was surprised he had not also woken early, but it was kind of pretty sounding, especially in the early morning sunshine. Even the crisp autumn air felt good.

"Wake up, pardner! It's time for some grub," said Ben, sticking his head into the tent. "You gonna sleep all day? Why the sun rose nearly an hour ago."

"What time is it?"

"Almost eight I reckon. Most of the men are done eatin'. I thought you could use a little extra sleep, but if you want some grub, you better get over there."

"All right," said Karl. The morning was cold, and he still felt tired, and he did not relish another grotesque meal courtesy of the camp cook. But Ben's boyish smile made him feel friendly. He crawled out of the bedroll and dug around for his pants and boots. A couple minutes later, he stepped outside to be bedazzled as never before. The sun was glimmering down through the tree branches, transforming every visible object in its golden haze. Karl looked up at the sun and felt dwarfed beside the towering jackpines that had reached into the sky for a century. He felt his mind spinning at the thought of their age and strength. Gosh, they were breathtaking. It would be a shame to cut them down. Everything in the woods was so glorious this morning as the colored leaves fell like confetti in the rustling breeze. Karl had never before been in the woods at such an early hour, never realized just how empowering a feeling the forest can create. He had often thought Lake Superior the most magnificent scene possible, but this sight surpassed even the Great Lakes.

"Here," said Ben, appearing from behind the tent with a plate. "I managed to grab you a biscuit and some eggs. I'm afraid the coffee's kinda watered down. That cook is pretty horrible, but on the bright side, I have known worse ones."

"Thanks," Karl replied, appreciating Ben's kindness. "I never noticed before how beautiful trees were. Seems almost a pity to cut them down."

"Yup, I know what you mean, but we don't get paid to look at 'em. That's just an added bonus."

Karl smiled.

"Beauty about trees," said Ben, "is that when you cut them down you can always plant more. The forests will always be here."

"I hope so," Karl replied.

"They say there's so many trees in these forests that we'll be logging here for a hundred years; so at least they won't be gone in our lifetimes."

"Still seems a shame though," Karl replied.

"Now listen," said Ben. "I know this is a tough job, but there ain't a better kind of life. A man can feel freer in the woods than he can any other place on earth. You're going to feel sore for a while until you get used to the work, but it'll make a man out of you. I can tell already you've got the makings of a good lumberjack."

"I don't know about that," said Karl.

"Trust me. I was just like you when I started. Young and smart and wanting a soft city life. I thought I was too smart for this kind of work, but brains have nothing to do with it. It's the soul that counts. Out here a man can find his soul."

Karl said nothing; the beautiful morning testified to Ben's words, but Karl could not imagine spending his life cutting down trees.

"You just wait a while. The bug will get you—and I'm not talking about just the mosquiteers, though they'll get you as well. No, it's the north-country bug, and once he bites you, he's poisoned your mind until you don't think you can be happy any place 'cept in the woods. Only way you can imagine wanting to die then is in a quick flash when a tree falls and takes you down in exchange for all the blows you've given 'em. And it's a fair exchange. I've seen it happen to a couple men, and they was some of the finest lumberjacks I've ever known. It's the best way to go after a long life of cutting and sawing in this paradise."

Yesterday, Karl would have thought this the dumbest speech he had ever heard, but he was surprised by the poetic touch on his partner's lips. He liked Ben all the more for loving these trees. He caught an unexpected glimpse of his possible future—of he and Ben developing a friendship while he grew to love being in these woods. The food was horrible out here, but the scenery might just make up for it.

1874

Montoni did not want to go, and that was fine with Molly. She was relieved to have a couple hours away from him. Last time Montoni had gone, Gerald had been polite to him, but Gerald clearly disliked her husband as much as she disliked Sophia. Montoni did not like the Hennings or the Whitmans; he preferred to sit in his saloon, chatting with his customers and counting his money. Molly would not even go except that Gerald would be disappointed, and she liked to see Agnes and her little girls.

The picnic, at Sophia's insistence, was to be held at Park Cemetery. The cemetery had originally belonged to the Episcopalians, but in 1858, it had been renamed and made available for all of Marquette's Protestant denominations—the Catholics, of course, had to have their own cemetery. Then in 1872, Peter White initiated a plan for Park Cemetery's improvement, including having it landscaped, plotted out, and cared for regularly. Plans were now in progress to dredge the ponds, build arched bridges to the little islands inside the ponds, and to improve the pathways. Slowly the cemetery was becoming as beautiful as any city park in the United States, and Marquette's residents frequently chose it as a place for Sunday picnics. Molly thought it gruesome to eat among the tombstones, but Sophia insisted family parties be held in the cemetery so Caleb could be included.

Molly and Kathy left home just before noon that day, lugging a picnic basket along with them. On Bluff Street, they met Jacob and Agnes and their two little girls coming out their front door. Agnes had thought the Brookfield farm too far from her family, so Jacob had built a house in town and found an overseer for the farm; he now walked a couple miles everyday to supervise the farming operations.

"It looks as if it's going to be a hot day," Jacob said as they all walked to the cemetery.

"Yes," said Molly. "It always surprises me how hot Marquette can get in the summers when in winter it can be forty below."

"True," said Jacob, "but it wasn't bad down by the lake this morning."

"Jacob was down there fishing this morning," Agnes explained.

"Did you catch anything?" asked Molly.

"No, I don't think the fish want to bite in this hot weather. I went with Charley Kawbawgam, and he didn't catch any either."

At this point, little Sylvia began whining that she could not walk anymore. She was two, and had insisted on walking, but now Agnes picked her up. Then her older sister, Mary, a big girl of four, insisted she be carried, and since Jacob had the Whitmans' picnic basket, Molly gave her basket to Kathy, and willingly picked up Mary, who then sulked because she wanted her father to carry her.

His daughters' whining distracted Jacob from the conversation. His morning fishing trip with Chief Kawbawgam, and now going to the cemetery, made him think of Caleb. He remembered the time he and Caleb had gone camping and fishing at Presque Isle. That was when they had first met Kawbawgam, from which time Jacob and the Chippewa chief had begun a friendship. Kawbawgam was not much of a talker, but he had taught Jacob more about fishing than Jacob's own father, and the two enjoyed each other's quiet company. Caleb had never gotten to know Kawbawgam because his mother would not let him. That Kawbawgam had saved Caleb's life during that fishing trip had not mattered to Sophia; she would not even speak to the chief when he came to Caleb's funeral. But Jacob had gone up to greet Kawbawgam, and he never forgot the chief's sad eyes when he said, "I could not save boy from falling this time." Jacob understood Kawbawgam's sadness; his having saved Caleb seemed futile since Caleb had died anyway by falling into the lake. Jacob had asked himself the same question—why had his cousin's life been saved only to be lost later; Jacob doubted he would ever quit mourning for his cousin and a life wasted.

Mary again fussed that she wanted her father to carry her, so Jacob and Molly exchanged burdens, although they were at the cemetery gate. Edna now spotted them and led them to where the rest of the party was situated.

"We're over by Caleb and Uncle George's graves," she said.

"I might have guessed," Jacob muttered.

It was still several hundred feet back to the graves in the humid heat.

"I'm sure the ice cream will be all melted, though I tried to pack it in plenty of ice," Agnes said. The heat was now becoming near unbearable, especially after the long walk to the cemetery.

"I always like my ice cream rather melted anyway," Molly said cheerfully.

"There they all are," Nathaniel said, coming to relieve Jacob and Agnes of his granddaughters. "Look what I've got for my girls," he added, reaching into his pocket and then keeping his palms closed as he held out his hands for them. "Each of you pick a hand."

"I want the right one," said Mary, while Sylvia just stared, too young to understand the process. Nathaniel opened his palms to reveal a piece of candy in each hand. Sylvia quickly unwrapped hers and popped it in her mouth, but Mary said, "Grandpa Henning always gives us nickels."

"Mary, what do you say?" Agnes scolded.

"Thank you," she muttered, then unwrapped her candy and also popped it into her mouth.

"Come here girls, we'll get you something to drink," said Cordelia. "I made plenty of lemonade."

"I could use some of that myself, Mother," said Jacob.

"Hello, Molly," said Gerald. "How are you?"

"I'm fine. Hello, Sophia."

"Hello, Mrs. Henning," added Kathy.

"Hello," Sophia replied. "Cordelia, don't give Sylvia too much lemonade. She'll only spill it."

"Why did you pick this spot?" Jacob asked his aunt; he knew the answer, but on hot days, he lacked sentiment. "There's more shade over by those trees."

"I thought if we sat here," Sophia replied, "it would be as if Caleb were joining us."

"As if he knows we're here," Jacob muttered; Agnes poked his arm to silence him. Jacob missed Caleb, but he could not help thinking his aunt ridiculous. Six years had passed, yet she still carried around her black parasol, and she always had some sort of black ribbon about her, although the rest of the family had removed their mourning two years after Caleb's death. Jacob knew his aunt had not mourned so much for her first husband or for either of her parents.

"Have you heard from Karl lately?" Gerald asked Molly.

"Not since he visited last month. He works so hard I imagine he's too tired to write."

"But he's not logging now, in the summer, is he?"

"No, he found a job building houses up in Calumet—his friend Ben knew a man up there who gave them work."

"He didn't want to come home for the summer?"

"He makes better money up there," Molly replied.

Gerald was tempted to say, "Money isn't everything," but he suspected money was not why Karl stayed away. Gerald equally had no desire to associate with Montoni, but for Molly's sake, he offered an occasional invitation to the couple. Changing the subject, he asked, "Is business prospering up in Calumet? There's been such a slow down in work since the Panic last fall. I'm surprised anyone can afford to build a house. I understand lots of the copper mines up there are laying off just like the iron mines here."

"I don't know," said Molly. "He says he's working pretty steady."

"Gerald is just a worrier," Sophia observed. "He looks for every possible sign of doom. I'm sure the country's financial situation is stable."

"When banks fail, it's hardly a good sign," Gerald replied. "Look at Philo Everett."

"Is it true," asked Jacob, "that Mr. Everett paid his depositors out of his own pocket when his bank failed?"

"Yes, Everett's an honest man if ever there was one," Gerald stated.

"He's getting back on his feet now," said Sophia. "Economic slowdowns are bound to happen. Why Gerald's father back in New England had some losses as well—what was his loss Gerald, four hundred thousand dollars?"

"Something like that," Gerald muttered, not wishing to flaunt his family's wealth before the others.

"He's already gained back half of it," said Sophia, "so I don't think there's anything to worry about."

Gerald thought there would be plenty to worry about if she kept wasting money on expensive clothes, but he kept silent in front of the company.

Madeleine had been occupied helping her Aunt Cordelia arrange the food, but now she added, "Grandpa Henning is so rich we have nothing to worry about, and we own lots of land to fall back on."

Gerald did not reply. Like her mother, Madeleine had everything she could desire, yet not one grain of business sense. How could she when her mother indulged her every whim without regard to family finances? He would have to teach Madeleine something about money soon because like Agnes, she would one day own half his company.

"Cordelia, that fried chicken looks scrumptious," said Molly. The comment was enough to get the food passed around, and soon everyone was indulging his taste buds; people stopped chewing only long enough to compliment the women on the dishes they had brought. Only Mary and Sylvia did not enjoy the food; they were finicky eaters who refused to eat anything except ice cream, which had sadly melted, so consequently, they slopped it all over themselves. Agnes did her best to wash up the girls, and then Molly suggested Kathy play with them. Soon the three girls were running about in a game of tag among the gravestones. Kathy asked Madeleine to play, but was told, "I'm not a tomboy and I don't want to soil my dress." At fourteen, Madeleine had reached that immature age when one is too old for children's games.

"There are some people wandering around over there," said Jacob, looking through the trees while the women cleaned up the dishes.

"Who would go walking through the cemetery in this heat?" Agnes asked.

"Who would have a picnic in this heat?" Cordelia laughed.

The party in question consisted of two middle-aged women and a gentleman. After a few minutes, the strangers approached the picnickers.

"Hello," said Gerald, rising and shaking hands with the gentleman. "Are you enjoying our warm weather?"

"We heard horror stories about how cold it was up here," the man replied. "We're from Detroit and just up visiting relatives, but we couldn't take the heat in the house anymore, so we thought we'd go for a walk. We were told how lovely your cemetery is, and we're pleased to see that's true."

"It's such a large cemetery with such pretty little lakes and trees," said one of the ladies.

"Elegant stones too," added the last of the party.

Sophia eagerly rose to her feet. "Did you see this stone?" she asked, pointing to the six-foot high marble pillar that marked Caleb's grave.

"Yes, it's lovely," said the first woman.

"Thank you," Sophia replied. "I chose it myself. It's my son's."

"Oh, I'm so sorry," said the second lady, noting the black lace trim on Sophia's dress. "Did you lose him recently?"

"Six years ago," Sophia replied, stepping closer to the stone while the two ladies and the gentleman followed her. Gerald returned to his dessert while Jacob, rolling his eyes, observed his aunt.

"Six years," said the first lady. "That's quite a while."

"It's a dreadful long while for a mother to be parted from her son," said Sophia. "Do you have children?"

"Yes, I and my husband here have six, all grown now and with their own families, and my sister here has three girls."

"Are they all living?" Sophia asked.

"Oh yes, fortunately," the woman replied.

"I did have one stillborn child," the second woman added.

"Oh, that's not the same. It's still sad, yes," said Sophia, "but not the same as losing your son after he's grown into manhood and you've spent so many years loving him and raising him up with hopes to see him married with his own children."

"Yes, that would be hard," the gentleman replied.

"My only consolation," said Sophia, "is that my boy died a hero's death."

Jacob grimaced.

"Oh, how did he die?" asked the second lady.

"Have you heard about the horrendous fire Marquette had back in '68?"

"Yes, our relatives here were telling us about it," said the man.

"Well, my son was helping to rescue people and carry their belongings out onto the docks. Everyone who saw him said he was doing a hero's job, but he fell off the dock and plummeted into the lake, and with all the commotion, no one saw him fall. They didn't find his body until the next day."

"Oh, isn't that awful!" said the first lady.

"So sad," the second replied.

The man respectfully bowed his head.

"Yes, as I said," Sophia added, taking out a handkerchief to wipe her eyes, "my only consolation is that he died a hero's death."

"Oh yes, think of the lives he saved," replied the first lady. "People must be extremely grateful to you for having such a brave son."

"Yes, he was a real hero," the second lady added.

"It is a consolation to me," Sophia repeated as she replaced her handkerchief in her pocket, "but I would not wish the loss of a child upon anyone."

"Well," said Gerald, seeing his wife's grief was making the visitors uncomfortable, "we hope you enjoy your stay in Marquette."

"Thank you. It's a beautiful city," said the man, using this opportunity to rush his party away, although the women would not be hurried as they paused at other gravestones, hoping to find more heroes like he who had died in the fire of '68.

That evening, when they were alone in their bedroom, Jacob said to Agnes, "Now Aunt Sophia thinks Caleb's a hero not only for helping during the fire but for saving people's lives."

"Jacob, let her mourn for Caleb in her own way," Agnes replied. She knew her stepmother was overreacting, but she also found it endearing that Sophia's grief expressed a tenderness the woman had not displayed prior to her son's tragic death.

"I don't doubt Caleb could be brave," said Jacob, "but I was there during the fire, and I never saw him once."

"Other people saw him," Agnes replied. "Why else would he have been on the dock if he weren't helping to rescue things?"

Jacob did not reply. He had never told anyone Caleb's plan to leave that night, and he would not now; he did not care how Caleb had died; he just wanted his cousin back. And sometimes Jacob wondered why the Lord had taken Caleb and left behind Aunt Sophia. It was a wicked thought, but Jacob could not help thinking it.

That autumn, Karl and Ben stayed with the Montonis for a few days before logging season began. Montoni was civil to the young men, although he was clearly eager for the visit to end. They had arrived unannounced, partly to surprise Karl's mother and partly so Montoni could not refuse their visit before they arrived. Their presence made Molly nervous until Montoni came home and merely grunted hello to them. He appraised his strapping stepson and his strapping stepson's even more strapping friend and decided it would not be a problem to put them up for a couple nights. For those two days, Molly knew a reprieve from her husband's temper. The visit was much too short for her; Karl promised to visit again on some future weekend, but soon he and Ben were back to work in the forests of Marquette County.

Over the past year, Karl and Ben had become such great friends that every logging boss knew one would not work without the other. No boss had a problem with this stipulation, for the partners were among the fastest and strongest laborers in the North country. Karl had quickly learned everything Ben knew about the woods until he equaled and in some ways surpassed his tutor. Karl found Ben to be a bright and jovial young man, but not one to talk about his past. He never mentioned his parents or even where he came from. Even when Karl invited him home, Ben made no mention of his family or extended a similar invitation for Karl to visit his parents.

One day as the partners were sawing down a giant jack pine, Karl heard a holler and turned to see his friend race across the woods to where a logger was beating a dog. Ben grabbed the other logger by the back and hurled him to the ground. The man jumped up and turned with his fist ready to swing until he saw who had assailed him.

"Go ahead and hit me just like you hit that poor dog of yours!" Ben said. "Only, remember, I hit back."

Meanwhile Karl ran to where the dog lay whimpering on the ground.

"He kicked the dog in the ribs," one bystander told Karl.

The dog's owner met Ben's eye, then turned away.

"A man ought to be allowed to do what he likes with his own mutt," he grumbled.

"A man ought to behave like a man and not hurt a helpless animal," Ben replied. He stepped over to the hurt animal, picked it up, and carried it into his tent.

No one dared object, least of all the dog's owner, who was unwilling to wrestle his property from Ben's corded arms.

"Ben, what'll you do with it?" Karl asked, following his partner into the tent.

"Take care of it," Ben replied as he tore a piece from his own shirt to bandage the dog's bleeding leg.

"It's just a dog, Ben. You can't risk making all the men in camp angry with you over a dog."

"What's wrong with your head, Karl? This dog's a living thing just like you and me."

Ben seethed with anger over the dog's condition. When Karl asked if he could be any help, Ben only replied, "Keep the jackass who did this away from me."

Never before had Karl heard his friend use abusive language, despite all their time spent with rough men in the woods. Karl returned to cutting down trees, all day waiting for Ben to rejoin him, but Ben remained in the tent, gently petting and talking to the dog. No one dared suggest he should be working instead.

That night, Ben told Karl, "I s'pose you think I'm nuts to care about a dog like this, so let me explain. I once had a dog of my own, and when my ma died, that dog was my only true friend. I had a father of course, but all he ever did was ignore me 'cept when he wanted someone to take out his anger on. He would leave me locked up all day in the cabin while he went off to work. I was just a little thing then—five or six—and that dog took better care of me than my own father did."

Karl listened quietly. Ben had never mentioned his family, and Karl did not want to ask questions that might make Ben clam up now.

"One day my damn father kicked that dog. I was twelve then and the dog was getting old, but he was still getting around okay. Yeah, he was blind in one eye, but he was still happy. I knew 'cause his tail was always wagging. My father did it one night when he was drunk. He said it was time to put the dog out of its misery. I tried to stop him but the drunk bastard walloped me into a corner, then pulled out a rifle and shot my dog right there in the cabin. I never forgot it. I ran away the next day. Never saw my old man again after that."

Ben's voice broke as he relived that awful moment from his childhood. After a deep sigh, he said, "I don't take kindly to anyone hurting an animal."

"I understand," Karl gulped. He had never seen such anger in a person's eyes, not even during one of his stepfather's most violent rages.

"People make their own problems," Ben said. "Most of the time they get what they deserve. But not animals. All they ask is that you love 'em, but instead people mistreat 'em. There's no excuse for it."

After a few minutes, Karl asked, "Will the dog be okay?"

"He'll be all right," said Ben. "Long as that jackass don't get near him again."

Karl did not object when the dog slept in the tent that night. From then on, it was their constant companion.

🍁   🍁   🍁

By December, the snow was already thick in the woods. Heavy snow was perfect for logging because then the sleighs could more easily pull the logs, but when the heavy snows began so early, it was a sure sign the winter would be wrought with many storms. Karl and Ben were working only twenty miles from Marquette that winter, so Karl hoped to go home for a day or two at Christmas if the weather were good. Today the sky was clear, so one of the men in the logging camp had been sent to town to fetch the mail. They all knew if a storm hit, it could be weeks before anyone could go again for the mail. The man returned the next day, having snowshoed to town and back. Karl was pleased to receive a letter from his mother, inviting him to come home for Christmas. Ben's letter, however, was more significant.

"It's from my cousin up in the Keweenaw," he told Karl as he ripped open the envelope. He read the letter, then passed it to Karl.

Copper Harbor, Michigan
December 10, 1874
Dear Ben,

Hope your well? Hows the work there in Marqette County? You loggers have easy winters there. We get more snow hear at the top of the Keweenaw than you get down there.

I wanted to let you know I'm in charge of things hear now. I became a partner a few months ago but my partner is moving to Minesota and wants to sell me his haf. I been saving up money for this vary thing. Now that I'm the boss I want you to come work for me. I ain't got the mind for bookwork like you so you can by into a partnership with me. Your the only family I got now that my father is gone. Were making lots of money hear. Enuf that you can find yourself a wife and by a house. Rite me back with your anser. You can come up to Copper Harbor then after the 1st of the year.

Your Cuzzin, Norman

"You're not going?" asked Karl.

"Well, I guess I will. He wants me to come right after Christmas. We'll be done here in a couple more weeks, so I might as well go then. I'm not going to turn down a chance to be a partner in my own operation. The opportunity might not come again."

"No, I guess not," said Karl.

"What are you looking so glum for?" laughed Ben. "You are a silly fool, Karl Bergmann. Of course you're coming with me."

Karl's face lit up. "Yeah?"

"Yeah. You'll be working for me now. Won't that be swell? Better than working for the boss we've got. And I promise I'll make sure we have a better cook."

But then Karl thought of his mother.

"Ben, I can't go."

"Why not? This is the opportunity of a lifetime."

"What about my mother and sister. Who'll look out for them?"

"You went to Calumet last summer, and they got along fine without you."

"Yeah, but that was only for a few months, not all year round. It's a long way to Marquette from Copper Harbor. I'd never see them, and you know I need to look after them."

"Karl," Ben sighed, "I've told you before. Your mother's married to that man, and there's nothing you can do about it. You know she won't leave him, and you also know she doesn't want to ruin your future for her sake. I'll be running my own operation and you'll be my right hand man. The two of us together know more about logging than the whole rest of these here numskulls we work with. Think of the profit we can make now that we're finally getting our big break."

"I know," said Karl, "but I can't help worrying about my mother."

"Well, you have a couple weeks to think about it," said Ben. "We won't be going until after Christmas. I'll write to my cousin tonight and tell him I'm coming and that you might come too. And if you decide not to come now, you're always welcome later. For the moment though, we better get back to work."

Karl went back to work, but while his hands sawed, his mind whirled with indecision. For the past year, he had lived day by day, not thinking about the future, but simply enjoying his independence from his stepfather. Now the future loomed up before him; he realized if he worked with Ben, he might make more money to care for his mother and sister—he knew money would not make his mother leave Montoni—she was too good a Catholic for that—but maybe he could use the money to support Kathy; maybe he could get his own place and she could come keep house for him so she need not marry just to escape from their stepfather. Yet Karl did not think he could bear to be so far from his family.

By Christmas, the decision became easier for Karl. He and Ben went to stay with his family for the holiday. Again his stepfather was polite yet distant. When Montoni saw Ben's dog, he made no comment, even when the dog slept on Ben's bed. Karl longed to talk to his mother about his dilemma but he never found a moment they could be alone. Then the day after Christmas, a man arrived at the house looking for Ben. "I went out to the logging camp this morning," the man said, "but they told me you were over here. I came down from Calumet looking for you. I'm afraid your cousin passed away a few days ago. He came down with pneumonia and died real sudden. I'm the executor of his will. I have it with me to read it to you, but basically, it makes you his sole heir."

Ben was thunderstruck. He had expected to work until he could buy into a partnership with his cousin, but now he was the head of a logging company, as well as owner of a small house in Copper Harbor and several thousand dollars in the bank.

"Of course, I feel sorry to lose him," Ben told Karl, "but we were never close. I feel lucky, but it'll be hard work. I'll need you more than ever now, Karl."

Molly had listened silently to the lawyer's briefing, but she heard Ben's offer with dread. She knew her son would leave, but she would not hold him back.

"It seems as if this were meant to be, Karl," she said. "I think you should go with Ben, and when you're both rich men, you can come and start up another logging company closer to Marquette. I'm glad you have this chance to make your fortune while you're still young. Remember how your father's health failed; you have to put away what money you can to be ready for the future."

Karl had not forgotten those many years of poverty before his mother married Montoni—they had been happier years despite the deprivation. But he knew his mother really meant, "Don't worry about me. I'll be fine." He kissed her goodbye the next morning, and then he and Ben departed for the Keweenaw. He hoped he would not return home someday to find that villain had killed his mother, but he also knew she had chosen her life. He must choose his life now, and if he worked hard, perhaps he could make enough money for them all to be happy again.

1875

"It's never going to happen," Nathaniel Whitman said, reading the *Journal's* election results. "No matter how we try, we'll never become a separate state from Lower Michigan."

"No, the Lower Peninsula won't support our cause so what hope do we have?" Gerald replied. He had stopped by the boarding house on his way home from the office to invite the Whitmans to Thanksgiving dinner. He and Nathaniel had immediately fallen into their usual conversation on politics and the economy. Last March, a meeting had been held in nearby Ishpeming to promote the cause of Upper Michigan's statehood; the Upper Peninsula's residents had greatly approved the move, but the rest of the state dismissed it without interest. Since then, the leading men of the Upper Peninsula had angrily but fruitlessly continued their efforts. Cordelia and Edna were sitting in the parlor today with the men, but both women felt they should not interfere in men's business so they simply listened.

"The politicians downstate know if the Upper Peninsula leaves Michigan, we'll take all the minerals with us," Nathaniel said. "They mock us for our smaller cities but between our mines, our shipping, and our logging, we're worth twice what they are."

"That's true," said Gerald. "There's no reason why we can't be our own state or join with part of Northern Wisconsin. The Upper Peninsula's the combined size of Massachusetts, Connecticut, Rhode Island and Delaware and our population keeps growing."

"I'm all for our statehood," said Nathaniel, "but it'll never happen if we have to depend on the Lower Peninsula's recommendation. Look at Peter White— he couldn't even get elected to the University of Michigan's Board of Regents because the people downstate are all prejudiced against us—they're too ignorant to admit or even realize what we're worth. We need to get some major state services up here, like a prison or a college. Then we'll get the attention we deserve."

"Chandler promises if he's elected as U.S. senator he'll fight for our statehood, but I don't think even he can help us," said Gerald. "The only time the Lower Peninsula is interested in us is when we send our tax dollars down to Lansing. If we became our own state, we'd have more control over our own industries and that would help increase our profits."

Edna had been quietly reading Emerson until Uncle Gerald's visit had destroyed her concentration. She was heartily sick of all this talk over politics and the economy. Daring to break her ladylike silence, she declared, "Father, you and Uncle worry too much about money."

"And what else should we worry about?" Nathaniel asked.

"What this town needs is more emphasis on the arts. Then people will respect us. We need theatres and libraries, museums and opera houses to impress the people downstate."

"Edna, you have no concept of money or business," her father replied. "All theatres and museums do is fill people's heads with fancy ideas to distract them from the real work of building this country."

Edna was about to retort when her mother took her father's side. "Edna, you do spend far too many hours with your nose in a book to know anything about business or politics."

"I work just as hard as anyone else around here," Edna replied.

"Yes, you are a help to me in running the boarding house, but you waste your spare time reading those books when you could be sewing or quilting. A little reading is all right, but you don't need to read a book every week."

"You'd do better to spend your time looking for a husband," Nathaniel added.

Edna did not answer but lowered her eyes in humiliation. She did not see what her reading or finding a husband had to do with politics.

"I better get going," said Gerald. "I'll see you all later."

Edna went up to her room while her parents saw her uncle out. She was embarrassed that at twenty-five years of age, her parents still treated her like a child. She knew they were worried that she had not yet married, and they only had her best interests in mind, but she also felt that no matter how much help she was around the boarding house, they considered her a burden. And even when she brought in a little extra money from working at the library a couple days a week, her parents thought her life meaningless without a husband and children. Not that Edna did not want to marry; she just had not yet seen a man in Marquette who fulfilled her vision of a husband. Her mother would have told her she might see a man if she took her nose out of her books. Her father would have added that the heroes in her books had made her want a man who could never be real.

Some days Edna admitted her life was dull and humdrum, but then her books let her escape this sad reality. Her favorite heroine was Josephine March in *Little Women*; Jo had refused Laurie without fear, so equally Edna saw no reason why she could not remain single. That Jo eventually married Professor Bhaer was something Edna chose to ignore. Jo had wanted to write and to found her own school, and her creator Louisa May Alcott was a writer and had been a nurse and had never married. Edna wanted an independent and meaningful life like Jo March and Miss Alcott's lives, but being a wife and mother was all the world offered to women; even the few women who became teachers quit their careers once they married. Being a wife and mother did not seem fulfilling to Edna. Books were the only freedom she could find from the restrictive life imposed upon her, from the deluge of voices constantly asking her, "When are you going to get married?"

Edna's parents might have been happier if Madeleine were their daughter. At fifteen, the girl already dreamt of marriage. But while Cordelia pushed Edna to find a husband, Sophia would soon be horrified to learn what man was interested in her daughter.

His name was Lazarus Carew, and despite the seventeen rough years that had marked his life, he was a youth of genuine virtue, a quality to please any mother in her prospective son-in-law. Madeleine was the first girl Lazarus had ever desired. That he had not pursued any other girls may have been due to his innocence, but more likely, because other girls did not find him attractive enough to encourage him. His looks were unremarkable; girls who did notice him thought him downright homely. He had been nearly invisible until last year when a growth spurt caused him to shoot up to three inches over six feet; then he was noticed as a gawkish fellow, thin as a broomstick, but with wiry arms that hung down a bit too far from his sloping shoulders. His long neck made his head look shrunken, and his hair would not comb down straight but stood up like a frazzled mop. His deep voice sometimes attracted attention, mainly because it was such a surprising contrast to the peach fuzz above his lips.

Lazarus's parents had emigrated from Cornwall, England to nearby Negaunee. Many of the Cornish were migrating to Upper Michigan, bringing with them their ancestors' mining expertise, much sought after in the local iron and copper industries. The Carews had arrived seven years ago with their ten-year old son. Four years later, Mr. Carew had died, forcing Lazarus to work in the mines to support his mother. The next winter, an attack of bronchitis caused Mrs. Carew to follow her husband to the grave; she left her only son alone in the world. Lazarus then moved to Marquette where he found work as a stable boy, with his room and board included in his wages. The job was not pleasant smelling, but he could see daylight outside the stable door, unlike in the mines' underground caverns. He determined from that point to save his wages until he could afford to go West.

Lazarus had one relative in the United States—a maternal uncle who had migrated to the Montana Territory where there were also large mining operations. To Lazarus, Montana seemed like the end of the earth, but he often thought about moving out West to be near the uncle he scarcely remembered from his childhood in Cornwall. He knew it might be many months before he could afford the trip to Montana, but he was too proud to ask his uncle for trainfare. He spent his days working, his nights dreaming of the Wild West. Then Madeleine Henning invaded his dreams.

They had met at the Hennings' Ridge Street mansion, but not at one of Sophia's evening soirees. Such a poor, ungainly youth without family or social connections and smelling of the stable never would have been admitted into either of Sophia's parlors. Lazarus came in by the back door, the appropriate entrance for servants and delivery men; he came one weekday morning with an urgent business message from his employer to Mr. Henning, who had a bad cold that kept him at home that day.

Lazarus had often walked past the grand homes on Ridge Street. He had often wondered what kind of people could afford such miniature palaces. Never had he dreamt he would meet these people, much less enter even one of their kitchens. That autumn day, the Hennings' cook and parlormaid were in their beds with the same ailment from which their master suffered. Sophia was in a tizzy, insisting the cook must make supper, whether ill or not, and she also wanted the laundry done, though reluctantly she found she must do it herself. Madeleine, despite the spoiled tendencies she had inherited, was blessed with her father's patience, so she was making what effort she could to keep the house running smoothly during this time of crisis; in other words, she was the only one available to answer the ringing service doorbell.

Madeleine was in a plain dress that day, for she had been dusting the parlors. On first seeing her, Lazarus thought her one of the servants. After he explained his mission, she asked him to wait while she delivered the message.

Upon returning, she said, "He asked whether you could wait about twenty minutes. He needs to write a letter to your boss as the nature of their agreement is rather complex. Would you like some coffee or some biscuits while you wait? I know it seems a long walk from downtown on a cold day like this."

"I'd be much honored, Miss," he replied, "provided the master or mistress don't mind none."

"Oh no, I may do as I please," she replied, setting the kettle on to boil.

Lazarus thought what a nice position this girl must have to work in a warm house and to drink coffee whenever she chose without her mistress chiding her.

Madeleine felt sorry for the still shivering young man, who looked only a couple years older than herself, despite his great height. After she made them coffee, she sat at the table with him and inquired about his welfare.

"What's your name?" she asked, followed by several more questions of a personal nature. Soon, he was pouring out his entire history, and since he was seventeen, that took less than ten minutes with time left over to tell his dreams of going to Montana and growing rich from cattle ranching. Most boys would have been disconcerted by Madeleine's inquisitiveness, even if she were a pretty girl, but Lazarus was so lonely he did not mind; the more attention she paid him, the more lovely she appeared. For the first time in his life, his heart stirred as he wondered whether she—if he should even dare to ask—whether she would go for a walk with him on Sunday.

"Miss Henning, your father asked me to bring this letter down to you," said the cook, having decided she would rather come downstairs to make supper than lose her position. Madeleine took the envelope and handed it to Lazarus. He was so astonished by the cook's revelation of Madeleine's identity that he scarcely thought to reach for the envelope. He stood up, nervously wanting to escape from the house, but first he had to put on his coat; as his arm came through the coat sleeve, he found Miss Henning shaking his hand and saying, "It's been a pleasure to meet you, Lazarus. I've never met anyone quite like you, and I wish you much luck in making your fortune."

"Thank you, Miss," he said. "I better be going."

"I hope I'll see you around town," she added. "You'd better button up your coat so you don't catch a cold."

Embarrassed by her attention, Lazarus did as told, then made his exit. He was soon far from the house, but its fair occupant remained in his thoughts.

Meanwhile, Madeleine went up to her room. She had a library book she had intended to read that afternoon because Edna had insisted it would be good for her. But Madeleine found herself listlessly reading the first sentence over and over as she remembered her conversation with Lazarus. She had meant it when she said she had never met anyone quite like him; the young men to whom her parents introduced her were all from good families; they were young men her mother continually mentioned would be good matches for her. Lazarus was so much more interesting than them; he was not waiting to enter the family business or go to an eastern college; he had real ambitions, while simultaneously reminding her of the poor characters in Dickens because of his Cornish accent and rough speech; still, there was charm in his speech, and he had treated her as a normal person, not as "Miss Henning"; she was tired of being "Miss Henning." He was different; she hoped that would help him succeed.

The following day two more odd men appeared on the Hennings' doorstep. They were separated by a few decades in age, yet resembled each other enough that if the older man had been younger, or if the younger man older, they might have been brothers. They were father and son. The first gentleman was in his early sixties, while the younger was just past thirty. To consider them "gentlemen" depends on how low one's standards are for the definition. They were not the type of gentlemen Sophia Henning would have invited to a dinner party. They were tall men, thin yet powerful in their figures; their demeanors gave every indication they were accustomed to hard work and manual labor. Further observation of them as male specimens was inhibited by their long fur coats, which appeared to be hand sewn from a variety of animal skins. The older man had a long beard, of salt and pepper coloring, and badly in need of grooming. His son found a mustache to be sufficient facial hair, allowing to be revealed a strong jaw, clever eyes, a thick neck, and a general air of capability. The men wandered around Marquette for a couple hours before they came to the Henning house. Further information about them may be gathered from the reception the Hennings gave them.

"I ain't seen nothing like this, Pa, not since I was in Washington D.C. during the war," said the younger man as they turned into the front yard.

Ridge Street was now a fashionable neighborhood of manicured lawns and imposing houses. The Gothic sandstone mansion rising up before the two men, complete with wood carvings, stained glass windows, and a towering turret impressed them greatly.

"Well, it ain't as grand as that temple in Salt Lake City they're building," replied the father.

"No, I guess not, but just think that she would live in a place like this."

"I wonder what she does here," mused the father. "That fellow we asked said this was the Henning place, so maybe she's their housekeeper. She probably works here to support her family cause that husband George of hers wasn't much good for anything from what I remember. Funny though how that man didn't direct us right to her and George's house."

"Maybe he knew they'd both be working," said the son as he rang the doorbell.

The parlormaid opened the door. She took one glance at the two men and stepped back in fear, thinking they looked just like the highwaymen she had read about in novels.

"Pardon me, ma'am," said the father, "but we're looking for Mrs. Rockford."

There was no response.

"Please, Miss, is Mrs. Rockford here?" asked the younger man.

"There's no one of that name here," replied the parlormaid. She grabbed the knob to shut the door, although she feared these wild men would break the door down if they were determined to abduct her.

"Why, we was told she was at the Henning house," said the older man. "Is that this place?"

"Yes, but there's no Mrs. Rockford here," repeated the maid.

She had only worked six months for the Hennings, and she had not inquired into her employers' personal histories; she had no idea Mrs. Henning had been previously married, and when she had overheard her employers mention Caleb, she assumed he had been the mutual son of her master and mistress.

"Well, this feller we met downtown said she'd be here. Do you know where we could find her then?"

"What is it, Emma?" asked Sophia, coming down the front hall stairs. She was alarmed to see such rough men on her front porch. Deliverymen were to use the back entrance. What if the Whites or the Calls should see them standing there? She was ready to reprimand them when the young man stepped inside and addressed her.

"Ma'am, we're looking for Mrs. Rockford," he said.

"Do you have business with my husband?" asked Sophia, confused to hear the name she had not used for years. Nor would she reveal her identity to strangers.

"Sophia!" shouted the older man, pushing aside the bewildered Emma to step inside.

"Stay back," Sophia exclaimed, retreating toward the staircase. "You have no right to come into my house and use my Christian name. Who are you?"

"Don't you know me, Sophia? It's Darius."

"I don't know anyone of that name," she said in panic.

"Darius. Your brother, Darius Brookfield. You don't know me?"

"Darius?" Sophia repeated, trying to understand. Her brother Darius? But Darius had—no one had heard from him in—"I haven't seen Darius in forty years!"

"That's true," said the stranger. "Last I saw you back in New York, you'd just gotten married and blossomed into womanhood, and now here you are working in a fine mansion in Michigan."

Brother or not, and Sophia was still uncertain this was her brother, she did not want to give the wrong impression about herself.

"This is my home. My husband's home."

"I thought it belonged to a family named Henning."

"I'm Mrs. Henning now," she said.

"Omelia never told me that I don't think," Darius replied.

"Now that I think of it, Pa, I recollect she did say Aunt Sophia had married again, though I'd forgotten her new husband's name."

"Then poor George is dead?" asked Darius.

"Ye-es," said Sophia, peering closely, almost fearing to recognize her long-absent brother in this ruffian.

"My goodness," said Darius, looking about the front hall. "Omelia said you was doing well out here, but not this well."

"When did you see Omelia?"

"Why we just came from New York by train. Oh, this here's my son Esau. Captain Esau Brookfield that is. Named him for Grampa."

"A captain?" Sophia felt some relief at this sign of respectability.

"You're still not sure it's me, are you, Sophia?" said Darius. "I guess if I didn't have this beard it might help, though I'm a might deal older now, but that's why I'm here. I've come to visit. I'm getting old and awful lonesome for family. All I have left in this world now is Esau here. My wife's been dead for years and years, and Omelia told me our parents are gone, but that you and

Cordelia were still alive and out here. I couldn't remember Cordelia's married name so I sought you ought first."

"But Darius. I mean. I—we thought you were dead. Where have you been all these years? Mother and Father—they—." But what was the use of explaining her parents' pain over his disappearance? It could not be helped now.

"Where haven't I been?" her brother laughed about his absenteeism. "I've been clear across the continent of North America, but mostly out West—California, Utah, Texas, Mexico, thereabouts. It's a long, long story."

"Why didn't you write to say you were coming?"

"I never was much with a pen," he replied. "We went to New York to see the family, but Omelia's the only one left there now, her and her brood that is. She wanted to send a letter, but I said we'd come out and surprise you and Cordelia. Tried to talk Omelia into coming too, but she said she's too old for traveling. She's younger than me, but then, age is a matter of spirit, not years."

"Well, I—I don't know what to say," Sophia said. "I'm so stunned to see you. We thought you must be dead since we never got any letters. Father, he—well, he and mother, they—" she tried to explain again but could not. "They—they'd be so happy to know you're still alive."

"Haven't felt more alive a day in my life."

"No, but when you went out to be an Indian scout, and then when we didn't hear from you, we figured, well, that the Indians had gotten you or—or—something. Oh!" Sophia recognized her brother's kind eyes. She felt an urge to fling her arms around him then—but—he looked so grubby—so strange in that animal skin coat—and with that mountain man's beard.

"Well, how long will you stay?" she asked, assessing Esau as moderately clean compared to his father.

"We heard," said Esau, "that the winters here are so fierce we might be snowed in until spring so we figured we'd stay that long if it's acceptable."

"Oh, well. I'm sure we'd love to have you. I'll bet Cordelia has a spare room in her boarding house for you. I don't know what—I guess we should go tell her you're here. I—"

Darius was about to ask why they couldn't stay in Sophia's enormous home, but just then Madeleine appeared on the landing. She had heard a loud man's voice downstairs so curiosity had brought her into the upstairs hall.

"Madeleine," said Sophia, calling her daughter down. "I want to introduce you to someone. This is my brother, your Uncle Darius, and his son, Captain Brookfield."

Sophia hoped the "Captain" would make her relatives appear more respectable to her well bred daughter. A sudden whiff of Darius's awful coat made her feel dizzy. Why hadn't Emma taken their coats? Couldn't she see they were important guests?

"Just call me Esau, Miss. Captain Brookfield's too formal for cousins," the young man replied, taking Madeleine's hand to shake it warmly.

"You're my cousin?" Madeleine repeated, trying to believe it.

"Yes, Miss."

"I didn't know I had any cousins, other than Jacob and Edna."

"I haven't seen my brother in many years," Sophia explained.

"She thought I was dead," Darius laughed. "But I'm here now, and this here's my son so now you've found a new cousin."

"Oh, I'm glad," said Madeleine. "Are you from New York?"

Sophia was struck by the pleasure in Madeleine's voice. How could her own daughter be more pleased than she was? She ran her eyes over Darius again. She had to admit he looked good for his age. Why he must be, what, sixty-one now? But why had he come? Not that she wasn't glad to see him; he was her brother. But why had he come now after all these years, especially after their parents were gone? She found it hard to believe he was alive, and what would the neighbors think to hear her long lost brother had suddenly appeared? Respectable people do not have missing relatives.

"Well, I was born in New York," Darius answered his niece, "but I left there 'bout forty years ago to go out West and make my fortune. Been traveling around ever since, and Esau here, he was born in Wisconsin Territory—before it was a state, that is."

"Really?" said Madeleine, delighted to meet people from faraway places. "And you came all this way just to visit us?"

"Yes, your ma and you and your Aunt Cordelia and her family too."

"We'll have to take you over to see Cordelia right away," Sophia repeated.

"Well, I imagine after all these years, we can wait an hour there, sister. Let's sit down an' have us a drink and hear all about you first. Why, your husband must be a rich man. What's his name again?"

"Gerald Henning."

"And your daughter here. Is she George's or the new husband's girl?"

"I'm a Henning," Madeleine smiled. "Emma, take their coats, and please bring us coffee in the parlor."

"Yes, Miss," the maid replied. She had been standing in the corner, listening to the conversation, all the while her jaw getting closer to the floor as she realized these uncouth mountain men were related to the refined Hennings.

Madeleine led her uncle and cousin into the west parlor with Sophia following in a daze.

"When did George pass on?" asked Darius, sitting down as Sophia winced to see his coarse denim pants touch her silk sofa. She painstakingly answered all his questions, describing her journey to Marquette over twenty years ago, telling him of George and their parents' deaths, of her marriage to Gerald, of how his nephew Caleb, whom he had never known, had drowned. Then she started in on the details of Cordelia's family.

"Jumpin' Jehoshaphat, but this is just too much to take in one sittin'," Darius said, standing up from the sofa. Sophia's eyes scanned for stains where he had sat. "We're gonna have ta stay six months just ta get ta know all these new relations and reminisce about our young days back in ole New York. I do want ta see where my ole folks are buried too, but right now, if my niece'll be so kind, could ya point me ta your outhouse?"

"We have an indoor washroom," Sophia said.

"Indoor! Why, now I've heard all!" Darius laughed.

"I'll show you where it is," said Madeleine, unable not to join in his laughter.

"Madeleine, ring for Emma to show him," said Sophia. She was afraid to be alone with her nephew. The maid came to lead Darius to the restroom while Madeleine quizzed her cousin.

"Esau, how did you become a captain?"

"I was in the army during the war," he replied.

"My cousin Jacob was in the war," said Madeleine. "He's the one who married my half-sister, Agnes."

"Is that right? Well, I imagine Jacob and I'll have plenty to talk about then."

"Yes, he must be about the same age as you," said Madeleine. "I'm a lot younger than my other cousins."

"Was all your military service during the war?" Sophia asked.

"No, ma'am. Actually, I rose up to lieutenant during the Civil War, but then during the Indian Wars out West, they made me a captain."

"You've seen Indians?" asked Madeleine with excitement; she had seen Indians around Marquette, but Indians weren't really interesting unless they were the scalping kind.

"Yes, Miss. I reckon you could say so. I've shot my share of them, though most of them are decent folk. Just fighting for their own land and that. You can't blame them for getting riled up, but I have to protect the settlers out there."

"I daresay," said Sophia, still unsure whether Esau were a desirable nephew. He was brave—that counted for something—but fighting Indians!

Gerald now arrived home from the office. He was astonished to see his wife and daughter in the parlor with a strange man. Madeleine ran to greet him, then pulled him into the room amid explanations. In another minute, Gerald was wringing his new nephew's hand, and then Darius returned from the restroom and also shook hands.

"Well, this is fine," said Gerald. "I was expecting a dull winter, but think of all the marvelous stories Darius and Esau can entertain us with now. Why I never imagined anything like it. I'd almost forgotten Sophia ever had a brother."

"I almost plumb forgot I had sisters," Darius chuckled. "But one day, I says to myself, I wonder what's happenin' back there in New York, I says, and then I decided to go and find out, and next thing I knows, here I am in Michigan."

Gerald roared with clear delight over these new—or rather old—additions to the family. "We'll have some fine times now. I'll send right over for Cordelia and Nathaniel to come for supper tonight, and Jacob and Agnes too. We'll have a real family reunion."

"Gerald, don't you think that's a bit much?" said Sophia. "Darius and Esau must be tired, and the cook isn't prepared for such a party."

"We'll just have supper a little later than usual," said Gerald, surprised by his wife's lack of enthusiasm.

"I appreciate your concern, Sophia, that I might be all tuckered out," said Darius, "but if I came all this way to see the family, I guess supper's as good a time as any."

When Edna first met her cousin and uncle, she could scarcely believe she was related to them. Uncle Darius seemed like a character out of a newspaper story about the Wild West; he only began to seem real after her mother told stories of his boyhood in New York, and then just as Edna started to feel comfortable around him, his bushy beard would frighten her all over again. When Madeleine later told Edna of the maid's original fear of Uncle Darius and Esau, Edna did not find it amusing. She seriously wondered whether had it been her, she would have opened the front door at all to the two men.

Fortunately, Edna had not had to open the boarding house's front door. Darius had insisted he wanted to surprise Cordelia just as he had surprised Sophia. Just then, Madeleine had spied Jacob walking down the street. She ran out to fetch her cousin, hurriedly explaining everything as they came up the walk into the house. Jacob thought Uncle Darius and Esau's sudden appearance a great joke, especially when he saw the outlandish figures they cut in his aunt's prim parlor. He would not have believed they were his relations except no other reason could exist for why Aunt Sophia had let them into her house.

"Go fetch your parents and Agnes and the girls," Gerald told his son-in-law. "Have them all come back for supper."

But before Jacob could reply, Darius said, "He ain't goin' ta fetch my sister 'less I go with 'im."

Then Jacob had a mischievous idea.

"You can come with me, only we won't tell my mother who you are," he said. "We'll say you're a prospective boarder, looking for a room to rent, and then we'll see how long it takes her to recognize you."

"All right," Darius laughed. "But that could take days 'cause I'm good at play actin'."

"Oh, don't be silly," said Sophia. "Seriously, Jacob, do you think your mother will have an extra room for Darius and Esau to stay in?"

"Don't bother asking, Jacob," Gerald said. "They'll stay here with us. We've plenty of room. Sixteen rooms to be exact, plus a couple over the carriage house."

"Jumpin' Jehoshaphat, but it'll be like stayin' in the White House ta sleep here," said Darius, clasping Gerald's hand in a hearty shake. "Thank ya very much. I can see we're gonna get along just as brothers should."

"I hope so; I always wanted a brother," Gerald replied. Sophia had never seen Gerald grin so much in his entire life.

Darius smiled, revealing a mouthful of brown teeth, minus four where empty holes separated them. Sophia shivered. To think this was her brother! Had she asked Darius, however, he would have told her how proud he was still to have his teeth. "It's cause I don't use all that sugar like most white men," he would have said; Sophia had eaten plenty of sugar; she never would have admitted it, but she had worn false teeth these past ten years.

Madeleine showed Esau up to one of the guest rooms while Jacob and Darius set out to hoodwink Cordelia. The Whitmans' boarding house was only a few blocks away, but in that time, Jacob heard enough of his uncle's Western exploits to feel great affection for the rough but kindhearted man, and the joy he knew his mother would soon experience only increased the pleasure of his uncle's company.

Edna did not answer the front door because Jacob freely entered, and standing in the front hall, hollered, "Mother!" while his uncle followed inside. When she heard her brother's voice, Edna popped her head out of the kitchen, and then her eyes nearly popped out of her head. Who was this grimy, furry, hairy mountain man with Jacob?

"Go fetch, Mother. I've brought her a new boarder," Jacob told Edna, while Darius grinned wide enough to expose his missing teeth. He was enjoying the gag immensely.

Edna ran upstairs, half in fright and half angry with Jacob.

"That's my sister, Edna," Jacob told his uncle.

"I knew it. Looks just like your mother did when a girl."

"Oh, Edna's no girl," Jacob laughed, then whispered into his uncle's ear. "She's twenty-five and resolved to die an old maid."

"Jacob? What is it?" Cordelia called as first her feet and then her head became visible on the stairs, followed by the feet and head of Edna.

"Mother, I got a boarder here for you. Mr.—"

"Jones," jumped in Darius.

"Mr. Jones, this is my mother, Mrs. Whitman."

Cordelia glared at her son as if to say, "How dare you bring such a man here?" Cordelia tried to be a good Christian and not judge people by appearances, but she had her limits; she was thankful she could honestly say, "I'm sorry, but all my rooms are full."

"I can sleep on the parlor sofa," Darius replied.

"Oh no, we couldn't have that," Cordelia frowned.

"I wouldn't mind none. Only I ain't got nothin' to pay with, but maybe I could help the young miss there with the cookin'."

"The cooking!" Edna gasped.

"Edna does need a lot of help with her cooking," Jacob said.

"I can cook up a mean possum pie," Darius added.

"I dare say," Cordelia replied, "but I'm afraid we don't have any space."

"Well, maybe I could bunk in with you and the Mister."

"Don't be impertinent," snapped Edna.

"Why not?" continued the pseudo Mr. Jones. "It's not as if I never slept with you before, Cordelia."

"What?" Cordelia exclaimed. "How dare you use my first name? Jacob, tell him to leave. Don't let him talk to your mother like that."

"It's no insult, Mother. He probably has slept with you."

"Jacob, really!" cried Edna, in disbelief that her brother would say such a thing.

Cordelia felt ready to cry that her son would treat her so. Darius, however, saw the tears coming and could pretend no longer.

"Cordelia, don't you know me?"

"I never saw you before in my life, and if you don't leave, I'll send for the policeman."

"You'll be causing a family scandal then."

"What are you talking about?" she demanded in fear he wished to soil her spotless reputation.

"You'll have to explain to the police why you want your brother thrown out."

"My brother? I—"

"Cordelia," he said, "I'm Darius."

She stood still, taking it in. Edna remained confused, but then a gasp broke from Cordelia's throat, and Darius found himself wrapped in her arms.

"It—it can't be true," she sobbed. "We thought you were dead. Why, after all these years—I can't—I can scarcely believe it."

"Come, Mother, let's sit down," said Jacob, separating her from his uncle and leading everyone into the dining room. "We didn't mean to upset you so much, just to surprise you."

"How do you expect me to feel when the dead come walking in my front door?" Cordelia laughed, wiping tears away with her handkerchief.

Darius stumbled to a chair beside his sister and clasped her hand. Speechless, Edna softened toward her reclaimed uncle by passing him her own handkerchief. She did not even mind too much when he used it to blow his nose. Then came more exclamations, followed by questions and answers and joy such as the family had not felt since Jacob returned home from the war.

"I better go fetch Agnes and the girls," said Jacob after fifteen minutes. "I'll see you all at Uncle Gerald and Aunt Sophia's at six o'clock. Are you all right, Mother?"

"Never better," she said, squeezing her brother's hand. Fortunately, it was a big strong hand because she would not leave off squeezing it for a good half hour. "Tell Gerald and Sophia we'll be over as soon as your father gets home, and we'll bring your uncle with us."

✦   ✦   ✦

Within the hour, the entire Brookfield, Whitman, and Henning clan were seated around Gerald and Sophia's long mahogany dining table.

"I still can't believe you're here," Cordelia kept repeating, still squeezing her brother's hand.

"I can scarce believe it myself," he replied. "Seems like just yesterday I left New York, and now here we all are with children older than we were when I went out West forty years ago."

"Where out West did you go?" asked Jacob.

"Oh, all over the place. I went out to Ohio first, then moved on to Wisconsin where I settled for a few years. Then I heard about people goin' out West on the Oregon Trail so I sailed down the Mississippi to St. Louis and then from there, I headed over the frontier as an Indian scout and guide for the settlers."

"The Oregon Trail!" exclaimed Edna. "I've read that book."

"I don't know nothin' 'bout a book, just the actual trip," Darius replied.

"The book's a classic. It's by Francis Parkman," said Edna, ever ready to bore others with her literary information.

"I remember when you left our town," Nathaniel told Darius. "I was eighteen and wanted to go West myself. I always wondered what would have happened if I had."

"You wouldn't have ended up with me," Cordelia replied.

"That's true," said Nathaniel. "I guess I made the right decision not to go."

"Where else have you been, Uncle Darius?" Madeleine asked.

"Oh, just about every place you can imagine. I met my wife when I was in Wisconsin, and that's where Esau here was born. She and I was complete opposites 'cause she didn't like ta move 'round, so once we got ta Oregon, she wanted ta stay put, but I just couldn't stand it and wanted ta keep on wanderin'. Then that first winter she got sick and up and died on me. Hurt like hell, pardon the expression, but it allowed me ta wander like I wanted. And I always was afraid when I was with her that someone would hurt her. I was always worryin' about Injuns getting her or some sickness or somethin'. Havin' ta protect a woman is an awful worry, ya see. Now Esau, he weren't no worry at all. Seems ta have the same wanderin' spirit as me, and tough too. Why, by the time he was ten, I reckon he coulda whooped half them Injuns by himself."

Esau looked embarrassed by the mention of his youthful prowess, but Edna noticed he did not deny it.

"So where did you go next?" asked Jacob.

"Well, Esau's mother passed away just in time for me ta go ta Californee. They'd just struck gold there, and I was aimin' to see for myself if I could find some. Well, I saw lots of fine country, but no gold."

"Is California as beautiful as they say?" asked Edna. "I've read about it in *Two Years Before the Mast.*"

"That must be another book I ain't never heard of, but it's a beautiful place all right. San Francisco Bay and the Gold Coast, where it's warm all winter and they only get rain but no snow. There's nothing I've seen ta match it."

"Did you stay in California then?" Jacob asked.

"No, it's beautiful there, but it didn't cure my roamin' spirit, and Esau here, I thought he was bored as well there—"

"Guess I'm just like my pa," said Esau.

"So we went out ta Texas next ta try our hands at ranchin' for a while. Then I thought I'd like ta see more of the South, so I ended up workin' on a riverboat goin' up and down the Mississippi. But when the war started, I knew I couldn't stay down South. I'd seen plenty of slavery, and it made my stomach sick, so Esau and I, we took a riverboat right back up the Mississippi ta Minnesota, and there I settled down while Esau went inta Wisconsin and signed up with the army."

"What regiment did you join?" Jacob asked his cousin.

"Wisconsin 37th."

"I was in the war too—the Michigan 27th," said Jacob.

"They was at Petersburg, wasn't they?" asked Esau, who received a nod in reply from his cousin. "We was too. That was a horrible campaign."

"Yeah. I got wounded there," said Jacob, "shot in the abdomen, but I've come through okay. Did you get hurt?"

"No, guess I was lucky; most everyone else I knew got killed or wounded there."

"Let's not talk about that horrid war," Sophia said. "It's been ten years now yet you soldiers just won't forget it."

Jacob was annoyed by his aunt's dismissal of the war; she had no idea what he had suffered during it, but he would not argue with her before company.

"You men can reminisce later," Agnes soothed her husband. But Edna wished they would keep talking about the war; she was glad to see Jacob forming a bond with Esau; she knew how much her brother needed a friend since Caleb had died; that Esau was a cousin like Caleb made him seem a good companion for Jacob.

"So what did you do then, Darius?" Cordelia asked.

"Well, after the war, Esau here got a job with the railroads, and then they took me on, ole man that I was by then. Pretty soon the railroads were crossin' the entire land, and I was seein' mighty pretty country wherever I went. Enjoyed it for a few years, but then started ta feel I was gettin' too old for all that travelin', so we settled down in Denver. But you guessed it, even when I was willin' ta rest my roamin' spirit was restless, so after a few months, we took off again and this time got as far as Salt Lake City where we settled last."

"Do you know any Mormons there?" asked Agnes.

"Heaps of 'em, everywhere you step. But they're fine people for the most part; a bit odd in some of their ways, but then we all is. Esau and me, we've got ourselves a ranch there and been doin' good business on it for a couple years now. But then Esau wanted ta roam again, so I suggested we look up my family back in New York. Left the ranch in good hands, we did, never thinkin' we'd be gone so long. Didn't know then we'd be comin' ta Michigan ta find my sisters. I woulda come ta see ya when we was livin' in Minnesota if I'd a known that."

"Well, I'm glad you came at all," said Cordelia.

"Are you going back to Salt Lake City then?" asked Jacob.

"Whatever Esau wants I guess," said Darius.

"I think so," his son replied. "I've had my share of wanderin' now I think. I'm gettin' ready to settle down."

"And get married? A handsome fellow like you should have a wife," said Cordelia, who now that she was used to her nephew, thought he was almost as good looking as her own son.

"Ain't never found the right woman," Esau replied.

"Aren't there any pretty girls in Utah?" asked Madeleine.

"Sure, but most of them are Mormons. I'd rather have a bride of my own persuasion—a good Methodist if possible."

"Darius, you still go to church then and raised your son Methodist?" asked Cordelia with delight.

"We go when there's a church near where we're livin'," Darius replied.

"Mother was always worried about your soul," Sophia said. "She used to worry whether you were dead, and whether you'd died in a state of grace, but now she'd be so proud to know she had nothing to worry about."

"I reckon her and Father would be proud of me," said Darius, wishing he had come sooner to see them. "Can't think of too many things I've done that

I'm ashamed of, and I made my fortune, so the Lord must of been smilin' on me."

"Are you rich then?" asked Sophia.

"Not anything like you and your mister, Sophia, but I'd say me and the boy have done well for ourselves."

Sophia remembered she had always expected Darius would succeed. He had always been her favorite sibling.

After dinner, Jacob and Esau retired to Gerald's smoking room. Gerald did not smoke himself so he declined the invitation—the room had only been built so he could entertain his gentlemen guests. The Brookfield sisters refused to part with their brother's company so the two male cousins talked and smoked privately.

The conversation centered upon their war experiences. During their talk, Jacob came to admire his cousin, and even more, to like him. He felt as if he had known Esau all his life, perhaps because they were cousins with similar ideas and personalities. At one point, Jacob raised his glass of lemonade—for temperance minded Sophia never would have allowed an alcoholic drink in her house and none of her guests would have dared request one—and peering over its rim, he saw only the upper half of his cousin's face, minus the mustache, mouth and chin. As if he had seen a ghost, he started to choke on his lemonade.

"You need a pat on the back?" Esau asked.

"No, it's just—well." Jacob set down his glass and cleared his throat, "did my Aunt Sophia tell you about her son who died?"

"The one that drowned. She mentioned him earlier."

"Yes, Caleb. We were the same age and more like brothers than cousins. There was something familiar about you I couldn't quite place before, but the truth is, without that mustache, you'd be the spitting image of him."

"You don't say? Well, I guess that's not so surprisin' since we'd be cousins too."

"It's surprising to me. For a minute there, I thought I was looking at the dead."

"I wish I could have met him," said Esau, responding to the pain in Jacob's eyes.

Jacob felt an urge to pour out the tale of Caleb's wasted life, but he could not articulate those painful memories; it hurt enough when his aunt spoke of Caleb, and if he did speak—but he would not speak ill of his aunt in her own home, especially not the first day he had met Esau. Instead, he said, "I think you and Caleb would have liked each other. He was my best friend, and you remind me a lot of him."

"Why's that?"

"We used to talk about going off to see the world, but when I joined the army, he stayed here to help the family. When I came back from the war, I had seen enough to want to stay settled in one place; sometimes I wish I had gone wandering with him. He would have loved your stories about all the places you've been."

"Seems like wandering is in this family's blood," said Esau. "But then, I guess us Americans are all wanderers at heart—we got it from our ancestors who crossed the ocean to the New World, and each generation moved a little farther West to explore and settle new lands until now we're clear to the Pacific Ocean."

"That's exactly something Caleb would have said," Jacob replied. "Seems like we've clear gone across the whole continent now. I remember hearing that after the Lewis and Clark expedition, President Jefferson said it would take Americans fifty generations to fill up this new land, but it looks like it'll be done in five."

"You're right," said Esau. "People are fillin' up the West at an amazing rate. It makes you wonder what'll be left for our grandchildren to explore—will they carry on the restless pioneer spirit of us Brookfields, or will they settle down in towns and stay put for generations like they do back in Europe."

"I don't know," said Jacob, "but because of the war, I saw enough of this country to know Marquette's the only place I want to be."

"Since you were at Petersburg, I don't blame you. It was Hell. I prefer quiet little towns myself."

"Cold Harbor was Hell too," said Jacob, puffing on his cigar as if to illustrate the smoke of cannons. Both could still hear the battlefield's roar in their ears.

Unknown to either man, Edna had been standing outside the door for the last couple minutes, listening to their conversation. She was glad they were getting along; she hoped Esau's friendship would heal the wound Caleb had left in Jacob's heart. Esau seemed a fine, stable man, despite his wandering spirit; unlike Caleb, he would never be a burdensome friend.

"Jacob, Esau," said Edna, hovering in the doorway of the room forbidden to women, "Aunt Sophia asked me to fetch you men back for dessert."

"All right," said Jacob.

Edna waited for the men to pass out of the room, then followed behind Esau, marveling, not for the first time, at how tall and strong he looked.

The family reunion was a happy one for everyone except Sophia. She went upstairs that night, feeling tired and vexed. Gerald was in a jovial mood by comparison as he went up two stairs at a time. He was surprised when he found his wife sitting at her vanity, her eyes swollen. She turned her head when he entered, and seeing the glow in his eyes, she said, "Oh, Gerald, not tonight."

For a moment, Gerald stood, unsure of himself, but compassion overcame his wounded pride. He shut the bedroom door, then asked what was wrong.

"Nothing," she replied.

"I thought you'd be happy your brother is here, especially after all these years you thought he was dead."

"I—I am happy," she said. "You wouldn't understand."

"Tell me what's wrong, Sophia."

She looked up at her husband. He was a good man, always genuinely concerned about her; he was not just trying to soothe her quickly so he could then get what he wanted as George would have done.

"I do love you, Gerald," she whispered.

He smiled. "What does that mean?"

She felt flustered and started to let down her hair. He pushed away her hands and undid the hairpins as he had when they were first married. No matter how Sophia irritated him, Gerald had never lost his fascination for her raven black hair; it stirred something in him that even Clara's unsurpassed beauty could not have done. Even now when Sophia was fifty-five, it remained purely black without a touch of grey, more than could be said about his own hair, speckled grey and brown despite his being four years younger than his wife.

"It means," said Sophia, "that you're the only one I've ever been able to depend on, and I appreciate it."

He kissed her cheek, then asked, "What's upset you this evening? Is it having Darius here?"

"Yes," she replied. "Let me put on my nightgown."

"Won't you tell me."

"As soon as I put on my nightgown."

She smiled at his reflection in the vanity mirror, then went into the bathroom to change her clothes. Meanwhile, Gerald quickly turned down the bedding before she would notice the maid had forgotten to do so. She came back a minute later with her hairbrush, and sat down on the bed beside him. He took the brush and stroked her hair while she opened her heart.

"When I was a girl, I idolized Darius," she said. "He was the oldest of us and the only boy, so naturally, I thought he could do anything. My father said Darius had a better head for money making than anyone else in the family. Then when my grandfather lost everything—" She broke off, remembering the pain of those years.

"Yes," Gerald said, "because of his drinking and gambling, right?"

"Yes, Grandfather just about lost his mind then, so he came to live with us, and when I saw how poor we had become because of his actions, I despised him. He had so many debts that he had to sell most of his land and was left with almost nothing. That was about the time Van Buren became president and money became tight. Perhaps you were too young or rich to remember, but those were hard times."

Gerald thought it could not have been much harder than the present. For two years now, business had slowed to a crawl, and he feared it might never recover. More than once he had thought he should return East to help his father consolidate their assets; their eastern offices were losing money, and Gerald felt if he were with his father, they might salvage something by abandoning their interests in Upper Michigan, but Gerald also loved this land he had helped to build up, so he kept putting off the subject of their moving. He tried now to put off worrying and listen to his wife.

"Since Darius was the boy in the family, I expected he would repair our fortunes," Sophia said. "He was young enough to work hard, and I thought him so clever. Instead, he decided there was nothing in New York worth staying for so he headed out West. I begged him to take me with him. I didn't see the rest of my family as amounting to much; my sisters could not make their own fortunes, and my grandfather was practically an imbecile by that point. I loved my parents, but the more money my father made, the more my mother gave to her charities."

"Then why didn't you go West with Darius?"

"He told me the West was no place for a young girl."

Gerald, recalling how Clara had died in a wilderness land, said, "He was probably right."

"Maybe," said Sophia. "Anyway, I made him promise that after he had made his fortune out West, he would come back to take care of us all. I figured it would take a year or two and then he'd be back. We hardly heard from him at all, and by the time he wrote and said he had married in Wisconsin Territory, I knew he wouldn't return. Then I finally gave in to George, who had been asking me to marry him for years. I didn't know what else to do. When I wrote to Darius about my marriage, he never even sent me a letter of congratulations. None of us ever heard from him after that."

"So naturally you thought he was dead?" said Gerald.

"Yes. We wrote him many more letters, and some came back while the rest he either got or they were just lost out West somewhere. I don't know. Anyway, it didn't take me long to realize George was lazy and unambitious, though I shouldn't speak ill of him now that he's gone. Still, it wasn't until I moved to Marquette that I started to work for myself and put behind me the feeling that my brother had betrayed me."

"And now that you're doing well, Darius had to return and bring up all those old hurts," said Gerald, laying down the hairbrush to put his arm around her.

"How could he be so selfish?" Sophia sobbed. "At least when I thought he was dead, I could forgive his faults, but I can't understand how he could just disappear without considering how we would worry. Even if he could be so coarse toward me, how could he do it to Mother and Father?"

Gerald wondered whether Darius had disappeared because he felt Sophia expected too much from him.

"I understand," he told his wife, "but now that he's returned and we know he's alive, maybe you can forgive him. You shouldn't give up the chance of knowing him in the future because of his mistakes in the past."

"I know you're right, but it still hurts," she replied.

"Remember the Bible story of the prodigal son," said Gerald. "When he came home, his brother sinned by not rejoicing that he had returned. You should forgive Darius and be glad he's back."

"I am glad to have him back, Gerald. But I don't feel I need him now that I have you."

She kissed his cheek, and he gave her a little squeeze.

"I mean it, Gerald. I know I'm not the easiest woman to live with, but I do try. I think I'm a better wife to you than I was to George, but that's easy because you're a better husband."

He said nothing, just buried his face in her intoxicating hair.

Sophia lay in Gerald's arms long after he fell asleep. He always tried to comfort her, sacrificing his own needs for hers. She could no longer be angry with Darius when Gerald had taken his place as a good provider and so much more for her. She told herself that from now on, she must try not to be so selfish but to think about Gerald's needs. Madeleine was fifteen and soon she would be married; Sophia realized that before long she and Gerald would be alone in the house; she wanted their last years together to be happy ones.

December 19, 1875
Marquette, Michigan
Dear Karl,

Merry Christmas to you. I hope you have a happy holiday in Calumet although your sister and I will miss you. Be sure to take a couple days off from work to enjoy the holiday season. Since I won't be seeing you at Christmas, I am sending your present with this letter. I know you said it could wait until the next time you came to Marquette, but I didn't want you to go without any Christmas presents. Please don't feel you have to send us anything. Just a letter is enough because we so seldom hear from you since you and Ben have become big wigs in the lumber business, but I understand you must make your own way in this world. I know your father would be very proud of your success and that you have found good companions to help you along in life. Your father and I came to America so our children could have better lives, and now I finally see our dream coming true.

I have something to tell you that might be of interest to you as a logger. I meant to tell you before, but forgot the last time I wrote. Mr. Harlow used a giant log to build an enormous wooden man and put it up in his yard. I don't know how many feet tall it is, but it towers way over everyone's heads. It even has arms, a beard and a hat and has become the marvel of all the town. Since he put it up in his yard, people have been streaming down there to see it. Everyone here thinks it a great joke and calls it Harlow's Wooden Man. Anyway, I thought you might like to know there are other uses for those logs you cut down.

All your old friends here are well. You will be surprised to hear that Mrs. Henning and Mrs. Whitman's brother and his son have recently appeared in Marquette. They were thought to be long dead as the family has not heard from them in something like thirty years, but now they are going to stay and visit throughout the winter. They have been living out West so long they are rather rough characters, but are nice and gentlemanly in their own way from what I could tell when I met them.

We are about to have a visitor of our own here in the spring. Your stepfather's sister is coming to visit all the way from Italy! She doesn't know a word of English, but she will stay for several months. She is much older than your stepfather and practically raised him after their parents died. He has not seen her since he came to the United States. He is hoping she will decide to live here, but since she has her own family in Italy, I doubt she will.

I will close now as I have Christmas packages to wrap. Kathy sends her love and wishes you a Merry Christmas and Happy New Year as does your stepfather. Give holiday wishes to Ben from us. We miss you and will be thinking of you on Christmas day.

Love, Mother

Molly sealed the envelope, while hoping the letter sounded cheerful. Montoni had not thought to send holiday wishes to Karl, but it did not hurt to write that he did. She knew her husband was actually relieved Karl would not spend Christmas with them, but he said nothing about it, and she would not bring up the subject. She tried to keep goodwill among all the family. She did not know, however, if she would manage to be cheerful when her sister-in-law arrived. She dreaded the thought of that woman. Molly did not doubt Montoni's sister would baby her little brother, and that would mean her trying to take over Molly's house and especially her kitchen. She would be horrified by Molly's poor Italian cooking, and that would only rile Montoni. But it would be months before her sister-in-law arrived; she would try to have a good Christmas for Kathy's sake, and hopefully, that would somehow compensate for whatever problems came in the spring with their foreign guest's arrival.

1876

Cordelia believed the New Year would be a happy one. Just since Christmas Day, Edna had asked three times for her mother's opinion on what to wear, something quite unusual for a girl who paid more attention to her books than her wardrobe. Neither had Cordelia failed to notice that on each of these occasions Edna was about to see Esau. Granted the two only met at family parties, but Cordelia was convinced Edna had fallen for her burly mountain man cousin, and as a mother, Cordelia was pleased. After years of worrying about her daughter, Cordelia now thought Edna's lack of interest in men seemed part of a predestined plan to keep her unattached until Esau entered her life. She hoped the cousins would marry, and that would give Darius an incentive to remain in Marquette. Her brother had no reason to return to Utah; he had plenty of money, and he could make himself comfortable here; he had said he was enjoying the winter immensely because it reminded him of his New York childhood, and his presence brought back to Cordelia her youthful memories and spirit; she did not want to lose her brother again, and she wanted a son-in-law. Now she just needed for Esau to state his intentions.

One day in early January, Cordelia and Nathaniel left the boarding house in Edna's care while they went shopping. Because of the holidays, many of their boarders had gone out of town so the house was quiet that morning. Edna had settled down in the parlor to sneak in a half hour of reading before she did the laundry, but Esau soon interrupted her solitude.

She did not hear him knock; she was too lost in one of Tennyson's poems, while curled up in an unladylike position on the sofa. She was unaware of his presence until from the corner of her eye, she saw an imposing figure in the doorframe.

"I'm sorry to disturb you," he said.

"Oh, no, it's all right," she replied, quickly shutting her book and sitting up straight to smooth her dress. She could feel her hair out of place, but she was too self-conscious to draw attention by patting it. "I'm afraid my parents aren't home."

"Oh, well—-" said Esau, awkwardly eyeing the chair across from her.

"Please sit down," said Edna; usually she was annoyed when interrupted during her meditative reading, but she thought the poems dull compared to talking with Esau.

"I'm sorry to disturb you," he repeated.

"It's all right; I was just reading, not anything important."

She had a fleeting, fearful thought that like her father, Esau might think women should not read many books, especially not poetry, but only religious tracts or moral novels such as *Uncle Tom's Cabin*; Edna hated that book after a childhood spent hearing her grandmother revere it.

"Do you like to read?" Esau asked.

She did not know how to answer. Did he ask out of politeness, or did he really want to know? What would he think if she answered "Yes"? Would she get a lecture on how reading would overstrain a woman's brain? But she was not given to lying, so after a moment, she admitted she did like books, then added, "Do you?"

"I'm usually too busy to read, but I like to when I get the chance. I don't have time to read whole books, but I like poetry now and then."

"I love poetry," Edna gushed.

"It sounds pretty," Esau replied, "though I don't always understand it. My father says he don't see much value in books, but then, most of the time he can barely make sense out of 'em. I think there's a lot you can learn in books, and in poetry, well, you don't learn things so much, but it makes you feel good and that seems worth it."

"Yes, poetry lifts the soul and leads the mind to beautiful thoughts," Edna spouted. "Some people read for entertainment, but I read to understand the human character."

Fortunately, her parents were not present to tell her she might learn as much about human character if she took her nose out of her books to observe the world around her. As for Esau, her explanation was far too intellectual for him to make an adequate reply, yet he was greatly impressed to meet such an educated young lady. "Do you write poetry too?" he asked.

Edna was silent. She had never expected such a question. Her parents had never thought to ask, so she had never been forced to confess it.

"Did you hear me, Edna? Maybe I've got a frog in my throat," Esau coughed.

"No, I—well, I write poetry a little bit," she said, "but not very well."

"I'll bet you do better than what I could. I sure do admire anyone who can make up rhymes, 'specially when most of us folks out West can't even talk proper."

"Your English isn't bad," said Edna. "It's much better than your father's."

Should she have said that? He might think she was insulting his family.

"What do you write about?" he asked.

"I don't know. I've only tried a few poems, and like I said, they aren't very good. I—I mostly scribble stories."

"Have you published 'em? Like in the newspaper here?"

"No, I've never shown them to anyone," she said, staring at the floor. "In fact, no one knows I write them. My parents would think I was wasting my time when I should instead be cleaning house or having a family."

"Perhaps you're one of those women who isn't supposed to have a family, but writes instead like some of them lady authors back East."

Edna had considered such a life, but somehow, she no longer wanted to be a spinster. "No," she replied, "sometimes I think I write just because I don't know what else to do."

She knew she sounded pathetic. She wanted to crawl into bed and pull the covers over her head. She was a twenty-five year old spinster living in a fantasy world of books because no man wanted her.

"Perhaps someday you'll write a story for me?" said Esau.

"Oh no, I couldn't."

"Why not? No one need ever read it but me, and I promise to be a kind critic."

"No, I don't think so."

Esau was not used to shy women. All the girls out West were rather forward, and consequently, his father had told him to stay away from them. Now he feared he was being forward in pestering Edna with questions. Was he ruining his chances? Maybe he should just ask before he lost all courage.

"I've come—"

"Would you like—" she said simultaneously. "I'm sorry, please speak first."

"No, go ahead."

"I just wondered if you would like some coffee? My parents will be back soon, so I'm sure they'll want some. I could make some for all of us."

Esau had not come to see his aunt and uncle, but he consented to coffee. He then searched for his courage while Edna was in the kitchen. He hoped her parents would not return home before she came back into the parlor. This courting was worse than going into battle! But he was determined when she returned, he would charge straight ahead and hope not to be shot down.

A few minutes later, the kitchen door opened, and Edna's return was announced by the jingling of the tea tray.

Before she could set down the tray or say one word, Esau jumped to his feet and boldly looked her in the eye. "I wondered whether you'd go to the dance with me Saturday evening."

Edna was so surprised, she set the tea tray on top of the piano before she dropped it. She told herself a girl in a novel would faint at such a proposition, but she did not feel like fainting. Instead, she let out a mousy, "Yes."

Her assenting squeak was the music of the spheres to Esau. He had never dreamt his wandering ways and increasing age could make a woman take interest in him, least of all his sophisticated, intellectual cousin.

"I'll come by for you a little after seven then."

"Yes, that will be fine."

"I'll see you then," he said, searching about for the hat he had placed on the sofa and then stumbling to the door. This giant warrior of a man had been defeated by the green eyes and pale face of a bookwormish girl. Life is all the more marvelous that such can happen.

Edna sat down and relived the moment over and over in her mind until her mother came home and demanded to know why the tea tray was sitting on the piano, and why a full pot of coffee had been allowed to grow cold. Edna ignored her mother's questions and told her news; then Cordelia needed no explanation about the coffee.

The next day, when she knew Esau would not be there, Edna went over to the Henning house, burdened with the terrifying question, "What will I wear to the dance?" She wanted to insure she would have Esau's attention all evening. She knew she would be the oldest single woman at the party, and far from the prettiest, and it would be Esau's first social gathering in Marquette, and he was so tall and handsome all the girls would flock to him. Among so many pretty faces, she feared he would notice Cousin Edna was a plain, frumpy old thing. So sucking in her pride, Edna went to her fashionable cousin for advice; Madeleine would have her own coming out party this winter, and according to Aunt Sophia, she was destined to be the leader of her social circle that season.

Madeleine willingly agreed to help; she had long felt embarrassed to have a dowdy old maid for a cousin, so she eagerly set about remedying the problem. She immediately marched Edna downtown and began a quest through all the shops for the perfect dress to metamorphose Edna into a beauty. Edna was unsure at first that the transformation could happen, but by the time they reached the bottom of Front Street's hill, Madeleine had her cousin almost convinced it was not too late for her to become ravishing.

As they passed a stable yard, Edna quickened her pace to avoid foul smells from interfering with her dream of silks, hoops, and bows. She was rather annoyed when Madeleine stopped to speak with a stable boy.

"Hello, Miss Henning," said a young man, stepping outside. Edna was no beauty, but she congratulated herself on being a rung above this gawkish creature.

"Hello, Lazarus. Please call me Madeleine. How are you?"

"Fine. Thank you, Madeleine," he said, exhilarated that she remembered him.

"How are things in the stable?" she asked despite Edna staring at her with a look that demanded, "Why are you speaking to him?"

"Good," Lazarus replied. "It's a bit cold, but I like the horses."

"I love horses."

Edna cleared her throat.

"This is my cousin, Edna Whitman."

"I'm pleased to meet you," said Lazarus.

"Did you have a nice Christmas?" asked Madeleine.

"Yes," he fibbed. He had spent Christmas alone without anything special to eat, but he did not seek sympathy. "Where are you off to today?"

"We're shopping for dresses," said Madeleine. "You know us women; we can never stop trying to look our best for you men."

"I'm sure, Madeleine," he said with all sincerity, "that you look beautiful no matter what you wear."

Edna thought this an impertinent remark from a stranger.

Madeleine blushed and said, "Thank you."

"Lazarus!" bellowed a man from inside the stable.

"I better be going."

"All right," Madeleine frowned. "I envy you getting to work with the horses."

"Would you like to come in and see them?" Lazarus asked.

Edna could not believe it when Madeleine consented. As the older cousin, she resigned herself to entering the stable as Madeleine's chaperone.

Lazarus was soon demonstrating how he groomed a horse.

"Oh, let me brush him," Madeleine begged. She had never shown interest when she had seen her father's groom brush the horses, but now she felt she had been missing a great form of excitement.

"No, this way," said Lazarus, placing his large bare hand over her gloved one to guide the brush down the horse's flank.

"His coat is so smooth," said Madeleine.

"Yes," said Lazarus, thinking the same of her glove.

"Madeleine, we really must be going," said Edna, resisting the urge to stamp her foot.

"Very well," said Madeleine. "Edna does badly need a dress."

Lazarus looked disappointed, but he tried to smile courteously.

"I'm sure I'll see you again soon," said Madeleine. "Maybe when spring comes you can take me out riding sometime?"

"I'd love to, Miss Henning—I mean Madeleine."

"Well, goodbye."

"Goodbye. It was nice to meet you, Miss Whitman."

Edna abruptly nodded, and the girls made their exit.

"Madeleine, you shouldn't speak to strange men," said Edna as soon as they were out of Lazarus's hearing.

"Oh, he's just a boy, hardly more than my age," said Madeleine. "He made a delivery at the house one day, and while he waited for Father to reply, we just talked. He's had a hard life so I feel I should be kind to him."

"He might interpret your kindness as something more."

"Do you think he's handsome?" Madeleine asked. "I know he's rather tall and ungainly looking, but don't you think his pale eyes give him a distinguished look?"

"I wouldn't know," said Edna. She thought Madeleine's remarks so trite, like something out of one of those cheap romance novels. True heroines like Jane Eyre or Lily Dale would never make such remarks.

"Did you decide what color dress you want?" Madeleine asked to change the subject.

❄   ❄   ❄

The evening of the dance, Madeleine insisted Edna dress at her house so she could assist. Edna knew her mother would prefer to help so she could see her daughter in the first dress ever worn while courting a man, but Madeleine was so used to getting her own way that Edna found it impossible to refuse. Cordelia settled for staying up late to see her daughter's dress when she came home from the party.

Only the youths of Marquette's finest families had been invited to the party. The hosts were the Hennings' new next-door neighbors, the Richardsons. They were snobs, and therefore, Sophia's ideal friends. Mr. Richardson was the son of a wealthy coal magnate in Pittsburgh who had come as attorney for one of the mines, while his wife was a Palmer of the Philadelphia Palmers. "Even their names sound rich," Sophia had said to Gerald, "Richard and Regina Richardson." Sophia would have thought her new neighbors flawlessly fastidious except that they built a house to rival her own in taste and expense, which she declared gauche. Still, they were the right kind of people for her daughter to associate with, so she did not complain when they acknowledged the Hennings as part of their desired social circle.

Gerald and Sophia waited downstairs to accompany Esau and the girls to the party. Darius sat with them, although he had refused the invitation the Richardsons had deemed necessary to send him. He felt too old for such gatherings, but he was pleased Esau was going with such a pretty girl. Sophia was a bit nervous her nephew would embarrass her, but when he came downstairs in a suit Jacob had loaned him, she thought him quite handsome, even with the enormous mustache she abhorred.

Then, as Madeleine hovered over the upstairs railing to peer at her creation, Edna descended the stairs in a light green gown that set off her eyes and dark brown hair. Esau was speechless at the laced and ribboned china doll before him, but her nervous smile encouraged him to step forward and take her hand. He led her to one of the sofas where they sat together, chatting in utter awkward contentment while Madeleine made her entrance.

"She grows more beautiful every day," said Gerald as his daughter descended the stairs.

"She's a woman now," Sophia replied. "She'll be sixteen soon."

Blue was Madeleine's color. Beneath her black hair shown out two striking blue eyes to complement her complexion. Her gown was deep blue, conjuring up images of a moonlit lake on a clear summer night.

"I never seen anyone so beautiful but once," Darius said, as Madeleine sat down beside the uncle who had quickly become a favorite of hers.

"Who dared to be as beautiful as I?" Madeleine teased.

"It was when I spent a winter in Nebraska, not far from the North Platte River where there was a small settlement," Darius said. "There was this young Indian maiden—couldn't have been much older than you, niece—she was the beauty of the area, like no woman I ever saw before."

"I hope, Darius," said Sophia, "that you are not comparing my daughter to an Indian squaw."

"Listen now, it's not a bad comparison by any means," Darius replied. "Even the white men longed for her favor. Poor girl ended up sadly though. One of the white soldiers finally got her to marry 'im, and he took her inta his home. Her people were against it, but she claimed she loved 'im, and when she had his child, people started ta accept the relationship. That all happened before I arrived there, but at the start a that winter, the major died and the woman went back to her people takin' the child with 'er. The commandin' officer sent a letter ta the major's parents informin' them of 'is death, and then in the spring, 'is parents showed up demandin' ta see their grandkid. The major had been their only child, and when they saw that grandkid, they swore he was the spittin' image of their son."

"But wasn't he awful dark skinned?" asked Sophia.

"Not too noticeably," said Darius. They decided they'd take the child back East with 'em and claim their son had been married to a white woman that died."

"Oh," said Edna, "how sad and unfair."

"It was for the Indian woman. And what could she do? The army hauled her inta the fort, then took that child away, tore it right outta her arms and sent it off on the next train with the grandparents before the Indians could stop 'em."

"What could they have done anyway?" asked Esau. "Most of the Indians are completely helpless and exploited by the U.S. government."

"The poor mother," said Gerald.

"She jus' couldn't bear it," Darius said. "She didn't know where the grand-parents went and she had no way ta follow 'em if she did know. A couple a the soldiers felt sorry for her, so they let her spend the night in her husband's old quarters. Next mornin', they found her hangin' from the rafters."

"Oh no!" cried Madeleine.

"I'm afraid so," said Darius. "I've seen lots of cruel things, even an Indian massacre, but I think that beautiful woman hangin' herself was the worst."

"Still," said Sophia, "that child will be better off with its grandparents, and think of their courage in taking on the burden of raising up a half-breed as if it were white. It just shows you that white people shouldn't marry into other races."

"It's no different than *Romeo and Juliet*," said Darius.

"Oh, have you read Shakespeare?" Edna asked her uncle.

"No, but I seen the play in Denver one time."

"How can you compare that story to Shakespeare?" Sophia asked.

"Romeo and Juliet's parents didn't approve of their marriage either," Edna replied, "so it ended in tragedy."

"Hmmph," Sophia sniffed, "as if its being like Shakespeare matters. I've heard his plays are full of indelicate innuendoes. I won't have such writings in my house."

"Beauty often results in tragedy—that's been my experience," said Darius.

"It was a beautiful story, Uncle," said Madeleine. "It's so true, so full of emotion. I think I would have acted the same way if I were that Indian woman."

"Madeleine!" Sophia frowned. "As if my daughter would ever act like an Indian."

"We better be going now," said Gerald, standing up and leading the party out the door.

The Richardsons' party was the typical social melee that composed Sophia's raison d'etre, the type of party Gerald tolerated for his wife's sake. Esau and Edna scarcely knew they were at a party—they spent the evening talking only to each other; once they found their tongues, they had no absence of topics to discuss. As for Madeleine, she later told her mother she had had a merry time, meaning she had danced with half a dozen eligible young bachelors, all of them relatively handsome, all of them well bred, all of them from well-to-do families, and one or two of them even prospective suitors in Sophia's eyes. But Madeleine was bored by them all. Each young man talked of nothing but going East to Harvard, of being on the college rowing team, of living in New York or Boston where he could meet the right people. The talk was the same tedious chatter she had heard everyday of her life.

Edna went home to fill her mother's ear with the evening's enchantments. Madeleine went home, wearily climbed the stairs, then lay with moonbeams streaming across her bed until she finally got up and looked out at the harbor and wondered if anything interesting would ever happen to her. The only memorable event in recent months had been her meeting Lazarus—he was so different from anyone else she knew. From her window, she tried to glimpse the stable where he worked, but even the moonlight did not make it visible.

She remembered when grooming that horse, how his large hands had covered hers. She told herself she had felt shivers then; she had felt nothing when any of the boys at the party had touched her. Those boys were merely polite and interested in themselves more than in her. Lazarus had wanted to please her by showing her the horses.

She was being silly—it was the moonlight, she told herself. But Lazarus was different from those other boys, with his tall figure and his Cornish accent, and his dreams of going out West to do real work on a ranch; she likened him to Uncle Darius or Cousin Esau who were so much more alive than the dull boys she had met tonight. Lazarus had gumption, and dreams beyond making money—he wanted to be his own man and live on his own ranch. He wanted happiness, not just money. Madeleine was so sick of hearing her mother talk about money.

Having grown up in an affluent home, Madeleine knew nothing of hunger or poverty, much less of how deprivation can eat away the soul. Her mother had always been too ashamed to tell her daughter about the difficult years of her own youth when the family was impoverished. Madeleine had no idea the majority of people spent their days just struggling to survive. She only knew she had always gotten whatever she wanted until now, when she wanted romance and adventure, and they were forbidden. She knew her mother would never approve of her desires, so she thought perhaps her mother need never know. Even if she could not be with Lazarus, what could it hurt if she occasionally walked downtown to catch a glimpse of him. If she just happened to cross his path, she could not be rude and ignore him. They were friends after all—nothing more. Nothing could be wrong with their just being friends.

❦   ❦   ❦

Lent arrived. Molly had to make her Easter duty by going to confession. She was ashamed to go, knowing that despite the screen separating them, the priest would recognize her voice. But it was her duty, and she needed God's forgiveness.

"Forgive me, Father, for I have sinned," she confessed to the dark screen. "It has been one month since my last confession."

"Yes, my child," the priest acknowledged her.

"I—I have feelings of hate—toward my husband."

"What causes these feelings, my daughter?"

"He is mean to me. He—he strikes me. Not often, but I hate him for it."

She had never admitted to anyone before that she was abused; she could only tell a priest because he was bound by his holy office not to reveal her confession.

"What have you done that your husband beats you?"

"I don't know," cried Molly.

"Are you disobedient to him?"

"I try not to be."

"Do you love your husband?"

"No."

"Why not?"

"Because he is cruel to me."

"There must be a reason why he is cruel."

"He doesn't like my cooking."

"I don't think you are telling me the whole truth, my child. Why did you marry him? Did you not know he was cruel?"

Molly trembled, wondering how to answer. Was Montoni's anger her fault?

"No, he only showed his violent temper after we married. I—I don't know why I married him."

"Didn't you love him?"

"I hoped to eventually. I—no, I didn't love him then. I needed to support my children. I was a widow, and I thought he would be a good provider."

"Then you married him for his money," the priest said.

"No, well, only for my children's sake."

"The love of money is the root of all evil," said the priest. "If you want him to treat you better, you need to love him better. If you did not love him when you married, then you sinned by lying to him."

"But Father, I want to love him. I just don't know how to when he's so cruel."

"If you love him, he'll see that and be kinder to you. You must go home and serve him, treat him with respect and kindness; as your husband, he deserves no less. Maybe then he will be kind to you, but whether or not he is, you will have done penance for your sins by trying."

"Ye-es, Father," Molly said.

"And I ask that you pray the rosary daily for the next month."

"Yes, Father."

She did not tell him that she already did pray the rosary daily; she prayed constantly to the Blessed Virgin to deliver her from her husband's abuse, but the prayers never seemed to work. Maybe the Virgin could not understand what it was like to have an abusive husband; how could she when St. Joseph had been a perfect spouse, never complaining, always willing to support her? How ironic, Molly thought, that her own Joseph was nothing like his namesake.

She tried to listen as the priest absolved her, but once she left the confessional, she could not help feeling annoyed. She would try to be a better wife, but whatever the priest implied, she would not blame herself for her marital woes.

That evening when Montoni was at the saloon, she took Kathy with her to visit Cordelia. The two women were scarcely more than acquaintances, but Molly felt Cordelia was the only Protestant woman she could talk to. Since Clara's death, she had not had any close female friends, and she knew the women at her church, being Catholic, would only tell her to obey the priest's dictate. Neither could she speak to Gerald, despite all his kindness; he was a man after all.

Molly was relieved to find Cordelia alone in the kitchen. Nathaniel had a cold and had gone to bed early, and Edna was gone to visit the Hennings. Cordelia was surprised to see her guest; they had known each other for years, through visits to Gerald and Sophia's house and when they had belonged to the Ladies' Literary Society, but they had never called on each other.

"I don't have anyone else to talk to," Molly explained when Cordelia commented on her red eyes—she had struggled to hold back her tears as Kathy held her hand on the walk there. Cordelia sat her down in the parlor, then made tea while Molly got control of her emotions. Kathy awkwardly sat in a corner, frightened by her mother's distress.

"I don't think I can do it any longer," Molly said once the tea was poured. "I hate him. He's horrible. I know it's a sin to hate anyone, but I hate him."

Cordelia did not need to ask who "he" was. Long ago, Molly's strained face had told Cordelia that the Montonis' marriage was unhappy.

"I'm so sorry," said Cordelia, "but what can you do, Molly?"

"Wish that he would die. That's about it."

"Molly!" gasped Cordelia, "you shouldn't say such things before your little girl."

"I wish he would die too," Kathy stated.

"But—but," Cordelia sought for words.

"I'm sorry, Cordelia, but I need to talk to someone. I know divorce is frowned on, and the Catholic Church would never permit an annulment even if we could afford it, and I don't know how I would live without a man to support me and Kathy, but how can God want me to live with this man?"

"I don't know, Molly. The ways of the Lord are strange. When we suffer, often it is so He can bring us closer to Him."

"But He ignores my prayers, and when I went to confession, the priest said it was my fault—that I must be doing something to anger Joseph. I know he doesn't like my cooking, but I do try, Cordelia. Sometimes I only have to say one word he doesn't like, and his fist flies into my face."

"Oh Molly—I—I didn't know he was that way." Cordelia shuddered.

"He isn't always but often enough. Especially when he's had too many drinks."

"Drunkenness is an evil," said Cordelia. "I have never understood why this town allows those saloons to stay open."

"If it weren't for the saloon, my children and I would have starved," said Molly.

"Better to starve than take part in the devil's ways." Rebecca Brookfield could be heard in her daughter's voice.

"But I can't stop him from drinking. What can I do?"

"Why do you want to leave now?" Cordelia asked. "You've been married to him for years—is it just getting bad now?"

"No, it's always been bad," said Molly. "It's just, I fear it'll get worse. His sister is coming to visit later this spring, and he thinks she's wonderful. She'll remind him of all the things I do wrong, like not cooking the way he wants, and then he'll mistreat me worse than ever."

"Maybe his sister will help you deal with him?"

"She practically raised him after their parents died," said Molly, "so I imagine he grew up to be just like her."

"She's a witch!" said Kathy.

"Kathy, hush," Molly warned. "I don't know anything about her except that Joseph says she's a saint, and that's enough to terrify me."

"If he respects her as a woman so much, he should be able to respect you."

"He never will. He hates me. He just wants me to be his maid and cook, and I'm sure his sister is a better housekeeper than me, which will make him hate me more. I bet she's a horrid fat Italian woman who reeks of garlic all the time. I think—"

"Molly, I've never seen you so spiteful. You used to be such a cheerful person. He must have really hurt you to make you like this."

"It's hard to be cheerful when everyday you're afraid your husband will knock your brains out."

"I guess I've been lucky," said Cordelia. "Nathaniel upsets me sometimes, such as when he tracks up my clean floors with his boots, or when he never puts things back where they belong, but he would never hit me. I can't imagine how awful it would be to live with a man like that."

"But what do I do, Cordelia? Can I leave him?"

"I don't know," Cordelia replied.

Molly began to cry; her life seemed so hopeless. Cordelia gave her a handkerchief, and Kathy put an arm around her mother's shoulder.

"Just be patient," Cordelia said. "God does not give us problems we cannot handle. Just keep having faith."

Both women knew these were just words of comfort; neither were sure they believed them after so many years of life's difficulties, of constant fear of death, loss of children or spouses, financial insecurity, illness, fire, and fierce winters. Little evidence existed that God had any plan for this world, but somehow they had managed to survive all those hardships. They kept trying to believe; they feared what life would be if they did not have hope.

"I'm sorry," said Molly. "He's not really such an awful husband. It's just that sometimes it becomes so hard to bear."

"I understand," said Cordelia. "We all need a good cry sometimes just to carry on."

"I should go before he gets home. Kathy, put on your coat."

Cordelia stood helplessly while her guests got ready to leave. Then she remembered the bread she had baked and left to cool on the kitchen counter. She ran into the kitchen, quickly wrapped up a loaf, and gave it to Molly.

"Here, I want you to have this," she said.

Molly did not know what to say. She did not want the bread, but she appreciated Cordelia's thoughtfulness.

"It will all work out," Cordelia said, "and you can come talk anytime."

"Thank you," said Molly. She went out into the cold, dark night, but the loaf of bread kept her hands warm until she reached home.

It was a wet day, but it was not rainy. It was one of those splendid spring days of forty degrees that begin the intense melting of heaps of snow. Three-foot snowbanks were suddenly transformed into shoveled out sidewalks, like canyons with little rivers trickling down them. The streets were flooded with puddles filled with chunks of floating ice. Mixed up in this watery mess was mud that once had been sand sprinkled to ward off the winter ice's slipperiness. Now it formed a chocolate colored slush that seeped through shoes and soaked into stockings, creating wet feet and the potential for pneumonia. It was forty degrees. It was a fine day.

That afternoon, Lazarus Carew stepped outside the stable for a little fresh air; the spring wind was blowing, but rather than airing out the pungent animal smells, it blew into the horse stalls, stirring up the straw to enhance the wreaking stench. Deeply inhaling the fresh outdoor air, Lazarus looked up the street to see a vision of beauty. Madeleine Henning was stepping out of a store, gingerly lifting up her skirts, daintily tiptoeing over the sidewalk's slimy slush. Suddenly, a bear of a man was behind her. He was wrapped in an animal fur coat, and he wildly grabbed her arm. She turned her head in surprise and nearly slipped on the ice. Her face filled with alarm.

Heedless of ice that might land him on his back with a broken skull, Lazarus tore up the street, grabbed the furcoated man and tried to throw him to the ground.

"Get your hands off the lady, you dirty old man!" he yelled.

Madeleine's assailant turned around, nearly whirling Lazarus through the air; Lazarus hung onto the man's shoulders, finding himself whipped around in a semicircle. Then the wild man reached back and grabbed Lazarus's wrist, crushing it in a grip so firm Lazarus nearly dropped to his knees as his feet slid on the ice.

"Watch it, boy!" Darius Brookfield warned and pushed Lazarus up against the wall.

"How dare you touch her!" said Lazarus. "You can't assault women on the street. Do you know who she is?"

"Calm down, boy."

"It's okay, Lazarus. He's my uncle. It's okay," Madeleine said.

Lazarus looked at her, then at Darius, trying to understand how such an animal could be uncle to this stunning beauty.

"It's all right, boy," said Darius. "Just don't attack me like that again."

"I'm sorry, sir," Lazarus replied as he was released from Darius's iron grip. He straightened his coat and looked oddly at Madeleine.

"It's sweet of you to come to my rescue," Madeleine smiled. "But I'm perfectly safe with Uncle."

"Darius Brookfield, boy," said the uncle, extending a hairy paw.

"Lazarus Carew," he replied.

Lazarus felt better when he saw his own gigantic hands were not lost in those of the bearish uncle.

"That's a good grip you have there, boy. Proud to meet anyone gallant 'nough to protect my niece."

"Thank you, sir."

"Thank you, Lazarus," said Madeleine. "I'll see you later."

He had been embarrassed by the old man's victory over him, but Madeleine's smile was fair compensation.

"All right," he replied, then stared stupidly as Darius assisted his niece in stepping over a giant mud puddle and climbing into the waiting carriage.

"Niece, am I right in guessin' you like that boy?" asked Darius after the carriage had pulled away from the curb.

"Why, I like him real fine," she teased by slipping into her uncle's jargon.

Darius smiled. "He seems a fine young man. A tad hotheaded maybe, but that's good when it comes ta takin' care a women. And he's not afraid ta get his hands dirty. That says alot for 'im."

Embarrassed, Madeleine said, "Please don't tell, Uncle. Mother and Father wouldn't approve."

"Never mind that," laughed Darius. "No one in this family was ever good at doin' what others thought was best. They told me not ta go out West, but I did, and now look at me. Got one of the biggest ranches out there. Maddie, in this life, ya gotta follow your heart. You do what's right for you, or else you'll grow old and bitter."

"It's not always easy to do what you think is best for yourself," said Madeleine.

"It's easier than livin' with knowin' you didn't do what was best."

Madeleine was too embarrassed to discuss the matter further, but she appreciated her uncle's words, and she remembered them.

❦   ❦   ❦

After her talk with Cordelia, Molly felt better, but she also felt a little guilty. She had spoken words she never should have, and even though Montoni did not know what she had said about him, she decided she would make reparation—or rather penance—by being kind to him.

She actually found it easier than she expected. Now that his sister was coming to visit, Montoni was more cheerful. Molly started to think he was not such a bad man, but that she had been unfair by not trying kindness sooner. At the same time, she feared any ground she might gain by her efforts would be lost when his sister visited.

Finally came the dreaded day of the sister's arrival. Molly took Kathy's hand and with Montoni, they dismally walked down to the harbor, then stood half an hour as the steamship came into view and pulled up at the dock. Molly strained her eyes to see the passengers aboard, anxiously watching each man, woman, and child come down the gangplank.

Molly knew the woman the moment she was visible. She was a great, tall, ugly creature. She had a typical, swarthy, Italian complexion with skin that looked as if it reeked of garlic and tomato sauce—Molly thought she could already smell her, though still a hundred feet away. The woman's Roman nose was turned up, her nostrils pulsing with disdain for all she saw. Her black eyes frowned, as if they would rather be blinded than lower themselves to look at Marquette. Her rigid figure was restricted by a formal black dress that clung tightly about her unnaturally ample bosom. Molly cringed.

Montoni shouted, "Therese!" and walked rapidly to the end of the dock. The horrid woman did not even look pleased. Her chilling eyes would smile for no one, least of all her brother.

Montoni rudely brushed past the ugly creature and continued down the dock. In confusion, Molly watched a little old lady, her cheeks blossoming into a smile, stretch out her arms in anticipation. Montoni reached down to meet the embrace, nearly picking her up; she was so short, barely five feet. Again he shouted her name, and the two burst into a flurry of Italian.

"Why!" thought Molly, "she's rather grandmotherly with that grey hair. She's not at all what I expected. I'm glad."

Molly stepped forward to greet her sister-in-law. Montoni had barely explained Molly was his wife before Therese threw arms around her, then continued to squeeze her hand as they returned up the dock, meanwhile smiling at Kathy and jabbering away in Italian, until Montoni explained that his sister had said Kathy was "adorable."

Molly suggested they hire a carriage since it was several blocks to the house and Therese was rather elderly. Montoni was delighted with this chance to be thoughtful toward his sister, but she vigorously protested; her legs had been too cramped up on the boats and trains and she needed a good walk; with her little stumps of legs, she nearly outwalked the rest of them. All the way home she and Montoni rambled away in Italian. Montoni was laughing and smiling more than Molly had ever seen. Every couple minutes, Therese turned to Molly or Kathy to say something in Italian, using her hands to explain, and Molly would smile good-naturedly, wishing Montoni would translate, but he was too happy to pay attention to his wife; Molly felt she liked Therese, but the sister's presence would not change how her husband treated her. How would she endure several months of this visit? Montoni had insisted Therese stay until mid-July, and it was only May now—how would she endure months of this nonsensical Italian tongue being bleated into her ears, and worse, what would she do when Montoni went to the saloon, leaving her alone with a woman who could not speak English?

It was late afternoon when they reached home. Molly got Therese a glass of water, showed her into the parlor, then excused herself to make supper. Montoni kept his sister occupied by conversing in Italian while Kathy shyly retreated to the kitchen with her mother. Now was the moment Molly most dreaded. She had to cook for this woman. Her hands shook so much that without Kathy's assistance, she might have burnt everything, but eventually supper was ready and only ten minutes late. She waited for Montoni to complain about her tardiness, but he was in such a jovial mood, he led his sister to the table, pulled out her chair for her, then sat down and smiled at his wife. Molly was so surprised she lowered her head in embarrassment.

Then she set the food on the table—she had made salads with salami chopped up in them, and she had made vermicelli, the only Italian dish Montoni had not yet tossed at the dining room wall. Tonight she was too nervous to try anything more fancy; she could not serve vermicelli at every meal, but she hoped she would be safe for tonight. Therese smiled as Molly scooped the noodles onto her plate, and she even pointed at the chinaware and managed to remember the English word "pretty." Then Montoni grabbed the vermicelli bowl and heaped his plate, barely leaving one serving to be shared between his wife and stepdaughter. Neither cared; they were thankful just to see him chew down the first bite of vermicelli without complaint.

Therese was bubbling with laughter. Montoni explained when she recalled a prank he played as a boy. "She says I was quite the brat," he laughed. "She remembers the time I held my little brother down and pissed on him."

He roared with laughter while Molly tried not to show her disgust. She was not at all surprised by the anecdote itself, but she thought her sister-in-law would have better sense than to mention such an incident at mealtime. Therese laughed and started to tell another story; Molly listened, thinking how beautiful Italian sounded, even when her husband spoke it.

Then Montoni's tone changed. He looked down at the vermicelli he had been shoveling into his mouth, and wrapping it around his fork, he demonstrably shook it in the air. Molly did not understand his Italian words, but she knew the crisis had come. He was complaining to Therese about his wife's cooking. Wincing, Molly steeled herself for when the two turned against her.

Montoni ranted for a couple minutes. Then Therese muttered a couple monosyllabic replies.

Molly saw Kathy start to tear up in fear.

"This is uneatable!" Montoni exploded in English. "You should apologize to my sister for giving her dog food her first night here."

"I'm sorry, Joseph. I tried my best. You know I can't get the same quality of noodles and spices they have in Italy."

"You could make your own noodles if you weren't so damn lazy!"

He jumped up from the table. The sudden action coincided with his letting out a terrific fart; the scene would have been comical if he were not so enraged. He picked up his plate and flung it upside down on the table; vermicelli dripped down the tablecloth onto the floor.

"Dog food! That's all this crap is! Dog food!"

He walked over to his sister, grabbed her plate and flung it upside down. "Don't eat this crap!" Then in Italian he repeated his words.

Therese sat quietly, listening to him rant.

He turned and stomped out of the house to go smoke on the porch.

Usually, Molly followed him outside with tearful apologies; she had learned that if she did not instantly beg forgiveness, he would return inside to give her a walloping. Her Irish pride never would have consented to such lowering of herself when she was married to Fritz, but fear had long ago conquered her pride. If she waited to apologize, his rage would boil until it reached a near volcanic eruption.

But tonight when Molly would go to her husband, Therese grasped her wrist. "No, no," said the little Italian woman.

"No, I have to. He'll hit me if I don't," Molly said, though she knew Therese could not understand her.

Therese did not understand English, but she understood the terror in her sister-in-law's eyes. The little woman got up and wrapped her arms around Molly. Molly trembled but did not pull away. Kathy looked down at her plate, afraid that any second Montoni would return. Then Therese pushed Molly back down into her chair, handed her a fork, and said, "Eat." Therese flipped her own plate over, scooped the vermicelli back onto it, and ate. After a few seconds, Kathy also started to eat, trying to pretend the horror had not happened. Molly began to wonder whether her husband would refrain from coming inside to strike her with his sister present.

Therese finished her meal, then pushed back her chair with a grating sound that made Molly jump. She watched with astonishment as Therese picked up Montoni's plate, scooped up the vermicelli from the floor and table, and carried it into the kitchen. Molly hesitated, then followed. She watched Therese scrape the food into the garbage. Then Therese fetched the other dishes from the table. Each one she scraped into the garbage. Montoni's vermicelli, his salad, his salami, and his bread, all went into the wastebasket. When finished, Therese turned to Molly and said, "He no eat; he no eat."

Molly understood, but she was still frightened.

"He'll be so upset," she pled, although it was too late now to retrieve the food.

Therese set the plates in the sink, then squeezed Molly's hand. "Mia show you."

The little woman went out on the porch to talk to her brother. Molly waited fearfully, but she heard no yelling except a few high pitched shouts from Therese, and muffled answers from Montoni. Half an hour later, her husband stomped down the porch steps to leave for the saloon. Therese returned inside and went upstairs to the guest room. She quickly returned and settled down in the parlor with her needlework. Kathy felt safe enough now to leave the dinner table. She found a book and nestled into a corner of the sofa.

Molly was at a loss for words. When she finished the dishes, she joined the others and tried to knit, but she kept making mistakes. She was relieved when bedtime arrived.

In the morning, she realized Montoni had not come to their bed. She hurriedly dressed, then went into the kitchen to make breakfast. Glancing at the clock, she saw she had overslept an hour. She had never failed to wake up in time to make her husband's breakfast. But this morning, Montoni was nowhere to be seen, and Kathy was eating pancakes at the table. Therese hovered over the stove, cooking up sausages while wearing Molly's apron. When she saw Molly, she wiped her hands on the apron, then ushered her sister-in-law to a chair, poured her a strong cup of coffee, chatted away in Italian and broken English, and placed a stack of pancakes before her.

"Eat. Eat," Therese ordered.

Molly obeyed until she could eat no more. Therese sat down to her own breakfast, but she only spared herself a couple minutes before she was up again to wash the dishes. When Molly finished eating, Therese declared, "Cooka vermicelli. Mia show you."

Molly had dreaded having her kitchen taken over by her sister-in-law, but now she saw Therese understood her dilemma and wanted to be a true sister; they were going to pull together to make their lives bearable in this male-dominated house. Molly learned that day how a woman can conquer a man by learning to the exact second how long to boil noodles, what is the exact measurement of spices for various sauces, how to knead bread properly, and how to make her own pasta. They spent the morning grocery shopping without thought to cost. They spent the afternoon cooking numerous dishes to satiate even Montoni's enormous appetite. Kathy assisted by writing down the recipes while Therese demonstrated them to Molly. The three women brought harmony to the Montoni household.

Molly had long felt that since she had come to Marquette, she had struggled through life on her own. She had loved both her husbands—today she could even be that charitable toward Montoni—and she loved her children—but none of them brought the joy of having another woman to help her. Clara had almost been Molly's sister, but then she had died before Molly had most needed her. Now here was Therese, scarcely knowing a word of English, but able to translate the language of food into love. The visit Molly had dreaded was suddenly a holiday from fear because she had a friend to share her burden; already she thought six months too short for Therese to stay.

July 4, 1876. The United States of America's one hundredth anniversary of independence.

Early that morning, Madeleine went for a walk with Lazarus. She had seen him downtown a couple days before, and he had asked to take her on a picnic or to the fireworks. Madeleine's day was already filled with a family picnic at noon and an afternoon boating excursion with several friends. She did not know if she would be back in time for the fireworks, and if she were, she knew she could not be alone with him at such a late hour, not even in a crowd. She did not want to disappoint him, however, so she compromised by suggesting they go for a walk that morning.

Lazarus was willing to accept what he could get. "It's not a big deal about the picnic or fireworks," he had said. "It's just you're the only one who's like a friend to me in this town, and I want to tell you something kind of important."

"Laz! Get in here right now!" his boss had shouted, ending their conversation.

"Meet me at the bottom of Ridge Street about seven in the morning," Madeleine said as her friend—he had just called her friend and she was pleased—disappeared into the stable. Lazarus did not have time to ask why such an early hour, but he would not argue.

Madeleine had chosen seven o'clock because her mother would not come down to breakfast until eight-thirty, which should give them a full hour and then some for their walk. They were only friends, but she knew her mother would still not approve.

As she had walked home, Madeleine had wondered what Lazarus wanted to tell her that was so important. He had called her friend, but she hoped he wanted to be more than a friend. Every time she heard his rich Cornish accent, it was like poetry in her ears. And he was so tall, towering above every other boy. She knew plenty of young men who were better looking, perhaps even smarter, but she had her heart set on Lazarus. To her, he was the kindest, finest looking man she had ever seen; her heart throbbed heavily when she thought of him, which was every moment possible.

Madeleine built up so much nervous anticipation for their secret morning assignation, that when Independence Day arrived, she had set herself up for disappointment. She was shaking with anxiety as she dressed quietly that morning. She feared her fidgeting would knock over some knickknack that would wake her parents, but she managed to put on her clothes, to primp a few minutes before her mirror, and then to slip downstairs and out the back door without being seen. All night she had agonized about which dress to wear, until she remembered Lazarus did not have nice clothes; then she settled on a simple pink dress to make her look feminine in the morning sunlight. She did not want him to feel intimidated or below her station if he felt the need to ask any important question. She wondered whether he would still be taller than her if he went down on one knee. What a prodigiously outstanding young man he was.

She found him at the bottom of the hill, walking along the lakeshore. She went to his side without a word. He looked troubled—she imagined he was nervous about his intended declaration. To soothe him, she slipped her hand into his; he seemed surprised, but he did not pull away when she gently led him north along the beach.

"Lazarus, you're shaking," she said to distract him from noticing her own tremors.

"I'm sorry," he said.

"It's okay."

She waited for the expected moment—after all, he was holding her hand. But he remained silent.

"You said you had something important to tell me?" she said.

"Yes, I—I don't know that it'll matter much to you. I hardly even know you, Madeleine, but well—" He stopped to take a deep breath. "You're the only one in this town who's taken time to get to know me—to see me for what I am—something more than just a stable boy. My boss, he just yells at me, and the people who come to the stables, they treat me no better than the horses. I hate it here."

"You must," she replied, less sympathetic than exhilarated that he was sharing his pain with her.

"I've decided," he stammered. "I've decided—"

"Yes, Lazarus," she said, standing still and looking in his face.

"Well, like I said, I don't know that it matters to you, but I've decided—well, I don't like it here, so I've decided it's best I go out West to be with my uncle."

Madeleine's face dropped; she had not expected this.

Lazarus saw her disappointment. He was pleased to think she would miss him.

"I'm sorry," he said. "It's just that—well, my uncle's my only family, and no one here cares for me."

"I do," she replied.

"Well, no one but you. My uncle wants me to come there, and I've saved up enough money to get me to Montana Territory now."

"Montana," she muttered. She knew his uncle lived there, but somehow it had never sunk into her that Lazarus's plans would mean he would move away. Now his life would begin; he would have wonderful adventures, become an even more fascinating man like Uncle Darius had become by going out West.

"Yeah, Montana. I think I'll like it. My uncle can get me a job in the mines there. I don't much like mining, but it'll be a start until I can save up money to buy a ranch."

"I'm going to miss you," she said. "I—"

"I appreciate that, Madeleine, but I'm not the right sort of friend for you anyway. Someday you'll own a grand house like your parents, and you'll know lots of fine folks, and have a rich husband, and then you'd be ashamed to have a friend like me even if I do become a cattle baron. It's best this way for both of us."

"I'd never be ashamed of you," said Madeleine. "I'm not like that."

"I know, but it's easier for me to go if I tell myself so. Otherwise I'd think about how much I'll miss you."

"Then don't go."

Lazarus was silent. He had made up his mind; he had spent many hours trying to persuade himself that Madeleine was sufficient reason for him not to leave Marquette; he would have stayed for her, but by the same token, for her sake, he had to go; he could never be part of her world. He knew she understood that.

"I'll miss you," she repeated.

They held hands, scarcely knowing they did so, as they walked silently back to town. When they reached the foot of Ridge Street's hill, Lazarus asked, "Can I walk you all the way home?"

"Yes," she said. It was not yet eight o'clock, and she was so disappointed that she did not care if anyone did see her. She had said she was not ashamed to be his friend, and she would not be.

"This'll probably be the last time I see you," he said.

"Why, you're not going already?"

"I'm leaving tomorrow. I quit at the stable yesterday, and I'll buy a train ticket first thing tomorrow morning."

This news hit her so hard she was silent until they reached her house. Then all she could manage to say was, "Goodbye, Lazarus. Good luck."

He squeezed her hand. Then she walked up the path to the house while he turned back down the street.

The second Madeleine entered the front hall, she was accosted by her mother.

"What were you doing holding hands with that boy, and at this hour of the morning!" Sophia demanded. "Who is he?"

"He's not a boy, Mother. He's eighteen," said Madeleine, although she felt too tired and disappointed to argue.

"That's even worse. The older the boy, the more experienced, and the more apt to take advantage of a young girl. Who are his parents? Your father will have a talk with them."

"His parents are dead."

"What does he do for a living?"

"He works at the stable on Front Street."

"A stable boy!" Sophia cried. "I can't believe this. Did he try to hurt you?"

"No, Mother, we're just friends. He came here one day to give Father a message, and I made him coffee and we talked while he waited for Father's reply. We're just friends is all."

"Why have you kept this from me?"

"There wasn't anything to keep from you. I don't know him that well."

"You must have been keeping it from me. Why else would you be out with a strange boy at this hour of the morning?"

"Mother, we just went for a walk. That's all."

"Do you know what those kinds of boys want? I'm not just talking about your father's money either."

"He just wants a friend to talk to. He doesn't know many people here."

"He's not going to know you anymore. Did he try anything? Did he touch you?"

"No, Mother," Madeleine repeated. "No. Don't say such awful things."

"You don't know what lower class boys are like. I forbid you to see him again."

Madeleine could have told her mother she would not see him again because he was moving away. But she was used to getting her own way, and when her mother yelled at her, she became obstinate.

"I'm sixteen now, and I can see whomever I want."

"Don't you sass me, young lady. If you say one more word, I'll lock you up in your room rather than let you go to the picnic or out with your friends. Wait until I tell your father about this."

Madeleine silently went into the dining room for breakfast. She was a spoiled girl, but she did not like to be disrespectful toward her parents; she especially did not want to hurt her father by being so. Yet she was stunned by her mother's anger. She remembered how Caleb had constantly felt their mother's tongue. She had been too young to understand then, but she knew how unhappy her brother had always been, and how her mother had always seemed angry in those years. Once when she had asked why Caleb had not gone to the war, her mother had snapped, "Do you think I would let my son go get shot?" Madeleine had long suspected her mother had dictated Caleb's life. She was not going to let her mother control hers. Lazarus was leaving, but since her mother refused to listen to her, she would not tell her the next time she met a boy. Her mother had no right to know anything if she would not trust her.

Jacob was irritable that morning. His war wound had troubled him all night so that he had barely slept; he was a gentle man, but when he ached, he tended to be sharp with his family.

"I suppose Aunt Sophia will bring that same disgusting cake she always has the cook make just because it's a French recipe," he grumbled to his wife that morning. "Funny she thinks French recipes are so "tres chic" as she says, yet she always belittled Suzanne for being French."

"Now Jacob, just be polite and eat the cake. It won't hurt you," Agnes replied.

"I sure don't understand what's wrong with her," Jacob continued. "My mother and Uncle Darius came from the same family and they don't put on airs. I'm sure my grandparents didn't raise her to be that way."

Agnes could not help a mischievous smile. "Just be thankful my father talked her into a picnic by the lake rather than at the cemetery."

"Come on, Mama!" Mary said, tearing into the kitchen. "We're gonna be late!"

She had been up since the crack of dawn, exasperating her parents with a six-year old's excitement; eight times that morning she had demanded noise-makers and explosives, which were denied, and she terrified her little sister with tales of how fireworks might land on them and blow them all to smithereens.

"Mary, if you don't stop running around the kitchen, there'll be no picnic for you!" said Jacob. "Go find your sister and tell her we're ready to go."

"Yes, Papa," Mary shouted, then bolted upstairs in a patriotic manner. "Oh say can you see! Oh say can you see! Over the land of the brave and the home of the free-ee! Sylvia, where are you? Can you see? Oh say can you see? Sylvia, can you see? Where are you? I can't see you? Oh say can you see?"

"That girl makes me wish the U.S. had stayed part of England," Jacob moaned.

"Don't say that, Jacob. You know we wouldn't trade our freedom for anything."

"What do you want me to carry?" he changed the subject.

"Just this," said Agnes, handing him a picnic basket. The girls ran downstairs, then rushed out the door, followed by their parents. They had barely reached the sidewalk when Sylvia demanded, "Daddy, carry me on your shoulders!"

"Not today, Sylvia."

"It's too far to walk."

"I'm afraid you'll have to."

"Why?"

"Daddy isn't feeling well," Agnes said.

"You don't look sick," said Mary.

"It's not that kind of sick," said Jacob. "My war wound is hurting."

"Can I see the wound?" Mary asked.

"No."

"Why not?"

"Because I said," Jacob replied. "Why don't you and Sylvia try being quiet until we reach your grandparents' house?"

"That game's no fun," Mary pouted, but when her parents ignored her, she glumly marched along, deciding this was the worst Fourth of July ever.

When they reached the boarding house, they found the men in the parlor. "We're waiting for the women," Jacob's father said. "You'd think that when it took Edna this many years to get a man interested in her, she wouldn't keep Esau waiting, but there's no understanding women."

Esau smiled without comment. He did not mind waiting for Edna. He had waited all his life for a woman like her.

"Cousin Esau, give me a piggy back ride!" Mary screamed.

"Me too!" yelled Sylvia.

"You don't have to Esau," said Jacob. "I refused to give them rides so now they're going to pester you."

"It's all right, but we'll have to go outside," said Esau.

"Thank you," Agnes whispered to him as he led the girls out the door. She was always grateful for a free moment from her children's boundless energy.

"How are you, Father?" Jacob asked, sitting down.

"Can't complain today. This is my favorite holiday you know."

"Yes," smiled Agnes, perching on the sofa. "You're just like my stepmother—you grandchildren of the Revolution. You all act as if your own individual soldier grandfather single-handedly won this country's independence."

Nathaniel chuckled, "Well, can you blame me when my grandfather raised me on stories of his war days?"

"No," said Agnes. "We should be proud. My father has told me that my mother's Grandfather Lyte fought at the Battle of Bunker Hill."

"Ouch," Jacob moaned as he readjusted his seat.

"Does it hurt much today, son?" Nathaniel asked.

"Something fierce," Jacob winced while crossing his legs.

"You should go to the doctor tomorrow," said Agnes.

"The doctor can't do much for me."

"It can't hurt for you to go," she replied. "Tell him, Nathaniel."

"We do hate to see you suffering," said his father.

"I suffer more from my wife telling me what to do," Jacob smirked.

"You can't help that," Nathaniel replied. "It's best just to do what she says. Otherwise, you never know what she might slip into your food for revenge."

"Nathaniel!" Agnes said.

Her father-in-law grinned while Jacob insisted, "The pain will go away in a day or two."

Cordelia had heard Nathaniel's last comment as she stepped into the room. "My husband likes to talk that way," she said, "but he knows he'd be lost without me."

"That I would," said Nathaniel. "Well, are we ready to go?"

"Just another moment. Edna's coming down."

"Do you think maybe today he'll—" Nathaniel asked.

"I hope so, but hush," said Cordelia.

Edna joined the family, but her eyes searched for Esau. She felt flustered until she was outside and he came to speak to her. Inflicted with Sylvia riding on Esau's shoulders, the couple led the party down to the lakeside picnic area.

Sophia greeted everyone who arrived. Even she found pleasure this holiday in bragging about her grandfather's heroic deeds as a boy of sixteen who had fought against the British. On Independence Day, she could even forgive her Grandfather Brookfield for drinking and gambling; his patriotic actions had instilled her with aristocratic pride. Sophia would never believe all men were created equal; on this day especially, she looked down on immigrants like the Montonis, who enjoyed American freedom, but whose ancestors had not fought and died for it.

Despite their lack of an illustrious Revolutionary War hero ancestry, Molly's family had been invited to the Hennings' picnic. Gerald had met Therese Montoni shortly after her arrival, and he had been charmed with her even though she could scarcely speak English. He was determined to show her the best of the American spirit on this most patriotic holiday. Montoni himself tended to avoid Gerald; he was not adverse to social climbing, but Gerald was too much the pillar of honesty for him to feel comfortable around; Montoni was not above a shady deal to advance his interests, and it irritated him that Gerald had prospered while playing by the rules. Montoni had only accepted this invitation to impress his sister with the quality of his acquaintances; Therese need not know the Hennings tolerated him only for his wife's sake.

Gerald was himself rather despondent today. When Sophia had told him about the incident with Madeleine that morning, he had not been troubled; he assumed his daughter was sensible, and he had met Lazarus down at the stable a few times and thought him a polite young man. Rather, his mind had been miles from Marquette ever since last week when word had arrived of his father's death. He had gone East to visit his father a few years ago, and he had intended to go again soon, but the economic slowdown since the Panic of '73 had made it difficult for him to leave his office. Now he had less to worry about since he had inherited his father's wealth, making him owner of a business empire that spread from New England to the Midwest. He did worry, however, about operating this empire from Marquette, even with several trusted advisors back East. Between grieving and trying to fill his father's shoes, Gerald had lately become oblivious to domestic concerns. Today was his first outing since the sad news, and he had to force himself to be jovial.

"My word, Karl," he said, shortly after the Montonis arrived, "I swear you've grown a foot taller and another six inches in the chest since last I saw you."

Karl grinned. He was proud of his size, though never as proud as he was of Ben's size; Ben could lick any man in Upper Michigan if you asked Karl.

"I guess I can't help getting stronger when I'm lifting logs all day," said Karl.

"Where are you boys logging now?" Gerald asked.

"Up around L'Anse," said Ben, "but we were glad to get away for the holiday."

"Boys worka too hard. Should geta wifes," Therese scolded.

"They haven't time," Molly said, "they're too in love with making money. That's the American way."

"They have plenty of time," said Nathaniel. "Both Edna and Esau are unmarried and they're far older."

"Not unmarried for long I hope," Darius whispered to Nathaniel, but not so low that half the party did not hear him.

"Excuse me, I think I'll go for a little walk," said Esau. "Edna, would you join me?"

She assented by standing up.

"Can I go too?" asked Mary.

"No, dear," said Agnes, clutching her daughter's skirt to stop her.

"Why not? Aunt Edna and me go for walks all the time."

"It's 'Aunt Edna and I,' dear, and no, today, you may not go."

"Why not!"

"Don't speak to me in that tone," Agnes replied. "I said you can't. That's sufficient reason."

"Sit down, Mary, and finish your cake," said Jacob. If he had to eat the horrid French cake, then so did naughty little girls.

"I want to go too!" Mary repeated

"Sit down, or I'll give you a spanking," Jacob replied.

Mary sat down but she refused to eat her cake. "It's nasty!" she said. That was enough. Jacob picked her up, war wounds or not, walked her off from the group and gave her a couple gentle slaps on her behind. But since the cake was nasty, he did not slap her hard enough to make her cry.

When Mary returned to the group, she dutifully ate her cake, after first apologizing to Grandma Henning for insulting the French delicacy.

"Poor thing," said Cordelia. "She's not old enough to understand why she can't join them for a walk."

"She's old enough to mind her father," said Jacob.

Meanwhile, Edna and Esau had retreated to a distant clump of trees. Esau stopped there and put his arm around Edna's waist. She had let him hold her hand twice, but never had they touched so intimately. She was afraid someone would see them; she was too naive to realize the entire family already knew her feelings and approved.

"Edna," Esau began, "perhaps this isn't the best moment, but it's been boiling up in me something fierce for months now, and I can't hold it in any longer."

"Esau, is something wrong?" she asked, pretending not to know what boiled within him.

"You know my Pa and me, we're going back West in a couple weeks. My life is out there. You know that. I like Marquette well enough, but it can't never be my home."

"I know that, Esau."

"I know that you—that you're a city woman in your heart. I know it's much to ask, but I'm asking anyway."

Edna said nothing. She hoped he was going to ask better than this; she couldn't say yes to something so vague. She wished this awkward moment were over so they could move on to being happy together.

"I want to ask you," he stumbled for words. "I know it's not right of me to presume, but I want to ask you—"

He removed his hand from around her waist and took her hand.

"I want to ask you whether you'll be my wife."

"Oh, Esau, I—" She started to cry; she could not remember a word of the speech she had rehearsed a hundred times just for this moment.

"You're welcome to think about it. I got a couple weeks before I—"

"Yes, Esau, yes. Of course I will," she said before he could talk her out of it.

"You mean 'yes' you'll marry me?"

"Yes, of course. I love you, Esau."

"I love you too," he said, and the words no longer sounded as odd as he had thought them before. Overcome by emotion, he stepped in front of her so his broad back would block everyone's view. Then his lips gently pressed against hers.

Edna felt surging emotions she had never dreamt could exist. Her fears of future spinsterdom vanished as she first felt herself on the threshold of womanhood.

No words were necessary when they returned to the others. Edna's glowing eyes and Esau's beaming smile explained everything. Cordelia jumped up to hug and kiss her daughter, while every man had to shake Esau's hand in congratulations.

Madeleine sat on the edge of the picnic cloth. She was glad that the party dress she had helped Edna choose had led to such a fortuitous conclusion. But her heart whispered, "Poor, Madeleine, you love a man just as handsome as Esau, just as deserving of love, but you will never have him."

"Madeleine, dear," said Sophia. "It's almost three o'clock. Isn't it time you go meet your friends? You don't want to be late. Tell Roger and Rowena Richardson to give my best to their parents."

"Yes, Mother," replied Madeleine, standing up to leave.

"And don't eat too much. Rowena eats like such a bird that you don't want Roger to compare you to his sister and think you unladylike."

Madeleine knew Roger Richardson was her mother's current favorite for her hand in marriage; the thought sickened her. Roger was not half so handsome as Lazarus; he was short and slightly chunky; he had an annoying laugh, and a ridiculous hair colic that would stand up whenever she danced with him; but none of that mattered when he had a trust fund of a hundred thousand dollars. Lazarus could barely afford a train ticket to Montana Territory.

"Have fun, dear," Gerald said, wishing he could be young and carefree like his daughter.

Madeleine found her friends gathered at the harbor. The pleasure party consisted of herself, Roger and Rowena Richardson, Madeleine's best friend Delia, and Delia's brother, Matthew. They were all within a year of Madeleine's age. The plan was for Matthew and Roger each to take a rowboat while the girls split up between them. They would row to Partridge Island, picnic there, and return by dark.

"You and I can ride together," Delia told Madeleine. The two girls climbed into an empty rowboat and waited for the others to situate themselves.

"I'm taking Madeleine and Delia," Roger said.

"Why?" Rowena asked.

"I only ride with pretty girls," he replied.

His sister ignored the insult and climbed into the other rowboat.

"Roger," asked Matthew, "are you sure you can row that boat with two extra passengers?"

"I row better than you," Roger replied; his scrawny arms suggested otherwise, but the lake was gentle today, and the others were all a little afraid of arguing with the aggressive temper he had developed to compensate for his short physique.

Madeleine and Delia had wanted Matthew to row them. Neither was fond of Roger, least of all Madeleine who was tired of hearing from her mother how wonderful he was.

Matthew pulled his rowboat out of the harbor, and Roger's boat followed. Roger was irritated with his sister today; the reason did not matter—it took little to irritate either of the quarrelsome Richardsons. After pulling his boat beside Matthew's, Roger tried to get back at Rowena by flattering Madeleine, and when his sister ignored him, he resorted to more desperate measures.

"Roger, you're splashing me!" cried Rowena, as spray hit her from her brother's oar.

"Am not."

"You are so," said Rowena, "and I know you're doing it on purpose."

"Knock it off, Roger," said Matthew. "You're getting us all soaked."

"What do you expect when we're out on the lake?" Roger asked. "Of course you're going to get wet. Don't be such a crybaby."

"Gentlemen don't splash ladies," Rowena said.

"What do you know about it? You don't have any gentleman callers. Only fellow who's ever taken an interest in you is the milk boy."

"That's not true!" Rowena cried.

"If it ain't, you wish it was. I've seen you staring out the window at him."

"Roger," Delia said, "you could at least try to be a gentleman."

Roger scowled, "You don't know anything more about gentlemen than Rowena. Your father's just a store clerk."

"He is not!" Delia replied. "We own that store."

"Well, he was just a store clerk before he came to Marquette. My father said so."

Matthew warned, "You'll lay off my father if you know what's good for you."

"It doesn't matter what a person does for a living," said Madeleine. "That's not what makes a gentleman."

"It doesn't?" laughed Roger. "Then I guess the milk boy will do for Rowena."

"That's not what I mean," Madeleine said.

"What do you mean?" Roger asked.

"I mean, a gentleman is defined by how he treats other people. He's polite to everyone, rich or poor, and even if others are rude to him, he's still pleasant and kind. He's concerned about other people's feelings before his own."

"Ha! That's good," Roger laughed. "You can speak your false sentiments, but I know you like what your money can buy. You won't marry any poor gentleman. You'd even marry a rich man you hated if he would buy you jewelry and pretty dresses. I wouldn't be surprised if I led you to the altar myself some day. You'd be just the girl to ornament my dinner parties."

"You are impertinent!" said Delia.

"We'll wait and see," Roger said.

"Whomever I marry," said Madeleine, "I can assure you his name won't be Roger Richardson!"

For all his ability to poke fun at others, Roger sulked if anyone laughed at him, and Madeleine's vehemence caused the others to roar. Angered, Roger quit rowing while Matthew and Rowena's boat drifted ahead, thus breaking off communication between the two groups until they reached Partridge Island. Madeleine and Delia exchanged grimaces over being alone with Roger. Then they stared with feigned interest at the towering cliffs of Presque Isle to avoid conversing with him.

The prolonged silence caused Madeleine to think back to the morning's argument with her mother; her anger rose up again at the thought that her mother disapproved of Lazarus, who was ten times more of a gentleman than Roger. Could her mother really expect her to marry someone like Roger? Nothing she said would ever make her mother understand. The more Madeleine considered her future, the bleaker it seemed; she could not even view her father as an effective ally. She vaguely remembered how he had fought for Caleb, only to lose the battle. She could not blame her parents for Caleb's death, but she suspected her mother had been the primary source of her brother's unhappiness. She had now lost Lazarus, and if she should ever love again, she knew her mother would spoil that as well.

"Madeleine, are you crying?" Delia asked.

"No, I have something in my eye. I think some water splashed into it."

The party soon reached the island, and the picnic was set up. Madeleine tried to divert her thoughts from Lazarus, but the harder she tried, the more his handsome face kept appearing in her mind. She found herself bored with these friends whose company she had enjoyed just a year before. Now she felt restricted in their society; they always expected her to be charming, beautiful, gracious, a near oracle on the rules of fashion and breeding. All her life she had participated in this masquerade, hiding her true nature to please everyone else. She felt like a performing marionette with her mother pulling the strings. Only when she met Lazarus had she begun to have her own personal feelings, to feel real. Her love for him had made her view her own performance, and she did not care for the drama any longer.

She felt consumed by misery while her companions laughed and joked. She was embarrassed when Matthew had to repeat a question because she was too self-absorbed to hear the conversation. She apologized by claiming she was admiring the scenery. She tried to compensate by joining in the chatter about meaningless frivolities, but secretly she yearned to escape all this artificiality that controlled her life.

The hours dragged on, but inevitably the sun began to set. No one else paid attention to the time until the island became illuminated by the declining sun's rays. Then they rushed to pack up the picnic supplies and embark in the rowboats to reach Marquette before dark. No one wanted to be on the lake at night when the wind and waves would be unpredictable.

The rowboats had not traveled far when dusk made the shoreline indiscernible. The girls grew nervous and their conversation dwindled into whispers. The boys kept sharp watch for hidden rocks in the black waters. They rowed slowly, and every few minutes, one of their oars scraped against a dangerous rock, warning the rower to move the boat farther out into the lake. The wind was picking up, causing the waves to increase in size and speed.

Then an inevitable scraping and cracking clamor. One end of Roger's rowboat tips up onto a rock, then swiftly slips off. In the sudden moment of tumult, Madeleine is projected overboard. Exclamations of surprised terror! Her friends cry out Madeleine's name. Roger is overcome with horror. He has rowed the boat onto a submerged rock. He had not seen it; the rock had seemingly sprung to life, rising out of the dark lake solely to tip the boat.

At first, Madeleine is too stunned to realize what is happening; then she splashes about in panic. She sinks beneath the surface. For a second, her head emerges above the pummeling waves, and she can hear her friends' cries. She tries to answer, but the water pours down her throat. She closes her mouth and struggles to keep her chin above water. Her arms desperately strike out to grasp the edge of the boat, but it is already several yards away. She grasps at a sinister rock rising up out of a wave, but its side is smooth and gripless. Her hand scrapes against it, then slides off as the waves mercilessly shove her toward the cliffs of Presque Isle. She kicks off her shoes to better fight the waves, but the lake's fury propels her forward. She prepares to be dashed against the rocks. She feels overcome with fear of drowning. She thinks, "This must be how Caleb felt." Then the pounding waves engulf her.

🍁   🍁   🍁

When the picnic was over, the Hennings and their guests were not ready to end the day's celebrations. Gerald proposed that everyone adjourn to the Henning house to engage in an evening of gaiety. Sophia arranged for refreshments of ice cream and lemonade, and she was in such good spirits that she catered to everyone; she even told the maid and cook they might have the evening off. Agnes was asked to play on the pianoforte while Jacob's strong baritone joined his wife's soprano voice to provide musical entertainment. But the surprise of the evening was when Therese Montoni pushed Jacob aside to belt out Italian airs from several Verdi operas. No one had guessed such a gigantic voice could exist in such a little woman; a standing ovation followed her performance, along with testimonies that such singing had never been heard in Marquette. "Fifty year," she explained, while Montoni translated that she had sung in her church choir for half a century. Sophia then engaged her guests in a riotous game of cards; Methodist upbringing or not, she enjoyed cardplaying, especially when she won, and this night her winning streak sustained her merriment. On this glorious national holiday, the adults were more energetic than the children, and soon Mary and Sylvia were thankfully exhausted. Agnes carried the girls upstairs to one of the beds while the grownups continued to tell stories, laugh, eat and drink without a care.

The party did not break up until darkness fell around ten o'clock. The Montonis and Bergmanns left first, with Karl and Ben resisting entreaties to stay longer by pleading they had to travel back to Calumet in the morning. Therese thanked her hosts with kisses on the cheek that even Sophia did not mind. Then Cordelia and Nathaniel departed so Esau could walk Edna home in private. But this night was not simply for young couples. In the gloaming, Nathaniel took Cordelia's hand as they went down the sidewalk; old married couples still have moments when love burns within them, and tonight they loved each other in the joyful knowledge that their daughter had successfully found a husband to ensure for her a happiness equal to their own. They had striven to raise their children properly, and now they remembered again that the Lord makes good on all His promises in His time.

"It's about time we go as well," said Jacob after Edna and Esau had departed homeward.

"I'll go wake the girls," said Agnes.

"I'll help you carry them down," Gerald said. "I know how heavy they can be when they're asleep."

Jacob waited downstairs and chatted with Uncle Darius while Sophia cheerfully cleared away the empty glasses scattered about her parlor.

At that moment, too upset to knock, Matthew burst into the house.

"Why, what?" said Sophia, startled by the intrusion into her parlor.

"My word, boy," said Jacob, "you're pale. Are you ill?"

Matthew had raced uphill from the harbor; despite his urgent mission, he was nearly breathless and struggling to find words.

"What's wrong?" Darius asked.

"Madeleine. There's been an accident. She—she fell into," he panted, "she fell out of the rowboat and into the lake. I don't know even how it happened, but—it's so dark—we don't know what happened to her. We—"

"Quick, get Uncle Gerald," said Jacob, but Gerald was already rushing down the stairs. The front door slamming open had alarmed him, and he had looked over the upstairs landing in time to hear the speech.

"We'll form a search party," he said. "Quickly, Darius, go for help."

He did not need to utter the command; Darius was already tearing out the door.

"Gerald!" cried Sophia, too aghast for further words.

"It'll be okay," he said, going to her and clutching her arms. "You stay here in case there's word."

"Can't I come?" she asked, afraid to be alone because of the shock.

"No, stay here. Let the men do this."

"Agnes will stay with you, Aunt," said Jacob. Agnes had come downstairs, leaving behind the sleeping children. She was also frightened, but she kept her wits about her enough to think of the others before herself.

"We'll be fine. Good luck," Agnes replied, quickly kissing her husband's cheek. Gerald and Jacob followed behind Darius, who was outside hollering, "Help!" to rouse the neighbors. Jacob explained the emergency as people rushed out of their homes.

"Oh, God," Sophia shrieked after the men left. "I don't know what to do. What can I do?"

"Just be patient," said Agnes, pulling her to the sofa. "Come and sit. Maybe it's not as bad as it sounds. When people get excited, they usually overreact."

"But I don't even know what's really happened," said Sophia, violently shaking as she gripped her skirt and tried to imagine the possible horror. "How can they leave me here? I'm her mother. She needs me."

"Please be calm, Mother. Take a few deep breaths and you'll feel better."

Agnes was terrified by her little sister's danger, but now she had a hysterical mother to soothe. She grasped Sophia's hand to focus her thoughts, then undid Sophia's collar so she could breathe better.

"Should I get the smelling salts?" Agnes asked.

Sophia breathed deeply for a moment, then said, "No, I'm okay. I just want to know what's happening. Why don't men ever let women do anything? She's my daughter after all."

"I know," said Agnes, equally longing to join the search. "It's hard to wait, but we can be strong for the men by not getting in their way. We need to be hopeful. If they were rowing near shore, then Madeleine might be okay. She's a strong swimmer. She might swim to shore or onto a rock until she can be rescued."

But despite her brave words, Agnes thought these possibilities unlikely; she remembered Caleb and began to wonder what curse had been inflicted upon the family that two children should drown.

"My poor baby," Sophia cried. "She'll be frozen. I remember that terrible time I fell out of Jay Morse's boat, and that lake is so cold. I can't bear to think of her sitting on a rock in the night air with her clothes soaked through."

"It's a warm night; I'm sure her clothes will dry quickly," said Agnes.

"Not when she fell into the lake. That cold water soaks right into the skin." Sophia's teeth chattered as she recalled her own traumatic experience the night she saw Mr. Maynard drown. That night she had at least had Gerald to console her—Madeleine was alone in the cold night. Her poor little girl, hardly more than a baby; how terrified she must be without her mother!

"Oh, why didn't those stupid boys pay attention to what they were doing?" Sophia asked. "They should have known better than to be out rowing on the lake so late. And why didn't they have any lanterns with them? Then they could have searched for her; young people are so foolhardy these days."

"I'm sure they did their best," said Agnes. "Poor things, I imagine they're as upset as we are."

"She'll never be found now," despaired the mother. "Too much time has passed. She's dead. I just know it. My poor Madeleine!"

She broke into such a wailing shriek that Agnes instinctively put her arm around her stepmother. She was relieved Sophia was letting out her agony now so she might be stronger and better able to wait through the long night.

"Take my handkerchief," said Agnes. "I'll make us some tea to calm your nerves."

"No, tea will keep me awake," said Sophia, wiping her eyes. "Not that I'll sleep tonight. Maybe tea would be good. I want to wait up until they return with some news."

Agnes and Sophia each had two cups of tea. Neither slept through the long night hours, though they sat beside each other on the sofa, sometimes nearly slumbering against each other, other times recalling incidents from Madeleine's life. At times, the chiming of the grandfather clock was the only break in the monotonous silence, and then one of them would feel the need to peer out the window in hopes someone would come with news. But dawn broke before Gerald returned.

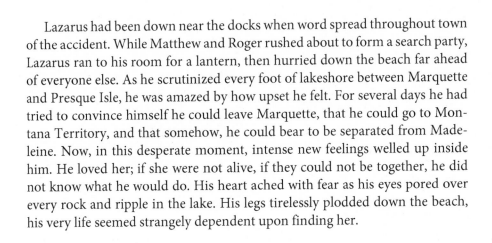

Lazarus had been down near the docks when word spread throughout town of the accident. While Matthew and Roger rushed about to form a search party, Lazarus ran to his room for a lantern, then hurried down the beach far ahead of everyone else. As he scrutinized every foot of lakeshore between Marquette and Presque Isle, he was amazed by how upset he felt. For several days he had tried to convince himself he could leave Marquette, that he could go to Montana Territory, and that somehow, he could bear to be separated from Madeleine. Now, in this desperate moment, intense new feelings welled up inside him. He loved her; if she were not alive, if they could not be together, he did not know what he would do. His heart ached with fear as his eyes pored over every rock and ripple in the lake. His legs tirelessly plodded down the beach, his very life seemed strangely dependent upon finding her.

Despite everyone's distress and the already common belief that Madeleine could not survive Lake Superior's fury, Nature saw fit to be kind. Madeleine Henning's nearly unconscious form was pushed by the strong currents toward the cove on Presque Isle's north side. She had been propelled along the cliffs and Black Rocks without any more damage than a few scrapes and bruises and a great deal of fright. These injuries were hardly worth noticing in exchange for the preservation of her life. The mysterious lake, now inexplicably benevolent when at other times so ruthless, washed her up into the shallow water of the cove, where she managed to scramble up the rocky shore onto dry ground. There in the cove's pebble bed, she collapsed exhausted and breathless. She coughed up a great deal of water, then lay, breathing deeply. Even when the water lapped at her feet, it was a long time before she found strength to move; she slipped into a half-dazed sleep of exhaustion, scarcely aware of the peril she had escaped.

She awoke around midnight, her head throbbing as she sat up. She began to shiver. In the darkness, she could not tell where she was, and the rocky cliffs made it impossible for her to find her way along the lakeshore, even if she knew in which direction lay home. She dared not venture into the forest because she had no idea how many miles she was from Marquette; she feared that being lost in the woods would be a worse ordeal than what she had already undergone.

She would have to remain here until the sun rose. She was not even quite sure where she was. She would have to walk along the shore until she saw something familiar to point her back toward Marquette. As her memory improved, she remembered hearing her friends' cries as she sunk beneath the waves. If they assumed she were dead, no one might be out searching for her body until morning. She worried about the pain her family and friends must be suffering, but still she dared not move while it was dark.

The stillness of night broke with a crashing in the trees behind her. Imagining a bear, she jumped to her feet and stumbled to the edge of the lake, hoping to find a place on the cliff where she could climb to safety. But she could see nothing. Fear started to paralyze her just as a lantern's light broke through the blackened forest.

"Lazarus!" she cried. He had rescued her.

Both were overjoyed as they ran forward into each other's arms. He had found her alive. He must love her to be out searching for her! Forgetting all decorum, she planted a kiss on her hero's lips while he let his arms linger around her in a manner he had never dared imagine.

"When I left town, they were forming a search party for you. Everyone thinks you're already dead, but I wouldn't believe it," he said. "I felt crazy, but I just knew I could find you. I left before anyone could—"

"Oh," she said, squeezing him with joy. "I'm so glad you found me."

"Madeleine, I—I thought I would die if anything happened to you. I love you, Madeleine. I know I'm not good enough, but—"

"You are, Lazarus. You rescued me. How much more good can anyone be?"

"But—but you have to understand. I can't go to Montana Territory now. I want to be with you—to marry you. I know it can never happen, but I want it so badly."

My parents won't approve," Madeleine replied, "so I don't know how we can—but—oh, Lazarus, I do love you, even if—"

"Now that you nearly drowned, your parents will be even more protective," said Lazarus. "But I can barely stand it. I think about you all the time. I walk by your house at night just hoping to catch a glimpse of you. I—"

"I know. I feel the same way," she said, feeling his arm still around her waist. She trembled, not from her wet clothes, but in disbelief that he could love her.

"If you had drowned, I don't know what I would have done," Lazarus said. "Go crazy I think. Maybe drowned myself so I could be with you that way. I can't bear it—I need you, Madeleine. But your parents—"

"Unless—" she mused.

"Your parents will never agree to our marrying."

"But," she said slowly, "Do they need to agree?"

"They'd lock you up before they'd let you marry me."

"My mother actually threatened to do that after she saw us together this morning," said Madeleine. "That's why we should get married."

"But how can we?"

"We can if we elope."

Lazarus was speechless.

"You said," Madeleine explained, "that everyone in Marquette thinks I'm dead."

"Yes, they'll think it a miracle to see you alive. No one thinks you can survive in the lake when it's dark out."

"Then maybe I should stay dead," she said. "Maybe we can run away and get married because they'll think I'm dead. Then we can go out to Montana as you planned. After we've been out there a few months, then I can always write and tell them the truth. By then, they'll be so happy to know I'm alive that they won't object to the marriage. Maybe we could even have a child before I reveal I'm alive so my parents can't try forcing us to divorce."

Lazarus's head was spinning.

"But Madeleine! It would be wrong! Think how your parents would suffer if they thought you dead. It's deceitful."

"I know. I hate to hurt them, but it's just for a little while, and we have a right to be happy, Lazarus. It's the only answer I can see for us."

She was a cajoling female, one gifted at manipulating words to make her wishes become everyone's.

It was too golden a fantasy for Lazarus to argue—he was already imagining this beautiful woman as his wife. Caught up in the dream, he said, "I think I have enough money to buy two train tickets to Montana."

"Good," she said. "You go back to Marquette and get the money. I'll hide here until you come back. Then maybe we can walk to Negaunee—we can't take the train from here in case someone sees us. You'll need to find me some shoes since I lost mine in the lake. I couldn't walk without them. Then once we're out of Michigan, we can get married."

"I love you, Madeleine," said Lazarus still in disbelief she wanted to be his wife. "But do you think you could live out West, so far from everything you know, and all the luxuries you have? It'll be a hard life out there."

"If I'm with you, none of that will matter," she said.

She was a young girl. She did not fear hardship because she had never known it. She was a romantic girl who believed she could do anything, and Lazarus was a foolish young man who let his emotions control him. Yet luck and love might see them through.

"Go now," she said. "I'll hide here until you come back, but hurry, and try not to let anyone see you leave town."

"I love you, Madeleine. I can't believe you can love a fellow like me."

Rather than reply, she gave him a peck on the lips. Then he disappeared into the woods. She found a little cluster of bushes to hide in until her lover returned.

She tried not to think about her parents; it would serve her nagging mother right to worry, yet at the same time, Madeleine hated to hurt her, or to hurt her father, who had never been anything but good to her. She loved them both, but she would not let her mother control her life. And she would only be hurting them for a short time. She had a right to love the man she chose, and if that meant eloping and moving to Montana Territory, then she would do it. After all, hadn't it just been Independence Day? This act would be her Declaration of Independence. She would be with Lazarus forever now. She would sit in this clump of bushes all night just to be with that darling man.

The search party traversed the beaches north of Marquette, but they ignored the forests. Madeleine heard their voices calling, and her heart yearned to save everyone the trouble of searching for her, but love was stronger than guilt. Lazarus soon returned for her, and then they vanished into the forest toward Negaunee.

Meanwhile Lake Superior grew placid, as though not a wave had disturbed it all night. By noon, hope had vanished and people talked of waiting for the lake to cast up the body, though for all anyone knew, it might wash up on the Canadian shore.

When Gerald returned home at daybreak, he felt completely helpless; he badly needed his wife's comfort, as she had sorely needed him all that night. But when his blank face told her his search had been useless, Sophia steeled her nerves and said, "Then I'll go out to help look."

Agnes protested that her stepmother had not slept, but Gerald was too tired and grief-stricken to object. He sank into a chair and stared out the window while the women stared at him.

"Give me five minutes to rest and then we'll go together," he told Sophia. "Agnes, Jacob said for you to go home, and he'll meet you there later. I would have kept searching with him, but he wanted me to let everyone know what is happening."

"Nothing's happening," said Sophia. "We can't sit any longer. We need to keep searching."

Gerald stood up, his wife's determination reinvigorating him. He could not rest until his daughter was found. Together the couple walked down to the harbor, then north along the lakeshore. Occasionally, Sophia expressed her fears, but restless energy kept her walking and searching, which she found easier than sitting and waiting. Gerald marveled as she trudged along the shoreline mile after mile without complaint of fatigue. She had often played the hypochondriac, the dainty female, but today she would willingly bear any strain except the loss of her child. For the first time, Gerald realized how heavily Caleb's death had weighed upon her, and he chided himself for often thinking she was simply seeking attention by her grief, and he knew her grief over Caleb's death would be nothing compared to the nightmare of her daughter's drowning.

When they had walked a mile past Partridge Island, Sophia consented to return to the house, but only to rest half an hour and eat a small lunch. Then she insisted they walk along the south beach all the way past Harvey, just in case Madeleine had been washed in that direction, beyond Marquette's harbor. Neither parent dared remark that if Madeleine had drifted so far, she would surely be dead.

Night fell before they returned home. The other search parties equally reported their efforts to have been fruitless. Then hope was finally given up.

"How could God take our child from us?" Sophia cried. "Are we such bad people that He punishes us like this?"

"No," Gerald said. "Not even a vengeful God could wish this suffering upon us."

"Then why?" Sophia repeated, but Gerald had no answer. Had he known Madeleine and Lazarus were on a train heading westward, the answer would have been no easier for him to find.

❦   ❦   ❦

After a week, Cordelia convinced Gerald that a funeral service had to be held. Sophia refused to attend the funeral, saying it was ridiculous when they had not yet found Madeleine's body. She would not even be comforted by the thought of wearing fashionable new mourning clothes. While the family attended the services, Molly stayed with Sophia. Molly would not have offered except out of kindness toward Gerald, but her own kindness was rewarded when Therese offered to go with her. Therese was to return to Italy the next day, so she wanted to say goodbye to Sophia, and although she could not converse with her, she pitied the grieving mother.

When Molly and Therese arrived, they found Darius, Gerald, and Esau waiting on the front porch to leave for the funeral.

"How is she today?" Molly asked.

"Never seen anyone so upset," said Darius.

"Poor, poor mama," Therese said, shaking her head.

"Thanks for helping out like this, Molly," said Gerald. "If you need anything, just let the maid know."

"Don't worry; we'll be fine," Molly replied.

But Molly was not so confident they would be fine once she saw Sophia. She had not met the grieving mother since the Fourth of July Picnic when Sophia had been exceptionally cheerful. Molly had baked a cake for the family the day after Madeleine's accident, but it had been left with Darius because Sophia would not receive visitors. Now Molly was surprised to see the grief-stricken mother's eyes sagging from excessive tears; she had always begrudgingly admired Sophia's raven black hair that even in her fifties had remained jet black, but now she saw several grey threads had seeped into it. Sophia had paid no attention to her toilet, but wore a wrinkled dress; even a stain from spilled coffee marked her bosom, but she was apparently unconcerned about such little matters.

"How are you doing, Sophia?" Molly asked while Therese squeezed the grieving mother's hand.

"I don't know," she said. "I couldn't go to that funeral. I don't know why Gerald consented to it when we aren't even certain that Madeleine's gone yet."

"I know, dear," said Molly. She thought Sophia should accept her daughter's death and go on with life, but she could not say so. She recognized the woman's spirit was broken, that she was unable to fight anymore. Molly had felt that way after Karl's departure and again before Therese's visit.

To divert Sophia's attention from her grief, Molly offered to read aloud to her.

"No, I couldn't concentrate on any book," Sophia replied.

"But you need to occupy yourself. Your pain will be easier to bear if you keep busy," Molly said.

Sophia stared at her, then replied, "You don't know anything about it."

Molly felt angry, but she held her tongue. She had never liked Sophia, but she would not be rude at this moment. Calmly, she replied, "I know when Fritz died, I had to live for my family. They needed me to be strong for them."

"My children are gone now," said Sophia. "I only have Gerald."

"He needs you, and so do your brother and sister and their families."

"I won't see much of them anymore," said Sophia.

"Of course you will."

"No, I won't," Sophia said. "We're leaving."

Molly was surprised. Gerald had not mentioned this to her.

"What do you mean, you're leaving?"

"I can't look at that hateful lake anymore. As soon as we can sell this house, we're moving back East. I'll start packing tomorrow."

"When did you decide this?" Molly asked.

"Last night," said Sophia. "I told Gerald I want to go away."

"Does he want to leave?"

"He understands, and since his father passed away, he thinks he should go to New York City to take over the main office there."

Molly could just imagine how Sophia, selfishly considering only herself, had talked Gerald into this move. She was both unaware of Gerald's guilt over not seeing his father before he died, and how determined he was to continue the family business in his father's memory.

Molly tried to change the subject until she could discuss it with Gerald, until she could persuade him not to leave.

"I understand that Gerald picked out a lovely casket," she said.

"What good is a casket when there's nothing to put in it?" Sophia snapped.

Silence followed for several minutes. Then Molly remarked on how lovely was the black crepe ribbon she had seen on the front door.

"Darius bought that," said Sophia. "The Richardsons sent us a ribbon as well, but I had the maid burn it. I don't want anything from those people after what their son did."

Molly only felt sorry for the Richardson boy, imagining how much guilt he must feel.

"I think I'll go lie down upstairs," Sophia said. "I have a headache."

"Can I do anything to make you comfortable?" Molly asked.

"No. I'll call the maid if I need anything."

"All right," said Molly, regretting that she had failed to bring comfort. Therese had not understood the conversation; she raised her eyebrows at Molly as Sophia climbed upstairs. Molly explained by gestures that Sophia was going to take a nap.

Time now passed uncomfortably. Therese occupied herself with the needle-work she had brought, but Molly stared out the window, grieving for the Henning family.

An hour later, Edna and Esau returned. Since the happy day of their engagement, that same sad day as Madeleine's accident, the lovers had rarely been apart.

"How was the funeral?" Molly asked when they came into the parlor.

"Very nice," Edna replied. "I wish Aunt Sophia had come. It might have helped her."

"How is she?" Esau asked.

"She went to take a nap," Molly said. "I'm afraid I wasn't much comfort to her."

"I'm sure you did your best," said Edna.

"Is it true what she told me? That she and Gerald are moving back East?"

"Yes," said Esau. "As soon as they sell the house."

"It's too bad," Molly said. "It must be disappointing for the two of you. I had imagined you would be married in this house as Jacob and Agnes were."

"Oh no," Edna replied. "We would rather be married in the new church."

The Methodists had undergone several disasters in the last few years while they tried to build their new church. First, their minister had humiliated the congregation by disappearing with their money from the building fund. Then when new funds were gathered and the building finally erected, a dedication ceremony was held, but during the service, the crowd in the church was so great it had caused the basement pillars to sink into the foundation. Neverthe-less, the Methodists had succeeded in completing their sandstone church, complete with stained glass windows and steeples at the corner of Ridge and Front Streets. Now it was only fitting that two grandchildren of Rebecca Brookfield should wed in the church that stood as a testament to the Method-ists' perseverance in Marquette for a quarter century.

"That will be nice; your new church is even more grand than St. Peter's Cathedral," Molly said. "It's good you can be married there since this house will be sold."

"I suppose we could still be married in the house if we wanted to," said Esau, "since we plan to be married in another week."

Molly expressed surprise the wedding would be held so soon after Madeleine's funeral.

"Aunt Sophia understands," said Edna. "We have to go back West before winter comes, and we want to be married so Uncle Gerald and Aunt Sophia can attend before they move East. It may be the last time all the family is together."

"I didn't know you were moving West, Edna?"

"Yes, she is," Esau replied. "She's going to be the mistress of my and Father's ranch."

Gerald now returned with the rest of the family.

"How is Sophia?" was his first concern.

"She's napping," Molly replied.

"I better check on her," he said and disappeared upstairs.

Molly noticed his ashen face and the lack of vitality in his step as he climbed the stairs. Therese collected her needlework and joined Molly in offering more condolences to the family, who responded with wishes for Therese to have a safe trip back to Italy.

As she walked home, Molly felt emotionally drained. The last week had been nearly unbearable as she watched her friends suffer. And now that Therese was leaving, she felt flooded with anxiety.

"Thank you for coming with me," Molly told her sister-in-law.

"Poor Sophia," Therese replied. "People no change. She normal soon."

Molly had come to understand her sister-in-law's broken English by the tone of her voice. Like Therese, she expected eventually Sophia would return to her interests in fashion and society. She just wished Sophia did not insist on recovering from her sorrow in the East. Molly would miss Gerald, just as she would now miss Therese. If as her sister-in-law said, people do not change, then what would happen to her after the peacemaker in her home had left?

"Therese, what will I do when you've gone back to Italy?" she asked as they climbed up the steps of Montoni's house. Therese smiled, "All good. Soon, all good." But Molly was not so sure. If Montoni returned to his old behavior, she thought she might be better off in the lake with Madeleine. But when Kathy greeted her at the door, Molly decided she would endure for her daughter's sake.

A week later, Sophia was in the middle of packing. Many of the books, knickknacks, and lesser necessities were already stored away. The maid had been ordered to pack Madeleine's room since Sophia refused to enter it. Madeleine's belongings were to be kept at the Whitmans' boarding house until the Hennings left Marquette; then the items would be distributed among the poor, but only after Sophia left so she would not have to see a stranger wearing her daughter's clothes.

That week, Gerald found a potential buyer for the house, a young lawyer and his wife named Smith.

"They wish to come this evening to see the place," he told Sophia.

"It seems a shame ta sell this house after all the money you've sunk into it," said Darius, shaking his head. But after dinner, he left the decision to the husband and wife, and promptly accompanied his son to spend an evening with the Whitmans.

"Oh, but Gerald," Sophia said as they waited for the Smiths to arrive, "how can we sell the house to them? They're Catholics, and she's a Southerner and Irish no less. I hate to think of such people in my home."

"Sophia, don't be unreasonable," Gerald replied. He loved his wife but between the strains of grieving and moving, Gerald had become irritable to her idiosyncrasies.

"Don't snap at me," she snapped back.

"Well, you are being unreasonable," he replied. "Mrs. Smith's parents left the South when she was a little girl and her family supported abolition before the War."

"I don't care if they did support abolition. Her parents were slaveowners before they came to Marquette, and I hear she's still prejudiced against the Negroes," Sophia said, despite her own dislike of Indians. "You can't consider that a good recommendation."

"Dear, we can't be picky," Gerald said. "The sooner we sell the house, the sooner we can move East."

"But," Sophia said, "you know how dirty and shiftless the Irish are. I just don't want my lovely home to fall into ruin."

"Molly is Irish," Gerald replied, "yet she's one of our closest friends, and her house is quite spotless."

Sophia knew better than to speak against Molly—she had never liked the woman, liked her all the less after she had come and jabbered away during Madeleine's funeral until Sophia had been forced to go upstairs, feigning a headache to escape the Irish woman's running tongue. Furthermore, because of Molly, Gerald had never been able to love her fully; Molly's presence always made him think of Clara. Once they were back East, Sophia would be relieved not to have that Irishwoman around, or her detestable Italian husband. But for now, she conceded, "Well, Molly is an exception. But I'm not sure a Catholic family will be accepted in this neighborhood."

"We won't be here, so it's no concern of ours," said Gerald. "Besides, Mr. Smith is one of the most respected lawyers in this town."

"But Gerald—" Sophia started, but the doorbell rang.

"That will be the Smiths," said Gerald. "Try to be civil."

"I'm always civil," Sophia snapped again. How could he think of selling their home to such people when she was already under such a strain?

The Smiths were little more than newlyweds and clearly in love. Sophia's heart ached in the glow of their happiness; they reminded her of the unfulfilled hopes for Madeleine's future marriage.

"Mr. and Mrs. Smith, this is my wife," said Gerald, introducing everyone.

"Hello," said Sophia as she accepted Mrs. Smith's hand.

"Hello. We've met before, but you probably don't remember," said Mrs. Smith. "My parents are Edmund and Dolly O'Neill; my mother was a member of your literary club. I was just a little girl back then."

"Oh yes, you're Carolina," Sophia said.

"Well," said Gerald. "It looks as if you ladies already have something in common. Shall we show them the house, Sophia?"

Sophia consented, but she did not like Carolina any better because her mother had belonged to the literary society; Sophia had barely spoken two words to Dolly O'Neill in the last ten years, and she had always thought Dolly preposterous for retaining her Southern accent after living in Marquette for twenty years.

As they wandered through the downstairs and then up to the bedrooms, Sophia followed halfheartedly, thinking Carolina's fashionable dress the only thing in the couple's favor.

Halfway through the second floor, Mr. Smith said to Gerald, "I think we've seen enough. We're very interested and wish to make an offer. Why don't we go downstairs to discuss the terms. Your wife can show Carolina the rest of the house."

Sophia did not argue but showed Carolina the servants' rooms while the men returned downstairs. Then, before the women went downstairs, Carolina asked, "Isn't there one other bedroom?"

"Yes, my daughter, Madeleine's," said Sophia, reluctant to show it. For a moment, she considered letting Carolina enter it by herself, but she did not like the thought of a stranger alone in her daughter's room.

"I'm sorry; I don't need to see it," Carolina said, recalling the Hennings' recent tragedy.

"No, you can; it's just—"

"I understand," said Carolina. "I'm sure it's a beautiful room from the good taste exhibited by the rest of the house, and no one could doubt your daughter would be like her mother in her decorative talents."

"Thank you," said Sophia, pleased even by praise from an Irish Catholic Southerner.

"I'm sure you don't want your daughter's privacy invaded."

"It's all right," said Sophia, leading Carolina to the room. "It's best you see the room now before it's completely empty so you can get some ideas for redecorating it."

As soon as they entered, Carolina began to praise the velvet colored silk wallpaper, the canopied bed, the vanity, the paintings on the wall, and through it all, she kept repeating, "It's so charming."

"Madeleine's favorite color was purple," Sophia said. "Her father said purple was the royal color, and she was our little princess."

"How sweet; she was rather like a princess," Carolina replied. She took every opportunity to flatter because Gerald had warned her husband how particular Sophia was about the purchaser of the house.

Sophia half held in a sob. "I'm sorry," she said, "but sometimes it's still so difficult for me to believe Madeleine is gone. She was so young and beautiful."

"I understand," Carolina replied. "The entire town mourns with you. We all feel the most beautiful girl in Marquette has been lost to us."

Sophia searched for her absent handkerchief; she had soaked so many lately that the maid could not keep up with washing them.

"Please, take mine," Carolina offered.

Sophia accepted, warming to Carolina's sympathy.

"I would like to think," said Carolina, "that if I were to live here, I might have a little girl someday who could enjoy this room as Madeleine must have."

"I think Madeleine would like that," said Sophia. "I bet you and Mr. Smith will have lovely children."

"Thank you," Carolina replied.

"I think it would give me comfort," Sophia said, "to think of another little girl living in this house. Gerald doesn't care who lives here, but I want to sell the house to someone who will appreciate it."

"I understand," Carolina said, "although I'm sure no one could fail to appreciate the finest home in Marquette."

"Do you think it is the finest?" asked Sophia. She had long wanted to affirm this, always fearing one of her neighbors' homes perhaps grander than her own.

"I don't think there's another home in the Upper Peninsula as well laid out or decorated, or with such a beautiful view," said Carolina, secretly redecorating in her mind; that horrid wallpaper in the east parlor, French or not, would have to go, and what sane person would want a velvet colored bedroom? She smiled. "It will be a sad day for Marquette when its finest family leaves."

"You're too kind," said Sophia, "but Gerald needs to take care of the business back East, and we'll be more comfortable there. This little town has always been rather a roughing it experience, you understand, for people of our social background. There are far more opportunities and so much more culture in New York City."

"I understand," said Carolina. "I envy you the opportunity."

"Let's go downstairs. Of course, it's Gerald's decision, but I'll try to convince him to sell the house to your husband."

"Thank you," Carolina beamed, delighted with her persuasive abilities.

Gerald was surprised when Sophia appeared and ordered the maid to bring in tea and cake for their guests.

"Sophia, Mr. Smith has made us an offer. Do you wish to discuss it first?"

"No, Gerald, I'm sure his price is acceptable. I'm just happy to think there will be children in the house again. I'm sure," she said, addressing the Smiths, "you'll have a large, happy family here."

"I hope we have a daughter," Carolina replied. "I've always liked the name Madeleine for a girl."

Sophia had met a woman after her own nature, the only kind who could have gotten the best of her. A year later, Carolina Smith gave birth to her only child, a daughter she named Jane.

❦   ❦   ❦

With their belongings packed and their furniture already shipped East, the Hennings made their last public appearance in Marquette at the First Methodist Church for Edna and Esau's wedding. It was a quiet little ceremony. Edna wore a simple dress appropriate for traveling; she and her husband would depart on the train that afternoon to return West with Darius. Most brides would not appreciate their father-in-laws accompanying them on their honeymoons, but Edna loved Uncle Darius almost as much as she loved Esau.

The day after the wedding, Gerald and Sophia also departed. From that time on, save for a few footnotes in the local history books referencing Marquette's earliest families, and some continually diminishing memories of relatives remaining in Marquette, the Henning family was almost completely forgotten. Their Ridge Street home soon became known as Judge Smith's house, and its new owners prospered as Marquette society leaders for decades to come.

"Don't cry, Cordelia," Nathaniel told his wife after their daughter had gone West and Gerald and Sophia had gone East. "They'll all write to us, and we can always go visit them."

"I know," said Cordelia, almost wishing her daughter had not married. "I'm happy for Edna, and I know Esau will take good care of her, but nothing will be the same again."

Much as she loved her daughter, Cordelia equally lamented the loss of her sister. For all their differences, she and Sophia had been the closest in age of their siblings, and scarcely a day of their lives had passed without them seeing one another. Many a day, Cordelia had been so angry with Sophia that she wished they lived farther apart, but now that they were parted, her heart softened and she thought Sophia a better sister than she had admitted before. Sophia had been the only one in Marquette who shared her childhood memories, but now as old age approached—when they would most need each other—they would be apart. Cordelia sympathized with her sister's pain over her children's deaths, but she wished Sophia had considered how this separation would hurt her.

"It's just too many changes all at once," Cordelia said.

"Life is full of changes," replied her husband.

"I know, but lately, it seems all the changes are bad ones."

"Then we should expect something good any time now," Nathaniel smiled.

1883

A cold December evening. As always, the snow was pummeling Marquette. Montoni hated winter. He had never known such bone-chilling cold in Italy; these frigid nights made him wonder whether he had been wrong to think life would be better in America. Occasionally he even told himself he should go back to Italy; he had often thought if he could save up a little more money, even if it meant leaving his wife behind, he might return home. His morbid thoughts matched the evening as he trudged through slushy streets in the falling darkness. He walked more slowly than usual, the scowl across his face resembling that of Ebenezer Scrooge, not that Montoni would have been familiar with that disreputable character. Yet he and Scrooge shared a misanthropic attitude and a sudden awareness of their own mortality.

Years ago, he had trained his wife to have supper on the table the minute he came home, but tonight she was not responsible for their late meal. Montoni came into the house, stood in the hallway, and waited for Molly to come brush the snow off his shoulders before she removed his coat. Usually, she would not speak until she had assessed his mood and could adapt her responses to it, but tonight, she dared ask, "Why are you so late?"

"Just tired I guess," he replied. He walked into the dining room and sat down at the table. Molly hung up his coat, then went into the kitchen and carried out the supper. Kathy, having heard the front door open, came quietly to the table, equally unwilling to speak until her stepfather had.

Molly served the food, while waiting for Montoni to burst into his usual self-absorbed conversation. When he said nothing, she could not bear the suspenseful silence.

"Did you see the doctor today?" she asked.

"Yes," he muttered, sticking his fork into the pasta.

"Did he have any idea why you've been feeling so tired lately?"

Montoni dropped his fork. Gruffly, he said, "I have cancer."

Silence. The women reacted with inner shock.

"Cancer," Molly whispered. "How bad?"

"It's fatal," said Montoni. "I'll only live a few more months."

"Is there anything that can be done?"

"No, it's in too late a stage," he replied.

"Well, what—what—" Molly did not know what to say. "I knew you should have gone to the doctor sooner."

"He said he couldn't a stopped it," Montoni replied. "I'm gonna die."

"Oh," said Molly. "But is—can I do anything to make it easier, less painful?"

"Yes, letta man be," he growled. "I don't need so many questions. If you need ta know somethin', I'll tell ya."

Until her husband came to terms with the situation, Molly decided it best to be silent. Kathy quickly ate her meal, then excused herself. Usually Montoni would not let anyone leave the table until he had finished eating, but tonight he did not care. He only cleared half his plate, then pushed it from him and sat silently for several moments. Unable to bear the tension, Molly stood up to clear the table.

"Why don't you go lay down for a little while?" she said.

"No, I'm goin' back ta the saloon."

"You shouldn't keep such long hours if you don't feel well. You—"

"I can take care a myself. I don't need ta be treated like a baby. I'm goin' back ta the saloon."

"All right," said Molly, going to fetch his coat. He was out the door a minute later. She went to wash the dishes.

Kathy, hearing her stepfather go out the door, now felt it safe to go downstairs.

"Mother," she said, stepping into the kitchen.

"Yes?" said Molly, scraping Montoni's leftovers from his plate. He had never before failed to clear his plate, except when he had thrown the food across the room.

"Is he really going to die?"

"I don't know."

"If he does—"

"We'll deal with that when it happens," said Molly. "I don't want to hear another word about it."

Kathy had not expected this reaction. Her mother knew what she would say; her mother must have the same idea. How could she help it? They had always felt the same about Montoni since Kathy had reached the age of reason. Did her mother not want him to die? Did she feel guilt? Kathy did not care. She returned to her room, and lying on the bed, imagined the future if everything worked out.

Molly did not blame the girl. In weak moments, she had given way to expressing the same wish Kathy held. But now that wish would be reality, and he was her husband, and it was wrong to wish ill even on your enemies. Now she would have to care for him until the end, but she feared that as caretaker she would gain mastery in the relationship. She might become vindictive in these last months of his life, repaying him for every blow, every abusive word, when he was too weak to retaliate. Was God testing her again? Hadn't He already tested her enough? Perhaps God was also testing her husband, warning him of his approaching death so he would have one last chance to attempt kindness. She doubted Montoni would learn anything from it, but if she were kind to him, perhaps she would be forgiven for the many evil thoughts she had held previously. Perhaps he would feel he did not deserve her kindness and then be kinder himself, and that would help them both.

She felt she was dreaming the impossible to think he would change in the slightest, but in either case, her suffering was almost over.

🍁   🍁   🍁

On cold, winter nights, Montoni preferred to stay late at work. The saloon was better lit and more cheerful than sitting at home with a wearisome wife who sewed but never spoke an interesting word, and a stepdaughter who preferred to sit in her room with a book than speak to the man who fed and clothed her.

The saloon was crowded tonight; Montoni was glad because the noise diverted his thoughts. In addition to the continual flow of customers seeking the quickest path to drunken oblivion, Montoni earned income from renting three spare rooms above the saloon. He had lived in those rooms until his marriage; then he had built a home for his unappreciative wife and stepchildren so he would appear a respectable family man; he did not care that owning a saloon detracted from that respectability. Nor did his avaricious soul have qualms about renting the upstairs rooms at exorbitant prices; the alcohol downstairs ensured the rooms were rarely empty of patrons too inebriated to walk out of the building. Tonight was no exception. Two of the rooms were rented early in the evening to men who intended to spend the night in drunken ecstasy.

Montoni stood at the bar pouring drinks, then washing and wiping beer glasses to fill them again. Whenever his mind had a free moment, he recalled his doctor's visit that afternoon. Like most abusive men, he was a coward. The thought of extended, intense suffering distressed him; he pondered buying a revolver to end it all now. But first, he would find a lawyer to change his Will so Therese would be his heir. He wouldn't let that bitch of a wife get anything. She'd sell the saloon first thing. Worse, that moron son of hers, that sonofabitch, might try to run the place; he'd probably be good at it too since he was prospering in the lumberjack business. Therese would have to inherit everything; he didn't know what she'd do with it, but he had come to America to help his family in Italy, and he would make his family his heirs.

"Hey, you got a spare room?"

Montoni looked up from the whiskey glass he was wiping to see a burly, bearded lumberjack and a lean, longhaired Indian.

"We don't serve his kind," Montoni told the white man while gesturing toward his companion.

"We need a room."

"There's only one left, and it's only got one bed."

"Then I guess we'll have to share," said the lumberjack. He opened his mouth and let fly a glob of tobacco juice into the spittoon at the end of the bar.

"You can sleep there, but your friend'll have ta find somewhere else."

"That ain't being very friendly, Mister."

"Them's the rules here," Montoni said.

"I thought this was America, where we're all equal."

"We is if we're Americans, but he ain't. He's a red blooded Injun."

"Seems to me he's more American than the rest of us."

"Now how'd you figure a stupid notion like that?"

"You callin' me stupid, Mister?"

"You must be if you don't know an Injun from an American."

"He was born in this country. Was you born in this country, Mister?"

"Don't mattuh."

"Where was ya born, Mister?"

Montoni set down the beer glass and towel and leaned his hands on the bar; his nose was only inches from that of his antagonist. He hated lumberjacks; his stepson was a lumberjack.

"Italy," he said.

"Italy?" said the lumberjack, spitting out another chew of tobacco. "I hears there's only dainty olive-skinned girls there. Ain't no men there."

"Italy's a bettuh country than this one."

"Then why the Hell don't you go back there, Signora? We don't need no Dagos here."

"This here's my saloon, and your friend ain't welcome here, so get him out."

"We ain't leavin' until mornin' after we've slept in that room."

"Ya stinkin' Injun," Montoni shouted, turning to the lumberjack's companion. "Get the hell outta my place, ya hear me. I don't want none of ya dirty vermin in here."

The Indian remained silent. He was used to discrimination and ready to leave without argument, but his friend felt otherwise.

"You don't talk to him like that, you Popish rat."

"I said get the hell outta here!" Montoni yelled.

"We won't," said the lumberjack, sitting down on a barstool. "Our money's good here. Give us a coupla beers."

Montoni, perhaps irked on by the ill tidings he had received that day, completely lost control. Picking up the stem of an empty whiskey bottle, he raised it above his head and charged around the bar, intending to whack open the Indian's head. But he had barely stepped around the bar when the logger grabbed him in midstride; lifting him with great might, the logger thrust Montoni backward until his spine snapped down over the bar. Then he flung him like a straw scarecrow over the bar and into the back mirror; Montoni collapsed into shattered glass, then lay helplessly on the floor.

The saloon was silent as everyone watched in disbelief. Before he could be stopped, the logger stepped behind the bar, yanked Montoni up by his collar, slammed his back against the bar, and decked his fist into Montoni's face. Montoni's jaw was bleeding; the blood streamed down the logger's fist and onto the bar. When the logger released his victim, he picked up the bar towel and wrapped his hand in it to stop his bleeding. Montoni slid back onto the floor.

Seeing everyone staring at him, including his Indian friend, who stood awkwardly by the saloon door, the logger said, "He came at us first. It was self-defense. You're all my witnesses."

After a moment of silence, everyone grunted in agreement. No man present had liked Montoni.

"See to 'im," the logger said, joining his friend at the door. "If the police need ta speak ta me, I'll be at the hotel down the street looking for a room."

Montoni's two employees now felt it safe to tend to him.

"He's hurt really bad," said one, patting Montoni's face to waken him. The two men tried to lift him, but the movement made Montoni scream in agony.

"Maybe his back's broken," said one man. "You better run for the doctor."

"Should I go get his wife too?" asked the second man.

"Yeah, after you fetch the doctor."

The young man ran out of the saloon, his speed resulting more from the excitement of the moment than from concern for Montoni. The doctor did not appreciate being woken, and even his duty to care for others did not prevent him from grumbling to his wife when he heard his patient's name. But the young man did not wait to hear the doctor grumble; he ran to notify Mrs. Montoni, whom he pitied more than her husband.

When he reached the house, he was so excited and out of breath it took Molly a couple minutes to understand and digest the information. Kathy understood more quickly; a queer tingle of hope passed through her as she ran to fetch her mother's overcoat and scarf, then threw on her own jacket and mittens to accompany her mother. The young man now wished he had not been the messenger when he saw the troubled look on Mrs. Montoni's face and realized he would have to walk back to the saloon with her. He awkwardly led the two women back through the streets, no one speaking along the way. He wondered that Mrs. Montoni did not ask more questions, while Kathy longed to know if her mother shared her thoughts. But Molly remained silent.

They arrived at the saloon to find that the other employee and several of the patrons had managed, with great care and trouble, to carry Montoni upstairs to the empty bed that, had the scene been played differently, might have been shared by the logger and his Indian friend. Molly went upstairs, but before she went into the room, the doctor pulled her aside. He had just arrived a few minutes before, but soon enough to gauge the situation.

"There's nothing I can do," he told her. "His back is broken irreparably. He only has minutes to live. I gave him morphine to lessen the pain, but all we can do now is hope he'll die quickly."

"Is it murder?" Kathy asked, surprising herself with the strange words.

"The witnesses claim Montoni attacked first, and the other man only acted in self-defense."

"He probably lost his temper," said Molly. "He told me he saw you this morning, Doctor, so you can understand why he might be so upset."

"Yes. Perhaps in some way, this is an unlooked for blessing. Now his suffering will not be as drawn out as if he had waited for the cancer to take him. Be strong for him now. Try to comfort him."

Molly went into the room where her husband lay dying. She searched for comforting words, but she could not help admitting to herself she was fortunate to be released from nursing him for the next several months.

Montoni lay on the bed with closed eyes, trying not to move. The young man who had fetched Molly placed a chair beside the bed so she could sit down. For a second she hesitated, then reached over to take her husband's hand. Montoni's eyes opened with surprise at the tender touch. He struggled to speak.

"Let's leave them alone," said the doctor, ushering everyone from the room. "I'll be in the hall if you need me, Mrs. Montoni."

Kathy followed the doctor out. She felt cowardly not to remain with her mother, but she did not feel sorry for her stepfather.

When the door had closed, Montoni asked, "I'm going to die now?"

Molly nodded. "Are you in much pain?"

"Yes," he groaned.

"The morphine should be starting to work."

"It still hurts."

Molly silently held his hand. Her own hand began to sweat, more from anxiety than heat, but she did not pull it away.

A painful, constricted look spread over Montoni's face. She thought she was losing him right then, but instead, he had a spasm, then spit out, "Forgive, Molly."

She had never expected such words. Before she could think how to reply, the door opened, and the doctor stuck in his head to announce that the priest had come.

Molly rose to give the priest her seat. Montoni was unwilling to release her hand, but she told him, "I won't leave. I'll stand beside you."

She watched from the corner, while her husband received extreme unction. She saw how the priest frightened him. Could he even realize the misery she and her children had suffered because of him? Did he now fear God's judgment? She wanted to believe he was sincere; she wanted the priest to finish quickly so she could say she forgave him. Even if he had not apologized, she felt she must forgive him before he died. She was astonished that after he had mistreated her for so many years, now she could pity him. She wondered whether his body or his spirit tormented him worse, and she wondered whether her forgiveness would bring him more relief than that of the Holy Church.

When the priest finished, she asked to be alone with her husband. She sat beside him and took his hand again. He looked questioningly at her.

"I forgive you," she said, "and I pray God does as well."

"I never deserved—Molly—never—." He struggled just to breathe and his words came out slowly between heaving sighs. "No other woman—would—put up—with—"

"Shh, it's all right," she said. "You took care of us. That's what matters."

She had not lied; he had been good at providing material things, and now she would still have those things when he was gone.

His eyes continued to plead with her. "I—if I could—again—I'd do better—"

"I know," she said, but she doubted him. Therese had told her people do not change. If he were to recover now, he would be his old hateful self in a few weeks. Yet she affirmed his lie, to comfort him into believing he had told the truth; now he could die repentant; she hoped God would be merciful, and that he would learn from what he had done.

He squeezed her hand, nearly crushing it as another violent spasm consumed him. His mouth opened in agony, and he struggled to breath. His head jerked up, then fell lifeless on the pillow.

The doctor, hearing Montoni's final groan, stepped into the room to close his eyes. Molly let go of the lifeless hand and stumbled to the doorway where Kathy stood. For a minute, they held each other. Then Kathy let out a hideous laugh from nervous relief; she could not believe their ordeal had ended.

"What do we do now?" Molly asked for both of them.

"Let's go home and get some sleep," said Kathy. "In the morning we can make the funeral arrangements."

Molly allowed her daughter to lead her home. Most wives would be grieving for their husbands, but Molly found herself asking, "What will I do now? I have a home and money and nothing to worry about." The future seemed unimaginably easy.

Everyone in town speculated over what would happen to the murderer. The logger willingly turned himself into the sheriff. Several witnesses made statements that he had acted in self-defense. A trial would be held, but most people were convinced the lumberjack would be acquitted. Molly was indifferent about the situation. She was sorry Montoni's life had ended violently, but she felt a sense of justice that he had died as he had lived. In the end, she pitied her husband; she knew what it was to be physically abused and could not even wish such a beating upon him. Yet, when the logger only served a short jail term, Molly did not feel the sentence unjust.

The funeral passed quietly. Not even Montoni's two bartenders attended. They had already heard rumors that Mrs. Montoni would sell the saloon, so they felt no obligation to pay their respects to maintain their jobs. The funeral mourners were limited to Molly and Kathy, the Whitmans, and a few ladies Molly knew from church. Karl telegrammed that he would come, but Molly telegrammed back that it was not necessary. Several neighbors sent sympathies along with excuses for their lack of attendance.

Christmas arrived almost immediately after the funeral. Molly and Kathy attended the special Mass that Christmas Eve in the basement of the new cathedral. In 1879, the old cathedral, which Bishop Baraga had consecrated, had burnt down and now a new one was slowly being raised. St. Peter's parishioners had been attending the French Catholic Church on Washington Street until the new cathedral would be completed, but for Christmas, although the walls were not yet raised, a roof had been placed over the basement so the parish family could celebrate Christmas Eve Mass together.

Molly's thoughts strayed throughout the Christmas service. Montoni would have attended with her tonight, but she felt it appropriate that he had died before ever entering the new cathedral. She had no evidence, but she had often suspected her husband's involvement in the cathedral's destruction. When Bishop Baraga had died, he had been succeed by Bishop Mrak; then in 1879, Bishop Mrak had left the office due to poor health, and Bishop Vertin had taken up the episcopal seat. Not long after his consecration, the new bishop had transferred the cathedral's pastor, Father Kenny, from Marquette to Mackinac Island. The congregation of St. Peter's, particularly the many Irish parishioners, had greatly loved Father Kenny, and his parting from them caused both sadness and anger. Many an unchristian word had been spoken in secret against the new bishop, and Montoni, one of those who attended church out of habit and always looked for a reason to complain, was among the dissidents. One evening, Molly had stopped by the saloon on an errand and found her husband and some of his cronies discussing Father Kenny's transferal. Two nights later, a roaring fire had reduced St. Peter's Cathedral to ashes. No one was ever accused, but rumors were rampant that the cathedral's destruction was an act of revenge against the bishop for transferring Father

Kenny. The fire was proven to have begun outside the church, and arson was suspected, but no one came forward with information to convict the arsonists.

Molly did not forget what she had overheard in the saloon, and the day after the church's destruction, she was struck by the conversation that ensued when she and Montoni met one of his friends on the street. When the fire was mentioned, Montoni had said, "Serves the bishop right. Who does he think he is ta come in and change things without the people's permission? This is America, ain't it? The church don't have that kind a power here."

"You got that right," his friend had replied.

Molly was not so sure. As a Catholic, she felt she should be obedient to the Church. She had been disappointed by Father Kenny's transfer, but she saw no reason to be insubordinate toward the diocese's shepherd. In a moment of weakness, she had obstinately replied, "If he's the bishop, he must know best."

"Ha!" Montoni had said. "We ain't gonna see another like old Baraga."

"No, he was a saint," Molly agreed, "but the new bishop means well."

Montoni had scowled. "That church wasn't much of a cathedral anyway. About time a new one was built. You should see the beautiful ones in Italy."

No, Molly thought that Christmas Eve, her husband did not deserve to celebrate the Christmas miracle in the new cathedral. Yet it felt strange not to have him stand beside her in church, or not to have his hulking form lying against her at night. She could not help missing him, and now that he had left her so well off, she was thankful, and perhaps kinder to his memory than he deserved.

1884

There was no absence of snow that January, and it was the best kind of snow—good for both sledding and snowshoeing. Agnes had already been out with the Marquette women's snowshoeing club a few times that winter, but somehow she had always been too busy to go sledding with her girls. A fresh snow had fallen the night before, and the day being a surprisingly warm twenty-five degrees, the afternoon was perfect sledding weather. She had to take the children sledding at least once this winter since her son Will was three years old now, and he had never gone before; she had always felt him too little in past years. And she might not have another chance to take him because she was expecting her fourth child; if it were not that bundling up in winter clothes hid what her figure otherwise made apparent, she would not have gone outside at all, but her winter coat would allow her to remain active for another month. Of course, she and Will would have to settle for a safe, small hill, but that was better than an entire winter without a sledding trip.

A good half hour was spent getting everyone ready. Will was her only child who needed help putting on his winter clothes, but Mary and Sylvia insisted on their mother's constant attention even for such little details as color coordinating their hats and scarves.

"We're only going sledding girls, not to a party," Agnes reminded.

"Yes, but you can never be too careful. A young lady must be prepared for every occasion," Mary replied.

Agnes usually ignored such affected comments from her daughters. Mary was the worst while Sylvia only followed her older sister's example. Agnes thought Sylvia would be more like herself if not so influenced by Mary, who sometimes reminded Agnes a lot of her own stepmother. She often wondered what kind of women her girls would be while she hoped Will would be as kind and handsome as his father.

"Are we all ready now?" Agnes asked, after helping Will put on his mittens. "Yes, Mother," Mary replied. "Hurry, I'm sweating in this warm coat."

But they were delayed another minute. Kathy Bergmann chose that moment to appear on the doorstep with a fruitcake from her mother.

"Mama meant to bring it over before Christmas," Kathy said, "but what with the funeral and everything, she didn't have time."

"I didn't expect her to give me anything," said Agnes, nonetheless touched to be remembered despite Molly's recent troubles. Except for Montoni's funeral, Agnes had rarely seen Molly lately. After Agnes's father and stepmother had moved back East, the Montonis and Whitmans had lost touch with each other. But Agnes knew Molly looked on her as a daughter because her mother and Molly had once been best friends. Agnes had found it hard to visit Molly after she married Montoni because she remembered Molly as a happy young woman, despite poverty and her first husband's ill health, and Molly's sadness in recent years had unnerved her into keeping her distance. Now Agnes wished she had done more than just attend Montoni's funeral and send a gift of money. She should have gone to visit, but Christmas and her pregnancy had kept her occupied. Agnes reminded herself that since her father had moved away, Molly was now the only one left in town who had known her mother well, and Agnes did not want to lose that connection; her memories of her mother were growing dim, and she had recently been surprised to realize she was now several years older than her mother had been when she died.

Agnes accepted the fruitcake, and feeling she should give something in return, offered, "Kathy, we were just about to go sledding. We would love to have you join us."

Before Kathy could reply, Will grabbed her skirt and shouted, "Do come! Please, Kathy!"

Kathy laughed, and picking up Will, she gave him a big hug. She was sixteen now, and the maternal instinct was strong in her. She yearned for a baby, one as cute as Will, but first she needed a husband. Not even her mother's second marriage had distorted her romantic notions; Montoni had been a bad man, but Kathy honored the memory of the father she had never known, and she idolized her brother. She even had a secret fondness for Ben, her brother's attractive business partner; she hoped someday he would notice her. But if not, other men existed who might make good husbands and fathers; she was becoming obsessed with the desire to find one.

"Kathy is going to join us," Agnes told her daughters as they continued to sweat in their winter clothes.

"Oh," Mary said. Sylvia sighed. Both noted Kathy's unfashionable coat.

Seeing that Agnes and Will wanted her to tag along, Kathy overlooked the girls' lack of enthusiasm and agreed to join the party.

"I don't think you'll be warm enough," Mary tried to dissuade her. "You're not dressed for sledding."

Kathy felt self-conscious then, and she hated that Mary, three years her junior, could make her feel that way. "I'll be warm enough," she replied.

"I have an extra scarf and some heavier mittens you can borrow," Agnes said.

"No, I'm fine. I don't mind the cold," said Kathy, already regretting that she had agreed to join them.

"Let's go!" Will screamed and wiggled until Kathy set him down. Then he grabbed her hand and tried to tug her toward the door.

"Girls, fetch your sleds out back. We'll wait out front for you," said Agnes.

A few minutes later, they had walked to the eastern end of Ridge Street, where the bluff sloped down toward the lake to make an excellent hill for sledding.

"That's my grandparents' house!" said Sylvia as they passed the Hennings' former home.

"They don't live there anymore," Agnes replied.

"No," said Mary, "they have an even bigger house in New York City because they're rich!"

Mary looked at Kathy as she spoke, but Kathy ignored the ostentatious child.

"Our grandparents always send us expensive Christmas presents," Mary said. "This year Sylvia and me each got a dress made in Paris."

"Sylvia and I," said Agnes.

"Mary," Sylvia said, "Kathy has probably never owned a store bought dress, much less one from Paris. I think her mother makes all her clothes."

"Girls, that's enough," Agnes said.

"How will she ever find a husband without a decent dress?" Mary asked.

"Maybe I don't need a husband," said Kathy, denying her dearest longing.

"That's good 'cause rich men don't like poor girls," Sylvia replied.

"I'm not poor," said Kathy, "and even if I were, didn't a prince marry Cinderella?" Despite this bold retaliation, Kathy was unnerved by the girls voicing her fears.

"Yeah, but Cinderella was at least beautiful," said Mary.

"Girls, that's enough," Agnes repeated. "Do you want to go back home instead of going sledding?"

"No!" cried Will. "Be good. Don't be bad," he implored his sisters.

"Apologize to Kathy," said Agnes.

Each girl muttered, "I'm sorry." Kathy tried graciously to accept their apologies, but she felt this much-needed festive excursion was spoiled.

They had now reached the top of the sledding hill.

"Girls," said Agnes, "why don't the three of you ride down on the big sled, and Will and I will use the small one."

Mary gave her mother a funny expression, making it clear she did not want Kathy on her sled, but when Agnes glared back, Mary said nothing. Kathy saw the facial exchange and again wished she had not come, but she would not embarrass Mrs. Whitman by acknowledging her daughters' rude behavior.

"No. Me and Kathy ride," said Will, unknowingly solving the problem.

"Kathy, do you mind going with Will?" asked Agnes.

"No, Will and I can have a good time by ourselves."

Mary and Sylvia, relieved of Kathy's company, climbed onto their sled, ready to go downhill.

"Thank you, Kathy," said Agnes, feeling more tired than usual from the walk to the hill. "I'm feeling a little worn out so I'll wait until later. You go without me."

"I don't mind," Kathy assured her.

Agnes stood at the top of the hill. She watched her girls, then Will and Kathy sail down the snow-covered street. She had looked forward to this outing, but her obstinate girls now made her thankful for a moment alone. She looked out at the lake, slowly freezing over as winter progressed. January was her favorite time of year because the snow completely covered the earth; December even in this northern land occasionally could be without snow, and Christmas was so much trouble—although in the end the children's pleasure made it worthwhile. But January was a month without the bother of holidays, a month that allowed a good long rest, a month to enjoy the snow before it piled up in February and March and seemed as if it would never end. January was the slow return of longer days, the month when each night a minute or two more daylight remained before you closed the curtains, a minute or two that reflected the promise of spring's inevitable return. Agnes found pleasure in these little things, in marking the rhythm and progression of the seasons; she never complained about the weather, but marveled over the daily variety as one season changed into another, accumulating into a lifetime of natural wonders.

The children were climbing back up the hill, but Agnes still had a couple minutes before they would reach her. She continued to look out at the half frozen, silent lake, so serene this afternoon; a flood of warm sunlight made its iced surface sparkle like diamonds. Some days that massive lake roared like a bellowing monster; some days it was cruel, as when it had taken Caleb and Madeleine. But the lake was a constant in Agnes's life, something that never failed to revive her spirits when all else came and went. The lake was always there, almost like a family member, someone to quarrel with one day, but ultimately, even if begrudgingly, to love as a familiar extension of herself, its very water flowing inside her. The lake was a part of her as was the snow, the trees, and these hills she loved so well.

She felt an especial fondness for this particular spot with its distinct view of the lake. She vividly remembered one summer day when she and her mother had stood on this hill to collect lady's slippers—they had filled a whole basket with the delicate flowers, and all the while, she remembered that in the distance, through the trees—trees that were now mostly gone and replaced with large prosperous homes—she had been able to see the lake; back then there had been no grand houses, no real streets, just a small collection of wooden buildings nearly hidden along the shore of Lake Superior. At that time, she had known few children to play with, so she had named many of the trees, pretending they were her friends as much as any little boy or girl in the village. In later years, her father had frequently told her how her mother had loved this land—she wondered whether her mother had also thought of the land as a friend, a real person, a very part of her soul. Agnes loved her hometown, but she liked to remember more what it had looked like nearly thirty years ago when she was a small girl. Everything had changed since that distant spring day when she had come here to pick flowers with her mother, yet for a moment she could forget it was winter and that she stood in the middle of a fashionable neighborhood; for a moment, she could imagine it was spring in the forest and her mother was with her, listening to her childish prattle.

"Mama! Mama! We went fast! Did you see, Mama?"

She awoke from the past and turned to her son.

"Was it fun, Will?" she asked as he ran up to her, his chubby cheeks glowing red from the cold.

"I wanna go again!" he screeched with delight.

"You don't have to take him if you don't want to," Agnes told Kathy.

"I don't mind," Kathy said.

"Just don't scare him by going too fast," Agnes replied.

She watched Kathy and Will go downhill again. Then Mary and Sylvia arrived at the top for their next trip down.

Agnes perched herself on a low snowbank, simply content to exist in this beautiful place where her mother had once watched her as she now watched her children.

When Will came back, he wanted her to ride with him, so she and Kathy started taking turns going downhill until Will's little legs became exhausted from climbing back up. Agnes hoped that meant he would take a nap when they got home. Finally, she and Kathy sat on a hard crunchy snowbank while Will curled up in his mother's lap and fell asleep. She wrapped him in her scarf to keep him warm. She considered taking him home, but the afternoon sun was causing icicles to drip off nearby houses, so she thought it warm enough to let the girls sled down the hill a few more times. Since Kathy waited with her, Agnes asked after Molly.

"Mama's fine," said Kathy, not wanting to confess how her mother had moped since the funeral.

"She must miss your stepfather?"

"I imagine so, but she doesn't really mention it."

"Do you think she'll marry again?"

"Not at her age," said Kathy.

"She isn't that old is she? Maybe fifty?"

"She'll be fifty-four this year."

"That's not so old," said Agnes.

"Two husbands were enough for her, especially considering what the last one was like."

Kathy regretted the words as soon as they were spoken, not wanting to shame her family.

"I always suspected she wasn't happy with your stepfather," Agnes replied, "but I remember your own father was a kind man."

"Yes, but he was always so sick Mama had to work to support us."

"Your mother did that out of love. It's worth it for a kind man."

"Is your husband kind?" Kathy asked. "I don't mean to be rude, but I want to know these things for when I get married someday."

"Yes, Jacob's a good man. He loves me and the children, and he works hard to give us more than we need. Even when he doesn't say so, I know he loves us by his deeds."

"I don't think I'll ever get married," Kathy said.

"You will when the time is right."

"No, I don't think I want to," she lied to deny her fear of being a spinster.

"You will when the right man comes along," said Agnes.

"No, no man will ever notice me," she said, thinking of how Ben ignored her. "I guess I'm not pretty enough."

"Of course you are."

"And I'm not rich or fashionable, just like Mary and Sylvia said."

"Mary and Sylvia are just silly young girls, and I apologize for their rudeness. I don't know where they get it from—not my side of the family," said Agnes. "But Kathy, in another year you'll be a blooming beauty. I was much more plain than you at sixteen, yet Jacob took an interest in me."

"I'll be seventeen in April."

"Then love could come anytime," said Agnes. "Just be patient. You don't want to rush it. Love comes at different times for everyone, but the wait is worth it when it does come."

Kathy thought it easy for Agnes to say such things when she had a husband and did not have to spend every day wondering whether she were destined for spinsterhood.

"We better move a little, or we'll freeze sitting here," said Agnes, trying to stand up without waking Will. "The girls are almost back up the hill now."

"We can lay Will in the sled to pull him home," said Kathy.

"That's a good idea. I'm glad you came, Kathy. It was the perfect day for an excursion. I hope your mother doesn't mind that you didn't come home sooner."

"Oh no, she won't be worried," said Kathy. "Thank you for inviting me." She did not add that she had not enjoyed herself.

"Hurry girls! We're freezing!" Agnes called to her daughters still a hundred feet down the hill. Then she took another gaze at the lake as the sun began to set. "Kathy, look at how beautiful the lake is with the sky all pink and reflecting on the ice. Even with the snow and cold, how could anyone want to live anywhere else?"

"Yes, it is pretty," said Kathy, but she was too worried about her future to appreciate the present moment's glory.

Agnes asked Kathy to come home for a cup of hot chocolate, but Kathy excused herself to turn down Front Street and walk south to her mother's house. She said she should get home before dark, but truthfully, she did not want to be around Mary and Sylvia any longer. She liked Agnes, but she had not found her comments on love very reassuring. She was terribly lonely, yet she preferred to be alone with her yearnings than to feel a lack of connection while speaking to others. She wanted to be needed, especially by a man, but everyone she knew already seemed to have a full life and not need her. Except for her mother, whose need scared her.

Molly had expected Kathy to return home directly; when three hours elapsed, she grew nervous. She was not worried; Marquette had no real crime, despite Montoni's tragedy, and today was too warm to worry about someone being lost in a snowstorm or suffering from frostbite. It was just that—up until now her life had always been full with just trying to survive, but now a tremendous loneliness, a boredom gnawed at her. She had never really loved Montoni, but she was used to having a husband, to spending a great deal of energy repressing her anger; now freed of caring for him, she did not know how to fill her time.

All these empty hours gave her time to think, to feel guilt, to ask herself had she been a better wife, would he have behaved differently? All the times she had wished for his death, she had never imagined it would happen so suddenly. And now that her wish was fulfilled, she felt how evil that wish had been; she doubted whether her forgiving him was enough for her to be forgiven as well.

She had privately wept a great deal since the funeral. Sometimes she wept tears of relief that years of unhappy marriage were over; other times she wished she had been given one last chance to show kindness as she had hoped to do when she learned he had cancer. Mostly she wept because the future was unknown. All her life she had given of herself—first taking care of Fritz, and then Karl and Kathy, and finally Montoni. Never before had she realized how badly she needed to care for people; even when she was poor, she had been happy to work to help her family, but now, with the small fortune Montoni had left her, what was left for her to do?

She had spent three hours sitting in front of the window, bored and pondering her future. When she finally saw Kathy coming down the street, she noticed her daughter's womanly shape. Soon Kathy would find a man and begin her own family, and then Molly feared she would be left alone completely.

When the door opened, all Molly's fears tumbled out of her.

"Where have you been?" she accosted her daughter. "I was getting worried."

"Oh," said Kathy as she pulled off her gloves and scarf, "Agnes asked me to go sledding with her and the children."

"Oh, did you have a good time?"

"Yes."

"Where did you go?"

"Down the hill on Ridge Street. What should we have for supper?"

They went into the kitchen and worked together to make the meal.

"What did you do all afternoon, Mother?" asked Kathy, pulling out the plates.

"Oh, I—well, I read some."

"Anything good?"

"No, not really. How is Agnes? Did she like the fruitcake?" Molly turned the conversation from herself. She did not want Kathy to know she had wasted three hours staring out the window in horror at a lonely future.

By the time supper was ready, it had been dark outside for nearly an hour. They had lit the lamps in the kitchen, but now Molly went into the dining room to light the candles and close the curtains. This was the worst part of the day—the need to create light in the evening. The arrival of dark meant another day lost and wasted; lighting candles meant the start of another long, lonely, winter evening. The dining room lamps cast shadows on the walls; because the light was not strong enough to brighten the entire room, Molly felt the vast emptiness of the house. She remembered how she and Fritz had crowded into a two room cabin when they came to Marquette, but the fireplace had been right beside the kitchen table, and it cast enough heat and light to make the entire house cozy and cheerful. Now she ate in a dining room separate from where the food was prepared, then sat in a parlor separate from the other two rooms, and at night, she and Kathy slept in separate rooms divided by a hallway. And Molly had to clean all these rooms. What did two women need with so much space? She missed the little cabin she and Fritz had built; she would move back to it except that it had been destroyed in the fire of '68, and after she married Montoni, he had sold the land and pocketed the money. She could not bear all this empty lonely space.

Supper was melancholy. Kathy barely spoke; she was wondering whether the Whitman girls had been right about how hard it would be for her to find a husband. Molly could see her daughters' thoughts were far away; she felt lonely, but she preferred to mope than ask what Kathy was thinking. She remembered being Kathy's age—she knew her daughter was old enough to dream of marriage and a house of her own, and a widowed mother would not be included in that dream.

When the meal ended, they did the dishes, then sat in the lonely parlor. Molly tried to sew while Kathy read one page of a novel over and over, her thoughts refusing to fix themselves on the story. Finally, out of sheer desire for the morbid day to end, Molly complained she was tired.

"All right, I'm tired too," said Kathy, rising to kiss her mother goodnight. "Oh, I meant to ask, when is Karl coming to visit again?"

"I don't know. He rarely comes in winter. Hopefully at Easter," Molly said; Easter was so far away.

Kathy wondered how she could wait that long to see Ben.

Both women went upstairs and closed themselves in their separate bedrooms.

Kathy stood by her window with the curtain pulled aside. She gazed out into the moonlit backyard, replaying one of her favorite memories. Karl and Ben had come to visit last summer. Ben had gone into the backyard to wash up. From this same window, Kathy had watched as Ben stripped to his waist, and with his hard, boyish body glistening in the sunlight, he had lathered himself with soap and water. Kathy had never seen a man's naked chest before, and she marveled, even feeling a bit nauseous at the sight of his large nipples and the way his chest spread to his shoulders from which hung his massive arms. The power of his body frightened yet fascinated her. After she had torn her eyes away and gone to lie on the bed, the image would not vanish from her mind. She had replayed that moment every day since last summer until she longed to be held up against his naked chest, to feel his powerful arms around her. Sometimes in her daydreams, she dared tell him he was the finest on earth and if he asked, she would be his. Then her soul would cry, "Ben!" and frustrated sobs were muffled into her pillow because he had not yet noticed her.

Sunday was Cordelia's day off. There was never any exception. Since her childhood, she had faithfully kept the Sabbath. Even without her Methodist upbringing, as daughter of the righteous New England Puritans, her conscience would not allow her to do otherwise. Boarding house or not, Cordelia would allow no one to work on this day. Work included cooking, and all her boarders understood this; when one boarder had objected that his mother had always cooked a chicken dinner on Sunday, Cordelia politely but firmly informed him she was not his mother, and he was free to room elsewhere. He backed down and lived with the Whitmans for two more years. Those boarders who wished to eat on Sunday were free to go into the kitchen and make themselves cold sandwiches, but Cordelia would feed no one who was not a family member, and she would not allow cooking under any circumstances.

Sunday was also a day for family. Unlike her stern parents and grandparents, who limited their children to reading the Bible and speaking in whispers, Cordelia wanted to please her family on Sunday. She felt most restful when her children and grandchildren surrounded her. The family always gathered at the boarding house for a cold Sunday dinner, and a cake Cordelia cleverly had baked the day before. Jacob and Agnes would follow his parents home from church, carting along their three children. When the family was lucky, Will would take a nap after dinner. Mary and Sylvia wished they could nap; they found Sunday dinner dull and an unfair robbery of their free time when one of two days they were free from school had to be taken up by church and family. But the adults enjoyed this time. Agnes would play the piano, although almost solely hymns. Jacob and Nathaniel would smoke their pipes. They would all sit around and talk and read the newspapers and point out interesting stories, and just enjoy conversing with each other. For Cordelia and Agnes, the day was best if there were letters to share. Letters were always read directly after the meal, and the children were not allowed to leave the table until after they were read. The girls found this ritual the dullest of all because most of the letters were from people they did not know, or some aunt, uncle, or cousin they could barely remember. On this particular Sunday, three letters were to be read. Agnes had received a letter from Edna, while Cordelia had received two letters, the first from Suzanne, the other from Gerald and Sophia.

It was generally agreed that Gerald and Sophia's letters were the most interesting, so they were always saved for last. Cordelia had not heard from Edna in weeks, so she insisted Agnes read her daughter's letter first. Had Mary and Sylvia been old enough to remember Aunt Edna vividly, they would have remarked that her letter was as dowdy as she had been. Instead, the girls expressed their boredom with loud sighs that caused icy glares from their father while their mother read aloud.

> January 2, 1884
> Salt Lake City, Utah
> Dear Jacob and Agnes,
>   I hope you had an enjoyable Christmas. I am sorry I am so bad at writing lately, but we have been very busy here. I am the only woman here and that means I have to run the house by myself, and it is quite a task. I have a hired boy who helps me, but between ourselves we can barely feed all the men at

the ranch here, and Christmas just caused my correspondence to get away from me. Of course, the children also keep me busy. Philip is hardly a baby anymore. He started to walk last month and is already becoming a trouble. Harry is doing quite well with learning to read. All this activity makes me a proud mother and wife, but it distracts me from the project I have thrown myself into.

Uncle Darius has been filling my head with tales of his adventures as a young man along the Oregon Trail, and I have continually thought what a shame it would be not to preserve these stories for his grandchildren, so I have begun to write them down. All over the house, I have scraps of paper and loose sheets with incidents scribbled on them and approximate dates of when they happened. I keep trying to organize them, but every time I get started, one of the children has a minor crisis needing my attention, and then, Uncle Darius keeps telling me new stories. He is a neverending source of entertainment. Ultimately, I hope I will find time to organize all his stories into a book, perhaps his life story so it will not be forgotten. He says he is "tickled" that I find his stories so interesting, and that he never thought his life all that remarkable. Esau is pleased by my intended project, and he constantly tells me how lucky he is to have such a "smart" wife. I guess that is my compensation for a lack of beauty, even though he tells me I am beautiful. He is very helpful with the project because he remembers dates better than his father, especially for events that happened during his own boyhood, while Uncle Darius seems to confuse all the years together.

We had a pleasant Christmas, although I don't think I will ever reconcile myself to Christmas without snow, but now that it's January, I imagine the snow is piling up all over Marquette and you are all wishing you were in a warmer climate. Uncle Darius insists that being in this warm, dry climate will make us all live longer. For me, only time will tell, but his health remains remarkable for his age, and he can keep up with almost any of the ranch hands, although he will be seventy this year.

I hope you all had a happy Christmas, and that the packages I sent arrived in time. Please tell Mother and Father I send my love, and I will write to them very soon. Even when I do not write, none of you are ever far from my thoughts. Esau and Uncle Darius send their love as well.

Your sister, Edna

"I wish I could go see her," said Cordelia. "But I'm too old to travel now."

"Why do you say that? We can go out West sometime," Nathaniel replied.

"No," said Cordelia. "I can't leave the boarding house."

"Well, maybe they'll come to visit again," Jacob said, knowing it was pointless to argue with his mother's dedication to her establishment.

"I barely even remember them," Sylvia said.

"I know," said Cordelia, "and I've never even seen those grandsons of mine."

"We will someday," Nathaniel said.

"Only if Edna comes to visit. Maybe when the baby is a little older. But I'm happy she's married and has children now. I used to worry she would never get married, and now here it's been seven and a half years already."

"Time does fly," said Jacob.

"Well, let's read the next letter," said Agnes, wanting to get past it to the letter her parents had written to Cordelia.

"Okay, here's Suzanne's," said Cordelia.

"Just who is Suzanne?" Mary asked.

"She's an old family friend. She came to visit last summer, remember?"

"No," said Sylvia. "Is she a relative?"

"By marriage. She was once married to your Great-Grandpa Brookfield."

"My great-grandpa?" said Sylvia. "How old is she, like a hundred?"

"Oh no," laughed Cordelia, "she's younger than me."

"How can that be?"

"She married young," Jacob replied. "She was my grandpa's second wife."

"And he was her second husband," said Agnes.

"How many wives and husbands did they each have?" Sylvia sighed.

"He only had two, but Suzanne is on her third marriage now because her first two husbands died," said Jacob.

"Where does she live?" asked Mary.

"In Green Bay, well, sort of, just listen," said Cordelia, unfolding the letter and putting on her spectacles.

January 4, 1884
Green Bay, Wisconsin
Dear Cordelia,

    I am sorry I did not write at Christmas, but we have been extremely busy lately. You may remember that when I came to visit last summer, I mentioned my husband's business might be expanding. We are now moving to Chicago where he is opening up a new store, so I have been occupied with packing everything in the house. I will miss this house because it is the longest I have ever lived in one place, but we have bought a beautiful, large home in Chicago, although now with most of the children grown, I don't know that we need such a large one, but my husband insists I have only the finest.

"Is she rich?" asked Mary.

"Yes, I believe so," Cordelia replied, "but it's impolite to interrupt."

Mary did not apologize. Cordelia continued to read anyway.

Only my two children by Frederick, Lucius and Frederick Jr., will be with us now since my daughters are all grown and married, and Gervase and Francois are moving to Menominee to begin their own store independent of Frederick and Amedee's. Amedee and Frederick will stay partners, Amedee taking over complete control of the Green Bay store while Frederick runs the store in Chicago. They also opened a store in Milwaukee this past autumn, so they are quite a company now. It amazes me that we prosper like this when I remember how little my Jean and I had when we lived in Marquette.

I think often about you all, although it is strange to think of Marquette now. I cannot believe how well the city has recovered and grown after the fire the year I moved away. Green Bay is a flourishing city, but I will always have an attachment to Marquette. I am excited about living in Chicago and hope I will be as happy there. It is so big and I am so used to smaller towns that I don't know how I will adjust.

I must get back to packing as we are taking the train to Chicago tomorrow, and a few things still must be done, but I did want to write and give you my new address. Give my love to all inquiring friends there. Please write when you are able, and I promise a longer letter soon. I hope you had a wonderful holiday season.

Love, Suzanne

"Gee, they own stores all over the place," said Sylvia.

"What kind of business do they have?" Mary asked.

"Several feed stores and a mercantile also I think," said Cordelia.

Mary turned up her nose. "I can't believe a relative of mine runs a feed store."

"She isn't a blood relative," Cordelia replied. "But she was my stepmother for a short time."

"How many kids does she have?" asked Sylvia. "It sounds like a lot."

"I think seven," Cordelia said, "from two different husbands."

"We don't have that many in our family."

"Well, they are Catholics," said Cordelia.

"Lots of families have more than us, and you might be one of seven yet," Jacob smiled and winked at Agnes.

"I don't want any more brothers or sisters," said Mary. "Will is enough trouble."

"Yeah," Sylvia agreed. "We especially don't want any brothers who grow up to own feed stores. How dreadful!"

"It's not much different than owning a farm like I do," Jacob told his daughters. "Besides, we've always been proud to consider Suzanne as family. She was very kind to my grandparents."

"That's true," said Cordelia. "She couldn't have loved them more if she had been their own daughter."

"If she was like his daughter, why'd Great-Grandpa marry her?" asked Sylvia.

"To help her out. Her first husband had just died," Cordelia said, "and your great-grandfather had just lost his wife, after Suzanne had helped to nurse her, so he married her and left her money in exchange for the good care she took of him."

"You mean she was his servant, but he married her to leave her money? Is that why she's richer than us?" asked Mary, feeling cheated out of an inheritance.

"No, dear, her husband and her brother earned their own fortunes, and my father left plenty behind for all of us."

Mary did not believe this. She begrudged the loss of money that would have trickled down to her if it had not been for this Suzanne woman.

"Can we read the last letter now?" asked Agnes.

"Of course," said Cordelia, passing it to her. "Why don't you read it to us?"

"Is it all written by my stepmother?"

"Yes, but she wrote some messages in it from your father, and he promises to write you soon."

Agnes was disappointed not to see her father's handwriting, but she read it anyway.

December 16, 1883
Paris, France
My dear Cordelia,
  Gerald and I arrived here in Paris yesterday from London. We had a miserable voyage over the channel. The waves were so intense, and the boat so small. You know I have always dreaded the sea, and I told you how I suffered from seasickness on the passage from New York to England. But I had no idea what suffering was. I was more miserable in the few hours spent crossing the English Channel than I was during the entire crossing of the Atlantic. I do not know how I ever let Gerald convince me to step on a boat again, but I have always dearly longed to see Paris, and now, here I am,

although I have barely gone anywhere yet, and so far, I am not impressed by what little I have seen.

I did nothing yesterday except rest and see that the rooms were properly cleaned and cared for. We have a pert little French maid, who, I fear, has a tendency to be saucy and smirk at my pronunciation. She is a very lazy and smelly girl, I might add. Indeed, the entire city smells of the gutters. We will attend the opera tonight, which is said to be a grand building, far surpassing that in New York. I forget the name of the performance, something in Italian I think. I mainly go to the Opera to see the latest Paris fashions and look up our American acquaintances who are here wintering. Gerald bought me a new light blue dress with velvet trim for this evening. He spoils me, and I willingly let him.

I must tell you more about London since the last letter I wrote was just after we arrived there. It is a beautiful city like I imagined. The monuments are impressive throughout, from Buckingham Palace to Westminster Abbey, but the weather is atrocious. It rained nearly everyday, and snowed some as well. Usually there was a thick heavy fog or mist that soaked you through to your bones, not even as pleasant as the long winters we have both known. I would have preferred a snowstorm. Of course, I found it disappointing that I did not even catch a glimpse of the Queen, but she never goes out much since her husband died, though it's been over twenty years. I made Gerald take me to the theatre many nights in hopes of catching a glimpse of the Prince of Wales, but we had no luck there either. There was a Duchess staying at our hotel for a few days, but she never came out of her room. Gerald and I spent many hours at the British Museum. He was utterly fascinated with the place, but to me, it was just a bunch of old ruins I knew nothing about. The food in London was terrible—everything I ate had cucumbers or eggs in it, and often we could not order a decent meal because we could not understand the waitress's poor English. I saw enough of London and am thankful now to be in Paris. I'm sure I'll find the French much more fashionable, and I cannot wait to go shopping and buy lovely trinkets and clothes.

I am tired now and sorely in need of an afternoon nap before dressing for dinner and the opera so I will close.

Love, Sophia

P.S. I will certainly send you a present, but I have not had the chance to look here in Paris yet. I saw nothing to suit you in London.

P.P.S. Gerald says to tell Agnes he will write her very soon. Business and taking me out keep him very busy, but I will make sure he writes.

Disappointed that the letter contained barely a word about her father, Agnes could not help remark, "It's not fair that people who don't appreciate London should get to see it." Many times she had dreamt of visiting the places Dickens and Jane Austen had written about, yet she doubted her stepmother had even bothered to glance at Dickens's grave in Westminster Abbey.

"I'm sure your father will write soon like he promised," said Jacob.

"This one just came on Friday," said Cordelia, "so probably by the end of next week there'll be a letter from Gerald."

"I'm happy for my stepmother," Agnes replied. "Now she has the fashionable life she always wanted."

"She does deserve some happiness," Cordelia said, "although Paris fashions will never make up for the children she lost."

Nathaniel winced. He knew Cordelia loved her sister and would speak no ill of her, but he often thought Sophia had cared more for her children after they were gone.

"Grandma, how come you've never been to Europe?" asked Sylvia.

"Because your grandpa and I are not rich."

"But you're not poor, Grandma?"

"No, but neither are we rich."

"Then what are you?"

"Middle class."

"Oh," said Sylvia, thinking how dull that seemed.

"I'm going to be rich when I'm older," said Mary.

"You'll have to marry a rich husband then," Nathaniel replied.

"No, Grandpa and Grandma Henning will leave me their money when they die."

"Mary, don't talk like that," Jacob scolded. "We hope they'll live for many years yet."

"Well, I don't see why my grandparents are rich and we're not. When can I go to Europe?"

"Never, if you continue with that attitude," said Jacob.

"But Marquette is so boring."

"Marquette is a fine city," Cordelia told her, "and you're better off here than in Europe. If Europe were so wonderful, Marquette wouldn't be full of so many people who came here from Europe."

"Who in Marquette came from Europe?"

"Well, Mrs. Montoni for example. She came here from Ireland and her first husband came from Germany and her second husband from Italy."

"Oh, those countries," moaned Mary. "They're not the same as England or France."

"There are plenty of people around here from Cornwall," Jacob replied.

"Where's that?" asked Mary.

"It's in England," said Agnes. "Really, don't you learn any geography at school?"

"Speaking of Molly," said Cordelia. "I wonder how she is. I haven't seen her since the funeral."

"Kathy came over to bring me a fruitcake a few days ago," said Agnes.

"Did she say how her mother is? I hear Molly has taken her husband's death very hard."

"I can't imagine why," Nathaniel grinned.

Cordelia gave him a glare that said, "Don't speak that way in front of the children."

"Kathy didn't say much at all," replied Agnes. "She went sledding with me and the children though. She seemed to be daydreaming a lot. I think she's at the age when girls start to think about love."

"Love?" said Mary. "Who'd ever love her with that hideous nose?"

"Nose? I never noticed anything wrong with her nose," said Cordelia.

"Neither have I," said Agnes.

"You haven't!" said Mary. "Why it's awful! It's all turned up and funny looking. It's very unfashionable."

"It's not as awful," said Jacob, "as rude girls who make fun of people's appearances. You are excused from the table, Mary. Go into the parlor and read one of the gospels for the next half hour, and I will come to quiz you on it."

"Fine," Mary replied, feigning relief to escape the dull adults.

"May I be excused too?" asked Sylvia.

"No," said Jacob, "you'll only distract your sister from her Bible lesson."

"Honestly, I don't know what gets into her," said Agnes after Mary had left the dining room. "We've tried to raise her to be kind and polite, but she thinks breeding is limited to fashionable clothes."

"She'll grow out of it," said Cordelia. "She's just at that age."

"Who's at the door?" Nathaniel wondered at the sound of a knock.

"I don't know," said Cordelia. "The boarders all know enough to walk right in."

Everyone listened to recognize the visitor's voice as Nathaniel went into the hall and opened the front door. They heard only muffled voices from the dining room. Then Nathaniel returned with a tall young man in a tattered jacket and cap. The stranger respectfully removed his cap at the sight of the ladies.

"Cordelia, we've got ourselves another boarder here," said Nathaniel.

"Oh," Cordelia replied, standing up and smoothing out her skirt as she assumed a business like air. "Are you looking for a room, young man?"

"Yes, please. I just arrived in town and need a place to stay."

Cordelia stated the cost and inquired whether he had work. She did not like to board unemployed people after she had once had a runaway in the night.

"No, but I will go out looking first thing in the morning," he said.

He had an Irish accent, which made Cordelia ask, "Do you have family here?"

"No, I don't know anyone here, but I thought I might find work in the mines."

"You're Irish?"

"Yes," he muttered, fearing she would now turn him away. He had learned in New York that the Irish were not wanted in America any more than in England.

"And you just arrived?"

"Yes, on the train from back East," he replied. "I do have some money. I can pay you in advance for a week, and then if I can't find work, I'll leave. I won't give you no trouble."

Cordelia looked him up and down as she considered. She noted fatigue from the long journey in his drooping face.

"I'm sure it'll be fine, Mother," Jacob decided for her. He stood up to shake the young man's hand. "Hello, I'm Jacob Whitman."

"Patrick O—McCarey," said the young Irishman.

"Well, Patrick, let me help you with your luggage," said Jacob, taking a bag from the young man's hand.

"Jacob, I don't know—" Cordelia began.

"I know, Mother; the room next to the Dalrymples is empty."

"Ye-es," she said. "I hope the room is okay. I'm afraid it's not large. The Dalrymples will be your next-door neighbors. They're a newly married couple."

"Thank you," said Patrick.

"Follow me," said Jacob. "I'll show you the way."

The young man went upstairs while the proprietress stood awkwardly in the dining room.

"It'll be okay," Agnes told her mother-in-law. "Jacob is a good judge of character."

"I hope so," said Cordelia. She had not liked what she thought was a shifty look in the Irishman's eye.

Five minutes later, Patrick O—McCarey was left alone in his new room. He sat on the bed, exhausted and nervous about how close he had come to slipping up. Why had he chosen a name starting with "Mc" and not "O"? It would have been easier to say then. Well, he didn't think they had suspected anything. He just hoped he could find work tomorrow because that Mrs. Whitman looked as if she could become unpleasant if he did not. She obviously did not want to take him in at all. Her son seemed real decent though. He thought of going back downstairs to ask whether they had any suggestions for where he might look for work. But they were apparently having some sort of family get together, so he did not want to disturb them further.

It upset him to see a happy family together; he did not need to see that now. Not after all he had gone through these past several months—and by himself; that was the worst part. If just one person from home had come with him—but there had been no time. And those cousins he had looked up in New York—they had been decent to him, but only decent, not friendly. Not like family as he had hoped they would be. They were sure he would bring them trouble, and that had scared Patrick, who did not think trouble would follow him over the ocean to another country. He had heard America was a land of freedom, but since he had gotten here, he had constantly looked over his shoulder. This town—Marquette—was remote though; he doubted anyone would trace him here.

He had experienced no amount of obstacles to get here. He had not bought any train tickets, just stowed away on several freight cars to wherever they led him. He had almost been caught in Cleveland. That had been close. If the police had nabbed him, they might have shipped him back to Ireland, and that would have been the death of him. For all he knew, they might even have shot him right here in America for theft since he had not paid for a train ticket.

God, what a mess he had gotten himself into. And now he had given that Mrs. Whitman the last of his money except for a dollar. He would have to stretch that to eat on until he found work. But at least he had a bed to sleep in. He would get some rest this next week and live like a human being again, and hopefully, he would find work and figure out whether it were safe to stay here or whether he should move on.

He stared out the window, wondering what it would be like to live in this town. It was horribly cold, and he had never seen so much snow. In Ireland, the county would have been shut down for a week with such a snowfall, yet here the train had sliced between the snowbanks without trouble. These Americans seemed miracle workers with all their industry. How brave these people must be to live in this cold, frozen land; no wonder they had their freedom; he felt warmer just to think freedom could exist here. He was still frightened, but if he could be free, he might still find happiness.

He had wanted to remain in New York or go to Chicago, but the Irish were all over those cities, and for now, he thought it best to hide out from his own people; he did not know what connections his countrymen here might have back in Ireland that could let the British find him. He was better off where no one would suspect his past. Even if the police learned what boat he had taken, and that he had arrived in New York, and even if among the Irish hordes in New York, his cousins were tracked down and interrogated, they did not know what train he had stowed away on, much less where he had switched trains. He could be anywhere in the United States, and millions of his countrymen were in this land; true many were second or third generation—he knew many had migrated during the potato famines, and unlike himself, they must have lost their Irish brogue, but the thousands of Irish here made it nearly impossible to track him. Surely, in a year or two the British would quit looking for him, and already several months had passed. He would be safe soon; he had to keep telling himself that or he would give himself up in panic.

He had better rest now and try to stop thinking about it. The landlady's son had said he could make himself a sandwich in the kitchen, but he was not even hungry—he just wanted to sleep. He would have to find work tomorrow, and prospective employers would ask the inevitable questions: where had he come from? why had he left home? why had he come here? what about his family? did he have relatives? were they also coming? Patrick was too tired right now to invent answers to all those questions. Instead, he pulled off his pants and shirt and crawled under the bedcovers, soon drifting into a deep and relatively peaceful sleep.

🍁　　　　🍁　　　　🍁

"If he's going to find a job, he had better get out of bed," Cordelia said about her new boarder the next morning.

"He must be tired after his long journey," said Nathaniel. "Besides, it's such a cold morning that you can't blame him for wanting to stay rolled up in those quilts."

"It's eight-thirty; I can't be making breakfast all morning."

"It can't hurt to wait a little longer, but I'll go up and see whether he's hungry."

Nathaniel found Patrick dressed and sitting on the edge of the bed, putting on his shoes.

"Breakfast is waiting."

"Thank you. I'll be right down," said Patrick. "Does it snow like this all the time?"

He had been staring out the window, where fluffy penny size snowflakes were steadily drifting down.

"Pretty often," smiled Nathaniel. "Didn't you notice how high the snow-banks are?"

"I never imagined there could be so much snow," said Patrick.

"Don't you get snow in Ireland?"

"Not like this."

"You'll see a lot more of it. Sometimes we even get snow in May."

Patrick followed his host downstairs to the table. Cordelia placed breakfast before him, but she failed to be her usual friendly self; she distrusted a man who had come here without purpose and had not acquired work beforehand. That he had messed up her morning schedule did not please her either. Patrick, noticing she seemed irritated, just assumed she was generally unfriendly. He ate in silence while Nathaniel regaled him with tales of the town's history, but when ten o'clock had come and Nathaniel had only reached the fire of '68, Patrick excused himself to go out and find work.

"If we have to throw him out at the end of the week," Cordelia warned her husband as she washed the breakfast dishes two hours behind schedule, "you're the one who'll have to tell him. You and Jacob insisted on letting him stay when I knew better."

Meanwhile, Patrick trudged through the snow, shivers running down his back as he gazed upon houses half buried in three-foot snowbanks. "The roads will practically be tunnels if this snow keeps up," he thought. Nathaniel had told him no boats could run on the lake during the winter, which made him fear he had arrived at the worst time of year to find work. In Ireland, he would have survived as a homeless man if worse came to worst, but he did not see how anyone could survive in this cold land without shelter, and he only had money enough to pay room and board for a few days. He could not even purchase a train ticket back to New York, or anywhere for that matter, and he was tired of being a stowaway.

When Patrick reached Marquette's business district, he soon learned no jobs were available. No clerks were needed at the First National Bank. No laborers were needed on the docks since no boats were running. The railroads did not need anyone to pound spikes. When he inquired, he learned no miners were currently being hired in nearby Negaunee, and he did not know whether he could afford to travel there anyway. None of the stores on Washington, Front, or Superior Streets needed workers, and none of the restaurants needed cooks—he could not cook, but in desperation, he lied to no avail. None of the saloons even needed bartenders.

By early afternoon, he had about given up. He thought of going back to the boarding house, but he did not want his landlady to know he had been unsuccessful. He was starving for lunch, but he knew she did not provide noontime meals, and he did not want to spend money he could not yet afford, so he continued to walk about the town, until he felt awkward from walking up and down the business streets, and a little dizzy because he was so hungry. To avoid everyone's eyes, he climbed uphill and walked through the residential neighborhoods of Bluff, Ridge, and Arch Streets.

After another hour of walking, he was so cold he was ready to return to the boarding house when he saw an old woman trying to shovel off her front steps. She looked as if she could barely lift the shovel, and she had only removed a couple feet of snow.

"Let me help you," he said.

"Oh, well—thank you," she replied. "I wouldn't mind a little help."

Patrick took the shovel and scooped part of the path while she stood and watched. He was surprised by the snow's wet heaviness, and it amazed him that this old woman had shoveled as much as she had. He had never seen such snow, never had to shovel it since in Ireland rarely more than an inch or two would fall at a time.

"I'd say we got a good eight inches last night," said the woman.

"Yes, I guess so," he replied.

"Where are you from?" she asked. "You sound English?"

Patrick was almost offended by the comment, but he suspected these Americans could not distinguish between accents. If he pretended to be English, maybe—but he had already told his landlord's family he was from Ireland.

"No, I'm Irish," he said.

"My son-in-law's Irish. Are you new in town? I don't recall seeing you around."

"I just arrived," he said. He did not want to give too much personal information, but he added, "I've been looking for a job."

"Oh, well—the young man who usually shovels me out has a bad case of bronchitis. There's a lot of people he shovels for. Maybe you could take over for him, just until he's better or you find something more steady?"

"Oh no, I was just trying to be helpful, I—"

"Now, I'm going to give you some money for helping me out, because I do appreciate it, and I certainly didn't want to do it myself. When you finish, you come inside and I'll pay you, and I'll give you that young man's address too; maybe you can help him out while he's ill."

"But I wouldn't want to take his business."

"Take his business? Why, he'll have no business if someone doesn't do the work for him. I'm sure he would rather someone help him until he feels better so he doesn't lose his customers. Besides, he's a nice young man, and he worries about us old folks when he can't take care of us. Now you finish up, and when you come in, I'll see whether I can't find you something warm to drink as well."

Patrick thought he might as well humor the lady. His fingers were numb and his nose was running from the cold, but he put all his strength into shoveling, soon finding it easiest to scoop half off the top of the little banks and toss the snow, then go back for the bottom layer rather than try to lift it all at once. He had never imagined snow could be so heavy.

"Now, here's the address," said the old lady, when he went inside. "You go straight over to his house and tell him I sent you. And here's some money for you," she said. "I usually pay a dime, but I'm giving you double just for your kindness to an old woman in need."

"Oh, no, I—"

"And here's a cup of hot chocolate."

He was too nervous to sit down, but she insisted. He feared she would be like the old women back home, ready to pry into his affairs, but instead she rattled on, telling him how she had come to Marquette from Ohio, where they hardly got any snow by comparison, and then she talked about how her husband had died two years ago, and about the Irishman her daughter had married that he would have to meet. Patrick found it hard to get away, but when the clock chimed out that it was only an hour until suppertime, he excused himself by saying he should go find the young man who did her shoveling. She wished him goodbye, and he promised to come back for the next snowfall. Even if shoveling snow only made him a dime or two, it might keep him from starving. If nothing else, he might shovel in exchange for meals.

The snow removal man looked deadly pale from his illness, but he was pleased by Patrick's proposition.

"I've got more customers than I can take care of as it is," he said. "Maybe we can form a partnership for the rest of the winter. We can divide up the customers to make sure everyone gets shoveled out. I have a regular job anyway, so I just do the shoveling on the side, and some of my customers get tired of waiting." He scribbled on a piece of paper for a minute, then handed it to Patrick. "You go visit these addresses tomorrow and do what you can for them. Most of the time, I can do a porch and sidewalk in twenty to thirty minutes depending on how big it is. I'll lend you my snowshovel for now, but you buy your own as soon as you're able."

Patrick hated the cold and the snow, and he was starting to think he hated this town, but any work was better than none, and even if he had to work out in the cold every day, at least if he made money, he could pay for a warm room to return to at night.

Cordelia met him at the boarding house door that evening.

"Why, you're soaked with snow. You better get those pants and that jacket off before they thaw, or you'll catch pneumonia."

"It's all right. I better get used to it," Patrick replied.

"We all have to get used to it with the winters here," she said, eyeing the snow melting all over her front hall.

"No, I mean, I got work shoveling snow for the rest of the winter."

"Oh," she said. "How will you support yourself when spring comes?"

"I don't know, but now you don't need to worry about my paying rent until the spring."

"Oh, I don't worry about that," she replied, as if his payments had never been a concern with her. "We're eating in a few minutes, so you better go upstairs and put on something dry."

Patrick went and changed into his only other pair of pants. They were his best pair, but he had no choice. He made a mental note to light his stove after supper so his work pants would dry; he would have to wear them again tomorrow.

He was cold and exhausted, but jubilant. He had survived his first day in this strange, frozen town, and even though his back, arms and legs ached from the unfamiliar exercise, he felt proud of the strength he had found to lift the snow and clear that kind lady's porch. He also reflected that it was when he had not been looking for work, but only intending to be kind, that he had found what he needed. He imagined he would be even more sore tomorrow after a full day's shoveling, but he knew his stamina would increase as his muscles accustomed themselves to the work. He was thankful just to have a job.

A few weeks later, Patrick found himself shoveling snow just down the street from St. Peter's Cathedral. He had not yet met the person he shoveled for, but his landlady had said the woman was a friend of hers, and she would appreciate him going to shovel her walk whenever more than six inches of snow fell since she was getting too old for such work and her daughter did not have the strength for it. This was Patrick's first visit to the house; he had been told by Mrs. Whitman to shovel and then go to the front door and he would be paid. He felt awkward shoveling the driveway without first speaking to the employer, but Mrs. Whitman promised him that Mrs. Montoni was a good honest woman.

As he shoveled, he could see the towers of the new St. Peter's Cathedral rising up high above all Marquette's other buildings.

"I wouldn't be surprised if by the end of winter," he thought, "those towers are the only things left sticking out of the snow. I don't think it will ever stop snowing here."

Yet he was thankful that the snow's constancy provided him with an income. Even on the rare day when it did not snow, he had plenty of work catching up with the previous day's accumulation. He found it hardest to adjust to the cold; despite long underwear and flannel beneath a heavy coat, a scarf, mittens, and a wool hat, he was still cold. Worse, when he shoveled, he began to sweat profusely, but once he unbuttoned his coat to cool off, he started to shiver. When he finished shoveling, the sweat drenched his clothes, then froze until ice chunks clung inside his coat. Then when he started to shovel out his next customer, he would get hot, melting the ice chunks in his coat, causing streams of water and sweat to run down his chest. Shoveling was the worst job he could imagine, more miserable than being down in the darkness of a mine. Sometimes he wondered whether being trapped in an English prison would not have been a lighter sentence than exile in this bitterly cold land.

As he shoveled today, he could not help looking up at the great cathedral. He had not prayed much since he arrived in America. Could he hear his landlady's nightly prayers, he would have been surprised that she believed him a great sinner because "all Irishmen are supposed to be strict Catholics, yet that one never goes to church." Patrick did not go to Mass because he had no great trust in God or the Church. But the sight of the cathedral made him think about religion and the Catholic Church that he had fled from just as much as he had fled from the British. The sandstone walls of St. Peter's suggested a warmth inside that was lacking in his own heart, but he could not bring himself to go inside, to become part of a faith community that would remind him of home.

"Even in this distant land," he thought, "the Church exists. I wonder whether it oppresses people here, or whether it actually carries out the good work for which it was intended."

Whatever the answer, Patrick was not inclined to find out. He had had enough of religion, and he felt in good conscience he could never set foot inside a church again.

That afternoon, Kathy walked home from visiting with her girlfriend Mary Mitchell; she had partly gone out of interest for Mary's older brother, Roger, but looking at him was only small compensation for the absence of Ben, and Roger paid even less attention to her. Despite her inability to attract the opposite sex, Kathy was not an unattractive young lady. Nor should it be assumed that because her brother was brawny and hulking from years of working in the woods, that she lacked a delicate womanly figure. Kathy's face was bony, but her skin was soft and her complexion slightly dark, perhaps from being offset by her deep brown hair that she had begun to wear up to proclaim her adulthood. If her nose were a tad turned up, as her detractor Mary Whitman had said, it was also delicate and small, and beneath it were beautifully formed lips eagerly awaiting love's first kiss.

As she approached home, Kathy was surprised to see a man shoveling her sidewalk. At first, she thought it might be Karl or Ben come to make a surprise visit; she knew they rarely visited in winter because it was the height of logging season, but the hope of seeing Ben made her walk quickly until she was standing behind the man. Then she tapped him on the shoulder and uttered a friendly, "Hello."

When a stranger turned around, she instantly stepped back with a surprised, "Oh!" followed by a hasty apology.

"I thought you were someone else."

Patrick paused to catch his breath in the bitter air, then said, "That's all right."

Kathy took a few seconds to look him over; she thought herself silly now because except for his height, he shared no similarities with Ben. This stranger's heavy winter overcoat made him appear more broad-shouldered than he really was, and now that he faced her, she could see he was rather thin. He did, however, have nice green eyes, and altogether, he was not too bad looking.

Patrick felt self-conscious as Kathy stared at him. To break the silence, he asked, "Are you Miss Montoni?"

"Oh no!" she said, caught between laughter and insult.

"I'm sorry. I thought this was the Montoni house."

"My mother is Mrs. Montoni," Kathy replied, "but I'm Miss Bergmann."

"It's nice to meet you, Miss Bergmann." He politely pulled off his knitted hat, then felt foolish because he realized his hair had stood straight up. "I'm Patrick."

"It's nice to meet you, Patrick. Aren't you boarding with the Whitmans?"

Kathy's mother had told her not to speak to strange men, but this one looked harmless, even vulnerable, as he nervously tried to smooth down his static-filled hair, which was impossible while he was still wearing his glove. She wished to put him at his ease, so she chatted a moment rather than going directly into the house as her mother would want.

"Yes, I live there," he replied, practically staring at her. He had never seen such a cute little nose. "What kind of name is Bergmann?"

"German."

"Oh," he said.

"You can call me Kathy if you like."

"All right."

He seemed nice, but shy, as if he wanted to talk but did not know what to say. "Have you met many people in Marquette?" she asked.

"No, just my landlords and their other boarders."

"The Whitmans are nice, but old—you probably want to meet younger people."

"I don't know," he said, afraid to agree to anything when he might have to flee town suddenly. "I'm not sure how long I'll be here."

"Why? Don't you like Marquette?"

"It's all right. There's a lot of snow."

"I love the snow," said Kathy, "but I was born here, so I guess I'm used to it."

"But how can you live like this? You're stuck in the house all winter."

"Oh no, we go sledding, snowshoeing, ice skating—winter gives us plenty to do."

Patrick had never heard of snowshoeing, and he did not know anyone in Ireland who could afford the luxury of ice skates.

"I've never gone ice skating," he said.

"A couple friends and I are going Saturday. You can come with us if you want."

He wanted to; then he imagined himself tumbling onto his face.

"I don't own any ice skates," he said.

"My brother probably has some you can use," she replied.

"Would he mind?"

"No, he doesn't live with us anymore, and he rarely comes home in winter. Besides, he's probably outgrown his old skates by now. I'm sure there are some old ones in the closet."

"Oh," Patrick considered. He would feel foolish if he showed up to go skating only to find her brother's skates did not fit him; then he would not be able to go after all. But he was lonely, and this little German girl was very attractive to a man who had not had a friend in several months.

"All right, I would like that," he said.

He hoped he would like it. He wondered how hard it was to ice skate.

"Stop by Saturday morning around nine-thirty. We're going for ten, but if you come early, then we can find a pair of skates to fit you."

"Thank you," he said, feeling his insides pulse rapidly at the thought that friends might be derived from this excursion.

"You're welcome," Kathy smiled. "I better go now or my mother will be worried that I'm home late."

"Goodbye then," said Patrick, retrieving the shovel he had stuck in the snowbank while talking to her.

"Goodbye. I'll see you Saturday," said Kathy, rushing up the path to the house. She had just caught a glimpse of her mother peeking out the window, so she prepared herself for her mother's worrisome questions, but she intended boldly to announce that she had invited her new friend to go ice skating.

Patrick finished his work while replaying in his mind all he could remember from his conversation with Kathy. When he was done shoveling, he went to the front door to receive his payment. Kathy smiled when she opened the door. She began to hand him the coins when from the kitchen, Patrick heard Mrs. Montoni yell, "Kathy! Can you come here right away!"

"Sorry," said Kathy. "I'll see you Saturday." She quickly placed the money in his hand, then shut the door, infuriated; she knew her mother intended to keep her from speaking to the young man.

Patrick did not mind her abruptness. He was elated just to have caught one more glimpse of the friendly "little German girl" as he already fondly thought of her.

That evening as usual, Patrick ate at the boarding house. His supper companions consisted of Nathaniel and Cordelia, their live-in kitchen girl who served the meal, a married couple named Dalrymple and the husband's father, old Mr. Dalrymple. The boarding house's other rooms were currently empty. Patrick was slowly becoming comfortable among the other boarders, and after Kathy's invitation for Saturday, he almost felt merry. Nevertheless, he said little during the meal until Mr. Whitman asked, "So Mr. McCarey, did you shovel out our friends today?"

"You mean the Montonis?" asked Patrick.

"Yes. Mrs. Montoni is a countrywoman of yours, you know."

Patrick was momentarily stunned. "I thought they were Italian, but I met the daughter who told me her name, Bergmann, was German. She looked German."

"Well, yes sort of," said Nathaniel, trying to think how to explain.

"Mrs. Montoni," Cordelia took over, not trusting a man to remember the details of relationships, "is Irish, but her first husband was a German, so the daughter, Kathy, is half-and-half, as is her older brother Karl, but then when Mr. Bergmann died, his wife married an Italian named Montoni, but she didn't have any children with him. Her second husband died just before Christmas. Poor thing, she's been rather depressed ever since."

"Imagine that," Patrick could not help remarking. "In this country, an Irishwoman can marry both a German and an Italian!"

"They're all Catholics, so it doesn't matter," said Cordelia.

Catholics or not, such differences were surprising to Patrick.

"This is an odd country," he said.

"Lots of Catholics live around here; many of them came for religious freedom just like you," said Cordelia; she was American enough to believe in religious freedom even for Catholics.

Patrick had not mentioned his religion since his arrival, and he felt annoyed by her assumptions.

"I'm not Catholic," he stated.

"Oh, I thought all Irish were Catholics? What are you then?" Cordelia asked.

He wanted to reply that he did not believe in God, but he feared he would be thrown out of his lodgings if he made such an answer to God-fearing Mrs. Whitman.

"Um, I'm Presbyterian," he lied.

"I was a Presbyterian before I married," said Mrs. Dalrymple.

"Oh," Patrick said. He knew nothing about Presbyterians; in fact, he rather thought of them as the enemy since there were lots of British ones in Ireland; now he had just created more trouble for himself.

Mrs. Dalrymple added, "But I became a Baptist like Charles when I married."

"And what religion are you?" Patrick asked his landlords to draw attention away from his own religious persuasion.

"We are Methodists," Nathaniel replied. "But my mother's family were Quakers."

"And my family were originally Puritans when they left England, like Nathaniel's father's family," said Cordelia.

Patrick had suspected these people were English; he feared they might still have friends in the mother country from whom they could learn he was a wanted man.

"Our families have changed religions over the years, but they're allowed to," said Nathaniel. "That's why they came here: for religious freedom."

"Do you know anyone in England?" Patrick asked.

"Oh no," said Nathaniel. "I wouldn't speak to an Englishman if I met one, not after how they acted in 1776 and 1812."

"Oh," said Patrick, ignorant of those dates' significance.

"Thankee, sir," roared out old Mr. Dalrymple. "I applaud you for that. Damn all the English. Damn them everyone to Hell. They drove me father out of the highlands of Scotland, and—"

"Oh father," moaned his son, "that was over seventy years ago."

"A Scot never forgets!" cried the old man. "We never can forget the crimes the bloody English inflicted upon our people!"

"I agree," said Patrick, suddenly feeling more at home in America. "The English have been cruel to the Irish as well."

Then he felt he had said too much. Would anyone suspect him now? But old Mr. Dalrymple was beaming at him with a glow of camaraderie. This America was a queer place. Everyone seemed to be allowed to say and think whatever he wanted. You could have been shot in Ireland for saying what any of them had said against the English tonight.

After supper, Patrick returned to his room and sat staring into the fire.

"Imagine that!" he kept repeating to himself. "An Irishwoman marrying a German and an Italian. Anything is possible in this country. The old rules from Europe don't seem to matter here."

For the first time since he had arrived in America, he began to ponder his future. The possibilities seemed endless. Just thinking of whom he might marry was dizzying. He had never imagined any wife but an Irish peasant girl. Now he might marry anyone he wished, even a German. German girls were rather pretty.

All week, Patrick looked forward to the skating party. Then Friday night, a blizzard sprung up and lake effect snow buried Marquette.

"I was supposed to go skating today," Patrick said to Mr. Dalrymple the next morning at breakfast.

"You can't go in this weather."

"Should I go over to the Montonis' house to say I can't go?"

"I doubt they'll expect you," said Mr. Whitman.

"What are you men discussing?" Mrs. Dalrymple asked, entering the room.

"Patrick here thinks he can still go ice skating today," said Mr. Dalrymple.

"Not unless he wants to be lost in a snowbank," Mrs. Dalrymple said. "I'd never go out in this horrible storm. Just the other day I heard about a man who died because he got lost during a blizzard while trying to walk from his barn to his house because he couldn't see the way back."

"No, you better not go out," Mr. Dalrymple said.

Patrick knew they were right, but he felt Nature had cheated him.

"Maybe you can go next week," Mrs. Dalrymple told him, but he spent a lonely, sad day after that.

Because of the blizzard, Patrick went to shovel for the Montonis on Monday, and as he had hoped, Kathy came outside to ask whether he could go skating the next Saturday.

"My brother just wrote to say he'll be coming to visit this weekend with his business partner, Ben, so you'll have a chance to meet them," she said.

Patrick nervously anticipated next Saturday. He felt he might finally make some friends close to his age. Mr. Dalrymple was close to his age, but he was married, and so while they were friendly, they could not be true chums. Perhaps Kathy's brother and his partner would befriend him, but Patrick was also nervous about meeting Kathy's brother; not that he had yet formed any clear intentions toward Kathy. In fact, when Mr. Whitman had told him, "Wait until you meet Karl Bergmann; he's a giant of a man," Patrick had thought it best not to have intentions.

He was nearly nauseous with anxiety when Saturday came. The morning was sunny, ideal for skating, but walking to the Montonis' house, he felt miserably warm. He was sweating profusely, and he guessed it was not because of his heavy overcoat.

"Oh good, you came," Kathy greeted him at the door. "Come in."

Patrick stepped inside the front hall; it was the loveliest hall he had ever seen. The soft green wallpaper suddenly made him homesick for Ireland. And wallpaper! He imagined how his mother's eyes would pop out at the sight of such elegance.

"This is my brother, Karl, and his friend, Ben," Kathy said, wondering why Patrick stared at the walls.

Patrick turned his head. What great men these were! How did wallpaper get his instant attention with these giants in front of him? Why, Karl's bullish shoulders filled the hallway, and with his burly beard, he looked completely unfit for such gentle surroundings. And then there was his friend, Ben, with a cherub's face, but strong enough to wrestle Michael the Archangel.

"Glad to meet you," said Karl, nearly crushing Patrick's hand, while Ben smiled and said, "Hello."

"Come on, we'll find you some skates," said Kathy, pulling Patrick back into the hallway. "My friends, the Mitchells, should be here any minute."

She opened a closet door and pulled out four pairs of skates. "Go ahead and try them on. I have to make Karl and Ben breakfast yet. Did you eat?"

"Yes," said Patrick.

"Okay, well, we won't be long. My mother would usually make breakfast, but she's upstairs still. She doesn't feel well today. She hasn't really since my stepfather died. And I'm the only woman poor Ben has to cook for him, other than my mother."

Patrick was left alone in the hall while Kathy made breakfast for the man she hoped would be her sweetheart. The skates all turned out to be too small, except the last pair which was far too large. Patrick did not know what to do. He hesitated to go into the breakfast room and interrupt a family meal. He dreaded being told that if none of the skates fit him, he could not join the party.

The front door opened, and two young ladies and a young man, intimate enough with the family not to knock, stepped inside.

"Hello," said the oldest girl. "I'm Mary; are you Patrick?"

"Yes," he replied.

"This is my sister, Florence, and this is our brother, Roger."

Roger Mitchell extended his hand. He was a pleasant looking young man, just a year or two younger than Patrick. Florence did not speak, but stood ill at ease, being at the awkward age of fourteen. Mary smiled and asked Patrick whether he were excited about going skating.

"Yes, but—I can't seem to find skates that fit."

"Are they too small?" asked Mary.

"No," said Patrick, but before he could explain, Kathy called, "Is that you, Mary?" and Mary disappeared with Florence into the dining room.

"It's all right if they're too big," said Roger. "We can stuff them with paper, or you can just wear double socks. It'll be cold anyway if we stay out all day. I'll go see whether Karl has some extra socks."

Patrick had no desire to wear anything more of Karl's; he already felt he was imposing by wearing Karl's old skates, but a minute later, Karl entered with thick wool socks.

"These should do for you," said Karl. Patrick thanked him.

A great bustle of getting ready occurred as everyone returned to the hall. Patrick offered to carry the lunch basket, trying to ingratiate himself with these strangers who made him nervous yet seemed friendly.

The party walked around the back of the house where Karl had parked his sleigh. Karl and Ben fetched the horses from the stable and hitched them to the sleigh while the girls piled in, and Roger and Patrick arranged the blankets around them. And then, a jolt, a burst of speed. What sheer delight! The sleigh was coursing down the streets of Marquette. The horses kept up a brisk trot, heading south of town; they were so used to pulling the full weight of sleighs loaded with giant pine logs that the weight of seven people, tightly packed, and all the warmer for it, was a light burden that made the horses dash merrily through the snow.

"You're sitting on my dress," Florence Mitchell told Patrick; instantly, he was embarrassed and tried to dislodge her skirt from under his legs. But soon the sheer crisp cool air and the nearly blinding sparkle of the sun on snow made him forget all cares in the thrill of this fast ride. And then they were in the woods, the first time Patrick had been outside the town since his arrival. Along an old road the sleigh coursed, between trees loaded down with snow from last week's storm. In the morning sun, snowballs fell from the trees, creating a pleasant, almost enchanting effect. Patrick had thought the snow overwhelming until today; now he felt as if he floated on clouds, the trees rising up through them. This pure white mystical forest seemed to be endless; he almost hoped the moment would last forever.

"The snow's at least three feet deep in these woods," Roger said.

The girls jabbered away, but on the edge of the sleigh, Patrick could scarcely hear the conversation. He found himself delighting more in the scenery than the human companionship he had so craved.

"Patrick, are you warm enough?" Kathy asked, leaning across Florence so he could hear her. He half-shouted a "yes," but then nodded instead when his voice was drowned out by the jingle bells around the horses' necks; what a delightfully loud jangle those bells made in the woods. Patrick did not even mind the cold; the numbness of his nose was a delight as was everything about this winter fairyland.

As they moved farther into the woods, the sleigh slowed down, the trail being less well groomed, and Karl wanted to be careful not to get the sleigh stuck. Conversation could now resume.

"Patrick," Mary asked, "do you like to ice skate?"

"I don't know. I've never gone," said Patrick.

"You've never gone ice skating!" said Florence.

"No, not in Ireland. The lakes and rivers near us didn't always freeze enough for it to be safe, and I didn't own any skates. None of us could afford them anyway."

"Did you at least get snow there?" Florence asked.

"We did, but never more than a couple inches at most."

"All this snow must be overwhelming for you," said Ben.

"Yes, when I'm shoveling it," said Patrick, "but I didn't realize it was so beautiful until we were out here in the forest."

"I bet Ireland's beautiful," said Karl. "You know, Kathy and I are Irish on our mother's side."

"Where in Ireland did your mother come from?" Patrick asked.

"We don't know," said Karl.

Kathy explained, "Mother never talks about Ireland. She says she lives in America now, so there's no point in talking about the past."

"Oh," said Patrick, thinking their mother was probably right.

"I'd love to see Ireland," said Kathy.

"Why?" asked Florence. "Everyone's poor there, and our neighbor says the Irish are dirty as dogs."

"Florence Anna Mitchell, you know better than to repeat such remarks," Roger told her.

"I'm half Irish," stated Kathy, "and I'm not dirty."

Despite the reprimanding of Florence, the damage was done. "Even here," Patrick thought, "among these nice people, the Irish are hated." He began to think things would be no better in America than they had been back home where the English and the Catholic Church oppressed the Irish.

"Just ignore her," Kathy told him, and she smiled so warmly Patrick nearly forgot the incident.

They were now coming down a hill; before them was a small lake, frozen, with snow and ice glistening on it, creating a crystal clearing in the winter woods.

Karl stopped the sleigh, and they all climbed out. Patrick put on his skates, observing how the others laced theirs. He was surprised it was not difficult to walk in the skates, but he was still walking on the snow. When he first stepped on the ice, he nearly fell over. Karl grabbed him before he slid on his face.

"Easy now," Karl said, helping him regain his balance.

"Here, take my hand and I'll help you," said Kathy. She ignored the disapproving look from her brother; she was at the age where he had become overprotective. Hesitantly, Patrick stepped forward as Kathy held his hand, innocently, through heavily knitted mittens.

Patrick had nothing to hang onto except Kathy. After a few seconds, it was obvious Kathy could not support his weight. After they both crashed to the ground, they gave up. Patrick was relieved; he had never held a girl's hand before, and he could not concentrate on his feet when she was touching him.

No nice Irish girl would have let him hold her hand, but he did not want to think harshly of her; he reminded himself this was America, so perhaps holding hands meant nothing here. Americans were maybe too friendly, and he felt uncomfortable not knowing the line between politeness and intimacy.

"I don't know how I can teach you," Kathy moaned.

"I'll help him," said Ben, skating up and taking Patrick's arm.

Patrick was intimidated by the lumberjack giant, but Ben was kind. He held onto Patrick's shoulders from behind and slowly pushed him forward, while grabbing him the couple times he nearly fell forward onto his face.

Kathy skated at their sides, telling Patrick he was doing well, and adding, "You're lucky. Ben is a good teacher. He actually taught me how to skate."

Then came the moment when Patrick, completely uncoordinated and thoroughly incompetent, was able to skate by himself. He found he could now keep his balance, even if he could only put one foot in front of the other in a plodding motion.

Karl built a fire, and Mary laid out lunch for everyone. Patrick was relieved when they stopped to eat, and he felt grateful they shared their food with him when he had not thought to bring anything. In Ireland, there had never been such a bounty of food, nor was it shared so willingly.

"After we eat," Roger told Patrick, "I'll teach you how to pick up speed."

"Take it easy on him," Karl said. "Don't push him if he's not ready."

Patrick wanted to protest he was ready, although he knew better. He longed to skate as well as Ben. He felt he would belong if he could skate better. Otherwise, he feared he would not be invited again because he was too much trouble.

Ben poured hot coffee for everyone, and Karl stoked the fire he had built to keep them warm for the day.

"Florence, you don't need anymore coffee," Mary told her sister.

"I do so. I'm cold."

"We have to share it, and you've had more than everyone else. Besides, it's not good for you when you're so young."

"I'm only three years younger than you," she said.

"Florence, you're being rude," said Roger.

Florence glared over her cup's brim as she gulped down more coffee.

Patrick felt Florence was one member of the party he had no desire to befriend. But her brother and sister were nice. He wanted to be invited back, even if Florence were included.

When lunch was over, Roger taught Patrick how to glide faster. Patrick found he could now walk on his own, even though he only took baby size steps; he longed to be graceful like his companions. Roger demonstrated how to thrust his feet forward in large strides while retaining his balance. Patrick took larger steps, while Roger skated in circles around him, showing off his ability to balance on one foot. Meanwhile, Kathy, Mary, and Florence formed a female skating party across the lake where Kathy and Mary appeared deep in conversation. Earlier, Patrick would have feared they were laughing at his lack of skill, but now his attention focused on increasing the speed and agility of his strides. He was beginning to feel comfortable.

Soon he had not fallen or lost his balance for ten minutes—he was doing almost as well as his new friends—acting as if he had skated all his life. He had never imagined winter could be so delightful—especially when he gained enough speed to glide halfway across the frozen lake. He reveled in the cool air brushing against his cheeks. He had hated the cold here since he had first stepped off the train. He hated the bitter subzero temperatures, and the even more bitter windchills. He hated being bundled in flannel shirts, long underwear, mittens, scarves, knitted hats, and heavy coats, and he hated how this multitude of garments made him sweat when he moved. But now as he glided along, the crisp air against his face turned his cheeks bright red, and his breath flowed visibly from his mouth. He had never known anything so delightfully refreshing as the winter air swooshing over his lips and creeping down into his throat.

Roger skated beside him. They circled the lake once, then not wanting to stop, began a second lap around. As they approached a corner of the lake, Roger swerved a bit too much to his right; Patrick tried to swerve to avoid Roger's sharp turn, but instead, kept going straight, colliding into his teacher. Patrick tilted left, then struggled to pull back, only to fall backward, his feet hitting Roger's legs. Together they tumbled into a jumble of arms and legs. Roger's skate sliced Patrick's pants and scratched his leg, causing it to bleed. Roger landed on his seat, his legs extended in the air. Patrick landed on his chest, his legs twisted beneath him.

"Are you all right?" Roger asked, struggling to his feet.

Patrick's breath was knocked out of him so he could not speak.

Ben skated over. "You fell so hard, it's a wonder the ice didn't crack beneath you. Are you all right?"

Patrick started to nod "yes" as the pain hit him. He tried to move his twisted ankle out from beneath his other leg, but the movement caused him to let out a girlish scream. Sympathetically, Ben picked him up under the arms as if he were a child. Once on his feet, Patrick found himself dizzy and drained of energy.

"Can you walk?" Ben asked.

Patrick scarcely heard the words. He felt like a fool. At that moment, Florence chose to skate over and laugh, "You looked so ridiculous when you flew up in the air with your legs over your head like that."

Patrick's eyes filled with tears as he thought of the grotesque picture he had presented; all his efforts to belong, only now to be alienated! Panic rose in his chest; he thought he would vomit, and not yet having gained his breath, he turned pale. His chest began to shake. Gurgles in his throat broke into a child's screeching sobs.

"Patrick, are you hurt that badly?" Kathy asked. She had not seen the accident, but had skated over when she saw him lying on the ice.

Karl led Patrick toward the shore. Patrick was embarrassed by his reaction. He wanted to shake Karl off, to run to shore and hide behind a tree. But he couldn't run—the skates would just make him fall, and his last fall had scared him so much he never wanted to skate again.

Tears streamed down his face, his pride more wounded than his body. Everyone was staring at him, which only made his tears all the more uncontrollable. He wished he were back in Ireland. He wished he had never come here.

"What's wrong with him?" asked Florence. "He's acting like a baby."

"Florence, shut up!" Mary said. She was not allowed to say "shut up" to her sister at home, but even Mary could lose her patience.

"Patrick, we're sorry," Kathy kept repeating as they reached the shore. Once off the ice, Karl let Kathy take Patrick's arm as she continued to apologize. "We're all sorry. We just wanted you to have a good time. We didn't want you to get hurt. Did you break or sprain anything?"

"Just leave me alone," he wailed. He did not mean to wail, but it came out that way.

"I'm so sorry, Patrick. We didn't want to ruin your day."

"No, no," he said, feeling guilty to have spoiled her fun as she led him from the others. "Just leave me alone."

"Don't be angry, Patrick. Anyone could have fallen. You'll learn to skate yet. You were doing really well before you fell. Please don't be upset. You can try again when you're ready. Next time you'll do better. The day isn't over yet."

"No," he said. "Everything's ruined."

How could he explain to her that this had been the finest day of his life—that he had not been so happy in months—to have friends, to have people be kind to him, people who actually cared and wanted him to have a good time—all this happiness had been almost more than he could bear. Then his tumble had exasperated all his conflicting fear and exhilaration. He had kept asking himself how he could be having fun when he had left his family behind in Ireland, and they could not share his pleasure. He had felt carefree today. He had been happy, yet saddened to find himself happy with people who were not his family.

"Are you hurt that badly?" Kathy asked.

"No, it's not that."

"What's wrong then?"

She got him to sit down on an overturned log halfway up a hill fifty feet from the lake.

"It's nothing. It's just—." He did not care what she thought. "I miss my family."

"Are they back in Ireland?"

"Yes."

"Didn't they want to come with you to America?"

"No."

"Then why did you come alone? Didn't you want to stay there?"

He wished he had not said anything. He could not hurt this innocent girl by telling her the misery he had known.

"Yes—but—I couldn't."

"Why not?"

"I can't say." He would not look at her, only at the snow beneath his feet.

"Why not?" she repeated.

"I just can't." His tone was angry enough to frighten her. She had never seen such an emotional display from a man. She had seen Montoni enraged, but that was almost normal compared to Patrick's mood.

"Is it something awful?" she asked. She was frightened, but she pitied him. She wanted them to be friends, and she hoped he would not say something so horrid she would have to stay away from him.

"I can't tell," he repeated.

Kathy thought it must be something awful then, but she only dared to ask, "Is it something you did wrong?"

"Yes, but I didn't mean to, and I didn't do it alone. There were others, but I don't know what happened to them."

"I'm sorry," she said after a minute, although she did not understand. She thought she should take his hand, but she was afraid. She knew she had been presumptuous to invite a stranger skating. Her brother might be angry if she took Patrick's hand now, and she feared anything she might do would upset Patrick further.

Roger walked up the hill.

"Do you want me to help you try it again, Patrick?" he asked.

Patrick stared up at him, his tears now dried, his eyes not as red anymore.

"All right," he said. He stood up and walked off with Roger.

Kathy watched them depart. After a minute, she also walked to the lake.

"What's wrong with him?" asked Mary, coming up to her. "I hate to agree with Florence, but he does seem awful moody."

"He's just homesick," said Kathy.

"I think it's more than that," said Karl.

"Kathy, I think you should stay away from him," said Ben. "I don't quite trust him."

Had these words come from her brother, Kathy would have understood their protective tone, but Kathy was irritated that Ben should speak them. "Ben, you aren't my brother so don't tell me what to do," she snapped. Then she skated onto the ice to join Patrick and Roger.

"What's wrong with her?" Ben asked.

"She's just stubborn," Karl replied.

Mary knew what was wrong with Kathy, but she did not think Ben deserved to know. She glided onto the ice to join her friend.

That both Roger and Kathy were still kind after his irrational outburst made Patrick feel reassured by the friendship of the group. The last couple hours of daylight passed rapidly as he skated around the lake, making jokes with Roger, Mary, and Kathy. They skated the rest of the afternoon, except for ten minutes spent by the fire to warm their fingers and toes. They all felt the day had passed too quickly when Karl said, "We better head home. It'll be dark soon."

Night fell as the party returned to town. Karl had a lantern attached to the sleigh to guide their way, but the night was nearly impenetrable as the tall pines and oaks, even with their leaves shed for winter, obstructed the moonlight. Patrick was thankful for the dark. That the excursion was almost over meant he would return to spend the evening in his lonely room. He felt homesick again and wondered how his parents were; he suffered to think they must miss him as fiercely as he missed them.

"It's too quiet," said Mary.

"Let's sing," Kathy replied.

"No, then the bears will know where we are," said Florence.

"They won't bother us," said Karl.

"Our singing will scare them away," Ben added.

"Yeah, especially if Florence is singing," said Roger, who was fortunate not to see the murdering scowl on his sister's face.

"What should we sing?" Mary asked.

"How about the "Lullaby"?

"Okay," said Mary. The two girls sang while everyone listened to their soft voices. When they had finished, Karl said, "Kathy, I never heard you sing that before."

"Agnes taught it to me a few weeks ago, and then I taught it to Mary. Can you guess why I like it so much?"

"No, why?"

"It's from a show in New York called, *Fritz, Our German Cousin*."

"You're kidding," laughed Karl. "I wouldn't be surprised if we did have a German cousin named Fritz."

"Our father," Kathy told everyone, "was named Fritz. Unfortunately, we don't know any of our cousins on either side of the family."

"Who's Agnes?" asked Florence, uninterested in the Bergmanns' family tree.

"Agnes Whitman. She's married to Jacob Whitman."

"Is she related to Mary Whitman?"

"Agnes is Mary's mother," said Kathy.

"Mary Whitman," said Florence, "is a total snob. All the Whitmans are stuck up. Just 'cause Mary's grandparents used to live in some dumb house on Ridge Street, she thinks she's Queen of Marquette."

"Her parents are nice," said Kathy, although she would not defend Mary Whitman. "Agnes plays the piano beautifully, and she's taught me lots of songs."

"So what?" said Florence. "Mary's still a snob. So's her sister, Sylvia."

Patrick felt like saying the Whitman girls' grandparents were also nice. He rather liked Mr. Whitman for his friendliness; Mrs. Whitman he hadn't quite figured out yet; she seemed suspicious of him, and perhaps overly concerned he would ruin her reputation as owner of "a respectable establishment," but she was always polite. And the couple times he had met Jacob and Agnes, they had seemed very pleasant.

"What should we sing next?" asked Mary.

"Patrick, do you sing?" Kathy asked.

"No, not really."

"Do you know any Irish songs?" Karl asked.

"Yes, but I don't have a good voice."

"Teach us some anyway," said Kathy. "I want to know what Ireland is like."

Patrick sighed, "It's a grand land, but it's in a terrible state. The people are very poor and oppressed."

"Why?" asked Kathy.

"Well, I'll tell you in a song," he said, and with more spirit than he had shown throughout the entire day, perhaps because he could not feel so ridiculous in the dark, he broke into a stirring rendition of "The Wearing of the Green." Even Florence was impressed by his deep bass voice. Patrick sang boldly of the injustices faced by his countrymen that had made Ireland "the most disgraceful country that ever yet was seen;/They're hanging men and women for the wearin' of the green."

When he finished, Kathy asked, "Is it really that bad in Ireland?"

"Yes," Patrick replied.

"No wonder you left," said Mary.

"But my mother always says it's a beautiful country," said Kathy.

"It's the most beautiful place in the world. I never realized just how beautiful until I came to America and had something to compare it with, though Marquette is beautiful too."

"Do you know any more Irish songs?" asked Mary.

"I'll sing one more," Patrick said. "This one will tell you how Ireland looks."

Take a blessing from my heart to the land of my birth,
And the fair hills of Eire, O!
Her woods are tall and straight, grove rising over grove;
Trees flourish, in her glens below and on her heights above.

"I thought you were going to sing about Ireland. I never heard of Eire," Florence said when he had finished.

"I did. Eire is the ancient name for Ireland," Patrick replied.

"It sounds lovely," said Kathy. "When you sing, I can tell how much you miss it."

Patrick said nothing, but he hoped now they understood him better and might forget his earlier outburst.

"You have a beautiful voice, Patrick," said Mary.

"Look at the moonlight!" said Roger. The sleigh had just broken out of the woods, and the clouds had opened so the moonbeams could shimmer across the snow. As the horses trotted into Marquette, the houses cast off a warm glow from their candlelit windows. The world felt suddenly warm and peaceful. When the sleigh drew up at Kathy's house, Patrick bid the rest of the party goodbye, while glowing inside as he had not done since a boy.

"We'll have to go again," said Kathy as he handed back the loaned ice skates.

"Yes, I'd like that," he replied.

"Glad to meetcha," Karl and Ben both said, shaking his hand, and Patrick believed they were sincere.

He walked up the hill, through downtown Marquette and back to the boarding house. He walked slowly to retain his happiness a little longer before returning to the loneliness of his solitary room. But when he entered the house, he found the Whitmans and Dalrymples in the parlor, and they all insisted he join them for a cup of hot chocolate and a cake Mrs. Whitman had just taken from the oven. Everyone wanted to hear about the skating excursion, and they were generally pleased he had experienced such a good time. When he went upstairs after a pleasant hour, he removed his frozen pants, now thawing out, and in his nightshirt, crawled into his warm bed; the smell of freshly washed and ironed linen soothed the aches caused by his skating tumbles. He had not felt so cheerful and contented since he had gone to sleep as a little boy in his parents' cottage.

In the weeks that followed, Patrick and Kathy saw more of each other, and Mary did not always accompany them. Kathy was unsure how her mother felt, but she mentioned the meetings to Molly, who made no comment. Kathy feared her mother was becoming indifferent to everything around her, but truthfully, Molly feared if she said anything, her opposition might only encourage her daughter.

If Molly had asked, Kathy would have said she only felt sorry for Patrick because he was lonely. Kathy's fancies still centered on Ben, who filled her thoughts on sleepless nights. She would lie awake, sighing over Ben's boyish face and muscular arms, and she would imagine a hundred little incidents she could arrange to make him notice her. When she dared, she tried to imagine how it would be when he declared his love and pressed his manly lips against her own small girlish ones. But weeks passed while Ben remained in the Copper Country with Karl, and she never heard a word from him; it was hard to keep up a passionate romance with an absent lover while she spent her free time with another young man; occasionally, that young man's face would even intrude when she was imagining Ben holding her in his arms. She was a bit irritated by the intrusion; she told herself Ben was the superior man, yet she could not rid her thoughts of Patrick, not when she saw him frequently. Ben might be stronger and better looking, but he treated her like a little girl, which to him she probably was, being a dozen years younger. Patrick was only five years older, and he seemed to like her company, and he was not far away. He paid attention to her.

One warm March evening, Kathy went walking with Patrick, Mary, and Florence.

"Finally, the snow is starting to melt," Mary said.

"What will you do now, Patrick?" Kathy asked. "You won't have a job when the snow's gone."

"Actually, Mr. Dalrymple said I can work for him. He's a carpenter and has some houses to build, and he said I can be a mason and help lay the foundations. He says it'll be steady work through the summer."

"Oh, good," said Kathy. "I was worried for you."

Patrick blushed; he hoped she really had cared enough to worry.

"Now that I have full time work," he said, "I was wondering—"

But then he closed his mouth. He would not speak in front of Mary or Florence.

"Wondering what?" asked Florence.

"Just, I was thinking I'll make more money so I can afford to buy us some candy or treats once in a while."

"I'm not allowed to take gifts from strange men," said Florence.

"Florence, really," Mary replied.

"I better get going," Patrick said, wanting to bolt. "It'll be dark soon."

"Oh no," said Kathy. "The days are getting longer."

"I'll see you sometime soon," Patrick replied, and abruptly took himself off.

"What's wrong with him?" asked Kathy. "Is he mad at me?"

"No, I think it's the opposite," said Mary. "Are you blind?"

"You mean he's in love!" said Florence. "He wouldn't presume—"

"Hush, Florence," Kathy snapped. "Don't say anything!"

Florence had never known Kathy's tongue to be harsh. The remark was so unexpected she could not help but be silent.

"I'm not kidding," Mary told her friend.

"Then why doesn't he say anything?" asked Kathy.

"I think he's just shy."

"And afraid of my mother," Kathy thought. "She always avoids him when he comes over. She's never even really met him."

"Do you like him?" asked Mary.

"I don't know," Kathy replied.

"Ben ain't ever going to love you," said Florence.

Kathy knew Ben was hopeless, although she had never expressed her feelings about him to anyone except Mary. Now she was too troubled by Patrick's feelings to be upset that Mary had told her greatest secret to her obnoxious little sister.

"I've never really thought about Patrick that way," she fibbed.

"What would your mother say if she knew he liked you?" Mary asked.

"I don't know. She hardly even talks to me anymore."

"Do you think you could love him?"

"I don't know. I guess—I mean I like him, but marry him—I don't know."

"Eventually he's going to ask you," Mary warned, "so you'd better figure it out."

That evening, Kathy thought long and hard about it. She knew she had feelings for Patrick, although she had tried to deny them. She thought it silly to think of marriage, but why else would a girl think of a young man? What should she do if he asked her? If she decided she loved him and said yes to his proposal, what would her mother say? Could she convince her mother? But why worry about that before she decided what she wanted?

What was there to decide? Ben was clearly not interested. And she wasn't getting any younger. If she didn't marry soon, what would become of her? In three short years, she would be twenty, and she could not still be single at that age. What if she got no more offers? Mary did not have a lover yet. She was certain Mary was destined to be an old maid, and while she loved Mary dearly, she did not want to be an old maid with her. If Patrick asked her, she would say yes. Unless Ben asked her first. Maybe if Patrick asked her, then Ben would notice her, and—

"Oh, stop being silly!" she told herself. "Ben will never ask you. He's too old for you anyhow."

So if she accepted Patrick, she would have to get her mother's approval. She knew her mother feared being left alone, but she was not going to be an old maid, not even for her mother's sake. So how could she convince her? Patrick was Irish; would that help any? It might. But did she really want to marry Patrick? How could she convince her mother before she convinced herself?

Kathy would wobble back and forth for days with these thoughts, trying to analyze every question and possible answer, but slowly she made up her mind.

🍁   🍁   🍁

Agnes loved her piano. Despite her stepmother's other flaws, Agnes always felt grateful that Sophia had insisted she study the piano as a young girl.

"Agnes must be taught the accomplishments belonging to a refined young lady of her station," she remembered her stepmother telling her father. She was only eight at the time, and she had long wanted to learn how to play the piano. Among her earliest memories was her mother playing the piano while she sat beneath the stool playing with her doll. That first piano had been shipped all the way from New York on a schooner when Agnes was no more than three. Carefully, it had been unloaded from the ship onto the dock, then gingerly rolled up the hill to the Henning house while Agnes watched, her hand in her mother's. Clara had begun to play it that very day. It had created the first real music Agnes had heard in the distant wilderness settlement of her childhood.

Sophia's musical talent was severely limited, but Agnes had a good ear, and once Sophia had taught her the scales and the basics of fingering, and ordered her to practice one hour every day, Agnes was able to progress by studying on her own. When she played, she lost herself in the music, the piano becoming a medium between herself and her mother's memory. Sophia had wanted Clara forgotten, but her insistence on Agnes's piano lessons only strengthened the girl's memories of her mother. While Sophia's domineering might have made Agnes timid and reclusive, Agnes's skill at the piano helped her gain friends who otherwise might have overlooked her. Marquette had little musical talent in its early days; most who could read music or play an instrument did so at an elementary level. Soon Agnes found her modest talent praised by small gatherings of family and friends. She did not know whether she were a good pianist, having no one to compare herself against, but while no great artist, she put a great deal of controlled emotion into her playing that made up for skill. While no one was ever crass enough to ask Agnes how she could bear to live with her stepmother, music provided her with an escape from the frustrations of her domestic situation; when she could not improve her life, she strove to improve her music.

When she married Jacob, Agnes had wanted to take her mother's old piano to her new home. Sophia had refused because she wanted Madeleine to learn how to play, and even though a grand piano was ordered for the parlor, Sophia wanted her daughter to practice on the old piano so the new one would not be scratched. When Madeleine became frustrated and refused to practice any longer, the piano remained at the Henning house. Agnes did not ask Jacob for a new piano—they could not afford it, and then once the girls were born, she had no time to play except during an occasional visit to her parents' house.

Then when Madeleine had drowned, and her father and stepmother had moved back east, Gerald took Agnes aside to say, "I'm leaving the piano here for you. Don't give in if your stepmother complains." By then, Sophia was too heartbroken to care about pianos; she wanted nothing that might remind her of Marquette, least of all something that had belonged to Gerald's first wife.

When Agnes rediscovered the piano, it released the grief she felt over the death of her half-sister and her absent father. More importantly, Agnes brought music into her husband's home. Her girls were not interested in learning to play, but when Will was born, Agnes found he shared her musical interests. He would sit on the floor at her feet and clap whenever she finished a song. He never obnoxiously wanted to "play" by banging his hands on the ivory keys. He sat quietly on the bench beside her and watched her fingers move from one key to the next; soon she hoped to teach him how to play. Winter would have been the perfect opportunity; the piano might have kept him from becoming rambunctious when he was cooped up in the house. But after a few simple lessons—his hands were still too small to play any chords— Agnes felt exhausted and found it difficult even to sit up straight at the piano bench. Several times during the day, she found she had to take breaks to sit or lie down. She knew a pregnancy could tire her out, but she had given birth three times before without trouble; of course, this child would be the first born after she had turned thirty so she had to admit she was not young anymore; that must be the difference.

When she confessed to Jacob that she was too tired to play the piano, he surprised her by bringing home a large crate. She opened it to find a shining Victrola with four records, one of Beethoven, then Chopin, Mozart, and Stephen Foster. It was the finest present she had ever received. Her stomach was too large now for her to go outside, so she escaped from the monotony of the household by lying on the sofa while the Victrola played. Will would build his blocks on the floor while she listened to the records over and over, occasionally dozing during the brilliant concertos or symphonies.

On one such musical afternoon, Kathy Bergmann stopped by. Agnes was too tired to answer the door, so Kathy let herself in.

"Kathy!" screeched Will when she came into the parlor. He hoped she would play with him; he did not understand why Mother had lately become no fun at all.

"I need to talk to you," said Kathy, sitting down across from the sofa and taking Will on her lap where he began to jabber about the new game he had made up.

Agnes sat up on the sofa. Kathy had arrived during her favorite symphony, and although she had listened to it fifty times since the Victrola arrived, she hated to have it interrupted. But she forgot all about it when Kathy declared the reason for her visit.

"I've fallen in love with a young man, and I know my mother won't approve so I need your help."

"Why Kathy!" was all Agnes could say at first. She thought Kathy far too young for love, but then she reminded herself she had been the same age when she fell in love with Jacob. Her conversation with Kathy from the day they went sledding returned to her; Agnes had hardly taken Kathy's remarks about love seriously then, but seeing the earnest look on the girl's face, she asked, "When did this happen? Tell me all about it."

"Mother won't like him, but I do, and I don't know how to tell her, and—"

"But who is he?" asked Agnes.

"It's Patrick."

"Patrick?" Agnes could not recall anyone by that name.

"Patrick McCarey," said Kathy. "The boarder at your mother-in-law's house."

"Oh." Agnes thought he hardly seemed attractive enough to steal a young girl's heart. He was so shy he was almost invisible. "He's rather old for you, isn't he?"

"No, he's twenty-two, and I'm about to turn seventeen."

"I see," said Agnes. When she was sixteen, Jacob had been twenty-four. "And does he love you?"

"I think so."

"Has he told you so?"

"No. He's too shy. I keep hoping he will, but he hasn't yet. Sometimes he's very moody, and I don't think he believes he deserves to be happy, but my friend Mary's brother, Roger, is hinting to get him to propose to me."

"But Kathy, you don't want a moody man. You'll only become unhappy with him." Agnes felt a headache coming on from having gotten up so suddenly when Kathy arrived. She was also a bit irritated from being so tired, and she found it hard to believe Kathy was one of those girls foolish enough to love the brooding, ornery type of man who only broke girls' hearts.

"He's not mean," Kathy said. "He's just shy, and I think he's very lonely. I guess he had a really hard life in Ireland, and he says he had to leave there, that he had no choice, but he misses his family."

"Why did he have to leave?" asked Agnes.

"I don't know. He won't tell me; his life there must have been horrible."

"I think," said Agnes, wincing from her headache, "that you need to make him tell you. You need to know what you'll be getting into if you marry him."

"I will marry him if he asks me," said Kathy, more interested in romance than in Patrick's troublesome past. "I love him and that can conquer anything."

"Yes," said Agnes, "it can, if you're willing to work at it, but most young girls don't know how much work love can be. I love Jacob, but there are days when I wish I could just be locked up in a tower somewhere all by myself and not have to deal with him."

"Agnes, you seem so sweet and calm all the time," said Kathy.

Agnes did not feel sweet and calm. She felt violently sick from the pounding in her head.

"No one is perfect," she said. "I'm sure you'll make a good wife, Kathy, but that's why you deserve to know whether Patrick will make a good husband."

Agnes wished Kathy had not had love troubles today, but she remembered many years ago when she had first confessed her love for Jacob to Kathy's mother, so she felt she must be helpful now.

Will chose this minute to lose his patience with the women's conversation.

"Kathy, play with me!" he shouted.

"Will," Agnes scolded, "Mama and Kathy are talking. She'll play with you when we're done. Go pick up your blocks."

"No! I want Kathy to play with me. You never will, Mama, so I want her to."

Agnes felt guilty; she had not been a good mother this last month, but she felt so tired.

"I'll come by and play with you some day soon, Will," said Kathy, "but I better go home now."

She stood up, feeling Agnes had not been any help.

"Kathy, wait, I—"

Kathy paused, trying to control her tongue. "All I want you to do is talk to my mother. She's been so strange since my stepfather died. I don't think she would like any boy I was interested in. Please talk to her."

"Has your mother said anything about him?"

"No, she's only said hello to him once, but from her manner I can see she doesn't like him."

"Mothers are wise—they sometimes see things—"

"No, Agnes," said Kathy. "She's just afraid of being alone, of losing me, but I can't live with her forever. I have a right to my own life."

Agnes could hear the pounding in her head.

"Well, your mother's having a hard time right now. Give her a little longer."

"Will you talk to her for me?" Kathy asked.

"Yes," Agnes sighed. "I'm sorry, Kathy. I'm just not feeling well. I know I'm not being much help, but yes, I'll talk to her. Just remember you're still young, and there are plenty of other young men who will be interested in you. You need to be certain Patrick is the right one, and if he's moody or depressed as you say, then—"

"He is the right one," said Kathy, hiding her own doubts.

"But will he make a good husband?" Agnes was tempted to ask whether he drank; didn't all the Irish drink? But she didn't want to upset Kathy any further.

"He's a hard worker, and he's kind to me," Kathy said. "He bought me chocolates just last week."

"Papa!" shouted Will as Jacob opened the door.

"Good, Jacob's home," thought Agnes. "Maybe he'll watch Will while I take a little nap before I make supper."

"Hello, Kathy," Jacob said as he picked up the little boy clinging to his leg.

"Hello," she said. "I better go. Promise, Agnes."

"Yes, I will."

Jacob looked askance at his wife as Kathy said, "Goodbye," and quickly left. Agnes was irritable, but she would not betray a fellow sister's heart, no matter how foolish she might think that heart to be. She distracted Jacob's attention away from the situation.

"Jacob, why are you home so early?"

"I came to check on you."

"I'm fine. Just a little tired."

Jacob offered to take Will for a walk to pick up the girls at school. Her husband was always so good to her. Agnes felt guilty for thinking a few minutes ago that sometimes she wished she had never had a family. She never would have thought such a thing if she felt like her normal self. She would have been terribly lonely if Jacob had not come to fill her life with his warm love.

Warm. That was how she felt as Jacob and Will departed. She climbed upstairs to her bedroom so she would not be disturbed when her family returned. She felt breathless when she reached the upstairs, and touching her forehead, she wondered whether she had a fever. No, it was just this sudden change from winter to spring weather. She never remembered such a warm spring. Or was she having hot flashes? But pregnant women didn't have those; she did not remember any during her first three pregnancies, but then, the baby was due any day. She even had some false labor pains yesterday. She hoped the baby would not come for another day or two. She was too tired to have a baby right now.

She crawled into bed, thankful for the chance to nap. She drew the quilt over her, but after a minute, she was sweating so she pushed everything but the sheet off her. When she still perspired, she struggled out of bed to crack open the window. My, but it was warm today! The snow was melting off the roof fast enough to make a little waterfall run down the eaves. Agnes lay back on the bed, breathing in the fresh smell of melting snow. It was the first time in months it had been warm enough to open the windows. Soon, it would be time for spring cleaning, but not until she had had her lying-in period after the baby was born.

She loved the music of the melting snow, the tinkling of it dripping off the roof. As the first harbinger of spring, the sound was almost more beautiful than the Victrola's melodies. A warm breeze provided background music to the drip-drop notes. Agnes drifted in and out of sleep to Nature's music until the front door slammed shut and she heard her family's footsteps in the front hall. Then came the pattering of unmistakable feet rushing upstairs.

"I saw fairy footprints in the snow!" Will yelled as he burst into the room. "I did really. They went under the porch steps. I saw them. Fairy footprints, Mama!"

"They're probably rabbit tracks," said Jacob, grabbing his son before he could jump on the bed.

"No, they were fairy feet!" Will insisted.

"I'm sure they were," Agnes smiled. "Come here, Will. It's okay, Jacob."

Her husband placed their son on the bed so he could cuddle against her.

"They were just rabbit tracks," said Mary, standing in the doorway.

"They were not!" Will shouted.

"That's enough, Mary," said Jacob. "Go do your chores and tell your sister to do hers."

Mary turned away, pouting.

"Mary?" Agnes called.

"What?"

"Did you have a good day at school?"

"I don't know," Mary huffed, then stomped downstairs.

Jacob shook his head.

"Do you need anything, dear?"

"No, I just want to rest a few minutes before I make supper."

"All right. Will, let's leave your mother alone."

"It's okay. He can stay," said Agnes. She saw he wanted to cuddle, and she had ignored him all afternoon. When she first knew she would be a mother, she had always thought she would love a daughter best, but it was Will who seemed most like her, perhaps because he was imaginative. Even with his excessive boyish energy, he was the easiest of her children to spend time with.

"Do you know what fairy footprints mean?" she asked him after Jacob left.

"No."

"It means the fairies are bringing us a present."

"A present? For me?" asked Will.

"No, not exactly."

"But I want a present, Mama."

"Well, it's not exactly a present. The fairies are bringing you a little brother or sister."

"Littler than me?"

"A baby," said Agnes.

"Do I get to play with it instead of Mary and Sylvia? They already have enough dolls, and you know, they don't play with them. They say they're too old."

"No, it's not a doll. It's a real baby and since it's closest to your age, yes, you'll have someone to play with."

"Can it be a boy?"

"I don't know. That's up to the fairies."

"I hope it's a boy," said Will.

Agnes felt a searing pain run through her, another contraction.

"If you want the baby to come," she said, "you must be good."

"Why?"

"Because otherwise the fairies won't bring it."

"Oh," said Will. He didn't like when things only happened if you were good. It was so hard to be good most of the time.

"Mama, do you think—"

But another jolt of pain made it impossible for Agnes to listen.

"Will, go get your father."

"First tell me about the fairies."

"Will, go get your father! Go now!"

Will scrambled downstairs, shouting that the fairies were bringing a baby.

"Jacob!" Agnes screeched, afraid her husband would think the boy was just talking nonsense.

When he heard his wife's cry, Jacob rushed up the stairs three at a time.

"Is it coming?"

"Yes," she grinned.

"I'll have the girls take Will over to my parents' house," Jacob said.

"Don't leave me."

"No, dear." He stooped to kiss her forehead. "I'll have the girls send my father for the doctor. I'll be back up in two minutes."

"All right," she said, trying to be brave. "I have time. It'll probably be hours yet."

Another pain shot through her as Jacob turned away. He went downstairs to explain the situation to the girls, then bundled them all off to their grandparents' house. For once, the girls did not argue with him; he felt they were good girls at heart. By the next contraction, Jacob was at Agnes's side, holding her hand. She knew she was a lucky woman, both in her husband and her children. Between pains, she spent a moment hoping Kathy would be so lucky.

🍁   🍁   🍁

"Hello," said Sylvia, answering the front door.

"Hello, Sylvia. I've come to see your mother and your new little brother."

"I'll see whether she's sleeping. Just a minute."

Sylvia was about to let the door slam shut, but fortunately, Jacob had heard Molly's voice and caught the door before it closed in her face.

"Come in, Molly. How are you?" he said cheerfully; he could not help being cheerful after the birth of his son, but he also hoped to cheer her since he knew she still deeply grieved for her husband.

"I'm all right," she said. "How are you?"

"Couldn't be happier," Jacob smiled. "Now I have an even number of boys and girls."

"Yes, isn't it wonderful," said Molly. "May I see the baby?"

"Yes, little Clarence is sleeping, but Agnes is awake. Come on in."

He led her into the parlor where Agnes lay on the sofa, cuddling her newborn.

"Oh, he's so precious," said Molly. "Let me hold him. It's been so long since I've held a baby."

Agnes handed little Clarence Whitman to Molly, her face lighting up the moment she held the blessing. "He's just beautiful," she said. "He's the most attractive baby I think I've ever seen! Oh, but don't tell my children I said that."

Agnes laughed and said, "He takes after his father," which made Jacob beam.

"He certainly is handsome," Molly said. "It's so wonderful to hold a baby; it just revives my spirits. And how are you, Agnes? Did everything go well?"

"I'm fine. More tired than I remember being when the other children were born, but I'm a lot older now."

"This is such a happy day for me," said Molly, sitting down in a chair, completely unwilling to surrender little Clarence to his parents. "I remember the day you were born, Agnes; I thought you were beautiful then, but of course, your mother was such a lovely woman. And now I've lived to see dear Clara's fourth grandchild."

Molly teared up a bit at the thought. Agnes wondered whether Molly just missed her mother or whether she regretted not yet having grandchildren of her own. "I'm sure you'll be a grandmother yourself before long," she said.

"Not unless Kathy or Karl get married," said Sylvia, having followed the grownups into the parlor.

"Sylvia," said Agnes, "will you go check on Will for me?"

"He's fine. He's upstairs with Mary."

"Would you go check anyway? I want to speak to Mrs. Montoni in private."

"Fine," Sylvia moaned.

"Sylvia, what did I tell you about using that tone of voice?" said Jacob.

"Sorry," she muttered as she vanished from the room.

Shaking her head, Agnes said to Jacob, "I hope Clarence doesn't take after his sisters."

"If he takes after his father, he'll break all the girls' hearts," said Molly as she rocked the baby.

"That's about all the complimenting a man can take in one day," said Jacob. "I'll leave you two women to your talk."

Jacob went upstairs. Molly continued to coo over Clarence, who was remarkably good to have remained asleep.

"How have you been, Molly?" asked Agnes, straightening herself on the sofa to prepare for the conversation she had promised Kathy she would have.

"I'm all right," said Molly. "Such a big boy too. I don't think even Karl was this big when he was born. It's so good to hold a baby again. I almost wish I could have another, but I don't even know whether I'll have grandchildren soon. Karl doesn't seem interested in marriage. All he wants to do is make money, although I don't know what good it will do him; not when he won't even buy a decent house to live in. He and Ben share an old cabin. They're typical bachelors, but I sure wish he'd find a wife to take care of him."

"Maybe Kathy will get married soon and give you grandchildren," said Agnes.

"Oh Kathy's just a girl," said Molly. "She's too young to think of marriage and children."

"Actually, Molly," Agnes said, taking a deep breath, "Kathy asked me to talk to you. She's in love with a young man, and she thinks he's going to ask her to marry him."

Molly lifted her head up from the baby to peer oddly at Agnes. After a moment, she let out a nervous laugh. "Oh, I know she has a crush on Ben, but he'll never marry her."

"No, not Ben. It's Patrick McCarey. She thinks he loves her, and she wants—"

"The boy who shovels our sidewalks?" Molly frowned.

"Yes, she says they're great friends, and they've spent a lot of time together."

"But they're just friends."

"She's convinced they're going to be more than that."

"Girls do have foolish notions," said Molly, wishing the baby would cry to end this conversation. She was tempted to give it a good poke.

"I think you need to talk to her," said Agnes.

"Why didn't she talk to me in the first place? Who keeps secrets from her mother?" But Molly knew why Kathy had not come to her even before Agnes tried to explain.

"She's afraid you won't approve."

"How can I approve when I don't know anything about this young man?"

"That's why you need to talk to her. He seems like a nice young man. I know Jacob's parents like him, but he seems to be—"

"What?"

"Well—moody or depressed. She didn't quite say so, but I think he's keeping something from her. I think he left Ireland because he was in some sort of trouble, and you need to find out what that is before you consent to her marrying him."

"I don't know what's gotten into her," Molly sighed. "She's just a girl."

"I was the same age when Jacob and I were engaged," said Agnes, "and I remember you approved of that. But even if you don't approve of her marrying

Patrick, you need to talk to her about men and being married. I know you've had a hard time since your husband died, but Kathy really needs you now."

Agnes had said these last words hesitantly, but even though they hurt, Molly knew Agnes was right. "I suppose I've been a bad mother," said Molly. "I haven't meant to be, but I know I've been ignoring her. I suspected she had feelings for this boy, but I hoped it was just a passing fancy; I'm just not ready for her to grow up yet." She could not yet admit she was afraid to be alone if Kathy married.

"You're a good mother," Agnes replied, "but sometimes being a good mother means letting go of your children. If Patrick's the right man, then I know you'll be happy for Kathy, but first you need to talk to them to find out whether he's suitable for her; you need to do that soon, before things become more serious between them."

Molly avoided Agnes's eyes by looking at the baby. Clarence's precious puffing little cheeks made her long for a grandchild.

"I'll talk to her," said Molly.

"Whatever happens," Agnes consoled, "it's all part of God's plan for us to be better people."

Molly knew that; she just did not understand why God's plans could never concur with her own.

Clarence now woke and gave out a little cry.

"There, there, Clarence; don't cry," Molly said. "Everything will be all right."

Molly had not been to confession since before Christmas. After Montoni had died, she did not have the heart to go, but now in need of guidance, she turned to the Church, the only real comfort in her life, with its exemplary saints, incense, hymns, Latin prayers, and reminders of her Irish childhood. She had long avoided confession because of her guilty feelings over Montoni's death. She had excused herself from going by pretending it was too hard to go to the cathedral when it was not finished and that it was too far to climb uphill to the French Catholic Church on Washington Street. But today was a beautiful spring day, and more importantly, she felt if everything were to go well when she talked to Kathy, first she needed forgiveness.

She climbed the hill to St. John the Baptist's, the French Catholic Church, hoping the priest there would not recognize her voice as the priests at the cathedral were sure to. She found only a few people in the darkened church, each praying in a pew while waiting his or her turn for confession. She knelt down and prayed the "Hail Mary" but her thoughts wandered to her daughter. She failed to notice that those who arrived after her went before her to speak with the priest. Finally, the church emptied out. When she was the last penitent remaining, still Molly did not feel ready, but she entered the confessional, afraid the priest might come out, thinking he was done, only to see her there. She did not want anyone to suspect what weighed upon her mind, and Catholic or not, she would not have gone to confession if the priest were able to see her face. She felt her sins were only between her and God, but to hear "You are forgiven" would help her believe in God's forgiveness, and the need to believe overcame her pride.

She stepped inside and knelt in the dark confessional. After a few seconds, the priest slid aside the little window, and through the grilled screen, Molly strained her eyes to see which priest it was, but she could not quite make out his profile.

"Yes, my child," he answered her silence. Neither did she recognize his voice.

"Forgive me, Father, for I have sinned. I made my last confession at Christmas."

"Why so long ago my child?"

Molly fumbled for words. She had many reasons, all of them selfish.

"I was ashamed, Father."

"God sees all our thoughts and deeds. He already knows your sins. You need only confess them. Were you not sorry for them before?"

"No, I mean I want to feel sorry, but I don't know how."

"Tell me these sins, my daughter."

"I hated my husband," she said; it was her worst sin, and she could not deny it. "He's dead now, but I still feel anger toward him."

"Why did you hate him?"

"Because he mistreated me. He abused me, and he was cruel to my children. But I stayed with him, Father, because I felt it was my duty."

"I see," said the priest.

His silence made her feel free to express the rest of her guilt without fear.

"And I'm selfish. I only married him to provide security for my children—he was my second husband, and my first husband left us impoverished when he died. I did not love my second husband; I sinned by being dishonest about why I married him. I tried to love him, but I couldn't when he abused me."

"He sinned against you as well by mistreating you," said the priest. "I know you are sorry for your sin of anger. The way he mistreated you was punishment enough for that. What else, my child?"

Molly was surprised, remembering how another priest had suggested she should treat her husband better. But she had tried, so perhaps now she deserved to be forgiven for her hatred.

"I knew he was committing evil acts, but I did not speak out against them."

"What evil acts?"

"He used to cheat people, and Father, he—I—I've kept it to myself all these years, but now that he's dead, I feel I have to say something."

The priest waited patiently.

"I think he—I think he knew something about, or was partly responsible for burning down the cathedral."

The priest cleared his throat, then asked, "Why did you say nothing, my child?"

"I was afraid he would hurt me or my daughter, and I worried about how we would survive if he were imprisoned, and, well, he was my husband, Father."

"So you wished to protect him?"

"Yes, him and—well, all my family."

"If you protected him, then you loved him. We can be frustrated with our family members, but deep down we do love them, even the most difficult ones."

Molly did not know whether this were true; she missed Montoni after being so used to caring for him, but had she loved him? Yet she would not contradict a priest.

"Is there anything else, my daughter?"

"Yes, I am selfish," said Molly, confessing what most weighed on her mind. "My daughter wants to marry, but I don't want her to because I'm afraid."

"Afraid of what?"

"I tell myself her husband might mistreat her as mine mistreated me."

"Is the man she loves a bad man?"

"No, I don't think so. I don't really know him."

"Then why do you fear this?"

"I—I don't know whether I do. I think it's just my excuse because really I'm afraid to be alone if she marries him."

"Why would you be alone? Will your daughter move away?"

"I don't know. It just won't be the same. I'll have to live alone."

"Your daughter will probably have children; how could you be lonely when she will only be adding people to your life?"

"I know; I've thought of that. Please tell me how to overcome my selfishness."

"You need to think less of yourself," said the priest. "Be generous, and if your daughter and this man love each other, be happy for them; help them. Be generous to everyone you meet, and put them before yourself. If you can do this, even if a little bit more each day, then you'll receive far more happiness than you can imagine. Let that become your life's purpose: generosity and love."

Molly's heart leapt at these words, yet she feared she could not accomplish what the priest said. "But tell me how to do this, Father?"

"You must pray, my child; if you truly want to be generous, the Lord will teach you how, and you'll find it's easier than you expect."

Molly wanted to ask more, but the priest began to absolve her. He told her to pray the rosary three times as penance and to ask for the Lord's guidance.

She stepped outside into the dazzling spring sunshine, but she did not feel enlightened. She had hoped to emerge with relief that her sins were forgiven, but she did not want to work at being better. Still, she knew God was generous in forgiving her; she wanted to cry to think he could still love her despite her many faults. She wanted to be as generous. Until now, she had thought herself generous, kind, loving, but inwardly, she knew she was being selfish in wanting Kathy to herself. Her generosity must begin there; she would have to talk with Kathy.

Agnes was enjoying her lying-in period, and this time, she felt she sorely needed it. After the other children had been born, she had rested only a week or two, and she would have been up sooner back then if only Edna or her mother-in-law had not insisted on doing the housework so she could rest. But Clarence's birth had left her completely exhausted.

In the mornings, she did not even get out of bed to make Jacob breakfast before he left for the farm. Jacob had hired a girl to come in and help her, and while Agnes soon determined the girl incompetent at housekeeping, she did not argue with her husband's attempted kindness.

Jacob was nevertheless disappointed that his wife remained in bed so long. That morning, she had wanted to make him breakfast; three times she had tried to get up, but she could barely open her eyes. She even dreamt she was making Jacob's breakfast, only then to wake and find herself still in bed. Jacob worried about her exhaustion, but gently kissing her on the cheek, let her sleep. The hired girl was late that morning—she was late every morning, so Jacob made breakfast for himself and the girls and sent them off to school. Will was still asleep and Clarence slept beside Agnes, so Jacob did not worry about leaving for work. He knew the hired girl would pass him on the street hurrying to the house. He would have waited for her, but this morning, he had some business to do for his father-in-law before he went to the farm; Gerald occasionally wrote to request he perform some bank transaction or sign some documents as proxy for him. Jacob told himself Agnes would be fine alone for just a couple minutes.

As he walked out the front door, he could see the hired girl coming down the street a couple blocks away. He set off in the opposite direction for the bank. She slowed down her walk, hoping Mr. Whitman would not stop to give her a reprimand.

Meanwhile, Agnes managed to open her eyes and crawl out of bed. She felt confused and dizzy, but she needed to use the chamber pot. She only got halfway across the room before she knew she should just go back to bed; she felt terribly warm; it was the warmest spring she ever remembered; she turned around by clutching onto the armoire; she saw Clarence lying in the bed, still asleep; she loved him, but she never wanted to have another baby if it would make her feel like this; she let go of the armoire and took a step forward, but her leg failed beneath her. She collapsed, reaching out but unable to grab anything to stop her fall.

The hired girl heard the thump as she opened the front door. In a few seconds, she had come to her mistress's aid.

"You're burning up, Mrs. Whitman," she said as she felt Agnes's forehead, but Agnes could not hear her; the fever had overcome her senses. The girl struggled and somehow managed to get Agnes back in bed. Then removing Clarence so he would not be endangered by the fever, she bundled up the baby, and took him with her. In a panic, she completely forgot about Will, who fortunately remained sleeping. She ran next door and within a couple minutes, the Whitmans' neighbor had gone to fetch the doctor.

Cordelia stared out the window while dawdling over her coffee. She had plenty to do, but at that moment, she did not have the gumption to finish the laundry. She was exhausted and deserved a break—it could not hurt to rest a few minutes.

She was not physically tired, just depressed. And worried. It was hard to believe it was June—already over a month since Agnes had died. She knew it was hard to recover from the loss of a loved one—that truthfully one never fully recovered—she knew because she still missed her parents after all these years. But never had she seen anyone suffer like Jacob. Sophia's crying fits had been excruciating after Madeleine's death. Even Molly's confused sadness after Montoni's death was understandable. But Jacob had always seemed strong enough to withstand anything. Now he sat, staring into space, oblivious of the world around him, forgetting even the children who needed him. Only now did Cordelia suspect the toll the Civil War had taken upon her son, and that much of his comfort and inner strength had sprung from Agnes's sustaining love.

A month had failed to relieve any of Jacob's pain; Cordelia grieved more for her son than for the daughter-in-law she had lost. The funeral had been so dismal. Agnes had been laid out in her own parlor during a hot, stormy spring night. During the wake, the girls had wept while Cordelia tried to comfort them and Nathaniel tried to keep Will and the baby from screaming. Jacob had sat silently, looking helpless and lost, unable to think of his children, unable to thank the guests for coming, unable—it sometimes appeared he was unable even to move or breathe. He scarcely ate for days after. He constantly complained he was tired, yet he would walk restlessly about the room, his footsteps speaking his unutterable agony.

After the funeral, Cordelia had suggested Jacob and the children stay at the boarding house for a while. Jacob had refused. Then she offered to have the children stay with her and Nathaniel until he felt better, but he said it did not matter. Nothing seemed to matter to him. Cordelia thought his attitude intolerable. She found herself caught between caring for two households while her granddaughters refused to help, and their father would not discipline them. Cordelia knew the girls' mother had taught them to cook and clean, but they were lazy without constant supervision, and Cordelia did not have the energy to control them. If Jacob did not snap out of it soon, Cordelia feared he would lose his mind, and then what would become of his children?

As she stared out the window, her sad thoughts were distracted by the sight of Nathaniel tramping up the road to the house. His figure looked more haggard and bent over than usual. She scolded herself for worrying so much about Jacob and her grandchildren to the neglect of her husband. Nathaniel had not complained, and he had helped her as much as a man can be of help to a woman, but she knew it was difficult for him to lack his wife's attention during these hard, sad days.

"I have the mail," he said when he came into the dining room. Cordelia jumped up from her chair so he would not suspect her laziness.

"Anything interesting?" she asked.

"A letter from your sister."

"Sophia? It's about time."

She had written to Gerald and Sophia the day after Agnes's death. She and Nathaniel had discussed sending a telegram, but they knew the funeral would take place before Agnes's parents could return from Europe, so a letter was sent instead; until today, no response had come.

Cordelia ripped the envelope open, while mumbling, "Poor Gerald, I'm sure he'll be devastated. His only child—"

She scanned the letter for news.

"Sophia wrote it," she said, skimming over several pages of minuscule handwriting. Nathaniel sat down at the table, waiting for her to read aloud.

"Listen to this," Cordelia said, almost angry enough to toss the letter into the stove. "This is all she wrote about poor Agnes: 'I am sorry to hear about Agnes's death. Gerald has been very upset and he says he will write to Jacob directly.'"

"That's all?" said Nathaniel.

"Yes. Can you believe it? But you know, if she were here, I don't think she would have bothered to say much more. She'd probably be more upset that the new house Mr. Swineford built for his daughter is larger than the one she and Gerald built. Can you believe her? Agnes was her stepdaughter, after all!"

"That's Sophia for you," said Nathaniel.

"It's not that I don't love my sister," Cordelia fumed, "but there are times— even taking her shortcomings into consideration—when she still might rise to the occasion."

"Maybe she's a comfort to Gerald in Paris," said Nathaniel, "even if only between shopping trips. She never was much of a letter writer anyway."

"She filled a full page telling me about her visit to Versailles."

"You know what she's like," Nathaniel replied. "You set yourself up for disappointment by expecting more from her."

"I guess I thought they would want to come home to spend time with the family."

"Gerald probably doesn't want to ruin Sophia's trip when she's looked forward to seeing Europe for so long. You know how attentive he is to Sophia, always putting her before himself. And she did vow she would never return to Marquette."

"She vowed that because her children died here," said Cordelia, "but it's precisely because she lost her children that she should be more sympathetic to Gerald and Jacob's loss."

"Well," said Nathaniel, "she said Gerald would write. Maybe she felt it wasn't her place to say more since it's his daughter. I'm sure we'll get a letter from him in a day or two."

Jacob received his father-in-law's letter the next day. When Cordelia came over that afternoon, he passed it to her without a word. Cordelia read quickly: Gerald was deeply grieved; he sent his sympathies to Jacob and his grandchildren; he could not disappoint Sophia by returning early to the States; returning would make no difference to poor Agnes now; he would like to come visit, but he could not bear to see Marquette yet when it held so many memories of his daughter.

"Sophia planted that idea into his head," Cordelia told Nathaniel that evening when she summarized the letter for him. "Gerald's so heartbroken he's letting Sophia take control of his life."

"Shh, the Dalrymples will hear you," Nathaniel said as their boarders came downstairs.

Cordelia buttoned her lip and went to make supper, but her anger remained. She knew she was taking out her anger on her sister for Agnes's death, but she was too grief-stricken to care if she were being unfair. "Just this one time," she thought, "I would really like to write and tell Sophia just what I think of her."

♣   ♣   ♣

"Mrs. Montoni?" said Patrick.

Molly had opened the door to find the young man on her front porch. She had been waiting for him to come any day now, but she had hoped Kathy would first give her notice. She did not at all feel ready for this conversation.

"Yes—um," she fumbled for words. Perhaps she should pretend she did not know why he had come. "Kathy isn't home. She's gone out with her friend, Mary, and I don't know when she'll be back, but you're welcome to stop by later."

She started to shut the door, not to be rude, but from a self-protective reflex.

"No, I came for you."

She hoped he did not notice how she was shaking. After she had lost Agnes, whom she had loved like a daughter, she again felt she was not ready to lose Kathy. She did not want to be hard, but she would need to have a long conversation with him before she consented to any marriage.

"Mrs. Whitman sent me," said Patrick.

"Why?" Molly was confused; why would Cordelia interfere in her affairs?

"It's Mrs. Dalrymple. She's about to have her baby. They can't afford a doctor. Mrs. Whitman says she can deliver the child, but she wants you to come help because," he smiled, "she says men are useless at times like these."

"Oh," said Molly, quickly understanding the urgency of the moment, yet feeling a baby was nothing to worry about compared to talking with Patrick about marriage. "Just a minute." She ran into the other room for her shawl, then reappeared.

"I'll walk back with you," said Patrick.

"All right, oh—I better leave a note for Kathy," she said, running back into the dining room. After a minute, she returned to find Patrick standing in the hall and staring into the parlor. She was suddenly embarrassed; she knew it was a fine parlor, quite an expensive and extravagant one, but Montoni had had a rich man's tastes. She suspected this young man beside her had been poor all his life, just as she had been at his age. He looked awkward standing in her elegant home; she understood; she still felt out of place amid all this finery.

"You have a beautiful home," he said when he turned around at her footstep.

"Thank you," she said. "My husband decorated it. It's a bit fancy for my tastes."

Patrick did not reply as they stepped outside. Once they were together on the porch, she turned around to lock the door.

"We never locked our doors in Ireland. We never had anything to lock up," Patrick said. Then he thought how ignorant and poor he must sound, how inappropriate as a lover for Kathy.

Molly said nothing but went down the porch steps and walked to the street. Patrick awkwardly followed.

"Mrs. Whitman said it might be several hours still," said Patrick as they turned onto Fourth Street. As they passed the Harlow house, Molly thought, "That house is larger and finer than mine," but she did not know how to explain that to Patrick. To make conversation, she remarked, "That's the Harlow house. Mr. Harlow is the founder of Marquette, you know."

"No, I didn't know that," said Patrick, wondering whether the house's owner was a better man than the horrible landowners he had known in Ireland.

Molly struggled to find something else to say, but nothing came to her. Silently they walked uphill, crossed Washington Street, then made their way to where the Whitmans had rebuilt their boarding house just down the street from Jacob and Agnes's home.

"Have you seen Jacob lately?" Patrick asked, as they passed his now melancholy house.

"No," said Molly. "Is he any better?"

"He hardly speaks a word. His parents are really worried about him."

"Poor Jacob," said Molly, shaking her head. "He's always been so good to everyone, his parents, his in-laws, his wife and children. He's the last person who deserved such a tragedy to happen to him."

"Kathy told me," Patrick replied, "that after her own mother, she thought Agnes the kindest person she ever knew."

Molly was embarrassed by the indirect compliment. Was this young man trying to flatter her? But there had been sincerity in his voice, as if, forgetting Kathy's mother walked beside him, he had solely intended to compliment Agnes's memory. Molly told herself to quit analyzing everything and focus on Mrs. Dalrymple's situation. She could not think about Kathy and Patrick now.

"Did Cordelia say whether everything was going well for Mrs. Dalrymple so far?"

"She said it may be difficult," replied Patrick; the thought of childbirth frightened him after what had happened to Agnes. "It'll be her first child."

"Yes," said Molly. "Sometimes that can make a difference."

Mr. Dalrymple met them at the door. Cordelia had ordered him out of the bedroom. Nathaniel had tried to help her, but Cordelia was relieved when a woman arrived who would know what to do. Then Nathaniel was also cast from the room.

Patrick and Nathaniel joined Charles Dalrymple and old Mr. Dalrymple in the parlor. The prospective father was terrified every time the slightest cry drifted downstairs.

"The first one is bound to be the hardest," said Nathaniel, as if he were an authority on childbirth.

"Yes," old Mr. Dalrymple told his son. "With your mother, the first child was the hardest, but all your other brothers and sisters were born with hardly any trouble at all."

"How many children do you have, Mr. Dalrymple?" Patrick asked the old man.

"Oh, let me think." He frowned and slowly counted on his fingers. "There's Mary Flora, and Barbara Allan, and William Wallace, and Robert Bruce, and—"

The list seemed endless.

"I didn't realize you had any children besides Charles here," said Nathaniel.

"Oh yes," said Mr. Dalrymple, still trying to count them all. "Let's see— twelve I guess."

"Where do they all live?" asked Nathaniel.

"Well, Charles is right here," laughed the old man. "Four of them have joined their mother in Heaven. But not one of them died at birth, my boy, so don't you worry none about it. Let's see, that leaves seven others. One of them, he moved back to Scotland, and five of them decided to stay in Nova Scotia, and then two of them are in Chicago. Does that make twelve?"

"Yes," said Nathaniel, unsure but not interested in hearing the list of names again if one were missing.

"No," said Charles Dalrymple. "Only Alexander is in Chicago now, Father. Remember, there were two of us there because I was one of them, but then you and I moved here."

"I didn't know you had lived in Chicago," said Patrick, only having a vague idea of where that great city was despite having passed through it as a stowaway on the train.

"Yes, we moved there after the great fire," said old Mr. Dalrymple. "We thought we'd find work helping to rebuild since both Charles and Alexander are carpenters. But then work slowed down during the Depression in the '70s, so we moved up to Wisconsin for the logging; then we came up here when Charles found carpenter work. Alexander didn't want to leave the city, so it's just me, Charles, and Christina now."

"And soon your grandchild," Nathaniel added.

The evening was long with anticipation, perhaps all the longer because old Mr. Dalrymple, excited by the prospective continuance of his family line, launched into tales of his ancestors, beginning with his life in Nova Scotia, and then how his father had migrated there from Scotland, then into the story of some ancestor who had fought with Bonnie Prince Charlie. Neither Nathaniel nor Patrick had any idea who that was, but Mr. Dalrymple revered the tragic prince as little less than a saint.

When it had been dark for hours, when Patrick was glowing with indignation from hearing how the English had forbidden the wearing of tartans in Scotland, and when Nathaniel could not keep his eyes open another minute to hear the details of the Battle of Bannockburn, Molly reappeared.

"You have a child, Mr. Dalrymple," she said. "Mrs. Whitman is washing it up, and then she'll bring it right down."

"And Christina?" asked the proud father, jumping to his feet.

"She's just fine. You can see her in a few minutes."

"Charles," said old Mr. Dalrymple, "you haven't asked whether it's a boy or a girl."

"It's a girl," said Molly.

"Margaret Dalrymple," the old man declared, christening the child before the father could speak. "That's what we agreed on. To name it for my mother if it were a girl. My mother, now she was named for St. Margaret, who was a Queen of Scotland, you know. She was married to King Malcolm III, the king who slew King MacBeth, whom I'm sure you're familiar with from Shakespeare's play, although the play is historically inaccurate. St. Margaret was herself a descendant of the English royal family, but we can forgive her for that because—"

But no one was listening to him. Instead, they all turned to see Cordelia come downstairs with the newborn and place it in its adoring father's arms.

For ten or fifteen minutes, exclamations of wonder followed over the child's beauty, healthy color, and size. Patrick thought the little girl looked beat red and bald, and the veins showing through her head were unsightly. He was a bit revolted, frankly; he was surprised to see Charles glow with pride, yet he wondered whether he and Kathy might not someday feel the same way about their own child, if he dared hope that—

"I'll be going home now," said Molly.

"Let me walk you home," Patrick offered.

"Oh no, it's too late."

"But it's the middle of the night," he replied. "I'd feel better if I went with you."

"Oh no, I've lived in this town for thirty-five years," said Molly. "I probably know Marquette's streets better than anyone, so I'm sure I'll find my way home all right. It's not as if there's any crime for us to worry about here."

"Ten years ago," said Nathaniel. "I would have also said I knew this town well, but the way it keeps growing, and the way I keep getting older, I can't keep up with it."

"We can't help getting old," said Molly, "but we should be glad to see Marquette grow and prosper. Well, good night everyone. Congratulations again, Mr. Dalrymple."

"Good night," everyone replied except Patrick who again asked and was again refused the opportunity of walking Molly home.

"That was a good night's work," Molly thought as she walked carefully in the dark. A warm night breeze filled the air with the scent of lilacs. It was not such a dark night, once her eyes adjusted; she was thankful summer had finally come because ice could make a winter night's walk quite treacherous. But she would have gone to help no matter what the weather or season. "I helped bring life into the world today," she commended herself. "That's about the most important thing anyone can do. It makes my life seem more meaningful to help others. The priest told me to be generous, and tonight I succeeded."

But then she wondered whether she had been selfish when she refused to let Patrick walk her home. "He must think I want to avoid him," she thought. "I think he's a little intimidated by me; that's probably why he didn't try to force the issue of his relationship with Kathy. It's been over a month now since I told her I would talk to him, and he still hasn't asked for her hand, but the couple times I've seen them together, it's clear they're smitten with each other. Maybe I should be the one to give things a little push; I'll ask Kathy to invite Patrick over for supper some night next week."

Patrick's stomach nearly dropped to the floor when Kathy told him he was invited for supper. He knew it meant Kathy's mother might be softening toward him, but with such hope, greater fear of rejection came. He did not even own a decent looking suit for dinner; he had to borrow one from Charles Dalrymple; it was terribly tight upon his broader back, and the sleeves ended a couple inches above his wrists.

"It's the best I can do," said Charles. "You're just too tall."

Patrick felt foolish in the suit; he had never worn anything so fine in his life, and he was already nervous enough without worrying that he looked ridiculous. And the evening was so humid, and the suit so unbearably warm, he feared he would ruin it by staining it with sweat. Still, he dared not appear on Mrs. Montoni's doorstep without showing the utmost respect in his personal appearance. He walked to the house, continuously mopping his forehead on the way until his handkerchief was drenched when he arrived; he wished he could have a glass of ice water before he rang the doorbell.

He was relieved when Kathy opened the door.

"Good, you're right on time. Oh, you look so handsome," she said.

The compliment only made Patrick more self-conscious.

"Don't worry," said Kathy. "Just be polite and don't contradict Mother on anything. Not that she's narrow-minded, but her Irish tongue does get out of control now and then."

Reminded that Kathy's mother was from his native land, Patrick became more nervous; what if she should ask him something about Ireland; she was bound to ask; what would he say?

Kathy showed him into the dining room, but he refused to sit down until her mother entered and seated herself. Molly then appeared, carrying in the mashed potatoes. She was highly irritable from the hot weather and had considered canceling the dinner until a cooler evening, but she did not wish her daughter to think she was rescinding on her agreement to talk with Patrick. After setting down the potatoes, she poured a glass of ice water for everyone while she greeted her guest.

"Hello, Patrick. We're glad you could come. It's horribly warm, isn't it?"

She passed him a glass of water and asked him to sit down. Then she slid into her own chair and gave thanks to the Lord for the meal.

Kathy began passing the food around the table. Patrick politely praised the appearance and smell of the various dishes, then helped himself to each.

When everyone's plate was full, an awkward moment followed until Molly opened the conversation.

"So, Patrick, do you like Marquette?" she asked, looking him straight in the eye while ham dangled from her fork, as though his answer were so important she must wait for it before she could eat.

"So far," he replied.

"You didn't mind the long cold winter?"

"It was the coldest I've ever known," he said, "especially since I worked outside most of the time. But spring and summer are sure beautiful here."

"Yes," said Molly, "but not as beautiful as in Ireland."

She lifted the fork to her mouth and bit off the piece of ham in a manner that made Patrick think she disapproved of his answer.

"Well," he said, his eyes pleading with Kathy for a hint on how to respond, "it's a different kind of beauty here. Ireland is really green—especially the grass, but here when I'm in the forest, the trees are so green I feel like Ireland was barely green at all."

"Hmm, well, the climate here isn't as good," said Molly. "In winter, it's colder than Ireland, and in summer, it's hotter."

"It is awfully warm today," said Patrick, unsure whether she wanted him to like Marquette or Ireland better.

"I'd love to see Ireland," Kathy said to help along the conversation, "but we are better off here. Ireland sounds like such a poor country."

"Yes," Molly replied, "but sometimes I think I'd rather be back in Ireland anyway. You probably understand that, Patrick. Kathy tells me you've been homesick since you've arrived here."

"I was at first," he said, "but I've made some good friends now."

"And Kathy says you've found steady work?"

Patrick explained that Mr. Dalrymple had found him work for the summer, and an opportunity existed for some indoor carpentry work next winter.

"I'm just doing bricklaying now," said Patrick, "but I'm hoping to learn about carpentry."

"And when you save up enough money, will you be sending for the rest of your family back in Ireland?"

"No," he said, surprised by the question.

"Why not?"

Patrick had persevered through the conversation until this question, but now he felt he was being interrogated; he little suspected Molly did not want him to send for other relatives; she wanted his money to go toward supporting his wife—contingent of course upon her giving him permission to marry Kathy.

"My family doesn't want to come here," he said, "but I think I'll have a better life in America."

"That's what we all thought when we came," said Molly.

"How is the Dalrymples' baby?" Kathy changed the subject.

Patrick detailed the baby's daily routine of eating and sleeping and how the Dalrymples delighted in their little daughter's every move. Molly appeared uninterested during the remarks, although she was proud she had assisted in the child's birth.

"What's the baby's name again?" Kathy asked.

"Margaret."

"It's a pretty name," said Kathy.

"I've always been partial to names beginning with M," Molly smiled for the first time during the meal.

"Patrick's last name begins with M," Kathy said.

"Kathy, I think we ate too much to have dessert yet," Molly replied. "Would you mind making some lemonade and then we can have it with our pie in the parlor? Patrick and I will join you there, but I wish to talk to him alone first."

"Mama," Kathy tried to object.

"Use the dessert plates in the left cupboard," Molly replied.

When Kathy had no choice but to leave him, Patrick felt like a mouse waiting for the cat to pounce. He was no more at ease when Molly got up to shut the door behind Kathy, then returned to the table.

Patrick nervously cleared his throat.

"Thank you for inviting me over," he said. "The meal was very good."

"Why do you want to marry my daughter?" Molly asked, tired of politeness, and too irritable from the humidity to waste time on pleasantries.

Patrick felt alarmed but collected himself enough to reply, "Because I love her."

"You haven't asked her yet, but it's clear you intend to."

"Yes," he said, wanting to look down yet holding his eye to hers, "but I wanted to ask your permission first."

"You sound doubtful that I'll approve," she replied, not breaking his stare.

Patrick did not know what to say.

"If you'll make Kathy happy, I have no reason to object," said Molly, but before Patrick could begin to smile, she added, "I do, however, have to be certain you can make her happy."

Patrick felt foolish. How could he convince her he would make her daughter happy—should he profess his undying love for Kathy? Wouldn't he just sound more foolish if he did?

"I say that," Molly continued, "because I've known my share of drunk and shiftless Irishmen. Your being my countryman isn't necessarily in your favor. I know Ireland is plagued with troubles so perhaps I need not question why you left, but Kathy has suggested it was for reasons beyond just hopes of a better life in America."

Patrick did not know what to say. Had he escaped the British only to have his own countrywoman betray him?

"Why did you leave Ireland, Patrick? Kathy cannot understand what Ireland is like, but I can, so I want the truth."

Patrick would have lied, but he sensed she would know he was lying. Her eyes had a cunning look born from the many difficulties she had faced and conquered.

"I—I—" he stuttered.

"Kathy says you will not speak about Ireland, and if that's the case, I'm guessing you're ashamed of your past. I don't want her to get involved with a troublemaker or a criminal, and if you love her, you'll want the best for her just as I do."

Patrick's anger rose up in him; he wanted to launch into denials, but he was less angry at Molly than at himself and his conscience that did label him as a criminal.

"Patrick, I need to hear what you did. I won't reveal your secret to Kathy, but I need to know before I give you permission to marry my daughter."

Whatever his guilt, he felt she had no right to judge him. Finally, his voice came to his defense.

"I love your daughter, and I swear I'll make her a good husband. I'm sorry for my past, and I won't repeat those mistakes, but I think the past should just rest."

"The past never rests," said Molly. "Whatever we do, we are marked by it for the rest of our lives. You know that, or you would not have fled Ireland."

"I came here to forget, to start a new life. Kathy is my hope for that new life."

"When I came to this land, I also had hope," said Molly, "but my hope has mostly been wasted. Still I've lived a hard life so my daughter can have a better one. I don't want my daughter's hopes destroyed because of your mistakes."

"I've suffered and I'm sorry for it," Patrick repeated. "What happened is between me and God."

"Patrick," she said, "do you love your pride more than my daughter? If you do love her, you will tell me this one thing for her sake."

This woman was manipulating him as if she were his own mother. Yet Patrick respected her protective instinct. He had sworn never to tell anyone of his hideous deed, yet his stomach was slowly being eaten away by the anxiety of keeping his secret.

"All right," he broke down. "But please don't tell Kathy."

"If we're to be a family, we need to trust each other. I promise not to repeat what you say if you tell me the truth."

He was shivering despite the constrictive heat of the stuffy room. Molly waited patiently for his confession.

"Mrs. Montoni, I am a criminal. I left Ireland to escape punishment for my crime."

"Tell me what you did, quickly, so it'll be out and we can move on."

"I—I didn't mean to do it—I mean, I didn't realize how horrible it would be. I—"

She steeled herself, fearing his secret.

"God forgive me," he broke into sobs. "I killed a man."

He waited to be cast from the room as Lucifer was cast from Heaven. "Why?"

"I didn't want to—it's just—things didn't work out the way we intended."

"Who is we?" Molly asked. "Was it an accident? Did you plan to murder, or was it done in self-defense?"

"It's hard to say. Several of us from my village were determined to help free Ireland from English rule. We went to work in Dublin and waited for the right time to act. We were going to make a statement, to blow up a government building. We wanted to drive out the English by frightening them. We weren't the only ones. Hundreds like me are willing to risk everything to free our people."

"Yes," said Molly. "I've read in the paper about the murders in Phoenix Park in Dublin. But whatever the situation, there's no excuse for murder. To kill is a mortal sin; as a Catholic, how could you act so?"

"I was raised Catholic," said Patrick, "but when God does not come to our aid, we need to act to protect our people. Mrs. Montoni, you have no idea how horrible it is back home; God does not answer our prayers, and the Church only tells us to submit to our oppressors. We're slaves in our own land. You can barely walk in the cities without a British soldier breathing down your neck."

"I wouldn't know," said Molly. "I grew up on a farm far from the cities. I never even saw an Englishman until we stopped in Liverpool on the way to America."

"Then you can't imagine the suffering, the brutalities our people now endure. Every single bloody day!"

He was overcome with indignation and despair. He wanted to shout and cry, to shock this woman into an understanding of the intolerable circumstances that caused his crime. In America, people had it so good; they might be poor or have hardships, but at least they were free and had the chance to better themselves; they did not have to starve, to obey their enemies, to live without hope.

"Tell me how the crime came about," said Molly, more frightened of what the experience may have done to this young man than by his actual deed.

"My friends and I, we had big plans," said Patrick. "We talked about blowing up a government building, but I don't know that we ever would have done it. Maybe we just wanted to believe we were heroic. Anyway, somehow the British found out about our plans. During one of our meetings, the soldiers came to arrest us. They broke down the door before we knew what was happening. Me and another bloke, we managed to get out the back window, but the other six were shot before they could escape. Even the two of us didn't get far. My friend was shot in the back as we ran down the street. I ducked around a corner before they could get me. I knew I couldn't outrun them, so I hid until a soldier came around the corner. Then I jumped him. I grabbed him around the neck, and somehow, I don't know how, I found the strength to strangle him with my bare hands."

Patrick stared at his hands, still in disbelief of their power.

"Then I—I panicked," he said, his voice shaking as he remembered the terror. "I didn't know what to do except run. I still have nightmares about it. I dream I'm holding that soldier's neck and then as he dies, I try to stop myself, and I wake up crying."

He paused to wipe his tears, then gazed up at her.

"I'm sorry," he sobbed.

"How did you get away?" asked Molly. "They must have searched all of Dublin for you."

"I went to my sister and brother-in-law. They live just outside Dublin. She gave me some money she had put aside, even though she and her husband have three children to support. Her husband sneaked me down to the docks, and bribed a sailor to hide me on a boat headed for America. Once I got to New York, I went to some cousins I had there, but when I told them my story, they wanted nothing to do with me. Then I saw an advertisement for work here in the iron mines, so I stowed away on a train and switched several cars to get here. I didn't want to stay in the big cities from fear the British had agents out looking for me. I don't know whether the soldiers could even identify me, but I was afraid to take any chances. I'm afraid even to write to my family in Ireland to tell them I'm all right; I'm afraid a letter from me will cause them trouble."

"No wonder you're homesick," sighed Molly.

Patrick had nothing more to say; he could only await her verdict.

"Well," Molly groaned, "it was self-defense. I can't blame you, Patrick. I almost think the British had it coming."

"They treat our people like dogs," said Patrick. "They grind us into the ground. They've repressed our every activity until we might as well be kept in cages. You can't imagine the suffering there."

"I can to some extent," Molly replied. "I lived during some hard years in Ireland myself."

"It's never been as bad as now," said Patrick. "And the people only make it worse by being afraid to act. They pray for miracles, even make up stories about them, but nothing changes. I don't believe in miracles."

"I do," said Molly. She remembered how Bishop Baraga had prayed to God to save Kathy's life, then laid his hands on her.

"Well, I don't," Patrick repeated. "The only good miracle would be to have the British drowned in the Irish Sea. Instead, we get a useless miracle like the one at Knock a few years ago."

"At Knock?" asked Molly, remembering that village had not been far from where she grew up. "What happened at Knock?"

"People claim a miracle happened, but I don't believe it. It makes no sense."

"What kind of a miracle?" asked Molly. "I never heard of a miracle happening in Ireland."

"Some of the villagers in Knock claim they saw an apparition."

"Really?" Molly pondered what this could mean for Ireland, if it were true. Was it a sign of peace, or of trouble to come? All her life, she had longed to see a vision, but she had never believed herself good enough to be so blessed. Having God intercede through Bishop Baraga to cure her daughter was in itself more than she had deserved.

"It happened about five years ago," said Patrick. "Near the church, some people saw three figures: the Blessed Virgin in the center, dressed in white and wearing a crown. On one side of her was St. Joseph and on her other side St. John the Baptist. The vision lasted for two hours; it was evening and dark because it was raining, yet the vision remained and supposedly no rain fell on it."

"Was a message given?" Molly knew visions and apparitions often resulted in tidings or miracles, as at Lourdes when the Virgin Mary had caused a healing spring to appear.

"No," said Patrick. "I don't believe in miracles anyway, but this vision or miracle or whatever you want to call it made no sense. My sister claims it was intended to comfort the poor and suffering of Ireland, but I don't see how they can be comforted when God and His Church improve nothing."

"Perhaps the miracle reminded people that God loves them, that they will have a better life in the hereafter," Molly replied; yet she wondered why a vision had not appeared in those hard years of the famine when her family had been forced to leave their home.

"My sister visited Knock not long after," Patrick said. "She claims you can sense you are on holy ground there, that the Holy Spirit fills the place. Tons of people now go there on pilgrimage. Some say the miracle occurred at Knock because the local priest is a holy man, but others say that because the priest did not witness it, Ireland is lost. Some claim the sick have been cured there, but I doubt there's any proof. Everyone is in disagreement about what happened and what it means, so it might as well have never happened for any difference it has made."

"We can't know that," said Molly. "Plenty of things happen that we question at the time, but years later when we look back, we find a meaningful pattern in them."

"The Irish want salvation from the English, but God sends them a vision that lasts for two hours and that only a handful witness. That makes no sense," Patrick repeated. "If you ask me, God has abandoned Ireland."

"Patrick," said Molly, less angered by his words than grieved by his lack of faith, "remember that people thought the Messiah would be a king, but instead, He was the Son of God who came to free men from their sins. Your experiences were horrible, but you do not yet know the full extent of suffering. Like you, whenever I've suffered, I've asked why, only to find later that I was the stronger for it. God knows your suffering is to your advantage, and someday you will come to know that too."

"With all due respect," Patrick said, "you may have suffered, but you haven't known the misery I have by being exiled from my family and having to live in daily fear."

Molly tried to control her voice. What did this young man know about her life?

"I have never been completely alone," she admitted, "but I have watched my loved ones suffer and stood by helpless. You are too young to know what my generation endured, but your parents or grandparents must have told you about the great famine."

"Of course," said Patrick, "but a famine is not the same as political oppression."

"No, it's much worse," said Molly. "We had no one to blame for it, not even the English. We could find no meaning or explanation for our misery. You don't know what it is to watch your loved ones starve to death, to know there is nothing you can do to help them, even to wonder if there were a morsel to eat, if you would have the decency to share it with your own mother or sister. Hunger can turn people into ravaging animals. It makes you completely helpless until even your mind is lost."

"Yes, but I don't think—"

"Don't interrupt me," said Molly. "I've not spoken of this for thirty-five years, but in all fairness, I think I owe you my story as well, and perhaps you're the only one who can understand or bear its horror."

Patrick shrunk back. The painful hunger in Molly's eyes looked as if it would devour him when unleashed.

"First," said Molly, "we heard rumors that the crops were blighted. Not long after, my father and brother dug up the potatoes. They stank; they were black, filled with disease. My father let up a wail unlike anything I had ever heard before in my life, not even from a woman. We ran to him in the fields, my mother, grandmother, sister, all of us, and we feverishly dug up every potato, hoping to spare a few. Not one potato was edible. Every single one was destroyed. We fell to the ground in tears. We held each other. We wept in the belief we would all die. Soon we had word that all our neighbors suffered the same catastrophe. There was no food to be found in the entire county. The few who were rich enough to own cattle, slaughtered and ate them, then starved to death when the meat was gone. Our neighbors resorted to eating grass. My grandmother—she became so weak we had no other option; we tried to get her to eat grass too, but she only vomited it all up. Can you imagine watching a good old woman suffering like that? And when she died—"

Molly broke into loud wailing sobs.

In the kitchen, Kathy heard her mother's tears and trembled. Yet she dared not enter the room.

Patrick waited as Molly wiped her tears. Once she regained control, she continued, "We dug my grandmother a grave. My father could not do it, not for his own mother; he was so weak from hunger he could barely stand. My brother and I dug the grave, knowing we would soon also dig one for my father. I wanted then to toss myself in the hole with my grandmother. I do not know to this day how I managed to live through that week.

"But then my uncle came to visit us from twenty miles away. His wife and his two small children had starved to death. My aunt had wanted to leave Ireland for England, but he had refused; he madly thought the government would help us. I don't know whether the English were at fault—I think they were at a complete loss what to do since the famine was so terrible. My uncle had some money; he wanted to save the rest of the family by sending us to England, but my father was stubborn. He refused to go to the enemy's land. Then my uncle became ill; he died quickly while my father continued to linger. We took the money from the pockets of my uncle's corpse, and my brother, sister, and I forced our parents to leave their home. We fled, leaving behind our land, our home, our friends and neighbors, leaving them all behind to die. Do you know the guilt I still feel over that? Do you know how many times I've wished I had been buried on the heath of my family's farm? How often I have asked myself if I deserved to live when so many of them died?"

She was practically screaming at Patrick, as if demanding an answer, demanding relief from her guilt.

"That wasn't even the end," she said. "My sister died on the boat to Liverpool; she gave my father her portions of food, never hinting how sick she was. My father recovered from his illness, but both my parents were broken after that. We barely had money for the passage to America. My brother had to steal food on the ship so we could eat. And then we came to America, and things were hardly better than in Ireland; we had to live in two cramped, sordid rooms in what they would call a tenement house today, and we could not find work for weeks. Finally, I got hired in a factory, long hours for slave wages; after six weeks, I was laid off—then I hired myself out as a maid. When I met Fritz, I agreed to marry him partly so I would not be a burden on the rest of my family. What else could I do? True, I was not alone. I was with my husband, and I loved him, but it was not the same as being with my family.

"Tell me, Patrick, the reason for all that suffering. What justice existed in my innocent grandmother dying like that? Why should my poor uncle save us with his money, yet never see America himself? And my poor sister, who sacrificed herself to starvation so my father could live. None of it should make any sense, Patrick. It would have made more sense if I had died with them, but that's precisely why it makes sense. I believe God preserved me for some reason. I don't know what it is; He does not let me know because it is beyond my understanding, but I believe it, maybe only because having something to believe keeps me sane, but I choose to believe anyway."

Patrick was silent after Molly's revelation. He was relieved when she quit talking, yet he hated the silence that followed. He could not find words to cast out her demons.

"You have the death of one man on your hands, Patrick. I have the death of half the Irish race on my conscience because I outlived them. That's suffering."

"You couldn't have done anything else," he said. "You wanted to die, but you knew your family needed you."

"But why did any of us have to suffer? What did we do to deserve it?"

"I don't know," said Patrick.

"I don't know either."

Patrick was sweating from the heat of her tale. He thought of his own grandparents; now he understood why they had never spoken of the famine. He had asked them about it a couple times, but they had always dismissed his questions. He imagined their pain must have been like that of his hostess.

"It's all right now, Mother," he said, placing his hand on her shoulder and giving her his handkerchief. "No one can blame you for any wrong. We're in a better land now, where we're safe, and where our children will have better lives. We should just be thankful."

"It is a better land," she said, wiping her eyes, then placing her hand in his. She was surprised that he addressed her as mother; had he done so from respect for her age, or from affection as her future son-in-law? It didn't matter; he had said it sincerely, not to butter her up. He was the only one she had ever told these horrors to—not even Fritz had known; she had not wished to burden her family with that misery, any more than she wanted her children to have empty stomachs.

"I'm sorry," she said, squeezing his hand. "I've tried to forget it all for so long that when I remembered it now, it seemed as awful as if I were living it all over again."

"It's all right," he soothed.

"A million people died, Patrick. Do you know that? One million people died during the famine. I could cry for years and never shed enough tears for them all."

Patrick said nothing, just allowed her to finish her thoughts.

"If I had stayed in Ireland, like your family did," she said, "I don't know whether I wouldn't be just as angry about the oppression. I try to be a good Catholic, but if I were a man, I might have done the same to that English soldier."

"Thank you," said Patrick, "for understanding."

"I'm glad we've had this talk," she said. She swallowed, trying to clear the dry throat caused by her sobbing. "You understand I had to know for Kathy's sake."

"Yes. You're a good mother to care so much about her."

"Kathy will be worried," she said, now feeling at peace with her decision. "You can go tell her I give you my consent. I need a moment alone now. I'll come join you in the parlor in a few minutes."

"Thank you," Patrick smiled, almost reluctant to leave this courageous woman.

Left alone, Molly thought, "The priest was right. If I try to be generous, I receive more. I'm glad I told Patrick; we trust each other now. I think he'll take good care of Kathy."

Patrick went into the parlor but found it empty. He wondered what to do until he saw Kathy's silhouette through the lace curtains. Then he went out onto the porch, welcoming the cool air, the smell of coming rain, the relief to the end of the heat and humidity.

Kathy was leaning against a pillar. She did not even tremble when the thunder clapped.

"Kathy," Patrick nearly whispered.

A flash of lightning showed him she had been crying.

"What's wrong?" he asked. For the first time he placed his arm around her waist. He marveled at how natural it felt to hold her. She did not shiver at his touch, but leaned back against his chest.

"Your mother gave us permission. Will you marry me, then?"

"Yes," she sighed.

"Are you happy?" he asked. "Why are you crying?"

"Yes, I'm happy," she said. "I love you."

"I love you," he replied, kissing her hair.

"I heard," she said, "what my mother told you."

"About what? The potato famine?"

He quivered, fearful she had heard his own tragic tale.

"I only heard when she raised her voice, talking about how her grandmother had died. I had no idea she went through that. Can you imagine, my great-grandmother having to eat grass, and then starving to death, and her poor uncle, and all his family, and her sister—her sister would have been my aunt if she had lived. I wish I could thank them all for what they suffered so my mother could come to America."

"You thank them everyday by living and being happy," said Patrick.

"I understand now why you left Ireland; if I had to live in such poverty, I would have left too. I'll never pester you again about it. I understand how awful it must be to speak of it."

He was glad she understood, without having heard the actual reason he had left.

His chin rested upon her head. The sudden cool air made the perfume of her hair all the sweeter. The rain broke. It came down in torrents. They stood watching it. Patrick remembered Molly saying she could never cry enough tears for the million who died in the famine. He felt as if Nature wept tonight for all those innocent lives.

"How can we live in America, knowing that others are suffering?" Kathy asked.

"By appreciating our good fortune and being happy."

"Happy?" she asked, feeling it impossible after years of living under her stepfather's oppression, after the suffering her mother had known. She feared to be happy from fear it would not last.

"Yes, happy," said Patrick. "All those people who suffered would want us to be happy, to live and marry and have children who will not know such pain. We are the extensions of our parents and grandparents and all those brave people; we're a continuation of their spirits, and our happiness helps to validate their struggles, to give meaning to their lives."

He only understood this truth as he spoke it, as he suddenly believed the world could be a wonderful place; that everything could work out for the best. He felt like an old Celtic bard who foresaw a hopeful future capable of washing away past grief.

"We should go inside," he said. "Your mother expects us to have dessert."

Autumn comes all too quickly after an Upper Michigan summer. Already the leaves began to turn color, and a cool, crisp smell filled the early morning air. Marquette's residents, keeping in mind that blizzards may come as early as October, began to pull out winter boots and coats and search for their snow-shovels. But this early autumn day, the onslaught of winter was forestalled by a warm Saturday of sunshine, making the autumn leaves glow brilliantly. Say what you will of New England autumns, the people of Marquette know their land surpasses all others in its fall colors.

This specific day might resemble a hundred other autumn days, but to Patrick and Kathy, today was the finest ever created; it was their wedding day. Neither rain, nor sleet, nor snow could have spoiled it; Mother Nature herself had come to the celebration, her wedding gift a color collage as decoration for the nuptials. A gentle breeze fluttered the first falling leaves about like confetti. Lake Superior murmured in its rolling waves, complete with festive whitecaps. Overhead, the Canadian geese bleated out a song of goodwill as they headed for warmer climes.

"It's the perfect day," Cordelia said as she walked with her family to St. Peter's Cathedral that wedding morn.

"They always say 'happy is the bride whom the sun shines upon'," Nathaniel replied.

"Father," asked Sylvia, "did the sun shine on your wedding day?"

"I don't remember," said Jacob.

"Your parents had a beautiful wedding," Cordelia said, hoping that to speak of happy memories might cheer her downcast son. "Your mother looked absolutely stunning in her dress. Your stepgrandmother had it sent for all the way from New York and Mrs. Montoni—she was still Mrs. Bergmann then—made the most beautiful lace veil for your mother, and since your Grandpa Henning had just finished building his new house, the wedding was held in the parlor."

"I wish I'd been there," said Sylvia.

"Well," chuckled her grandfather, "you couldn't have been; your parents had to marry before they could have children."

"No they didn't," said Mary. "People don't have to marry to have—"

"That's enough, Mary," Cordelia snapped; if her granddaughter knew enough to realize children could be born outside wedlock, she did not want to hear it.

"I don't recall whether that day was sunny," said Jacob, "but I do remember that night was the great fire."

"That's right; it was," said Nathaniel.

"What was the great fire?" Sylvia asked.

Her grandfather described the devastating fire of '68 that had burned down half of Marquette. "Your father was quite the hero, fighting the flames on his wedding night."

"Yes," said Jacob, "we had to cancel our honeymoon. I guess I should have realized then the fire was a bad omen for my and Agnes's future."

"Let's hope then," said Cordelia, "that this beautiful day is a sign of good fortune for Kathy and Patrick. I like to see young people happy."

Jacob remembered he and Agnes had been happy when they were young. He could not claim to be young anymore; sixteen years of marriage had passed far too quickly.

"Cheer up, son. We're going to a wedding, not a funeral," said Nathaniel.

"I'm sorry," Jacob replied. "I'm just a little cranky because my old war wound is acting up again."

Cordelia was usually concerned about her son's health, but she knew he used his old war wound as an excuse today; attending a wedding was difficult for him when he showed little sign of moving past his overwhelming grief. Agnes may have been Jacob's greatest happiness, but Cordelia knew he had to count his remaining blessings.

"Look at that giant maple tree," she said to change the subject. "It must be older than me, yet its colors are so radiant. It's a true miracle. So much beauty!"

Everyone's attention turned toward this tree before the cathedral; this single tree was perhaps more magnificent than the entire cathedral, still being built, but soon to contain intricate stained glass windows, carved stone, and marble pillars.

"Seeing a tree like that makes all life's hardships seem bearable," Cordelia said.

"Grandma, it's just an old tree," Mary rolled her eyes.

"Maybe to you," said Cordelia, "but someday you'll understand it's part of God's magnificent artwork, a sure proof of His existence. Nothing that beautiful could happen accidentally, despite what that apostate Darwin says."

Mary did not know who Darwin was—had she known, her grandmother would have been more alarmed than by what Mary knew about the birds and the bees. Mary only knew Grandmother must be getting soft in the head to get that excited over a tree.

The Whitmans now entered the cathedral. St. Peter's walls were still being raised, so the wedding would be held in the basement, but the immensity of the basement alone was astonishing compared to the fine yet much smaller Methodist church the Whitmans attended.

"My gosh," gasped Sylvia. "Our whole church could fit inside here!"

"It's going to be gigantic," Cordelia agreed. "Popery is always extravagant."

"Now I know why people are Catholics," said Mary, as they slid into their seats. "It's worth it because their churches are so much prettier. I hear there'll be gold trim upstairs. Our church doesn't have anything as grand as that."

"No, and I hope it never will," Cordelia whispered, aware she was now surrounded by Roman Catholics. "What a gaudy waste of money that could have gone to help the poor."

"The intent of such decoration is to honor God," said Nathaniel.

"No," said Cordelia, "it's intended to show off the local bishop's importance."

"Bishop Vertin is said to be a very good man," Jacob replied with goodwill.

"His parishioners must not have thought so, or they wouldn't have burned down his old cathedral," said Cordelia. "But then, the whole Roman hierarchy is corrupt. I've never been in a Catholic Church before, and I don't intend to be in one again; I only came today out of respect for Patrick and Kathy. I don't need an ostentatious temple in which to worship my God."

"What's ostentatious?" asked Sylvia.

"It means showing off," Mary said.

"Shh," said Jacob.

The wedding procession began.

First Molly came down the aisle. She had made Kathy's wedding gown and veil, but she had failed to leave time to make her own dress. Karl had then found reason to treat his mother to a new store bought gown. Molly did not think the new dress fit her as well as if she had made it herself, but it could have been ten sizes too large and no one would have noticed since she came in on the arm of the gorgeous Ben. Few had self-control enough not to stare at his handsome face, his innocence shining through despite what the worst blows of life had inflicted upon him. If these townspeople thought him handsome today, how sad they never saw him walking through the forest, breaking through the trees with ax over his shoulder, his smile elevating all he looked upon as if he were the forest god himself. Even Sylvia felt a tingling desire she had never known until that moment; for the remainder of the day, she would cast shy glances toward Ben.

Next came Mary Mitchell, maid of honor, on the arm of Roger Mitchell, best man.

"That's my brother and sister," said Florence Mitchell, seated in front of the Whitmans. She despised Mary Whitman so she wanted to brag today, thinking herself superior because her siblings were in the wedding.

"We know," Mary snapped. "Turn around."

"Mary, shh," said Cordelia.

Florence did not turn around because she caught sight of the bride. Kathy had entered the church on Karl's arm.

For a moment, the audience was distracted by Karl's enormous beard, but then complete attention centered on the masterpiece created by Molly's countless hours of sewing. The gown was simple enough, but pink rosebuds trimmed the neckline and the hem, emphasizing the rest of the gown's simplicity and offsetting the bride's complexion and hair. Through a graceful, yet transparent veil could be seen Kathy's pert little nose, her dark brown hair, and the smile that spread across her face when Patrick turned around to see the great joy of his life.

In a moment, she was beside Patrick; her brother gave her away, then stepped back, leaving the bride and groom to the full attention of the congregation.

No one could help but be happy for these newlyweds. Even though the service was long, even though Sylvia and Mary were distracted by sneaking glances at Ben, even though Cordelia refused to kneel during the communion prayers for fear it would be idolatry, the ceremony was perfect.

Molly cried unashamedly during the Mass. Tears ran down her face until her handkerchief was soaked, and Karl had to give her his. She cried as much for her daughter's happiness, as she cried because God had allowed her to overcome her selfishness so this happy day could occur. The only thing perhaps more surprising to Molly than her daughter being old enough to marry was that the giant beside her had once been her little Karl. She still found it hard to believe she was a day over thirty, and today she felt so young that when she glanced out the corner of her eye, she could just imagine it was not Karl, but her dear Fritz beside her, watching the marriage of the daughter he had never known.

The ceremony was over all too soon. Already the bride and groom were walking down the aisle, and then Karl escorted his mother from the church. Molly found herself outside, receiving congratulations along with the newlyweds. Wedding photos followed, first of the bride and groom, then of the entire wedding party. Molly was saddened to be the only parent to stand with the couple, but she promised she would be parent to them both; they would all manage together; as long as they loved one another, they would get by, just as she and Fritz had.

Molly felt Fritz's presence throughout the ceremony, but one other departed soul also came to her mind today. When the photographs were finished, she told Kathy she would walk home to set up for the afternoon reception; first however, she found her way back into the church to where a tomb had been built for Bishop Baraga, the holy man who was already a legend. The older members of the diocese spoke with pride when they recalled a kind word he had spoken to them or the honor of having received the Eucharist from his hand. Molly felt an even deeper connection to him, and today she came to thank him personally.

"If you had been here to counsel me," she said, kneeling before the tomb of the saintly man, "I might not have been so foolish for so long. God once saved my child by your hand, and then you told me He must have a plan for my Kathy, or He would not have preserved her life. I cannot comprehend God's plans, but I trust you understood them better than I. Good Bishop, I know now that God's plans will work out no matter what I or Kathy do. I thank God again for preserving her life through you, and that He let me live long enough to see her happiness today."

Molly rose from her knees and exited the cathedral. As she walked home, her thoughts returned to Fritz and her own wedding day, the start of many hard years, but not as hard as they might have been without a husband to love. She believed Kathy and Patrick shared a love as strong as Fritz and hers. That they would have each other made Molly think this day the happiest of her life.

🍁   🍁   🍁

When the wedding was over, the Whitmans returned to Jacob's house until it was time for the afternoon reception. Jacob was anxious about Will and Clarence, who had been left with the rather absent-minded maid, but when he found them perfectly safe, he could not excuse himself from the reception by pleading the maid's incompetence; retreating to the old excuse of his war wound hurting, he decided he would not attend the reception.

"Mary and Sylvia will be disappointed if you don't go," said Cordelia.

"No, they'll only be disappointed if they don't get to go," Jacob replied.

"They can come with us," said Nathaniel.

"Of course they can," said Cordelia, "but we would like Jacob to come too."

"I just feel too tired. I need a little rest," Jacob replied.

"You won't get any rest with Will and Clarence to look after," said Cordelia.

The maid offered to stay and watch the children while Jacob napped; she could always use the extra money, and she had some vague notion that if she took good care of the war hero's house, he might someday look upon her as a future wife. Jacob was still handsome enough to attract women half his age, but the hired girl was too self-absorbed to realize he had no intention of ever replacing his Agnes.

Unable to persuade her son, Cordelia ushered the family off to the reception.

"If you feel better, maybe you can come later," she told Jacob.

As they walked to the reception, Mary said, "I thought Catholics were usually poor because they didn't have our Protestant work ethic, but now I think it's because they spend all their money to decorate their churches."

"No," said Cordelia. "The Catholic Church takes all their money so its priests can feast while leaving its people poor."

"They take all your time too," Sylvia said. "I didn't think that service would ever end. Why can't they talk in English?"

"Latin is just another way they brainwash people," Cordelia replied. "The people think it's some sacred language that God prefers, so they're ignorant of just how many blasphemies are said during the services."

"Well, I enjoyed the music at least," said Nathaniel.

"Fancy music hardly compensates for the loss of your soul," Cordelia frowned.

"Grandma, do you think Ben's Catholic?" Mary asked. She knew her family would oppose her marrying a Catholic.

"I don't know. Why?" asked Cordelia.

"I just wondered since he's Karl's friend, and Karl's Catholic."

"I know nothing of his religious beliefs," said Cordelia.

"I think Ben and Karl both worship money," Nathaniel replied. "Molly says all they do is work to get rich, but she doesn't see what good it does them."

"They both need to find a wife," said Cordelia.

Mary agreed; she was willing to help Ben out in the matter.

"How old is Ben?" she asked.

"I'd guess about thirty," said Cordelia.

Thirty! His youthful face made Mary think him not a day over twenty. Thirty was really old. But Ben looked so young and strong, and he was rich. Thirty was at least younger than her father, and Ben was still handsome. In two more years, she would be sixteen, and he would be thirty-two, and that wasn't too old for him to marry her.

"Kathy kind of looked pretty," Sylvia said, "but you could tell her dress was homemade."

"Why does Karl wear that shaggy looking beard?" asked Mary.

"It's horrible, just like a bear's," Sylvia added.

"Shh, someone will hear you," said Cordelia as they caught sight of the wedding guests gathered on Molly's front lawn.

"It's such a beautiful day I thought we'd have an outdoor picnic," Molly greeted them at the front gate.

"Good idea," said Nathaniel, "especially since this'll probably be our last warm day before the snow flies."

"Make yourselves comfortable. I'll have the food brought out in a few minutes."

Cordelia congratulated Molly once again on her daughter's marriage, and she apologized for Jacob's absence. The Whitmans then found seats beside the Dalrymples.

"Sit down girls," Cordelia said, taking a chair between Nathaniel and Christina Dalrymple.

"All right," said Mary. She had hoped to sit next to Ben, but she did not see him anywhere.

"How is baby Margaret today?" Cordelia asked her boarders. "Can I hold her?"

"She's fine; she didn't cry once during the wedding," said Christina, passing the child into Cordelia's arms.

"I'm sure Jacob would have let you leave her with the maid if you had wanted."

"Oh no, I'm still too attached to be parted from her for more than a few minutes," said the doting mother.

Sylvia saw no reason to fuss over the baby; it hardly even had hair yet. She hoped she never had a baby. Watching her brother Clarence was enough trouble.

"Wasn't it a beautiful ceremony?" said Cordelia.

"Yes," Charles Dalrymple agreed.

"It looks as if Mrs. Montoni has outdone herself with the wedding banquet," Christina added.

"Oh, it's well enough, I guess," old Mr. Dalrymple said, "but it breaks my heart that weddings are not what they used to be."

"What do you mean?" asked Cordelia. Old Mr. Dalrymple was no more than ten years older than her, yet Cordelia did not remember any major changes in wedding ceremonies during her lifetime.

"My father," he replied, "used to tell me about the wonderful wedding celebrations they had in Scotland back in the old days."

"How are Scottish weddings different?" Nathaniel asked.

"Why, in the Highlands, there are games, and all the people come from far and near; all the people are decked out in their clan tartans, and the dancing, the kicking of the heels—marvelous to behold! Yes, I do feel I miss the good old days."

"Father," said his son, "how can you miss them when you've never even seen a real Scottish wedding?"

"Charles," chided Christina, thinking it best to indulge the old man's fancies.

"Maybe not," Arthur Dalrymple said, "but my parents and grandparents saw those ceremonies, saw the clans wearing their tartans, until the tartans were outlawed by the bloody English. I dream of Scotland at night because memories of the mother land were passed on in my blood, just the same as if I'd been born and raised there."

"I understand," Cordelia said. "My mother used to tell me what Boston was like when she was a little girl; sometimes I think I know just what it was like to live in that great city at the turn of the century."

"Yes, yes, you see," Arthur Dalrymple told his son. "Mrs. Whitman understands."

"How is everyone?" Karl asked, stepping up behind them.

"Just fine, thank you," said Nathaniel.

"These are the Dalrymples," Cordelia introduced, "and this is their little girl, Margaret, the one your mother helped bring into the world."

"Glad to meet you. I'm Karl Bergmann," he said, shaking everyone's hand.

Mary looked around, suspecting wherever Karl was, Ben could not be far away.

"Mother instructed me to tell everyone we can start eating," said Karl. He then passed on to greet the other guests while the Whitmans and Dalrymples made their way to the picnic tables laid out with food. Mary's heart fluttered when she found herself in line behind Ben.

"Molly has a good size house in case it rains," said Cordelia, as she filled her plate, "but I think this picnic style is much nicer."

"Who would want to be indoors today?" Ben replied. "It's such a beautiful day, as if the very trees dressed up in their finest to celebrate the wedding."

Mary had earlier rolled her eyes when her grandmother raved about trees, but when Ben spoke, she thought him poetic. Using all her coquettish wiles—she had so many at fourteen—she asked Ben to put a scoop of potato salad on her plate.

"Oh, not so much," she cried. "I don't have an appetite like you big strong lumberjacks."

Ben smiled, then offered to scoop some for old Mr. Dalrymple. Mary felt annoyed that he would pay equal attention to that old Scottish coot. She tried to think of something else to say so he would notice her, but by the time she thought to ask whether he would want a big church wedding like Kathy and Patrick, he had already plopped Mr. Dalrymple's potato salad on a plate, then walked off to sit with Karl. Mary considered following him, but she knew her grandmother would object if she did not sit with the rest of her dull family.

Molly was pleased by her guests' delight over all the food she had prepared. She waited by the gate until they had all filled their plates, content to have for herself whatever was left over. Because she was the only one unoccupied, she was the first to see Jacob approach the house.

"Hello," she said, meeting him at the gate. "I'm glad you came. I hope you're feeling better."

"I had a headache," he said, "but it went away after I lay down for a little while."

He had never had a headache; he had simply found it more difficult to be alone than to be surrounded by a joyous crowd. He never felt happy these days—only lonely; neither solitude nor a crowd could change that. He had only decided to come to the reception so he would not hurt Molly's feelings, and because Agnes would have wanted to attend.

"How are you managing?" Molly asked. "I know a celebration must be hard for you when you're still in mourning."

He sighed and stared at the ground, unsure how to answer; he feared if he began to discuss it, he would break down.

"Agnes wouldn't want you to be unhappy; she loved you too much for that," Molly said. "Time heals all wounds. Trust me; I know."

He had nearly forgotten Molly's own loss, not so many months before his own. And now her daughter had married, leaving her alone.

"Will you be lonely now that Kathy is married?" he asked.

"No, that's why I'm selling the house; it's too gigantic for just me."

"Gigantic? It's a good size, but hardly gigantic compared to the one Mr. Swineford has put up."

"What he built is hardly a house," said Molly. "It's more like a castle. I understand there's an elevator in that four-story tower. I'd hate to have to clean the place."

"I'm sure they have a maid," said Jacob.

"I've always felt," Molly replied, "that if you need someone else to clean your house, then it's just too big. Sometimes I think I was a lot happier in my parents' old dirt floor cottage than I am in this fancy house."

Jacob could not imagine being content with a dirt floor, nor did he remind Molly that he had hired a maid for Agnes just before she died.

"Where will you live then?" he asked.

"I'm also selling that horrid old saloon of my late husband's," said Molly. "I've bought two plots near the cathedral. One has a house on it that will be perfect for Kathy and Patrick, and next door, I'm going to build a little widow's home; that way I can be near them without being in the way. Then I think I'll start doing some charity work to keep myself occupied since I don't have to look after a family anymore."

"That sounds like a good plan," said Jacob. "Did my mother tell you the children and I are also moving?"

"No, where to?"

"My farm. Our house here in town has too many memories, and since I work on the farm everyday, it'll be more convenient just to live there."

"But it's so far from town," said Molly.

"Only a couple miles; not a long walk at all. The girls are so spoiled that I hope living in the country and having some farm work to do will build their characters, and the boys need a place to run around. My cousin Caleb and I had the best times as boys at that farm, and I want my children to have equally happy memories."

Molly could not imagine Sylvia and Mary enjoying farm life, but Jacob might be right that it would cure them of their spoiled tempers.

"I'm sure your grandparents would be happy to see what good care you've taken of their farm," Molly replied.

They stood awkwardly then, neither knowing what to say. Jacob's grief was so apparent Molly felt an urge just to hug him. But after a minute, Jacob said, "I suppose we'll be celebrating Karl's wedding next?"

"I wouldn't count on it," Molly sighed. "Karl's only interested in working, not that I know what good it does him. I've been to his and Ben's house in Calumet, and it's really such a mess. Those boys need a couple good women to take care of them."

"At least Karl will be able to provide for a family when the time comes."

"True. I'm hoping his sister's wedding will put ideas into his head," Molly smiled. "I see your mother looking this way, Jacob. I bet she's glad you decided to come. Why don't you get something to eat and join your family."

Jacob headed toward the food while Molly noted that Karl and Ben were sitting across from two pretty girls and their mother, all friends of hers from church. The girls were obviously flirting with the handsome Ben, but since Ben could only marry one girl, Molly hoped Karl might have a chance with the other.

"Both you boys are bachelors, hey?" asked the matron at Karl and Ben's table.

"Yes," Karl said.

"Don't you boys want a nice wife?" asked Ernestine, a buxom girl of twenty-two.

"Haven't seen one yet to suit me," Ben smiled, melting the girls' hearts.

"There's lots of pretty girls here," said Hilda, who at nineteen still aspired to her sister's full figure.

"You boys can't wait forever," said Hilda and Ernestine's eager mother.

"I'll wait until the right one comes along," Ben joked. "And I don't imagine that'll be any time soon."

A mother who has daughters to marry is not easily put off by a jest.

"A handsome young man like you can't stay single for long," she said. "I'm sure you'll be snapped up before you're twenty-five."

"I doubt that," laughed Ben. "I'm nearly thirty now."

"You look so young," said Ernestine.

"Girls generally do prefer mature men," the mother assured Ben.

"I'm not the marrying type," he replied. "Excuse me."

He escaped from the table, under the pretense of clearing away empty plates.

Karl did not understand how Ben could leave when Hilda was such an attractive woman in everything but her name.

"You know," Karl told Hilda, "I don't feel about marriage as he does."

"That's nice," she said; she noticed he had potato salad caught in his beard; she hoped he was not trying to flirt with her; she let her eyes roam across the lawn to follow the gorgeous Ben.

Karl did not know how to flirt. He realized Hilda was not interested in him. He tried to think of something charming to say to Ernestine; she was not quite as pretty as Hilda, but she was a woman, and Karl rarely saw a woman out in the woods. He would like a woman to be tender toward. Ben was a fine companion, but he was not a tender, soft woman. Karl had always thought he had plenty of time to marry, but he had recently turned thirty, and after that significant birthday, a man starts to worry he's getting too old for any woman to want him.

Later that night, after the wedding guests had departed, after the dishes had been washed, after the newlyweds had gone to their hotel honeymoon suite, and after the mother of the bride had gone to bed, exhausted but happy, Karl and Ben sat up in the parlor smoking cigars. They were not men of many words. They had spent so much time together that they needed little speech to communicate. But tonight, Karl's tongue burned with a question.

"Ben," he said, trying to sound casual by stopping to take a puff on his cigar, "do you ever think about getting married?"

"No," Ben shook his head. "I told those silly girls today I'm not the marrying kind."

"Why's that?" asked Karl, blowing out a ring of smoke.

"Only girl I was ever foolish enough to take an interest in—she didn't like that I was always off in the woods. Way I see it, there's a time to work and a time for love, but it seemed as if she wanted love all the time. I had other things to do than keep her happy. I was awful young then—figured I was just too young for marriage; now I figure I must be too old, or I'd have gotten mixed up with a woman by now."

"I don't think thirty's too late," said Karl.

"I wouldn't even think about it," said Ben. "Way I see it, you and me, we've got some kind of impediment against marrying. Everyone's got an impediment, sort of like what St. Paul said about having a thorn in his flesh, but our impediment is also the source of our strength. I figure I wouldn't be much of a logger if I had a wife. My heart would always be hankering after a woman, and I'd be thinking less about profits."

"But what's the point of making money if you have no one to spend it on?"

"Karl, you've seen how some of the men are," said Ben. "They work all month to earn a few dollars, then they go to town and blow it all in one weekend on whiskey and women. That's just throwing away your life. You've got to save for your future."

"But what good's a future if you never have any fun?"

"Thing is," said Ben, "I've got the best job in the world, being out in those woods. For me, work and play are the same thing. Money doesn't even matter to me. It's freedom I love. Most people aren't lucky enough to have a job like that. There's nothing like the smell of a fresh cut jackpine. If you made me stay indoors, I'd pine away the first week. Besides, the best friend I ever found was out in the woods; you're so easy to get along with; I'd rather cut down a tree with you, than have some woman kiss me one minute and nag me the next."

Karl liked working in the woods, but he remembered he had only gone out there to escape his stepfather; sometimes he also thought he had purposely avoided marriage because he saw how it had made his mother unhappy; he had worked so hard, hoping to care for his mother and sister so they would be better off. But now Kathy had a husband to care for her, and his mother could live the rest of her life off Montoni's money. Now no one needed him; Ben enjoyed his company, but he was too self-sufficient to need him. Karl thought he might like a wife to care for, but he wondered whether Ben would forgive him if he found one.

"I'm off to bed," said Ben, crushing out his cigar. "We've got a long trip back to Calumet in the morning."

"I'll be up in a minute, soon as I finish this one," said Karl. But after Ben went upstairs, Karl lit another cigar; he sat wondering whether he had strayed down the wrong path in life, and whether he could still get onto that other path that led to a wife and children. Could he still find some more happiness before he was too old?

"You coming up?" Ben asked, returning downstairs when he saw the lamp was still lit. "I have a hard time sleeping in this house, especially when you're not snoring in the next room like at home."

"I'm coming." Karl stood up to stretch. "I guess I kind of drifted off."

"You're lucky you didn't set the house on fire."

"What?" asked Karl, but he did not hear Ben repeat the comment. He was tired; it had been a long day; he told himself that was why he had such strange thoughts tonight; in the morning, he would be his old self again.

If romance had led to naught for most people this day, perhaps that was because today had been Kathy and Patrick's day for love. After all their sufferings—tragic flight from a homeland, a tyrannical stepfather, loneliness and fear of ever being loved—they deserved all their marital happiness. In their honeymoon hotel room, Patrick held Kathy in his arms; he marveled at her beauty, and for the first time since he had left Ireland, he felt God had not completely abandoned him; perhaps it had all been planned that his desperate flight to America would result in his calling this "little German girl" his own. From that night on, he was not homesick for Ireland; he did not care where he lived if only Kathy were there. He laid his head against her own. The scent of her hair brought contentment. Home was with Kathy.

1895

On a Saturday in April, Jacob and Will went fishing. Clarence had been invited to join them, but he preferred to spend the day with his grandparents. Since Jacob and Will were going to the Dead River, and they had to pass through town on the way, they took the wagon and deposited Clarence on his grandparents' doorstep, then continued on their father-son excursion.

When Clarence arrived at his grandparents' house, it was midmorning, but because Nathaniel had been ill with pneumonia the past couple weeks, he was still resting in bed. Cordelia greeted her grandson at the door. "I'm glad you're here, Clarence. Your grandpa's been awful lonesome while cooped up in the house. I know he's looking forward to your company."

"Is he feeling any better, Grandma?"

"Yes, he's just mainly tired now. I imagine it'll be a couple more weeks before he feels like his old self again. This warm spring weather helps, but it takes longer to recover at his age."

"How old is Grandpa?"

"Seventy-seven," said Cordelia. "Now, I know it's early yet, but I just baked a cake. Would you like a slice? You can have another later when we have lunch."

"How old are you, Grandma?"

"Would you like some cake?" she repeated to avoid the question.

"What kind is it?" asked Clarence, as if an eleven-year old boy would ever refuse cake.

"Chocolate of course. I know that's your favorite."

"Okay," said Clarence, "but Grandma, you didn't say how old you are."

"A lady does not reveal her age, and it's not polite to ask," Cordelia said, trying to laugh off the question while ensuring he would not ask again. "I'm not as old as your grandfather; I will tell you that much."

Clarence had followed Cordelia into the kitchen as they talked, and she had begun slicing the cake. When she had two pieces on plates, she said, "Let me go see whether your grandpa's awake. Maybe he'll get up to eat with us, or you could go sit in his room with him. No matter how sick he's been, I know he won't turn down cake. All you Whitmans have the same sweet tooth."

"We can't all have the same tooth," Clarence laughed. "Otherwise, we'd have to take it out and share it with each other the way those witches did with their eye in the Greek myths."

"You know what I mean," stated Cordelia before disappearing upstairs. Clarence waited quietly in the kitchen. The entire house was quiet. The Whitmans had worked and scrimped and saved for many years, and now in their old age, they had closed the boarding house and bought a smaller home where they set about enjoying their retirement. But Cordelia was glad when the grandchildren came over; otherwise, the house was just too quiet with only Nathaniel for her to look after.

"He said to give him a minute and he'd be down," said Cordelia when she returned to the kitchen.

"Grandpa and Grandma Henning sent me a birthday present," Clarence said while his grandmother cut a slice of cake for her husband.

"That's good," said Cordelia, setting the plates on the table before pouring glasses of milk. She did not bother to ask what the gift was; she knew Clarence would tell her anyway.

"It's clothes," said Clarence, unenthused. "A suit jacket made in New York City."

"Do you like it?" she asked as she sat down opposite him.

"I'd rather have had a bicycle."

"Those contraptions are too dangerous. I don't know how anyone can ride them."

"Everyone has them nowadays, Grandma."

"In my day, people had more sense, especially the girls. I can't imagine any self-respecting young lady riding such a thing, especially when she has to wear a short skirt so it doesn't get caught in the chain. Be thankful you got a suit jacket. You'd probably kill yourself on a bicycle."

"No I wouldn't. A boy at school let me ride his, and I didn't fall off. I can even ride it without using my hands."

"You're giving me shivers," said Cordelia. "Anyway, you should have your photograph taken in that suit. I'm sure my sister would like to see you in it."

"Grandma, why are you and Grandma Henning sisters? A person's grandmas aren't usually sisters."

"No, your Grandma Henning is actually your stepgrandmother. Your real grandmother died when your mother was a little girl, and then your Grandpa Henning married my sister for his second wife."

"My real grandma died when my ma was little? Kind of like my ma died when I was little?"

"Yes," said Cordelia.

"Then I'm not really related to my Grandma Henning?"

"She's not your blood grandmother," Cordelia said, "but because she's my sister, she's your great-aunt as well as being your stepgrandmother."

"That's too confusing," said Clarence. "But how come I've never met her and Grandpa Henning?"

"Because they live in New York and that's a long way off."

"They could come to visit."

"It's too far," Cordelia repeated. She thought Clarence too young for her to explain that Sophia would not come back to Marquette because Madeleine and Caleb had drowned in the lake. If the boy were to know such things, Jacob would have to tell him.

"I don't see what good grandparents are if instead of coming to visit, they only send you suits in the mail."

Cordelia knew she and Nathaniel were good grandparents, but the poor boy should not be deprived of all four grandparents. Then again, how many children were even lucky enough to know one single grandparent?

Nathaniel now cluttered down the stairs, clutching the banister as he came.

"Nat, are you okay?" Cordelia called.

"Yes!" he yelled back with irritation.

"Why aren't you using your cane?" she demanded when he entered the kitchen.

"I don't need that blasted thing. I ain't crippled yet."

Cordelia saw he was in one of his moods when she could not reason with him. He looked worn out just from the climb downstairs as he collapsed into a chair.

"Grandpa, did you know your grandparents when you were my age?"

For all his fatigue, Nathaniel picked up his fork and eagerly started on his cake.

"Not all of them," he said. "My mother's parents were both dead before I was born, but I did know my Grandpa and Grandma Whitman."

"That's just like me," said Clarence, "I mean, I know my Grandpa and Grandma Whitman, but my other grandma is dead, and I've never met my other grandpa, so he might as well be dead."

"Clarence, don't say such things," said Cordelia, but Nathaniel replied, "Yes, as seldom as we hear from Gerald, he might as well be."

"Nathaniel, really!" Cordelia snapped.

"Well, the boy ought to know his other grandparents. There's no reason why they can't come to visit except for your sister's orneriness."

"He's lucky he knows two grandparents. I only knew one of mine," said Cordelia. "Back then, people didn't live as long. Those early pioneers had to work so hard they died young, or they moved West and left their families behind. But one good grandparent, like my Grandpa Brookfield," she said, long ago having forgiven her grandfather's faults, "can fill the absence of the others."

"Yes, not many of our grandparents' generation lived to be old," said Nathaniel. "Too many of them gave their lives to free this land from the British, and then they and their children built America."

"And their grandchildren," said Cordelia. "We came as pioneers to help build this city."

"Grandpa, what do you mean they helped to free America?" asked Clarence. "Do you mean they fought in the American Revolution?"

"Oh yes," said Nathaniel. "Hasn't anyone told you that? Why, both of my grandfathers and your grandmother's grandfathers were in the Revolution. That's four ancestors you can claim who fought in that war."

"I think one of Gerald's grandfather's fought as well," said Cordelia, "but I'm not sure about Clara's family."

Clarence had never fully realized that the Revolutionary War had been real, not until now when he learned he was connected to it by no less than five great-great-grandfathers.

"I know about the American Revolution from school," he said. "We read all about George Washington crossing the Delaware, and the Battle of Bunker Hill, and Thomas Jefferson writing the Declaration of Independence."

"That's good," said Nathaniel, "but when I was a boy, we didn't just read about the Revolution. We heard stories of its battles all the time because several of the soldiers were still alive."

"Kind of like how Pa fought in the Civil War," Clarence boasted, "only he never talks about it."

"You shouldn't expect him to," Cordelia said.

"No, the battles your father faced were pure nightmares," said Nathaniel. "Especially Cold Harbor and Petersburg where he was wounded. We're lucky he even lived."

"That makes Pa a hero, right? Because he was wounded?"

"Any man who fights for his country is a hero," Nathaniel replied, "but let me finish telling you about my Grandfather Whitman's involvement in the American Revolution. He was a merchant marine and captain of his own ship before the war broke out. He used to make trips to England and back, bringing new settlers to New York as well as carrying all kinds of goods from the old country. If you think about it now, there must be hundreds if not thousands of people in this country who would not live here today if my grandfather had not brought their ancestors here on his ship."

"He was really a ship captain?" asked Clarence; he was highly impressed; he loved tales of the sea; his eyes were always fixed on the harbor, its docks and ships, whenever he was near Lake Superior.

"Yes," said Nathaniel. "So when the American Revolution broke out, my grandfather decided he would help the cause by enlisting his ship as part of the navy. He told me he fought in many battles, until finally the British sunk his ship one day, but he managed to escape in a rowboat with a group of his men. They had to paddle for a whole day before they finally reached the mainland."

"He's lucky," said Cordelia, "that he didn't drown or get lost at sea."

"What else did he do, Grandpa?" asked Clarence.

"Well, when the war ended, he kept on sailing ships, back and forth from England just as always, although he didn't like going there so well after the war. He took journeys other places too but I don't rightly know where. Somewhere in the Mediterranean I think—Italy or Greece or somewhere."

"So he was Captain Whitman?"

"Yes," said Nathaniel. "And my mother's father also fought in the war, only I didn't know him so I don't know much about the family except that they were one of those old Dutch families who settled New Amsterdam before the British took it over and made it New York."

"Did Captain Whitman ever meet John Paul Jones?" asked Clarence, only interested in his seafaring ancestors.

"I don't know," said Nathaniel. "He might have since he was in the navy, but I don't recall him ever mentioning it."

"Did he ever sail to the South Seas or the Sandwich Islands?" Clarence asked. He didn't know where those places were, but he knew people sailed to them.

"That I don't know either," said Nathaniel. "Although my father did say my grandfather once brought home a pineapple, so maybe."

"Did he ever meet any cannibals?" asked Clarence.

Nathaniel laughed. "I doubt it."

"Was he ever in a storm at sea?"

"I imagine he was probably in lots of them, but I don't know for sure," said Nathaniel. "I was too young and rambunctious to sit and listen to all his stories, and by the time I was old enough to be really interested, he had passed away."

"Think of all the stories he had to tell," said Cordelia. "It's a shame no one wrote them down like Edna is writing down Darius's stories."

"I guess no one in my family was much for writing," said Nathaniel.

"I hate writing," said Clarence. "If I was a sailor, I'd never have to write."

"If you were a sailor," said Cordelia, getting up to collect the empty plates, "you would still have to write home to tell us how you were. But you don't want to be a sailor; it's a hard and dangerous life. You're better off to work hard at your schooling so you can find safer work than being a sailor."

"Being a sailor is more fun though," grinned Nathaniel.

"You can romanticize it all you want," Cordelia replied, "but a sailor's life is a hard one; he's always at the mercy of the elements, and he's all alone and lonely out at sea."

"However hard it is, there've been some awful fine stories about sailor life," said Nathaniel.

"What stories?" asked Clarence.

"Come in the other room and I'll show you."

Cordelia's frown warned Nathaniel he should not encourage the boy's foolish dreams.

Nathaniel added, "Clarence, maybe you could read some of the stories out loud to your old grandfather, while I rest in my chair."

Cordelia knew Nathaniel was trying to compromise with her by turning the stories into reading practice for Clarence. She was not placated, however, when she heard Clarence slaughtering the exquisite lines of *The Rime of the Ancient Mariner*. "People should not be allowed to read poetry aloud until they know how," she thought as she washed up the breakfast dishes.

❦   ❦   ❦

While Clarence reveled in the Ancient Mariner's encounters with slimy sea serpents and ghost ships, Jacob and Will discovered the Dead River, despite its name, was sorely lacking in sea serpents, but its trout were abundant. Jacob was surprised that his younger son's interest in the sea did not extend to fishing, but Will made up for it by being an enthusiastic fisherman, and as he grew into a young man, Jacob found his oldest son an enjoyable companion. By comparison, his daughters had always been nearly impossible to speak with; he loved the girls, but he had been relieved when they married and moved into town; they had always complained of his cooking, yet they were unwilling to cook themselves, and he could scarcely get them to do any chores; keeping after them had only created more work for him. He did not imagine his daughters made very good housewives, but life was far more peaceful once he and the boys were alone on the farm. They lived like true bachelors now, the boys content to eat just about anything as long as plenty of sweets were in the house, for Cordelia was correct: all the Whitmans had been born with the same sweet tooth; even on this short fishing expedition, Jacob had brought along a sack of sugar cookies to share with Will. Best of all, Jacob found his boys easy to talk to, and now that they were older, while he still would not speak to them of the war, they knew well how much he had loved both their mother and his best friend Caleb.

Today's fishing catch was a good one, but Jacob always had to tell tales of the giant catches he, Caleb, and his father used to make when he was a boy.

"Didn't Caleb's father go fishing too?" asked Will.

"Yes, my Uncle George fished, but he died when I was only twelve, so I don't remember too many trips with him."

"Weren't you fishing with Caleb the first time you met Chief Kawbawgam?" asked Will. He already knew his father's stories, but these fishing trips had a pattern to be adhered to, which included tales of the glories of fishing trips long ago.

"Yes," said Jacob. "That was the same day my Uncle George passed away. Caleb almost died that day too. He fell off the cliff but Chief Kawbawgam saved his life."

"And after that you started to go fishing with Chief Kawbawgam?"

"Yes, but Caleb never went with us. Usually it was just Kawbawgam and me, but my pa came along a few times."

"Why didn't Caleb go with you?"

"My Aunt Sophia wouldn't let him. She doesn't like Indians."

"Oh," said Will. No one had ever said so directly, but from various comments he had heard from family members, Will suspected Aunt Sophia was little short of being an old witch. He also understood it was her fault he had never seen his other grandfather.

"It was just as much your Grandfather Henning's decision to move away," Grandma Whitman had once told him, but Will was still too young to understand how adults make choices and learn to compromise.

"Speaking of Chief Kawbawgam," said Jacob. "I think we've caught enough trout here to give your grandparents some, and maybe bring some over to the Chief as well; he was the one who taught me what to use to catch them."

"He was?" said Will, who had never been told this impressive fact.

"Yes, so let's repay him the favor. It won't take long to go visit him."

"Where does he live?" asked Will.

"That little cabin just before you get to Presque Isle. You've seen it. Peter White built it for him."

"Oh," said Will, having some idea from storybooks that Indians only lived in teepees. Plenty of the Chippewa were still in the area, but their lodgehouses were a more rare sight now, and Will had grown up woefully ignorant of their way of life. Neither had he ever spoken to Chief Kawbawgam, only met him downtown a couple times when his father had stopped to exchange greetings with the old man. Will had never imagined he would be in an Indian's home; the thought made him somewhat nervous, but also curious. Everyone in Marquette retained great respect for the chief, rumored to be ninety years old now; he was considered the last Chief of the Chippewa since the tribe, with the coming of the white settlers, had abandoned much of their traditional lifestyle and many natives had gone to live on the reservations or blend in with the white people. The migration of whites to the area had been mostly peaceful, largely because of the goodwill of Chief Kawbawgam and his people, despite how certain whites, including a now deceased saloon owner, had treated them.

When Jacob and Will arrived at the old chief's house, they were greeted at the door by his wife, Charlotte. She was the daughter of Chief Marji Gesick, the man who had first led the white men to the beds of iron ore where now stood the town of Negaunee. From that event, the mining of iron ore in Upper Michigan had begun, and the city of Marquette consequently founded as a port from which to ship the ore. Will looked at Charlotte Kawbawgam, now nearly blind, and at her husband, his birth date lost to history. What incredible changes this couple had seen, Will thought. In their childhoods, to see a white man must have been a rarity, and now the white population outnumbered them. When they had been Will's age, Charles and Charlotte Kawbawgam had not known of stone buildings, but only their seasonal lodge houses. There had been no steamboats then, no railroads, no ore cars, no docks in the harbor, and the land was still being fought over by the Americans and the British. Michigan was decades away from statehood. Since those wilderness days, Marquette had grown and prospered to become the greatest city on Lake Superior's southern shore. Will found it hard to imagine a time before his city had existed, but these people could remember the time long before.

Once inside the Kawbawgams' home, Will discovered he and his father were not the couple's only guests. The old chief's brother-in-law, Jacques LePique, of mixed French and Indian blood, was visiting, and so was another young man, not more than twenty, who introduced himself as Homer. Jacob explained to Will that Homer was the son of Mr. Kidder who lived on Ridge Street near Peter White.

Kawbawgam greeted his new guests with smiles and nods, but he was a man of few words, especially English ones, so he allowed his guests to dominate the conversation.

"I've been writing down the old Chippewa legends," Homer Kidder told Jacob. "I want to preserve them for posterity, and the Kawbawgams and Monsieur LePique have been kind enough to tell me many of them."

"Our young people, they are trying to be white men," Jacques LePique said, "so they don't appreciate the old tales. After my generation is gone, we must ensure the old ways are not forgotten."

Jacob smiled approvingly.

"Will you tell us one of the stories?" Will asked.

"Chief Kawbawgam is telling them right now, and Mr. LePique is translating them for me," Homer replied. "In fact, the Chief was just about to tell me one about Jacques's grandfather."

Will and Jacob sat down to hear a good yarn. Before they left, they would listen to many tales, but later Will would remember one in particular. That tale was of a man who tried to capture a flock of swans by swimming in the lake and tying all their feet together. Unfortunately, the swans decided to fly away, and when they flew up in the air, they carried the man with him. Finally, the man could hold onto the rope no longer; he fell and landed inside a stump. It was a fanciful tale and highly unlikely, but Will found it amusing and fascinating as he heard it spoken in the Chippewa tongue, then translated into English by Jacques LePique with his mixed French and Indian accents. Each tale took quite a while to relate because it had to be translated, and Mr. Kidder kept interrupting the translation with questions to ensure the stories were recorded accurately; for Will, these interruptions only built up the suspense and excitement of the tales. Will and Jacob laughed throughout the tellings, finding each story as amusing as any European fairy tale. But the time came to leave. Charlotte Kawbawgam pressed them to stay and share the fish they had brought, but Jacob politely declined because his parents expected Will and him for supper.

Will left reluctantly. Chief Kawbawgam shook his hand goodbye, and Will found the grasp strong and firm, despite the carved wrinkles in the elderly man's face. He thought again how Chief Kawbawgam seemed almost ancient, like the repository of the Great Lakes' entire past. Mr. Kidder had said many of the chief's oral stories were doubtless hundreds of years old, having been passed down from one generation to the next. Will was glad they would now be preserved in writing. He felt sad to think the Chief would eventually join his ancestors, their ancient traditions forgotten. If that was the way of the world, it was a sad way.

"Your grandparents will be pleased with our catch," said Jacob as he and his son rode back into town.

"I hope so," Will replied, thoughtfully staring out at Lake Superior. The waves' peaceful roar was suddenly broken by the clanging bell of a streetcar, the hideous sound of modern life, and for a moment, Will hated the civilized world that had so quickly changed this land he loved. Yet if civilization had not arrived, he would not have been born here. He felt torn in his feelings; his own family had helped contribute to these changes, to the building up of the city, to the gradual wiping away of the ancient Indian traditions that had existed here before them. Will felt haunted by the old chief's wrinkled face, and he marveled at how Kawbawgam's good nature had resigned itself to the changes seen during his lifetime. Will had a strange notion that he would cry the day he heard the last Chief of the Chippewa had passed on.

Jacob noticed his son's somber demeanor but did not question him. He knew Will would speak if he wished, and Jacob, content with his fine catch of fish, and the conviviality of having seen his old friend, was now looking forward to a good meal.

Cordelia and Nathaniel greeted the catch of fish with exclamations. Cordelia immediately started to clean the fish, and Nathaniel said he was so hungry that he set to work helping her. Meanwhile, Clarence dragged Will into the parlor to show him the fascinating illustrations from *The Rime of the Ancient Mariner.*

Jacob offered to help prepare supper, but Cordelia handed him the mail she had picked up for him at the post office that week since he did not live in town.

"There's a letter there from Gerald. Why don't you tell us what it says?"

Jacob ripped open the envelope and skimmed over the contents.

"You won't believe this," he said. "Uncle Gerald says he's coming to visit. He'll be here in a few weeks."

"Why would he come now, after all these years?" Nathaniel asked.

"He says he wants to see his grandchildren. He's never even met the boys." Cordelia asked, "Is Sophia coming?"

"If she is, she must have softened in her old age," said Nathaniel.

"No, Uncle Gerald says she won't come," Jacob read on. "She says she's too old to travel so far, and the fast trains make her nervous."

"Any excuse," muttered Cordelia. She badly wanted to see Sophia, especially since their sister Omelia had died last month; that sadness had made Cordelia fear she would never see her other siblings again; Sophia had not even bothered to write since Omelia's death, and Cordelia felt badly hurt by her neglect.

"Who's coming?" asked Clarence. The boys, hearing excitement in their father's voice, came into the kitchen.

"Your Grandfather Henning," said Cordelia, still stunned by the news.

"He is?" said Clarence. "Grandma, you said he lived too far away."

"He lives in New York. That's pretty far," said Will.

"He must be rich then to travel this far," said Clarence.

"You don't have to be rich to travel on a train, silly," Will replied.

"But you have to be rich to own a telephone. Grandma said he has one of those."

"Actually, they have two telephones," said Cordelia, wondering why anyone would want such a cantankerous invention.

"He must be really rich then," said Clarence. "I'm glad he's coming."

"You boys will have to help me straighten up the house," Jacob said. "Your grandfather is used to a neat place. He has servants, you know, who keep things nice for him and your grandmother."

"Is she coming to?" asked Will, curious to see the notorious woman.

"No," said Jacob.

"She could if she wanted to," Nathaniel said.

"Molly will have to be told. She'll want to see Gerald," Cordelia said to change the subject from her sister.

"Who's Molly?" asked Clarence.

"Mrs. Montoni. She was good friends with your Grandmother Henning, your grandfather's first wife. Maybe we could plan a picnic at Presque Isle for everyone."

"It'll be just like the old days," Nathaniel smiled.

Cordelia reflected that you could not bring back the old days. But she had not known that so painfully until she had heard Sophia would not come. "Maybe I should write to Edna," she said. "She, Esau, and Darius might want to come too. It could be a true family reunion."

"That's a good idea," said Jacob. "Edna's only visited once since she moved away, and I still have a niece I've never met."

"I'll write to her tonight," said Cordelia, "but for now I better fry these fish."

Jacob was both pleased and uneasy about his father-in-law's prospective visit. He and Gerald had always been on good terms; they had shared a deep love for Agnes, and they had helped each other through their shared grief over Caleb's loss. But Agnes's death had left Jacob somewhat angry with his father-in-law. Granted, Gerald and Sophia had been in Europe at the time, but Jacob had expected they would visit shortly after they returned to the States. Since then, Gerald had continually pled that his work kept him too busy to travel, but all the Whitmans suspected Sophia would not let Gerald come to visit. Jacob could not understand how any self-respecting man would let a woman control his life in such a manner. Still, he would try to enjoy this visit for the sake of his sons who had never met their grandfather.

❦   ❦   ❦

May 10, 1895
Salt Lake City, Utah
Mrs. Esau Brookfield to Mrs. Nathaniel Whitman
Dear Mother,

As always, I was happy to receive your letter. We are all well, and glad to hear you are the same. I was very worried about father when you wrote last month that he had pneumonia, but I am relieved that he has recovered.

I am sure by now you are beginning to enjoy a long awaited spring there. I remember those six foot snowbanks of my childhood and the relief we always felt the first time we saw grass after many months of snow cover, and I miss the sound of snow melting off the roof in spring. We never see a snowflake here, rarely even rain. I especially miss the snow around Christmas. I don't think I'll ever adjust to this warm climate. Esau just laughs at me. He's always telling the children about the terrible winter he spent in Marquette. I tell him it couldn't have been that terrible since he got a wife out of it.

But enough of the weather. You are awaiting an answer from me. I'm afraid the answer is no. We would all love to visit Marquette and see Uncle Gerald, but Uncle Darius is just too frail to travel that far anymore. For years, he has been hale and strong and for a long time, we thought he would live forever, but this past year, he has become quite shaky and his eyes are failing; in fact, he is almost completely blind in his right eye. We think the strain of the journey would be too much for him now that he is eighty-one. Esau and I would come, but we cannot leave just the children to look after him. Mother, I know how much you love your brother. I want to prepare you that he may not be with us much longer. It will be especially hard for me since I've cared for him these last couple years, helping him with little things he cannot do so well on his own anymore. He can scarcely even coordinate his brittle fingers to button his shirts. It is difficult, to say the least, to watch such frailty happen to a man who used to have perfect accuracy as a sharpshooter. I am thankful I have written down his stories so they will remain to comfort us when he is gone. I am sure my children will appreciate his tales when they are older if only as a means to remember their grandfather.

The children are all fine. Harry will be seventeen next month, and he is already as tall as his father. Philip is not far behind him. Young Tom takes after his mother, always with his nose in a book. We are all proud of how well our little Celia did during her first year at school.

I have to make this short because I must attend a benefit this afternoon for the new library. I am chairwoman of the book purchasing committee and hope to buy as many books for the lowest price possible to fill the library's shelves. I guess I finally must take after Grandmother Brookfield in my community involvement. All those years of helping you with the boarding house cured me of wanting only a domestic life. I love my family, but it's good to have a reason to get out of the house. Our maid Anna has to do almost everything I'm afraid, but then, she does a much better job of it than I would. I'm always nervous to leave Uncle Darius alone, but it is only for a couple hours, and we are only a few blocks from the library. Esau is talking about putting a telephone in so we can call for help in the middle of the night if Uncle Darius has any trouble.

Give my love to everyone there. Tell Jacob I promise to write to him soon. I hope he and his children and his little grandson are all doing well. Give my love to Uncle Gerald when he comes. I hope he has a wonderful visit with you and does not feel a moment's guilt about coming without Aunt Sophia. Write again soon.

Love, Edna

Cordelia's heart was heavy after reading her daughter's letter. She was already disappointed that Sophia would not come. She had known Darius was getting older, but she could not imagine him unable to button a shirt, much less slowly going blind. But then, even with her remarkable eyesight, she had consented to wearing glasses after she turned sixty. Suddenly everyone she knew seemed to be old—here was Nathaniel, cluttering around the house with a cane, when she could convince him to use it. And she would never get used to the fact that she had recently become a great-grandmother. Time had somehow gotten away from them all.

"Hello, Cordelia. I guess you didn't hear me knock, but I came in because I saw the light on in the dining room."

"Yes, I often have lights on during the day now. My eyes don't see as well as they used to," Cordelia replied.

"We're all getting older," said Molly, sitting down at the table. "How are you?"

"I'm not in the grave yet," said Cordelia. "I guess that's all I can hope for."

"You sound rather down today, Cordelia?"

"I'm sorry. I'm just a little disappointed. Edna wrote to say they won't come because Darius is too frail for the trip, and I've already felt so disappointed that Sophia won't come."

"At least Gerald is coming. We can be thankful for that."

"Yes," said Cordelia. "But it's not the same as having my sister here."

Molly had never liked Sophia; she doubted she ever could, but while she had buried two husbands, she had never known the grief of losing a child; Sophia had twice known that sorrow, so Molly would say nothing ill about her.

"Well," said Molly, "is there any reason why you can't go visit her?"

Cordelia considered, but no, it was impossible. "Nathaniel's too old to travel now."

"I think he could make it," Molly said. "And if not, can't you go without him?"

"No, I couldn't leave him. I—"

"He could stay with Jacob. I remember your father went out East when he was older than you are, and the trains are faster and more comfortable than back then."

Cordelia was surprised by the thought of such a journey. Was it possible? Could she convince Nathaniel to let her go?

"Maybe next year," she said more to herself than to Molly.

"You could go back with Gerald," said Molly. "Then you would only have to return by yourself."

"Then I could see Omelia's family too," Cordelia replied. "I haven't seen her children since they were little. Oh, but Darius and Edna and Esau, wouldn't they be jealous that I—"

"They'd understand. The bond between sisters is a special one."

Cordelia sighed. "I would so like to see Sophia."

"You should go," said Molly. "It might cheer her as much as it will you."

"That's true," said Cordelia. "I wouldn't be surprised if Sophia were lonely for her family too, although she never admits it."

"Well, I just stopped to say hello for a minute, so I better be going," said Molly. "I promised Dolly O'Neill I would visit her. The poor dear, she's not much older than me, yet she's nearly blind now, so she can use the company."

"Wasn't that her daughter who bought Gerald and Sophia's house?"

"Yes, Carolina—she's married to Judge Smith," said Molly. "But I'm afraid she's not too thoughtful of her mother. Dolly and I kind of understand each other, she being from the South, which is almost another country compared to here, and me being from Ireland, and Dolly's husband was Irish. Since her husband died, Dolly's been lonely, and I know what that's like."

"Molly, you seem to understand what everyone needs," said Cordelia. "If all the Catholics were as kindhearted as you, there would be no strife between denominations."

Molly knew Cordelia meant this remark kindly, despite its prejudiced implications. Over the years, she had grown to respect Cordelia's devotion to her Methodism, even if it made no room for "popery." Cordelia had been too staunch a friend for Molly to let her comments rile her now.

"Thank you, Cordelia, but I'm not really all that good."

"You are, dear," said Cordelia. "Look how you just cheered me up."

"I imagine Gerald's visit will cheer us all," Molly smiled, then said goodbye.

As she walked to Dolly O'Neill's house, Molly meditated on Cordelia's compliment. "I'm not that good," she thought, "but I try to do what I can for others. Life is so hard for most people, and when I look back on my life, I see

I've been far luckier than most. Poor Mrs. O'Neill; what do I know about suffering compared to her dealing with near blindness and a neglectful daughter, yet she stays patient and good-natured. It's far easier for me to be good when I no longer have any great trials in my life."

❦   ❦   ❦

When Gerald stepped off the train, he looked about in confusion. At first, he scarcely recognized his son-in-law, and Jacob scarcely recognized him. Gerald had grown a beard since he left Marquette, and that beard had grown snowy white. In his imagination, Jacob had forgotten to age Gerald, and the elderly man who stood before him, once so lively and capable, made Jacob feel all the more keenly his own fifty-two years.

"Jacob," Gerald smiled; his voice was enthusiastic even if his step were not. He shook his son-in-law's hand, then peered over Jacob's shoulder at two young men, who awkwardly waited to be noticed.

"Are these my grandsons? They're both so tall I'm not sure which is the oldest."

"I am," said Will, asserting his birthright with a manly handshake.

"I'm only two inches shorter even if Will's four years older," Clarence stated.

"And where are your sisters?" Gerald asked his handsome grandsons.

"Oh, well, they were too busy to come, being married now you know," said Jacob. "But we've arranged a family picnic at Presque Isle, so you'll see them then."

"At Presque Isle?" asked Gerald, who remembered that little peninsula as being nearly inaccessible.

"Sure," Jacob replied. "Everyone has picnics there now."

"Do we have to take a boat?" asked Gerald, not sure he was up to trudging through the bog that separated Presque Isle from the mainland. He remembered picnics being held near the lakeshore, or sometimes in Park Cemetery.

"No," said Jacob. "The streetcar runs out there now. Peter White bought Presque Isle and donated it to the city as a park."

"Oh!" said Gerald, surprised by such a change, and surprised by this different family before him, not to mention the unfamiliar buildings all around him.

"We thought we'd just have a quiet meal at the farm tonight," said Jacob. "We figured you'd be too tired from traveling to visit anyone before tomorrow."

"That suits me," said Gerald. "I am a little tired, but the trip was easy compared to that first trip I remember taking to Marquette. The train only took a few days, but back then I remember we spent weeks traveling by stagecoach and schooner."

"You came here on a boat once?" asked Clarence. He had never been on a real boat, only a canoe. But a real big schooner or a steamboat—that seemed the ultimate experience to this future mariner.

"By boat was the only way to get here back then. There weren't any railways or scarcely even a road in Upper Michigan," said Gerald. "Marquette appears to have changed quite a lot since then."

"Let me take your bag," said Jacob, removing it from his father-in-law's hand. "We'll take you out to the farm so you can wash up and rest before supper time."

"I don't want to be a bother," said Gerald. "I could stay in a hotel."

"Don't be silly," Jacob replied. "We've been looking forward to your staying with us. Will is going to let you have his room while he bunks in with Clarence."

"Thank you, Will," said Gerald.

"You're welcome," Will replied, embarrassed to have his generosity acknowledged. He had insisted his grandfather have his room; he wanted to do everything for this grandfather he had never met but always wanted to know, and he already felt this visit would not be a disappointment.

Gerald began asking more questions than anyone could answer as the wagon drove away from the train depot and headed west toward the farm. Many new sights aroused his curiosity while familiar ones led to inquiries about old friends and neighbors. The Harlow house made him ask after Marquette's founding family; with sadness, Gerald learned Amos Harlow, the city father, had passed away in 1890. "I'll have to call on Mrs. Harlow," he said. The height of St. Peter's towers astonished him, making them "fit for New York City," in his opinion. The city's extensive westward growth made him exclaim, "Marquette must have doubled in size since I left!"

"Yes, you founding families made it such a fine town that people keep wanting to live here," Jacob replied.

But once they were outside the city and passing through a stretch of woods halfway to the farm, silence overcame them. Gerald felt troubled by the now unfamiliar trees; they were more lovely and peaceful than he remembered, and in their boughs he could hear the birds singing, their music undisturbed by New York's elevated railroad, that whizzing, rattling noisemaker, invented by Marquette's own Charles Harvey. In these deep Michigan woods were no train whistles, no racket of a thousand carriages busily clattering down Broadway or Forty-Second Street. Then, breaking through the trees into a clearing, the wagon came in sight of the old Brookfield farm, and memories surged up in Gerald of his deceased parents-in-law, Lucius and Rebecca Brookfield, Jacob's grandparents.

"Your grandfather would be pleased with how well you've cared for the old place," Gerald told Jacob.

"Did you know my Great-Grandfather Brookfield?" Clarence asked.

"Oh yes," said Gerald. "We were partners in a forge we built when we first came to Marquette. And your great-grandmother was one of Marquette's great ladies. She was always performing good deeds, whether they were wanted or not."

Jacob smiled, fondly remembering his grandmother's lovable, if sometimes aggravating, efforts to reform the new community and spread the gospel of temperance in its streets.

Once inside the farmhouse, Gerald continued to comment upon its wonderful upkeep and preservation, although its lack of feminine touches somewhat saddened him. It was clearly a man's house, a sore reminder that his grandsons had been raised without a mother. His heart ached for the boys, such that he would not let his suitcase be carried to his room without first opening it and pulling out the presents he had brought. "I have packages for the girls and your parents as well," he told Jacob, "but the boys won't want to wait until tomorrow to open theirs." A leather baseball glove and a ball for Will won enthusiastic thank you's from their new owner while Clarence was pleased with a compass. "It's just like the ones I bet the sailors use," the recipient informed his grandfather. Gerald had thought presents might be necessary for an estranged grandfather to gain acceptance, but immediately he felt the boys' affection for him. Not a minute after Gerald placed his things in his room, Will and Clarence had him by the hands and were pulling him all over the farm, showing him the cow, the carrots and tomato plants, the plow and scarecrow, and all their places to hike, to fish, to read, and to daydream, even those sacred places kept secret from their father. Boys know grandfathers keep better secrets than parents; grandfathers have survived life's struggles, and in their golden years, they are ready to enjoy once more boyhood's dreams and pastimes.

When supper had ended and bedtime came, Will said, "Grandpa, I'm glad you've come," and Clarence insisted on kissing his grandfather's cheek. The boys then skedaddled upstairs to bed, while Gerald barely held in the tears springing to his eyes; it took several minutes of staring into the fire, and silently thanking God that he had been able to return home one last time, before he regained his composure.

The next morning, Gerald said he wished to visit Park Cemetery. He and Sophia had left Marquette before the stone for Madeleine's grave had been placed there; although Madeleine's body had never been recovered from Lake Superior, her parents had wanted a stone so she would be remembered. Gerald also wanted to see Agnes's resting place, so he could pay respects to his daughter. And he wanted once more to see where Clara lay. He never would have told Sophia this, for she would think him unfaithful just to remember his first wife, but Clara had been the love of Gerald's youth, perhaps of his entire life, although so many years later, he often found it difficult to believe he had once been so happily married to such a pretty young girl.

Jacob excused himself from going with Gerald since he had so much work to do on the farm, and he thought the boys could show their grandfather their mother's grave and thereby also spend some time alone with him. Truthfully, Jacob did not wish to witness Gerald's sadness at Agnes's grave from fear it would open the floodgates of his own grief. He did, however, dig up several batches of pansies from the garden for his father-in-law to plant at the cemetery.

Gerald and his grandsons departed in the wagon, with Will insisting on driving to impress his grandfather with his mature, responsible nature; the boy scarcely needed to try; Gerald was completely captivated with these grandsons he had only known as names from Jacob's letters. He was proud Will could handle horses with such expertise; he was proud to see how carefully Clarence held the box of flowers all the way to the cemetery; he was proud that the older brother looked after the younger, that they did not quarrel, that they were such strong, healthy, happy boys. Their brotherly bond reminded Gerald of the one he had once witnessed between Jacob and Caleb; he made a mental note to visit Caleb's grave as well since it was near Madeleine's.

"There's the cemetery," said Gerald as they neared Seventh Street. He had almost thought they had missed it because it had once been on the far end of town, but now houses surrounded it. One day, Gerald imagined it would be in the city's center from the way Marquette was moving westward from the lake. The cemetery as the city's heart would be appropriate, since here lay its pioneer families, those who had sacrificed to build Marquette. Few of those first settlers were still alive; Gerald was of that minority, yet he and Sophia would never rest beside the cemetery's beautiful lilypad filled ponds. Sophia wanted to be buried in New York.

Will drove the wagon through the cemetery gate, and then they all climbed out. Instinctively, Gerald started in the direction of Clara's grave, but Clarence clutched his hand and said, "No, Grandpa, Mama's grave is this way."

Gerald allowed himself to be led. He had wanted to see Agnes's stone last, expecting it would affect him the most, but he was touched by his grandsons' need to see the grave of the mother they had hardly known. When he stood before his daughter's stone, when he saw engraved upon it "Agnes Whitman, beloved wife and mother" and thought how the attribute did not include "beloved daughter," he struggled to hold back his tears. He was surprised to see the date that confirmed eleven years had passed since her death, yet the stone looked new, well cared for by a husband and children who continually visited it, continually planted flowers before it, and always felt the absence it represented in their family circle. Trying to hide his emotions, Gerald knelt without heed to his rheumatism, then took the spade from Will's hand, and dug away the earth to plant the flowers.

"Mama always liked pansies," said Clarence. "That's what Pa says. That's why he sent these with us."

"Yes, I remember she liked pansies," Gerald replied, "but I think she loved lady's slippers best because they're so delicate, yet wild and free. In fact, she told me she liked them because her most vivid memory of her own mother was once when they went picking flowers in the woods, on the hill where Ridge Street now is. She told me they brought home a whole basket of lady's slippers that day."

"I like pansies," said Clarence, "because my mother liked them."

"What was my mother like?" Will asked. "I only have a couple vague memories of her, and Clarence can't remember her at all."

"She was short and somewhat plain," said Gerald. "I'm afraid she took after me more than her beautiful mother; she usually wore her hair up in a bun after she married your father. But she had a smile that made everyone feel especially welcomed. She was always calm and patient with everyone. She was a gentle spirit."

"I remember she used to sing me to sleep," said Will.

"Yes, she liked to sing, and she played the piano splendidly. Most of the time she was shy and did not speak much in a crowd, but she did not mind displaying her musical talents when we had company over. She was quite accomplished considering how remote Marquette was and that she had to teach herself. I think she let all her frustrations out in her music, and her hopes and dreams as well, and that allowed her to be patient with people. She took care of everyone around her, myself, your father, you children, and she never asked thanks for her kindnesses."

"She was an only child," said Will. "Maybe that's why she was so quiet. She didn't have a brother or sister to talk to like me and Clarence."

"Well, she had her stepbrother, Caleb, and her half-sister, Madeleine, though she was several years apart from both of them. Still, she took care of them as much as she could."

"Where are Aunt Madeleine and Uncle Caleb buried?" asked Clarence.

"Caleb wasn't our uncle," Will told his brother. "He was Pa's cousin."

"But he was Mama's stepbrother, and Pa says he and Caleb were just like brothers, so I like to call him uncle. I bet he would have been a good uncle if I had known him."

"He would have been a splendid uncle to you boys," said Gerald, imagining how Caleb would have loved these nephews, maybe even finally found hope in that love. "Come, I'll show you where their stones are."

Gerald rose and brushed the dirt off his knees. He was sad to think how he was visiting the graves of three people, so much younger than himself, yet gone so many years before that even these tall boys could not remember them.

They crossed the cemetery's path and walked past a few trees, down a sloping hill before arriving at Caleb and Madeleine's graves. Caleb's name was on a tall pillar shaped memorial, making the stone beside it of his father, George Rockford, look mighty humble. On the other side of Caleb's stone was Madeleine's, identical in shape and size but of glorious red polished sandstone with a cherub carved at the top above Madeleine's name. Sophia had insisted on this ornate stone. Gerald looked with surprise at the dates of his stepson and daughter's deaths, 1868 and 1876. In each of those years, he had been so bitterly hurt that he thought his life could not go on, and each time he had rallied his spirits to console Sophia. He wondered now for what practical purpose he and Sophia had so long outlived their children.

"Madeleine's stone is so pretty," said Clarence.

"It fits her," said Gerald. "She was a beautiful girl. Caleb's stone is grand too; it reflects the potential he sadly never realized."

This time Will and Clarence knelt and planted the flowers before Madeleine's stone. When they had finished, Will asked, "We should have brought extra flowers for Caleb, but we only have enough left for Grandmother's grave."

"It's all right," Gerald replied. "Caleb does not need flowers; he's in a better place now."

"Grandpa, you sound so sad," said Clarence.

"Well, I am," said Gerald, repressing a sob. "It's hard to lose the people you love, especially your own children; that's just unnatural."

"You still have us, Grandpa. We love you."

Gerald put his arm around Clarence's shoulder. He had not had so many simultaneously conflicting emotions in years. He loved these grandsons of his; he wondered whether he had been wrong to let Sophia talk him into moving back East. Had they remained in Marquette, maybe being surrounded by the family would have made their grief more bearable. "We better go to your Grandma Henning's stone now," he said.

"Where is it, Grandpa?" asked Will. "Pa never showed us."

Gerald was momentarily surprised, but then realized Jacob had no reason to show them the grave. Jacob had been a boy when Clara died, and if Agnes had ever shown him her mother's grave, he must have forgotten about it.

Clara's plot had long been neglected. The flat stone had cracked and grass grew up in its middle; rain and snow had obscured its words, and moss grew in the engraved dates. Gerald knelt for the second time that day. With the spade, he scraped away the moss, while careful not to damage the stone further. Silently, he told Clara she was the true love of his life; perhaps he betrayed Sophia with such feelings, but with Clara, he would be honest. He loved Sophia, had cared for her all these years, but in old age, honesty won out. If Clara had lived, how much happier he would have been; life might have been so different, but his great love lay beneath the earth, nearly forgotten by all save himself, and perhaps it was right she was gone when he had always felt he never deserved such a lovely woman.

"It looks like I'll have to order a new stone for your grandmother," he said as he stood back up.

He knew the boys were staring at him in concern. Clara's memory was almost forgotten, but Gerald could see she lived on in her grandsons' innocent faces. Later, he would have to tell the boys about their grandmother, but he was not ready to speak of her at this moment.

"Let's go," he told them.

"All right," said Will, half-understanding his grandfather's feelings.

"Where are we going? Back home?" asked Clarence.

"Why don't I take you boys out to lunch since you've been so good at humoring an old man this morning. Where's the best place in town to eat?"

"The Hotel Superior," said Clarence.

"Where is it?" Gerald asked.

"We can't go there," said Will. "It's too expensive."

"Have you ever eaten there?" Gerald asked.

"No," the boys said in unison.

"Then how do you know whether it's too expensive?" Gerald smiled. "Drive me all around Marquette, Will; give me the grand tour. I want to see how my favorite city has changed, and then afterwards, we'll go to the Hotel Superior for lunch."

Will drove the wagon out of the cemetery and across Seventh Street onto Ridge, moving east toward the fashionable part of town.

"Let me see my old house, first," Gerald said, "and then go downtown."

Soon the wagon was passing the Methodist church and across from it now rose up the new Baptist Church. Farther down the street stood the Episcopal Church, where Gerald and Clara had gone before Gerald had married Sophia and converted to Methodism. A new church had just been built the year before he moved away, but since then attached to it had been a chapel, built by Peter White in memory of his son, Morgan, who had died. Saddened to think his old acquaintance had also lost a child, Gerald silently rode past the White house. Then he saw his own impressive home, well kept up by its present owners, and surrounded by several equally fine homes. A couple blocks farther down the road rose up the Longyear mansion, dwarfing every other home in Marquette. John Munro Longyear had come to the Upper Peninsula during the Panic of 1873; when so many others had fled Marquette during those economically troubled times, Mr. Longyear had remained to transform a meager living into an enormous fortune. Now, an entire city block was consumed by his newly built palatial home, the largest residence the Upper Peninsula had ever known, the one house in Marquette everyone longed to receive an invitation to enter. The large Swineford home nearby, only a decade before considered the most impressive in Marquette, was now a mere cottage beside it.

"My word," said Gerald. "I haven't seen anything like this short of the Vanderbilts' homes in New York and Newport."

Next Will drove the wagon downhill toward the lake, and then beside the bustling harbor, filled with boats and docks beyond the dreams of Marquette's first entrepreneurs. The success of the iron industry was manifested in the buildings Gerald saw spread throughout downtown. The Savings Bank building on the corner of Front and Washington Streets was Marquette's first true skyscraper, five stories high on Front Street, six stories on Washington, and seven stories at its back facing the lake. Its crowning jewel was the ornate clock tower the residents of Marquette swore could rival London's Big Ben. On Washington Street, replacing the small time theatricals performed in private homes, stood a magnificent opera house, the finest north of Chicago; here people were enticed from across the peninsula to attend such favorite performances as *Uncle Tom's Cabin*, thereby establishing Marquette as the region's cultural metropolis. Farther down the street was the towering Post Office, and beside it, a robust new domed city hall built of Lake Superior Sandstone.

"These city buildings are as fine as any in New York," Gerald praised. He looked about but found no evidence of the flimsy wooden structures that had been tacked together before the great fire of 1868 had resulted in a city ordinance that all structures in the business district be built of stone.

"We were just a struggling village back then," he mused. "Now Marquette is an impressive city. God bless this town that has survived despite all the adversities of fire, blizzard, and its remote location. The people here have more gumption than in any other place I've known."

The city had a special grace, a richness in minerals, but also in nature; the city had grown, but the lakeshore had remained scenic; cool breezes blew off the lake to make the air pure and invigorating; trees had been preserved to keep the city lush and green, rather than turning it into a stone desert. Even the brown sandstone, not necessarily attractive in itself, had been carved into beautiful structures, public buildings to testify to the inhabitants' determination, and churches to honor the God who shed special blessings on the town.

Gerald had missed watching all these changes. All these magnificent buildings were new, mostly built in the last decade, and there was promise of more grand structures to come. Here were all the advantages of the large cities, without the crime, the poverty, the filth of New York and other industrial metropolises.

"Thank you for showing me around," Gerald told the boys. "Now let's go eat."

Will turned the wagon south onto Third Street. Gerald looked up at the towers of St. Peter's Cathedral, already considered the world's most beautiful sandstone building. Then Will drove the wagon down what was once Superior Street, now renamed Baraga Avenue to honor the saint who had labored in this land. Finally, as Gerald and the boys turned again to ride parallel to the deep blue lake, a large European-looking castle rose up out of the cliff.

"There's the Hotel Superior!" shouted Clarence.

"That's a hotel?" asked Gerald as Will turned the wagon up its driveway.

"Yes," said Will. "It was built to be a fashionable health resort. Marquette is considered to have the healthiest climate in the world because of its fresh air and clean water, so people come from all over the country to spend summers here."

"I can see why," said Gerald, straining his head to see the top of the Hotel Superior. "It looks like you could fit the entire population of Marquette into this hotel—probably all the livestock from the surrounding farms as well."

"Only the richest people can stay or eat here," said Clarence.

"Well," said Gerald, raising his eyebrows, "I hope they'll let us in then."

The Hotel Superior was magnificent, more so than any hotel in the North. Its enormous tower rose up two hundred feet, while its pointed arches resembled a Bavarian castle. Inside, visitors were treated to the latest innovations in plumbing and electric lighting. Even Turkish baths were available. When Gerald and his grandsons climbed the front steps, they found themselves on a spacious porch, sixteen feet wide, which reminded Gerald of the fine hotels he had visited in Europe. The boys had never been in a hotel before, so rather than immediately eat, they insisted on walking up and down the winding porch. From there, they could look down at scenic Lake Superior, at Marquette's homes, at the common people bustling about the prosperous city.

"These gardens are amazing," said Gerald, thinking only the grounds of Hampton Court or Versailles more exquisite.

When the charms of the porch and gardens were exhausted, the trio confessed their hunger. They stepped into the elaborately decorated hotel and sat down to the most elegant meal the boys had ever experienced.

Once they had been shown to their table and had placed their orders, the boys stared about in wonder, thrilled to be among so many fine people, and feeling a tad guilty that their father had not joined them. Gerald thought how much Sophia would prefer this new Marquette full of prosperity and splendor compared to the little village they had once known. He overheard snatches of conversation from the nearby tables, informing him the other diners were guests, many of them millionaires from Chicago, Detroit, or New England, all come to partake of the area's healthy climate. He felt a bit bewildered that his little village of a hundred inhabitants had grown into a city of ten thousand, with not one familiar face in this dining room. He had once been a major contributor to the city's prosperity; now he was a stranger here.

"Why, is it Gerald? Gerald Henning!" a man cried from the dining room's entrance. Gerald looked about, thinking the voice familiar, but unable to place it. A rotund, bearded man approached with smiling eyes.

"You haven't changed a bit," said the man, grasping his hand. "You don't recognize me. It's Peter. Peter White."

"Peter," Gerald laughed, standing up to greet his old friend. "How are you?"

"Fine, just fine. When did you get into town?"

"Just yesterday. I'm staying with my son-in-law. These are my grandsons."

"Pleased to meet you," said Peter, shaking Will and Clarence's hands.

"Would you like to have lunch with us?" Gerald asked.

Peter pulled up a chair as if eating with Gerald were an everyday occurrence, while Will and Clarence exchanged glances that said, "Pa will never believe we had lunch with the Honorable Peter White."

Peter was now Marquette's grand old man. The community's most celebrated citizen, he had done more than anyone else for the city's political and economic advancement; he had built up a real estate and banking empire, funded the library that bore his name, given Chief Kawbawgam a home in his old age, and as his crowning glory, secured Presque Isle as a city park to be treasured for generations by all who would call Marquette home.

A prodigious figure throughout the state of Michigan, the Honorable Peter White numbered among his friends several senators, governors, and more than one United States president. This titan now sat and shared humorous tales with Gerald of the old days when he had bathed cholera victims, been lost in the woods, snowshoed to Green Bay to retrieve Marquette's mail, and been, along with Gerald, a victim of the *Jay Morse*'s sinking. For these old men the past sprang to life again as if it were only yesterday. Will and Clarence reveled in their elders' conversation, scarcely tasting their food as they listened, although in later years, they would elaborate upon every detail of this encounter, including the delectable meal they would not remember eating.

Too soon came the moment when Peter White said, "Well, I better be going. I have a bank appointment, but I'd like to see you again before you leave, Gerald. Have you heard about our new fishing and hunting club up in the Huron Mountains? Maybe I could take you up there before you go."

"I hadn't heard about it," Gerald replied, "but I'd enjoy making the trip."

"It's a bit of a ride, but worth the trouble. Several of us have built little getaway cabins up there. I'll send one of my staff over to your son-in-law's place to let you know when would be a good day."

"Fine, fine," said Gerald. "I'm looking forward to our further reminiscing."

"Well, we're about the only ones left who remember the early days now. Amos Harlow, Robert Graveraet, Bishop Baraga, all of them have passed on."

"It won't be long before I have too," said Gerald. "That's why I wanted to make one last trip back here."

"I don't blame you; it's the finest place on God's good earth," said Peter. "It was great seeing you Gerald. Give my best wishes to your wife. And I'm sure I'll be seeing you handsome boys around town."

Clarence blushed at the compliment while Will felt completely charmed by their illustrious dinner companion.

"Wait until we tell Pa about this," Clarence whispered to Will. "And it never would have happened if Grandpa hadn't come." Having a grandfather was splendid!

Following Sunday church services, Gerald and the Whitman clan congregated at Cordelia and Nathaniel's house and waited for Molly's family to join them. Greetings, preparations, and explanations ensued before embarking on the picnic. Sylvia explained that her husband, Harry Cumming, had refused to come because he was going to dinner at his parents' house. Mary frowned at her brother-in-law's selfishness, since he had not yet met his wife's Grandpa Henning, but there was no understanding Sylvia's husband. Mary's husband, Reuben Feake, had no qualms about coming to the picnic, or bringing their six month old baby, Virgil. Cordelia and Nathaniel then had a little spat about Nathaniel bringing his cane along; he argued it would take up too much room on the streetcar; Cordelia insisted he would find walking at Presque Isle too strenuous without it. Finally, Jacob was called in to arbitrate, and he convinced his father to bring along what the old man called "the dang nuisance" which made Cordelia declare "such language sets a bad example for the children." Molly's family arrived and the expedition set off for the streetcar, but on the way, Patrick and Kathy's youngest, four year old Jeremy McCarey, had a temper tantrum and seven year old Frank McCarey told his little brother "You're being a brat," for which Frank was scolded.

Gerald enjoyed every minute of all this fussing, all this typical family loving. Usually, only Sophia fussed at him, and there just being the two of them, their life was quiet and rather dull. Here was the fullness of life, complete with joy and irritation.

Once on the streetcar, Gerald found a seat beside his old friend, Molly.

"I see what they say is true," Molly told him. "Men only get more handsome with age."

Gerald laughed, enjoying Molly's Irish lilt, still there despite the hard years she had known. He could not return the compliment without her thinking she was being flattered; her face had aged rapidly in recent years from too many cares regarding others, but her eyes shone brightly.

"Thank you," he said. "But I'm afraid we're all getting older."

"Older but wiser," she replied.

"I hope so. The world certainly has changed since we first knew each other." As he spoke, he stared out at the city that whizzed by as the streetcar took them north through town to Presque Isle. "I can't get over how Marquette has changed. It looks so prominent compared to the handful of little cabins we had that first winter."

"You know," said Molly, "there are days I walk down Baraga or Front Street and don't see a face I recognize, although I must know a couple thousand people in town."

"At least Marquette's not so big you can get lost in a maze of streets like in New York."

"But I'm sure you and Sophia love New York," said Molly. "We have nothing to compare to the museums and theatres and the high society there."

"Those are advantages perhaps," said Gerald, "but I'm rather tired of it all; I wouldn't mind moving back here."

Molly knew Sophia would never consent to such a move. Cordelia and Molly had often debated whether Gerald would ever return to Marquette, and they had always arrived at the same conclusion. But Molly saw no reason not to try persuading him.

"I know your family would love to have you here again."

"Sophia would never come," said Gerald, "but I have persuaded Cordelia to come visit us next summer."

Molly smiled but did not mention she had set the groundwork for his persuasion.

"It would be nice to be near my grandchildren," Gerald added. "I barely know them now. I never even saw the boys until this visit."

"I scarcely recognize your grandsons myself," said Molly. "I see Cordelia and Nathaniel fairly regularly, but since Jacob moved out to the farm, I've kind of lost touch with him and his children."

"How are your children doing?" asked Gerald.

"Fine," she said, glancing to the rear of the streetcar where her daughter's family was seated. "Patrick's a good husband to Kathy; he's got a good, steady job at the prison."

"The prison? Where's that?"

"Oh, it's a state branch prison. It was built just south of town maybe half a dozen years ago. It's a large sandstone building, quite impressive. You should drive past it before you leave."

Gerald shook his head in wonder. "A state prison here in Marquette. I can't believe it."

"They built it here because we're so remote from the rest of the state. Most of the prisoners come from Lower Michigan, and if they break out, they only get lost in the woods, especially in winter, so they're soon caught. Even if the prisoners got out of the Upper Peninsula, they'd have to travel through Wisconsin to get back downstate."

"They might make it across the Straits of Mackinac, but I suppose the police would be watching for them," said Gerald. "When I went to buy my train tickets, I thought I would have to go through Chicago, but the man at the ticket counter told me I could take a train over the Straits since a ferry now carries trains across. I could scarcely believe it. The changes in transportation have been incredible during our lifetime. We didn't even have railroads when I was born."

"Or streetcars," said Molly as the vehicle clanged around a corner. "I still feel nervous riding this thing."

"So how is Karl?"

"He's fine. He still logs all over the Keweenaw Peninsula. He and his friend Ben have both made their fortunes twice over now."

"Is he married yet?"

"No, I doubt he ever will be, but Patrick and Kathy will supply me with enough grandchildren. I've got two and I doubt they're done yet."

"I'm happy for you, Molly. I know you had many rough times, but now it seems you've finally gotten your reward. It must be a comfort to know you'll spend your old age surrounded by your loving family."

"Yes, I'm very lucky," said Molly, well aware that her constant faith had resulted in many blessings.

"I wish," Gerald said, "that I could be near my grandchildren like you are."

"Why can't you, Gerald? You've made your money. There must be younger men who can run the business for you, and Sophia should understand your need to be near your family. If you asked her, I bet—"

"Mother!" Kathy yelled. "Catch him."

Four-year old Jeremy had escaped from his parents. He was running toward his grandmother, but you never knew what a four year old intended; he might be planning to jump off the streetcar! But Gerald saw him coming and nabbed him before he could go farther.

"Stay here, Jeremy," said Molly, taking him on her lap. "Stay with Grandma until we get off. We're going to have a picnic. Won't you like that?"

Gerald watched his old friend with her little grandson. His grandsons would never be that small again; he had completely missed watching them grow up, missed a thousand special moments in their lives. He did not want to miss another, especially now that he had a great-grandson. He did not want his family to be strangers.

"Grandpa," called Will from across the aisle. "There's the river where Pa and I caught those trout I told you about, and there's Chief Kawbawgam's house."

Gerald barely had time to look as the streetcar whizzed over the very ground where once the bog had cut Presque Isle off from the mainland. The day before, Gerald had visited with Peter White and made the trip up to the Huron Mountain Club. On the way, Peter had told Gerald how he had purchased the land of Presque Isle from the federal government, then built the road to it, lining it with Lombardy poplars to make the shoreline picturesque. Presque Isle would now be preserved as a park for all those who were to call Marquette home. Forever protected would be its towering cliffs, its rich vegetation, its wandering deer, its marvelous black rocks. Gerald had been delighted by Peter's public benefaction; he only wished he had thought to make an equally grand gesture toward Marquette.

But no time now for regrets. They had arrived at Presque Isle. The streetcar stopped; picnic baskets and small children were handed out as everyone disembarked; then in a troop they all made their way across a grassy field surrounded by birch, pine, and oak trees with a splendid view of Lake Superior.

Gerald had barely yet spoken to his granddaughters, so he made a point of sitting near the young women he only remembered as very little girls. Once the picnic cloths were laid, the food arranged, once everyone was seated and plates filled to contentment with sandwiches and potato salad, Gerald tried to speak to the girls—not girls, but married women now. Yet Mary was distracted with trying to feed little Virgil so her husband, Reuben, could eat without disturbance. Sylvia enviously watched Mary's child, imagining the joys of motherhood that would be hers by Christmas. Since she had no husband to wait on, she offered to hold her nephew while Mary ate.

"It's hard to believe my granddaughters are now having babies of their own," Gerald said. "It seems just yesterday you were newborns in my arms."

Mary smiled awkwardly while Sylvia was too occupied with Virgil to listen.

"What's hard for me to believe," Cordelia frowned, "is that my grand-daughters want to move away."

"Move away? Where?" asked Gerald. No one had told him this before.

"I'm the only one who's moving," said Mary. "Sylvia refuses to."

"Well," said Sylvia, used to defending herself from Mary's constant criticism. "It's not that I don't want to go to Chicago—it's that Harry doesn't want to."

"Chicago? But why there?" Gerald asked.

"That's where I'm from," said Reuben. "My brother found me a job there in his office. It will be much better pay. Mary and I are moving there next month."

"Money isn't always worth moving for," said Cordelia. She was not particularly close to Mary, but the loss of any family member saddened her. Cordelia had not heard until now, however, that Sylvia had decided to stay in Marquette, so she felt a little cheered.

"But listen to Sylvia and Harry's reason for not moving," Mary tattled.

Sylvia was reluctant to speak, especially since it was Harry's decision not to move, but as his wife, she had to defend him.

"Harry says the cost of living is higher in Chicago, and it would be expensive to move there, so we're better off here."

"But the job would pay more," said Mary.

"But with the cost of living, it would probably average out the same," Cordelia said, more to convince Sylvia than to aid her argument.

"I for one," said Gerald, "don't understand why anyone would want to leave Marquette. Even New York's Central Park cannot surpass this beauty." And he waved his arm about to encompass the entire park and the lake.

"Scenery don't put food on the table," said Reuben. "We ain't all rich enough to do as we please."

"Maybe I could help you and Mary out," said Gerald. "Give you a loan to start your own business or—"

"I ain't looking for handouts," Reuben grunted, then jumped up and walked over to join Patrick and Jacob's conversation.

Gerald felt the reproach keenly. He had worked hard many years to ensure his family was comfortable. But what right did he have to interfere, trying to help people he had ignored all these years? Still, what did that young man know? He was jealous of Gerald's wealth, yet going to Chicago to make his own fortune at the cost of tearing his wife and child from their family. Gerald thought the young too often equated money with happiness. During his own lifetime, Gerald had watched moneymaking become the primary obsession of the nation, bringing in the gilded age, to the disregard of all morals and values; Gerald knew well the old adage "All that glitters is not gold." He remembered a time, or so he told himself, when loving your family and your God had been the two most important concerns in a man's life, and making money was done out of love for your family. All his money had made little impact on his happiness; it had been people, and mostly those in this little town, who had brought him the greatest happiness; if there were any conceivable way to return here, he would relinquish his wealth; he would trade it all just to live in that little cabin again with Clara.

He remembered one day in early May, when the green buds were just springing out of the trees, pollen floating in the air, when he and Clara had walked together in the forest. Unexpectedly, a fawn had stepped out in front of them, and rather than run away, it had stared at them curiously, never having seen a human before. The moment had seemed endless, a moment free of fear, free of awkwardness on the part of human or animal; Clara, he, and the deer stood mutually admiring the wonder of creation attested by one another's presence. Then the fawn's mother had stepped into the clearing, and the little creature had scampered after her, leaving Clara and Gerald breathless. They had felt honored by such intimate awareness of another being, separate from them, yet equally part of the Creation. Gerald remembered then how Clara had taken his hand, both of them too overwhelmed to speak, as they continued down the rough Indian trail amid budding trees and tiny, star-shaped may-flowers. That poignant memory had come back to him many times over the years; it was a memory of complete union with life, a moment of peace he had sought for but never known since.

"Here, Sylvia, I'll take the baby back now," said Mary.

"Let me hold him a moment," Gerald said, taking Virgil on his lap.

"Our first great-grandchild, Gerald," observed Cordelia.

"Yes, yours and Nathaniel's, and mine and—" but he did not say her name. He smiled into the child's tiny eyes, its little fist squeezing his finger. How could its parents take it to be imprisoned in Chicago? This child should be allowed to wander through the beautiful forests, to learn to swim amid Lake Superior's waves, to learn Nature's priceless lessons.

· Virgil began to cry. Mary reached over to take him from Great-Grandpa Henning. Gerald had finished eating. Jacob, Reuben, and Patrick were talking. Molly and Kathy were cleaning up the plates. Cordelia was fussing at Nathaniel for dropping potato salad on his pants. Gerald was included in none of this chatter; he loved them all, but he felt separated from them.

"I think I'll go for a little walk," he said. "I need one after eating so much."

"Can I go too, Grandpa?" asked Will.

"And me?" asked Clarence.

"All right," Gerald smiled. He had thought he wanted a moment alone, but he would have other times alone; he did not want to lose a moment of his grandsons' company.

The three of them climbed up a hill, then took a wooded path into the heart of the island; the forest here was so thick they could not see the lake, even though they were high above it.

"We need walking sticks," declared Will, picking up a hefty tree branch.

Gerald looked about him, spying a thick solid stick. Clarence picked up a dead pine tree branch with orange needles still clinging to its tip.

"That looks silly," Will told his brother. "Walking sticks don't have pine needles on them."

Clarence dropped it awkwardly and looked for another.

"I think it's a fine stick myself," said Gerald, retrieving the stick and handing it to his youngest grandson. "Always go with your heart, Clarence."

Clarence smiled and proudly reclaimed it.

"Come on then, let's go," said Will. "But you know, Moses wouldn't have had a staff like that."

"Maybe Joseph would have," Clarence replied. "He was second to the Pharaoh of Egypt so he would have had a fancy one."

The boys began to debate the possible staffs of their biblical heroes. Clarence suggested the orange pine needles might mean his staff was made from the burning bush while Will wished he could make his own staff turn into a snake.

Gerald let the boys play their game, following behind as they raced up and down the trail, waiting for him to catch up. After about twenty minutes, Will said, "Grandpa, we're coming to a clearing. I can see the lake up ahead."

"Come on, Grandpa," called Clarence. "There's a big cliff that's a great lookout."

"Go on. I'll be there in a minute," Gerald replied, too old to rush for anything. He stopped to take out his handkerchief and wipe the sweat from his forehead. It was humid inside the forest; the lake breezes did not penetrate there. He wished he were beside the lake to dip in his hands for a drink.

He heard a crackling sound, and turning his head, he saw a little chipmunk, sitting on a log, chewing away at a nut. The forest creature was either unaware or indifferent to Gerald's presence as it nibbled its snack. Gerald was struck by how simple the creature's life must be, its only worry to find food and avoid dangerous animals, and in this remote island in summer, neither worry was great. Gerald felt the same should be true for him; he only needed food and shelter, but he had toiled all his life for money, first because his father had expected it of him, then to please Sophia with material things. He had rarely if ever lived just to enjoy life.

He wondered why most people spent their lives grasping for things that never made them happy. What was it he had once read in Carlyle, something about, oh yes—"the Fraction of Life can be increased in value not so much by increasing your Numerator, as by lessening your Denominator." He did not care now whether he ever earned another dollar. He had enough already for several lifetimes. He wished to be like a chipmunk, content with a little nut, needing no table but a log with a shady evergreen branch overhead.

"Grandpa, come look! There's an ore boat coming into the harbor!"

Gerald looked up to see Clarence pointing toward the lake. If he could only convince Sophia to come back here. He yearned for such a happy ending, here in this peaceful place. But he would never be able to explain what he wanted so Sophia would understand.

"Grandpa, are you coming?" Will called.

"Coming!" he replied. He glanced back at the log. The chipmunk had scampered away. Gerald put his handkerchief back in his pocket and hurried down the trail; perhaps he might still glimpse Clarence's ore boat before it was too late.

Months later, Sophia Henning wrote the following letter to her sister.

December 3, 1895

Dear Cordelia,

Thank you for your kind letter of condolence. I know you and Nathaniel loved Gerald almost as much as I did. Give my sympathies to Jacob and the children. Nearly three weeks have now passed, but I still find it difficult to believe my husband of nearly forty years is gone. I'm thankful he went in his sleep, although I wish I'd had some warning to prepare myself better. I was comforted by your descriptions of the memorial ceremony in Marquette when his body was buried. I would have liked to attend, but you understand I cannot return there.

I cannot help feeling jealous that Gerald asked to be buried in Marquette beside his first wife. I thought when the time came, we would be buried together, here in New York. Now I don't know where I will finally rest since I buried Caleb in my plot beside his father. I should not complain when Gerald made me so happy for so many years, but it is hard to be alone now. You spoke of coming to visit me in the spring, but I don't think I could bear to be alone here even until then.

I have written to Darius, and he wishes me to go out West and spend my last days there with his family. I scarcely know Omelia's children, and I cannot return to Marquette, so to be near our brother, and Edna and Esau and their children seems the best choice for me. I feel no bond to New York anymore, and the climate of the Southwest might be good for my old bones. Perhaps in the spring, you can come to visit all of us in Utah.

"She doesn't say much else," said Cordelia, not sharing the rest of the letter. She sat with Nathaniel, Jacob, and her grandsons around her dining room table.

"I'm surprised she's not more upset that Gerald wanted to be buried beside Clara," Nathaniel said.

"She's taking it very well, I think," said Cordelia.

"Gerald always did love it here, so I don't think it's surprising he would want to be buried in Marquette," Jacob said.

"Sophia is probably consoled enough in inheriting all his money," said Nathaniel.

"I am surprised," said Cordelia, "that Gerald made no provisions for his grandchildren. I imagine he intended to but never got around to it."

"It doesn't matter," Jacob replied, although he had wondered the same thing. "My children will have plenty when I'm gone, and Mary's husband now has a good job in Chicago. I want my children to be self-reliant."

"I'm going to get rich by being a merchant marine," Clarence said.

"No," Jacob replied. "I'm sending you boys to college. That way you won't have to work as hard as your parents and grandparents have."

"I wonder how Edna will feel about Sophia living with her," said Nathaniel. "They were never very close."

"No, but Sophia and Darius always were," said Cordelia. "I'm glad they'll have each other now. I just hope I can visit them this spring."

1897

Margaret Dalrymple had been born in a boarding house. She attributed all the misfortunes of her thirteen years to that initial tragedy, and she could not understand why such a fate had been cast upon her. Other girls were born in houses—she even knew a girl who had been born in a hospital—but to be born in a boarding house was decidedly common. She secretly believed she was not at all common, and her grandfather's constant stories of the Dalrymple family's former importance testified that she was intended for a much greater life. In fact, Margaret's imagination had been so colored by her grandfather's tales of Scotland's ancient glory that she found her dull life in Marquette nearly intolerable.

Margaret's grandfather had been born in Nova Scotia, the son of Scottish immigrants who had settled there in the late eighteenth century. Old Arthur Dalrymple had never been to Scotland, never seen it with his own eyes, but his father had told him of it, and more importantly, he had read and reread the novels of Sir Walter Scott until the fictions of that famed author had distorted his sense of self-importance. From Sir Walter Scott, Arthur Dalrymple had learned of the royal house of Stewart's plight, its being cast from Scotland, and its tragic end when Bonnie Prince Charlie failed to regain his rightful throne at the Battle of Culloden. Arthur's mother's maiden name had been Stewart, and although no proven connection existed between her ancestry and that of the infamous Scottish royalty, old Arthur Dalrymple flattered himself that he must be born from an offshoot of that illustrious yet unfortunate house. What her grandfather pondered as a possibility, Margaret had digested as her indisputable pedigree.

"To think," Margaret would brood, "that I have royal blood in my veins, yet I was born in a boarding house."

Her consolation over such a mortifying beginning was to remember King Charles I had suffered greater ignominy by hiding in a tree and then being beheaded by his enemies. He had been avenged when his son, Charles II, had taken the throne in 1660. The family had later been cast from the throne again, but someday, Margaret believed, the Stewart family would be vindicated, and who knew but that her own family branch might then be in line for the throne. If only she could get to Scotland, she might find proof of her denied heritage. She had no idea, at age thirteen, how to verify her ancestry, but she was certain some document, perhaps hidden away in a castle tower or monastery, would bear evidence of her birthright, and once found, she could rightfully reclaim her family's rank and heritage.

With such grand thoughts floating about in her childish mind, Margaret Dalrymple found it hard to appreciate the little town of Marquette, where nothing interesting ever happened, where she was stuck because she was a child. One day indignation over her circumstances rose up in her; she had been listening to her grandfather tell of how Sir Walter Scott had rediscovered the royal Scottish regalia in Edinburgh Castle; then she told her parents she wished she had been born in Scotland and that she hated America.

"Don't ever say that again," her father replied. "This is the best country there ever was, and your mother and I are proud to live here. You have no idea what freedoms we have here that we would lack in any other land."

"Like what?" Margaret demanded. Why live in this remote town when you could live in Edinburgh Castle?

"We have our own house," replied her father. "In some countries, people can't even own property."

Margaret was not convinced. Her family did not have much of a house, just a tiny thing with a narrow staircase and three bedrooms, one of which she had to share with her sister Sarah; Grandpa Dalrymple had his own room, while her parents and baby brother, Charles, slept in the largest bedroom. In a Scottish castle, they might each have an entire wing to themselves. Margaret did not understand how her parents could be so dull, so willing to settle for so little; had they never dreamt or wanted something more, something worthwhile from life? Only her grandfather understood her, and he was too old now to improve their lot. She was the one who would have to raise up the family when she was older. She was determined to do so.

On certain days, she came close to despair, but then she would look at herself in the mirror, and remind herself who she truly was, and of what fine lineage she came. Even if she had no documentation of her royal blood, she had a Roman nose, and fine straight teeth, an aristocratic chin, and a natural inclination toward fine things that placed her above the humdrum world of Marquette. One day she would startle the dull people of this little town by showing them her true magnitude.

For obvious reasons, Margaret was not popular with her classmates. She knew everyone could not be so refined as herself, and she took this deficiency into consideration when dealing with other children, but she could not help feeling superior to them. And they could not help thinking her the biggest snob they had ever known. Margaret comforted herself when her classmates avoided or mocked her by believing that to befriend such common people would only impede her from fulfilling her destiny.

Today Margaret was to know a temporary respite from the tedium of her life. The City of Marquette had declared a holiday for the unveiling of a statue of the city's namesake, the Jesuit priest who had arrived on these shores over two centuries before. Marquette's residents knew their city's fiftieth birthday was not far away; they were equally conscious that a new century would soon begin. Throughout the nineteenth century, the people of Marquette had survived many toils and tribulations, yet they had never relinquished their dream to be the Queen City of the North, and now as they neared their half-century mark, they felt confirmed that their city would endure for years to come. No better declaration of their solidity and perseverance could be chosen than a permanent statue of Father Marquette, one of the first Europeans to cross Lake Superior, a man who embodied the city's pioneer spirit. Peter White had commissioned the statue, and a great celebration was planned for its unveiling. The day's festivities would begin with a parade, led by the Keweenaw Peninsula's Calumet and Hecla Marching Band, famous for having won an international championship. The parade would pass through the main streets to the site of the statue, while the city's loyal citizens followed close behind. Speeches were to follow, a reenactment of Father Marquette's landing on the shore where now the city stood, and the unveiling of the statue itself. All these "big doings" as Margaret's father, to her annoyance, insisted on vulgarly calling the celebrations, were well and fine in Margaret's opinion, but it was the gala ball to be held that evening at the Hotel Superior that most enticed her imagination.

The rest of Marquette was most interested in the statue itself. Curiosity about its appearance circulated among the residents for weeks preceding the auspicious event. Much discussion had already taken place as to the statue's location, with Walnut Street, overlooking the harbor and Iron Bay, finally being chosen so the statue would receive a prominent place beside the city's newly built sandstone Waterworks building. Until the ceremony, it would remain a secret whether the statue would face the lake, as if Father Marquette were looking out over the great path of his journeys, or if he would face inland, as though blessing the city that bore his name.

As the Dalrymples walked to the site of the unveiling, Margaret's parents discussed what would be the best position for the statue, while her grandfather insisted the statue could never be as impressive as the Sir Walter Scott monument in Edinburgh. Although he had never seen the Scott monument, he never failed to find some way to affirm Scotland's preeminence among the nations.

Usually, Margaret would have requested further details about the famous Sir Walter Scott monument, but at the moment, she was not listening to her grandfather. She walked slightly behind her family, unwilling to speak with her obnoxious sister, whose meaningless babble would otherwise distract her from admiring the Longyear mansion as she passed it.

Not all the Waverley novels Sir Walter Scott had penned could work on Margaret's imagination as did this Marquette home. The Longyear mansion filled a block between Ridge and Arch streets, looking out over the lake and dwarfing all its neighbors. Inside were sixty-five elegant rooms and a bowling alley. The house perched on the top of the hill, like a castle whose owners could glance down upon the commoners living below.

Margaret had never met any of the Longyears, but she knew they must be genteel people. She had a notion that if she could get inside the mansion and meet the family, they would have the breeding and taste to realize she was of their kind. They would recognize her natural attributes and help her realize her dreams. If she could only get inside that house—but Margaret had never gotten further than peering through the front gate and pondering which windows were for the servants' rooms, and which were for the family's rooms, and which one belonged to the guest room where one day she would stay. Going up to the front door was something even a girl with her grandiloquent notions would not consider, but if she stood at the gate enough, one day Margaret was certain some elegant person inside would look out a window and wonder, "Who is that lovely girl?" Then a maid or footman would be sent out to fetch her, to bring her inside, to a luxurious parlor where Mrs. Longyear would receive her. The mistress of the house would recognize by Margaret's speech and manners that she was a fitting companion for her own daughters, and then Margaret would be adopted and given her own room in the house. Never would the Longyears consider the horror of making her return to her parents' cramped house, the dingy room she had to share with her unfastidious nine year old sister who lacked even the good taste to wash behind her ears at night, despite the number of times Margaret told her what an embarrassment she was. No, once she was inside the house, the Longyears would love her as part of the family, probably even send her to a private school with their own daughters, or better yet, take her with them to Europe, where she was certain to meet a Duke or Count—living in Marquette with the Longyears would be grand at first, but ultimately, she would need to marry a Scottish peer so she could restore her family's fortune to that of its former illustrious heritage. Not that Margaret necessarily wanted her family to live in Scotland with her— Sarah's dirty ears would not touch the silk pillows in her Scottish castle—but she would send her family expensive presents for Christmas and their birthdays, and occasionally, she would return to visit so the common people of Marquette would stare and bow, and her schoolmates would regret having been mean to her. Margaret would not condescend to notice any of them then. If only she could—

"Quit dawdling, Margaret. We're going to be late," her mother said. Margaret had actually come to a standstill before the Longyear mansion, forgetting to walk because she was so occupied with her daydream.

"Margaret always makes us late," Sarah whined.

"I'm coming," said Margaret. She skipped a few yards to catch up with her family. She had no desire to see the statue of Father Marquette, but she reminded herself that the city's most prominent citizens would be at the ceremony; if the Longyears attended, then perhaps today her fortunes might change.

Unlike the Dalrymples, most of Marquette's residents had followed the Calumet and Hecla band through the city streets to the site of the new statue. Consequently, a mass of people were now flooding onto Walnut Street, causing immediate confusion as Margaret's family merged into the crowd encircling the statue.

"Hello," said Mrs. Montoni, as the Dalrymples passed by her. "How are you all?"

"Fine, thank you," Mrs. Dalrymple replied.

"Is this Margaret?" asked Mrs. Montoni. "My, you've grown so much."

"Hello," Margaret muttered. She hated Mrs. Montoni. The old woman thought that because she had served as midwife when Margaret was born in that horrid boarding house, she had the right to take a patronizing tone with her. A couple winters ago, Mrs. Montoni had even gone so far, when

Margaret's father had been out of work for several months, to give Margaret some of her married daughter's girlhood clothes, clothes that were twenty years out of fashion.

"I won't wear those old things!" Margaret had yelled at her mother. "You can't make me!"

"But honey, they're lovely. Look at the pretty pink ribbon on this one," her mother had replied.

"No, I won't! I'll kill myself before I wear someone's castoffs."

"Don't talk like that, Margaret. You know it's wicked to speak of killing yourself."

"I don't care. I will kill myself if you make me wear those old things. It won't be as wicked as you trying to humiliate your daughter."

Mrs. Dalrymple had not known how to reason with the child. Her father-in-law was of no assistance, and she hated to trouble her husband when he was having enough trouble finding work.

Margaret had stormed into her room, slamming the door and leaning against it to prevent it being opened.

"Margaret, please, don't have a temper tantrum," Mrs. Dalrymple had begged from outside the closed door.

"You don't know what it's like!" Margaret sobbed. "You don't know how embarrassing it is to have to wear old castoffs!"

Mrs. Dalrymple was the third girl born in her family. She had worn plenty of castoffs in her day. "The girl is just too sensitive," she said to herself. But after more pleadings, which caused Margaret to sob violently and her mother to fear she would make herself sick, Mrs. Dalrymple whispered through the door.

"Margaret, dear, I have a little money put aside. Maybe I could buy some cloth to make you a couple new dresses, and Sarah can probably fit into the ones Mrs. Montoni sent us. But Margaret, Mrs. Montoni was only trying to be kind."

"I don't want her pity!" said Margaret.

"All right, dear. I'll buy material to make you some lovely new dresses. It'll be all right. Don't cry, dear. It doesn't matter that much. Please let me in."

Margaret had then stepped away from the door, and her mother had entered to embrace the exhausted child and rock her gently in her arms until she quit crying.

Since that day, Mrs. Dalrymple had realized Margaret was not like other girls. She tried to explain this difference to her husband, who only muttered, "the girl is spoiled." Mrs. Dalrymple persisted in believing Margaret was overly sensitive so she went out of her way to please her daughter; Mr. Dalrymple thought this attention only made Margaret "all the more spoiled."

Margaret could barely look at Mrs. Montoni without resentment. She was glad when the woman did not stop to chat further but quickly disappeared into the crowd.

Now came the great moment of the unveiling. First there were eloquent speeches to which Margaret scarcely listened. She was busy looking around to see who else had attended the celebration. The crowd was full of familiar faces, including several of the snotty girls from her school. The only likable member of her class whom she saw was Clarence Whitman. While the other boys generally tormented her, Clarence had always been polite and kind, and she claimed him as a friend. He would have claimed her simply as a girl he knew at school. But Margaret felt they shared a bond. Clarence had a noble, dreamy air about him that bespoke his deserving more than to live on a farm, even though Margaret knew his father was a very prosperous farmer. Sometimes, Margaret felt conflicted in liking him because she had been born in his grandparents' boarding house, but she knew he could not help his family's shortcomings anymore than she could. She was certain he was also destined for something better than their current humdrum lives. Perhaps someday he would make his fortune; perhaps someday he would even make her his own; of course, he did not have a noble title, but he had once told her he wanted to be a sailor, and Margaret, confident he would succeed in any undertaking, believed that being Mrs. Admiral Whitman would not be wholly unattractive.

"Margaret," said her mother, turning Margaret's gaze from Clarence. "Pay attention. They're about to unveil the statue."

In another second, the figure of Father Marquette was clearly revealed to all the residents of his namesake city. The crowd applauded and the people murmured with delight that the statue faced the town. The figure of the Jesuit priest stood atop a pedestal of sandstone, and on its base was a relief of Father Marquette preaching to the Indians at Lighthouse Point. But most striking was the statue itself. Father Marquette stood looking about him with wonder, as though admiring the beauty of the land he had visited; his brow spoke of determination to carry out his Christian mission to the Indians. His bearded face and large forehead suggested wisdom beyond his years. History had lost all record of the Jesuit missionary's appearance, only knowing he had died at the young age of thirty-eight, but here he was portrayed as a figure of indestructible and eternal force. His left hand clutched his robe, as if he had just stepped out of a canoe and was steeling himself against a harsh northern wind; in one hand he held a piece of paper, perhaps Marquette's city charter.

Margaret looked at the statue and saw a romantic hero, but the older residents of Marquette saw a pioneer like themselves; someone with a harsh, grim look who had known years of hardship; Father Marquette was one of them, the very first to experience the rigors of this land. Molly Montoni looked at the statue and remembered her first husband who like Father Marquette had also died young, but who would be proud of the community's survival. Charles Kawbawgam saw in the statue a symbol of how much his world had changed, and that change had begun with the coming of this black robe. Jacob Whitman looked at the statue and saw the immigrant spirit of all those pioneers, his parents and grandparents, his in-laws, cousins, aunt and uncle, his precious Agnes, and even himself, when he had come as a boy to a village of a few wooden buildings on the shores of Lake Superior. That moment of the statue's unveiling seemed a little eternity as everyone contemplated the changes of Marquette's half century.

When the ceremonies were over, Cordelia, Jacob, and his sons bumped into Molly and her family.

"Isn't it a beautiful statue?" said Cordelia. "I wish Nathaniel had come to see it."

"Why didn't he?" Molly asked.

"He was afraid the crowd and the walking would be too much of a strain for him. He rarely leaves the house now."

"I'm sorry," said Molly. "Tell him I'll stop by to cheer him up sometime soon."

"Molly, are you going to the midnight ball at the Hotel Superior?" Jacob asked.

"No, Patrick is working the night shift at the prison, and Kathy thinks the children are too young to go."

"You could still come," Cordelia said.

"I'd be happy to pick you up," said Jacob. "Mother and Will and I are going."

"Please come," Cordelia said. "Clarence doesn't want to go; he's agreed to stay with Nathaniel this evening, so there'll be plenty of room for you."

"Oh, I'd like to if it's not too much trouble," said Molly.

"No trouble at all. I'll come by for you half an hour beforehand," Jacob replied.

"Thank you. I'll be ready."

The Whitmans turned to leave when a shout of "Clarence!" resounded through the crowd.

Margaret Dalrymple had called out his name. Clarence turned awkwardly and said, "Hello," pretending to be glad to see her. Since summer had begun, he had scarcely seen any of his classmates, so he felt shy to see the one he was least interested in meeting.

"Are you going to the ball tonight?" she asked. "My mother says I can go, although she thinks I'm too young. If you're going, maybe we can dance together?"

"No," said Clarence. "I'm not going. I don't really want to."

"Oh, you should; I need someone there to talk to."

"I can't. I promised to stay with my grandpa so my grandma can go to the party." His father and grandmother were now busy speaking to Margaret's parents. He was thankful they had not heard him; his grandmother might insist she could stay with his grandfather so he could go. He had no desire to talk to Margaret at the party or anywhere for that matter; she usually talked so much it was all he could do not to tell her to be quiet.

"Can't you get out of it?" she asked.

"No," he said, then changed the subject. "Did you enjoy the speeches?"

"No, they were boring. Especially Peter White's."

"No, it wasn't," Clarence replied. "My grandpa was friends with Peter White."

"Your Grandpa Whitman?" asked Margaret. She doubted the Whitmans were rich enough to know Peter White.

"No, my other grandfather," said Clarence.

Margaret didn't know Clarence had another grandfather, but if he knew Peter White, he must be rich, so Margaret was impressed. Peter White's speech had still been boring, but he was prominent, and if Clarence's family knew him, that was one more sign Clarence came from a good family and was eligible as a future husband.

"Clarence, we're leaving now," said Will, coming over to him.

"I gotta go," said Clarence, thankful for the chance to escape.

"All right," Margaret replied. Now who would talk to her at the ball? Since her parents were not going, she had been forced to ask the neighbor girl whether she could go with her family; Margaret did not like the neighbors, but she felt sometimes a woman has to put up with unpleasant people to further her interests. Margaret knew her attendance at this ball was crucial, not only to see the beautifully dressed ladies and the handsome gentleman, but to learn the proper etiquette of such functions so she would be prepared to attend much grander royal balls in Europe. She would face whatever necessary to achieve her destiny, but it would be easier if a friend like Clarence were around.

When she went home that afternoon, Margaret tried to decide what to wear; she fretted and stared at her clothes; not one dress appeared elegant enough. In her indecision, she sat down and started to scribble, to write her name—Miss Margaret Dalrymple—Mrs. Admiral Clarence Whitman—Mrs. Dr. Clarence Whitman—after all, he had told her he would go to college so he might be a doctor. Mrs. President Clarence Whitman—that was a bit of a stretch, but one never knew. But most of all, she wanted to be Lady Margaret Dalrymple, the grand title she would receive when her Scottish ancestral lands were restored to her. Then if she married Clarence, of course, he would be Lord Clarence, but he would have to take the name of Dalrymple so their children could inherit her estate. Yes, Lord and Lady Clarence Dalrymple. Hadn't there once been a Lord Clarence in history? It sounded so aristocratic, and Lady Margaret was certainly a regal name—there had been St. Margaret, Queen of Scotland, for whom her grandfather said she had been named.

"Whatcha doing?" asked Sarah, bursting into their room.

Margaret quickly shoved her scribbling between the pages of Jane Porter's *The Scottish Chiefs*.

"Sarah, you know you're not allowed to come in unless you knock first," she snapped.

"It's my room too," said Sarah. "Did you pick out a dress for the party yet? I don't think it's fair I can't go to the ball."

"You weren't invited."

"Everyone else in Marquette is going, so I don't see why I can't."

"The neighbors didn't invite you. That's why."

"That's not a good enough reason," said Sarah. Margaret ignored her. She had to get ready. She only had forty-five minutes left, and she suspected a proper lady spent two hours to prepare her toilette. Margaret felt so flustered and hurried that she madly pulled her chiffon dress over her head, then ran downstairs so her mother could put up her hair.

Will Whitman had never before attended a ball. He had never even danced before. His grandmother had told him how handsome he looked, but his suit and the silk tie he wore only made him feel constricted and foolish. Mrs.

Montoni told him he was certain to have a good time, and no doubt a pretty girl would catch his eye. That remark only made Will more nervous; he always felt awkward around pretty girls.

He also felt foolish to be accompanied by a group of elderly people who would not dance. His grandmother did not approve of dancing, and she had almost decided not to attend the ball because of her religious convictions. Mrs. Montoni said her dancing days were over. Will's father would not dance because it would exacerbate his war wounds; just last month Will's father had spent a day completely bedridden after overworking in the fields.

When they reached the party, the three older folks found themselves seats against the wall, content to "watch the young people enjoy themselves." Since only three chairs were available, Will stood awkwardly beside them.

"Don't you see anyone you know, Will?" asked his grandmother.

"There must be some pretty girl here for you to dance with," said Molly.

"I don't know anyone here except a couple boys from school," Will replied.

"Why don't you go talk to them?" said Jacob.

"Maybe later," said Will. He saw the other boys were talking to girls Will did not know, so he felt too nervous to approach them.

"Maybe you could get your grandmother and Mrs. Montoni some punch?" his father said.

"Does it have alcohol in it?" asked Cordelia, who had never once swayed from her temperance upbringing and would not start now.

"I doubt it, Mother," said Jacob, "but Will can check it out for us."

"You ask someone, Will, but don't you taste it until you know for sure," his grandmother said. "Remember, liquor is the devil's agent."

Will was hurt by the reprimand. He was seventeen and old enough not to do anything to shame his Methodist family. Molly Montoni was not beyond drinking a glass of wine, but she agreed to settle for fruit punch in deference to her companions.

Will unwillingly walked over to the beverage table. A couple girls, whom he did not know, lingered by the punch bowl. They looked about thirteen years old. He hoped they would not speak to him.

"I like your silk tie," said the taller girl. She was so thin she reminded Will of an ostrich.

"It's really elegant," replied the second girl. Will thought she had an awfully pouty looking chin.

"Thank you," he replied. He was a bit flattered. The tie had belonged to his Grandpa Henning; Grandma Henning had recently sent it to him. "Do you know whether there's alcohol in the punch?"

"I don't think so," said the tall girl.

"You're Clarence's brother, aren't you?" asked the younger.

"Yes."

"I know Clarence. He's in my class at school. I'm Margaret Dalrymple," she said, thinking but not adding, "your future sister-in-law."

"It's nice to meet you," said Will, wondering whether he could carry four glasses so he would not have to make two trips and continue to make small talk with these girls.

"I'm Lizzie," said Margaret's friend. "Do you dance?"

"Not very well," he replied. "I was just getting drinks for my family."

"Where are they?" asked Lizzie. When Will pointed out his family, Margaret asked, "Are you related to Mrs. Montoni?"

"No, she's a family friend."

"Oh," said Margaret. Admiral's wife or not, she would not marry any member of that woman's family.

"Hello, Will. Do you remember me? I'm Sam Sheldon's sister?"

All three heads turned at the new voice. A beautiful young woman stood before them. She was older and more developed than Margaret or Lizzie, as both self-consciously noted. She had the tiniest waist Margaret had ever seen.

"Hi, Lorna," Lizzie said.

"Hi, Lizzie, how are you?" Lorna asked, but she had not come to speak to Lizzie. "Do you remember me, Will?"

"Of course," he said. He had met her a couple times at his friend Sam's house. The last time had been during the winter. He was stunned by how much she had developed in the past year. How radiant and glowing she looked in her rose-colored gown with her hair fixed up special for the party.

Margaret and Lizzie sized up Lorna. They could spot where her hair was out of place and that she had many split ends; they could see her dress was cheaply made, and they suspected she stuffed her bosom. But Will was ignorant of such feminine wiles.

"Won't you ask me to dance, Will?" Lorna asked.

"Um, well, I need to bring these drinks over to my family," he hemmed.

"I'll help you carry them. You're always so thoughtful of others. Then we'll dance after we deliver the drinks."

Will had been lassoed and pulled up tight. He could not deny he rather liked being captured by this beautiful woman. Every boy at the party would want to dance with her, but he feared once he was on the dance floor, she would think him a clod. He walked across the room, too nervous to speak, with her helping him to carry the punch glasses.

"Hello, I'm Lorna Sheldon," she introduced herself to Molly and the Whitmans.

"Hello," each replied and thanked her for the drinks.

"Will and I are going to dance," she said, taking his arm before anyone could say another word.

The young coquette led Will to the dance floor. He tried not to tremble or perspire. For the first time in his life, he felt he must be the center of attention. Every young man in the room must be jealous that he had such an alluring dance partner. Will felt his first tingling thrill at being a man.

Back at the punch bowl, Lizzie whispered to Margaret.

"Lorna's such a hussy."

"I can tell," said Margaret. She did not quite know what a hussy was, but she thought she understood from the tone in Lizzie's voice.

"What kind of name is Lorna anyway?" Lizzie said.

"Maybe she's named after Lorna Doone," said Margaret.

"Who's Lorna Doone?" asked Lizzie.

"It's the name of a book," said Margaret, remembering Lizzie knew nothing about literature or anything elegant, despite being Margaret's senior by two years. Margaret knew that book well; her grandfather had read it to her many times—it was one of the few English novels allowed in the house, accepted because of its Scottish characters.

"Lorna was never anything to look at until she filled out this year," said Lizzie. "I still don't think she's all that pretty."

Margaret thought Lorna very pretty, but because Will was Clarence's brother, she worried Lorna was far too glamorous; she would doubtless steal attention from Margaret when invited to the Scottish court. No, Lorna would not be a desirable sister-in-law.

"Isn't that your sister?" Lizzie asked.

"What?" said Margaret, her daydream interrupted. Lizzie pointed across the dance floor to where Sarah Dalrymple was filling a plate at the dessert table.

"What's she doing here?" said Margaret. "How did she even get in?"

Margaret did not wait for Lizzie to reply. She marched across the room to her prodigal sibling, noticing her sister had dared to come wearing nothing better than gingham. Was there to be no end to her embarrassment?

"What are you doing here?" Margaret demanded.

Sarah turned, stuffing an hors d'oeuvre in her mouth. She chewed and swallowed, momentarily ashamed she was caught, although she had known she would be.

"I have just as much right to be here as you," she said.

"How did you get here? Do Mother and Father know? Did they bring you?"

Margaret was furious. It was bad enough a hussy was dancing with Will Whitman, but now her sister had come to ruin her evening completely.

"Isn't it a wonderful party?" said Sarah. "Everyone is so elegant looking, and aren't there so many good things to eat?"

"First of all, it's not a party; it's a ball," said Margaret. "And secondly, how did you get here?"

"I told the man at the door that I had just stepped out for some air and that my parents were inside, so he let me in."

"But where are Mother and Father?"

"At home. They think I'm sleeping. I climbed down the tree outside our window and walked here."

"In the dark!"

"Yes. Please let me stay, just for a little while, Margaret. I wanted to come so bad, and I'm so glad I did. It's the best party I've ever been too."

"It's not for children," Margaret said.

"Well, I won't go home. It was scary walking here in the dark, and I can't do it again. If you send me home by myself, I'll tell Mother and then she'll be mad at you. The only way I'll go home is if you walk back with me."

Margaret debated. She had to admit she was not enjoying herself. If only Clarence were here to dance with, or even if Will asked her to dance, but he was dancing with—

"Just let me stay for a little while," said Sarah. "At least let me finish my cookies and punch. Then I'll go home. I just wanted to hear the music and see all the beautiful dresses. I've never even been in the Hotel Superior before, and it's so superior to everything else, isn't it?"

"All right," said Margaret. "You can stay for a little while, but then I'll have to take home. I'll have to tell Lizzie's parents I can't go back with them."

"Oh no," said Lizzie, arriving at the end of the sisters' spat. "Don't go, Margaret."

"I have to," Margaret replied. "My parents will worry if they discover Sarah's gone. Can you watch that Sarah doesn't get into trouble while I find your mother?"

Lizzie agreed, but she felt her evening was spoiled. Sarah offered her a cookie, but Lizzie refused. Sarah chatted happily about the music, the decorations, the beautiful gowns, and she set to devouring appetizers in a most unladylike manner.

❦   ❦   ❦

"They make a cute couple," said Molly, observing Will and Lorna dancing.

"Do you know her family?" Cordelia asked.

"No, I don't recognize her at all," said Molly. "I wish Karl would have come to town this week. Maybe he could have met a nice girl here."

"How is Karl?" Jacob asked, but he was only being polite. He did not feel much like making conversation; he was suddenly feeling ill. He told himself maybe there had been alcohol in that punch, although he knew the tremors in his side were not caused by liquor. He recognized the familiar spasms, a sign that his aging body was still fighting the Civil War and losing the battle.

"Karl's fine," Molly replied. "Every time I hear from him, he or Ben have sold another forty acres worth of lumber or added another thousand dollars to their bank accounts. But I don't know what good all that money does them without families."

"They'll marry when they're ready," said Cordelia.

"Karl's forty-three now so I rather doubt it," Molly replied, "but at least Kathy and Patrick are giving me grandchildren."

"Mother, I'm going to step outside a minute for some fresh air," said Jacob, slowly standing up.

"Are you all right, Jacob?" asked Cordelia. "You look kind of pale."

"I'm fine. Just a little warm," he said, trying to keep his voice steady as his head started to whirl.

"It's been a warm day," Molly said as Jacob meandered along the edge of the dance floor to the entrance.

He stepped onto the front porch, then stumbled to a pillar near the stairs. For a second, he clutched the pillar as the pain surged through his back. He was thankful no young lovers were about, spooning on the porch.

He knew he should not complain; the pain would pass in a minute. He had not had a bad day in weeks, but with all of these festivities, of course he had overexerted himself and inflamed his old wounds. He would have to take it easy tomorrow, maybe sleep late, something he had not done in years. Will and Clarence were good about looking after the livestock. They were good boys, not anywhere near the trouble his girls had been. They understood their father was no longer young. He could not have asked for better sons. The pain was not that bad; worth it really in exchange for the pleasure of today's celebration.

From the porch, Jacob could see Marquette's twinkling lights reflecting off the tranquil lake. He had never been this high above the city since electricity had been installed. All those lights sparkled like a queen's tiara. When he was a boy, he never would have dreamed of such inventions as electric lights and streetcars; how much the city had changed, and how much more it would change during his sons' lives. He imagined himself only the first of many generations who would look out at Marquette's harbor and feel enchanted by the electric lights reflecting through the gaps in the ore docks onto the lake. Soon it would be the twentieth century; what new marvels would appear then?

The pain was gone now. He should go back inside before his mother started to worry, but he wanted just one more minute in the refreshing cool air. He stepped down the porch steps and onto the drive. The sky was clear, the stars shining brightly. He did not think he had ever seen them shine so bright. He remembered long ago looking up at the stars when he and Caleb had gone camping at Presque Isle. Often he had recalled that camping trip, just him and his best friend together. The only days that had surpassed it were his wedding day, and the day on which each of his children had been born.

The pain returned, shooting through his left side. He felt as if the bullet were surging through him all over again. He wanted to sit down, but he was too far from the porch steps. Then his legs collapsed beneath him. Falling to the ground, he imagined how his mother would fret when he got grass stains all over his coat. Then a sudden spasm. He struggled to breathe, and lost consciousness.

"Oh, Margaret, look at that couple," Sarah said, pointing to Will and Lorna. It was time to leave, but Sarah was using any excuse to prolong her stay. Meanwhile, Lorna's beguiling beauty had kept Will on the dance floor. "I think they're the most handsome couple in the room. Don't you, Margaret?"

"No," Margaret replied. "Come on."

"Margaret, at least admit her dress is beautiful."

"She's just a hussy," said Margaret, leading her sister out the door.

"What's that?" asked Sarah.

"Never mind. You're too young to understand," Margaret said to avoid explaining what she did not fully understand herself.

"Is 'hussy' a bad word?" asked Sarah as she followed her sister down the porch steps. "If it is a bad word, I'll tell Mother on you."

"Sarah, after all the trouble you're in for sneaking out of the house, I don't think anything will make Mother angry with me. I hope you're happy that you've completely ruined my evening!"

Sarah considered crying to make her sister feel guilty and keep from tattling, but then she was distracted by a faint groan.

"What's that sound?" she asked.

"What sound?" Margaret snapped.

"It sounds like someone's hurt."

They looked around until they saw, just off the road a couple yards before them, a man lying on the grass.

For a second, Margaret did not move. Then she said, "Sir? Sir?" When there was no answer, she found the courage to walk over and shake him gently. He did not respond.

"It's Mr. Whitman. Quick, Sarah. Run inside for help."

Sarah was too frightened to disobey. She ran into the hotel and told the doorman. He shouted for a doctor, then ran outside to the unconscious man.

Within a minute, Margaret was pushed away from the scene and stood back watching. In another minute, she saw old Mrs. Whitman hovering over the man while Will stood by helplessly.

"Margaret!"

It was Mrs. Montoni's voice.

"Margaret, you know where the Whitmans live, don't you?" Mrs. Montoni asked.

Margaret nodded.

"Jacob's son and father are there. Go warn them what has happened so they'll be prepared before the body is brought home."

Margaret grasped her sister's hand and turned away. "Sarah, come on. We have to go tell Clarence."

They hurried down the hill, overwhelmed by their mission.

"Margaret, was he dead?" Sarah asked.

"The doctor said he had a stroke, but I guess so. He wasn't moving."

Before the Dalrymple girls reached the Whitman house, the doctor confirmed that Jacob Whitman had breathed his last. The Confederate army had finally gotten him. He left behind him two elderly parents, two married daughters, and most importantly, two sons who would now have to make their own way in the world.

BE SURE TO READ THE REST OF THE MARQUETTE TRILOGY!

🍁   🍁   🍁

THE QUEEN CITY
The Marquette Trilogy: Book Two

During the first half of the twentieth century, Marquette grows into the Queen City of the North. Here is the tale of a small town undergoing change as its horses are replaced by streetcars and automobiles, and its pioneers are replaced by new generations who prosper despite two World Wars and the Great Depression. Margaret Dalrymple finds her Scottish prince, though he is neither Scottish nor a prince. Molly Bergmann becomes an inspiration to her grandchildren. Jacob Whitman's children engage in a family feud. The Queen City's residents marry, divorce, have children, die, break their hearts, go to war, gossip, blackmail, raise families, move away, and then return to Marquette. And always, always they are in love with the haunting land that is their home.

🍁   🍁   🍁

SUPERIOR HERITAGE
The Marquette Trilogy: Book Three

The Marquette Trilogy comes to a satisfying conclusion as it brings together characters and plots from the earlier novels and culminates with Marquette's sesquicentennial celebrations in 1999. What happened to Madeleine Henning is finally revealed as secrets from the past shed light upon the present. Marquette's residents struggle with a difficult local economy, yet remain optimistic for the future. The novel's main character, John Vandelaare, is descended from all the early Marquette families in *Iron Pioneers* and *The Queen City*. While he cherishes his family's past, he questions whether he should remain in his hometown. Then an event happens that will change his life forever.

🍁   🍁   🍁

To learn more about Tyler R. Tichelaar's novels and to order autographed copies, visit: **www.MarquetteFiction.com**

Made in the USA
San Bernardino, CA
20 June 2017